Praise for
Harry Turtledove's
Worldwar novels

"Readers will have a perfectly delightful time....Turtledove's storytelling and historiography now march in perfect step. World War II buffs will have a particular romp."
—*Chicago Sun-Times*

"Unexpected twists and turns...Readers will be looking forward eagerly to the next [book]....[Harry Turtledove is] a Hugo-winning master of alternative SF."
—*Publishers Weekly*

"A feast for history buffs as well as SF fans."
—*Library Journal*

"Totally fascinating...Triumphant...Possibly the most ambitious in the subgenre's history and definitely the work of one of alternate history's authentic modern masters...."
—*Booklist*

By Harry Turtledove
Published by Ballantine Books

Departures
Guns of the South
How Few Remain
Krispos Rising

The American Empire Saga:
Blood and Iron
The Center Cannot Hold

The Colonization Series:
Second Contact
Down to Earth
Aftershocks

The Great War:
American Front
Walk in Hell
Breakthroughs

The Videssos Cycle:
Misplaced Legion
An Emperor for the Legion
Legion of Videssos
Swords of the Legion

The World War Saga:
In the Balance
Tilting the Balance
Upsetting the Balance
Striking the Balance

Edited by Harry Turtledove
Best Alternate History Stories of the 20th Century
Counting Up, Counting Down

Edited with Martin H. Greenberg
Best Military Science Fiction of the 20th Century

WORLDWAR: STRIKING THE BALANCE

Harry Turtledove

A Del Rey® Book
BALLANTINE BOOKS • NEW YORK

A Del Rey® Book
Published by Ballantine Books
Copyright © 1997 by Harry Turtledove

All rights reserved under the International and Pan-American Copyright Conventions. Published in the United States by Ballantine Books, a division of Random House, Inc., New York, and simultaneously in Canada by Random House of Canada Limited, Toronto.

Del Rey and colophon are registered trademarks of Random House, Inc.

www.delreydigital.com

Library of Congress Catalog Number: 97-91912

ISBN 0-345-41208-7

Map by Christine Levis

Manufactured in the United States of America

First Hardcover Edition: December 1996
First International Mass Market Edition: July 1997
First Domestic Mass Market Edition: September 1997

OPM   10   9   8

DRAMATIS PERSONAE

(Characters with names in CAPS are historical, others fictional)

HUMANS

ANIELEWICZ, MORDECHAI	*Jewish fighting leader, Lodz, Poland*
Apfelbaum, Moisei	*Colonel Skriabin's clerk, gulag near Petrozavodsk, USSR*
Auerbach, Rance	*U.S. Army cavalry captain, Lamar, Colorado*
Avram	*Partisan near Hrubieszów, Poland*
Bagnall, George	*Flight engineer, Pskov, USSR*
Beck	*Wehrmacht captain, Riga, Latvia*
BEGIN, MENACHEM	*Jewish guerrilla, Haifa, Palestine*
Birkenfeld, Oskar	*Jewish Order Service policeman, Lodz, Poland*
Boleslaw	*Pole in Lodz, Poland*
Borcke, Martin	*Wehrmacht captain, Pskov, USSR*
BRADLEY, OMAR	*U.S. Army lieutenant general, outside Denver*
BROCKDORFF-AHLEFELDT, WALTER VON	*Wehrmacht lieutenant general, Riga, Latvia*
Casimir	*Partisan leader outside Hrubieszów, Poland*
Chaim	*Jewish guard, Lodz, Poland*
CHILL, KURT	*Wehrmacht lieutenant general, Pskov, USSR*
Daniels, Peter ("Mutt")	*U.S. Army second lieutenant, Chicago*
Dölger, Hans	*Wehrmacht captain and adjutant, Pskov, USSR*
DONOVAN, WILLIAM ("WILD BILL")	*U.S. Army major general, Hot Springs, Arkansas*
Donskoi, Yakov	*Soviet interpreter, Cairo*

Drucker, Johannes	*Panzer driver north of Lodz, Poland*
Easter	*British Army colonel, Haifa, Palestine*
EDEN, ANTHONY	*British foreign secretary*
Embry, Ken	*RAF pilot, Pskov, USSR*
Fleishman, Bertha	*Jewish fighter, Lodz, Poland*
Fritz	Wehrmacht *ammunition hauler north of Lodz, Poland*
Fyodorov, Ivan	*Soviet prisoner in transit*
GERMAN, ALEKSANDR	*Partisan brigadier, Pskov, USSR*
GODDARD, ROBERT	*Rocket scientist, Hot Springs, Arkansas*
Goldfarb, David	*RAF radarman, Dover, England*
Gorbunova, Ludmila	*Red Air Force senior lieutenant, Pskov, USSR*
Grabowski	*U.S. Army corporal, Hot Springs, Arkansas*
Grillparzer, Gunther	Wehrmacht *gunner outside Lodz, Poland*
GROVES, LESLIE	*U.S. Army brigadier general, Metallurgical Laboratory, Denver*
Gruver, Solomon	*Jewish fighter, Lodz, Poland*
Hanrahan	*U.S. Army captain, outside Fordyce, Arkansas*
Hawkins	*U.S. Army lieutenant, Hot Springs, Arkansas*
Hines, Rachel	*U.S. Army cavalry private, Lamar, Colorado*
Hsia Shou-Tao	*Communist guerrilla leader, Peking*
HULL, CORDELL	*President of the United States*
Ignacy	*Partisan leader outside Warsaw*
Irma	*Waitress, Lamar, Colorado*
Jäger, Heinrich	Wehrmacht *panzer colonel outside Lodz, Poland*
Joachim	Wehrmacht *ammunition hauler north of Lodz, Poland*
Jones, Jerome	*RAF radarman, Pskov, USSR*
Jordan, Constantine	*RAF flight lieutenant, Dover, England*

Kagan, Max	*American nuclear physicist, north of Moscow*
Kapellmeister	*Wehrmacht major, Kristianstand, Norway*
Kaplan, Naomi	*Barmaid, White Horse Inn, Dover, England*
Karol	*Farmer north of Lodz, Poland*
KURCHATOV, IGOR	*Nuclear physicist, north of Moscow*
Kurowski	*U.S. Army private, Chicago*
Lidov, Boris	*NKVD colonel, Moscow*
Liu Han	*Ex-peasant woman; guerrilla, Peking*
Liu Mei	*Liu Han's daughter*
Logan	*Radioman near Fall Creek, Illinois*
Magruder, Bill	*U.S. Army cavalry lieutenant, Lamar, Colorado*
MAO TSE-TUNG	*Communist Party leader, Peking*
Marchenko	*NKVD captain, gulag outside Petrozavodsk, USSR*
MARSHALL, GEORGE	*U.S. Secretary of State*
Mather, Donald	*Captain, SAS, Dover, England*
Mavrogordato, Panagiotis	*Captain of the freighter* Naxos
Maxi	*SS officer north of Lodz, Poland*
McBride	*RAF flying officer, Dover, England*
Mehler, Karl	*Panzer loader north of Lodz, Poland*
Mendel	*Jewish guard, Lodz, Poland*
Mieczyslaw	*Farmer north of Lodz, Poland*
Mikhailov, Anton	*Zek in gulag near Petrozavodsk, USSR*
MOLOTOV, VYACHESLAV	*Foreign commissar, USSR*
Mori	*Japanese Army major, west of Peking*
Muldoon, Herman	*U.S. Army sergeant, Chicago*
NIEH HO-T'ING	*Guerrilla leader, Peking*
Nussboym, David	*Political prisoner in transit*
Osborne, Andy	*Guide near Karval, Colorado*
Palchinsky, Yuri	*Guard, gulag near Petrozavodsk, USSR*

PATTON, GEORGE	*U.S. Army lieutenant general near Fall Creek, Illinois*
Peterson, Richard	*Technician, Metallurgical Laboratory, Denver*
Pirogova, Tatiana	*Red Army sniper, Pskov, USSR*
Rasmussen	*U.S. Army lieutenant, Chicago*
RIBBENTROP, JOACHIM VON	*German foreign minister*
Rita	*Madam, Elgin, Ilinois*
Roundbush, Basil	*RAF flight lieutenant, Dover, England*
Rudzutak, Stepan	*Gang boss in* gulag *near Petrozavodsk, USSR*
Russie, Moishe	*Jewish leader, approaching Palestine*
Russie, Reuven	*Moishe and Rivka Russie's son*
Russie, Rivka	*Moishe Russie's wife*
Saul	*Jewish guard, Lodz, Poland*
Schultz, Georg	*German mechanic attached to Red Air Force, Pskov, USSR*
Sholom	*Partisan outside Hrubieszów, Poland*
SKORZENY, OTTO	SS *Standartenführer, North of Lodz, Poland*
Skriabin	*NKVD colonel,* gulag *outside Petrozavodsk, USSR*
Smithson, Hayward	*U.S. Army major, Medical Corps, Karval, Colorado*
STALIN, IOSEF	*General Secretary, Communist Party, USSR*
Stefania	*Partisan outside Hrubieszów, Poland*
STERN	*Jewish guerrilla leader, Jerusalem*
Summers, Penny	*Refugee, Lamar, Colorado*
Su Shun-Ch'in	*Muslim* qadi, *Peking*
Suzie	*Whore, Elgin, Illinois*
Sylvia	*Barmaid, White Horse Inn, Dover, England*
Szymanski, Stan	*U.S. Army captain, Elgin, Illinois*
Tadeusz	*Farmer outside of Lodz, Poland*
TOGO, SHIGENORI	*Japanese foreign minister*

VASILIEV, NIKOLAI — *Partisan brigadier, Pskov, USSR*

Witold — *Blacksmith, Hrubieszów, Poland*

Wladeslaw — *Partisan near Hrubieszów, Poland*

Yeager, Barbara — *Sam Yeager's wife*

Yeager, Jonathan — *Sam and Barbara Yeager's son*

Yeager, Sam — *U.S. Army sergeant, Hot Springs, Arkansas*

Yitzkhak — *Jew in Lodz, Poland*

Zelkowitz, Leon — *Jewish fighter, Lodz, Poland*

THE RACE

Aaatos — *Intelligence operative, Florida*

Atvar — *Fleetlord, conquest fleet of the Race*

Bunim — *Regional subadministrator, Lodz, Poland*

Chook — *Small-unit group leader near Fall Creek, Illinois*

Essaff — *Guard and interpreter, Peking*

Fsseffel — *Headmale, Race Barracks One, gulag near Petrozavodsk, USSR*

Gazzim — *Prisoner and interpreter, Moscow*

Kirel — *Shiplord, 127th Emperor Hetto*

Mzepps — *Prisoner, Dover, England*

Nikeaa — *Infantry officer outside Pskov, USSR*

Oyyag — *Prisoner, gulag near Petrozavodsk, USSR*

Ppevel — *Assistant administrator, eastern region, main continental mass, Peking*

Pshing — *Atvar's adjutant, Cairo*

Ristin — *Prisoner, Hot Springs, Arkansas*

Saltta — *Psychological researcher, Canton, China*

Straha	*Tosevite propagandist, Hot Springs, Arkansas*
Strukss	*Tosevite liaison officer, Cairo*
Teerts	*Killercraft flight leader, Florida*
Tessrek	*Researcher in tosevite behavior*
Ttomalss	*Researcher in tosevite behavior, Peking*
Uotat	*Atvar's interpreter, Cairo*
Ullhass	*Prisoner, Hot Springs, Arkansas*
Ummfac	*Aircraft armorer, Florida*
Ussmak	*Mutineer outside Tomsk, USSR*
Zolraag	*Negotiator with Jewish guerrillas, Jerusalem*

☆ **I** ☆

In free fall, Atvar the fleetlord glided over to the hologram projector. He poked the stud at the base of the machine. The image that sprang into being above the projector was one the Race's probe had sent back from Tosev 3 eight hundred local years earlier.

A Big Ugly warrior sat mounted on a beast. He wore leather boots, rusty chainmail, and a dented iron helmet; a thin coat woven from plant fibers and dyed blue with plant juices shielded his armor from the heat of the star the Race called Tosev. To Atvar, to any male of the Race, Tosev 3 was on the chilly side, but not to the natives.

A long, iron-pointed spear stood up from a boss on the contraption the warrior used to stay atop his animal. He carried a shield painted with a cross. On his belt hung a long, straight sword and a couple of knives.

All you could see of the Tosevite himself were his face and one hand. They were plenty to show he was almost as fuzzy as the beast he rode. Thick, wiry yellow fur covered his jaws and the area around his mouth; he had another stripe above each of his flat, immobile eyes. A thinner layer of hair grew on the back of the visible hand.

Atvar touched his own smooth, scaly skin. Just looking at all that fur made him wonder why the Big Uglies didn't itch all the time. Leaving one eye turret aimed at the Tosevite warrior, he swung the other in the direction of Kirel, shiplord of the *127th Emperor Hetto*. "This is the foe we thought we were opposing," he said bitterly.

"Truth, Exalted Fleetlord," Kirel said. His body paint was almost as colorful and complex as Atvar's. Since he commanded

1

the bannership of the conquest fleet, only the fleetlord out-ranked him.

Atvar stabbed at the projector control with his left index claw. The Big Ugly warrior vanished. In his place appeared a perfect three-dimensional image of the nuclear explosion that had destroyed the Tosevite city of Rome: Atvar recognized the background terrain. But it could as easily have been the bomb that vaporized Chicago or Breslau or Miami or the spearhead of the Race's assault force south of Moscow.

"As opposed to the foe we thought we faced, this is what we are actually dealing with," Atvar said.

"Truth," Kirel repeated, and, as mournful commentary, added an emphatic cough.

Atvar let out a long, hissing sigh. Stability and predictability were two of the pillars on which the Race and its Empire had flourished for a hundred thousand years and expanded to cover three solar systems. On Tosev 3, nothing seemed predictable, nothing seemed stable. No wonder the Race was having such troubles here. The Big Uglies did not play by any of the rules its savants thought they knew.

With another hiss, the fleetlord poked at the control stud once more. Now the threatening cloud from the nuclear blast vanished. In a way, the image that replaced it was even more menacing. It was a satellite photograph of a base the Race had established in the region of the SSSR known to the locals as Siberia, a place whose frigid climate even the Big Uglies found appalling.

"The mutineers still persist in their rebellion against duly constituted authority," Atvar said heavily. "Worse, the commandants of the two nearest bases have urged against committing their males to suppress the rebels, for fear they would go over to them instead."

"This is truly alarming," Kirel said with another emphatic cough. "If we choose males from a distant air base to bomb the mutineers out of existence, then, will it truly solve the problem?"

"I don't know," Atvar said. "But what I really don't know, by the Emperor"—he cast down his eyes for a moment at the mention of his sovereign—"is how the mutiny could have happened in the first place. Subordination and integration into the greater scheme of the Race as a whole are drilled into our males from hatchlinghood. How could they have overthrown them?"

Now Kirel sighed. "Fighting on this world corrodes males' moral fiber as badly as its ocean water corrodes equipment. We are not fighting the war that was planned before we set out from Home, and that by itself is plenty to disorient a good many males."

"This is also truth," Atvar admitted. "The leader of the mutineers—a lowly landcruiser driver, if you can image such a thing—is shown to have lost at least three different sets of crewmales: two, including those with whom he served at this base, to Tosevite action, and the third grouping arrested and disciplined as ginger tasters."

"By his wild pronouncements, this Ussmak sounds like a ginger taster himself," Kirel said.

"Threatening to call in the Soviets to his aid if we attack him, you mean?" Atvar said. "We ought to take him up on that; if he thinks they would help him out of sheer benevolence, the Tosevite herb truly has addled his wits. If it weren't for the equipment he could pass on to the SSSR, I would say we should welcome him to go over to that set of Big Uglies."

"Given the situation as it actually is, Exalted Fleetlord, what course shall we pursue?" Kirel's interrogative cough sounded vaguely accusing—or maybe Atvar's conscience was twisting his hearing diaphragms.

"I don't know yet," the fleetlord said unhappily. When in doubt, his first instinct—typical for a male—was to do nothing. Letting the situation come nearer to hatching so you could understand it more fully worked well on Home, and also on Rabotev 2 and Halless 1, the other inhabited worlds the Race controlled.

But waiting, against the Tosevites, often proved even worse than proceeding on incomplete knowledge. The Big Uglies *did things*. They didn't fret about long-term consequences. Take atomic weapons—those helped them in the short run. If they devastated Tosev 3 in the process—well, so what?

Atvar couldn't leave it at *so what*. The colonization fleet was on the way from Home. He couldn't very well present it with a world he'd rendered uninhabitable in the process of overcoming the Big Uglies. Yet he couldn't fail to respond, either, and so found himself in the unpleasant position of reacting to what the Tosevites did instead of making them react to him.

The mutineers had no nuclear weapons, and weren't Big Uglies. He could have afforded to wait them out . . . if they hadn't threatened to yield their base to the SSSR. With the Tosevites involved, you couldn't just sit and watch. The Big Uglies were never content to let things simmer. They threw them in a microwave oven and brought them to a boil as fast as they could.

When Atvar didn't say anything more, Kirel tried to prod him:

"Exalted Fleetlord, you can't be contemplating genuine negotiations with these rebellious—and revolting—males? Their demands are impossible: not just amnesty and transfer to a warmer climate—those would be bad enough by themselves—but also ending the struggle against the Tosevites so no more males die 'uselessly,' to use their word."

"No, we cannot allow mutineers to dictate terms to us," Atvar agreed. "That would be intolerable." His mouth fell open in a bitter laugh. "Then again, by all reasonable standards, the situation over vast stretches of Tosev 3 is intolerable, and our forces seem to lack the ability to improve it to any substantial extent. What does this suggest to you, Shiplord?"

One possible answer was, *a new fleetlord.* The assembled shiplords of the conquest fleet had tried to remove Atvar once, after the SSSR detonated the first Tosevite fission bomb, and had narrowly failed. If they tried again, Kirel was the logical male to succeed Atvar. The fleetlord waited for his subordinate's reply, not so much for what he said as for how he said it.

Slowly, Kirel answered, "Were the Tosevites factions of the Race opposed to the general will—not that the Race would generate such vicious factions, of course, but speaking for the sake of the hypothesis—their strength, unlike that of the mutineers, might come close to making negotiations with them mandatory."

Atvar contemplated that. Kirel was, generally speaking, a conservative male, and had couched his suggestion conservatively by equating the Big Uglies with analogous groupings within the Race, an equation that in itself made Atvar's scales itch. But the suggestion, however couched, was more radical than any Straha, the shiplord who'd led the effort to oust Atvar, had ever put forward before deserting and fleeing to the Big Uglies.

"Shiplord," Atvar demanded sharply, "are you making the same proposal as the mutineers: that we discuss with the Tosevites ways of ending our campaign short of complete conquest?"

"Exalted Fleetlord, did you yourself not say our males seem incapable of effecting a complete conquest of Tosev 3?" Kirel answered, still with perfect subordination but not abandoning his own ideas, either. "If that be so, should we not either destroy the planet to make sure the Tosevites can never threaten us, or else—" He stopped; unlike Straha, he had a sense of when he was going too far for Atvar to tolerate.

"No," the fleetlord said, "I refuse to concede that the commands of the Emperor cannot be carried out in full. We shall defend ourselves in the northern portion of the planet until its dreadful winter

weather improves, then resume the offensive against the Big
Uglies. Tosev 3 *shall* be ours."

Kirel crouched into the Race's pose of obedience. "It shall be
done, Exalted Fleetlord."

Again, the response was perfectly subordinate. Kirel did not ask
how it should be done. The Race had brought only so much
matériel from Home. It was of far higher quality than anything the
Tosevites used, but there was only a limited quantity of it. Try as
they would, the Race's pilots and missile batteries and artillery
had not managed to knock out the Big Uglies' manufacturing
capacity. The armaments they produced, though better than those
they'd had when the Race first landed on Tosev 3, remained infe-
rior . . . but they kept on making them.

Some munitions could be produced in factories captured from
the Tosevites, and the Race's starships had their own manufacturing capacity that would have been significant . . . in a smaller
war. When added to what the logistics vessels had brought from
Home, that still left the hope of adequacy for the coming campaign . . . and the Big Uglies were also in distress, no doubt about
that. Victory might yet come.

Or, of course . . . but Atvar did not care to think about that.

Even under a flag of truce, Mordechai Anielewicz felt nervous
about approaching the German encampment. After starving in the
Warsaw ghetto, after leading the Jewish fighters of Warsaw
who'd risen against the Nazis and helped the Lizards drive them
out of the city, he was under no illusions about what Hitler's
forces wanted for his people: they wanted them to vanish from the
face of the earth.

But the Lizards wanted to enslave everybody, Jews and *goyim*
alike. The Jews hadn't fully realized that when they rose against
the Nazis. Had they, it wouldn't have mattered much. Measured
against extermination, enslavement looked good.

The Germans were still fighting the Lizards, and fighting hard.
No one denied their military prowess, or their technical skill.
From afar, Anielewicz had seen the nuclear bomb they'd touched
off east of Breslau. Had he seen it close up, he wouldn't be coming
here to dicker with the Nazis.

"Halt!" The voice might have come out of thin air. Mordechai
halted. After a moment, a German wearing a white camouflage
smock and a whitewashed helmet appeared as if by magic from
behind a tree. Just looking at him made Anielewicz, who had Red
Army *valenki* on his feet and was dressed in Polish Army trousers,

a *Wehrmacht* tunic, a Red Army fur hat, and a sheepskin jacket of civilian origin, feel like a refugee from a rummage sale. He needed a shave, too, which added to his air of seediness. The German's lip curled. "You are the Jew we were told to expect?"

"No, I'm St. Nicholas, here late for Christmas." Anielewicz, who had been an engineering student before the war, had learned fluent standard German. He spoke Yiddish now, to annoy the sentry.

The fellow just grunted. Maybe he didn't think the joke was funny. Maybe he hadn't got it. He gestured with his Mauser. "You will come with me. I will take you to the colonel."

That was what Anielewicz was there for, but he didn't like the way the sentry said it even so. The German spoke as if the universe permitted no other possible outcome. Maybe it didn't. Mordechai followed him through the cold and silent woods.

"Your colonel must be a good officer," he said—softly, because the brooding presence of the woods weighed on him. "This regiment has come a long way east since the bomb went off near Breslau." That was part of the reason he needed to talk with the local commandant, though he wasn't going to explain his reasons to a private who probably thought he was nothing but a damn kike anyway.

Stolid as an old cow, the sentry answered, *"Ja,"* and then shut up again. They walked past a whitewashed Panther tank in a clearing. A couple of crewmen were guddling about in the Panther's engine compartment. Looking at them, hearing one grumble when the exposed skin between glove and sleeve stuck to cold metal, you might have thought war no different from any other mechanical trade. Of course, the Germans had industrialized murder, too.

They walked by more tanks, most of them also being worked on. These were bigger, tougher machines than the ones the Nazis had used to conquer Poland four and a half years before. The Nazis had learned a lot since then. Their panzers still didn't come close to being an even match for the ones the Lizards used, though.

A couple of men were cooking a little pot of stew over an aluminum field stove set on a couple of rocks. The stew had some kind of meat in it—rabbit, maybe, or squirrel, or even dog. Whatever it was, it smelled delicious.

"Sir, the Jewish partisan is here," the sentry said, absolutely nothing in his voice. That was better than the scorn that might have been there, but not much.

Both men squatting by the field stove looked up. The older one got to his feet. He was obviously the colonel, though he wore a plain service cap and an enlisted man's uniform. He was in his forties, pinch-faced and clever-looking despite skin weathered from a lifetime spent in the sun and the rain and, as now, the snow.

"You!" Anielewicz's mouth fell open in surprise. "Jäger!" He hadn't seen this German in more than a year, and then only for an evening, but he wouldn't forget him.

"Yes, I'm Heinrich Jäger. You know me?" The panzer officer's gray eyes narrowed, deepening the network of wrinkles around their outer corners. Then they went wide. "That voice . . . You called yourself Mordechai, didn't you? You were clean-shaven then." He rubbed his own chin. Gray mixed with the brownish stubble that grew there.

"You two know each other?" That was the moon-faced younger man who'd been waiting for the stew to finish. He sounded disbelieving.

"You might say so, Gunther," Jäger answered with a dry chuckle. "Last time I was traveling through Poland, this fellow decided to let me live." Those watchful eyes flicked to Mordechai. "I wonder how much he regrets it now."

The comment cut to the quick. Jäger had been carrying explosive metal stolen from the Lizards. Anielewicz had let him travel on to Germany with half of it, diverting the other half to the United States. Now both nations were building nuclear weapons. Mordechai was glad the U.S.A. had them. His delight that the Third *Reich* had them was considerably more restrained.

Gunther stared. "*He* let *you* live? This ragged partisan?" Anielewicz might as well not have been there.

"He did." Jäger studied Mordechai again. "I'd expected more from you than a role like this. You should be commanding a region, maybe the whole area."

Of all the things Anielewicz hadn't expected, failing to live up to a Nazi's expectations of him ranked high on the list. His shrug was embarrassed. "I was, for a while. But then not everything worked out the way I'd hoped it would. These things happen."

"The Lizards figured out you were playing little games behind their backs, did they?" Jäger asked. Back when they'd met in Hrubieszów, Anielewicz had figured he was no one's fool. He wasn't saying anything now to make the Jew change his mind. Before the silence got awkward, he waved a hand. "Never mind. It isn't my business, and the less I know of what isn't my business, the better for everyone. What do you want with us here and now?"

"You're advancing on Lodz," Mordechai said.

As far as he was concerned, that should have been an answer sufficient in and of itself. It wasn't. Frowning, Jäger said, "Damn right we are. We don't get the chance to advance against the Lizards nearly often enough. Most of the time, they're advancing on us."

Anielewicz sighed quietly. He might have known the German wouldn't understand what he was talking about. He approached it by easy stages: "You've gotten good cooperation from the partisans here in western Poland, haven't you, Colonel?" Jäger had been a major the last time Mordechai saw him. Even if he hadn't come up in the world, the German had.

"Well, yes, so we have," Jäger answered. "Why shouldn't we? Partisans are human beings, too."

"A lot of partisans are Jews," Mordechai said. The easy approach wasn't going to work. Bluntly, then: "There are still a lot of Jews in Lodz, too, in the ghetto you Nazis set up so you could starve us to death and work us to death and generally slaughter us. If the *Wehrmacht* goes into Lodz, the SS follows twenty minutes later. The second we see an SS man, we all go over to the Lizards again. We don't want them conquering you, but we want you conquering us even less."

"Colonel, why don't I take this mangy Jew and send him on his way with a good kick in the ass?" the younger man— Gunther—said.

"Corporal Grillparzer, when I want your suggestions, be sure I shall ask for them," Jäger said in a voice colder than the snow all around. When he turned back toward Mordechai, his face was troubled. He knew about some of the things the Germans had done to the Jews who'd fallen into their hands, knew and did not approve. That made him an unusual *Wehrmacht* man, and made Anielewicz glad he was the German on the other side of the parley. Still, he had to look out for the affairs of his own side: "You ask us to throw away a move that would bring us advantages. Such a thing is hard to justify."

"What I'm telling you is that you would lose as much as you gain," Mordechai answered. "You get intelligence from us about what the Lizards are doing. With Nazis in Lodz, the Lizards would get intelligence from us about you. We got to know you too well. We know what you did to us. We do sabotage back of the Lizards' lines, too. Instead, we'd be raiding and sniping at you."

"Kikes," Gunther Grillparzer muttered under his breath. "Shit, all we gotta do is turn the Poles loose on 'em, and that takes care of that."

Jäger started to bawl out his corporal, but Anielewicz held up a hand. "It's not that simple any more. Back when the war just started, we didn't have any guns and we weren't much good at using them, anyhow. It's not like that now. We've got more guns than the Poles do, and we've stopped being shy about shooting when somebody shoots at us. We can hurt you."

"There's some truth in this—I've seen as much," Jäger said. "But I think we can take Lodz, and it would make immediate military sense for us to do just that. The place is a Lizard forward base, after all. How am I supposed to justify bypassing it?"

"What's that expression the English have? Penny wise and pound foolish? That's what you'd be if you started your games with the Jews again," Mordechai answered. "You need us working with you, not against you. Didn't you take enough of a propaganda beating when the whole world found out what you were doing here in Poland?"

"Less than you'd think," Jäger said, the ice in his voice now aimed at Anielewicz. "A lot of the people who heard about it didn't believe it."

Anielewicz bit his lip. He knew how true that was. "Do you suppose they didn't believe it because they didn't trust the Lizards to tell the truth or because they didn't think human beings could be so vile?"

That made Gunther Grillparzer mutter again, and made the sentry who'd brought Mordechai into camp shift his *Gewehr* 98 so the muzzle more nearly pointed toward the Jew. Heinrich Jäger sighed. "Probably both," he said, and Mordechai respected his honesty. "But the whys here don't much matter. The whats do. If we bypass Lodz north and south, say, and the Lizards slice up into one of our columns from out of the city, the *Führer* would not be very happy with that." He rolled his eyes to give some idea of how much understatement he was using.

The only thing Adolf Hitler could do to make Anielewicz happy would be to drop dead, and to do that properly he would have had to manage it before 1939. Nevertheless, he understood what Jäger was saying. "If you bypass Lodz to north and south, Colonel, I'll make sure the Lizards can't mount a serious attack on you from the city."

"You'll make sure?" Jäger said. "You can still do so much?"

"I think so," Anielewicz answered. *I hope so.* "Colonel, I'm not going to talk about you owing me one." Of course, by saying he wasn't going to talk about it, he'd just talked about it. "I will say, though, that I delivered then and I think I can deliver now. Can you?"

"I don't know," the German answered. He looked down at the pot of stew, dug out a mess kit and spoon, and ladled some into it. Instead of eating, he passed the little aluminum tub to Mordechai. "Your people fed me then. I can feed you now." After a moment, he added, "The meat is partridge. We bagged a couple this morning."

Anielewicz hesitated, then dug in. Meat, kasha or maybe barley, carrots, onions—it stuck to the ribs. When he was done, he gave the mess kit and spoon back to Jäger, who cleaned them in the snow and then took his own share.

Between bites, the German said, "I'll pass on what you've told me. I don't promise anything will come of it, but I'll do my best. I tell you this, Mordechai: if we do skirt Lodz, you'd better come through on your promise. Show that dealing with you people has a good side to it, show that you deliver, and the people above me are more likely to want to try to do it again."

"I understand that," Anielewicz answered. "The same goes back at you, I might add: if you break faith with us after a deal, you won't like the partisans who show up in your backyard."

"And I understand that," Jäger said. "Whether my superiors will—" He shrugged. "I told you, I'll do what I can. My word, at least, is good." He eyed Anielewicz, as if daring him to deny it. Anielewicz couldn't, so he nodded. The German let out a long, heavy sigh, then went on, "In the end, whether we go into Lodz or around it won't matter, anyhow. If we conquer the territory around the city, it will fall to us, too, sooner or later. What happens then?"

He wasn't wrong. That made it worse, not better. Anielewicz gave him credit: he sounded genuinely worried. Gunther Grillparzer, on the other hand, looked to be just this side of laughing out loud. Let a bunch of Nazi soldiers like him loose in Lodz and the results wouldn't be pretty.

"What happens then?" Mordechai sighed, too. "I just don't know."

Ussmak sat in the base commandant's office—*his* office now, even if he still wore the body paint of a landcruiser driver. He'd killed Hisslef, who had led the Race's garrison at this base in the region of the SSSR known as Siberia. Ussmak wondered if *Siberia* was the Russki word for *deep freeze*. He couldn't tell much difference between the one and the other.

Along with Hisslef, a lot of his chief subordinates were dead, too, hunted down in the frenzy that had gripped the rest of the males after Ussmak fired the first shot. Ginger had had a lot to do with both the shooting and the frenzy that followed it. If Hisslef had just had the sense to let the males gathered in the communal chamber yell themselves out complaining about the war, about Tosev 3, and about this miserable base in particular, he probably still would have been alive. But no, he'd come storming in, intent on stamping this out no matter what ... and now his corpse lay stiff and cold—in Siberian winter, very stiff and very cold—outside the barracks, waiting for the weather to warm up enough for a cremation.

"And Hisslef was legitimate commandant, and see what happened to him," Ussmak muttered. "What will end up happening to *me*?" He had no millennia of authority to make his orders obeyed almost as if by reflex. Either he had to be obviously right, or else he had to make the males in the base obey him out of fear of what would happen if they didn't.

His mouth fell open in a bitter laugh. "I might as well be a Big Ugly ruling a not-empire," he said to the walls. They had to rule by fear; they had no tradition to give them legitimate authority. Now he sympathized with them. He understood in his gut how hard that was.

He opened a drawer in what had been Hisslef's desk, pulled out a vial of powdered ginger. That was *his*, by the Emperor (the Emperor against whose officers he'd mutinied, though he tried not to think about that). He yanked off the plastic stopper, poured some of the powder into the palm of his hand, and flicked out his long forked tongue again and again, till the herb was gone.

Exhilaration came quickly, as it always did. In moments after tasting the ginger, Ussmak felt strong, fast, clever, invincible. In the top part of his mind, he knew those feelings, save perhaps for heightened reflexes, were an illusion. When he'd driven the landcruiser into combat, he'd held off on tasting till he got out again: if you felt invincible when you really weren't, you'd take chances that were liable to get you killed. He'd seen that happen to other males more times than he cared to recall.

Now, though— "Now I taste all I can, because I don't want to think about what's going to happen next," he said. If the fleetlord wanted to blast this base from the air, Ussmak and his fellow mutineers had no antiaircraft missiles to stop them. He couldn't surrender to the authorities; he'd put himself beyond the pale when he shot Hisslef, as his followers had with the killings that followed.

He couldn't hold out indefinitely here, either. The base would run short of both food and hydrogen for fuel—and for heat!—before long. No supplies were coming in. He hadn't worried about such things when he raised his personal weapon against Hisslef. He'd just worried about making Hisslef shut up.

"That's the ginger's fault," he said querulously—even if his brain was buzzing with it while he complained. "It makes me as shortsighted as a Big Ugly."

He'd threatened to yield the base and everything in it to the Big Uglies of the SSSR. If it came down to that, he didn't know whether he could make himself do it. The Russkis made all sorts of glowing promises, but how many would they keep once they had their claws on him? He'd done too much fighting against the Big Uglies to feel easy about trusting them.

Of course, if he didn't yield the base to the Russkis, they were liable to come take it away from him. They minded cold much less than the Race did. Fear of Soviet raiders had been constant before the mutiny. It was worse now.

"No one wants to do anything hard now," Ussmak muttered. Going out into the bitter cold to make sure the Russkis didn't get close enough to mortar the barracks wasn't duty anyone found pleasant, but if the males didn't undertake it, they'd end up dead. A lot of them didn't seem to care. Hisslef had got them out there, but he'd enjoyed legitimate authority. Ussmak didn't, and felt the lack.

He flicked on the radio that sat on his desk, worked the search buttons to go from station to station. Some of the broadcasts the receivers picked up came from the Race; others, mushy with static, brought him the incomprehensible words of the Big Uglies. He didn't really want to hear either group, feeling dreadfully isolated from both.

Then, to his surprise, he found what had to be a Tosevite transmission, but one where the broadcaster not only spoke his language but was plainly a male of the Race: no Tosevite was free of accent either annoying or amusing. This fellow was not just one of his own but, by the way he spoke, a male of considerable status:

"—tell you again, this war is being conducted by idiots with fancy body paint. They anticipated none of the difficulties the Race would confront in trying to conquer Tosev 3, and, when they found those difficulties, what did they do about them? Not much, by the Emperor! No, not Atvar and his clique of cloaca-licking fools. They just pressed on as if the Big Uglies were the sword-swinging savages we'd presumed them to be when we set out from Home. And how many good, brave, and obedient males have died on account of their stupidity? Think on it, you who still live."

"Truth!" Ussmak exclaimed. Whoever this male was, he understood what was what. He had a grasp of the big picture, too. Ussmak had heard captive males broadcasting before. Most of them just sounded pathetic, repeating the phrases the Tosevites ordered them to say. It made for bad, unconvincing propaganda. This fellow, though, sounded as if he'd prepared his own material and was enjoying every insult he hurled at the fleetlord.

Ussmak wished he'd caught the beginning of this transmission, so he could have learned the broadcaster's name and rank. The fellow went on, "Here and there on Tosev 3, males are getting the idea that continuing this futile, bloody conflict is a dreadful mistake. Many have thrown down their weapons and yielded to the Tosevite empire or not-empire controlling the area in which they were assigned. Most Tosevite empires and not-empires treat prisoners well. I, Straha, shiplord of the *206th Emperor Yower*, can personally attest to this. Atvar the brain-addled fool was going to destroy me for daring to oppose his senseless policies, but I escaped to the United States, and have never regretted it even for an instant."

Straha! Ussmak swung both eye turrets to focus sharply on the radio. Straha had been the third-ranking male in the conquest fleet. Ussmak knew he'd fled to the Big Uglies, but hadn't known much about why: he hadn't caught any of the shiplord's earlier broadcasts. He clawed at a sheet of paper, slicing it into strips. Straha had told the truth and, instead of being rewarded as was proper, had suffered for it.

The refugee shiplord went on, "Nor is yielding to the Tosevites your only choice. I have heard reports of brave males in Siberia who, tired at last of endless orders to do the impossible, struck a blow for freedom against their own misguided commanders, and who now rule their base independent of foolish plans formulated by males who float in comfort high above Tosev 3 and who think that makes them wise. You who hear my voice, ignore orders whose senselessness you can see with one eye turret and with the nictitating membrane over that eye. Remonstrate with your officers. If all else fails, imitate the brave Siberians and reclaim liberty for yourselves. I, Straha, have spoken."

Static replaced the shiplord's voice. Ussmak felt stronger, more alive, than even ginger could make him. However much he enjoyed that intoxication, he knew it was artificial. What Straha had said, though, was real, every word of it. Males on the ground had been treated shabbily, had been sacrificed for no good purpose—for no purpose at all, as far as Ussmak could tell.

Straha had also told him something he badly needed to know. When he'd spoken with the males up in orbit, he'd threatened to surrender the base to the local Big Uglies if the Race didn't meet his demands or attacked him. He'd hesitated about doing anything more than threatening, since he didn't know how the Soviets would treat males they captured. But Straha had set his mind at ease. He didn't know much about Tosevite geography, but he did know the United States and the SSSR were two of the biggest, strongest not-empires on Tosev 3.

If the United States treated its captured males well, no doubt the SSSR would do the same. Ussmak hissed in satisfaction. "We now have a new weapon against you," he said, and turned both eye turrets up toward the starships still in orbit around Tosev 3.

His mouth dropped open. Those males up there certainly didn't know much about the Big Uglies.

Sam Yeager looked at the rocket motor painfully assembled from parts made in small-town machine shops all over Arkansas and southern Missouri. It looked—well, *crude* was the politest word that came to mind. He sighed. "Once you see what the Lizards can do, anything people turn out is small potatoes alongside it. No offense, sir," he added hastily.

"None taken," Robert Goddard answered. "As a matter of fact, I agree with you. We do the best we can, that's all." His gray, worn face said he was doing more than that: he was busy working himself to death. Yeager worried about him.

He walked around the motor. If you set it alongside the pieces of the one from the Lizard shuttlecraft that had brought Straha down to exile, it was a kid's toy. He took off his service cap, scratched at his blond hair. "You think it'll fly, sir?"

"The only way to find out is to light it up and see what happens," Goddard answered. "If we're lucky, we'll get to test-fire it on the ground before we wrap sheet metal around it and stick some explosives on top. The trouble is, test-firing a rocket motor isn't what you'd call inconspicuous, and we'd probably have a visit from the Lizards in short order."

"It's a straight scaledown from the motor in the Lizard shuttlecraft," Yeager said. "Vesstil thinks that should be a pretty good guarantee it'll work the right way."

"Vesstil knows more about flying rockets than anyone human," Goddard said with a weary smile. "Seeing as he flew Straha down from his starship when he defected, that goes without saying. But Vesstil doesn't know beans about engineering, at least the cut-and-try kind. Everything else changes when you scale up or down, and you have to try the new model to see what the devil you've got." He chuckled wryly. "And it's not *quite* a straight scaledown anyhow, Sergeant: we've had to adapt the design to what we like to do and what we're able to do."

"Well, yes, sir." Sam felt his ears heat with embarrassment. Since his skin was very fair, he feared Goddard could watch him flush. "Hell of a thing for me to even think of arguing with you." Goddard had more experience with rockets than anybody who wasn't a Lizard or a German, and he was gaining on the Germans. Yeager went on, "If I hadn't read the pulps before the war, I wouldn't be here working with you now."

"You've taken advantage of what you read," Goddard answered. "If you hadn't done that, you wouldn't be of any use to me."

"You spend as much time bouncing around as I've done, sir, and you know that if you see a chance, you'd better grab for it with both hands, 'cause odds are you'll never see it again." Yeager scratched his head once more. He'd spent his whole adult life, up till the Lizards came, playing minor-league ball. A broken ankle ten years before had effectively ended whatever chance he'd had of making the majors, but he'd hung in there anyhow. And on the endless bus and train trips from one small or medium-sized town to the next, he'd killed time with *Astounding* and any other science-fiction magazines he'd found on the newsstands. His teammates had laughed at him for reading about bug-eyed monsters from another planet. Now—

Now Robert Goddard said, "I'm glad you grabbed this one, Sergeant. I don't think I could have gotten nearly so much information out of Vesstil with a different interpreter. It's not just that you know his language; you have a real feel for what he's trying to get across."

"Thanks," Sam said, feeling about ten feet tall. "Soon as I got the chance to have anything to do with the Lizards besides shooting at 'em, I knew that's what I wanted. They're—fascinating, you know what I mean?"

Goddard shook his head. "What they know, the experience they have—that's fascinating. But them—" He laughed self-consciously. "A good thing Vesstil's not around right now. He'd be insulted if he knew he gave me the creeps."

"He probably wouldn't, sir," Yeager said. "The Lizards mostly don't make any bones about us giving them the creeps." He paused. "Hmm, come to think of it, he might be insulted at that, sort of like if a Ku-Kluxer found out some Negroes looked down their noses at white men."

"As if we don't have the right to think Lizards are creepy, you mean."

"That's right." Sam nodded. "But snakes and things like that, they never bothered me, not even when I was a kid. And the Lizards, every time I'm with one of them, I'm liable to learn something new: not just new for me, I mean, but something nobody, no human being, ever knew before. That's pretty special. In a way, it's even more special than Jonathan." Now he laughed the nervous laugh Goddard had used before. "Don't let Barbara found out I said that."

"You have my word," the rocket scientist said solemnly. "But I do understand what you mean. Your son is an unknown to you, but he's not the first baby that ever was. Really discovering something for the first time is a thrill almost as addictive as—as ginger, shall we say?"

"As long as we don't let the Lizards hear us say it, sure," Yeager answered. "They sure do like that stuff, don't they?" He hesitated again, then went on, "Sir, I'm mighty glad you decided to move operations back here to Hot Springs. Gives me the chance to be with my family, lets me help Barbara out every now and then. I mean, we haven't even been married a year yet, and—"

"I'm glad it's worked out well for you, Sergeant," Goddard said, "but that's not the reason I came down here from Couch—"

"Oh, I know it's not, sir," Sam said hastily.

As if he hadn't spoken, Goddard went on, "Hot Springs is a decent-sized city, with at least a little light manufacturing. We're not far from Little Rock, which has more. And we have all the Lizards at the Army and Navy General Hospital here, upon whom we can draw for expertise. That has proved much more convenient than transferring the Lizards up to southern Missouri one by one."

"Like I said, it's great by me," Yeager told him. "And we've moved an awful lot of pieces of the Lizard shuttlecraft down here so we can study 'em better."

"I worried about that," Goddard said. "The Lizards always knew about where Vesstil brought Straha down. We were lucky we concealed and stripped the shuttlecraft as fast as we did, because they tried their hardest to destroy it. They easily could have sent in troops by air to make sure they'd done the job, and we'd have had the devil's own time stopping them."

"They don't go poking their snouts into everything the way they did when they first landed here," Sam said. "I guess that's because we've hurt 'em a few times when they tried it."

"A good thing, too, or I fear we'd have lost the war by now." Goddard rose and stretched, though from his grimace that hurt more than it made him feel good. "Another incidental reason for coming to Hot Springs is the springs. I'm going to my room to draw myself a hot bath. I'd gotten used to doing without such things, and almost forgot how wonderful they are."

"Yes, sir," Yeager said enthusiastically. The fourth-floor room in the Army and Navy General Hospital he shared with Barbara—and now Jonathan—didn't have a tub of its own; washing facilities were down at the end of the hall. That didn't bother him. For one thing, Goddard was a VIP, while he was just an enlisted man doing what he could for the war effort. For another, the plumbing on the Nebraska farm where he'd grown up had consisted of a well and a two-holer out back of the house. He didn't take running water, cold or especially hot, for granted.

Walking up to his room was a lot more comfortable in winter than it had been in summertime, when you didn't need to soak in the local springs to get hot and wet. As he headed down the hall toward room 429, he heard Jonathan kicking up a ruckus in there. He sighed and hurried a little faster. Barbara would be feeling harassed. So would the Lizard POWs who also lived on this floor.

When he opened the door, Barbara sent him a look that went from hunted to relieved when she saw who he was. She thrust the baby at him. "Would you try holding him, please?" she said. "No matter what I do, he doesn't want to keep quiet."

"Okay, hon," he said. "Let's see if there's a burp hiding in there." He got Jonathan up on his shoulder and started thumping the kid's back. He did it hard enough to make it sound as if he were working out on the drums. Barbara, who had a gentler touch, frowned at that the way she usually did, but he got results with it. As now—Jonathan gave forth with an almost baritone belch and a fair volume of half-digested milk. Then he blinked and looked much happier with himself.

"Oh, good!" Barbara exclaimed when the burp came out. She dabbed at Sam's uniform tunic with a diaper. "There. I got most of it, but I'm afraid you're going to smell like sour milk for a while."

"World won't end," Yeager said. "This isn't one of your big

spit and polish places." The smell of sour milk didn't bother him any more. It was in the room most of the time, along with the reek that came with the diaper pail even when it was closed—that reminded him of the barnyard on his parents' farm, not that he ever said so to Barbara. He held his little son out at arm's length. "There you go, kiddo. You had that hiding in there where Mommy couldn't find it, didn't you?"

Barbara reached for the baby. "I'll take him back now, if you want."

"It's okay," Sam said. "I don't get to hold him all that much, and you look like you could use a breather."

"Well, now that you mention it, yes." Barbara slumped into the only chair in the room. She wasn't the pert girl Sam had got to know; she looked beat, as she did most of the time. If you didn't look beat most of the time with a new kid around, either something was wrong with you or you had servants to look beat for you. There were dark circles under her green eyes; her blond hair—several shades darker than Sam's—hung limp, as if it were tired, too. She let out a weary sigh. "What I wouldn't give for a cigarette and especially a cup of coffee."

"Oh, Lord—coffee," Yeager said wistfully. "The worst cup of joe I ever drank in the greasiest greasy spoon in the lousiest little town I ever went through—and I went through a lot of 'em . . . Jeez, it'd go good right now."

"If we had any coffee to ration, we ought to share it between soldiers in the front lines and parents with babies less than a year old. No one else could possibly need it so badly," Barbara said. Frazzled as she was, she still spoke with a precision Sam admired: she'd done graduate work at Berkeley in medieval English literature before the war. The kind of English you heard in ballparks didn't measure up alongside that.

Jonathan wiggled and twisted and started to cry. He was beginning to make different kinds of racket to show he had different things in mind. Sam recognized this one. "He's hungry, hon."

"By the schedule, it's not time to feed him yet," Barbara answered. "But do you know what? As far as I'm concerned, the schedule can go to the devil. I can't stand listening to him yell until the clock says it's okay for him to eat. If nursing makes him happy enough to keep still for a while, that suits me fine." She wriggled her right arm out of the sleeve of the dark blue wool dress she was wearing, tugged the dress down to bare that breast. "Here, give him to me."

Yeager did. The baby's mouth fastened onto her nipple. Jonathan sucked avidly. Yeager could hear him gulping down the milk. He'd felt funny at first, having to share Barbara's breasts with his son. But you couldn't bottle-feed these days—no formula, no easy way to keep things as clean as they needed to be. And after you got used to breast-feeding, it didn't seem like such a big thing any more, anyhow.

"I think he may be going to sleep," Barbara said. The radio newsman who'd announced Jimmy Doolittle's bomber raid over Tokyo hadn't sounded more excited about a victory. She went on, "He's going to want to nurse on the other side too, though. Help me out of that sleeve, would you, Sam? I can't get it down by myself, not while I'm holding him."

"Sure thing." He hurried over to her, stretched the sleeve out, and helped her get her arm back through past the elbow. After that, she managed on her own. The dress fell limply to her waist. A couple of minutes went by before she shifted Jonathan to her left breast.

"He'd better fall asleep pretty soon," Barbara said. "I'm cold."

"He looks as if he's going to," Sam answered. He draped a folded towel over her left shoulder, not so much to help warm her as to keep the baby from drooling or spitting up on her when she burped him.

One of her eyebrows rose. " 'As if he's going to'?" she echoed.

He knew what she meant. He wouldn't have said it that way when they first met; he'd made it through high school, then gone off to play ball. "Must be the company I keep," he replied with a smile, and then went on more seriously: "I like learning things from the people I'm around—from the Lizards, too, it's turned out. Is it any wonder I've picked things up from you?"

"Oh, in a way it's a wonder," Barbara said. "A lot of people seem to hate the idea of ever learning anything new. I'm glad you're not like that; it would make life boring." She glanced down at Jonathan. "Yes, he is falling asleep. Good."

Sure enough, before long her nipple slipped out of the baby's mouth. She held him a little longer, then gently raised him to her shoulder and patted his back. He burped without waking up, and didn't spit up, either. She slid him back down to the crook of her elbow, waited a few minutes more, and got up to put him in the wooden crib that took up a large part of the small room. Jonathan sighed as she laid him down. She stood there for a moment, afraid he would wake. But when his breathing steadied, she straightened and reached down to fix her dress.

Before she could, Sam stepped up behind her and cupped a

breast in each hand. She turned her head and smiled at him over her shoulder, but it wasn't a smile of invitation, even though they had started making love again a couple of weeks before.

"Do you mind too much if I just lie down for a while?" she said. "By myself, I mean. It's not that I don't love you, Sam—it's just that I'm so tired, I can't see straight."

"Okay, I understand that," he said, and let go. The soft, warm memory of her flesh remained printed on his palms. He kicked at the linoleum floor, once.

Barbara quickly pulled her dress up to where it belonged, then turned around and put her hands on his shoulders. "Thank you," she said. "I know this hasn't been easy for you, either."

"Takes some getting used to, that's all," he said. "Being in the middle of the war when we got married didn't help a whole lot, and then you were expecting right away—" As best they could tell, that had happened on their wedding night. He chuckled. "Of course, if it hadn't been for the war, we never would have met. What do they say about clouds and silver linings?"

Barbara hugged him. "I'm very happy with you, and with our baby, and with everything." She corrected herself, yawning: "With almost everything. I could do with a lot more sleep."

"I'm happy with just about everything, too," he said, his arms tightening around her back. As he'd said, if it hadn't been for the war, they wouldn't have met. If they had met, she wouldn't have looked at him; she'd been married to a nuclear physicist in Chicago. But Jens Larssen had been away from the Met Lab project, away for so long they'd both figured he was dead, and they'd become first friends, then lovers, and finally husband and wife. And then Barbara had got pregnant—and then they'd found out Jens was alive after all.

Sam squeezed Barbara one more time, then let her go and walked over to the side of the crib to look down at their sleeping son. He reached out a hand and ruffled Jonathan's fine, thin head of almost snow-white hair.

"That's sweet," Barbara said.

"He's a pretty good little guy," Yeager answered. *And if you hadn't been carrying him, odds are ten bucks against a wooden nickel you'd have dropped me and gone back to Larssen.* He smiled at the baby. *Kid, I owe you a big one for that. One of these days, I'll see if I can figure out how to pay you back.*

Barbara kissed him on the lips, a brief, friendly peck, and then walked over to the bed. "I *am* going to get some rest," she said.

"Okay." Sam headed for the door. "I guess I'll find me some

Lizards and chin with them for a while. Do me some good now, and maybe even after the war, too, if there ever is an 'after the war.' Whatever happens, people and Lizards are going to have to deal with each other from here on out. The more I know, the better off I'll be."

"I think you'll be just fine any which way," Barbara answered as she lay down. "Why don't you come back in an hour or so? If Jonathan's still asleep, who knows what might happen?"

"We'll find out." Yeager opened the door, then glanced back at his son. "Sleep tight, kiddo."

The man who wore earphones glanced over at Vyacheslav Molotov. "Comrade Foreign Commissar, we are getting new reports that the *Yashcheritsi* at the base east of Tomsk are showing interest in surrendering to us." When Molotov didn't answer, the technician made so bold as to add, "You remember, Comrade: the ones who mutinied against their superiors."

"I assure you, Comrade, I am aware of the situation and need no reminding," Molotov said in a voice colder than Moscow winter—colder than Siberian winter, too. The technician gulped and dipped his head to show he understood. You were lucky to get away with one slip around Molotov; you wouldn't get away with two. The foreign commissar went on, "Have they any definite terms this time?"

"*Da*, Comrade Foreign Commissar." The fellow at the wireless set looked down at the notes he'd scribbled. His pencil was barely as long as his thumb; everything was at a premium these days. "They want pledges not only of safe conduct but also of good treatment after going over to us."

"We can give them those," Molotov said at once. "I would think even the local military commander would have the wit to see as much for himself." The local military commander should also have had the wit to see that such pledges could be ignored the instant they became inconvenient.

On the other hand, it was probably just as well that the local military commander displayed no excessive initiative, but referred his questions back to Moscow and the Communist Party of the Soviet Union for answers. Commanders who usurped Party control in one area were only too likely to try to throw it off in others.

The wireless operator spoke groups of seemingly meaningless letters over the air. Molotov sincerely hoped they were meaningless to the Lizards. "What else do the mutineers want?" he asked.

"A pledge that under no circumstances will we return them to the Lizards, not even if an end to hostilities is agreed to between the peace-loving workers and peasants of the Soviet Union and the alien imperialist aggressors from whose camp they are trying to defect."

"Again, we can agree to this," Molotov said. It was another promise that could be broken at need, although Molotov did not see the need as being likely to arise. By the time peace between the USSR and the Lizards came along, he guessed the mutineers would be long forgotten. "What else?"

"They demand our promise to supply them with unlimited amounts of ginger, Comrade Foreign Commissar," the technician replied, again after checking his notes.

As usual, Molotov's pale, blunt-featured face revealed nothing of what was in his mind. In their own way, the Lizards were as degenerate as the capitalists and fascists against whom the glorious peasants and workers of the USSR had demonstrated new standards of virtue. Despite their high technology, though, the Lizards were in social terms far more primitive than capitalist societies. They were a bastion of the ancient economic system: they were masters, seeking human beings as slaves—so the dialecticians had decreed. Well, the upper classes of ancient Rome had been degenerates, too.

And, through degeneracy, the exploiters could be exploited. "We shall certainly make this concession," Molotov said. "If they want to drug themselves, we will gladly provide them with the means to do so." He waited for more code groups to go out over the air, then asked again, "What else?"

"They insist on driving the tanks away from the base themselves, on retaining their personal weapons, and on remaining together as a group," the wireless operator answered.

"They *are* gaining in sophistication," Molotov said. "This I shall have to consider." After a couple of minutes, he said, "They may drive their vehicles away from their base, but not to one of ours: the local commandant is to point out to them that trust between the two sides has not been fully established. He is to tell them they will be divided into several smaller groups for efficiency of interrogation. He may add that, if they are so divided, we shall let them retain their weapons, otherwise not."

"Let me make sure I have that, Comrade, before I transmit it," the technician said, and repeated back Molotov's statement. When the foreign commissar nodded, the man sent out the appropriate code groups.

"Anything more?" Molotov asked. The wireless operator shook

his head. Molotov got up and left the room somewhere deep under the Kremlin. The guard outside saluted. Molotov ignored him, as he had not bothered giving the man at the wireless a farewell. Superfluities of any sort were alien to his nature.

That being so, he did not chortle when he went upstairs. By his face, no one could have guessed whether the Lizard mutineers had agreed to give up or were instead demanding that he present himself for immediate liquidation. But inside—

Fools, he thought. *They are fools.* No matter that they'd become more sophisticated than before: the Lizards were still naive enough to make even Americans seem worldly by comparison. He'd seen that before, even among their chiefs. They had no notion of how to play the political games human diplomates took for granted. Their ruling assumption had plainly been that they would need no such talents, that their conquest of Earth would be quick and easy. Now that that hadn't happened, they were out of their depth.

Soldiers snapped to attention as he strode through the halls of the Kremlin. Civilian functionaries muted their conversations and gave him respectful nods. He did not acknowledge them. He barely noticed them. Had he failed to receive them, though, he would have made sharp note of that.

The devil's cousin or some other malicious wretch had dumped a stack of papers on his desk while he went down to bring himself up to date on the talks with the mutinous Lizards. He had high hopes for those talks. The Soviet Union already had a good many Lizard prisoners of war, and had learned some useful things from them. Once Lizards surrendered, they seemed to place humans in the positions of trust and authority their own superiors had formerly occupied for them.

And to lay hold of an entire base full of the equipment the alien aggressors from the stars manufactured! Unless Soviet intelligence was badly mistaken, that would be a coup neither the Germans nor the Americans could match. The British had a lot of Lizard gear, but the imperialist creatures had done their best to wreck it after their invasion of England failed.

The first letter on the pile was from the Social Activities Committee of *Kolkhoz* 118: so the return address stated, at any rate. But the collective farm not far outside of Moscow was where Igor Kurchatov and his team of nuclear physicists were laboring to fabricate an explosive-metal bomb. They'd made one, out of metal stolen from the Lizards. Isolating more of the metal for themselves was proving as hard as they'd warned Molotov it would—harder than he'd wanted to believe.

Sure enough, Kurchatov now wrote, "The latest experiment, Comrade Foreign Commissar, was a success less complete than we might have hoped." Molotov did not need his years of reading between the lines to infer that the experiment had failed. Kurchatov went on, "Certain technical aspects of the situation still present us with difficulties. Outside advice might prove useful."

Molotov grunted softly. When Kurchatov asked for outside advice, he didn't mean help from other Soviet physicists. Every reputable nuclear physicist in the USSR was already working with him. Molotov had put his own neck on the block by reminding Stalin of that; he shuddered to think of the risk he'd taken for the *rodina*, the motherland. What Kurchatov wanted was foreign expertise.

Humiliating, Molotov thought. The Soviet Union should not have been so backwards. He would never ask the Germans for help. Even if they gave it, he wouldn't trust what they gave. Stalin was just as well pleased that the Lizards in Poland separated the USSR from Hitler's madmen, and there Molotov completely agreed with his leader.

The Americans? Molotov gnawed at his mustache. Maybe, just maybe. They were making their own explosive-metal bombs, just as the Nazis were. And if he could tempt them with some of the prizes the Lizard base near Tomsk would yield . . .

He pulled out a pencil and a scrap of paper and began to draft a letter.

"Jesus, God, will you lookit this?" Mutt Daniels exclaimed as he led his platoon through the ruins of what had been Chicago's North Side. "And all from one bomb, too."

"Don't hardly seem possible, does it, Lieutenant?" Sergeant Herman Muldoon agreed. The kids they were leading didn't say anything. They just looked around with wide eyes and even wider mouths at their fair share of a few miles' worth of slagged wreckage.

"I been on God's green earth goin' on sixty years now," Mutt said, his Mississippi drawl flowing slow and thick as molasses in this miserable Northern winter. "I seen a whole lot o' things in my time. I fought in two wars now, and I done traveled all over the U.S. of A. But I ain't never seen nothin' like this here."

"You got that right," Muldoon said. He was Daniels' age, near enough, and he'd been around, too. The men alongside them in the ragged skirmish line didn't have that kind of experience, but they'd never seen anything like this, either. Nobody had, not till the Lizards came.

Before they came, Daniels had been managing the Decatur Commodores, a Three-I League team. One of his ballplayers had liked reading pulp stories about rocketships and creatures from other planets (he wondered if Sam Yeager was still alive these days). Mutt pulled an image from that kind of story now: the North Side reminded him of the mountains of the moon.

When he said that out loud, Herman Muldoon nodded. He was tall and thick-shouldered, with a long, tough Irish mug and, at the moment, a chin full of graying stubble. "I heard that about France back in nineteen an' eighteen, and I thought it was pretty straight then. Goes to show what I knew, don't it?"

"Yeah," Daniels said. He'd seen France, too. "France had more craters'n you could shake a stick at, that's for damn sure. 'Tween us and the frogs and the limeys and the *Boches*, we musta done fired every artillery shell in the world 'bout ten times over. But this here, it's just the one."

You could tell where the bomb had gone off: all the wreckage leaned away from it. If you drew a line from the direction of fallen walls and houses and uprooted trees, then went west a mile or so and did the same thing, the place where those lines met would have been around ground zero.

There were other ways of working out where that lay, though. Identifiable wreckage was getting thin on the ground now. More and more, it was just lumpy, half-shiny dirt, baked by the heat of the bomb into stuff that was almost like glass.

It was slippery like glass, too, especially with snow scattered over it. One of Mutt's men had his feet go out from under him and landed on his can. "Oww!" he said, and then, "Ahh, shit!" As his comrades laughed at him, he tried to get up—and almost fell down again.

"You want to play those kind o' games, Kurowski, you get yourself a clown suit, not the one you're wearin'," Mutt said.

"Sorry, Lieutenant," Kurowski said in injured tones that had nothing to do with his sore fundament. "It ain't like I'm doing it on purpose."

"Yeah, I know, but you're still doin' it." Mutt gave up ragging him. He recognized the big pile of brick and steel off to the left. It had come through the blast fairly well, and had shielded some of the apartment houses behind it so they weren't badly damaged at all. But the sight of upright buildings in the midst of the wreckage wasn't what made the hair stand up on the back of his neck. "Ain't that Wrigley Field?" he whispered. "Gotta be, from where it's at and what it looks like."

He'd never played in Wrigley Field—the Cubs had still been out at old West Side Grounds when he came through as a catcher for the Cardinals before the First World War. But seeing the ballpark in ruins brought the reality of this war home to him like a kick in the teeth. Sometimes big things would do that, sometimes little ones; he remembered a doughboy breaking down and sobbing like a baby when he found some French kid's dolly with its head blown off.

Muldoon's eyes slid over toward Wrigley for a moment. "Gonna be a long time before the Cubs win another pennant," he said, as good an epitaph as any for the park—and the city.

South of Wrigley Field, a big fellow with a sergeant's stripes and a mean expression gave Daniels a perfunctory salute. "Come on, Lieutenant," he said. "I'm supposed to get your unit into line here."

"Well, then, go on and do it," Mutt said. Most of his men didn't have enough experience to wipe their asses after they went and squatted. A lot of them were going to end up casualties because of it. Sometimes all the experience in the world didn't matter, either. Mutt had scars on his backside from a Lizard bullet—luckily, a through-and-through flesh wound that hadn't chewed up his hipbone. A couple, three feet up, though, and it would have hit him right in the ear.

The sergeant led them out of the blast area, down through the Near North Side toward the Chicago River. The big buildings ahead stood empty and battered, as meaningless to what was happening now as so many dinosaur bones might have been—unless, of course, they had Lizard snipers in them. "We shoulda pushed 'em farther back," the sergeant said, spitting in disgust, "but what the hell you gonna do?"

"Them Lizards, they're hard to push," Daniels agreed glumly. He looked around. The big bomb hadn't leveled this part of Chicago, but any number of small bombs and artillery shells had had their way with it. So had fire and bullets. The ruins gave ideal cover for anybody who felt like picking a line and fighting it out there. "This here's a lousy part of town for pushin' 'em, too."

"This here's a lousy part of town, period—sir," the sergeant said. "All the dagos used to live here till the Lizards ran 'em out—maybe they did somethin' decent there, you ask me."

"Knock off the crap about dagos," Daniels told him. He had

two in his platoon. If the sergeant turned his back on Giordano and Pinelli, he was liable to end up dead.

Now he sent Mutt an odd glance, as if wondering why he didn't agree: no pudgy old red-faced guy who talked like a Johnny Reb could be a dago himself, so what was he doing taking their part? But Mutt was a lieutenant, so the sergeant shut up till he got the platoon to its destination: "This here's Oak and Cleveland, sir. They call it 'Dead Corner' on account of the da—the Eyetalian gents got in the habit of murdering each other here during Prohibition. Somehow, there never were any witnesses. Funny how that works, ain't it?" He saluted and took off.

The platoon leader Daniels replaced was a skinny blond guy named Rasmussen. He pointed south. "Lizard lines are about four hundred yards down that way, out past Locust. Last couple days, it's been pretty quiet."

"Okay." Daniels brought field glasses up to his eyes and peered down past Locust. He spotted a couple of Lizards. Things had to be quiet, or they never would have shown themselves. They were about the size of ten-year-olds, with green-brown skin painted in patterns that meant things like rank and specialization badges and service stripes, swively eyes, and a forward-leaning, skittery gait unlike anything ever spawned on Earth.

"They sure are ugly little critters," Rasmussen said. "Little's the word, too. How do things that size go about making so much trouble?"

"They manage, that's a fact," Mutt answered. "What I don't see is, now that they're here, how we ever gonna get rid of all of 'em? They've come to stay, no two ways about that a-tall."

"Just have to kill 'em all, I guess," Rasmussen said.

"Good luck!" Mutt said. "They're liable to do that to us instead. Real liable. You ask me—not that you did—we got to find some other kind of way." He rubbed his bristly chin. "Only trouble is, I ain't got a clue what it could be. Hope somebody does. If nobody does, we better find one pretty damn quick or we're in all kinds of trouble."

"Like you said, I didn't ask you," Rasmussen told him.

☆ II ☆

High above Dover, a jet plane roared past. Without looking up, David Goldfarb couldn't tell whether it was a Lizard aircraft or a British Meteor. Given the thick layer of gray clouds hanging low overhead, looking up probably wouldn't have done him any good, either.

"That's one of ours," Flight Lieutenant Basil Roundbush declared.

"If you say so," Goldfarb answered, tacking on "Sir" half a beat too late.

"I do say so," Roundbush told him. He was tall and handsome and blond and ruddy, with a dashing mustache and a chestful of decorations, first from the Battle of Britain and then from the recent Lizard invasion. As far as Goldfarb was concerned, a pilot deserved a bloody medal just for surviving the Lizard attack. Even Meteors were easy meat against the machines the Lizards flew.

To make matters worse, Roundbush wasn't just a fighting machine with more ballocks than brains. He'd helped Fred Hipple with improvements on the engines that powered the Meteor, he had a lively wit, and women fell all over him. Taken all in all, he gave Goldfarb an inferiority complex.

He did his best to hide it, because Roundbush, within the limits of possessing few limits, was withal a most likable chap. "I am but a mere 'umble radarman, sir," Goldfarb said, making as if to tug at a forelock he didn't have. "I wouldn't know such things, I wouldn't."

"You're a mere 'umble pile of malarkey, is what you are," Roundbush said with a snort.

Goldfarb sighed. The pilot had the right accent, too. His own, despite studious efforts to make it more cultivated, betrayed his East End London origins every time he opened his mouth. He hadn't had to exaggerate it much to put on his 'umble air for Roundbush.

The pilot pointed. "The oasis lies ahead. Onward!"

They quickened their strides. The White Horse Inn lay not far from Dover Castle, in the northern part of town. It was a goodly hike from Dover College, where they both labored to turn Lizard gadgetry into devices the RAF and other British forces could use. It was also the best pub in Dover, not only for its bitter, but also for its barmaids.

Not surprisingly, it was packed. Uniforms of every sort— RAF, Army, Marines, Royal Navy—mingled with civilian tweed and flannel. The great fireplace at one end of the room threw heat all across it, as it had been doing in that building since the fourteenth century. Goldfarb sighed blissfully. The Dover College laboratories where he spent his days were clean, modern—and bloody cold.

As if in a rugby scrum, he and Roundbush elbowed their way toward the bar. Roundbush held up a hand as they neared the promised land. "Two pints of best bitter, darling!" he bawled to the redhead in back of the long oaken expanse.

"For you, dearie, anything," Sylvia said with a toss of her head. All the men who heard her howled wolfishly. Goldfarb joined in, but only so as not to seem out of place. He and Sylvia had been lovers a while before. It wasn't that he'd been mad about her; it wasn't even that he'd been her only one at the time: she was, in her own way, honest, and hadn't tried to string him along with such stories. But seeing her now that they'd parted did sometimes sting—not least because he still craved the sweet warmth of her body.

She slid the pint pots toward them. Roundbush slapped silver on the bar. Sylvia took it. When she started to make change for him, he shook his head. She smiled a large, promising smile—she was honestly mercenary, too.

Goldfarb raised his mug. "To Group Captain Hipple!" he said. He and Roundbush both drank. If it hadn't been for Fred Hipple, the RAF would have had to go on fighting the Lizards with Hurricanes and Spitfires, not jets. But Hipple had been missing since the Lizards attacked the Bruntingthorpe research station during their invasion. The toast was all too likely to be the only memorial he'd ever get.

Roundbush peered with respect at the deep golden brew he was quaffing. "That's *bloody* good," he said. "These handmade bitters often turn out better than what the brewers sold all across the country."

"You're right about that," Goldfarb said, thoughtfully smacking his lips. He fancied himself a connoisseur of bitter. "Well hopped, nutty—" He took another pull, to remind himself of what he was talking about.

The pint pots quickly emptied. Goldfarb raised a hand to order another round. He looked around for Sylvia, didn't see her for a moment, then he did; she was carrying a tray of mugs over to a table by the fire.

As if by magic, another woman materialized behind the bar while his head was turned. "You want a fresh pint?" she asked.

"Two pints—one for my friend here," he answered automatically. Then he looked at her. "Hullo! You're new here."

She nodded as she poured beer from the pitcher into the pint pots. "Yes—my name's Naomi." She wore her dark hair pulled back from her face. It made her look thoughtful. She had delicate features: skin pale without being pink, narrow chin, wide cheekbones, large gray eyes, elegantly arched nose.

Goldfarb paid for the bitter, all the while studying her. At last, he risked a word not in English: *"Yehudeh?"*

Those eyes fixed on him, sharply. He knew she was searching his features—and knew what she'd find. His brown, curly hair and formidable nose had not sprung from native English stock. After a moment, she relaxed and said, "Yes, I'm Jewish—and you, unless I'm wrong." Now that he heard more than a sentence from her, he caught her accent—like the one his parents had, though not nearly so strong.

He nodded. "Guilty as charged," he said, which won a cautious smile from her. He left her a tip as large as the one Basil Roundbush had given Sylvia, though he could afford it less well. He raised his mug to her before he drank, then asked, "What are you doing here?"

"In England, do you mean?" she asked, wiping the bar with a bit of rag. "My parents were lucky enough, smart enough—whatever you like—to get out of Germany in 1937. I came with them; I was fourteen then."

That made her twenty or twenty-one now: *a fine age,* Goldfarb thought reverently. He said, "My parents came from Poland before the First World War, so I was born here." He wondered if he should have told her that; German Jews sometimes looked down their noses at their Polish cousins.

But she said, "You were very lucky, then. What we went

through . . . and we were gone before the worst. And in Poland, they say, it was even worse."

"Everything they say is true, too," David answered. "Have you ever heard Moishe Russie broadcast? We're cousins; I've talked with him after he escaped from Poland. If it hadn't been for the Lizards, there wouldn't be any Jews left there by now. I hate being grateful to them, but there you are."

"Yes, I have heard him," Naomi said. "Terrible things there—but there, at least, they're over. In Germany, they go on."

"I know," Goldfarb said, and took a long pull at his bitter. "And the Nazis have hit the Lizards as many licks as anyone else, maybe more. The world's gone crazy, it bloody well has."

Basil Roundbush had been talking with a sandy-haired Royal Navy commander. Now he turned back to find a fresh pint at his elbow—and Naomi behind the bar. He pulled himself straight; he could turn on two hundred watts of charm the way most men flicked on a light switch. "Well, well," he said with a toothy smile. "Our publican's taste has gone up, it has indeed. Where did he find you?"

Not sporting, Goldfarb thought. He waited for Naomi to sigh or giggle or do whatever she did to show she was smitten. He hadn't seen Roundbush fail yet. But the barmaid just answered, coolly enough, "I was looking for work, and he was kind enough to think I might do. Now if you will excuse me—" She hurried off to minister to other thirst-stricken patrons.

Roundbush dug an elbow into Goldfarb's ribs. "Not sporting, old man. You have an unfair advantage there, unless I'm much mistaken."

Damn it, he *was* sharp, to have identified the accent or placed her looks so quickly. "Me?" Goldfarb said. "You're a fine one to talk of advantages, when you've got everything in a skirt from here halfway to the Isle of Wight going all soppy over you."

"Whatever could you be talking about, my dear fellow?" Roundbush said, and stuck his tongue in his cheek to show he was not to be taken seriously. He gulped down his pint, then waved the pot at Sylvia, who had at last come back. "Another round of these for David and me, if you please, darling."

"Coming up," she said.

Roundbush turned back to the Royal Navy man. Goldfarb asked Sylvia, "When did she start here?" His eyes slid toward Naomi.

"A few days ago," Sylvia answered. "You ask me, she's liable to be too fine to make a go of it. You have to be able to put up with the drunken, randy sods who want anything they can get out of you—or into you."

"Thanks," Goldfarb said. "You've just made me feel about two inches high."

"Blimey, you're a gent, you are, next to a lot of these bastards," Sylvia said, praising with faint damn. She went on, "Naomi, her way looks to be pretending she doesn't notice the pushy ones, or understand what they want from her. That's only good for so long. Sooner or later—likely sooner—somebody's going to try reaching down her blouse or up her dress. Then we'll—"

Before she could say "see," the rifle-crack of a slap cut through the chatter in the White Horse Inn. A Marine captain raised a hand to his cheek. Naomi, quite unperturbed, set a pint of beer in front of him and went about her business.

"Timed that well, I did, though I say so my own self," Sylvia remarked with more than a little pride.

"That you did," Goldfarb agreed. He glanced over toward Naomi. Their eyes met for a moment. He smiled. She shrugged, as if to say, *All in a day's work.* He turned back to Sylvia. "Good for her," he said.

Liu Han was nervous. She shook her head. No, she was more than nervous. She was terrified. The idea of meeting the little scaly devils face-to-face made her shiver inside. She'd been a creature under their control for too long: first in their airplane that never came down, where they made her submit to one man after another so they could learn how people behaved in matters of the pillow; and then, after she'd got pregnant, down in their prison camp not far from Shanghai. After she'd had her baby, they'd stolen it from her. She wanted her child back, even if it was only a girl.

With all that in her past, she had trouble believing the scaly devils would treat her like someone worth consideration now. And she was a woman herself, which did nothing to ease her confidence. The doctrine of the People's Liberation Army said women were, and should be, equal to men. In the top part of her mind, she was beginning to believe that. Down deep, though, a lifetime of teachings of the opposite lesson still shaped her thoughts—and her fears.

Perhaps sensing that, Nieh Ho-T'ing said, "It will be all right. They won't do anything to you, not at this parley. They know we hold prisoners of theirs, and what will happen to those prisoners if anything bad happens to us."

"Yes, I understand," she said, but she shot him a grateful glance anyhow. In matters military, he knew what he was talking about. He'd served as political commissar in the first detachment of Mao's revolutionary army, commanded a division in the Long March, and been an army chief of staff. After the Lizards came, he'd led resistance against them—and against the Japanese, and against the counterrevolutionary Kuomintang clique—first in Shanghai and then here in Peking. And he was her lover.

Though she'd been born a peasant, her wits and her burning eagerness for revenge on the little devils for all they'd done to her had made her a revolutionary herself, and one who'd risen quickly in the ranks.

A scaly devil emerged from the tent that his kind had built in the middle of the *Pan Jo Hsiang Tai*—the Fragrant Terrace of Wisdom. The tent looked more like a bubble blown from some opaque orange shiny stuff than an honest erection of canvas or silk. It clashed dreadfully not only with the terrace and the walls and the elegant staircases to either side, but also with everything on the *Ch'iung Hua Tao*, the White Pagoda Island.

Liu Han stifled a nervous giggle. Peasant that she was, she'd never imagined, back in the days before the little scaly devils took hold of her life and tore it up by the roots, that she would find herself not just in the Imperial City inside Peking, but on an island the old Chinese Emperors had used as a resort.

The little devil turned one turreted eye toward Liu Han, the other toward Nieh Ho-T'ing. "You are the men of the People's Liberation Army?" it asked in fair Chinese, and added a grunting cough at the end of the sentence to show it was a question: a holdover from the usages of its own language. When neither human denied it, the scaly devil said, "You will come with me. I am Essaff."

Inside the tent, the lamps glowed almost like sunlight, but slightly more yellow-orange in tone. That had nothing to do with the material from which the tent was made; Liu Han had noticed it in all the illumination the little scaly devils used. The tent was big enough to contain an antechamber. When she started to go through the doorway, Essaff held up a clawed hand.

"Wait!" he said, and tacked on a different cough, one that put special emphasis on what he said. "We will examine you with our machines, to make sure you carry no explosives. This has been done to us before."

Liu Han and Nieh Ho-T'ing exchanged glances. Neither of them said anything. Liu Han had had the idea of sending beast-show men whose trained animals fascinated the scaly devils to perform for them—with bombs hidden in the cases that also held their creatures. A lot of those bombs had gone off. Fooling the little devils twice with the same trick was next to impossible.

Essaff had the two humans stand in a certain place. He examined images of their bodies in what looked like a small film screen. Liu Han had seen its like many times before; it seemed as common among the little devils as books among mankind.

After hissing like a bubbling pot for a minute or two, Essaff said, "You are honorable here in this case. You may go in."

The main chamber of the tent held a table with more of the scaly devils' machines at one end. Behind the table sat two males. Pointing to them in turn, Essaff said, "This one is Ppevel, assistant administrator, eastern region, main continental mass—China, you would say. That one is Ttomalss, researcher in Tosevite—human, you would say—behavior."

"I know Ttomalss," Liu Han said, holding emotion at bay with an effort of will that all but exhausted her. Ttomalss and his assistants had photographed her giving birth to her daughter, and then taken the child.

Before she could ask him how the girl was, Essaff said, "You Tosevites, you sit down with us." The chairs the scaly devils had brought for them were of human make, a concession she'd never seen from them before. As she and Nieh Ho-T'ing sat, Essaff asked, "You will drink tea?"

"No," Nieh said sharply. "You examined our bodies before we came in here. We cannot examine the tea. We know you sometimes try to drug people. We will not drink or eat with you."

Ttomalss understood Chinese. Ppevel evidently did not. Essaff translated for him. Liu Han followed some of the translation. She'd learned a bit of the scaly devils' speech. That was one reason she was here instead of Nieh's longtime aide, Hsia Shou-Tao.

Through Essaff, Ppevel said, "This is a parley. You need have no fear."

"You had fear of us," Nieh answered. "If you do not trust us, how can we trust you?" The scaly devils' drugs did not usually work well on people. Nieh Ho-T'ing and Liu Han both knew that. Nieh added, "Even among our own people—human beings, I mean—we Chinese have had to suffer under unequal treaties. Now we want nothing less than full reciprocity in all our dealings, and give no more than we get."

Ppevel said, "We are talking with you. Is this not concession enough?"

"It is a concession," Nieh Ho-T'ing said. "It is not enough." Liu Han added an emphatic cough to his words. Both Ppevel and Essaff jerked in surprise. Ttomalss spoke to his superior in a low voice. Liu Han caught enough to gather that he was explaining how she'd picked up some of their tongue.

"Let us talk, then," Ppevel said. "We shall see who is equal and who is not when this war is over."

"Yes, that is true," Nieh Ho-T'ing agreed. "Very well, we shall talk. Do you wish this discussion to begin with great things and move down to the small, or would you rather start with small things and work up as we make progress?"

"Best we start with small things," Ppevel said. "Because they are small, you and we may both find it easier to give ground on them. If we try too much at the beginning, we may only grow angry with each other and have these talks fail altogether."

"You are sensible," Nieh said, inclining his head to the little scaly devil. Liu Han listened to Essaff explaining to Ppevel that that was a gesture of respect. Nieh went on, "As we have noted"— his voice was dry; the People's Liberation Army had noted it with bombs—"we demand that you return the girl child you callously kidnapped from Liu Han here."

Ttomalss jumped as if someone had jabbed him with a pin. "This is not a small matter!" he exclaimed in Chinese, and added an emphatic cough to show he meant it. Essaff was put in the odd position of translating for one little devil what a different one said.

Nieh Ho-T'ing raised an eyebrow. Liu Han suspected the gesture was wasted on the scaly devils, who had no eyebrows—nor any other hair. Nieh said, "What would you call a small matter, then? I could tell you I find the stuff from which you have made this tent very ugly, but that is hardly something worth negotiating. Compared to having all you imperialist aggressors leave China at once, the fate of this baby is small, or at least smaller."

When that had been translated, Ppevel said, "Yes, that is a small matter compared to the other. In any case, this land is now ours, which admits of no discussion—as you are aware."

Nieh smiled without replying in words. The European powers and the Japanese had said such things to China, too, but failed in their efforts to consolidate what they had taken at bayonet point. Marxist-Leninist doctrine gave Nieh a long view of history, a view he'd been teaching to Liu Han.

But she knew from her own experience that the little scaly devils had a long view of history, too, one that had nothing to do with Marx or Lenin. They were inhumanly patient; what worked against Britain or Japan might fail against them. If they weren't lying, even the Chinese, the most anciently and perfectly civilized nation in the world, might have been children beside them.

"Is my daughter well?" Liu Han asked Ttomalss at last. She dared not break down and cry, but talking about the girl made her nose begin to run in lieu of tears. She blew between her fingers before going on, "Are you taking good care of her?"

"The hatchling is both comfortable and healthy." Ttomalss took out a machine of a sort Liu Han had seen before. He touched a stud. Above the machine, by some magic of the scaly devils, an image of the baby sprang into being. She was up on all fours, wearing only a cloth around her middle and smiling wide enough to show two tiny white teeth.

Liu Han did start to weep then. Ttomalss knew enough to understand that meant grief. He touched the stud again. The picture vanished. Liu Han didn't know whether that made things better or worse. She ached to hold the baby in her arms.

Gathering herself, she said, "If you talk to people as equals or something close to equals, you do not steal their children from them. You can do one or the other, but not both. And if you do steal children, you have to expect people to do everything they can to hurt you because of it."

"But we take the hatchlings to learn how they and the Race can relate to each other when starting fresh," Ttomalss said, as if that were almost too obvious to need explanation.

Ppevel spoke to him in the scaly devils' tongue. Essaff declined to translate what he said. Nieh looked a question to Liu Han. She whispered, "He says one thing they have learned is that people will fight for their hatchlings, uh, children. This may not have been what they intended to find out, but it is part of the answer."

Nieh neither replied nor looked directly at Ppevel. Liu Han had enough practice at reading his face to have a pretty good notion that he thought Ppevel no fool. She had the same feeling about the little devil.

Ppevel's eye turrets swung back toward her and Nieh Ho-T'ing. "Suppose we give back this hatchling," he said through Essaff, ignoring another start of dismay from Ttomalss. "Suppose we do this. What do you give us in return? Do you agree to no more bombings like those that marred the Emperor's birthday?"

Liu Han sucked in a long breath. She would have agreed to anything to have her baby back. But that decision was not hers to make. Nieh Ho-T'ing had authority there, and Nieh loved the cause more than any individual or that individual's concerns.

Abstractly, Liu Han understood that that was the way it should be. But how could you think abstractly when you'd just seen your baby for the first time since it was stolen?

"No, we do not agree to that," Nieh said. "It is too much to demand in exchange for one baby who cannot do you any harm."

"Giving back the hatchling would harm our research," Ttomalss said.

Both Nieh and Ppevel ignored him. Nieh went on, "If you give us the baby, though, we will give you back one of your males whom we hold captive. He must be worth more to you than that baby is."

"Any male is worth more to us than a Tosevite," Ppevel said. "This is axiomatic. But the words of the researcher Ttomalss do hold some truth. Disrupting a long-term research program is not something we males of the Race do casually. We require more justification for this than your simple demand."

"Does child-stealing mean nothing to you as a crime?" Liu Han said.

"Not a great deal," Ppevel answered indifferently. "The Race does not suffer from many of the fixations on other individuals with which you Tosevites are so afflicted."

Worst, Liu Han realized, was that he meant it. The scaly devils were not evil, not in their own strange eyes. They were just so different from mankind that, when they acted by their own standards of what was right and proper, they couldn't help horrifying the people on whom they inflicted those standards. Understanding that, though, did nothing to get her daughter back.

"Tell me, Ppevel," she asked with a dangerous glint in her eye, "how long have you been assistant administrator for this region?"

Nieh Ho-T'ing's gaze slid toward her for a moment, but he didn't say anything or try to head her off. The Communists preached equality between the sexes, and Nieh followed that preaching—better than most, from what she'd seen. Hsia Shou-Tao's idea of the proper position for women in the revolutionary movement, for instance, was on their backs with their legs open.

"I have not had this responsibility long," Ppevel said. "I was previously assistant to the assistant administrator. Why do you ask this irrelevant question?"

Liu Han did not have a mouthful of small, sharp, pointed teeth, as the little scaly devils did. The predatory smile she sent Ppevel showed she did not need them. "So your old chief is dead, eh?" she said. "Did he die on your Emperor's birthday?"

All three scaly devils lowered their eyes for a moment when

Essaff translated "Emperor" into their language. Ppevel answered, "Yes, but—"

"Who do you think will replace you after our next attack?" Liu Han asked. Interrupting at a parley was probably bad form, but she didn't care. "You may not think stealing children is a great crime, but we do, and we will punish all of you if we can't reach the guilty one"—she glared at Ttomalss—"and you don't make amends."

"This matter requires further analysis within the circles of the Race," Ppevel said; he had courage. "We do not say yes at this time, but we do not say no. Let us move on to the next item of discussion."

"Very well," Nieh Ho-T'ing said, and Liu Han's heart sank. The little scaly devils were not in the habit of lying over such matters, and she knew it. Discussion on getting her daughter back would resume. But every day the little girl was away would make her stranger, harder to reclaim. She hadn't seen a human being since she was three days old. What would she be like, even if Liu Han finally got her back?

From the outside, the railroad car looked like one that hauled baggage. David Nussboym had seen that, before the bored-looking NKVD men, submachine guns in hand but plainly sure they wouldn't have to use them, herded him and his companions in misfortune into it. Inside, it was divided into nine compartments, like any passenger car.

In an ordinary passenger car, though, four to a compartment was crowded. People looked resentfully at one another, as if it was the fault of the person on whom the irritated gaze fell that he took up so much space. In each of the five prisoner compartments on this car . . . Nussboym shook his head. He was a scrupulous man, a meticulous man. He didn't know how many people each of the other compartments held. He knew there were twenty-five men in his.

He and three others had perches—not proper seats—upon the baggage racks by the ceiling. The strongest, toughest prisoners lay in relative comfort—and extremely relative it was, too—on the hard middle bunk. The rest sat jammed together on the lower bunk and on the floor, on top of their meager belongings.

Nussboym's rackmate was a lanky fellow named Ivan Fyodorov. He understood some of Nussboym's Polish and a bit of Yiddish when the Polish failed. Nussboym, in turn, could follow

Russian after a fashion, and Fyodorov threw in a word of German every now and again.

He wasn't a mental giant. "Tell me again how you're here, David Aronovich," he said. "I've never heard a story like yours, not even once."

Nussboym sighed. He'd told the story three times already in the two days—he thought it was two days—he'd been perched on the rack. "It's like this, Ivan Vasilievich," he said. "I was in Lodz, in Poland, in the part of Poland the Lizards held. My crime was hating the Germans worse than the Lizards."

"Why did you do that?" Fyodorov asked. This was the fourth time he'd asked that question, too.

Up till now, Nussboym had evaded it: your average Russian was no more apt to love Jews than was your average Pole. "Can't you figure it out for yourself?" he asked now. But, when Fyodorov's brow furrowed and did not clear, he snapped, "Damn it, don't you see I'm Jewish?"

"Oh, that. Yeah, sure, I knew that," his fellow prisoner said, sunny still. "Ain't no Russian with a nose that big, anyhow." Nussboym brought a hand up to the offended member, but Ivan hadn't seemed to mean anything by it past a simple statement of fact. He went on, "So you were in Lodz. How did you get *here*? That's what I want to know."

"My chums wanted to get rid of me," Nussboym said bitterly. "They wouldn't give me to the Nazis—even they aren't that vile. But they couldn't leave me in Poland, either; they knew I wouldn't let them get away with collaborating. So they knocked me unconscious, took me across Lizard-held country till they came to land you Russians still controlled—and they gave me to your border patrols."

Fyodorov might not have been a mental giant, but he was a Soviet citizen. He knew what had happened after that. Smiling, he said, "And the border patrol decided you had to be a criminal—and besides, you were a foreigner and a *zhid* to boot—and so they dropped you into the *gulag*. Now I get it."

"I'm so glad for you," Nussboym said sourly.

The window that looked out from the compartment to the hallway of the prison car had crosshatched bars over it. Nussboym watched a couple of NKVD men make their way toward the compartment entrance, which had no door, only a sliding grate of similar crosshatched bars. The compartment had no windows that opened on the outside world, just a couple of tiny barred blinds that might as well not have been there.

Nussboym didn't care. He'd learned that when the NKVD men walked by with that slow deliberate stride, they had food with them. His stomach rumbled. Spit rushed into his mouth. He ate better in the prison car—a Stolypin car, the Russians universally called it—than he had in the Lodz ghetto before the Lizards came, but not much better.

One of the NKVD men opened the grate, then stood back, covering the prisoners with a submachine gun. The other one set down two buckets. "All right, you *zeks*!" he shouted. "Feeding time at the zoo!" He laughed loudly at his own wit, though he made the joke every time it was his turn to feed the prisoners.

They laughed too, loudly. If they didn't laugh, nobody got anything to eat. They'd found that out very fast. A couple of beatings soon forced the recalcitrant ones into line.

Satisfied, the guard started passing out a chunk of coarse, black bread and half a salted herring apiece. They'd got sugar once, but the guards said they were out of that now. Nussboym didn't know whether it was true, but did know he was in no position to find out.

The prisoners who reclined on the middle bunk got the biggest loaves and fishes. They'd enforced that rule with their fists, too. Nussboym's hand went to the shiner below his left eye. He'd tried holding out on them, and paid the price.

He wolfed down the bread, but stuck his bony fragment of herring in a pocket. He'd learned to wait for water before he ate the fish. It was so salty, thirst would have driven him mad till he got something to drink. Sometimes the guards brought a bucket of water after they brought food. Sometimes they didn't. Today they didn't.

The train rumbled on. In summer, having two dozen men stuffed into a compartment intended for four would have been intolerable—not that that would have stopped the NKVD. In a Russian winter, animal warmth was not to be despised. In spite of being cold, Nussboym wasn't freezing.

His stomach growled again. It didn't care that he would suffer agonies of thirst if he ate his herring without water. All it knew was that it was still mostly empty, and that the fish would help fill it up.

With a squeal of brakes, the train pulled to a halt. Nussboym almost slipped down onto men below. Ivan had done that once. They'd fallen on him like a pack of wolves, beating and kicking him till he was black and blue. After that, the fellows perched on the baggage racks had learned to hang on tight during stops.

"Where are we, do you think?" somebody down below asked.

"In hell," somebody else answered, which produced laughs both more bitter and more sincere than the ones the guard had got for himself.

"This'll be Pskov, I bet," a *zek* in the middle bunk declared. "I hear tell we've cleared the Lizards away from the railroad line that leads there from the west. After that"—he stopped sounding so arrogant and sure of himself—"after that, it's north and east, on to the White Sea, or maybe to the Siberian *gulags*."

Nobody spoke for a couple of minutes after that. Winter labor up around Archangel or in Siberia was enough to daunt even the heartiest of spirits.

Small clangs and jerks showed that cars were either being added to the train or taken off it. One of the *zeks* sitting on the bottom bunks said, "Didn't the Hitlerites take Pskov away from the *rodina*? Shit, they can't do anything worse to us than our own people do."

"Oh yes, they can," Nussboym said, and told them about Treblinka.

"That's Lizard propaganda, is what that is," the big-mouthed *zek* in the middle bunk said.

"No," Nussboym said. Even in the face of opposition from the powerful prisoner, about half the *zeks* in the car ended up believing him. He reckoned that a moral victory.

A guard came back with a bucket of water, a dipper, and a couple of mugs. He looked disgusted with fate, as if by letting the men drink he was granting them a privilege they didn't deserve. "Come on, you slimy bastards," he said. "Queue up—and make it snappy. I don't have all day."

Healthy men drank first, then the ones with tubercular coughs, and last of all the three or four luckless fellows who had syphilis. Nussboym wondered if the arrangement did any good, because he doubted the NKVD men washed the mugs between uses. The water was yellowish and cloudy and tasted of grease. The guard had taken it from the engine tender instead of going to some proper spigot. All the same, it was wet. He drank his allotted mug, ate the herring, and felt, for a moment, almost like a human being instead of a *zek*.

Georg Schultz spun the U-2's two-bladed wooden prop. The five-cylinder Shvetsov radial caught almost at once; in a Russian winter, an air-cooled engine was a big advantage. Ludmila Gorbunova had heard stories about *Luftwaffe* pilots who had to light fires on the ground under the nose of their aircraft to keep their antifreeze from freezing up.

Ludmila checked the rudimentary collection of dials on the *Kukuruznik*'s instrument panel. All in all, they told her nothing she didn't already know: the Wheatcutter had plenty of fuel for the mission she was going to fly, the compass did a satisfactory job of pointing toward north, and the altimeter said she was still on the ground.

She released the brake. The little biplane bounced across the snowy field that served as an airstrip. Behind her, she knew, men and women with brooms would sweep snow over the tracks her wheels made. The Red Air Force took *maskirovka* seriously.

After one last jounce, the U-2 didn't come down. Ludmila patted the side of the fuselage with a gloved but affectionate hand. Though designed as a primary trainer, the aircraft had harassed first the Germans and then the Lizards. *Kukuruznik*'s flew low and slow and, but for the engine, had almost no metal; they evaded the Lizards' detection systems that let the alien imperialist aggressors hack more sophisticated warplanes out of the sky with ease. Machine guns and light bombs weren't much, but they were better than nothing.

Ludmila swung the aircraft into a long, slow turn back toward the field from which she'd taken off. Georg Schultz still stood out there. He waved to her and blew her a kiss before he started trudging for the pine woods not far away.

"If Tatiana saw you doing that, she'd blast your head off from eight hundred meters," Ludmila said. The slipstream that blasted over the windscreen into the open cockpit blew her words away. She wished something would do the same for Georg Schultz. The German panzer gunner made a first-rate mechanic; he had a feel for engines, the way some people had a feel for horses. That made him valuable no matter how loud and sincere a Nazi he was.

Since the Soviet Union and the Hitlerites were at least formally cooperating against the Lizards, his fascism could be overlooked, as fascism had been overlooked till the Nazis treacherously broke their nonaggression pact with the USSR on 22 June 1941. What Ludmila couldn't stomach was that he kept trying to get her to go to bed with him, though she had about as much interest in sleeping with him as she did with, say, Heinrich Himmler.

"You'd think he would have left me alone after he and Tatiana started jumping on each other," Ludmila said to the cloudy sky. Tatiana Pirogova was an accomplished sniper who'd shot at Nazis before she started shooting at Lizards. She was at least as deadly as Schultz, maybe deadlier. As far as Ludmila could see, that was what drew them together.

"Men," she added, a complete sentence. Despite enjoying Tatiana's favors, Schultz still kept trying to lay her, too. Under her breath, she muttered, "Damned nuisance."

She buzzed west across Pskov. Soldiers in the streets, some in Russian khaki, others in German field-gray, still others in winter white that made their nationality impossible to guess, waved at her as she flew by. She didn't mind that at all. Sometimes, though, human troops would fire at her in the air, on the assumption that anything airborne had to belong to the Lizards.

A train pulled out of the station, heading northwest. The exhaust from the locomotive was a great black plume that would have been visible for kilometers against the snow had the low ceiling not masked it. The Lizards liked shooting up trains whenever they got the chance.

She waved to the train when she came closest to it. She didn't think anyone on board saw it, but she didn't care. Trains pulling out of Pskov were a hopeful sign. During the winter, the Red Army—*and the Germans*, Ludmila thought reluctantly—had pushed the Lizards back from the city, and back from the railroad lines that ran through it. These days, you could, if you were lucky, get through to Riga by train.

But you still needed luck, and you still needed time. That was why Lieutenant General Chill had sent his despatch with her—not only did it have a better chance of getting through, it would reach his Nazi counterpart in the Latvian capital well before it could have got there by rail.

Ludmila skinned back her teeth in a sardonic grin. "Oh, how the mighty Nazi general wished he could have sent a mighty Nazi flier to carry his message for him," she said. "But he didn't have any mighty Nazi fliers, so he was stuck with me." The expression on Chill's face had been that of a man biting into an unripe apple.

She patted the pocket of her fur-lined leather flying suit in which the precious despatch rested. She didn't know what it said. By the way Chill had given it to her, that was a privilege she didn't deserve. She laughed a little. As if he could have stopped her from opening the envelope and reading what was inside! Maybe he thought she wouldn't think of that. If he did, he was stupid even for a German.

Perverse pride, though, had made her keep the envelope sealed. General Chill was—formally—an ally, and had entrusted her with the message, no matter how reluctant he was about it. She would observe the proprieties in return.

The *Kukuruznik* buzzed along toward Riga. The countryside over which it skimmed was nothing like the steppe that surrounded Kiev, where Ludmila had grown up. Instead of endless empty kilometers, she flew above snow-dappled pine woods, part of the great forest that stretched east to Pskov and far, far beyond. Here and there, farms and villages appeared in the midst of the forest. At first, the human settlements in the middle of the wilderness almost startled Ludmila. As she flew on toward the Baltic, they grew ever more frequent.

Their look changed about halfway to Riga, when she crossed from Russia into Latvia. It wasn't just that the buildings changed, though plaster walls and tile roofs took the place of wood and sometimes thatch. Things became more orderly, too, and more conservative of space: all the land was used for some clearly defined purpose—cropland, town, woodlot, or whatever it might have been. Everything plainly was being exploited, not lying around waiting in case some use eventually developed for it.

"It might as well be Germany," Ludmila said aloud. The thought gave her pause. Latvia had only been reincorporated into the Soviet Union a little more than a year before the Hitlerites treacherously invaded the *rodina*. Reactionary elements there had welcomed the Nazis as liberators, and collaborated with them against Soviet forces. Reactionary elements in the Ukraine had done the same thing, but Ludmila tried not to think about that.

She wondered what sort of reception she'd get in Riga. Pskov had had Soviet partisans lurking in the nearby forests, and was now essentially a codominion between German and Soviet forces. She didn't think any significant Soviet forces operated anywhere near Latvia—farther south, maybe, but not by the Baltic.

"So," she said, "there soon will be a significant Soviet force in Latvia: me." The slipstream blew away the joke, and the humor from it.

She found the Baltic coast and followed it south toward Riga. The sea had frozen some kilometers out from the shore. The sight made her shiver. Even for a Russian, that was a lot of ice. Smoke rose from Riga harbor. The Lizards had been pummeling harbors lately. When Ludmila approached the docks, she started drawing rifle fire. Shaking her fists at the idiots who took her biplane for a Lizard aircraft, she swung away and looked around for someplace to land the *Kukuruznik*.

Not far from what looked like the main boulevard, she spied a park full of bare-branched trees. It had enough empty space—snow and dead, yellow-brown grass—and to spare for the biplane. No sooner had she slid to a jerky stop than German troops in field-gray and white came running up to her.

They saw the red stars on the *Kukuruznik*'s wings and fuselage. "Who are you, you damned Russian, and what are you doing here?" one of them shouted.

A typically arrogant German, he assumed she spoke his language. As it happened, he was right this time. "Senior Lieutenant Ludmila Gorbunova, Red Air Force," Ludmila answered in German. "I have with me a despatch for General Brockdorff-Ahlefeldt from General Chill in Pskov. Will you be so kind as to take me to him? And will you camouflage this aircraft so the Lizards cannot spot it?"

The Hitlerite soldiers drew back in surprise to hear her voice. She was sitting in the cockpit, and her leather flying helmet and thick winter gear had effectively disguised her sex. The German who'd spoken before leered now and said, "We've heard of pilots who call themselves Stalin's Hawks. Are you one of Stalin's Sparrows?"

Now he used *du* rather than *Sie*. Ludmila wasn't sure whether he intended the familiar intimacy or insult. Either way, she didn't care for it. "Perhaps," she answered in a voice colder than the weather, "but only if you're one of Hitler's Jackasses."

She waited to see whether that would amuse or anger the German. She was in luck; not only did he laugh, he threw back his head and brayed like a donkey. "You have to be a jackass to end up in a godforsaken place like this," he said. "All right, *Kamerad*—no, *Kameradin*—Senior Lieutenant, I'll take you to headquarters. Why don't you just come along with me?"

Several Germans ended up escorting her, maybe as guards, maybe because they didn't want to leave her alone with the first one, maybe for the novelty of walking along with a woman while on duty. She did her best to ignore them; Riga interested her more.

Even after being battered by years of war, it didn't look like a godforsaken place to her. The main street—Brivibas Street, it was called (her eyes and brain needed a little while to adjust to the Latin alphabet)—had more shops, and smarter-looking ones, than she'd seen in Kiev. The clothes civilians wore on the street were shabby and none too clean, but of better fabric and finer cut than would have been usual in Russia or the Ukrainian Soviet Socialist Republic.

Some of the people recognized her gear. In spite of her German escort, they yelled at her in accented Russian and in Latvian. She knew the Russian was insulting, and the Latvian sounded less than complimentary. To rub in the point, one of the Germans said, "They love you here in Riga."

"There are plenty of places where they love Germans even more," she said, which made the Nazi shut up with a snap. Had it been a chess game, she would have won the exchange.

The *Rathaus* where the German commandant had his headquarters was near the corner of Brivibas and Kaleiyu Streets. To Ludmila, the German-style building looked old as time. Like the *Krom* in Pskov, it had no sentries on the outside to give away its location to the Lizards. Once inside the ornately carved doors, though, Ludmila found herself inspected by two new and hostile Germans in cleaner, fresher uniforms than she was used to seeing.

"What do you have here?" one of them asked her escort.

"Russian flier. She says she has a despatch from Pskov for the commanding general," the talky soldier answered. "I figured we'd bring her here and let you headquarters types sort things out."

"She?" The sentry looked Ludmila over in a different way. "By God, it is a woman, isn't it? Under all that junk she's wearing, I couldn't tell."

He plainly assumed she spoke only Russian. She did her best to look down her nose at him, which wasn't easy, since he was probably thirty centimeters the taller. In her best German, she said, "It will never matter to you one way or the other, I promise you that."

The sentry stared at her. Her escorts, who'd been chatting with her enough to see her more or less as a human being—and who, like any real fighting men, had no great use for headquarters troops—suppressed their snickers not quite well enough. That made the sentry look even less happy. In a voice full of winter, he said, "Come with me. I will take you to the commandant's adjutant."

The adjutant was a beefy, red-faced fellow with a captain's two pips on his shoulder straps. He said, "Give me this despatch, young lady. *Generalleutnant Graf* Walter von Brockdorff-Ahlefeldt is a busy man. I shall convey to him your message as soon as it is convenient."

Maybe he thought the titles and double-barreled name would impress her. If so, he forgot he was dealing with a socialist. Ludmila stuck out her chin and looked stubborn. *"Nein,"* she said. "I was told by General Chill to give the message to your commandant, not to anyone else. I am a soldier; I follow orders."

Red-Face turned redder. "One moment," he said, and got up from his desk. He went through a door behind it. When he came out again, he might have been chewing on a lemon. "The commandant will see you."

"Good." Ludmila headed for that door herself. Had the adjutant not hastily got out of her way, she would have walked right over him.

She'd expected an overbred aristocrat with pinched features, a haughty expression, and a monocle. Walter von Brockdorff-Ahlefeldt had pinched features all right, but plainly for no other reason than that he was a sick man. His skin looked like yellow parchment drawn tight over bones. When he was younger and healthier, he'd probably been handsome. Now he was just someone carrying on as best he could despite illness.

He did get up and bow to her, which took her by surprise. His cadaverous smile said he'd noticed, too. Then he surprised her again, saying in Russian, "Welcome to Riga, Senior Lieutenant. So—what news do you bring me from Lieutenant General Chill?"

"Sir, I don't know." Ludmila took out the envelope and handed it to him. "Here is the message."

Brockdorff-Ahlefeldt started to open it, then paused and got up from his chair again. He hurriedly left the office by a side door. When he came back, his face was even paler than it had been. "I beg your pardon," he said, finishing the job of opening the envelope. "I seem to have come down with a touch of dysentery."

He had a lot more than a touch; by the look of him, he'd fall over dead one fine day before too long. Intellectually, Ludmila had known the Nazis clung to their posts with as much courage and dedication—or fanaticism, one—as anyone else. Seeing that truth demonstrated, though, sometimes left her wondering how decent men could follow such a system.

That made her think of Heinrich Jäger and, a moment later, start to blush. General Brockdorff-Ahlefeldt was studying General Chill's note. To her relief, he didn't notice her turning pink. He grunted a couple of times, softly, unhappily. At last, he looked up from the paper and said, "I am very sorry, Senior Lieutenant, but I cannot do as the German commandant of Pskov requests."

She hadn't imagined a German could put that so delicately. Even if he was a Hitlerite, he was *kulturny*. "What does General Chill request, sir?" she asked, then added a hasty amendment: "If it's not too secret for me to know."

"By no means," he answered—he spoke Russian like an

aristocrat. "He wanted me to help resupply him with munitions—" He paused and coughed.

"So he would not have to depend on Soviet equipment, you mean," Ludmila said.

"Just so," Brockdorff-Ahlefeldt agreed. "You saw the smoke in the harbor, though?" He courteously waited for her nod before continuing, "That is still coming from the freighters the Lizards caught there, the freighters that were full of arms and ammunition of all sorts. We shall be short here because of that, and have none to spare for our neighbors."

"I'm sorry to hear that," Ludmila said, and found she was not altogether lying for the sake of politeness. She didn't want the Germans in Pskov strengthened in respect to Soviet forces there, but she didn't want them weakened in respect to the Lizards, either. Finding a balance that would let her be happy on both those counts would not be easy. She went on, "Do you have a written reply for me to take back to Lieutenant General Chill?"

"I shall draft one for you," Brockdorff-Ahlefeldt said. "But first—Beck!" He raised his voice. The adjutant came bounding into the room. "Fetch the senior lieutenant here something from the mess," Brockdorff-Ahlefeldt told him. "She has come a long way on a sleeveless errand, and she could no doubt do with something hot."

"Jawohl, Herr Generalleutnant!" Beck said. He turned to Ludmila. "If you would be so kind as to wait one moment, please, Senior Lieutenant Gorbunova." He dipped his head, almost as if he were a maitre d' in some fancy, decadent capitalist restaurant, then hurried away. If his commander accepted Ludmila, he accepted her, too.

When Captain Beck came back, he carried on a tray a large, steaming bowl. *"Maizes zupe ar putukrejumu,* a Latvian dish," he said. "It's corn soup with whipped cream."

"Thank you," Ludmila said, and dug in. The soup was hot and thick and filling, and didn't taste that alien. Russian-style cooking used a lot of cream, too, though sour as often as sweet.

While Ludmila ate, Beck went out to his own office, then came back a couple of minutes later to lay a sheet of paper on General Brockdorff-Ahlefeldt's desk. The German commander at Riga studied the message and glanced over at Ludmila, but kept silent until, with a sigh, she set down the bowl. Then he said, "I have a favor to ask of you, if you don't mind."

"That depends on what sort of favor it is," she answered cautiously.

Graf Walter von Brockdorff-Ahlefeldt's smile made him look like a skeleton that had just heard a good joke. "I assure you, Senior Lieutenant, I have no improper designs upon your undoubtedly fair body. This is a purely military matter, one where you can help us."

"I didn't think you had designs on me, sir," Ludmila said.

"No?" The German general smiled again. "How disappointing." While Ludmila was trying to figure out how to take that, Brockdorff-Ahlefeldt went on, "We are in contact with a number of partisan bands in Poland." He paused for a moment to let that sink in. "I suppose I should note, this is partisan warfare against the Lizards, not against the *Reich*. The bands have in them Germans, Poles, Jews—even a few Russians, I have heard. This particular one, down near Hrubieszów, has informed us they could particularly use some antipanzer mines. You could fly those mines to them faster than we could get them there any other way. What say you?"

"I don't know," Ludmila answered. "I am not under your command. Have you no aircraft of your own?"

"Aircraft, yes, a few, but none like that Flying Sewing Machine in which you arrived," Brockdorff-Ahlefeldt said. Ludmila had heard that German nickname for the U-2 before; it never failed to fill her with wry pride. The general went on, "My last Fieseler *Storch* liaison plane could have done the job, but it was hit a couple of weeks ago. You know what the Lizards do to larger, more conspicuous machines. Hrubieszów is about five hundred kilometers south and a little west of here. Can you do the job? I might add that the panzers you help disable will probably benefit Soviet forces as much as those of the *Wehrmacht*."

Since the Germans had driven organized Soviet forces—as opposed to partisans—deep into Russia, Ludmila had her doubts about that. Still, the situation had grown extremely fluid since the Lizards arrived, and a senior lieutenant in the Red Air Force did not know all there was to know about deployments, either. Ludmila said, "Will you be able to get word to Lieutenant General Chill without my flying back to give it to him?"

"I think we can manage that," Brockdorff-Ahlefeldt answered. "If it's all that stands in the way of your flying this mission, I'm sure we can manage it."

Ludmila considered. "You'll have to give me petrol to get there," she said at last. "As a matter of fact, the partisans will have to give me petrol to let me get back. Have they got any?"

"They should be able to lay their hands on some," the German general said. "After all, it hasn't been used much in Poland since the Lizards came. And, of course, when you return here, we will give you fuel for your return flight to Pskov."

She hadn't even asked about that yet. In spite of that forbidding name and those titles, *Generalleutnant Graf* Walter von Brockdorff-Ahlefeldt was indeed a gentleman of the old school. That helped Ludmila make up her mind to nod in agreement to him. Later, she would decide she should have picked better reasons for making up her mind.

Richard Peterson was a decent technician but, as far as Brigadier General Leslie Groves was concerned, a hopeless stick-in-the-mud. He sat in the hard chair in Groves' office in the Science Building of the University of Denver and said, "This containment scheme you have in mind, sir, it's going to be hard to maintain it and increase plutonium production at the same time."

Groves slammed a big, meaty fist down on the desk. He was a big, meaty man, with short-cropped, gingery hair, a thin mustache, and the blunt features of a mastiff. He had a mastiff's implacable aggressiveness, too. "So what are you telling me, Peterson?" he rumbled ominously. "Are you saying we're going to start leaking radioactives into the river so the Lizards can figure out where they are? You'd better not be saying that, because you know what'll happen if you are."

"Of course I know." Peterson's voice went high and shrill. "The Lizards will blow us to kingdom come."

"That's just exactly right," Groves said. "I'm damn lucky I wasn't in Washington, D.C., when they dropped their bomb there." He snorted. "All they got rid of in Washington was some Congresscritters—odds are, they helped the war effort. But if they land one on Denver, we can't make any more nuclear bombs of our own. And if we can't do that, we lose the war."

"I know that, too," Peterson answered. "But the reprocessing plant can only do so much. If you get more plutonium out of it, you put more byproducts into the filters—and if they make it through the filters, they go into the South Platte."

"We have to have more plutonium," Groves said flatly. "If that means putting in more filters or doing more scrubbing of the ones we have, then take care of it. That's what you're for. You tell me you can't do it, I'll find somebody who can, I promise you that. You've got top priority for getting materials, not just from Denver but from all over the country. Use it or find another job."

Behind his horn-rimmed glasses, Peterson looked like a

puppy who'd got a kick in the ribs for no reason at all. "It's not the materials, General. We're desperately short of trained personnel. We—"

Groves glowered at him. "I told you, I don't want excuses. I want results. If you don't have enough trained men, train more. Or else use untrained men and break all your procedures down into baby steps any idiot can understand: if this happens when you do that, then go on and do this next thing. If something else happens, do that instead and try the procedure again. And if *that* or *that* happens, yell for your boss, who really knows what's going on. Takes a while to draft procedures like that, so you'd better get cracking on it."

"But—" Peterson began. Groves ignored him—ostentatiously ignored him, picking up the topmost sheet from his overflowing IN basket. The technician angrily got up and stomped out of the office. Groves had all he could do not to laugh. He'd seen furious stomps much better done. He made a mental note to keep an extra close watch on the plutonium reprocessing plant over the next few weeks. Either Peterson would get production up without releasing radioactive contamination into the river, or somebody else would get a crack at the job.

The sheet Groves had picked up was important in its own right, though, important even by the standards of the moment, where everything in any way connected with atomic weapons had top priority. He rubbed his chin. This one was routed through the Office of Strategic Services, which was something he didn't see every day.

"So the damn Russians want our help, do they?" he muttered. He didn't think much of the Russians, either their politics or their engineering ability. Still, they'd made the first human-built atomic bomb, even though they had used fissionables they'd stolen from the Lizards. That showed they had more on the ball than he'd given them credit for.

Now, though, they were having trouble turning out their own radioactives, and they wanted somebody to get over there some kind of way and give them a hand. If it hadn't been for the Lizards, Groves would have reacted to that with all the enthusiasm of a man who'd had a rattlesnake stuck in his skivvies. But with the Lizards in the picture, you worried about them first and only later about the prospect of Uncle Joe with an atomic bomb, or rather a whole bunch of atomic bombs.

Groves leaned back in his swivel chair. It squeaked. He wished for a cigarette. *While you're at it, why not wish for the moon?*

Instead of worrying about the moon, he said, "I wish Larssen were still with us. He'd be the perfect guy to ship off to Moscow."

Larssen, though, was dead. He'd never been the same after his wife took up with that Army fellow—Yeager, that was his name. Then, even after Larssen made it to Hanford, Washington, and back, nobody'd wanted to disrupt work at the Metallurgical Laboratory by relocating. That had been a hell of a trip; too bad it was wasted. When it came to coping with the travails of the open road, Larssen was top-notch.

What he couldn't handle were his own inner demons. Finally, they must have got the better of him, because he'd shot a couple of men and headed east, toward Lizard-held territory. If he'd sung a song for the aliens, as Groves had feared he might, nuclear fire would have blossomed above Denver. But the cavalry had hunted him down before he could go over to the enemy.

"Well, who does that leave?" Groves asked the office walls. Trouble was, the memorandum he'd got didn't tell him enough. He didn't know where the Reds were having trouble. Did they even have an atomic pile going? Was separating plutonium from an active pile their problem? Or were they trying to separate U-235 from U-238? The memo didn't say. Trying to figure out what to do was like trying to put together a jigsaw puzzle when you didn't have all the pieces and weren't sure which ones were missing.

Since they were Russians, he had to figure their problems were pretty basic. His own problem was pretty basic, too: could he spare anybody and ship him halfway around the world in the middle of war, with no guarantee he'd get there in one piece? And if he could, who did he hate enough to want to send him to Moscow, or wherever the Russians had their program?

He sighed. "Yeah, Larssen would have been perfect," he said. Nothing he could do about that, though. Nothing anybody could do about it, not till Judgment Day. Groves was not the sort to spend time—to waste time, as he would have thought of it—on something he couldn't do anything about. He realized he couldn't decide this one off the top of his head. He'd have to talk things over with the physicists.

He looked at the letter from the OSS again. If somebody went over to lend the Russians a hand, the U.S.A. would get paid back with gadgets taken from a Lizard base that had mutinied and surrendered to the Soviet Army.

"Have to make sure the Reds don't cheat and give us stuff that doesn't work or that we've already got," he told the walls. The one thing you could rely on about the Russians was that you couldn't rely on them.

Then he stopped and read the letter again. He'd missed something there by letting his worries about the Russians blind him to the other things that were going on.

"A Lizard base up and mutinied?" he said. He hadn't heard of anything like that happening anywhere else. The Lizards made for solid, disciplined troops, no matter how much they looked like chameleons with delusions of grandeur. He wondered what had driven them far enough over the edge to go against their own officers.

"Damn, I wish Yeager and those Lizard POWs were still here," he muttered. "I'd pump 'em dry if they were." Inciting Lizards to mutiny had nothing to do with his current assignment, but, when curiosity started itching at him, he felt as if he had to scratch or die.

Then, reluctantly, he decided it was just as well Yeager hadn't been around when Jens Larssen got back from Hanford. Larssen probably would have gone after him and Barbara both with that rifle he carried. That whole mess hadn't been anybody's fault, but Larssen hadn't been able to let go of it, either. One way or another, Groves was sure it had flipped him over the edge.

"Well, no point in worrying about it now," he said. Larssen was dead, Yeager and his wife were gone to Hot Springs, Arkansas, along with the Lizard POWs. Groves suspected Yeager was still doing useful things with the Lizards; he'd had a real flair for thinking along with them. Groves didn't know exactly what that said about Yeager's own mental processes—nothing good, odds were—but it was handy.

He dismissed Yeager from his thoughts as he had Larssen. If the Russians were willing to pay to get the knowledge they needed to build atomic bombs, they needed it badly. On the other hand, Lenin had said something about the capitalists' selling the Soviet Union the rope the Reds would use to hang them. If they got nuclear secrets, would they think about using them against the United States one fine day?

"Of course they will—they're Russians," Groves said. For that matter, had the shoe been on the other foot, the U.S.A. wouldn't have hesitated to use knowledge in its own best interests, no matter where that knowledge came from. That was how you played the game.

The other question was, did such worries really matter? It was short-term benefits versus long-term risks. If the Russians had to bail out of the war because they got beat without nuclear weapons, then worrying about what would happen down the line was foolish. You'd fret about what a Russia armed with atomic bombs could do to the United States after Russia had done everything it could do to the Lizards.

From all he'd learned—Yeager and the Lizard prisoners came back to mind—the Lizards excelled at long-term planning. They looked down their snouts at people because people, measured by the way they looked at things, had no foresight. From a merely human perspective, though, the Lizards were so busy looking at the whole forest that they sometimes didn't notice the tree next door was in the process of toppling over and landing on their heads.

"Sooner or later, we'll find out whether they're right or we are, or maybe that everybody's wrong," he said.

That wasn't the sort of question with which he was good at dealing. Tell him you needed this built within that length of time for the other amount of money and he'd either make it for you or tell you it couldn't be done—and why. Those were the kinds of questions engineers were supposed to handle. *You want philosophy,* he thought, *you should have gone to a philosopher.*

And yet, in the course of his engineering work for this project, he'd listened to a lot of what the physicists had to say. Learning how the bomb did what it did helped him figure out how to make it. But when Fermi and Szilard and the rest of them got to chewing the fat, the line between engineering and philosophy sometimes got very blurry. He'd always thought he had a good head for math, but quantum mechanics made that poor head spin.

Well, he didn't have to worry about it, not in any real sense of the word. What he did have to worry about was picking some luckless physicist and shipping him off to Russia. Of all the things he'd ever done in his nation's service, he couldn't think of one that roused less enthusiasm in him.

And, compared to the poor bastard who'd actually have to go, he was in great shape.

☆ **III** ☆

Panagiotis Mavrogordato pointed to the coastline off the *Naxos'* port rail. "There it is," he said in Greek-accented German. "The Holy Land. We dock in Haifa in a couple of hours."

Moishe Russie nodded. "Meaning no offense," he added in German of his own, with a guttural Yiddish flavor to it, "but I won't be sorry to get off your fine freighter here."

Mavrogordato laughed and tugged his flat-crowned black wool sailor's cap down lower on his forehead. Moishe wore a similar cap, a gift from one of the sailors aboard the *Naxos*. He'd thought the Mediterranean would be warm and sunny all the time, even in winter. It was sunny, but the breeze that blew around him—blew through him—was anything but warm.

"There's no safe place in a war," Mavrogordato said. "If we got through this, I expect we can get through damn near anything, *Theou thelontos*." He took out a string of amber worry beads and worked on them to make sure God would be willing.

"I can't argue with you about that," Russie said. The rusty old ship had been sailing into Rome when what had been miscalled the eternal city—and was the Lizards' chief center in Italy— exploded in atomic fire. The Germans were still bragging about that over the shortwave, even though the Lizards had vaporized Hamburg shortly afterwards in retaliation.

"Make sure you and your family are ready to disembark the minute we tie up at the docks," Mavrogordato warned. "The lot of you are the only cargo we're delivering here this trip, and as soon as the Englishmen pay us off for getting you here in one piece, we're heading back to Tarsus as fast as the *Naxos* will take us." He stamped on the planking of the deck. The *Naxos* had seen better decades. "Not that that's what you'd call fast."

"We didn't bring enough to have to worry about having it out of

55

order," Moishe answered. "As long as I make sure Reuven isn't down in the engine room, we'll be ready as soon as you like."

"That's a good boy you have there," the Greek captain answered. Mavrogordato's definition of a good boy seemed to be one who got into every bit of mischief imaginable. Moishe's standards were rather more sedate. But, considering everything Reuven had been through—everything the whole family had been through—he couldn't complain nearly so much as he would have back in Warsaw.

He went back to the cabin he shared with Reuven and his wife Rivka, to make sure he'd not been telling fables to Mavrogordato. Sure enough, their meager belongings were neatly bundled, and Rivka was making sure Reuven stayed in one place by reading to him from a book of Polish fairy tales that had somehow made the trip first from Warsaw to London and then from London almost to the Holy Land. If you read to Reuven, or if he latched onto a book for himself, he'd hold still; otherwise, he seemed a perpetual-motion machine incarnated in the shape of a small boy—and Moishe could think of no more fitting shape for a perpetual-motion machine to have.

Rivka put up the book and looked a question at him. "We land in a couple of hours," he said. She nodded. She was the glue that held their family together, and he—well, he was smart enough to know it.

"I don't want to get off the *Naxos*," Reuven said. "I like it here. I want to be a sailor when I grow up."

"Don't be foolish," Rivka told him. "This is Palestine we're going to, the Holy Land. Do you understand that? There haven't been many Jews here for hundreds and hundreds of years, and now we're going back. We may even go to Jerusalem. 'Next year in Jerusalem,' people say during the High Holy Days. That will really come true for us now, do you see?"

Reuven nodded, his eyes big and round. Despite their travels and travails, they were bringing him up to understand what being a Jew meant, and Jerusalem was a name to conjure with. It was a name to conjure with for Moishe, too. He'd never imagined ending up in Palestine, even if he was being brought here to help the British rather than for any religious reason.

Rivka went back to reading. Moishe walked up to the bow of the *Naxos* and watched Haifa draw near. The town rose up from the sea along the slopes of Mount Carmel. Even in winter, even in cold, the Mediterranean sun shed a clearer, brighter light than he was used to seeing in Warsaw or London. Many of the houses and other buildings he saw were whitewashed; in that penetrating sunlight, they sparkled as if washed with silver.

Mixed among the buildings were groves of low, spreading trees with gray-green leaves. He'd never seen their like. When Captain Mavrogordato came up for a moment, he asked him what they were. The Greek stared in amazement. "You don't know olives?" he exclaimed.

"No olive trees in Poland," Moishe said apologetically. "Not in England, either."

The harbor drew near. A lot of the men on the piers wore long robes—some white, others bright with stripes—and headcloths. *Arabs*, Moishe realized after a moment. The reality of being far, far away from everything he'd grown up with hit him like a club.

Other men wore work clothes of the kind with which he was more familiar: baggy pants, long-sleeved shirts, a few in overalls, cloth caps or battered fedoras taking the place of the Arabs' kerchiefs. And off by themselves stood a knot of men in the khaki with which Moishe had grown so familiar in England: British military men.

Mavrogordato must have seen them, too, for he steered the *Naxos* toward the pier where they stood. The black plume of coal smoke that poured from the old freighter's stacks shrank, then stopped as the ship nestled smoothly against the dockside. Sailors and dockworkers made the *Naxos* fast with lines. Others dropped the gangplank into place. With that thump, Moishe knew he could walk down to the land of Israel, the land from which his forefathers had been expelled almost two thousand years before. The hair at the back of his neck prickled up in awe.

Rivka and Reuven came out on deck. Moishe's wife was carrying one duffel bag; a sailor had another slung over his shoulder. Moishe took it from the man, saying, "*Evkharisto poly*—thanks very much." It was almost the only Greek he'd picked up on the long, nervous voyage across the Mediterranean, but a useful phrase to have.

"*Parakalo,*" the sailor answered with a smile: "You're welcome."

The uniformed Englishmen walked toward the *Naxos*. "May I—may we—go to them?" Moishe asked Mavrogordato.

"Go ahead," the captain said. "I'm coming, too, to make sure I get paid."

Moishe's feet thudded on the gangplank. Rivka and Reuven followed closely, with Mavrogordato right behind them. Moishe took one last step. Then he was off the ship and onto the soil—well, the docks—of the Holy Land. He wanted to kneel down and kiss the dirty, creosote-stained wood.

Before he could, one of the Englishmen said, "You would be Mr. Russie? I'm Colonel Easter, your liaison here. We'll get you in contact with your coreligionists as soon as may be. Things have been rather dicey lately, so your assistance will be most welcome. Having everyone pulling in the same direction will help the war effort, don't you know?"

"I will do what I can," Moishe answered in his slow, accented English. He studied Easter without much liking: the man plainly saw him as a tool, nothing more. That was how the Lizards had seen him, too. He liked the British cause better than he had that of the aliens, but he was sick of being anyone's tool.

Off to one side, a British officer handed Panagiotis Mavrogordato several neat rolls of gold sovereigns. The Greek beamed from ear to ear. He didn't think of Moishe as a tool: he thought of him as a meal ticket, and made no bones about it. That struck Moishe as a more honest approach than the one Easter showed.

The Englishman said, "If you'll come with me, Mr. Russie, you and your family, we have a buggy waiting down past the end of the dock. Sorry we can't lay on a motorcar for you, but petrol is in rather short supply these days."

Petrol was in short supply all over the world. Colonel Easter hardly needed to be polite in mentioning its absence. He ignored politeness at a much more basic level: neither he nor any of his men made any move to take the duffel bags from Moishe and Rivka. You worried about whether guests were comfortable. Tools—who cared about tools?

The buggy was a black-painted English brougham, and might have been preserved in cotton wool and tinfoil for the past two generations. "We'll take you to the barracks," Easter said, getting aboard with the Russies and an enlisted man who picked up the reins. The rest of the officers climbed into another, almost identical carriage. Easter went on, "We'll get you something to eat and drink there, and then see what sort of quarters we can arrange for the lot of you."

If they'd cared about anything more than using him, they would have had quarters ready and waiting. At least they did remember that he and his family needed food and water. He wondered if they'd remember not to offer him ham, too. The driver flicked the reins and clucked to the horses. The wagon rattled away from the harbor district. Whatever the British had in mind for him, he'd soon find out about it.

He stared wide-eyed at the palm trees like huge feather dusters, at the whitewashed buildings of mud brick, at the mosque the buggy rolled past. Arab men in the long robes he'd already seen and Arab women covered so that only their eyes, hands, and feet showed watched the wagons as they clattered through the narrow, winding streets. Moishe felt very much an interloper, though his own folk had sprung from this place. If Colonel Easter had the slightest clue that God had not anointed him to rule this land, he gave no sign of it.

Suddenly, the buildings opened out onto a marketplace. All at once, Moishe stopped feeling like an alien and decided he was at home after all. None of the details was like what he'd known back in Warsaw: not the dress of the merchants and the customers, not the language they used, not the fruits and vegetables and trinkets they bought and sold. But the tone, the way they haggled—he might have been back in Poland.

Rivka was smiling, too; the resemblance must also have struck her. And not all the men and women in the marketplace were Arabs, Moishe saw when he got a closer look. Some were Jews, dressed for the most part in work clothes or in dresses that, while long, displayed a great deal of flesh when compared to the clothes in which the Arab women shrouded themselves.

A couple of Jewish men carrying brass candlesticks walked by close to the wagon. They were talking loudly and animatedly. Rivka's smile disappeared. "I don't understand them," she said.

"That's Hebrew they're speaking, not Yiddish," Moishe answered, and shivered a little. He'd caught only a few words himself. Learning Hebrew so you could use it in prayer and actually speaking it were two different things. He'd have a lot to pick up here. He wondered how fast he could do it.

They passed the market by. Houses and shops closed in around them again. At bigger streetcorners, British soldiers directed traffic, or tried to: the Arabs and Jews of Haifa weren't as inclined to obey their commands as the orderly folk of London might have been.

A couple of blocks past one thoroughfare, the road all but doubled back on itself. A short young fellow in a short-sleeved shirt and khaki trousers stepped out in front of the wagon that held the Russies. He pointed a pistol at the driver's face. "You will stop now," he said in accented English.

Colonel Easter started to reach for his sidearm. The young man glanced up to the rooftops on either side of the road. Close to a dozen men armed with rifles and submachine guns, most of them wearing kerchiefs to hide their faces, covered both wagons heading back to the British barracks. Very slowly and carefully, Easter moved his right hand away from his weapon.

The cocky young fellow in the street smiled, as if this were a social occasion rather than—whatever it was. "Ah, that's good, that's very good," he said. "You are a sensible man, Colonel."

"What is the point of this—this damned impudence?" Easter demanded in tones that said he would have fought had he seen the remotest chance for success.

"We are relieving you of your guests," the hijacker answered. He looked away from the Englishman and toward Moishe, dropping into Yiddish to say, "You and your family, you will get out of the buggy and come with me."

"Why?" Moishe said in the same language. "If you are who I think you are, I would have been talking with you anyhow."

"Yes, and telling us what the British want us to hear," the fellow with the pistol said. "Now get out—I haven't got all day to argue with you."

Moishe climbed down from the buggy. He helped his wife and son down, too. Gesturing with the pistol, the hijacker on the street led him through a nearby gate and into a courtyard where a couple of other men with guns waited. One of them set down his rifle and efficiently blindfolded the Russies.

As he tied a cloth over Moishe's eyes, he spoke in Hebrew—a short sentence that, after a moment, made sense to Moishe. It was, in fact, much the same sort of thing he might have said had he been blindfolder rather than blindfoldee: "Nice job, Menachem."

"Thanks, but no chatter," the man who'd been on the street said in Yiddish. He was Menachem, then. He shoved Russie lightly in the back; someone else grabbed his elbow. "Get moving." Having no choice, Russie got.

Big Uglies pushed munitions carts toward Teerts' killercraft. Most of them were of the dark brown variety of Tosevite, not the pinkish-tan type. The dark brown ones on this part of the lesser continental mass were more inclined to cooperate with the Race than the lighter ones; from what the flight leader had gathered, the lighter ones had treated them so badly, rule by the Race looked good in comparison.

His mouth fell open in amusement. As far as he was concerned, a Big Ugly was a Big Ugly, and no more needed to be said. The Tosevites themselves, though, evidently saw things differently.

These Tosevites had stripped off the tunics that covered the upper parts of their bodies. The metabolic water they used for bodily cooling glistened on their hides. As far as they were concerned, it was hot.

To Teerts, the temperature was comfortable, though he found the air far too moist to suit him. Still, the humidity in this Florida place was the only thing about its weather he didn't care for. He'd spent winters in Manchuria and Nippon. Next to them, Florida seemed wonderful.

A couple of armorers began loading the munitions onto Teerts' killercraft. He looked at the load. "Only two air-to-air missiles?" he said unhappily.

The senior armorer said, "Be thankful you've got two, superior sir." He was a solid fellow named Ummfac. Though he was nominally subordinate to the killercraft pilots, wise ones treated him and his ilk as equals—and often got better loads because of it. Now he went on, "Pretty soon it'll be nothing but cannon fire, we and the Big Uglies hammering away at each other from short range."

"There's a nasty thought," Teerts said. He sighed. "You're probably right, though. That's the way the war seems to be going these days." He patted the skin of the killercraft's fuselage. "The Emperor be praised that we still fly superior aircraft."

"Truth," Ummfac said. "There's the question of spares even with them . . ."

Teerts climbed up into the cockpit and snuggled down in the armored, padded seat as if he were a hatchling curling up inside the eggshell from which he'd just emerged. He didn't want to think about problems with spares. Already, the Big Uglies were flying aircraft far more dangerous to his machine than they had been when the Race first came to Tosev 3.

He laughed again, bitterly. The Big Uglies weren't supposed to have been flying any aircraft. They were supposed to have been pretechnological barbarians. As far as he was concerned, barbarians they were: no one who'd ever been in Nipponese captivity could possibly argue with that. Pretechnological, however, had turned out to be another matter.

He went through his preflight checklist. Everything was as it should have been. He stuck a finger into the space between a loose piece of padding and the inner wall of the cockpit. No one had found his vial of ginger. That was good. The Nipponese had addicted him to the herb while he lay in their hands. After he'd escaped from captivity, he'd discovered how many of his fellow males tasted it of their own accord.

He called the local flight controller, got permission to take off. The twin turbofans in the killercraft roared to life. The vibration and noise went all through him, a good and familiar feeling.

He taxied down the runway, then climbed steeply, acceleration shoving him back hard into his seat. His horizon expanded marvelously, as it did whenever he went airborne. He enjoyed that expansion less than he had from other bases, though, for it soon brought into view the ruins of Miami.

Teerts had been flying down to Florida when that area went up in an appalling cloud. Had he been a little ahead of himself, the fireball might have caught him, or the blast might have wrecked his killercraft or flipped it into a spin from which it never would have recovered.

Even thinking about that squeezed an alarmed hiss from him. Of itself, his hand started to reach for the little plastic vial of powdered ginger. When he was reassigned to the lesser continental mass, he'd wondered if he would still be able to get the powdered herb he craved. But a good many males on the Florida base used it, and the dark-skinned Big Uglies who labored for the Race seemed to have an unending supply. They hadn't yet asked him for anything more than trinkets, little electronic gadgets he could easily afford to give up in exchange for the delights ginger brought him.

But— "I will not taste now," he said, and made his hand retreat. However good ginger made him feel, he knew it clouded his judgment. Engaging the Big Uglies wasn't so easy or so safe as it had once been. If you went at them confident you'd have things all your own way no matter what, you were liable to end up with your name on the memorial tablet that celebrated the males who had perished to bring Tosev 3 into the Empire.

Rabotev 3 and Halless 1 had such tablets at their capitals; he'd seen holograms of them before setting out from Home. The one on Halless 1 had only a few names, the one on Rabotev 2 only a few hundred. Teerts was sure the Race would set up memorial tablets for Tosev 3; if they'd done it on the other worlds they'd conquered, they'd do it here. If you didn't maintain your traditions, what point to having a civilization?

But the memorial tablets here would be different from those of the other two habitable worlds the Race had conquered. "We can set up the tablets, then build the capital inside them," Teerts said.

In spite of himself, his mouth fell open. The image was macabre, but it was also funny. The memorial tablets to commemorate the heroes who fell in the conquest of Tosev 3 would have a *lot* of names on them.

Teerts flew his prescribed sweep, north and west over the lesser continental mass. A lot of the territory over which he passed was still in the hands of the local Big Uglies. Every so often, antiaircraft fire would splotch the air below and behind him with black puffs of smoke. He didn't worry about that; he was flying too high for the Tosevites' cannon to reach him.

He did keep a wary eye turret turned toward the radar presentation in his head-up display. Intelligence said the Americans lagged behind the British and the Deutsche when it came to jet aircraft, and they mostly used their piston-and-airfoil machines for ground attack and harassment duties, but you never could tell ... and Intelligence wasn't always as omniscient as its practitioners thought. That was another painful lesson the Race had learned on Tosev 3.

Here and there, snow dappled the higher ground. As far as Teerts was concerned, that was as good a reason as any to let the Big Uglies keep this part of their world. But if you let them keep all the parts where snow fell, you'd end up with a depressingly small part of the world to call your own.

He drew nearer the large river that ran from north to south through the heart of the northern half of the lesser continental mass. The Race controlled most of the territory along the river. If his aircraft got into trouble, he had places where he could take refuge.

The large river marked the westernmost limit of his planned patrol. He was about to swing back toward Florida, which, no matter how humid it was, did at least enjoy a temperate climate, when his forward-looking radar picked up something new and hideous.

Whatever it was, it took off from the ground and rapidly developed more velocity than his killercraft had. For a moment, he wondered if something inside his radar had gone wrong. If it had, would the base have the components it needed to fix the problem?

Then his paradigm shifted. That wasn't an aircraft, like the rocket-powered killercraft the Deutsche had started using. It was an out-and-out rocket, a missile. The Deutsche had those, too, but he hadn't known the Americans did. From his briefings, he didn't think Intelligence knew it, either.

He flicked on his radio transmitter. "Flight Leader Teerts calling Florida base Intelligence," he said.

Satellite relay connected him almost as quickly as if he'd been in the next room. "Intelligence, Florida base, Aaatos speaking. Your report, Flight Leader Teerts?"

Teerts gave the particulars of what his radar had picked up, then said, "If you like, I have fuel enough to reach the launch site, attack any launcher or Tosevite installation visible, and still return to base."

"You are a male of initiative," Aaatos said. Among the Race, the phrase was not necessarily a compliment, though Teerts chose to take it as one. Aaatos resumed: "Please wait while I consult my superiors." Teerts waited, though every moment increased the likelihood that he would have to refuel in the air. But Aaatos was not gone long. "Flight Leader Teerts, your attack against the Tosevite installation is authorized. Punish the Big Uglies for their arrogance."

"It shall be done," Teerts said. The computers aboard the killer-craft held the memory of where radar had first picked up the missile. They linked to the satellite mappers the Race had orbiting Tosev 3 and guided Teerts toward the launch site.

He knew the Race was desperately low on antimissile missiles. They'd expended a lot of them against the rockets the Deutsche hurled at Poland and France. Teerts had no idea how many—if any—were left, but he didn't need to wear the fleetlord's body paint to figure out that, if the Race had to start using them here in the United States, whatever remaining reserves there were would vanish all the sooner.

He skimmed low over the woods west of the great river, and over a clearing where, if his instruments didn't lie, the American missile had begun its flight. And, sure enough, he spotted a burned place in the dead grass of the clearing. But that was all he saw. Whatever launcher or guide rails the Big Uglies had used, they'd already got them under cover of the trees.

Had he had an unlimited supply of munitions, Teerts would have shot up the area around the clearing on the off chance of hitting worthwhile. As things were . . . He radioed the situation back to the Florida air base. Aaatos said, "Return here for full debriefing, Flight Leader Teerts. We shall have other opportunities to make the Big Uglies look back in sorrow upon the course they have chosen."

"Returning to base," Teerts acknowledged. If the American Tosevites were starting to use missiles, the Race would have plenty of chances to attack their launchers in the future, anyhow. Whether that was just what Aaatos had meant, Teerts didn't know.

Holding his white flag of truce high, George Bagnall moved out into the clearing in the pine woods south of Pskov. His *valenki* made little scrunching noises as he walked through the packed snow. The big, floppy boots put him in mind of Wellingtons made of felt; however ugly they were, though, they did a marvelous job of keeping his feet warm. For the rest of him, he wore his RAF fur-and-leather flying suit. Anything that kept him from freezing above Angels Twenty was just about up to the rigors of a Russian winter.

On the far side of the clearing, a Lizard came into sight. The alien creature also carried a swatch of white cloth tied to a stick. It too wore a pair of *valenki*, no doubt plundered from a dead Russian soldier; in spite of them, in spite of layers of clothes topped by a *Wehrmacht* greatcoat that fit it like a tent, it looked miserably cold.

"Gavoritye li-vui po russki?" it said with a hissing accent. *"Oder sprechen Sie deutsch?"*

"Ich spreche deutsch besser," Bagnall answered, and then, to see if he was lucky, added, "Do you speak English?"

"Ich verstehe nicht," the Lizard said, and went on in German, "My name is Nikeaa. I am authorized to speak for the Race in these matters."

Bagnall gave his name. "I am a flight engineer of the British Royal Air Force. I am authorized to speak for the German and Soviet soldiers defending Pskov and its neighborhood."

"I thought the Britainish were far from here," Nikeaa said. "But it could be I do not know as much of Tosevite geography as I thought."

What *Tosevite* meant came through from context. "Britain is not close to Pskov," Bagnall agreed. "But most human countries have allied against your kind, and so I am here." *And I bloody well wish I weren't.* His Lancaster bomber had flown in a radar set and a radarman to explain its workings to the Russians, and then been destroyed on the ground before he could get back to England. He and his comrades had been here a year now; even if they had established a place for themselves as mediators between the Reds and the Nazis—who still hated each other as much as either group hated the Lizards—it was a place he would just as soon not have had.

Nikeaa said, "Very well. You are authorized. You may speak.

Your commanders asked this truce of us. We have agreed to it for now, to learn what the reason is for the asking. You will tell me this *sofort*—immediately." He made *sofort* come out as a long, menacing hiss.

"We have prisoners captured over a long time fighting here," Bagnall answered. "Some of them are wounded. We have done what we can for them, but your doctors will know better what to do with them and how to treat them."

"Truth," Nikeaa said. He moved his head up and down in a nod. For a moment, Bagnall took that for granted. Then he realized the Lizard had probably had to learn the gesture along with the German and Russian languages. His respect for Nikeaa's accomplishments went up a peg.

What he'd told the Lizard was indeed true. From everything he'd heard, the troops around Pskov treated Lizard prisoners far better than the Germans had treated their Russian captives, or vice versa. Being hard to come by, Lizard prisoners were valuable. The Nazis and Reds had had plenty of chances to take each other's measure.

"In return for giving these wounded males back to the Race, you want what?" Nikeaa asked, and made a queer coughing noise that sounded like something left over from his own language. "We also have captives, Germans and Russians. We have no Britainish here, this I tell you. We do not harm these captured ones after we have them. We give them for yours. We give ten for one, if you like."

"Not enough," Bagnall said.

"Then we give twenty for one," Nikeaa said. Bagnall had heard from others who'd dealt with the Lizards that they were not good bargainers. Now he saw what they'd meant. Human negotiators would not have backpedaled so readily.

"Still not enough," he said. "Along with the soldiers, we want a hundred of your books or films, and two of your machines that play the films, along with working batteries for them."

Nikeaa drew back in alarm. "You want us to give you our secrets?" He made that coughing noise again. "It cannot be."

"No, no. You misunderstand," Bagnall said hastily. "We know you will not give us any military manuals or things of that sort. We want your novels, your stories, whatever science you have that will not let us build weapons with what we learn from it. Give us these things and we will be content."

"If you cannot use them immediately, why do you want them?" Reading tone into a Lizard's voice probably told you more about yourself than about the Lizard, but Bagnall thought Nikeaa sounded suspicious. The alien went on, "This is not how Tosevites usually behave." Yes, he was suspicious.

"We want to learn more about your kind," Bagnall answered. "Eventually, this war will end, and your people and mine will live side by side."

"Yes. You will be our subjects," Nikeaa said flatly.

But Bagnall shook his head. "Not necessarily. If your conquest were as easy as you'd thought it was going to be, it would have been finished by now. You'll need to be dealing with us more nearly as equals at least until the end of the war, and maybe afterwards as well. And we with you—the same does apply. I gather you've been studying us for a long time. We're just beginning to learn about you."*And most of what we have learned, I don't fancy.*

"I have not the authority to decide this on my own," Nikeaa said. "It is not a demand we were prepared for, and so I must consult with my superiors before replying."

"If you must, then you must," Bagnall said; he'd already noted—and he was sure he was far from the only one who had—that the Lizards were not good at deciding things on the spur of the moment.

He'd tried to put disappointment in his own voice when he replied, though he doubted whether Nikeaa recognized it. Even inserting it wasn't easy. If the Lizards did come up with the books and films and readers, they wouldn't stay in Pskov. Half of them would go to Moscow, the other half to . . . no, not to Berlin, which was ruined, but to some town in Germany. The NKVD, no doubt, would pore over one set, and the *Gestapo* over the other. No matter how much he wanted mankind to defeat the Lizards, Bagnall had a devil of a time finding much enthusiasm for the notion of the Bolsheviks and Nazis getting a leg up on England and the United States in understanding the alien invaders. He'd seen Hitler and Stalin's men in action, and had more often been horrified than impressed.

Nikeaa said, "I will report this condition of yours and will make my reply when my superiors determine what the correct response should be. Shall we meet again in fifteen days? I hope to have their decision by that time."

"I had not expected so long a delay," Bagnall said.

"Decisions should not be made hastily, especially those of such importance," Nikeaa said. Was that reproach he was trying to convey? Bagnall had trouble being sure. The Lizard added, "We are not Tosevites, after all, to rush into everything." Yes, reproach, or perhaps just scorn.

"Fifteen days, then," Bagnall said, and made for the woods where his escort—a mixed party, or rather two separate parties, one German, the other Russian—awaited his return. He glanced back over his shoulder. Nikeaa was hurrying away toward his own folk. Bagnall's sigh sent a plume of fog out ahead of him. But for Ken Embry the pilot and Jerome Jones the radarman, his folk were far from Pskov.

Captain Martin Borcke was holding Bagnall's horse. The *Wehrmacht* man spoke fluent English; Bagnall thought he was in Intelligence, but wasn't certain. In English, he asked, "Have we got the exchange agreement?"

Bagnall wished Borcke hadn't used English, as if expecting a reply in the same tongue—one the Russians did not know. Keeping the two alleged allies from each other's throats was anything but easy. The RAF man answered in German, which many of the Red Army men could follow: "No, we have no agreement yet. The Lizards need to talk to their superiors before they decide whether they can give us the books we want."

The Russians accepted that as a matter of course. To their way of thinking, moving an inch past the orders you had was dangerous. If anything went wrong, the blame landed squarely on you. Borcke snorted in contempt; the *Wehrmacht* let people do more thinking for themselves. "Well, it can't be helped," he said, and then turned that into Russian: *"Nichevo."*

"Nichevo, da," Bagnall said, and swung up onto the horse. Riding it wasn't as pleasant as being in a heated motorcar, but it did keep his legs and thighs warm. That was something. He hadn't been on horseback above half a dozen times before he came to Pskov. Now he sometimes felt ready to ride in the Derby. Intellectually, he knew that wasn't so, but the strides he had made in equitation encouraged him in the fancy.

After a cold night encampment, he got back into Pskov the next afternoon. He went over to the *Krom*, the medieval stone castle, to report the delay to Lieutenant General Kurt Chill and to Brigadiers Nikolai Vasiliev and Aleksandr German, the German and Russian officers commanding in the city. With them, as he'd expected, he found Ken Embry. The RAF men, being relatively disinterested, served as lubricant between *Wehrmacht* and Red Army personnel.

After Bagnall made his report, he and Embry headed back to the wooden house they shared with Jerome Jones. When they drew near, they heard a dish shatter with a crash, and then angry voices, two men's and a woman's, shouting loudly.

"Oh, bugger, that's Tatiana!" Ken Embry exclaimed.

"You're right," Bagnall said. They both started to run. Panting, Bagnall added, "Why the devil couldn't she leave Jones alone after she took up with that Jerry?"

"Because that would have been convenient," Embry answered. Ever since he'd been pilot and Bagnall flight engineer aboard their Lancaster, they'd had a contest to see who could come up with the most casually cynical understatements. For the moment, Embry had taken the lead.

Bagnall, though, was a better runner, and got to the door a couple of strides ahead of his comrade. He would willingly have forgone the honor. All the same, he threw the door open and rushed inside, Embry right behind him.

Georg Schultz and Jerome Jones stood almost nose-to-nose, screaming at each other. Off to one side, Tatiana Pirogova had a plate in her hand, ready to fling. By the shards, she'd thrown the last one at Jones. That didn't mean this one wouldn't fly at Schultz's head. At that, Bagnall was glad Tatiana was still flinging crockery instead of reaching for the scope-sighted Mosin-Nagant sniper's rifle she wore slung on her back.

She was a striking woman: blond, blue-eyed, shapely—altogether lovely, if face and body were all you cared about. She'd made advances to Bagnall, not so long ago. That she'd been Jones' lover at the time hadn't been the only reason he'd declined. It would have been like bedding a she-leopard—probably fun while it lasted, but you could never afford to turn your back afterward.

"Shut up, all of you!" he shouted now, first in English, then in German, and finally in Russian. The three squabblers didn't shut up, of course; they started yelling at him instead. He thought the fair Tatiana was going to let fly with that plate, but she didn't, not quite. *Good sign,* he thought. Having them scream at him was another good sign. Since he wasn't *(thank God!)* sleeping with any of them, they might be slower to get lethally angry at him.

Behind him, Ken Embry said, "What the devil is going on here?" He used the same mixture of Russian and German he did with Lieutenant General Chill and the Russian partisan brigadiers. Their squabbles sometimes came near to blows, too.

"This bastard's still fucking my woman!" Georg Schultz shouted, pointing at Jerome Jones.

"I am not your woman. I give my body to whom I please," Tatiana answered, just as hotly.

"I don't want your body," Jerome Jones yelled in pretty fluent Russian; he'd studied the language in his undergraduate days at Cambridge. He was a thin, clever-looking fellow in his early twenties, about as tall as Schultz but not nearly so solidly made. He went on, "Christ and the saints, how many times do I have to tell you that?"

His picturesque oath meant nothing to Tatiana, or even less. She spat on the floorboards. "That for Christ and the saints! I am a Soviet woman, free of such superstitious twaddle. And if I want you again, little man, I will have you."

"What about me?" Schultz said, like the others conducting the argument at the top of his lungs.

"This will be even more delightful to mediate than the generals' brawls," Bagnall murmured in an aside to Ken Embry.

Embry nodded, then grinned impudently. "It's rather more entertaining to listen to, though, isn't it?"

"—have been sleeping with you," Tatiana was saying, "so you have no cause for complaint. I do this even though, last time you got on top of me, you called me Ludmila instead of my own name."

"I what?" Schultz said. "I never—"

"You did," Tatiana said with a certainty that could not be denied—and an obvious malicious pleasure in that certainty. "You can still think about that soft little Red Air Force pilot you pined for like a puppy with its tongue hanging out, but if I think of anyone else, it's like you think your poor mistreated cock will fall off. If you think I mistreat your cock when it's in there, it can stay out." She turned to Jones, swinging her hips a little and running her tongue over her lips to make them fuller and redder. Bagnall could see exactly what she was doing, but that didn't mean he was immune to it.

Neither was the British radarman. He took half a step toward Tatiana, then stopped with a very visible effort. "No, dammit!" he yelled. "This is how I got into trouble in the first place." He paused and looked thoughtful, so well that Bagnall wondered if the expression was altogether spontaneous. And when Jones spoke again, he made a deliberate effort to turn the subject: "Haven't seen Ludmila about for the past few days. She's overdue from her last flight, isn't she?"

"*Ja,*" Schultz said. His head bobbed up and down. "She flew last to Riga, and should have been back soon."

"No, not necessarily," Bagnall said. "General Chill got a message answering whatever query he'd sent with her, and saying also that the soldier commanding in Riga was taking advantage of her light airplane for some mission of his own." Now he had trouble keeping his face straight. He'd been interested in Ludmila Gorbunova, too, but she hadn't been interested back.

"Ah, that is good; that is very good," Schultz said. "I had not heard it."

Tatiana started to smash the plate over his head. He was fast; he knocked it out of her hand so that it flew across the room, hit the timbers of the wall, and broke there. Tatiana cursed him in Russian and in the bad German she'd picked up. When she'd run through all her invective once—and the choicer bits twice—she shouted, "Since no one cares about me, to the devil's uncle with the lot of you." She stormed out of the house, slamming the door behind her loud enough, probably, to make the neighbors think an artillery round had hit it there.

Georg Schultz surprised Bagnall by starting to laugh. Then Schultz, a farmerly type, surprised him again by quoting Goethe: "*Die ewige Weibliche*—the eternal feminine." The German shook his head. "I don't know why I get myself into such a state over her, but I do."

"Must be love," Ken Embry said innocently.

"God forbid!" Schultz looked around at the shattered crockery. "Ah, the hell with it." His gaze fixed on Jerome Jones. "And the hell with you, too, *Engländer*."

"From you, that's a compliment," Jones said. Bagnall took a step over to the radarman's side. If Schultz wanted to try anything, he wouldn't be going against Jones alone.

But the German shook his head again, rather like a bear bedeviled by bees, and left the house. He didn't slam the door as hard as Tatiana had, but broken pieces of dishes jumped all the same. Bagnall took a deep breath. The scene hadn't been as bad as combat, but it hadn't been any fun, either. He clapped Jerome Jones on the back. "How the devil did you ever get tangled up with that avalanche who walks like a man?"

"The fair Tatiana?" Now Jones shook his head—ruefully. "She doesn't walk like a man. She walks like a woman—that was the problem."

"And she doesn't want to give you up, even though she has her dashing Nazi, too?" Bagnall said. *Dashing* wasn't the right word to describe Georg Schultz, and he knew it. *Capable* fit pretty well.

Dangerous was in there, too, perhaps not as overtly as with Tatiana Pirogova, but part of the mix nonetheless.

"That's about it," Jones muttered.

"Tell her to go away often enough and she'll eventually get the message, old man," Bagnall said. "You do *want* her to go away, don't you?"

"Most of the time, of course I do," Jones answered. "But sometimes, when I'm—you know—" He glanced down at the crockery-strewn floor and didn't go on.

Bagnall did it for him: "When you're randy, you mean." Jones nodded miserably. Bagnall looked at Ken Embry. Embry was looking at him. They both groaned.

The coming of the Lizards had brought ruin to hundreds of towns for every one it helped. Lamar, Colorado, though, was one of the latter. The prairie town, a no-account county seat before the aliens invaded, had become a center for the defense against them. People and supplies had flowed into it rather than streaming away, as was the usual case.

Captain Rance Auerbach thought about that as he watched mutton chops sizzle on the grill of a local cafe. The fire that made them sizzle was fueled by dried horse dung: not much in the way of timber around Lamar, and coal was in short supply and natural gas unavailable. There were, however, plenty of horses around— Auerbach himself wore a cavalry captain's bars.

A waitress with a prizefighter's beefy arms set down three mugs of home brew and a big bowl of boiled beets—beets being one of the leading local crops. She too glanced at the chops. "Uh-*huh*," she said, as much to herself as to Auerbach. "Timed that about right—those'll be ready in just a couple minutes."

Auerbach slid one of the mugs of beer down the counter to Rachel Hines, who sat on his left, and the other to Penny Summers, who sat on his right. He raised his own mug. "Confusion to the Lizards!" he said.

"Hell with 'em," Penny agreed, and gulped down half of what her mug held. With her flat Midwestern accent, she could have been a native of Lamar; Auerbach's Texas drawl proclaimed him an outsider every time he opened his mouth. Neither Penny nor Rachel was from Lamar, though. Auerbach and his men had rescued both of them from Lakin, Kansas, when his company raided the base the Lizards had set up there.

After a moment's hesitation, Penny Summers softly echoed, "Confusion to the Lizards," and also sipped at her beer. She did everything softly and slowly these days. In the escape from Lakin, her father had been blown to sloppily butchered raw meat before her eyes. She'd never been quite the same since.

The waitress went around the counter, stabbed the mutton chops with a long-handled fork, and slapped them onto plates. "There y'go, folks," she said. "Eat hearty—y'never know when you'll get another chance."

"Ain't that the truth," Rachel Hines said. She attacked the mutton with knife and fork. Her blue eyes glowed as she gulped down a big bite. She hadn't been the same since she got out of Lakin, either, but she hadn't withdrawn into herself the way Penny had. These days, she wore the same khaki uniform Auerbach did, though with a PFC's single chevron rather than his captain's badges. She made a pretty fair trooper; she could ride, she could shoot, she didn't mouth off (too much), and the rest of the company paid her what had to be the ultimate compliment: for the most part, they treated her like one of the boys.

She cut off another bite, frowning a little as she transferred the fork to her left hand so she could use the knife. "How's your finger doing?" Auerbach asked.

Rachel looked down at her hand. "Still missing," she reported, and spread the hand so he could see the wide gap between middle finger and pinkie. "Now if I'd been shot by a Lizard, it would have been one thing," she said. "Having that crazy son of a bitch nail me, though, that just makes me mad. But it could have been worse, I expect, so I've got no real kick coming."

Few men Auerbach knew could have talked about a wound so dispassionately. If Rachel was one of the guys, she was a better one than most. Auerbach said, "That Larssen fellow was supposed to be going over to the Lizards with stuff they weren't supposed to know. He'd shot two men dead, too. He had what he got when we caught up with him coming, you ask me. I'm just sorry we took casualties bringing him down."

"Wonder what it was he knew," Rachel Hines said.

Auerbach shrugged. His troopers had been asking that question since the order to hunt down Larssen came out of Denver. He didn't know the answer, but he could make some pretty fair guesses, ones he didn't share. Back a while before, he'd led the cavalry escort that got Leslie Groves into Denver, and Groves had been carrying something—he wouldn't say what—he treated as just a little more important than the Holy Grail. If it didn't have something to do with the atomic bombs that had knocked the

Lizards for a couple of loops, Auerbach would have been mightily surprised.

Penny Summers said, "I spent a lot of time praying everyone would come through the mission safe. I do that every time people ride out of here."

"It's not the worst thing to do," Auerbach said, "but coming out and cooking or nursing or whatever you want wouldn't hurt, either." Since she'd come to Lamar, Penny had spent a lot of time in a little furnished room in an overcrowded apartment house, brooding and reading the Bible. Getting her out for mutton chops was something of a triumph.

Or so he thought, till she shoved her plate away and said, "I don't like mutton. It tastes funny and it's all greasy. We never had it much back in Lakin."

"You should eat," Auerbach told her, knowing he sounded like a mother hen. "You need it." That was true; Penny was rail-thin. She hadn't been that way when she came to Lamar, but she hadn't been the same in a lot of ways since Wendell Summers got himself messily killed.

"Hey, it's food," Rachel Hines said. "I don't even mind the beets, not any more. I just shovel it all down; I quit worrying about it as soon as I put on the uniform."

She filled out that uniform in a way the Army bureaucrats who'd designed it hadn't had in mind. Despite her talk of gluttony, she wasn't the least bit fat. If she hadn't been so all-around good-natured, she would have had half the men in the company squabbling over her. There were times when Auerbach had been tempted to pull rank himself. Even if she'd been interested, though, that would have created as many problems as it solved, maybe more.

He glanced over to Penny again. He felt responsible for her, too. He also had the feeling more was there than met the eye. With Rachel, what you saw was what you got—he couldn't imagine her holding anything back. With Penny, he got the feeling her present unhappiness masked something altogether different. He shrugged. The other possibility was that his imagination had gone and run away with him. *Wouldn't be the first time,* he thought.

To his surprise, she did take back the plate and start eating again, not with any great enthusiasm but doggedly, as if she were fueling a car. With what she'd been giving herself lately, a car would long since have run out of gas. He didn't say anything. That might have broken the spell.

Rachel Hines shook her head. She'd cropped her hair into a

short bob, the better to have it fit under a helmet. She said, "Going off and giving secrets to the Lizards. I purely can't fathom that, and there's a fact. But plenty of people in Lakin got on with 'em just fine and dandy, like they were the new county commissioners or something."

"You're right." Penny Summers' face twisted into an expression both fierce and savage, one altogether unlike any Auerbach had seen on her since she'd come to Lamar. "Joe Bentley over at the general store, he sucked up to them for all he was worth, and when Edna Wheeler went in there and called them a bunch of goggle-eyed things from out of a freak show, you tell me he didn't go trotting off to them fast as his legs could take him. And the very next day she and her husband and both their kids got thrown out of their house."

"That's so," Rachel said, nodding. "It sure is. And Mel Six-killer, I guess he got sick of folks calling him half-breed all the time, on account of he'd even make up tales to take to the Lizards, and they'd believe 'em, too. He got a lot of people in trouble like that. Yeah, some people were mean to him, but you don't go getting even by hurting 'em that kind of way."

"And Miss Proctor, the home economics teacher at the high school," Penny said. "What was it she always called the Lizards? 'The wave of the future,' that was it, like we couldn't do anything about 'em no matter what. And then she'd go out and make sure we couldn't do anything."

"Yeah, she sure did," Rachel said. "And . . ."

They went on for another five or ten minutes, talking about the collaborators back in their little hometown. Auerbach sat quietly, drinking his beer, finishing his supper (he didn't mind mutton, but he could have lived for a long time without looking another beet in the eye) and listening. He'd never seen Penny Summers so lively, and he'd never seen her finally clean her plate, either—she didn't seem to notice she was doing it. Complaining about the old neighbors got her juices flowing as nothing else had.

The brawny waitress came by. "Get you folks some more beer, or are you gonna sit there takin' up space?"

"I'll have another one, thanks," Auerbach said. To his surprise, Penny nodded before Rachel did. The waitress went away, came back with fresh mugs. "Thanks, Irma," Auerbach told her. She glowered at him, as if doing her job well enough to deserve thanks showed she'd somehow failed at it.

"You've raided Lakin since you got us out, haven't you, Captain?" Rachel asked.

"Sure we have," Auerbach answered. "You weren't along for that, were you? No, you weren't—I remember. We hurt 'em, too; drove 'em clean out of town. I thought we'd be able to keep it, but when they threw too much armor at us—" He spread his hands. "What can you do?"

"That's not what she meant," Penny said. "I know what she meant."

Auerbach stared at her. She surely hadn't been this animated before. "What did she mean?" he asked, hoping to keep her talking—and, more than that, hoping to keep her involved with the world beyond the four walls within which she'd chosen to shut herself away.

It worked, too; Penny's eyes blazed. "She meant, did you settle up scores with the quislings?" she said. Rachel Hines nodded to show her friend was right.

"No, I don't think we did," Auerbach said. "We didn't know just who needed settling back then, and we were too busy with the Lizards to risk putting anybody's nose out of joint by getting the locals mad at us for giving the wrong people a hard time."

"We're not going back to Lakin any time soon, are we?" Rachel asked.

"Not that I know of, anyhow," Auerbach said. "Colonel Nordenskold might have a different idea, but he hasn't told me about it if he does. And if he gets orders from somewhere up the line—" He spread his hands again. Above the regimental level, the chain of command kept getting broken links. Local commanders had a lot more autonomy than anybody had figured they would before the Lizards started plastering communications.

"The colonel needs to get word to the partisans," Rachel said. "Sooner or later, those bastards ought to get what's coming to 'em." She brought out the word as casually as any cavalry trooper might have; Auerbach didn't think of it as a woman swearing till he listened to the sentence over again inside his head. Even if she had curves, Rachel was a cavalryman, all right.

"That's what needs doing," Penny Summers said with a vigorous nod. "Oh yes indeed."

"Seems funny, talking about American partisans," Rachel said. "I mean, we saw the Russians hiding in the woods in the newsreels before the Lizards came, but to have to do that kind of stuff ourselves—"

"Funny to you, maybe, but you're from Kansas," Auerbach answered. "You come from Texas the way I do, or from Virginia like Lieutenant Magruder, and you'll know about bushwhacking, 'cause odds are you're related to somebody who did some of it during the States War." He touched his sleeve. "Good thing this uniform isn't blue the way it used to be. You come out of the South, your part of the country's been invaded before."

Rachel shrugged. "For me, the Civil War's something out of a history book, that's all."

"Not to Southerners," Auerbach said. "Mosby and Forrest are real live people to us, even nowadays."

"I don't know who they are, but I'll take your word for it," Penny said. "Thing of it is, if we can do that, we ought to. Can Colonel Nordenskold get in touch with the partisans?"

"Oh, yeah," Auerbach said, "and do you know how?" He waited for her to shake her head, then set a finger by the side of his nose and grinned. "Carrier pigeons, that's how. Not even any radio for the Lizards to intercept, and they haven't figured it out yet." He knew he was talking too much, but the chance to see Penny Summers act like a real live human being led him to say a little more than he should.

She bounced up off her stool now. "That's terrific. Let's go talk with the colonel right this minute." It was as if she'd flicked a switch inside herself, and everything she'd turned off over the past months came back to life all at once. It was quite a thing to see. *Hell of a woman there,* Auerbach thought, and then, a moment later, *and she's a civilian, too.*

Colonel Morton Nordenskold made his headquarters in what still said it was Lamar's First National Bank. Back in the twenties, some sort of spectacular robbery had happened there; Lamar natives talked about it even now. There weren't a lot of Lamar natives left any more, though. Soldiers and refugees dominated the town now.

No sentries stood outside the bank. Half the town away, a couple of dummies from Feldman's tailor shop, dressed in Army uniform from helmet to boots, guarded a fancy house. If the Lizards came by with bombers, the hope was that they'd hit there instead of the real HQ. So far, they hadn't bothered either one.

Inside, where reconnaissance couldn't spot them, two real live soldiers came to attention when Auerbach walked through the door with Rachel and Penny. "Yes, sir, you can see the colonel now," one of them said.

"Thanks," Auerbach said, and headed for Nordenskold's office.

Behind him, one of the sentries turned to the other and said, not quite quietly enough, "Look at that lucky son of a bitch, will you, walkin' out with two o' the best-lookin' broads in town."

Auerbach thought about going back and calling him on it, then decided he liked it and kept on toward the colonel's office.

The Tosevite hatchling made a squealing noise that grated in Ttomalss' hearing diaphragms. It reached up for the handle of a low cabinet, grabbed hold on about the third try, and did its best to pull itself upright. Its best wasn't good enough. It fell back down, splat.

Ttomalss watched curiously to see what it would do next. Sometimes, after a setback like that, it would wail, which he found even more irritating than its squeals. Sometimes it thought a fall was funny, and let out one of its annoyingly noisy laughs.

Today, rather to Ttomalss' surprise, it did neither of those. It just reached up and tried again, as deliberate and purposeful an action as he'd ever seen from it. It promptly fell down again, and banged its chin on the floor. This time, it did start to wail, the cry it made to let the world know it was in pain.

When it did that, it annoyed everyone up and down the corridor of the starship orbiting above Tosev 3. When the other males researching the Big Uglies got annoyed, they grew more likely to side against Ttomalss in his struggle to keep the hatchling and keep studying it rather than returning it to the female from whose body it had emerged.

"Be silent, foolish thing," he hissed at it. The hatchling, of course, took no notice of him, but continued to make the air hideous with its howls. He knew what he had to do: he stooped and, being careful not to prick its thin, scaleless skin with his claws, held it against his torso.

After a little while, the alarming noise eased. The hatchling liked physical contact. Young of the Race, when newly out of the eggshell, fled from anything larger than they were, instinctively convinced it would catch and eat them. For the first part of their lives, Big Uglies were as immobile as some of the limestone-shelled creatures of Home's small seas. If they got into trouble, the females who'd ejected them (and a hideous process *that* was, too) had to save them and comfort them. With no such female available here, the job fell to Ttomalss.

The hatchling's cheek rubbed against his chest. That touched off its sucking reflex. It turned its head and pressed its soft, wet mouth against his hide. Unlike a Tosevite female, he did not secrete nutritive fluid. Little by little, the hatchling was realizing that faster than it had.

"A good thing, too," Ttomalss muttered, and tacked on an

emphatic cough. The little Tosevite's saliva did unpleasant things to his body paint. He swung down an eye turret so he could look at himself. Sure enough, he'd have to touch up a spot before he was properly presentable. He hadn't intended to demonstrate experimentally that body paint was not toxic to Big Uglies, but he'd done it.

He turned the other eye turret down, studied the hatchling with both eyes. It looked up at him. Its own eyes were small and flat and dark. He wondered what went on behind them. The hatchling had never seen itself, nor its own kind. Did it think it looked like him? No way to know, not until its verbal skills developed further. But its perceptions would have changed by then, too.

He watched the corners of its absurdly mobile mouth curl upwards. Among the Tosevites, that was an expression of amiability, so he had succeeded in making it forget about its hurt. Then he noticed the cloth he kept around its middle was wet. The Tosevite had no control over its bodily function. Interrogations suggested Big Uglies did not learn such control for two or three of their years—four to six of those by which Ttomalss reckoned. As he carried the hatchling over to a table to clean it off and set a new protective cloth in place, he found that a very depressing prospect.

"You *are* a nuisance," he said, adding another emphatic cough.

The hatchling squealed, then made a noise of its own that sounded like an emphatic cough. It had been imitating the sounds Ttomalss made more and more lately, not just emphatic and interrogative coughs but sometimes real words. Sometimes he thought it was making those noises with deliberate intent. Tosevites could and did talk, often to excess—no doubt about that.

When the hatchling was clean and dry and content, he set it back down on the floor. He tossed the soaked cloth into an airtight plastic bin to prevent its ammoniacal reek from spreading, then squirted cleansing foam on his hands. He found the Tosevites' liquid wastes particularly disgusting; the Race excreted neat, tidy solids.

The hatchling got up on all fours and crawled toward the cabinets again. Its quadrupedal gait was much more confident than it had been at the beginning; for a couple of days, the only way it had been able to get anywhere was backwards. It tried pulling itself erect—and promptly fell down once more.

The communicator chimed for attention. Ttomalss hurried over to it. The screen lit, showing him the image of Ppevel, assistant administrator for the eastern region of the main continental mass.

"I greet you, superior sir," Ttomalss said, doing his best to hide nervousness.

"I greet you, Research Analyst," Ppevel replied. "I trust the Tosevite hatchling whose fate is now under discussion with the Chinese faction known as the People's Liberation Army remains healthy?"

"Yes, superior sir," Ttomalss said. He turned one eye turret away from the screen for a moment, trying to spot the hatchling. He couldn't. That worried him. The little creature was much more mobile than it had been, which meant it was much more able to get into mischief, too ... He'd missed some of what Ppevel was saying. "I'm sorry, superior sir?"

Ppevel waggled his eye turrets ever so slightly, a sign of irritation. "I said, are you prepared to give up the hatchling on short notice?"

"Superior sir, of course I am, but I do protest that this abandonment is not only unnecessary but also destructive to a research program vital for the successful administration of this world after it is conquered and pacified." Ttomalss looked around for the hatchling again, and still didn't see it. In a way, that was almost a relief. How could he turn it over to the Chinese if he didn't know where it was?

"No definitive decision on this matter has yet been made, if that is your concern," the administrator said. "If one is reached, however, rapid implementation will be mandatory."

"At need, it shall be done, and promptly," Ttomalss said, hoping he could keep relief from his voice. "I understand the maniacal stress the Big Uglies sometimes place on speedy performance."

"If you do understand it, you have the advantage over most males of the Race," Ppevel said. "The Tosevites have sped through millennia of technical development in a relative handful of years. I have heard endless speculation as to the root causes of this: the peculiar geography, the perverse and revolting sexual habits the Big Uglies practice—"

"This latter thesis has been central to my own research, superior sir," Ttomalss answered. "The Tosevites certainly differ in their habits from ourselves, the Rabotevs, and the Hallessi. My hypothesis is that their constant sexual tensions, to use an imprecise simile, are like a fire continually simmering under them and stimulating them to ingenuity in other areas."

"I have seen and heard more hypotheses than I care to remember," Ppevel said. "When I find one with supporting evidence, I shall be pleased. Our analysts these days too often emulate the Tosevites not only in speed but also in imprecision."

"Superior sir, I wish to retain the Tosevite hatchling precisely so I can gather such evidence," Ttomalss said. "Without studying the Big Uglies at all stages of their development, how can we hope to understand them?"

"A point to be considered," Ppevel admitted, which made Ttomalss all but glow with hope; no administrator had given him so much reason for optimism in a long time. Ppevel continued, "We—"

Ttomalss wanted to hear more, but was distracted by a yowl—an alarmed yowl—from the Big Ugly hatchling. It also sounded oddly far away. "Excuse me, superior sir, but I believe I have encountered a difficulty," the researcher said, and broke the connection.

He hurried along the corridors of his laboratory area, looking to see what the hatchling had managed to get itself into this time. He didn't see it anywhere, which worried him—had it managed to crawl inside a cabinet? Was that why its squawks sounded distant?

Then it wailed again. Ttomalss went dashing out into the corridor—the hatchling had taken it into its head to go exploring.

Ttomalss almost collided with Tessrek, another researcher into the habits and thought patterns of the Big Uglies. In his arms, none too gently, Tessrek carried the wayward Tosevite hatchling. He thrust it at Ttomalss. "Here. This is yours. Kindly keep better track of it in future. It came wandering into my laboratory chamber, and, I assure you, it is not welcome there."

As soon as Ttomalss took hold of it, the hatchling stopped wailing. It knew him, and knew he cared for it. He might as well have been its mother, a Tosevite term with implications far more powerful than its equivalent in the language of the Race.

Tessrek went on, "The sooner you give that thing back to the Big Uglies, the happier everyone else along this corridor will be. No more hideous noises, no more dreadful stenches—a return to peace and quiet and order."

"The hatchling's ultimate disposition has not yet been determined," Ttomalss said. Tessrek had always wanted the little Tosevite gone. Its jaunt today would only give him fresh ammunition.

"Getting rid of it will improve my disposition," he said, and let his mouth fall open in appreciation of his own joke. Then he grew serious once more: "If you must have it, keep it in your own area.

I cannot answer for its safety if it invades my laboratory once more."

"Like any hatchling, it is as yet ignorant of proper behavior," Ttomalss said coldly. "If you ignore that obvious fact and deliberately mistreat it, I cannot answer for *your* safety." To make sure he'd made his point, he turned and carried the hatchling back into his own chamber. With one eye turret, he watched Tessrek staring after him.

☆ **IV** ☆

An ugly little tracked ammunition carrier came *put-putting* up to the Panthers halted in the forest north of Lodz. The front hatch of the French-built machine—booty from the triumphant campaign of 1940—opened and a couple of men scrambled out, calling, "Here, lads! We've got presents for you."

"About time," Heinrich Jäger said. "We were down to our last few rounds for each panzer."

"That's not where you want to be against the Lizards, either," Gunther Grillparzer added. The gunner went on, "Their armor is so good, you can waste a lot of hits before you get one penetration."

The ammunition haulers grinned. They wore one-piece coveralls like the panzer crewmen, but in the field-gray of self-propelled gun units rather than panzer black. One of them said, "New toys for you here—a notion we borrowed from the Lizards and put into production for ourselves."

That was plenty to get the panzer men crowding around them. Jäger took shameless advantage of his rank to push his way to the front. "What do you have?" he demanded.

"We'll show you, sir," the fellow who'd spoken before answered. He turned to his companion. "Show them, Fritz."

Fritz went around to the back of the Lorraine hauler, undid the whitewashed canvas tilt on top of the storage bin at the rear of the machine. He reached in and, grunting a little at the weight, drew out the oddest-looking shell Jäger had ever seen. "What the devil is it?" half a dozen men asked at once.

"You tell 'em, Joachim," Fritz said. "I never can say it right."

"Armor-piercing discarding sabot," Joachim said importantly. "See, the aluminum sabot fits your gun barrel, but as soon as it gets out, it falls off, and the round proper goes out with a lot more

83

muzzle velocity than you can get any other way. It's capped with wolfram, too, for extra penetration."

"Is that so?" Jäger pricked up his ears. "My brother is a panzer engineer, and he says wolfram is in short supply even for machine tools. Now they're releasing it for antipanzer rounds?"

"I don't know anything about machine tools, *Herr Oberst*," Joachim said, and Fritz's head solemnly bobbed up and down to signify he didn't know anything, either. "But I do know these shells are supposed to give you half again as much penetration as you get with regular capped armor-piercing ammunition."

"Are supposed to give you." That was Karl Mehler, Jäger's loader. Loaders had an inherently pessimistic view of the world. When panzers were moving, they didn't see much of it. They stayed down in the bottom of the turret, doing what the gunner and the commander ordered. If you were a loader, you never had a clue before a shell slammed into your machine. One second, you'd be fine; the next, butchered and burnt. Mehler went on, "How good are they really?"

Fritz and Joachim looked at each other. Fritz said, "They wouldn't issue them to front-line units if they didn't think they'd perform as advertised, would they?"

"You never can tell," Mehler said darkly. "Some poor slobs have to be the guinea pigs, I suppose. We must have drawn the short straw this time."

"That's enough, Karl," Jäger said. The rebuke was mild, but plenty to make the loader shut up. Jäger turned to the men with the munitions conveyor. "Do you have any of our conventional armor-piercing rounds to use in case these things aren't as perfect as the people away from the firing line seem to think?"

"Uh, no, sir," Joachim answered. "This is what came off the train, so this is what we have."

The mutters that rose from the panzer crewmen weren't quite rumbles of mutiny, but they weren't rapturous sighs, either. Jäger sighed, also not rapturously. "Well, we all still have a few rounds of the old issue, anyhow. We know what that will do—and what it won't. Tell me one thing right now, you two: is this new round supposed to be able to pierce the frontal armor of a Lizard panzer?"

Regretfully, the ammunition resupply men shook their heads. "*Herr Oberst*, the next round that can do that will be the first," Joachim said.

"I was afraid you were going to say as much," Jäger answered. "The way things are now, it costs us anywhere between six and ten panzers, on average, for every Lizard machine we manage to kill—that's just panzer against panzer, mind you. It would be even worse if we didn't have better crews than they do—but we've lost so many veterans that our edge there is going. The thing that would help us most is a gun that would let us meet them face-to-face."

"The thing that would help us most is another one of those bombs that they set off outside of Breslau and Rome," Gunther Grillparzer put in. "And I know just where to set it, too."

"Where's that?" Jäger asked, curious to see what his gunner used for a sense of strategy.

"Lodz," Grillparzer answered promptly. "Right in the middle of town. Blast all the Lizards and all the kikes there to kingdom come, just like that." He was wearing gloves, so instead of snapping his fingers he spat in the snow.

"Wouldn't mind getting rid of the Lizards," Jäger agreed. "The Jews—" He shrugged. "Anielewicz said he'd keep the Lizards from mounting a counterattack out of the city, and he's done it. He deserves the credit for it, too, if you ask me."

"Yes, sir." The gunner's round, fleshy face went sullen, not that Grillparzer didn't look a little sullen most of the time. He knew better than to argue with his regimental commander, but he wasn't about to think warm, kind thoughts about any Jews, either.

Jäger glanced around the rest of the panzer crewmen. Nobody disagreed with him, not out loud, but nobody sprang up to say anything nice about the Jews in the Lodz ghetto. That worried Jäger. He wasn't massively enamored of Jews himself, but he'd been horrified when he learned what German forces had done to them in the areas the *Reich* had conquered. He hadn't wanted to learn about such things, but he'd had his nose rubbed in them, and he was not the sort of man who could pretend he was blind when he wasn't. A lot of German officers, he'd found to his dismay, had no trouble at all managing that.

Right this second, though, he didn't have to think about it. "Let's share out what they've brought us," he told his men. "If all you've got is a dead pig, you eat pork chops."

"This stuff is liable to turn us all into dead pigs," Karl Mehler muttered under his breath, but that didn't keep him from taking his fair share of the newfangled rounds. He stowed them in the Panther's ammunition bins. "It doesn't look right," he grumbled when he scrambled back out of the panzer. "It looks funny. We've never had anything like it before."

"Intelligence says one of the reasons we drive the Lizards crazy is that we keep coming up with new things," Jäger said. "They don't change, or don't change much. Do you want to be like them?"

"Well, no, sir, but I don't want to change for the worse, either, and not for the hell of it," Mehler said. "These things look like a sausage sticking out of a bun, like some engineer is having a joke with us."

"They don't pay off on looks," Jäger answered. "If these new shells don't work the way they're supposed to, then somebody's head rolls. First, though, we have to find out."

"If these new shells don't work the way they're supposed to, our heads roll," Karl Mehler said. "Maybe somebody else's head rolls afterwards, but we won't get to watch that."

Since Mehler was right, the only thing Jäger could do was glare at him. With a shrug, the loader climbed back into the turret. A moment later, Gunther Grillparzer followed him. Jäger climbed in, too, and flipped up the lid to the cupola so he could stand up and see what he was doing. The driver, Johannes Drucker, and the hull gunner, Bernhard Steinfeldt, took their positions at the front of the Panther's fighting compartment.

The big Maybach petrol engine started up. Steam and stinking exhaust roared from the tailpipe. All through the clearing, Panthers, Tigers, and Panzer IVs were coming to life. Jäger really thought of it that way: they seemed like so many dinosaurs exhaling on a cold winter's morning.

Drucker rocked the Panther back and forth, going from low gear to reverse and back, to break up the ice that accumulated overnight between the panzer's interleaved road wheels. That freeze-up problem was the only drawback to the suspension; it gave a smooth ride over rugged terrain. But sometimes even rocking the panzer wouldn't free up the road wheels. Then you had to light a fire to melt the ice before you could get going. If the enemy attacked you instead of the other way around, that could prove hazardous to your life expectancy.

But today, the Germans were hunters, not hunted—at least for the moment. The panzers rolled out of the clearing. With them came a few self-propelled guns and a couple of three-quarter-tracked carriers full of infantrymen. Some of the foot soldiers carried hand-held antipanzer rockets—another idea stolen from the Lizards. Jäger thought about remarking on that to his crewmen, but decided not to bother. They were doing fine as things stood.

Against the Poles, against the French, against the Russians, the *Wehrmacht* panzers had charged out ahead of the infantry, cutting great gaps in the forces of the enemy. Do that against the Lizards and your head would roll, sure as sure. The only way you had any hope of shifting them was with a combined-arms operation—and even then, you'd better outnumber them.

Jäger would have been just as well content to find no trace of the aliens. He knew how many times he'd been lucky. Christ crucified, he'd killed a Lizard panzer with the 50mm gun of a Panzer III back in the days when the Lizards had just come to Earth, and if that wasn't luck, he didn't know what was. And here he was, almost two years later, still alive and still unmaimed. Not many who'd seen as much action could say the same.

Up ahead, the trees thinned out. He got on the all-vehicles wireless circuit. "We'll halt at the forest's edge to reconnoiter." Charge out into open country and you deserved to get slaughtered.

Foot soldiers in winter white got down from their carriers and trotted ghostlike out across the snow-covered fields. A couple of them had rocket launchers (also whitewashed) on their backs; the rest carried MP-40 submachine guns. Jäger had heard Hugo Schmeisser wasn't involved with the design of that weapon, but it got called a Schmeisser just the same.

From behind a barn, a machine gun started chattering, kicking up clumps of snow. The *Wehrmacht* men out in the open dove for whatever cover they could find. Two panzers fired high-explosive shells at the barn to flush out the Lizards in back of it. Not ten seconds later, one of those panzers brewed up, flame and smoke spurting from every hatch and out the top of the cupola.

Jäger's mouth went dry. "That's a Lizard panzer there," he shouted into the microphone to his wireless set. It was stating the obvious—overstating the obvious—but it had to be said.

"Armor-piercing," Gunther Grillparzer said to Karl Mehler. "Give me one of the new rounds—we'll see what they can do."

"If they can do anything," Mehler said gloomily, but he slammed one of the aluminum-sabot rounds into the breach of the Panther's long 75mm cannon. With a clang, Grillparzer closed it.

"Range?" Jäger asked.

"Long, sir," the gunner answered. "Better than fifteen hundred meters."

Jäger grunted. He didn't see any other good hiding places for panzers ahead, but that didn't mean there weren't any. Even against the one, sending his own panzers out to flank it was more likely to get them picked off one at a time than anything else. The Lizard panzer's turret had a powered traverse, about which Jäger was fearfully jealous.

He couldn't just sit here, either. Even if he'd bumped into the last of the Lizard rear guard, that panzer could call down artillery on his head or maybe even summon a helicopter or two. With their rockets, Lizard helicopters made nasty antipanzer weapons, and they chewed up infantry like teething biscuits.

The barn started to burn, the sole result of the high-explosive shells the Germans had thrown at it. That was a break; the smoke would screen his panzers from the Lizards' eyes, at least until they shifted position. And, set alongside his other options, flanking out the Lizard panzer didn't look so bad after all.

He was off to the right of the barn. He ordered out a Tiger from off to the left and a Panzer IV from right out in front. That done, he spoke to the driver of his own machine: "Come on, Hans—time to earn our pay. Forward!"

"Jawohl!" Johannes Drucker sped out into the open country. The Panzer IV fired at the Lizard panzer. Its gun wasn't much worse than the Panther's, but at long range its odds of doing anything useful were slim indeed.

A shell knocked down a tree behind the Panzer IV. When the Lizards missed, it was commonly because they couldn't see well. Their panzer did move out into the open. The Tiger fired at it. The 88 scored a clean hit, but the Lizard panzer kept moving. It was unfair, how tough they were.

The cannon in that panzer spoke. The Tiger's turret flew off, shells inside exploding as it crashed to the ground five or six meters away from the stricken panzer. The chassis burned merrily, too. All five crewmen had to be dead. An infantryman fired an antipanzer rocket at the Lizard machine. He hit it right in the glacis plate, but the Lizard panzer's frontal armor—from what Jäger had heard, it wasn't just steel—defeated the shaped-charge warhead. The machine gun kept searching for Germans on foot.

"Range?" Jäger said again.

"Down under five hundred meters, sir," Gunther Grillparzer answered.

"Driver halt," Jäger said, and then, "Fire!"

Because he was still standing up in the cupola rather than sheltered in the turret, the noise was like the end of the world. A tongue of flame spurted from the cannon's muzzle.

Flame and smoke spurted from the Lizard panzer, too. "Hit!" everybody in Jäger's panzer screamed together. Jäger listened to the breech clang shut on another round. The long 75mm gun bellowed again—another hit. Hatches popped open in the Lizard machine. The Panther's hull-mounted machine gun started barking in short, precise bursts. In moments, the three Lizards who'd bailed out lay motionless on the ground, their all too humanly red blood staining the snow. Their panzer kept on burning.

Very seriously, Gunther Grillparzer said, "Sir, this is good ammunition. We can get good use from it."

"Even if it looks funny?" Jäger teased.

"Even so."

The west wind brought the yellow dust of the Gobi with it. The dust left a thin film over everything, you could taste it if you smacked your lips a couple of times. Nieh Ho-T'ing was used to it. It came with life in and around Peking.

Major Mori rubbed at his eyes. The dust bothered him. In fair Chinese, he asked Nieh, "So—what do you want from me now? More timers? I hear you did well with the last batch."

"No, not this time," Nieh answered. His first thought was that the Japanese major was a fool if he thought a trick would work against the Lizards twice running. But the eastern devil could not have been a fool, not if he'd kept his force in being this long even with the Lizards, the People's Liberation Army, the troops loyal to the Kuomintang reactionary clique, and the Chinese peasantry all arrayed against him.

What then? Nieh's lips skinned back from his teeth in a grin that showed scant amusement. The likeliest explanation was that Major Mori hoped he'd try the same trick twice in a row—and get smashed as a result. In Mori's boots, Nieh would have hoped for something like that.

"Well, what *are* you after now?" Mori demanded. Although the troops he led were hardly more than a guerrilla band, he kept all the arrogance the Japanese had shown when they held the whole of northeastern China and coastal enclaves elsewhere—and could push forward as they wished, even if they couldn't always hold the gains they'd made.

"Artillery shells would be useful about now," Nieh said musingly.

"Maybe so, but you won't get them from us," Mori said. "We still have some 75mm guns in commission, though I won't tell you where."

Nieh Ho-T'ing knew where the Japanese were concealing those cannon. Going after them struck him as being more trouble than it was worth, since they were far more likely to be turned on the Lizards than on his own men. He said, "Soldiers can be coolies and haul 75mm guns from one place to another. As you say, they are also easy to hide. But the Japanese Army used to have heavier artillery, too. The scaly devils destroyed those big guns, or else you've had to abandon them. But you still should have some of the ammunition left. Do you?"

Mori studied him for a while before answering. The eastern devil was somewhere not far from forty, perhaps a couple of years older than Nieh. His skin was slightly darker, his features slightly sharper, than a Chinese was likely to have. That didn't bother Nieh nearly so much as Mori's automatic assumption of his own superiority. *Barbarian,* Nieh thought scornfully, secure in his knowledge that China was the one true home of culture and civilization. But even a barbarian could be useful.

"What if we do?" Mori said. "If you want one of those shells, what will you give us for it?"

Capitalist, Nieh thought. *Imperialist. If all you care about is profit, you don't deserve even that.* Aloud, though, he answered, "I can give you the names of two men you think reliable who are in fact Kuomintang spies."

Mori smiled at him. It was not a pleasant smile. "Just the other day, the Kuomintang offered to sell me the names of three Communists."

"It wouldn't surprise me," Nieh said. "We have been known to give the names of Japanese sympathizers to the Kuomintang."

"Miserable war," Mori said. Just for a moment, the two men understood each other completely. Then Mori asked. "And when you dicker with the little devils, whom do you sell to them?"

"Why, the Kuomintang, of course," Nieh Ho-T'ing answered. "When the war with you and the scaly devils is over, the reactionaries and counterrevolutionaries will still be here. We shall deal with them. They think they will deal with us, but the historical dialectic shows they are mistaken."

"You are mistaken if you think Japanese cannot enforce on China a government friendly to its wishes—leaving the little scaly devils out of the picture, of course," Major Mori said. "Whenever your troops and ours meet in battle, yours always come off second best."

"And what has that got to do with the price of rice?" Nieh asked in honest bewilderment. "Eventually you will get sick of winning expensive battles and being nibbled to death inside areas you think you control, and then you will go away and leave China alone. The only reason you win now is that you started using the machines of the foreign devils"—by which he meant

Europeans—"before we did. We will have our own factories one day, and then—"

Mori threw back his head and laughed, a deliberate effort to be insulting. *Go ahead,* Nieh thought. *Laugh now. One fine day the revolution will cross the sea to your islands, too.* Japan had a large urban proletariat, exploited workers with nothing to offer but their labor, as interchangeable to a big capitalist as so many cogs and gears. They would be dry tinder for the flame of class warfare. But not yet—the Lizards remained to be beaten first.

Nieh said, "Are we agreed on the price of one of these shells?"

"Not yet," the Japanese answered. "Information is useful, yes, but we need food, too. Send us rice, send us noodles, send us *shoyu*, send us pork or chicken. Do this and we will give you as many 150mm shells as you can use, whatever you plan to do with them."

They started dickering about how much food would buy Nieh how many shells, and when and how to arrange deliveries. As he had before, Nieh kept the contempt he felt from showing. On the Long March, he'd dickered with warlords' officers and bandit chieftains over things like this. In China now, though, what survived of the once-mighty Imperial Japanese Army was reduced to bandit status; the Japanese couldn't do much more than prey on the countryside, and they didn't even do that well, not if they were trading munitions for food.

Nieh resolved not to tell Liu Han any details about how he was negotiating with the Japanese. Her hatred for them was personal, as it was for the little devils. Nieh hated the Japanese and the scaly devils, too, with an ideological purity his woman could never hope to match. But she had imagination, and came up with ways to hurt the enemies of the People's Liberation Army and the Communist Party that he would never have dreamt of. Success, especially among those who did not form large-scale policy, could make up for a lack of ideological purity—for a while, anyhow.

Major Mori was not the best bargainer Nieh had ever faced. Two Chinese out of three could have got more supplies from him than Mori did. He gave a mental shrug. Well, that was Mori's fault, for being a barbarous eastern devil. The Japanese made good soldiers, but not much else.

As far as he was concerned, the same went for the little scaly devils. They could conquer, but seemed to have no idea how to hold down a rebellious land once under their control. They didn't even use the murder and terror the Japanese had taken for granted.

As far as Nieh could tell, all they did was reward collaborators, and that was not enough.

"Excellent!" Major Mori exclaimed when the haggling was over. He slapped his belly. "We will eat well for a time." The military tunic he wore hung on him like a tent. He might once have been a heavyset man. No more.

"And we will have a present for the little devils one day before too long," Nieh replied. Even if he could do what he hoped with the 150mm shells, he aimed to try to blame it on the Kuomintang. Liu Han would not approve of that; she'd want the Japanese to receive the scaly devils' wrath. But, as Nieh had said, the Kuomintang was more dangerous in the long run.

So long as the little scaly devils did not blame the People's Liberation Army for the attacks, talks with them could go on unimpeded. Those talks had been building in size and importance for some time now; they needed to continue. Something of greater substance might come from them than the stalled negotiations about Liu Han's baby. Nieh hoped so, at any rate.

He sighed. If he'd had his choice, the People's Liberation Army would have driven the Japanese and the scaly devils out of China altogether. He didn't have his choice, though. If he'd ever needed reminding of that, the Long March would have given it to him. You did what you had to do. After that, if you were lucky, you got the chance to do what you wanted to do.

He bowed to Major Mori. The major returned the compliment. "Miserable war," Nieh said again. Mori nodded. *But the workers and peasants will win it, here in China and all over the world,* Nieh thought. He glanced at the Japanese officer. Maybe Mori was thinking victorious thoughts, too. Well, if he was, he was wrong. Nieh had the dialectic to prove it.

Mordechai Anielewicz stepped out onto the sidewalk in front of the building on Lutomierska Street. "I can deal with my enemies," he said. "The Nazis and Lizards are not a problem, not like that. My friends, now—" He rolled his eyes in theatrical despair. *"Vay iz mir!"*

Bertha Fleishman laughed. She was a year or two older then Mordechai, and normally so colorless that the Jewish resistance of Lodz often used her to pick up information: you had trouble noticing she was there. But her laugh stood out. She had a good laugh, one that invited everybody around to share the joke.

Now she said, "Actually, we've done pretty well, all things considered. The Lizards haven't been able to get much through Lodz to throw at the Nazis." She paused. "Of course, not everyone would say this is a good thing."

"I know." Anielewicz grimaced. "I don't say it's a good thing myself. This is even worse than being caught between the Nazis and the Russians. Whoever wins, *we* lose."

"The Germans are living up to their promise not to attack Lodz so long as we keep the Lizards from mounting any moves from here," Bertha said. "They haven't thrown any of their rocket bombs at us lately, either."

"For which God be thanked," Anielewicz said. Before the war, he'd been a secular man. That hadn't mattered to the Nazis, who'd dumped him into the Warsaw ghetto all the same. What he'd seen there, what he'd seen since, had left him convinced he couldn't live without God after all. What would have been ironic in 1938 came out sincere today.

"We're useful to them at the moment." Bertha Fleishman's mouth turned down. "Even that's progress. Before, we were working in their factories, making all kinds of things for them, and they slaughtered us anyhow."

"I know." Mordechai kicked at the paving stones. "I wonder if they tried out their poison gas on Jews before they started using it against the Lizards." He didn't want to think about that. If he let himself brood on it, he'd wonder why he was helping Hitler, Himmler, and their henchmen against the Lizards. Then he'd take a look at Bunim and the other Lizard officials in Lodz and be sure he couldn't help them beat the Germans and, in so doing, subject all of mankind.

"It isn't fair," Bertha said. "Has anyone since the world began ever been in such a predicament?"

"We're the Chosen People," Anielewicz answered with a shrug. "If you think I'd be just as glad if we hadn't been chosen for this, though, you're right."

"Speaking of which, aren't the Lizards supposed to be moving a convoy of lorries through town in about half an hour?" Bertha asked. Since she was the one who'd come up with that bit of intelligence, the question was rhetorical. She smiled. "Shall we go watch the fun?"

The convoy was supposed to head north up Franciszkanska Street, to bring reinforcements to the Lizards who were trying to cut the base off one of the German prongs advancing to either side of Lodz. The Lizards had not had much luck with their counter-movements. What they would do when they figured out why would be interesting—and likely unpleasant.

Jews and Poles stood on the corner of Inflancka and Franciszkanska and in the streets themselves, chatting, chaffering, and carrying on their business as they would have on any other day. It was a scene that might almost have come from the time before the war, save that so many of the men—and a few of the women—had rifles on their backs or in their hands. Cheating, these days, was liable to meet with swift and summary punishment.

About fifteen minutes before the convoy was due to come through, human policemen, some Jews, some Poles, began trying to clear the street. Anielewicz watched them—especially the Jews—with undisguised loathing. The Jewish police—thugs would have been a better word for them—owed allegiance to Mordechai Chaim Rumkowski, who had been Eldest of the Jews when the Lodz ghetto was in Nazi hands and still ran it for the Lizards. They still wore the long coats, shiny-brimmed caps, and red-white-and-black rank armbands the Germans had given them, too. Maybe it made them feel important. It made everyone else despise them.

They didn't have much luck with their street clearing, either. They were armed with nothing better than truncheons. That had been intimidating back in the days when the Nazis held Lodz. It did not do much, though, to shift men with rifles. Anielewicz knew the Jewish police had been screaming at the Lizards for guns of their own. What had been in place before the Lizards arrived, though, seemed to be like the Torah to them: not to be changed or interfered with by mere mortals. The police remained without firearms.

An old Jewish man driving a horse-drawn wagon that carried tables stacked four and five high tried to cross Franciszkanska on Inflancka just as a Polish lorry-driver rumbled down Franciszkanska with a load of empty tin milk cans. The Pole tried to slow down, but seemed to be having trouble with his brakes. His lorry crashed into the old Jew's wagon.

The racket that immediately followed the collision was louder than the crash itself. The rear gate of the lorry hadn't been well secured, so milk cans clattered down onto the pavement and started rolling away. As best Mordechai could see, the load of tables hadn't been secured at all. They landed in the street, too. Some of them broke, some didn't.

By what looked like a miracle, the wagon driver hadn't been hurt. Surprisingly agile for an old man, he jumped down from his beast and ran up to the driver's side of the lorry, screaming abuse in Yiddish.

"Shut up, you damned kike!" the Pole answered in his own language. "Stinking old Christ-killer, you've got your nerve, yelling at me."

"I'd yell at your father, except even your mother doesn't know who he is," the Jew retorted.

The Polish lorry-driver jumped out of the cab and grabbed the Jew. In a moment, they were wrestling on the ground. Jews and Poles both ran toward the altercation. Here and there, some of them bumped into one another and started fresh trouble.

Policemen—Jews and Poles—blew furiously on whistles and waded into the crowd, trying to clear it. Some of them got drawn into fistfights, too. Mordechai Anielewicz and Bertha Fleishman watched the unfolding chaos with eyebrows raised high.

Into the chaos came the Lizards' motor convoy. Some of their lorries were of their own manufacture, others human products they'd appropriated. A Lizard lorry horn made a noise that reminded Mordechai of what you'd get if you dropped a bucket of water onto a red-hot iron plate. When you added in the klaxons from the Opels and other human-made lorries, the din became truly dreadful.

No one in the street paid the least attention to it. As far as the Jews and Poles were concerned, the impatient Lizards might have been back on the far side of the moon, or wherever it was they came from. "What a pity," Mordechai said. "It looks like the Lizards are going to be delayed."

"That's terrible," Bertha said in the same solemn tones he'd used. Without warning, both of them started to laugh. In a low voice, Bertha went on, "This worked out even better than we thought it would."

"So it did," Anielewicz agreed. "Yitzkhak and Boleslaw both deserve those statues the Americans give their best cinema actors every year."

Bertha Fleishman's brown eyes twinkled. "No, they couldn't have played that much better if they'd rehearsed it for years, could they? The rest of our people—and also the *Armija Krajowa* men," she admitted, "are doing nicely, too."

"Good thing most of the people at this corner really do belong to us or the Polish Home Army," Mordechai said. "Otherwise we'd have a real riot on our hands, not a scripted one."

"I am glad no one's decided to pull a rifle off his back and use it," Bertha said. "Not everybody here knows we're playing a game."

"That's true," Anielewicz said. "The police don't, and the

Lizard lorry drivers don't, either." He pointed back to the rear of the long, stalled column of motor vehicles. "Oh, look. Some of them look like they're trying to turn around and use a different route to get out of town."

Bertha shaded her eyes so she could see better. "So they are. But they seem to be having some trouble, too. I wonder who started an argument way down there. Whoever it was, he certainly managed to pull a lot of people into the street in a hurry."

"He certainly did." Mordechai grinned at her. She was grinning back. Maybe she wasn't beautiful, but he certainly liked the way she looked when she was happy like this. "I don't think those poor Lizard lorries will be able to go anywhere for quite a while."

"I'm afraid you're right." Bertha sighed theatrically. "Isn't it a pity?" She and Mordechai laughed again.

Lizards weren't what you'd call big to begin with. Even as Lizards went, Straha was on the shortish side; a husky nine-year-old would have overtopped him. With Lizards as with people, though, size had little to do with force of personality. Whenever Sam Yeager got to talking with the former shiplord of the *206th Emperor Yower*, he needed only a couple of minutes to forget that Straha was hardly more than half his size.

"By not falling at once, you Big Uglies presented Atvar the brain-addled fleetlord with a problem he will not be able to solve," Straha declared. "At the time, I urged him to strike a series of blows against you so strong that you would have no choice but to yield to the Race. Did he heed me? He did not!" Straha's emphatic cough was a masterpiece of rudeness.

"Why didn't he?" Yeager asked. "I've always wondered about that. The Race never seemed to want to turn up the pressure more than one notch at a time. That let us—how would I say it?—I guess *adapt* is the word I want."

"Truth," Straha said, with another emphatic cough. "One thing we did not realize until far later than we should have was how adaptable you Tosevites are. Fool that he is, Atvar always intended to come as close as he could to the campaign we would have fought had you been the preindustrial savages we expected you to be. Even his eye turrets are not entirely locked in place, and he did conclude a greater effort would be called for, but he always did his best to keep the increases to a minimum, so as to have the least possible distortion in the plan with which we came to Tosev 3."

"Most of you Lizards are like that, aren't you?" Sam used

mankind's disparaging name for the Race as casually as Straha used the Race's handle for humanity. "You don't much care for change, do you?"

"Of course not," Straha said—and, for a Lizard, he was a radical. "If you are in a good situation where you are, why, if you have any sense, would you want to alter it? It would be only too likely to get worse. Change must be most carefully controlled, or it can devastate an entire society."

Sam grinned at him. "How do you account for us, then?"

"Our scholars will spend thousands of years attempting to account for you," Straha answered. "It could be that, had we not arrived, you would have destroyed yourselves in relatively short order. You were, after all, already working to develop your own atomic weapons, and with those you would have had no trouble rendering this planet uninhabitable. Almost a pity you failed to do so."

"Thanks a lot," Yeager said. "We really love you Lizards a whole bunch, too." He added an emphatic cough to that, even though he wasn't sure whether the Race used them for sardonic effect. Straha's mouth dropped open in amusement, so maybe they did—or maybe the ex-shiplord was laughing at the way Sam mangled his language.

Straha said, "Like most males of the Race, Atvar is a minimalist. You Big Uglies, now, you are maximalists. In the long term, as I pointed out, this will probably prove disastrous for your species. I cannot imagine you Tosevites building an empire stable for a hundred thousand years. Can you?"

"Nope," Sam admitted. The years Straha used were only about half as long as their earthly equivalents, but still— Fifty thousand years ago, people had been living in caves and worrying about mammoths and saber-tooth tigers. Yeager couldn't begin to imagine what things would be like in another fifty years, let alone fifty thousand.

"In the short term, though, your penchant for change without warning presents us with stresses our kind has never before faced," Straha said. "By the standards of the Race, I am a maximalist—thus I would have been well suited to lead us against your kind." By human standards, Straha was more mossbound than a Southern Democrat with forty-five years' seniority, but Yeager didn't see any good way to tell him so. The Lizard went on, "I believe in taking action, not waiting until it is forced upon me, as Atvar and his clique do. When the Soviets' nuclear bomb showed us how disastrously we'd misjudged your kind, I tried to have

Atvar the fool ousted and someone more suitable, such as myself, raised to overall command. And when that failed, I took the direct action of fleeing to you Tosevites rather than waiting for Atvar to have his revenge upon me."

"Truth," Yeager said, and it was truth—maybe Straha really was a fireball by Lizard standards. "There's more 'direct action' from you people these days, isn't there? What are the mutineers in Siberia doing, anyhow?"

"Your radio intercepts indicate they have surrendered to the Russkis," Straha answered. "If they are treated well, that will be a signal for other disaffected units—and there must be many—to realize they, too, can make peace with Tosevites."

"That would be nice," Sam said. "When will the fleetlord realize he needs to make peace with us, that he can't conquer the whole planet, the way the Race thought it would when you set out from Home?"

Had Straha been a cat, he would have bristled at that question. Yes, he despised Atvar. Yes, he'd defected to the Americans. Somewhere down in his heart of hearts, though, he was still loyal to the Emperor back on Tau Ceti's second planet; the idea that a scheme the Emperor had endorsed might fail gave him the galloping collywobbles.

But the shiplord countered gamely, asking in return, "When will you Big Uglies realize that you cannot exterminate us or drive us off your miserable, chilly planet?"

Now Yeager grunted in turn. When the U.S.A. had been fighting the Nazis and the Japs, everybody had figured the war would go on till the bad guys got smashed flat. That was the way wars were supposed to work, wasn't it? Somebody won, and he took stuff away from the guys who had lost. If the Lizards came down and took part of Earth away from humanity, didn't that mean they'd won?

When Sam said that out loud, Straha waggled both eye turrets at him, a sign of astonishment. "Truly you Big Uglies are creatures of overweening pride," the shiplord exclaimed. "No plan of the Race has ever failed to the extent of our design for the conquest of Tosev 3 and its incorporation into the Empire. If we fail to acquire the whole of the planet, if we leave Big Ugly empires and not-empires intact and independent upon it, we suffer a humiliation whose like we have never known before."

"Is that so?" Yeager said. "Well, if we think letting you have anything is a mistake, and if you think letting us keep anything is an even bigger mistake, how are Lizards and people ever going to get together and settle things one way or the other? Sounds to me like we're stuck."

"We might not be, were it not for Atvar's stubbornness," Straha said. "As I told you before, the only way he will consent to anything less than complete victory is to become convinced it is impossible."

"If he hasn't gotten that idea by now—" But Sam paused and shook his head. You had to remember the Lizards' point of view. What looked like disastrous defeats from up close might seem only bumps in the road if considered in a thousand-year context. Men prepared for the next battle, the Lizards for the next millennium.

Straha said, "When he does get that idea—if ever he does—he will do one of two things, I think. He may try to make peace along the lines you and I have been discussing. Or he may try to use whatever nuclear arsenal the Race has left to force you Tosevites into submission. This is what I would have done; that I proposed it may make it less likely now."

"Good," Yeager said sincerely. He'd been away from the American nuclear-bomb program for a while now, but he knew the infernal devices didn't roll off the assembly line like so many De Sotos. "The other thing holding him back is your colonization fleet, isn't it?"

"Truth," Straha replied at once. "This consideration has inhibited our actions in the past, and continues to do so. Atvar may decide, however, that making peace with you will leave the Race less of the habitable surface of Tosev 3 than he could hope to obtain by damaging large portions of the planet on our behalf."

"It wouldn't keep us from fighting back, you know," Sam said, and hoped he wasn't whistling in the dark.

Evidently Straha didn't think he was, because the shiplord said, "We are painfully aware of this. It is one of the factors that has to this point deterred us from that course. More important, though, is our desire not to damage the planet for our colonists, as you have noted."

"Mm-hmm," Sam said, tasting the irony of Earth's safety riding more on the Lizards' concern for their own kind than on any worries about human beings. "We've got what, something like eighteen years, before the rest of your people get here?"

"No, twice that," Straha answered. Then he made a noise like a bubbling teakettle. "My apologies—if you are using Tosevite years, you are correct."

"Yeah, I was—I'm a Tosevite, after all," Yeager said with a

wry grin. "What are your colonists going to think if they come to a world that isn't completely in your hands, the way they thought it would be when they set out from Home?"

"The starship crews will be aware of changed conditions when they intercept our signals beamed back toward Home," Straha said. "No doubt this will fill them with consternation and confusion. Remember, we of the conquest fleet have had some time now to try to accommodate ourselves to the unanticipated conditions on Tosev 3. These will be new for them, and the Race does not adapt well. In any case, there will be little they can do. The colonization fleet is not armed; the assumption was that we of the conquest fleet would have this world all nicely pacified before the colonists arrived. And, of course, the colonists themselves are in cold sleep and will remain ignorant of the true situation until they are revived upon the fleet's arrival."

"They'll get quite a surprise, won't they?" Sam said, chuckling. "How many of them are there, anyhow?"

"I do not know, not in precise figures," Straha replied. "My responsibility, after all, was with the conquest fleet. But if our practice in colonizing the worlds of the Rabotevs and Hallessi was followed back on Home—as it almost certainly would have been, given our fondness for precedent—then we are sending here something between eighty and one hundred million males and females . . . Those coughs mean nothing in my language, Samyeager." He pronounced Yeager's name as if it were one word. "Have they some signification in yours?"

"I'm sorry, Shiplord," Sam said when he could speak coherently again. "Must have swallowed wrong, or something." *Eighty or a hundred* million *colonists?* "The Race doesn't do things by halves, does it?"

"Of course not," Straha said.

"One mortification after another," Atvar said in deep discontent. From where he stood, the situation down on the surface of Tosev 3 looked gloomy. "Almost better we should have expended a nuclear device on those mutineers than let them go over to the SSSR."

"Truth," Kirel said. "The loss of the armaments is bad. Before long, the Big Uglies will copy whatever features they can figure out how to steal. That has happened before, and is happening again: we have recent reports that the Deutsche, for instance, are beginning to deploy armor-piercing discarding sabot ammunition against our landcruisers."

"I have seen these reports," the fleetlord agreed. "They do not inspire me with delight."

"Nor me," Kirel answered. "Moreover, the loss of the territory formerly controlled by the base whose garrison mutinied has given us new problems. Though weather conditions in the area remain appallingly bad, we have evidence that the SSSR is attempting to reestablish its east-west rail link."

"How can they do that?" Atvar said. "Surely even Big Uglies would freeze if forced to work in such circumstances."

"From what we have seen in the SSSR, Exalted Fleetlord, it would appear hardly more concerned about the well-being of its laborers than is Deutschland," Kirel said mournfully. "Getting the task done counts for more than the number of lives expended in the process."

"Truth," Atvar said, and then added, "Madness," and an emphatic cough. "The Deutsche sometimes appear to put expending lives above extracting labor. What was the name of that place where they devoted so much ingenuity to slaughter? Treblinka, that was it." The Race had never imagined a center wholly devoted to exterminating intelligent beings. Atvar would have been as glad never to have been exposed to some of the things he'd learned on Tosev 3.

He waited for Kirel to mention the most important reason why the fall of the Siberian base was a disaster. Kirel didn't mention it. All too likely, Kirel hadn't thought of it. He was a good shiplord, none better, when someone told him what to do. Even for a male of the Race, though, he lacked imagination.

Atvar said, "We now have to deal with the problem of propaganda broadcasts from the mutineers. By all they say, they are cheerful, well fed, well treated, with plenty of that pernicious herb, ginger, for amusement. Transmissions such as these are liable to touch off not only further mutinies but also desertions by individual males who cannot find partners with whom to conspire."

"What you say is likely to be correct," Kirel agreed. "It is to be hoped that increased vigilance on the part of officers will help to allay the problem."

"It is to be hoped, indeed," Atvar said with heavy sarcasm. "It is also to be hoped that we shall be able to keep from losing too much ground in this northern-hemisphere winter, and that guerrilla raids against our positions will ease. In some places—much of Italia springs to mind—we are unable to administer or control territory allegedly under our jurisdiction."

"We need more cooperation from the Tosevite authorities who

yielded to us," Kirel said. "This is true all over the planet, and especially so in Italia, where our forces might as well be at war again."

"Most of the Italian authorities, such as they were, went up with the atomic bomb that destroyed Roma," Atvar answered. "Too many of the ones who are left still favor their overthrown notemperor, that Mussolini. How I wish the Deutsch raider, that Skorzeny, hadn't succeeded in stealing him and spiriting him off into Deutschland. His radio broadcasts, along with those of our former ally Russie and the traitor Straha, have proved most damaging of all counterpropaganda efforts against us."

"That Skorzeny has been a pin driven under our scales throughout the campaign of conquest," Kirel said. "He is unpredictable even for a Tosevite, and deadly as well."

"I wish I could dispute it, but it is truth," the fleetlord said sadly. "In addition to all the other harm he has inflicted on our cause, he cost me Drefsab, the one intelligence officer we had who was both devious and energetic enough to match the Big Uglies at their own primary traits."

"Wherefore now, Exalted Fleetlord?" Kirel asked.

"We carry on as best we can," Atvar answered, a response that did not satisfy him and plainly did not satisfy Kirel. Trying to amplify it, he went on, "One thing we must do is increase security around our starships. If the Big Uglies can smuggle nuclear weapons within range of them, rather than of cities, they potentially have the ability to hurt us even worse than they have already."

"I shall draft an order seeking to forestall this contingency," Kirel said. "I agree; it is a serious menace. I shall also draft procedures whose thorough implementation will make the order effective."

"Good," Atvar said. "Be most detailed. Allow no conceivable loopholes through which a careless male might produce disaster." All that was standard advice from one male of the Race to another. After a moment, though, the fleetlord added in thoughtful tones, "Before promulgating the order and procedures, consult with males who have had experience down on the surface of Tosev 3. They may possibly make your proposed procedures more leakproof against the ingenious machinations of the Big Uglies."

"It shall be done, Exalted Fleetlord," Kirel promised. "May I respectfully suggest that none of us up here in orbit has enough firsthand experience with conditions down on the surface of Tosev 3?"

"There is some truth in what you say," Atvar admitted. "Perhaps we should spend more time on the planet itself—in a reasonably secure area, preferably one with a reasonably salubrious climate." He called up a flat map of the surface of Tosev 3 on a computer screen. One set of color overlays gave a security evaluation, with categories ranging from unconquered to pacified (though depressingly little of the planet showed that placid pink tone). Another gave climatological data. He instructed the computer to show him where both factors were at a maximum.

Kirel pointed. "The northern coastal region of the subcontinental mass the Tosevites term Africa seems as near ideal as any region."

"So it does," Atvar said. "I have visited there before. It *is* pleasant; parts of it could almost be Home. Very well, Shiplord, make the requisite preparations. We shall temporarily shift headquarters to this region, the better to supervise the conduct of the conquest at close range."

"It shall be done, Exalted Fleetlord," Kirel said.

Ludmila Gorbunova wanted to kick *Generalleutnant Graf* Walter von Brockdorff-Ahlefeldt right where it would do the most good. Since the damned Nazi general was in Riga and she was stuck outside Hrubieszów, that wasn't practical. In lieu of fulfilling her desire, she kicked at the mud instead. It clung to her boots, which did nothing to improve her mood.

She hadn't thought of Brockdorff-Ahlefeldt as a damned Nazi when she was in Riga herself. Then he'd seemed a charming, *kulturny* general, nothing like the boorish Soviets and cold-blooded Germans it had mostly been her lot to deal with.

"Fly me one little mission, Senior Lieutenant Gorbunova," she muttered under her breath. "Take a couple of antipanzer mines to Hrubieszów, then come on back here and we'll send you on to Pskov with a pat on the fanny for your trouble."

That wasn't exactly what the *kulturny* general had said, of course, and he hadn't tried to pat her on the fanny, which was one of the things that made him *kulturny*. But if he hadn't sent her to Hrubieszów, her *Kukuruznik* wouldn't have tried to taxi through a tree, which would have meant she'd still be able to fly it.

"Which would have meant I wouldn't be stuck here outside of Hrubieszów," she snarled, and kicked at the mud again. Some of it splashed up and hit her in the cheek. She snarled and spat.

She'd always thought of U-2s as nearly indestructible, not least because they were too simple to be easy to break. Down in the

Ukraine, she'd buried one nose-first in the mud, but that could have been fixed without much trouble if she hadn't had to get away from the little biplane as fast as she could. Wrapping a *Kukuruznik* around a tree, though—that was truly championship-quality ineptitude.

"And why did the devil's sister leave a tree in the middle of the landing strip?" she asked the God in whom she did not believe. But it hadn't been the devil's sister. It had been these miserable partisans. It was *their* fault.

Of course she'd been flying at night. Of course she'd had one eye on the compass, one eye on her wristwatch, one eye on the ground and sky, one eye on the fuel gauge—she'd almost wished she was a Lizard, so she could look every which way at once. Just finding the partisans' poorly lit landing strip had been—not a miracle, for she didn't believe in miracles—a major achievement, that's what it had been.

She'd circled once. She'd brought the Wheatcutter down. She'd taxied smoothly. She'd never seen the pine sapling—no, it was more than a sapling, worse luck—till she ran into it.

"Broken wing spars," she said, ticking off the damage on her fingers. "Broken propeller." Both of those were wood, and reparable. "Broken crankshaft." That was of metal, and she had no idea what she was going to do about it—what she *could* do about it.

Behind her, someone coughed. She whirled around like a startled cat. Her hand flew to the grip of her Tokarev automatic. The partisan standing there jerked back in alarm. He was a weedy, bearded, nervous little Jew who went by the name Sholom. She could follow pieces of his Polish and pieces of his Yiddish, and he knew a little Russian, so they managed to make themselves understood to each other.

"You come," he said now. "We bring blacksmith out from Hrubieszów. He look at your machine."

"All right, I'll come," she answered dully. Yes, a U-2 was easy to work on, but she didn't think a blacksmith could repair a machined part well enough to make the aircraft fly again.

He was one of the largest men she'd ever seen, almost two meters tall and seemingly that wide through the shoulders, too. By the look of him, he could have bent the crankshaft back into its proper shape with his bare hands if it had been in one piece. But it wasn't just bent; it was broken in half, too.

The smith spoke in Polish, too fast for Ludmila to follow. Sholom turned his words into something she could understand:

"Witold, he say if it made of metal, he fix it. He fix lots of wagons, he say."

"Has he ever fixed a motorcar?" Ludmila asked. If the answer there was yes, maybe she did have some hope of getting off the ground again after all.

When he heard her voice, Witold blinked in surprise. Then he struck a manly pose. His already huge chest inflated like a balloon. Muscles bulged in his upper arms. Again, he spoke rapidly. Again, Sholom made what he said intelligible: "He say, of course he do. He say, for you he fix anything."

Ludmila studied the smith through slitted eyes. She thought he'd said more than that; some of his Polish had sounded close to what would have been a lewd suggestion in Russian. Well, if she didn't understand it, she didn't have to react to it. She decided that would be the wisest course for the time being.

To Sholom, she said, "Tell him to come look at the damage, then, and see what he can do."

Witold strutted along beside her, chest out, back straight, chin up. Ludmila was not a tall woman, and felt even smaller beside him. Whatever he might have hoped, that did not endear him to her.

He studied the biplane for a couple of minutes, then asked, "What is broken that takes a smith to fix?"

"The crankshaft," Ludmila answered. Witold's handsome face remained blank, even after Sholom translated that into Polish. Ludmila craned her neck to glare up at him. With poisonous sweetness, she asked, "You do know what a crankshaft is, don't you? If you've worked on motorcars, you'd better."

More translation from Sholom, another spate of fast Polish from Witold. Ludmila caught pieces of it, and didn't like what she heard. Sholom's rendition did nothing to improve her spirits: "He say he work on car springs, on fixing dent in—how you say this?—in mudguards, you understand? He not work on motor of motorcar."

"*Bozhemoi,*" Ludmila muttered. Atheist she might be, but swearing needed flavor to release tension, and so she called on God. There stood Witold, strong as a bull, and, for all the use he was to her, he might as well have had a bull's ring in his nose. She rounded on Sholom, who cringed. "Why didn't you find me a real mechanic, then, not this blundering idiot?"

Witold got enough of that to let out a very bull-like bellow of rage. Sholom shrugged helplessly. "Before war, only two motor mechanics in Hrubieszów, lady pilot. One of them, he dead now—forget whether Nazis or Russians kill him. The other one, he licks the Lizards' backsides. We bring him here, he tell Lizards everything. Witold, he may not do much, but he loyal."

Witold followed that, too. He shouted something incendiary and drew back a massive fist to knock Sholom into the middle of next week.

The Jewish partisan had not looked to be armed. Now, with the air of a man performing a conjurer's trick, he produced a Luger apparently from thin air and pointed it at Witold's middle. "Jews have guns now, Witold. You'd better remember it. Talk about my mother and I'll blow your balls off. We don't need to take *gówno* from you Poles any more." In Polish or in Russian, shit was shit.

Witold's pale blue eyes were wide and staring. His mouth was wide, too. It opened and closed a couple of times, but no words emerged. Still wordlessly, he turned on his heel and walked away. All the swagger had leaked out of him, like the air from a punctured bicycle tire.

Quietly, Ludmila told Sholom, "You've just given him reason to sell us out to the Lizards."

Sholom shrugged. The Luger disappeared. "He has reason to want to breathe more, too. He keep quiet or he is dead. He knows."

"There is that," Ludmila admitted.

Sholom laughed. "Yes, there is that. All Russia is that, yes?"

Ludmila started to make an angry retort, but stopped before the words passed her lips. She remembered neighbors, teachers, and a couple of cousins disappearing in 1937 and 1938. One day they were there, the next gone. You didn't ask questions about it, you didn't talk about it. If you did, you would disappear next. That had happened, too. You kept your head down, pretended nothing was going on, and hoped the terror would pass you by.

Sholom watched her, his dark, deep-set eyes full of irony. At last, feeling she had to say something, she answered, "I am a senior lieutenant in the Red Air Force. Do you like hearing your government insulted?"

"*My* government?" Sholom spat on the ground. "I am Jew. You think the Polish government is mine?" He laughed again; this time, the sound carried the weight of centuries of oppression. "And then the Nazis come, and make Poles look like nice and kindly people. Who thinks anyone can do that?"

"So why are you here and not with the Lizards inside Hrubieszów?" Ludmila asked. A moment later, she realized the question was imperfectly tactful, but she'd already let it out.

"Some things are bad, some things are worse, some things are worst of all," Sholom answered. He waited to see if Ludmila followed the Polish comparative and superlative. When he decided she did, he added, "For Jews, the Nazis are worst of all. For people, the Lizards are worst of all. Am I a person first, or am I a Jew first?"

"You are a person first," Ludmila answered at once.

"From you, it sounds so easy," Sholom said with a sigh. "My brother Mendel, he is in Hrubieszów." The Jew shrugged yet again. "These things happen."

Not knowing what to say, Ludmila kept quiet. She gave her U-2 one more anxious glance. It was covered up so it would be hard to spot from the air, but it wasn't concealed the way a Red Air Force crew would have done the job. She did her best not to worry about it. The guerrillas remained operational, so their camouflage precautions were adequate.

In some way, their *maskirovka* was downright inspired, with tricks like those she'd seen from her own experience. A couple of kilometers away from their encampment, large fires burned and cloth tents simulated the presence of a good-sized force. The Lizards had shelled that area a couple of times, while leaving the real site alone.

Fires here were smaller, all of them either inside tents or else hidden under canvas sheets held up on stakes. Men went back and forth or sat around the fires, some cleaning their weapons, others gossiping, still others playing with packs of dog-eared cards.

With the men were a fair number of women, perhaps one in six of the partisans. Some, it seemed, were there for little more than to cook for the men and to sleep with them, but some were real soldiers. The men treated the women who fought like any other fighters, but towards the others they were as coarse and scornful as peasants were to their wives.

A fellow who wore a German greatcoat but who had to be a Jew got up from his card games to throw some powdered herbs into a pot and stir it with a wooden-handled iron spoon. Catching Ludmila's eye on him, he laughed self-consciously and said something in Yiddish. She got the gist of it: he'd been a cook in Hrubieszów, and now he was reduced to this.

"Better a real cook should cook than someone who doesn't know what he's doing," she answered in German, and set a hand on her stomach to emphasize what she meant.

"This, yes," the Jew answered. He stirred the pot again. "But that's salt pork in there. It's the only meat we could get. So now we eat it, and I have to make it tasty, too?" He rolled his eyes up to heaven, as if to say a reasonable God would never have made him put up with such humiliation.

As far as Ludmila was concerned, the dietary regulations he agonized over transgressing were primitive superstitions to be ignored by modern, progressive individuals. She kept that to herself, though. Even the Great Stalin had made his peace with the Orthodox patriarch of Moscow and enlisted God on the side of the Red Army. If superstition would serve the cause, then what point to castigating it?

She was young enough that such compromises with medievalism still struck her as betrayals, in spite of the indoctrination she'd received on the subject. Then she realized the Jew undoubtedly thought cooking salt pork and, worse yet, eating it, was a hideous compromise with godlessness. He was wrong, of course, but that did not make him insincere.

When she got a bowl of the pork stew, she blinked in amazement at the flavor. He might have thought it an abomination, but he'd given it his best.

She was scrubbing out her bowl with snow when one of the camp women—not one of the ones who carried a rifle—came up to her. Hesitantly, in slow Russian, the woman (girl, really; she couldn't have been more than seventeen) asked, "You really flew that airplane against the Lizards?"

"Yes, and against the Nazis before them," Ludmila answered.

The girl's eyes—very big, very blue—went wide. She was slim and pretty, and would have been prettier if her face hadn't had a vacant, cowlike expression. "Heavens," she breathed. "How many men did you have to screw to get them to let you do that?"

The question was innocent, candid. Somehow, that made it worse. Ludmila wanted to shake her. "I didn't screw anybody," she said indignantly. "I—"

"It's all right," the girl—Stefania, that's what her name was—interrupted. "You can tell me. It's not like it's something important. If you're a woman, you have to do such things now and again. Everybody knows it."

"I—didn't—screw—anybody," Ludmila repeated, spacing out the words as if she were talking to a half-wit. "Plenty of men have tried to screw me. I got to be a Red Air Force pilot because I'd been in the *Osoaviakhim*—the state pilot training program—before the war. I'm good at what I do. If I weren't, I'd have got killed twenty times by now."

Stefania studied her. The intent look on the Polish girl's face made Ludmila think she'd made an impression on her. Then Stefania shook her head; her blond braids flipped back and forth. "We know what we get from Russians—nothing but lies." As Witold had, she walked away.

Ludmila wished she were pointing a pistol at the stupid little bitch. She finished cleaning her bowl. This was her second trip outside the Soviet Union. Both times, she'd seen how little use foreigners had for her country. Her immediate reaction to that was disdain. Foreigners had to be ignorant reactionaries if they couldn't appreciate the glorious achievements of the Soviet state and its promise to bring the benefits of scientific socialism to all mankind.

Then she remembered the purges. Had her cousin, her geometry teacher, and the man who ran the tobacconist's shop across from her block of flats truly been counterrevolutionaries, wreckers, spies for the Trotskyites or the decadent imperialists? She'd wondered at the time, but hadn't let herself think about it since. Such thoughts held danger, she knew instinctively.

How glorious were the achievements of the Soviet state if you didn't dare think about them? Frowning, she piled her bowl with all the rest.

☆ V ☆

Ussmak didn't think he'd ever seen such a sorry-looking male in all his days since hatchlinghood. It wasn't just that the poor fellow wore no body paint, although being bare of it contributed to his general air of misery. Worse was the way his eye turrets kept swiveling back toward the Big Ugly for whom he was interpreting, as if that Tosevite were the sun and he himself only a very minor planet.

"This is Colonel Boris Lidov," the male said in the language of the Race, although the title was in the Russki tongue. "He is of the People's Commissariat for the Interior—the NKVD—and is to be your interrogator."

Ussmak glanced over at the Tosevite male for a moment. He looked like a Big Ugly, and not a particularly impressive one: skinny, with a narrow, wrinkled face, not much fur on the top of his head, and a small mouth drawn up even tighter than was the Tosevite norm. "That's nice," Ussmak said; he'd figured the Big Uglies would have questions for him. "Who are you, though, friend? How did you get stuck with this duty?"

"I am called Gazzim, and I was an automatic riflemale, second grade, before my mechanized infantry combat vehicle was destroyed and I taken prisoner," the male replied. "Now I have no rank. I exist on the sufferance of the Soviet Union." Gazzim lowered his voice. "And now, so do you."

"Surely it's not so bad as that," Ussmak said. "Straha, the shiplord who defected, claims most Tosevite not-empires treat captives well."

Gazzim didn't answer. Lidov spoke in the local language, which put Ussmak in mind of the noises a male made when choking on a bite too big to swallow. Gazzim replied in what

110

sounded like the same language, perhaps to let the Tosevite know what Ussmak had said.

Lidov put the tips of his fingers together, each digit touching its equivalent on the other hand. The strange gesture reminded Ussmak he was indeed dealing with an alien species. Then the Tosevite spoke in his own tongue once more. Gazzim translated: "He wants to know what you are here for."

"I don't even know where I am, let alone what for," Ussmak replied with more than a hint of asperity. "After we yielded the base to the soldiers of the SSSR, we were packed first into animal-drawn conveyances of some sort and then into some truly appalling railroad cars, then finally into more conveyances with no way of seeing out. These Russkis are not living up to their agreements the way Straha said they would."

When that was translated for him, Lidov threw back his head and made a peculiar barking noise. "He is laughing," Gazzim explained. "He is laughing because the male Straha has no experience with the Tosevites of the SSSR and does not know what he is talking about."

Ussmak did not care for the sound of those words. He said, "This does not strike me as the place of honor we were promised when we agreed on surrender terms. If I didn't know better, I would say it reminded me of a prison."

Lidov laughed again, this time before Ussmak's words were translated. *He knows some of our language,* Ussmak thought, and resolved to be more wary about what he said. Gazzim said, "The name of this place is Lefortovo. It is in Moskva, the capital of the SSSR."

Casually, without even seeming to think about it, Lidov reached out and smacked Gazzim in the snout. The paintless male cringed. Lidov spoke loudly to him; had the Big Ugly been a male of the Race, no doubt he would have punctuated his speech with emphatic coughs. Gazzim flinched into the posture of obedience.

When Lidov was done, the interpreter said, "I am to tell you that I am allowed to volunteer no further information. This session is to acquire knowledge from you, not to give it to you."

"Ask your questions, then," Ussmak said resignedly.

And the questions began—they came down like snow in the Siberian blizzards Ussmak had grown to hate. At first, they were the sort of questions he would have asked a Tosevite collaborator whose background he did not know well: questions about his military specialty and about his experience on Tosev 3 since being revived from cold sleep.

He was able to tell Colonel Lidov a lot about landcruisers. Crewmales of necessity had to know more than their own particular specialties so they could continue to fight their vehicles in case of casualties. He talked about driving the vehicle, about its suspension, about its weapons, about its engine.

From there, Lidov went on to ask him about the Race's strategy and tactics, and about the other Big Uglies he had fought. That puzzled him; surely Lidov was more familiar with his own kind than Ussmak could hope to be. Gazzim said, "He wants you to rank each type of Tosevite in order of the fighting efficiency you observed."

"Does he?" Ussmak wanted to ask Gazzim a couple of questions before directly responding to that, but didn't dare, not when the Big Ugly interrogator was likely to understand the language of the Race. He wondered how candid he should be. Did Lidov want to hear his own crewmales praised, or was he after real information? Ussmak had to guess, and guessed the latter: "Tell him the Deutsche fought best, the British next, and then Soviet males."

Gazzim quivered a little; Ussmak decided he'd made a mistake, and wondered how bad a mistake it was. The interpreter spoke in the croaking Russki tongue, relaying his words to Colonel Lidov. The Tosevite's little mouth pursed even tighter. He spoke a few words. "Tell him why," Gazzim said, giving no indication what, if anything, Lidov thought of the answer.

Your egg should have been addled instead of hatching, Gazzim, Ussmak thought. But, having begun his course, he saw no choice but to run it through to the end: "The Deutsche keep getting new kinds of equipment, each better than the last, and they are tactically adaptable. They are better tactically than our simulators back on Home, and almost always surprising."

Lidov spoke again in the Russki language. "He says the SSSR also discovered this, to their sorrow. The SSSR and Deutschland were at peace, were friends with each other, and the cowardly, treacherous Deutsche viciously attacked this peace-loving not-empire." Lidov said something else; Gazzim translated: "And what of the British?"

Ussmak paused to think before he answered. He wondered what a Deutsch male would have said about the war with the SSSR. Something different, he suspected. He knew Tosevite politics were far more complicated than anything he was used to, but this Lidov had slammed home his view of the situation like a landcruiser gunner shelling a target into submission. That argued he wouldn't care to hear anything unpleasant about his own group of Big Uglies.

Still, his question about the British gave Ussmak some time to prepare for what he would say about the SSSR. The former land-cruiser driver (who now wished he'd never become anything but a landcruiser driver) answered, "British landcruisers do not match those of Deutschland or the SSSR in quality. British artillery, though, is very good, and the British were first to use poisonous gases against the Race. Also, the island of Britain is small and densely settled, and the British showed they were very good at fighting in built-up areas. They cost us many casualties on account of that."

"Tak," Lidov said. Ussmak turned one eye toward Gazzim—a question without an interrogative cough.

The interpreter explained: "This means 'so' or 'well.' It signifies he has taken in your words but does not indicate his thoughts on them. Now he will want you to speak of the males of the SSSR."

"It shall be done," Ussmak said, politely responding as if Lidov were his superior. "I will say these Russki males are as brave as any Tosevites I have encountered. I will also say that their land-cruisers are well made, with good gun, good engine, and especially good tracks for the wretched ground conditions so common on Tosev 3."

Lidov's mouth grew a little wider. Ussmak took that as a good sign. The male from the—what was it? the NKVD, that was the acronym—spoke in his own language. Gazzim rendered his words as, "With all these compliments, why do you place the glorious soldiers of the Red Army behind those of Deutschland and Britain?"

Ussmak realized his attempt at flattery had failed. Now he would have to tell the truth, or at least some of it, with no reason to be optimistic that Lidov would be glad to hear it. The males of the SSSR had been skillful at breaking the rebellious Siberian males into smaller and smaller groups, each time with a plausible excuse. Now Ussmak felt down to his toes how alone he really was.

Picking his words with great care, he said, "From what I have seen in the SSSR, the fighting males here have trouble changing their plans to match changing circumstances. They do not respond as quickly as the Deutsche or the British." In that way, they were much like the Race, which was probably why the Race had had such good success against them. "Communications also leave a good deal to be desired, and your landcruisers, while stoutly made, are not always deployed to best advantage."

Colonel Lidov grunted. Ussmak didn't know much about the noises the Big Uglies made, but that one sounded like what would have been a thoughtful hiss from a male of the Race. Then Lidov said, "Tell me of the ideological motivations behind your rebellion against the oppressive aristocracy which had controlled you up to the point of your resistance."

After Gazzim translated that into the language of the Race, Ussmak let his mouth fall open in a wry laugh. "Ideology? What ideology? I had a head full of ginger, my crewmales had just been killed, and Hisslef wouldn't stop screaming at me, so I shot him. After that, one thing led to another. If I had it to do over again, I probably wouldn't. It's been more trouble than it's worth."

The Big Ugly grunted again. He said, "Everything has ideological underpinnings, whether one consciously realizes it or not. I congratulate you for the blow you struck against those who exploited your labor for their own selfish benefit."

All that did was convince Ussmak that Lidov didn't have the slightest idea of what he was talking about. All survivors of the conquest fleet—assuming there were survivors from the conquest fleet, which looked imperfectly obvious—would be prominent, well-established males on the conquered world by the time the colonization fleet arrived. They'd have years of exploiting its resources; the first starship full of trade goods might well have headed Homeward before the colonists got here.

Ussmak wondered how much clandestine ginger would have been aboard that first starship. Even if the Big Uglies had been the animal-riding barbarians everyone thought they were, Tosev 3 would have been trouble for the Race. Thinking of ginger made Ussmak wish he had a taste, too.

Colonel Lidov said, "You will now itemize for me the ideologies of the progressive and reactionary factions in your leadership hierarchy."

"I will?" Ussmak said in some surprise. To Gazzim, he went on, "Remind this Tosevite"—he remembered not to call the Big Ugly a Big Ugly—"that I was only a landcruiser driver, if you please. I did not get my orders straight from the fleetlord, you know."

Gazzim spoke in the Russki tongue. Lidov listened, replied. Gazzim translated back the other way: "Tell me whatever you know of these things. Nothing is of greater importance than ideology."

Offhand, Ussmak could have come up with a whole long list of things more important than ideology. Topping the list, at that moment, would have been the ginger he'd thought of a moment before. He wondered why the Big Ugly was so obsessed with an abstraction when there were so many genuinely important things to worry about.

"Tell him I'm sorry, but I don't know how to answer," Ussmak said to Gazzim. "I was never a commander of any sort. All I did was what I was told."

"This is not good enough," Gazzim answered after Lidov had spoken. The male sounded worried. "He believes you are lying. I must explain, so you will understand why, that a specific ideological framework lies under the political structure of this notempire, and serves as its center in the same way as the Emperor does for us."

Lidov did not hit Gazzim, as he had before; evidently he wanted Ussmak to have that explanation. As he had been conditioned to do, Ussmak cast down his eyes—this in spite of having betrayed the Emperor first by mutiny and then by surrender to the Tosevites.

But he answered in the only way he could: "I cannot invent bogus ideological splits when I know of none."

Gazzim let out a long, hissing sigh, then translated his reply for the male from the NKVD. Lidov flicked a switch beside his chair. From behind him, a brilliant incandescent lamp with a reflector in back of it glared into Ussmak's face. He swung his eye turrets away from it. Lidov flicked on other switches. More lights to either side burned at Ussmak.

The interrogation went on from there.

"Good God almighty damn," Mutt Daniels said with reverent irreverence. "It's the country, bread me and fry me if it ain't."

" 'Bout time they took us out o' line for a while, don't you think, sir?" Sergeant Herman Muldoon answered. "They never kept us in the trenches so long at a stretch in the Great War— nothin' like what they put us through in Chicago, not even close."

"Nope," Mutt said. "They could afford to fool around in France. They had the men an' they had the initiative. Here in Shytown, we was like the Germans Over There—we was the ones who had to stand there and take it with whatever we could scrape together."

"I wouldn't exactly call Elgin the country." To illustrate what he meant, Captain Stan Szymanski waved his arm to take in the factories that checked the town's grid of streets. The wave took in what had been factories, anyhow. They were ruins now, jagged and broken against the gray sky. Every one of them had been savagely bombed. Some were just medium-sized hills of broken bricks and rubble. Walls and stacks still stood on others. Whatever they had made, though, they weren't making it any more. The seven-story clock tower of the Elgin Watch factory, which had made a prime observation post, was now scarcely taller than any other wreckage.

Mutt pointed westward, across the Fox River. "But that's farm country out there yonder, sir," he said. "Ain't seen nothin' but houses and skyscrapers and whatnot when I look out for a long time. It's right nice, you ask me."

"What it is, Lieutenant, is damn fine tank country," Szymanski said in a voice that brooked no argument. "Since the Lizards have damn fine tanks and we don't, I can't get what you'd call enthusiastic about it."

"Yes, sir," Daniels said. It wasn't that Szymanski wasn't right—he was. It was just the way these young men, born in this century, looked at the world. Born in this century, hell—odds were Szymanski'd still been pissing his drawers when Mutt climbed on a troopship to head Over There.

But no matter how young the captain was on the outside, he had a cold-blooded way of evaluating things. The farmland over across the river was good tank country and the Lizards had good tanks, so to hell with the whole landscape. One of these days, there might not be a war going on. When Mutt looked at farmland, he thought about that, and about what kind of crops you'd get with this soil and climate, and how big your yield was liable to be. Szymanski didn't care.

"Where they gonna billet us, sir?" Muldoon asked.

"Just off of Fountain Square, not far from the watch factory," Szymanski answered. "We're taking over a hotel that hasn't been bombed to smithereens: the three-story red brick building over there." He pointed.

"Fountain Square? Yeah, I been there." Sergeant Muldoon chuckled. "It's a triangle, and it ain't got no fountain. Great little place."

"Give me a choice between a hotel an' the places we been stayin' at in Chicago, an' I ain't gonna carry on a whole lot," Mutt said. "Nice to lie down without worryin' about whether a sniper can pick up where you're sleepin' and blow your head off without you even knowin' the bastard was there."

"Amen," Muldoon said enthusiastically. " 'Sides which—" He glanced over at Captain Szymanski, then decided not to go on.

Mutt wondered what that was all about. He'd have to wander over to Fountain Square himself and see what he could see.

Szymanski didn't notice Muldoon's awkward pause. He was still looking westward. "No matter what they do and what kind of armor they might bring up, the Lizards would have a tough time forcing a crossing here," he observed. "We're nicely up on the bluffs and well dug in. No matter how hard they pasted us from the air, we'd still hurt their tanks. They'd have to try flanking us out if they wanted to take this place."

"Yes, sir," Muldoon said again. The brass didn't think the Lizards would be trying to take Elgin any time soon, or they wouldn't have sent the company here to rest and recuperate. Of course, the brass wasn't always right about such things, but for the moment no bullets were flying, no cannon bellowing. It was almost peaceful enough to make a man nervous.

"Come on, Lieutenant," Muldoon said. "I'll show that there hotel and—" Again, he didn't go on; he made a production of not going on. What the devil had he found over by Fountain Square? A warehouse full of Lucky Strikes? A cache of booze that wasn't rotgut or moonshine? Whatever it was, he sure was acting coy about it.

For a Midwest factory town, Elgin looked to be a pretty nice place. The blasted plants didn't make up a single district, as they did so many places. Instead, they were scattered among what had been pleasant homes till war visited them with fire and sword. Some of the houses, the ones that hadn't been bombed or burned, still looked comfortable.

Fountain Square hadn't been hit too badly, maybe because none of the town buildings was tall enough to draw Lizard bombers. God only knew why it had the name it did, because, as Muldoon had said, it was neither square nor overburdened with fountains. What looked to be a real live working saloon greeted GIs with open doors—and with a couple of real live working MPs inside those open doors to make sure rest and recuperation didn't get too rowdy.

Was that what Muldoon had had in mind? He could have mentioned it in front of Szymanski; the captain didn't mind taking a drink now and then, or even more often than that.

Then Mutt spotted the line of guys in grimy olive drab snaking their way down a narrow alley. He'd seen—hell, he'd stood in— lines like that in France. "They got themselves a whorehouse goin'," he said.

"You betcha they do," Muldoon agreed with a broad grin. "It

ain't like I need to get my ashes hauled like I did when I was over in France, but hell, it ain't like I'm dead, neither. I figure after we got our boys settled in at the hotel, maybe you an' me—" He hesitated. "Might be they got a special house for officers. The Frenchies, they done that Over There."

"Yeah, I know. I remember," Mutt said. "But I doubt it, though. Hell, I didn't figure they'd set up a house a-tall. Chaplains woulda given 'em holy hell if they'd tried it back in 1918."

"Times have changed, Lieutenant," Muldoon said.

"Yeah, a whole bunch of different ways," Daniels agreed. "I was thinkin' about that my own self, not so long ago."

Captain Szymanski's was not the only company billeted at the Gifford Hotel. Along with the beds, there were mattresses and piles of blankets on the floor, to squeeze in as many men as possible. That was fine, unless the Lizards scored a direct hit on the place. If they did, the Gifford would turn into a king-sized tomb.

When things were going smoothly there, Mutt and Muldoon slid outside and went back to Fountain Square. Muldoon gave Daniels a sidelong look. "Don't it bother you none to have all these horny kids watch you gettin' in line with 'em, Lieutenant?" he asked slyly. "You're an officer now, after all."

"Hell, no," Mutt answered. "No way now they can figure I ain't got any balls." Muldoon stared at him, then broke up. He started to give Mutt a shot in the ribs with an elbow, but thought better of it before he made contact. As he'd said, even in a brothel line an officer was an officer.

The line advanced steadily. Mutt figured the hookers, however many there were, would be moving the dogfaces through as fast as they could, both to make more money and to give themselves more breathers, however brief, between customers.

He wondered if there'd be MPs inside the place. There weren't, which probably meant it wasn't quite official, just winked at. He didn't care. As his foot hit the bottom of the stairway that led up to the girls, he noticed nobody was coming downstairs. They had a back exit, then. He nodded. Whether this crib was official or not, it was certainly efficient.

At the top of the stairs sat a tough-looking woman with a cash box—and a .45, presumably to keep the wages of sin from being redistributed. "Fifty bucks," she told Mutt. He'd heard her say that a dozen times already, all with the exact same intonation; she might have been a broken record. He dug in his hip pocket and peeled greenbacks off a roll. Like a lot of guys, he had a pretty good wad of cash. When you were up in the front lines, you couldn't do much spending.

A big blond GI who didn't look a day over seventeen came out of one of the doors down the hall and headed, sure enough, toward a back stairway. "Go on," the madam told Mutt. "That's Number 4, ain't it? Suzie's in there now."

Anyway, I know whose sloppy seconds I'm gettin', Mutt thought as he walked toward the door. The kid hadn't looked like somebody with VD, but what did that prove? Not much, and who could guess who'd been in there before him, or before that guy, or before the fellow ahead of *him?*

The door did have a tarnished brass 4 on it. Daniels knocked. Inside, a woman started laughing. "Come on in," she said. "It sure as hell ain't locked."

"Suzie?" Mutt said as he went into the room. The girl, dressed in a worn satin wrap, sat on the edge of the bed. She was about thirty, with short brown hair and a lot of eye makeup but no lipstick. She looked tired and bored, but not particularly mean. That relieved Mutt; some of the whores he'd met had hated men so much, he never could figure out why they'd lie down with them in the first place.

She sized him up the same way he did her. After a couple of seconds, she nodded and tried a smile on for size. "Hello, Pops," she said, not unkindly. "You know, maybe only one guy in four or five bothers with my name. You ready?" She pointed to a basin and a bar of soap. "Why don't you wash yourself off first?"

It was a polite order, but an order just the same. Mutt didn't mind. Suzie didn't know him from Adam, either. While he was tending to it, she shrugged the wrap off her shoulders. She wasn't wearing anything underneath it. She wasn't a Vargas girl or anything, but she wasn't bad. She lay back on the narrow mattress while Mutt dried himself off and got out of the rest of his clothes.

He couldn't tell if the moans she made while he was riding her were genuine or professional, which meant odds were good they were professional. She had hellacious hip action, but then she'd naturally try to bring him off in a hurry. He would have come pretty damn quick even if she'd just lain there like a dead fish; he'd been without for a long time.

As soon as he was done, he rolled off her, got up, and went over to the basin to soap himself off again. He pissed in the chamber pot by the bed, too. *Flush the pipes,* he thought. "You don't take chances, do you, Pops?" Suzie said. That could have come out nasty, but it didn't; it sounded more as if she approved of him for knowing what he was doing.

"Not a whole bunch, anyways," he answered, reaching for his skivvies. If he hadn't taken any chances, he wouldn't have gone in there with her in the first place. But since he had, he didn't want to pay any price except the one from his bankroll.

Suzie sat up. Her breasts, tipped with large, pale nipples, bobbed as she reached for the wrap. "That Rita out there, she keeps most of what you give her, the cheap bitch," she said, her voice calculatedly casual. "Twenty for me sure would come in handy."

"I've heard that song before," Mutt said, and the hooker laughed, altogether unembarrassed. He gave her ten bucks even if he had heard the tune; she'd been pretty good, and friendlier than she had to be in an assembly-line operation like this. She grinned and stuck the bill under the mattress.

Mutt had just set his hand on the doorknob when a horrible racket started outside: men shouting and cursing and bellowing, "No!" "What the hell's goin' on?" Mutt said. The question wasn't rhetorical; it didn't sound like any brawl he'd ever heard.

Through the shouts came the sound of a woman weeping as if her heart would break. "My God," Suzie said quietly. Mutt looked back toward her. She was crossing herself. As if to explain, she went on, "That's Rita. I didn't think Rita would cry if you murdered whatever family she's got right in front of her face."

Fists pounded, not on the door but against the wall. Mutt went out into the hallway. GIs were sobbing unashamed, tears cutting winding clean tracks through the dirt on their faces. At the cash box, Rita had her head buried in her arms. "What the hell is going on?" Mutt repeated.

The madam looked up at him. Her face was ravaged, ancient. "He's dead," she said. "Somebody just brought news he's dead."

By the way she said it, she might have been talking about her own father. But if she had been, none of the dogfaces would have given a damn. All they were here for was a fast fuck, same as Mutt. "Who's dead?" he asked.

"The President," Rita answered, at the same time as a corporal choked out, "FDR." Mutt felt as if he'd been kicked in the belly. He gaped for a moment, his mouth falling open like a bluegill's out of water. Then, to his helpless horror, he started bawling like everybody else.

* * *

"Iosef Vissarionovich, there is no reason to think the change in political leadership in the United States will necessarily bring on a change in American policy or in the continuation of the war against the Lizards," Vyacheslav Molotov said.

"Necessarily." Iosef Stalin spoke the word in a nasty, mocking singsong voice. "This is a fancy way to say you haven't the faintest idea what will happen next as far as the United States is concerned."

Molotov scribbled something on the pad he held in his lap. To Stalin, it would look as if he was taking notes. Actually, he was giving himself a chance to think. The trouble was, the General Secretary was right. The man who would have succeeded Franklin D. Roosevelt, Henry Wallace, was dead, killed in the Lizards' nuclear bombing of Seattle. The Foreign Commissariat was, however, quite familiar with Cordell Hull, the new President of the United States.

The foreign commissar trotted out what they did know: "As Secretary of State, Hull consistently supported Roosevelt's fore-doomed effort to reinvigorate the oppressive structure of American monopoly capitalism, forging trade ties with Latin America and attempting financial reform. As you well know, he also strongly supported the President in his opposition to fascism and in his conduct of the war first against the Hitlerites and then against the Lizards. As I say, I think it reasonable to assume he will continue to carry out the policies his predecessor initiated."

"If you want someone to carry out a policy, you hire a clerk," Stalin said, his voice dripping scorn. "What I want to know is, what sort of policies will Hull set?"

"Only the event will tell us," Molotov replied, reluctant to admit ignorance to Stalin but more afraid to make a guess that would prove wrong soon enough for the General Secretary to remember it. With his usual efficiency, he hid the resentment he felt at Stalin's reminding him he was hardly more than a glorified clerk himself.

Stalin paused to get his pipe going. He puffed in silence for a couple of minutes. The reek of *makhorka*, cheap harsh Russian tobacco, filled the little room in the basement of the Kremlin. Not even the head of the Soviet Union enjoyed anything better these days. Like everyone else, Stalin and Molotov were getting by on borscht and *shchi*—beet soup and cabbage soup. They filled your belly and let you preserve at least the illusion that you were being nourished. If you were lucky enough to be able to put meat in them every so often, as the leaders of the Soviet Union were, illusion became reality.

"Do you think the death of Roosevelt will affect whether the Americans send us assistance for the explosive-metal bomb project?" Stalin asked.

Molotov started scribbling again. Stalin was coming up with all sorts of dangerous questions today. They were important; Molotov couldn't very well evade them; and he couldn't afford to be wrong, either.

At last he said, "Comrade General Secretary, I am given to understand that the Americans had agreed to assign one of their physicists to our project. Because of the increase in Lizard attacks on shipping, however, he is coming overland, by way of Canada, Alaska, and Siberia. I do not believe he has yet entered Soviet territory, or I should have been apprised of it."

Stalin's pipe emitted more smoke signals. Molotov wished he could read them. Beria claimed he could tell what Stalin was thinking by the way the General Secretary laughed, but Beria claimed a lot of things that weren't—necessarily—so. Telling the NKVD chief as much carried its own set of risks, though.

Hoping to improve Stalin's mood, Molotov added, "The takeover of the Lizard base near Tomsk will ease our task in transporting the physicist once he does arrive on our soil."

"If he does arrive on our soil," Stalin said. "If he is still in North America, he is still subject to recall by the new regime." Another puff of smoke rose from the pipe. "The tsars were fools, idiots, imbeciles to give away Alaska."

That might or might not have been true, but Molotov couldn't do anything about it any which way. Stalin often gave the impression that he thought people were persecuting him. Given the history of the Soviet Union, given Stalin's own personal history, he often had reason for that assumption, but *often* was not *always*. Reminding him of that was one of the more delicate tasks presenting itself to his aides. Molotov felt like a man defusing a bomb.

Carefully, he said, "It is in the Americans' short-term interest to help us defeat the Lizards, and when, Iosef Vissarionovich, did you ever know the capitalists to consider their long-term interest?"

He'd picked the right line. Stalin smiled. He could, when he chose, look astonishingly benevolent. This was one of those times. "Spoken like a true Marxist-Leninist, Vyacheslav Mikhailovich. We shall triumph over the Lizards, and then we shall proceed to triumph over the Americans, too."

"The dialectic demands it," Molotov agreed. He did not let his voice show relief, any more than he had permitted himself to reveal anger or fear.

Stalin leaned forward, his face intent. "Vyacheslav Mikhailovich, have you been reading the interrogation reports from the Lizard mutineers who gave that base to us? Do you credit them? Can the creatures be so politically naive, or is this some sort of *maskirovka* to deceive us?"

"I have indeed seen these reports, Comrade General Secretary." Molotov felt relief again: at last, something upon which he could venture an opinion without the immediate risk of its blowing up in his face. "My belief is that their naïveté is genuine, not assumed. Our interrogators and other experts have learned that their history has been unitary for millennia. They have had no occasion to acquire the diplomatic skills even the most inept and feckless human government—say, for example, the quasi-fascist clique formerly administering Poland—learns as a matter of course."

"Marshal Zhukov and General Koniev also express this view," Stalin said. "I have trouble believing it." Stalin saw plots everywhere, whether they were there or not: 1937 had proved that. The only plot he hadn't seen was Hitler's in June 1941.

Molotov knew that going against his chief's opinion was risky. He'd done it once lately, and barely survived. Here, though, the stakes were smaller, and he could shade his words: "You may well be right, Iosef Vissarionovich. But if the Lizards were in fact more politically sophisticated than they have shown thus far, would they not have demonstrated it with a better diplomatic performance than they have given since launching their imperialist invasion of our world?"

Stalin stroked his mustache. "This could be so," he said musingly. "I had not thought of it in those terms. If it is so, it becomes all the more important for us to continue resistance and maintain our own governmental structure."

"Comrade General Secretary?" Now Molotov didn't follow.

Stalin's eyes glowed. "So long as we do not lose the war, Comrade Foreign Commissar, do you not think it likely we will win the peace?"

Molotov considered that. Not for nothing had Stalin kept his grip on power in the Soviet Union for more than two decades. Yes, he had shortcomings. Yes, he made mistakes. Yes, you were utterly mad if you pointed them out to him. But, most of the time, he had an uncanny knack for finding the balance of power, for judging which side was stronger—or could become so.

"May it be as you say," Molotov answered.

Atvar hadn't known such excitement since the last time he'd smelled the pheromones of a female during mating season. Maybe ginger tasters knew something of his exhilaration. If they did, he came closer to forgiving them for their destructive addiction than he ever had before.

He turned one eye turret toward Kirel and away from the reports and analyses still flowing across his computer screen. "At last!" he exclaimed. "Maybe I needed to come down to the surface of this planet to change our luck. That luck has been so cruel to us, it is time and past time for it to begin to even out. The death of the American not-emperor Roosevelt will surely propel our forces to victory in the northern region of the lesser continental mass."

"Exalted Fleetlord, may it be as you say," Kirel answered.

"May it be? *May* it be?" Atvar said indignantly. The air of this place called Egypt tasted strange in his mouth, but it was warm enough and dry enough to suit him—quite different from that of so much of this miserable world. "Of course it will be. It must be. The Big Uglies are so politically naive that events cannot but transpire as we wish."

"We have been disappointed in our hopes here so many times, Exalted Fleetlord, that I hesitate to rejoice before a desired event actually does take place," Kirel said.

"Sensible conservatism is good for the Race," Atvar said, a truism if ever there was one. He needed Kirel's conservatism; if Kirel had been a wild radical like Straha, he wouldn't be fleetlord now. But he went on, "Consider the obvious, Shiplord: the United States is not an empire, is it?"

"Indeed not," Kirel said; that was indisputable.

Atvar said, "And because it is not an empire, it by definition cannot have the stable political arrangements we enjoy, now can it?"

"That would seem to follow from the first," Kirel admitted, caution in his voice.

"Just so!" Atvar said joyfully. "And this United States has fallen under the rule of the not-emperor called Roosevelt. Thanks in part to him, the American Tosevites have maintained a steadfast resistance to our forces. Truth?"

"Truth," Kirel said.

"And what follows from this truth does so as inevitably as a statement in a geometric proof springs from its immediate predecessor," Atvar said. "Roosevelt is now dead. Can his successor take his place as smoothly as one Emperor succeeds another? Can his successor's authority be quickly and smoothly recognized as legitimate? Without a preordained imperial succession, how is this possible? My answer is that it is impossible, that the American Tosevites are likely to undergo some severe disorders before this Hull, the Big Ugly who claims authority, is able to exercise it, if he ever is. So also state our political analysts who have been studying Tosevite societies since the beginning of our campaign here."

"This does seem to be reasonable," Kirel said, "but reason is not always a governing factor in Tosevite affairs. For instance, do I not remember that the American Big Uglies are among the minority who attempt to govern their affairs by counting the snouts of those for and against various matters of interest to them?"

Atvar had to glance back through the reports to see whether the shiplord was right. When he had checked, he said, "Yes, that appears to be so. What of it?"

"Some of these not-empires use snoutcounting to confer legitimacy on leaders in the same way we use the imperial succession," Kirel answered. "This may tend to minimize the disruption that will arise in the United States as a result of the loss of Roosevelt."

"Ah, I see your point," Atvar said. "Here, though, it is not valid; Roosevelt's viceregent, a male named Wallace, also chosen through the snoutcounting farce, has predeceased him: he died in our bombing of Seattle. No not-empirewide snoutcounting has ever been perpetrated for this Hull. He must surely be reckoned an illegitimate usurper. Perhaps other would-be rulers of America will rise in various regions of the not-empire to contest his claim."

"If that comes to pass, it would indeed be excellent," Kirel said. "I admit, it does fit with what we know of Tosevite history and behavior patterns. But we have been disappointed so often with regard to the Big Uglies, I find optimism hard to muster these days."

"I understand, and I agree," Atvar said. "In this case, though, as you note, the Big Uglies' irksome proclivities work with us, not against us as they do on most occasions. My opinion is that we may reasonably expect control over major areas of the not-empire of the United States to fall away from its unsnoutcounted leader, and that we may even be able to use the rebels who arise for our own purposes. Cooperating with the Big Uglies galls me, but the potential profit in this case seems worthwhile."

"Considering the use the Big Uglies have got out of Straha, using their leaders against them strikes me as fitting revenge," Kirel said.

Atvar wished Kirel hadn't mentioned Straha; every time he thought of the shiplord who'd escaped his just punishment by fleeing to the American Tosevites, it was as if he got an itch down under his scales where he couldn't scratch it. Despite that, though, he had to admit the comparison was fair.

"At last," he said, "we shall find where the limits of Tosevite resilience lie. Surely no agglomeration of Big Uglies lacking the stability of the imperial form can pass from one rule to another in the midst of the stress of warfare. Why, we would be hard-pressed ourselves if, during such a crisis, the Emperor happened to die and a less experienced male took the throne." He cast down his eyes, then asked, "Truth?"

"Truth," Kirel said.

Leslie Groves sprang to his feet and forced his bulky body into as stiff a brace as he could take. "Mr. President!" he said. "It's a great honor and privilege to meet you, sir."

"Sit down, General," Cordell Hull said. He sat down himself, across from Groves in the latter's office. Just seeing a President of the United States walk into that office jolted Groves. So did Hull's accent: a slightly lisping Tennessee drawl rather than the patrician tones of FDR. The new chief executive did share one thing with his predecessor, though: he looked desperately tired. After Groves was seated, Hull went on, "I never expected to be President, not even after Vice President Wallace was killed and I knew I was next in line. All I ever wanted to do was go on doing my own job the best way I knew how."

"Yes, sir," Groves said. If he'd been playing poker with Hull, he would have said the new President was sandbagging. He'd been Secretary of State since Roosevelt became President, and had been Roosevelt's strong right arm in resisting first the human enemies of the United States and then the invading aliens.

"All right, then," Hull said. "Let's get down to brass tacks."

That didn't strike Groves as sounding very presidential; to him, Hull looked more like an aging small-town lawyer than a President, too: gray-haired, bald on top with wisps combed over to try to hide it, jowly, dressed in a baggy dark blue suit he'd plainly been wearing for a good many years. Regardless of whether he looked like a President or sounded like one, though, he had the job. That meant he was Groves' boss, and a soldier did what his boss said.

"Whatever you need to know, sir," Groves said now.

"The obvious first," Hull answered. "How soon can we have another bomb, and then the one after that, and then one more? You have to understand, General, that I didn't know a thing, not one single solitary thing, about this project until our first atomic bomb went off in Chicago."

"Soourity isn't as tight now as it used to be, either," Groves answered. "Before the Lizards came, we didn't want the Germans or the Japs to have a clue that we thought atomic bombs were even possible. The Lizards know that much."

"Yes, you might say so," Hull agreed, his voice dry. "If I hadn't happened to be out of Washington one fine day, you'd be having this conversation with someone else right now."

"Yes, sir," Groves said. "We don't have to conceal from the Lizards that we're working on the project, just where we're doing it, which is easier."

"I see that," the President said. "As may be,' though; President Roosevelt chose not to let me know till the Lizards came." He sighed. "I don't blame him, or anything of the sort. He had more important things to worry about, and he worried about them— until it killed him. He was a very great man. Christ"—he pronounced it *Chwist*—"only knows how I'll fill his shoes. In peacetime, he would have lived longer. With the weight of the country—by God, General, with the weight of the world—on his shoulders, moving from place to place like a hunted animal, he just wore out, that's all there is to it."

"That was the impression I had when he came here last year," Groves said, nodding. "The strain was more than his mechanism could take, but he took it anyhow, for as long as he could."

"You've hit the nail on the head," Hull said. "But, speaking of nails, we've forgotten about the brass tacks. The bombs, General Groves—when?"

"We'll have enough plutonium for the next one in a couple of months, sir," Groves answered. "After that, we'll be able to make several per year. We've about come to the limit of what we can do here in Denver without giving ourselves away to the Lizards. If we do need a lot more production, we'll have to start a second facility somewhere else—and we have reasons we don't want to do that, the chief one being that we don't think we can keep it secret."

"This place is still secret," Hull pointed out.

"Yes, sir," Groves agreed, "but we had everything set up and going here before the Lizards knew we were a serious threat to build nuclear weapons. They'll be a lot more alert now—and if they catch us at it, they bomb us. General Marshall and President Roosevelt never thought the risk was worth it."

"I respect General Marshall's assessment very highly, General Groves," Hull said, "so highly that I'm naming him Secretary of State—my guess is, he'll do the job better than I ever did. But he is not the Commander-in-Chief, and neither is President Roosevelt, not any more. I am."

"Yes, sir," Groves said. Cordell Hull might not have expected to become President, he might not have wanted to become President, but now that the load had landed on his shoulders, they looked to be wide enough to carry it.

"I see two questions in the use of atomic bombs," Hull said. "The first one is, are we likely to need more than we can produce here at Denver? And the second one, related to the first, is, if we use all we produce, and the Lizards retaliate in kind, will anything be left of the United States by the time the war is done?"

They were both good questions. They went right to the heart of things. The only trouble was, they weren't the sort of questions you asked an engineer. Ask Groves whether something could be built, how long it would take, and how much it would cost, and he'd answer in detail, whether immediately or after he'd gone to work with a slide rule and an adding machine. But he had neither the training nor the inclination to deal with the imponderables of setting policy. He gave the only answer he could: "I don't know, sir."

"I don't know, either," Hull said. "I'll want you to be prepared to split off a team from this facility to start up a new one. I don't know whether I'll decide to do that, but if I do, I'll want to be able to do it as quickly and efficiently as I can."

"Yes, sir," Groves repeated. As a contingency plan, what the new President proposed made good sense: you wanted to keep as many options as possible open for as long as you could.

"Good," Hull said, taking it for granted that Groves would do as he'd been told. The President stabbed out a blunt forefinger. "General, I'm still getting into harness here. What should I know about this place that maybe I don't?"

Groves chewed on that for a minute or so before he tried answering. It was another good question, but also another open-ended one: he didn't know what Hull did or didn't know. At last, he said, "Mr. President, it could be that nobody's told you we've detached one of our physicists from the facility and sent him off to the Soviet Union to help the Russians with their atomic project."

"No, I didn't know that." Hull clicked his tongue between his teeth. "Why do the Russians need help? They set off their atomic bomb before we did, before the Germans, before anybody."

"Yes, sir, but they had help." Groves explained how the Russians had built that bomb out of nuclear material captured from the Lizards, and how some of that same material had also helped the Germans and the United States. He finished, "But we—and the Nazis, too, by the look of things—have been able to figure out how to make more plutonium on our own. The Russians don't seem to have managed that."

"Isn't that interesting?" Hull said. "Under any other circumstances, I can't think of anybody I'd less rather see with the atomic bomb than Stalin—unless it's Hitler." He laughed unhappily. "And now Hitler has it, and if we don't help Stalin, then odds are the Lizards beat him. All right, we're helping him blow the Lizards to kingdom come. If we win that one, then we worry about him trying to blow us to kingdom come, too. Meanwhile, I don't see what choice we have but to help him. What else is there that I ought to know?"

"That was the most important thing I could think of, sir," Groves said, and then, a moment later, "May I ask you a question, Mr. President?"

"Go ahead and ask," Hull said. "I reserve the right not to answer."

Groves nodded. "Of course. I was just wondering . . . It's 1944, sir. How are we going to hold an election this November with the Lizards occupying so much of our territory?"

"We'll probably hold it the same way we held Congressional elections November before last," Hull answered, "which is to say, we probably won't. The officials we have will go on doing their jobs for the duration, and that looks like it will include me." He snorted. "I'm going to stay unelected a good while longer, General. It's not the way I'd like it, but it's the way things are. If we win this war, the Supreme Court is liable to have a field day afterwards. But if we lose it, what those nine old men in black robes think will never matter again. I'll take the chance of their crucifying me, so long as I can put them in a position of being able to do so. What do you think of that, General?"

"From an engineering standpoint, it strikes me as the most

economical solution, sir," Groves answered. "I don't know for a fact whether it's the best one."

"I don't, either," Hull said, "but it looks like it's what we're going to do. The old Romans had dictators in emergencies, and they always thought the best ones were the ones most reluctant to take over. I qualify there, no two ways about it." He got to his feet. He wasn't very young and he wasn't very spry, but he did manage. Again, seeing a President not only upright but mobile in that position reminded Groves things would never be the same again.

"Good luck, sir," he said.

"Thank you, General; I'll take all of that I can get." Hull started to walk toward the door, then stopped and looked back at Groves. "Do you remember what Churchill told Roosevelt when Lend-Lease was just getting rolling? 'Give us the tools and we will finish the job.' That's what the United States needs from the Metallurgical Laboratory. Give us the tools."

"You'll have them," Groves promised.

The white cliffs of Dover stretched a long way, and curved as they did. If one—or even two—walked along them, that one—or those two—could look down at the sea crashing against the base of those cliffs. David Goldfarb had read somewhere that, if the wave action continued with no other factor to check it, in some millions of years—he couldn't remember how many—the British Isles would disappear and the waters of the North Sea and the Atlantic commingle.

When he said that aloud, Naomi Kaplan raised an eyebrow. "The British Isles have plenty of things to worry about before millions of years go by," she said.

The wind from off the North Sea tried to blow her words away. It did the same for her hat. She saved that with a quick grab and set it more firmly on her head. Goldfarb didn't know whether to be glad she'd caught it or sorry he hadn't had the chance to be gallant and chase it down. Of course, the wind might have turned and flung it over the cliff, which wouldn't have done his chances for gallantry much good.

Feigning astonishment, he said, "Why, what ever can you mean? Just because we've been bombed by the Germans and invaded by the Lizards in the past few years?" He waved airily. "Mere details. Now, if we'd had one of those atomic bombs or whatever they're called dropped on us, the way Berlin did—"

"God forbid," Naomi said. "You're right; we've been through quite enough already."

Her accent—upper-crust British laid over German—fascinated him (a good many things about her fascinated him, but he concentrated on the accent for the moment). It was a refined version of his own: lower-middle-class English laid over the Yiddish he'd spoken till he started grammar school.

"I hope you're not too chilly," he said. The weather was brisk, especially so close to the sea, but not nearly so raw as it had been earlier in the winter. You no longer needed to be a wild-eyed optimist to believe spring would get around to showing up one of these days, even if not right away.

Naomi shook her head. "No, it's all right," she said. As if to give the lie to her words, the wind tried to flip up the plaid wool skirt she wore. She smiled wryly as she grabbed at it to keep it straight. "Thank you for inviting me to go walking with you."

"Thanks for coming," he answered. A lot of the chaps who visited the White Horse Inn had invited Naomi to go walking with them; some had invited her to do things a great deal cruder than that. She'd turned everybody down—except Goldfarb. His own teeth were threatening to chatter, but he wouldn't admit even to himself that he was cold.

"It is—pleasant—here," Naomi said, picking the adjective with care. "Before I came to Dover, I had never seen, never imagined, cliffs like this. Mountains I knew in Germany, but never cliffs at the edge of the land, straight down for a hundred meters and more and then nothing but the sea."

"Glad you like them," Goldfarb said, as pleased as if he were personally responsible for Dover's most famous natural feature. "It's hard to find a nice place to take a girl these days—no cinema without electricity, for instance."

"And how many girls did you take to the cinema and other nice places when there was electricity?" Naomi asked. She might have made the question sound teasing. David would have been easier about it if she had. But she sounded both curious and serious.

He couldn't fob her off with a light, casual answer, either. If he tried that, she could get the straight goods—or a large chunk of them—from Sylvia. He hadn't taken Sylvia to the cinema, either; he'd taken her to bed. She was friendly enough to him now when he dropped into the White Horse Inn for a pint, but he couldn't guess what sort of character she'd give him if Naomi asked. He'd heard women could be devastatingly candid when they talked with each other about men's shortcomings.

When he didn't answer right away, Naomi cocked her head to one side and gave him a knowing look that made him feel about two feet high. But, instead of pounding away at him on the point, as he'd expected her to do, she said, "Sylvia tells me you did something very brave to get one of your—was it a cousin? she wasn't sure—out of Poland."

"Does she?" he said in glad surprise; maybe Sylvia hadn't given him such a bad character after all. He shrugged; having been born in England, he'd taken as his own at least part of the notion of British reserve. But if Naomi already knew some of the story, telling more wouldn't hurt. He went on, "Yes, my cousin is Moishe Russie. Remember? I told you that back at the pub."

She nodded. "Yes, you did. The one who broadcast on the wireless for the Lizards—and then against them after he'd seen what they truly were."

"That's right," Goldfarb said. "And they caught him, too, and clapped him in gaol in Lodz till they figured out what to do with him. I went over with a few other chaps and helped get him out and spirited him back here to England."

"You make it sound so simple," Naomi said. "Weren't you frightened?"

That fight had been his first taste of ground combat, even if it had only been against Lizard and Polish prison guards too taken by surprise to put up all the resistance they might have. Since then, he'd got sucked into the infantry when the Lizards invaded England. That had been much worse. He couldn't for the life of him imagine why some men presumably in their right minds chose the infantry as a career.

He realized he hadn't answered Naomi's question. "Frightened?" he said. "As a matter of fact, I was ruddy petrified."

To his relief, she nodded again; he'd been afraid his candor would put her off. "When you tell me things like this," she said, "you remind me you are not an Englishman after all. Not many English soldiers would admit to anyone who is not one of their— what do you call them?—their mates, that is it—that they feel fear or much of anything else."

"Yes, I've seen that," Goldfarb said. "I don't understand it, either." He laughed. "But what do I know? I'm only a Jew whose parents got out of Poland. I won't understand Englishmen down deep if I live to be ninety, which doesn't strike me as likely, the way the world wags these days. Maybe my grandchildren will have the proper stiff upper lip."

"And my parents got me out of Germany just in time," Naomi said. Her shiver had nothing to do with the sea breeze. "It was bad there, and we escaped before the *Kristallnacht*. What—" She hesitated, perhaps nerving herself. After a moment, she finished the question: "What was it like in Poland?"

Goldfarb considered that. "You have to remember, the Nazis had been out of Lodz for a year, more or less, before I went in there." She nodded. He went on, "Keeping that in mind, I think about what I saw there and I try to imagine how it was when the Germans were there."

"*Nu?*" Naomi prodded.

He sighed. His breath smoked in the chilly air. "From everything I saw, from everything I heard, there might not be any Jews left alive there by now if the Lizards hadn't come. I didn't see all of Poland, of course, only Lodz and the road to and from the sea, but there might not be any Jews left in the whole country if the Lizards hadn't come. When the Germans said *Judenfrei*, they weren't joking."

Naomi bit her lip. "This is what I have heard on the wireless. Hearing it from someone I know who has seen it with his own eyes makes it more real." Her frown deepened. "And the Germans, the wireless says, are pushing deeper into Poland again."

"I know. I've heard that, too. My friends—my *goyishe* friends—cheer when they hear news like that. When I hear it, I don't know what to think. The Lizards can't win the war, but the bloody Nazis can't, either."

"Shouldn't," Naomi said with the precision of one who had learned English from the outside instead of growing up with it. "They can. The Lizards can. The Germans can. They shouldn't." She laughed bitterly. "When I was a little girl going to school, before Hitler came to power, they taught me I was a German. I believed it, too. Isn't that peculiar, thinking about it now?"

"It's more than peculiar. It's—" Goldfarb groped for the word he wanted. "What do they call those strange paintings where it's raining loaves of bread or you see a watch dribbling down a block as if it were made of ice and melting?"

"Surreal," Naomi said at once. "Yes, that is it. That is it exactly. Me—a German?" She laughed again, then stood to attention, her right arm rigidly outstretched. "*Ein Volk, ein Reich, ein Führer!*" she thundered in what wasn't the worst imitation of Hitler he'd ever heard.

He thought it was meant for a joke. Maybe she'd thought the same thing when she started it. But as her arm fell limp to her side, she stared at it as if it had betrayed her. Her whole body sagged. Her face twisted. She began to cry.

Goldfarb took her in his arms. "It's all right," he said. It wasn't all right. They both knew it wasn't all right. But if you let yourself think too much about the way it was, how could you go on doing what needed doing? With that thought, David realized he was closer to understanding the British stiff upper lip than he'd imagined.

Naomi clung to him as if he were a life preserver and she a sailor on a ship that had just taken a torpedo from a U-boat. He held her with something of the same desperation. When he tilted her face up to kiss her, he found her mouth waiting. She moaned deeply in her throat and put her hand on the back of his head, pulling him to her.

It might have been the oddest kiss he'd ever known. It didn't stir him to lust, as so many less emphatic kisses with girls about whom he cared less had done. Yet he was glad to have it and sorry when it was over. "I ought to walk you back to your digs," he said.

"Yes, maybe you should," Naomi answered. "You can meet my mother and father, if you like."

He'd fought the Lizards gun to gun. Would he quail from such an invitation now? By the slimmest of margins, he didn't. "Capital," he said, doing his best to sound casual. Naomi slipped her arm in his and smiled up at him, as if he'd just passed a test. Maybe he had.

A large group of dark-skinned Big Uglies formed ragged lines on a grassy meadow next to the Florida air base. Teerts watched another Tosevite of the same color stomp his way out in front of them. The pilot shivered. In his no-nonsense stride and fierce features, the Big Ugly with three stripes on each sleeve of his upper-body covering reminded him of Major Okamoto, who'd been his interpreter and keeper while the Nipponese held him captive.

The male with the stripes on his sleeve shouted something in his own language. "Tenn-*hut*!" was what it sounded like to Teerts. The rest of the Tosevites sprang to stiff verticality, their arms pressed tight against their sides. Given Teerts' forward-slung posture, that only made them seem more ridiculous to him, but it seemed to satisfy, or at least to mollify, the Big Ugly with the striped upper-body covering.

That male shouted again, a whole string of gibberish this time. Teerts had picked up a good deal of Nipponese in captivity, but it didn't help him understand the Florida locals. The Empire's three worlds all used the same language; encountering a planet where tens of different tongues were spoken required a distinct mental leap for males of the Race.

The dark-skinned Big Uglies marched this way and that across the grassy field, obeying the commands the male with the stripes gave them. Even their feet went back and forth in the same rhythm. When that didn't happen, the male in command screamed abuse at those who were derelict. Teerts did not have to be a savant of other-species psychology to figure out that the commanding male was imperfectly pleased.

He turned to another male of the Race who was also watching the Tosevites at their evolutions. The fellow wore the body paint of an intelligence specialist. His equivalent rank was about the same as Teerts'. The pilot asked, "Can we truly trust these Big Uglies to fight on our behalf?"

"Our analysis is that they will fight bravely," the male from Intelligence said. "The other local Tosevites so mistreated them that they will see us as a superior alternative to the continued authority of the lighter-skinned Big Uglies."

Teerts tried to place the other male's voice. "You are Aaatos, not so?" he asked hesitantly.

"Truth," the male answered. "And you are Teerts." Unlike Teerts', his voice held no doubts. If he didn't know who was who around the base, he wouldn't be earning his keep—or preserving Intelligence's reputation for omniscience.

That reputation had taken a beating since the Race came to Tosev 3. A lot of reputations had taken a beating since the Race came to Tosev 3. Teerts said, "I hope you will forgive me, but I will always be nervous in the presence of armed Big Uglies. We have given arms to the natives of other parts of this planet and, from what I have heard, the results have often left much to be desired." He could think of no politer way to say that the Big Uglies had the habit of turning their guns against the Race.

Aaatos said, "Truth," again, but went on, "We are improving control procedures, and will not permit these Tosevites to travel independently in large numbers while under arms: we shall always use significant cadres of males of the Race with them. They are intended to supplement our security details, not to supplant them. Thus we shall not be troubled by embarrassments such as the ones you mention—the case of Poland springs prominently to mind."

"Poland—yes, that is one of the names I have heard," Teerts said. He would have had trouble placing it on a map; but for Manchukuo and Nippon, which he knew in detail more intimate than he had ever wanted to acquire, his familiarity with Tosevite geography was limited.

"Nothing like that can happen here," Aaatos said, and gave an emphatic cough to show he meant it.

"May you be proved correct." Teerts let it go at that. What he had seen on Tosev 3 left him convinced of two things: that the Big Uglies were more devious than most males of the Race could grasp till they got their snouts rubbed in the fact, and that trying to convince those males of that fact before their snouts were rubbed in it was a losing proposition from the start.

Out on the meadow, the Big Uglies marched and marched, now reversing their course, now shifting at right angles. The male with stripes on his sleeves marched right along with them, berating them into performance ever more nearly perfect. Eventually, all of their legs were moving as if under the control of a single organism.

"This is intriguing to watch," Teerts said to Aaatos, "but what is its function? Any males who implemented these tactics in actual ground combat would be quickly destroyed. Even I, a killercraft pilot, know males are supposed to spread wide and seek cover. This is only common sense." He let his mouth fall open. "Not that common sense is common among the Big Uglies."

"This marching, I am given to understand, promotes group solidarity among the Tosevites," the male from Intelligence answered. "I do not understand exactly why this is so, but that it is so appears undeniable: every native military uses similar disciplinary techniques. One theory currently popular as to the reason why is that the Big Uglies, being a species less inherently disciplined than the Race, employ these procedures to inculcate order and conformity to commands."

Teerts thought about that. It made more sense than a lot of theories he'd heard from Intelligence. That didn't necessarily mean it was true—nothing necessarily meant anything on Tosev 3, as far as he could tell—but he didn't have to keep from laughing in Aaatos' face.

He went back to watching the marching Tosevites. After a while, they stopped marching and stood in a neat grid, still stiffly erect, as the male with stripes on his sleeves harangued them. Every so often, they would break in with chorused responses. "Do you understand their language?" Teerts asked Aaatos. "What are they saying?"

"Their leader is describing the attributes of the fighting males he wants them to become," Aaatos said. "He is asking them whether they desire to possess and do possess these attributes. They answer in the affirmative."

"Yes, I can see that they might," Teerts said. "We have never had cause to doubt the fighting attributes of the Tosevites. But still I persist in wondering: will these attributes be employed for us or against us in the end?"

"I do not think the danger is so great as you fear," Aaatos said, "and, in any case, we must take the chance or risk losing the war." Teerts had never heard it put so bluntly. He started worrying in earnest.

☆ **VI** ☆

One of the nice things about Lamar, Colorado, was that when you'd gone a mile past the outskirts of town, the place might as well not have existed. There was nothing but you, the prairie, a million stars shining down on you from a sky clearer and blacker than the sky had any business being—and the person who'd walked a mile past the outskirts of town with you.

Penny Summers snuggled against Rance Auerbach and said, "I wish I'd joined the cavalry, the way Rachel did. Then I'd be riding out with you tomorrow instead of staying stuck back here."

He slipped his arm around her waist. "I'm glad you're not," he answered. "If I were giving you orders, it wouldn't be fair for me to do something like this." He bent down and kissed her. The kiss went on for a long time.

"You wouldn't need to give me orders to get me to want to do that," she said breathlessly when their lips separated at last. "I like it." Then she kissed him.

"Hoo!" he said after a while—a noisy exhalation that sent breath smoking from his lungs. Spring was coming, but the nights didn't know it yet. That it was cold gave him another excuse to hold her tight against him.

After one more kiss, Penny threw back her head and stared up at the night sky through half-closed eyelids. She couldn't have sent him a fancier invitation if she'd had one engraved. The sweet curve of her neck was pale as milk in the starlight. He started to bend to kiss it, then checked himself.

She noticed that. Her eyes opened all the way again. "What's the matter?" she asked, her voice no longer throaty but a little cross.

"It's chilly out here," he said, which was true, but only part of an answer.

Now she exhaled—indignantly. "Wouldn't be *that* chilly," she said, " 'specially while we were doin'—you know."

He wanted her. They both had on long, heavy coats, but he knew she knew: she wouldn't have needed to be the heroine in the story of the princess and the pea to tell. But, even though she wasn't under his command, hauling her denims down and screwing her in the dirt wasn't what he had in mind, no matter how much he'd been thinking about it when he'd asked her to go walking with him.

He tried to put that into words, so it would make sense to him as well as to her. "Doesn't seem quite fair somehow, not when you were so poorly for so long. I want to make sure you're all right before I—" *Before I what?* If all he'd wanted to do was lay her, that would have been simple. Crazy how being interested in her as herself made him—not less interested in her as a naked girl, but not so interested in that just for its own sake.

She didn't get it. "I'm fine," she said indignantly. "Yeah, it hit me hard when my pa got killed, but I'm over that now. I'm as good as I'm ever going to be."

"Okay," he said. He didn't want to argue with her. But when people went from down in the dumps to up in the clouds too darn quick, that didn't mean they got off the roller coaster and stayed up there. From what he'd seen, the ride kept right on going.

"Well, then," she said, as if it were all settled.

"Look, here's what we'll do," he told her. "Wait till I come back from this next mission. That'll be plenty of time to do whatever we want to do." *And you'll have had more of a chance to sort yourself out, make sure you're not just throwing yourself at the first guy who's handy.*

She pouted. "But you're going away for a long time. Rachel says this next mission isn't just a little raid. She says you're going out to try and wreck one of the Lizards' spaceships."

"She shouldn't have told you that," Auerbach answered. Security came natural to him; he'd been a soldier all his adult life. He knew Penny wouldn't run off and blab to the Lizards, but who else had Rachel told about the planned strike? And who had they told? The idea of humans collaborating with the Lizards had been slow to catch on in the United States, at least in the parts that were still free, but such things did happen. Rachel and Penny both knew about them. Yet Rachel had talked anyway. That wasn't so good.

"Maybe she shouldn't have, but she did, so I know about it," Penny said with a toss of the head that seemed to add, *So there.*

"What if I go and find somebody else while you're gone, Mr. Rance Auerbach, sir? What about then?"

He wanted to laugh. Here he was trying to be careful and sensible, and where was it getting him? Into hot water. He said, "If you do that, you wouldn't want to tell him about a time like this, would you?"

She glared at him. "You think you've got all the answers, don't you?"

"Shut up," he said. He didn't aim to stop a fight, or to make one worse; he spoke the words in a tone of voice entirely different from the one he'd been using.

Penny started to reply sharply, but then she too heard the distant roar in the sky. It grew louder with hideous speed. "Those are Lizard planes, ain't they?" she said, as if hoping he'd contradict her.

He wished he could. "They sure are," he said. "More than I've heard in a while, too. Usually they fly higher when they're on their way to a target, then go down low to hit it. Don't know why they're acting different this time, unless—"

Before he could finish the sentence, antiaircraft guns east of Lamar, and then in the town itself, started pounding away. Tracers and shell bursts lit up the night sky, dimming the multitude of stars. Even well outside of Lamar, the din was overwhelming. Shrapnel started pattering down like hot, jagged hail. If that stuff came down on your head, you could end up with a fractured skull. Auerbach wished he were wearing a tin hat. When you took a pretty girl out for a walk, though, you didn't worry about such things.

He never saw the Lizard warplanes till after they'd bombed and rocketed Lamar, and then only the flames shooting out of their tailpipes. After their run, they stood on their tails and climbed like skyrockets. He counted nine of them, in three flights of three.

"I've got to get back," he said, and started toward Lamar at a trot. Penny came right with him, her shoes at first thumping on dirt and then clunking along the blacktop like his.

The Lizard planes returned to Lamar before the two of them got there. They gave the town another pounding, then streaked off toward the east. The antiaircraft guns kept firing long after they were gone. That was a universal constant of air raids, from everything Auerbach had seen and heard. Another constant was that, even when the guns were blazing away at real live targets, they hardly ever hit them.

Penny was panting and gasping before she and Auerbach got to the outskirts of Lamar, but she gamely stayed with him. He said, "Go on over to the infirmary, why don't you? They're sure to need extra hands there."

"Okay," she answered, and hurried off. He nodded to her back. Even if she remembered later on that she was supposed to be mad at him, it was better to see her up and doing things than tucked away in her miserable little room with nothing but a Bible for company.

No sooner had she disappeared round a corner than he forgot all about her. He made his way toward the barracks through chaos in the streets. Bucket brigades poured water on the fires the air attack had started. Some of those fires would burn for a long time, and were liable to spread; Lamar depended on wells for its water these days, and well water and buckets weren't going to be enough to douse the flames.

Wounded men and women cried and screamed. So did wounded horses—at least one bomb had hit the stables. Some of the horses had got out. They were running through the streets, shying from the fires, lashing out in panic with their hooves, and making life more difficult for the people who were trying to help them and help put Lamar back together.

"Captain Auerbach, sir!" somebody bawled, right in Rance's ear. He jumped and whirled around. His second-in-command, Lieutenant Bill Magruder, stood at his elbow. The firelight showed Magruder's face covered with so much soot, he might have been in blackface. He said, "Glad to see you're in one piece, sir."

"I'm okay," Auerbach said, nodding. Absurdly, he felt guilty for not having been on the receiving end of the punishment the Lizards had dished out. "What's the situation here?" That was as discreet a way as he could find of saying he didn't have the slightest idea what the hell was going on.

"Sir, not to put too fine a point on it, we've taken a hell of a licking: men, horses—" He waved at a horse that ran past, its mane smoldering. "The ammo we've been stockpiling got hit goddamn hard, too. Those bastards never pounded on Lamar like this before." He stuck his hands on his hips, as if to say the Lizards had no business pulling a rabbit out of a hat.

Auerbach understood that. Because the aliens didn't do new things very often, you could get the idea they never did anything new at all. If you did, though, it might be the last mistake you ever made.

Losing the ammunition hurt. "We can forget about tomorrow's mission, sounds like," Auerbach said.

"I'm afraid so, Captain." Magruder grimaced. "Be a while before we can think about it again, too." His soft Virginia accent made him sound all the more mournful. "Don't know what's going on with production, but getting the stuff from one place to another isn't easy any more."

"Tell me something I don't know," Auerbach said. He slammed a fist into the side of his thigh. "Damn it, if we could have blown up one of their spaceships, we really would have given them something to think about."

"I know it, too," Magruder answered. "Somebody's got to do it—I agree with you there. Just doesn't look like it's going to be us." He quoted a military maxim: "No plan survives contact with the enemy."

"And isn't that the sad and sorry truth?" Auerbach said. "The enemy, that dirty dog, he goes and has plans of his own." He laughed, even if it hurt. "You just can't trust the son of a bitch that way."

"Sure can't." Magruder looked around at the wreckage that had been Lamar. "Other thing is, his plan tonight, it worked out fine."

Lamar was a mess, no two ways about it. "Isn't that the truth?" Auerbach said again.

The *zeks* who'd been up at the *gulag* near Petrozavodsk for a while described the weather as nine months of winter and three of bad skiing. And they were Russians, used to winters far worse than David Nussboym was. He wondered if the sun ever came out, if the snow ever stopped falling.

Nights were bad. Even with a fire in the stove in the center of the barracks, it stayed bitterly cold. Nussboym was a new fish, a political prisoner as opposed to an ordinary thief, and a Jew to boot. That earned him a top-level bunk far away from the stove and right next to the poorly chinked wall, so that a frigid draft constantly played on his back or his chest. It also earned him the duty of getting up and feeding the stove coal dust in the middle of the night—and earned him a beating if he stayed asleep and let everyone else get as cold as he usually was.

"Shut your mouth, you damned *zhid*, or you'll be denied the right to correspondence," one of the *blatnye*—the thieves—warned him when he groaned after a kick in the ribs.

"As if I have anyone to write to," he said later to Ivan Fyodorov, who'd made the trip to the same camp and who, being without connections among the *blatnye* himself, also had an unenviable bunk site.

Naive as the Russian was, though, he understood camp lingo far better than Nussboym did. "You are a dumb *zhid*," he said, without the malice with which the *blatnoy* had loaded the word. "If you're deprived of the right to correspond, that means you're too dead to write to anybody anyhow."

"Oh," Nussboym said in a hollow voice. He hugged his ribs and thought about reporting to sick call. Brief consideration was plenty to make him discard that idea. If you tried to report sick and the powers that be weren't convinced, you got a new beating to go with the one you'd just had. If they were convinced, the borscht and *shchi* in the infirmary were even thinner and more watery than the horrible slop they fed ordinary *zeks*. Maybe the theory was that sick men couldn't digest anything with actual nourishment in it. Whatever the theory, if you weren't badly sick when you went into the infirmary, odds were you would be by the time you got out—if you got out alive.

He huddled in his clothes under the threadbare blanket and did his best to ignore both the pain in his ribs and the lice that swarmed over him. Everybody had lice. There was no point in getting upset about it—except that it disgusted him. He'd never thought of himself as particularly fastidious, but his standards, he was learning, differed from those of the *gulag*.

Eventually, he drifted down into a light, uneasy sleep. The horn that announced morning roll call made him jerk as if he'd grabbed hold of an electrified fence—not that the camp near Petrozavodsk boasted any such luxury, barbed wire being reckoned plenty to contain the likes of him.

Coughing and grunting and grumbling under their breaths, the *zeks* lined up so the guards could count them and make sure no one had vanished into thin air. It was still black as pitch outside, and cold as the devil's wife, as the Russians said: Petrozavodsk, the capital of the Karelian Soviet Socialist Republic, lay well north of Leningrad. Some of the guards couldn't count their fingers and get the same answer twice running, too. All that made roll call even longer and more miserable than it might have been otherwise. The guards didn't much care. They had warm clothes, warm barracks, and plenty to eat. Why should they worry?

When it left the camp kitchen, the *shchi* Nussboym gulped down might have been hot. By the time it got ladled from the pot into his tin cup, it was tepid going on cold. In another fifteen minutes, it would be cabbage-flavored ice. He got a lump of hard, coarse black bread to go with it—the regulation ration: not enough. He ate some and stuck the rest in the knee pocket of his padded pants for later.

"Now I'm ready to go out and chop wood," he declared in a ringing voice that would have sounded false even if he'd just feasted on all the beefsteak and eggs he could hold. Some of the *zeks*, those who understood his Polish, laughed. It *was* funny. It would have been even funnier if what he'd just eaten hadn't been starvation rations even for a man who didn't have to do hard physical labor.

"Work detail!" the guards bawled. They sounded as if they hated the prisoners they'd have to watch. Likely they did. Even if they didn't have to work, they did have to go out into the cold forest instead of back to the barracks.

Along with the rest of the men in his gang, Nussboym shuffled over to get an axe: a big, clumsy one with a heavy handle and a dull blade. The Russians would have got more labor from the *zeks* had they given them better tools, but they didn't seem to care about such things. If you had to work a little longer, you had to work a little longer. And if you lay down in the snow and died, another prisoner would take your place come morning.

As the *zeks* slogged out toward the forest, Nussboym thought of a riddle he'd heard one German guard in Lodz tell another, and translated it into a Soviet equivalent: "An airplane carrying Stalin, Molotov, and Beria crashes. No one lives. Who is saved?"

Ivan Fyodorov's brow furrowed. "If no one lives, how can anybody be saved?"

"It's a joke, fool," one of the other *zeks* hissed. He turned to Nussboym. "All right, Jew, I'll bite. Who?"

"The Russian people," Nussboym answered.

Fyodorov still didn't get it. The other *zek*'s pinched, narrow face stretched to accommodate a grin. "Not bad," he said, as if that were a major concession. "You want to watch your mouth, though. Tell that one where too many politicals can hear it and one of 'em'll rat on you to the guards."

Nussboym rolled his eyes. "I'm already here. What else can they do to me?"

"Ha!" The other *zek* snorted laughter. "I like that." After a moment's thought, he stuck out his gloved hand. "Anton Mikhailov." Like most prisoners in the camp, he didn't bother with patronymics.

"David Aronovich Nussboym," Nussboym answered, trying to

stay polite. He'd been able to make himself prominent in the Lodz ghetto. Maybe he could manage the same magic here.

"Come on!" shouted Stepan Rudzutak, the gang boss. "We don't make our quota, we starve even worse than usual."

"*Da*, Stepan," the prisoners chorused. They sounded resigned. They were resigned, the ones who'd been in the *gulags* since 1937 or even longer more so than new fish like Nussboym. Even the regular camp ration wasn't enough to keep a man strong. If they cut it because you didn't meet your norm, pretty soon they'd throw you in the snow, to keep till the ground got soft enough for them to bury you.

Anton Mikhailov grunted. "And if we work like a pack of Stakhanovites, we starve then, too."

"Which is *meshuggeh*," Nussboym said. You did get your bread ration increased if you overfulfilled your quota; Mikhailov was right about that. But you didn't come close to getting enough extra to make up for the labor you had to expend to achieve that overfulfillment. Coming close enough to quota to earn regular rations was hard enough. Six and a half cubic yards of wood per man per day. Wood had been something Nussboym took for granted when he was burning it. Producing it was something else again.

"You talk like a *zhid, zhid*," Mikhailov said. Above the face cloth he wore to keep his nose and mouth from freezing, his gray eyes twinkled. Nussboym shrugged. Like Fyodorov, Mikhailov spoke without much malice.

Snow drifted around treetrunks, high as a man's chest. Nussboym and Mikhailov stomped it down with their *valenki*. Without the thick felt boots, Nussboym's feet would have frozen off in short order. If you didn't have decent boots, you couldn't do anything. Even the NKVD guards understood that much. They didn't want to kill you right away: they wanted to get work out of you first.

Once they got the snow down below their knees, they attacked the pine with their axes. Nussboym had never chopped down a tree in his life till he landed in Karelia; if he never chopped down another one, that would suit him fine. No one cared what he thought, of course. If he didn't chop wood, they'd dispose of him without hesitation and without remorse.

He was still awkward at the work. The cotton-padded mittens he wore didn't help with that, although, like the *valenki*, they did keep him from freezing as he worked. Even without them, though, he feared the axe would still have turned every so often in his inexpert hands, so that he hit the trunk with the flat of the blade rather than the edge. Whenever he did it, it jolted him all the way up to the shoulder; the axe handle might have been possessed by a swarm of bees.

"Clumsy fool!" Mikhailov shouted at him from the far side of the pine. Then he did it himself and jumped up and down in the snow, howling curses. Nussboym was rude enough to laugh out loud.

The tree began to sway and groan as their cuts drew nearer each other. Then, all at once, it toppled. "Look out!" they both yelled, to warn the rest of the gang to get out of the way. If the pine fell on the guards, too damn bad, but they scattered, too. The thick snow muffled the noise of the pine's fall, although several branches, heavy with ice, snapped off with reports like gunshots.

Mikhailov clapped his mittened hands together. Nussboym let out a whoop of glee. "Less work for us!" they exclaimed together. They'd have to trim the branches from the tree; any that broke off of their own accord made life easier. In the *gulag*, not much did that.

What they still had left to trim was quite bad enough. Finding where the branches were wasn't easy in the snow, lopping them off wasn't easy, dragging them through the soft powder to the pile where everybody was stacking branches was plenty to make your heart think it would burst.

"Good luck," Nussboym said. The parts of him exposed to the air were frozen. Under his padded jacket and trousers, though, he was wet with sweat. He pointed to the snow still clinging to the green, sap-filled wood of the pine boughs. "How can you burn those in this weather?"

"Mostly you don't," the other *zek* answered. "Used to be you'd just get them to smoke for a while so the guards would be happy and say you'd fulfilled your norm there. But the Lizards have a habit of bombing when they spot smoke, so now we don't do that any more."

Nussboym didn't mind standing around and talking, but he didn't want to stiffen up, either. "Come on, let's get a saw," he said. "The quicker we are, the better the chance for a good one."

The best saw had red-painted handles. It was there for the taking, but Nussboym and Mikhailov left it alone. That was the saw Stepan Rudzutak and the assistant gang boss, a Kazakh named Usmanov, would use. Nussboym grabbed another one he remembered as being pretty good. Mikhailov nodded approval. They carried the saw over to the fallen tree.

Back and forth, back and forth, bend a little more as the cut got deeper, make sure you jerk your foot out of the way so the round of wood doesn't mash your toe. Then move down the trunk a third of a meter and do it again. Then again, and again. After a while, you might as well be a piston in a machine. The work left you too busy and too worn for thought.

"Break for lunch!" Rudzutak shouted. Nussboym looked up in dull amazement. Was half the day gone already? The cooks' helpers were grumbling at having to leave the nice warm kitchens and come out to feed the work gangs too far away to come in, and they were yelling at the *zeks* to hurry up and feed their ugly faces so these precious, delicate souls could get back in away from the chill.

Some of the men in the work gang screamed abuse at the cooks' helpers. Nussboym watched Rudzutak roll his eyes. He was a new fish here, but he'd learned better than that in the Lodz ghetto. Turning to Mikhailov, he said, "Only a fool insults a man who's going to feed him."

"You're not as dumb as you look after all," the Russian answered. He ate his soup—it wasn't *shchi* this time, but some vile brew of nettles and other weeds—in a hurry, to get whatever vestigial warmth remained, then took a couple of bites out of his chunk of bread and stuck the rest back in the pocket of his trousers.

Nussboym ate all his bread. When he got up to go back to his saw, he found he'd gone stiff. That happened every day, near enough. A few minutes at the saw cured it. Back and forth, back and forth, bend lower, jerk your foot, move down the trunk—His mind retreated. When Rudzutak yelled for the gang to knock off for the day, he had to look around to see how much wood he'd cut. Plenty to make quota for him and Mikhailov—and the rest of the gang had done fine, too. They loaded the wood onto sledges and dragged it back toward the camp. A couple of guards rode with the wood. The *zeks* didn't say a word. It would have been their necks if they had.

"Maybe they'll mix some herring in with the kasha tonight," Mikhailov said. Nussboym nodded as he trudged along. It was something to look forward to, anyhow.

Someone knocked on the door to Liu Han's little chamber in the Peking roominghouse. Her heart leaped within her. Nieh Ho-T'ing had been out of the city for a long time, what with one thing and another. She knew he'd been dickering with the Japanese, which revolted her, but she hadn't been able to argue him out of it before he left. He put what he thought of as military necessity before anything else, even her.

He was honest about it, at any rate. Given that, she could accept that he wouldn't yield to her, and yet go on caring about him. Most men, from all she'd seen, would promise you they'd never do something, go ahead and do it anyway, and then either deny that they'd promised or that they'd done it or both. *Usually both,* she thought with a curl of her lip.

The knock came again, louder and more insistent. She scrambled to her feet. If Nieh was knocking like that, maybe he hadn't bedded down with the first singsong girl he'd seen after his prong got heavy. If so, that spoke well for him—and meant she ought to be extra grateful now.

Smiling, she hurried to the door, lifted the bar, and opened it wide. But it wasn't Nieh standing in the hall, it was his aide, Hsia Shou-Tao. The smile slid from her face; she made haste to stand straight like a soldier, abandoning the saucy tilt to her hip that she'd put on for Nieh.

Too late. Hsia's broad, ugly features twisted into a lecherous grin. "What a fine-looking woman you are!" he said, and spat on the floor of the hall. He never let anyone forget he was a peasant by birth, and took any slight trace of polite manners as a bourgeois affectation and probably the sign of counterrevolutionary thought.

"What do you want?" Liu Han asked coldly. She knew the most probable answer to that, but she might have been wrong. There was at least a chance Hsia had come up here on Party business rather than in the hope of sliding his Proud Pestle into her Jade Gate.

She didn't stand aside to let him into the room, but he came in anyway. He was blocky and broad-shouldered and strong as a bullock—when he moved forward, he would walk right over you if you didn't get out of his way. Still trying to keep his voice sweet, though, he said, "You did a fine job, helping to blow up the little scaly devils with those bombs in the gear the animal-show men used. That was clever, and I admit it."

"That was also a long time ago now," Liu Han said. "Why pick this time to come and give me a compliment?"

"Any time is a good time," Hsia Shou-Tao answered. Casually, he kicked the door shut behind him. Liu Han knew exactly what that meant. She started to worry. Not many people were in the roominghouse in the middle of the afternoon. She wished she hadn't opened the door. Hsia went on, "I've had my eye on you for a long time, do you know that?"

Liu Han knew it only too well. She said, "I am not your woman. I am partnered to Nieh Ho-T'ing." Maybe that would make him remember he had no business being up here sniffing after her. He did respect Nieh, and did do as Nieh ordered him—when those orders had nothing to do with women, at any rate.

Hsia laughed. Liu Han did not think it was funny. Hsia said, "He is a good Communist, Nieh is. He will not mind sharing what he has." With no more ado than that, he lunged at her.

She tried to push him away. He laughed again—he was much stronger than she was. He bent his face down to hers. When he tried to kiss her, she tried to bite him. Without any visible show of anger, he slapped her in the face. His erection, big and thick, rammed against her hipbone. He shoved her down onto the thick pile of bedding in a corner of the room, got down beside her, and started pulling off her black cotton trousers.

In pain, half stunned, for a moment she lay still and unresisting. Her mind flew back to the bad days aboard the little scaly devils' airplane that never came down, when the little devils had brought men into her metal cell and they'd had their way with her, whether she wanted them or not. She was a woman; the scaly devils starved her if she did not give in; what could she do?

Then, she'd been able to do nothing except yield. She'd been altogether in the little scaly devils' power—and she'd been an ignorant peasant woman who knew no better than to do whatever was demanded of her.

She wasn't like that any more. Instead of fear and submission, what shot through her was rage so raw and red, she marveled it didn't make her explode. Hsia Shou-Tao yanked her trousers off over her ankles and flung them against the wall. Then he pulled down his own, just halfway. The head of his organ, rampantly free of its foreskin, slapped Liu Han's bare thigh.

She brought up her knee and rammed it into his crotch as hard as she could.

His eyes went wide and round as a foreign devil's, with white all around the iris. He made a noise half groan, half scream, and folded up on himself like a pocketknife, his hands clutching the precious parts she'd wounded.

If she gave him any chance to recover, he'd hurt her badly, maybe even kill her. Careless that she was naked from the waist down, she scrambled away from him, snatched a long sharp knife out of the bottom drawer of the chest by the window, and went back to touch the edge of the blade to his thick, bull-like neck.

"You bitch, you whore, you—" He took one hand away from his injured privates to try to knock her aside.

She bore down on the blade. Blood trickled from the cut. "Hold very still, *Comrade*," she hissed, loading what should have been an honored title with every ounce of scorn she could. "If you think I wouldn't like to see you dead, you're even stupider than I give you credit for."

Hsia froze. Liu Han pressed the knife in a little deeper anyhow. "Careful," he said in a tiny, strangled voice: the more he made his throat move, the more the knife cut him.

"Why should I be careful?" she snarled. It was, she realized, a good question. The longer this tableau held, the better the odds Hsia Shou-Tao would find a way to turn the tables on her. Killing him now would make sure he didn't. If she left him alive, she'd have to move fast, while he was still too shocked and in too much pain to think clearly. "Are you ever going to do that to me again?" she demanded.

He started to shake his head, but that made the knife blade move in his flesh, too. "No," he whispered.

She started to ask if he would ever do such a thing to any other woman again, but changed her mind before the words crossed her lips. He would say no to that, too, but he would undoubtedly be lying. Thinking of one lie would make it easier for him to think of others. Instead, she said, "Get on your hands and knees—slowly. Don't do anything to get yourself bled out like a pig."

He managed. He was awkward not just because of his battered testicles but also because his trousers were still in disarray, impeding his movement. That was one of the things Liu Han counted on: even if he wanted to grab her, having his pants around his ankles would slow him up.

She took the knife away from his neck, stuck it in the small of the back. "Now crawl to the door," she said. "If you think you can knock me down before I shove this all the way in, go ahead and try."

Hsia Shou-Tao crawled. At Liu Han's order, he pulled the door open and crawled out into the hall. She thought about kicking him again as he left, but decided not to. After the humiliation from that, she would have to kill him. He hadn't cared what humiliation he might visit on her, but she couldn't afford to be so cavalier.

She slammed the door after him, let the bar down with a thud. Only then, after it was over, did she start to shake. She looked down at the knife in her hand. She could never leave the room unarmed, not now. She couldn't leave the knife in a drawer while she slept any more, either. It would have to stay in the bedding with her.

She walked over, got her trousers, and started to put them back on. Then she paused and threw them down again. She took a scrap of rag, wet it in the pitcher on the chest of drawers, and used it to scrub at the spot where Hsia Shou-Tao's penis had rubbed against her. Only after that was done did she get dressed.

A couple of hours later, someone knocked on the door. Ice shot up Liu Han's back. She grabbed the knife. "Who is it?" she asked, weapon in hand. She realized it might not do her any good. If Hsia had a pistol, he could shoot through the door and leave her dead or dying at no risk to himself.

But the answer came quick and clear: "Nieh Ho-T'ing." With a gasp of relief, she unbarred the door and let him in.

"Oh, it's so good to be back in Peking," he exclaimed. But as he moved to embrace her, he saw the knife in her hand. "What's this?" he asked, one eyebrow rising.

What it was seemed obvious. As for why it was—Liu Han had thought she'd be able to keep silent about Hsia's attack, but at the first question the tale poured forth. Nieh listened impassively; he kept silent, except for a couple of questions to guide her along, till she was through.

"What do we do about this man?" Liu Han demanded. "I know I am not the first woman he has done this to. From the men in my village, I would have expected nothing different. Is the People's Liberation Army run like my village, though? You say no. Do you mean it?"

"I do not think Hsia will bother you again, not that way," Nieh said. "If he did, he would be a bigger fool than I know him to be."

"It is not enough," Liu Han said. The memory of Hsia Shou-Tao tearing at her clothing brought almost as much fury as had the actual assault. "It's not me alone—he needs to be punished so he never does this to anyone."

"The only sure way to manage that is to purge him, and the cause needs him, even if he is not the perfect man for it," Nieh Ho-T'ing answered. He held up a hand to forestall Liu Han's irate reply. "We shall see what revolutionary justice can accomplish. Come down to the meeting of the executive committee tonight." He paused thoughtfully. "That will also be a way of getting your views heard there more often. You are a very sensible woman. Perhaps you will be a member before too long."

"I will come," Liu Han said, concealing her satisfaction. She had come before the executive committee before, when she was advocating and refining her plan for bombing the little scaly devils at their feasts. She hadn't been invited back—till now. Maybe Nieh had ambitions of using her as his puppet. She had ambitions of her own.

Much of the business of the executive committee proved stupefyingly dull. She held boredom at bay by glaring across the table at Hsia Shou-Tao. He would not meet her eye, which emboldened her to glare more fiercely.

Nieh Ho-T'ing ran the meeting in ruthlessly efficient style. After the committee agreed to liquidate two merchants known to be passing information to the little devils (and also known to be backers of the Kuomintang) he said, "It is unfortunate but true that we of the People's Liberation Army are ourselves creatures of flesh and blood, and all too fallible. Comrade Hsia has provided us with the latest example of such frailty. Comrade?" He looked toward Hsia Shou-Tao like—the comparison that sprang to Liu Han's mind was *like a landlord who's caught a peasant cheating him out of his rents.*

Like that guilty peasant, Hsia looked down, not at his accuser. "Forgive me, Comrades," he mumbled. "I confess I have failed myself, failed the People's Liberation Army, failed the Party, and failed the revolutionary movement. Because of my lust, I tried to molest the loyal and faithful follower in the revolutionary footsteps of Mao Tse-Tung, our soldier Liu Han."

The self-criticism went on for some time. Hsia Shou-Tao told in humiliating detail how he had made advances to Liu Han, how she rebuffed him, how he tried to force her, and how she defended herself.

"I was in error in all regards in this matter," he said. "Our soldier Liu Han had never shown signs of being attracted to me in any way. I was wrong to try to take her for my own pleasure, and wrong again to ignore her when she made it plain she did not want me. She did right to rebuff me, and right again in courageously resisting my treacherous assault. I am glad she succeeded."

The oddest part of it was, Liu Han believed him. He would have been glad in a different way had he raped her, but his ideology drove him toward recognizing that what he had done was wrong. She didn't know for certain whether that made her respect the ideology more or frightened her green.

When Hsia Shou-Tao completed the self-criticism, he glanced toward Nieh Ho-T'ing to see whether it had been adequate. *No,* Liu Han thought, but it was not her place to speak. And, after a moment, Nieh said in a stern voice, "Comrade Hsia, this is not your first failing along these lines—your worst, yes, but far from your first. What have you to say of that?"

Hsia bowed his head again. "I admit it," he said humbly. "I shall be vigilant from now on in eliminating this flaw from my character. Never again shall I disgrace myself with women. If I should, I am ready to suffer the punishments prescribed by revolutionary justice."

"See to it that you remember what you have said here today," Nieh Ho-T'ing warned him in a voice that tolled like a gong.

"Women, too, are part of the revolution," Liu Han added, which made Nieh, the other men of the executive committee, and even Hsia Shou-Tao nod. She didn't say anything more, and everyone nodded again: not only did she say what was true, she didn't rub people's noses in it. One day, probably one day before too long, the executive committee would need a new member. People would recall her good sense. With that, and with Nieh backing her, she would gain a regular seat here.

Yes, she thought. *My time will come.*

George Bagnall stared in fascination at the gadgets the Lizards had turned over along with captive Germans and Russians to get their own prisoners back. The small disks were plastic of some sort, with a metallic finish that somehow had shifting rainbows in it. When you put one into a reader, the screen filled with color images more vivid than any he'd ever seen in the cinema.

"How the devil do they do it?" he asked for what had to be the tenth time.

Lizard talk came hissing out of the speakers to either side of the screen. Small as they were, those speakers reproduced sound with greater fidelity than any manufactured by human beings.

"You're the bleeding engineer," Ken Embry said. "You're supposed to tell the rest of us poor ignorant sods how it's done."

Bagnall rolled his eyes. How many hundreds of years of scientific progress for humanity lay between the aircraft engines he'd monitored and these innocent-looking, almost magical disks? Hundreds? Maybe how many thousands.

"Even the alleged explanations we get from Lizard prisoners don't make much sense—not that anyone here in Pskov speaks their language worth a damn," Bagnall said. "What the bleeding hell is a *skelkwank* light? Whatever it is, it pulls images and sounds out of one of these little blighters, but I'm buggered if I know how."

"We don't even know enough to ask the right questions," Embry said in a mournful voice.

"Too right we don't," Bagnall agreed. "And even though we see the stories and hear the sounds that go with them, most of the time they still don't make any sense to us: the Lizards are just too strange. And do you know what? I don't think they'll be a farthing's worth clearer to the Jerries or the Bolsheviks than they are to us."

"For that matter, what would a Lizard make of *Gone With the Wind*?" Embry said. "He'd need it annotated the way we have to put footnotes to every third word in Chaucer, but even worse."

"That bit in the one story where the Lizard kept doing whatever he was doing—looking things up, maybe—and the images appeared one after another on the screen he was watching . . . What the devil was that supposed to mean?"

Embry shook his head. "Damned if I know. Maybe it was supposed to be all deep and symbolic, or maybe we don't understand what's going on, or maybe the Lizard who made the film didn't understand what was going on. How can we know? How can we even guess?"

"Do you know what it makes me want to do?" Bagnall said.

"If you're anything like me, it makes you want to go back to our house and drink yourself blind on that clear potato spirit the Russians brew," Embry said.

"You've hit it in one," Bagnall said. He hefted another story disk and watched the shimmering rainbows shift. "What worries me most about having all these go to the Nazis and the Reds is that, if they do manage to decipher them better than we can in this one-horse town, they'll learn things we won't know in England."

"This thought has crossed my mind," Embry admitted. "Do recall, though, the Lizards must have left all sorts of rubbish behind when their invasion failed. If we don't have a goodly number of these *skelkwank* readers and the disks that go with them, I'll be very much surprised."

"You have a point," Bagnall said. "The trouble is, of course, it's rather like—no, it's exactly like—having a library scattered at random across the landscape. You never can tell beforehand which book will have the pretty picture you've been looking for all along."

"I'll tell you what I'd like." Embry lowered his voice; some Red Army men and a fair number from the *Wehrmacht* could follow English. "I'd like to see the Germans and the Russians—to say nothing of the bloody Lizards—scattered at random across the landscape. You couldn't make me much happier than that."

"Nor me." Bagnall looked around at the map-lined chamber where they regularly kept the Nazis and Bolsheviks from going for each other's throats. The readers and disks were stored there not least because it was tenuously neutral ground, with neither side likely to try to steal everything for itself from it. He sighed. "I wonder if we'll ever see England again. Not likely, I'm afraid."

"I fear you're right." Embry sighed, too. "We're doomed to grow old and to die in Pskov—or, more likely, doomed not to grow old and to die in Pskov. Only blind luck's kept us intact thus far."

"Blind luck and not getting infatuated with any snipers of the female persuasion, unlike poor Jones," Bagnall said. He and Embry both laughed, though it wasn't funny, not really. Bagnall added, "Being around the fair Tatiana is likelier to make certain you don't grow old and die in Pskov than any other single thing I can think of offhand."

"How right you are," Embry said feelingly. He would have gone on in that vein for some time, but Aleksandr German chose that moment to walk into the chamber. He went from English to halting Russian: "Good day, Comrade Brigadier."

"Hello." German did not look like a brigadier. With his red mustache, long, unkempt hair, and blazing black eyes, he looked half like a bandit, half like an Old Testament prophet (which occasionally made Bagnall wonder how much distinction there was between those two). Now he looked over at the Lizards' reading machines. "Marvelous devices." He said it first in Russian, then in Yiddish, which Bagnall followed better.

"That they are," Bagnall answered in German, which German the partisan leader also understood.

The brigadier tugged at his beard. He continued in Yiddish, in musing tones: "Before the war, you know, I was not a hunter or a trapper or anything of the sort. I was a chemist here in Pskov, making medicines that did not so much good." Bagnall hadn't known that; Aleksandr German usually said but little of himself. His eyes still on the reader, he went on, "I was a boy when the first airplane came to Pskov. I remember the cinema coming, and the wireless, and the talking cinema. How could anything be more modern than the talking cinema? And then the Lizards come and show us we are children, playing with children's toys."

"I had this same thought not long ago," Bagnall said. "I also had it when the first Lizard fighter plane flew past my Lancaster. It was worse then."

Aleksandr German stroked his beard again. "That is right; you are a flier." His laugh showed bad teeth and missing ones. "Very often I forget this. You and your comrades"—he nodded to Embry, and with the plural included Jones, too—"have done such good work here keeping us and the Nazis more angry at the Lizards than at each other that I do not recall it is not why you came to Pskov."

"Sometimes we have trouble remembering that ourselves," Bagnall said. Embry nodded emphatically.

"They have never tried to involve you with the Red Air Force?" German said. Before either Englishman could speak, he answered his own question: "No, of course not. The only aircraft we've had around these parts are *Kukuruzniks*, and they wouldn't bother foreign experts over such small and simple things."

"I suppose not," Bagnall said, and sighed. The biplanes looked as if they flew themselves, and as if anyone with a spanner and a screwdriver could repair them. Having him work on one would have been like calling out the head of the Royal College of Surgeons for a hangnail, but he wouldn't have minded fiddling about with any kind of aircraft.

Aleksandr German studied him. He'd had a lot of Russians and Germans study him since he'd got to Pskov. Most of the time, he had no trouble figuring out what they were thinking: *how can I use this chap for my own advantage?* They were usually so obvious about it, it wasn't worth getting annoyed over. He couldn't so readily fathom the partisan brigadier's expression.

At last, perhaps talking as much to himself as to Bagnall, Aleksandr German said, "If you cannot use your training against the Lizards here, you might do well with the chance to use it someplace else. So you might."

Again, he didn't wait for a reply. Scratching his head and muttering under his breath, he strode out of the chamber. Bagnall and Embry both stared after him. "You don't suppose he meant he could get us back to England—do you?" Embry whispered, sounding afraid to mention the thought aloud.

"I doubt it," Bagnall answered. "More likely, he's just wondering if he can turn us into a couple of Stalin's Hawks. Even that wouldn't be so bad—bit of a change from what we've been doing, what? As for the other—" He shook his head. "I don't dare think about it."

"Wonder what's left of Blighty these days," Embry murmured.

Bagnall wondered, too. Now he knew he would keep on wondering, and wondering if there really was a way to get home again. No point dreaming about what you knew you couldn't have. But if you thought you might somehow—Hope was out of its box now. It might disappoint him, but he knew he'd never be without it again.

The Tosevite hatchling was out of its box again, and all-seeing spirits of Emperors past only knew what it would get into next. Even with his swiveling eye turrets, Ttomalss had an ever more difficult time keeping track of the hatchling when it started crawling on the laboratory floor. He wondered how Big Ugly females, whose vision had a field of view far more limited than his own, managed to keep their hatchlings away from disaster.

A lot of them didn't. He knew that. Even in their most technologically sophisticated not-empires, the Big Uglies lost appalling numbers of hatchlings to disease and accident. In the less sophisticated areas of Tosev 3, somewhere between a third and a half of the hatchlings who emerged from females' bodies perished before the planet had taken one slow turn around its star.

The hatchling crawled out to the doorway that opened onto the corridor. Ttomalss' mouth dropped open in amusement. "No, you can't get out, not these days," he said.

As if it understood him, the hatchling made the irritating noises it emitted when frustrated or annoyed. He'd had a technician make a wire mesh screen he could set in the doorway and fasten to either side of it. The hatchling wasn't strong enough to pull down the wire or clever enough to unscrew the mounting brackets. It was, for the moment, confined.

"And you won't risk extermination by crawling off into Tessrek's area," Ttomalss told it. That could have been funny, but wasn't. Ttomalss, like most males of the Race, had no particular use for Big Uglies. Tessrek, though, had conceived a venomous hatred for the hatchling in particular, for its noise, for its odor, for its mere existence. If the hatchling went into his territory again, he might bring himself to the notice of the disciplinarians. Ttomalss didn't want that to happen; it would interfere with his research.

The hatchling knew none of that. The hatchling knew nothing about anything; that was its problem. It pulled itself upright by clinging to the wire and stared out into the corridor. It made more little whining noises. Ttomalss knew what they meant: *I want to go out there.*

"No," he said. The whining noises got louder; *no* was a word the hatchling understood, even if one it usually chose to ignore. It whined some more, then added what sounded like an emphatic cough: *I really want to go out there.*

"No," Ttomalss said again, and the hatchling went from whining to screaming. It screamed when it didn't get what it wanted. When it screamed, all the researchers along the whole corridor joined in hating both it and Ttomalss for harboring it.

He went over and picked it up. "I'm sorry," he lied as he carried it away from the door. He distracted it with a ball he'd taken from an exercise chamber. "Here, you see? This stupid thing bounces." The hatchling stared in evident amazement. Ttomalss knew relief. It wasn't always easy to distract any more; it remembered what it had been doing and what it wanted to do.

But the ball seemed interesting. When it stopped bouncing, the hatchling crawled over to it, picked it up, and stuck it up against its mouth. Ttomalss had been sure it would do that, and had washed the ball beforehand. He'd learned the hatchling would stick anything it could into its mouth, and learned not to let it get its hands on things small enough to go inside there. Sticking his hand into its slimy little maw to retrieve this or that was not something he relished, and he'd already had to do it more than once.

The communicator squawked for his attention. Before going to answer, he quickly scanned the area where the Tosevite sat to make sure nothing swallowable was close by. Satisfied over that, he answered the instrument.

Ppevel's face stared out of the screen at him. "Superior sir," he said, activating his own video.

"I greet you, Psychologist," Ppevel said. "I am to warn you that there is an increased probability you will be required to turn over the Tosevite hatchling upon which you are currently conducting research to the Big Ugly female from whose body it emerged. Do not merely be prepared for this eventuality; anticipate it as near-term reality."

"It shall be done," Ttomalss said; he was, after all, a male of the Race. Even as he pledged obedience, though, he knew a sinking feeling. He did his best not to show it as he asked, "Superior sir, what has led to this hasty decision?"

Ppevel hissed softly; *hasty* was a term of condemnation among the Race. But he answered civilly enough: "The female from whose body this hatchling came has acquired increased status in the People's Liberation Army, the Tosevite group in China responsible for most of the guerrilla activity against us there.

Thus, propitiating her is of increased priority when compared to its importance a short while ago."

"I—see," Ttomalss said slowly. As he tried to think, the Tosevite hatchling started whimpering. It got nervous now when he was out of its sight for very long. Doing his best to ignore the little squalling nuisance, he tried to keep his wits on the course they had begun. "If this female's status in the outlaw organization is lowered, then, superior sir, the pressure to turn over the hatchling also lessens once more, is that not correct?"

"In theory, yes," Ppevel replied. "How you can hope to turn theory to practice in this particular instance is difficult for me to comprehend. Our influence over any Tosevite groups, even those allegedly favoring us, is more limited than we would like; our influence over those in active opposition to us is, for all practical purposes, nil except for measures military."

He was right, of course. The Big Uglies were prone to believe that what they wanted would come true merely because they wanted it. The delusion afflicted the Race to a lesser degree. *And yet,* Ttomalss thought, *there ought to be a way.* It wasn't as if the female Liu Han had had no contact with the Race before giving birth to this hatchling. The small creature had been conceived in an orbiting starship; its mother had been part of the Race's initial study cadre on the bizarre nature of Tosevite sexuality and mating patterns.

All at once, Ttomalss' mouth fell open. "Are you laughing at me, Psychologist?" Ppevel asked, his voice soft and dangerous.

"By no means, superior sir," Ttomalss answered hastily. "I do believe, however, that I have devised a way to lower the status of the female Liu Han. If successful, as you say, this will lower her rank and prestige in the People's Liberation Army and will allow my vital research program to continue."

"My belief is that you place higher priority on the second than on the first," Ppevel said. Since that was true, Ttomalss did not reply. Ppevel went on, "I forbid military action against or assassination of the female in question. Either of these tactics, even if successful, will raise rather than lower her status. Some males have fallen into the slipshod Tosevite habit of obeying only such orders as suit them. You would be most unwise, Psychologist, to number yourself among them in this particular case."

"It shall be done as you say in every particular, superior sir," Ttomalss promised. "I have no plans for violence against the Big Ugly in question. I plan to reduce her status through ridicule and humiliation."

"If this can be done, well enough," Ppevel said. "Getting the Big Uglies even to notice they have been humiliated, though, is a difficult undertaking."

"Not in all instances, superior sir," Ttomalss said. "Not in all instances." He made his good-byes, checked the hatchling—which, for a wonder, hadn't got into any mischief—and then went to work on the computer. He knew just where to look for the data sequences he had in mind.

Nieh Ho-T'ing turned south off *Chang Mên Ta*—the street that led into the Chinese city of Peking from the Western Gate—and onto *Niu Chieh*. The district that centered on Cow Street was where the Muslims of Peking congregated. Nieh did not normally think much of Muslims; their outmoded faith blinded them to the truth of the dialectic. But, against the little scaly devils, ideology could for the moment be overlooked.

He was reasonably well fed, which made the curio-shop owners standing in the doorways of their establishments shout and wave with particular vigor as he walked past. Nine out of every ten of that breed were Muslims. Given the trash they sold, that helped reinforce the view most Chinese had of the Muslim minority: that their honesty was not always above reproach.

Further down *Niu Chieh*, on the eastern side of the street, stood the largest mosque in Peking. Hundreds, maybe thousands, worshiped there every day. The *qadis* who led them in prayer had a potentially large group of recruits ready to hand, recruits who could also give good service to the People's Liberation Army—if they would.

A large crowd of men stood around . . . "No, they aren't outside the mosque, they're in front of it," Nieh said aloud. He wondered what was going on, and hurried down Cow Street to find out.

As he drew nearer, he saw that the scaly devils had set up in the street one of their machines that could make three-dimensional pictures appear in the air above it. They sometimes tried broadcasting their propaganda on those machines. Nieh had never bothered suppressing their efforts; as far as he was concerned, the scaly devils' propaganda was so laughably bad that it served only to estrange them from the people.

Now, though, they were up to something new. The images floating in midair above the machine weren't propaganda at all, not in any conventional sense of the word. They were just pornography: a Chinese woman fornicating with a man who was too hairy and who had too big a nose to be anything but a foreign devil.

Nieh Ho-T'ing walked down Cow Street toward the display. He was a straitlaced sort himself, and wondered if the little devils hoped to provoke their audience into degeneracy. The show they were putting on here was disgusting but, if that wasn't what they intended, apparently pointless.

As Nieh drew nearer the picture machine, the foreign devil, who had had his head lowered for a while so he could tease the woman's nipple with his tongue, raised it again. Nieh stopped in his tracks, so suddenly that a laborer behind him carrying two buckets on a shoulder pole almost ran into him and shouted angrily. Nieh ignored the fellow. He recognized the foreign devil. It was Bobby Fiore, the man who had put Liu Han's baby into her.

Then the woman whose straining thighs clenched Bobby Fiore's flanks turned her face toward Nieh, and he saw that she was Liu Han. He bit his lip. Her features were slack with lust. The pictures had sound accompanying them. He listened to her little gasps of pleasure, just as he had when he held her in his arms.

In the pictures, Liu Han moaned. Bobby Fiore grunted like a stuck pig. Both of them glistened with sweat. A Chinese man—a running dog for the little scaly devils—spoke over their ecstatic noises, explaining to the crowd what it was watching: "Here we see the famous people's revolutionary Liu Han as she relaxes between her murders. Aren't you proud to have this kind of person claiming to represent you? Don't you hope she gets everything she wants?"

"Eee," said one of the men around the picture machine, "I think she is getting everything she wants. That foreign devil, he's made like a donkey." Everyone who heard him laughed—including Nieh Ho-T'ing, though stretching his mouth into the proper shape and making the right sounds come out of his throat hurt as if he were being flayed with knives.

The machine started a new film of Liu Han—with a different man this time. "Here is true Communism," the narrator said. "From each according to his abilities, to each according to his needs."

The crowd of loafers guffawed at that, too. Again, Nieh Ho-T'ing made himself join the men around him. The first rule was not to look conspicuous. As he laughed, though, he noted that the narrator was probably a Kuomintang man—you had to be familiar with Marxist rhetoric to use it so effectively in burlesque form. He also noted that man down for assassination, if he could find out who he was.

After Nieh had stood around for a couple of minutes, he went on to the mosque. He was looking for a man named Su Shun-Ch'in, and found him sweeping the prayer area clean. That bespoke sincerity and dedication. Had Su Shun-Ch'in been at his trade merely for profit, he would have had an underling do the unpleasant parts of the job.

He looked at Nieh with something less than perfect liking. "How can you expect us to work with folk who are not only godless but who put sluts in positions of authority?" he demanded. "The scaly devils are right to scorn you for that."

Nieh did not mention that he and Liu Han were lovers. Instead, he said, "This poor woman was captured by the little scaly devils and forced to give her body to these men or be starved. Is it any wonder that now she burns for revenge against them? They seek to discredit her, to lower her effectiveness as a revolutionary leader."

"I have seen some of these pictures the little devils show," Su Shun-Ch'in answered. "In one or two, the woman Liu Han looks to be forced, yes. In others, though—the ones with the foreign devil with the fuzzy back and chest—she is doing nothing but enjoying herself. This is very plain."

Liu Han had fallen in love with Bobby Fiore. At first, maybe, it had been nothing more than two miserable people thrown together in a situation where they had no relief save each other, but it had grown to more than that. Nieh knew it. He also knew, from his time with Bobby Fiore on the road and in Shanghai, that the foreign devil had loved her, too, even if he hadn't bothered being faithful to her.

No matter how true all that was, none of it would matter to the *qadi*. Nieh tried a different tack: "Whatever she did in the past that the little devils show, she did only because without doing it she would have been starved to death. Possibly she did not hate all of it; possibly this foreign devil was decent to her in a place where anything decent was hard to find. But whatever she did, it is the scaly devils' fault, not hers, and she repents of having done it."

"Maybe," Su Shun-Ch'in said. By Chinese standards, his face was long and craggy; he might have had a foreign devil or two in his distant ancestry. His features lent themselves to stern disapproval.

"Do you know what else the scaly devils did to the woman Liu Han?" Nieh said. When the *qadi* shook his head, he went on.

"They photographed her giving birth to a child, and photographed that child coming forth from between her legs. Then they stole it, to use it for their own purposes as if it were a beast of burden. You will not see them showing pictures of that, I would wager."

"This is so?" Su Shun-Ch'in said. "You Communists, you are good at inventing lies to advance your cause."

Nieh reckoned all religion a lie to advance a cause, but did not say so. "This *is* so," he answered quietly.

The *qadi* studied him. "You are not lying to me now, I do not think," he said at last.

"No, I am not lying to you now, Nieh agreed. He wished he had not tacked on the last word. Then he saw Su Shun-Ch'in nodding soberly, perhaps pleased he was acknowledging he did sometimes lie. He went on, "In truth, the woman Liu Han gains face from these pictures the scaly devils show; she does not lose it. They prove that the little devils fear her so much, they need to discredit her by whatever means they can."

Su Shun-Ch'in chewed on that like a man working meat from a chunk of pork that was mostly gristle. "Perhaps there is some truth in this," he said after a long pause. Nieh had to work hard not to show the relief he felt as the *qadi* continued, "I will present your interpretation of these pictures to the men who believe as I do, at any rate."

"That will be very fine," Nieh said. "If we stand together in a popular front, we may yet defeat the little scaly devils."

"Perhaps there is some truth in this," Su repeated, "but here, only some. When you say a popular front, you mean a front you will lead. You do not believe in equal partnerships."

Nieh Ho-T'ing put as much indignation as he could into his voice: "You are wrong. That is not true."

To his surprise, Su Shun-Ch'in started to laugh. He waggled a finger in Nieh's face. "Ah, now you are lying to me again," he said. Nieh started to deny it, but the *qadi* waved him to silence. "Never mind. I understand you have to say what you have to say to support your cause. Even if I know it is wrong, you think it is right. Go now, and may God, the Compassionate, the Merciful, someday put wisdom into your heart."

Sanctimonious old fool, Nieh thought. But Su Shun-Ch'in had shown he wasn't a fool, and he was going to work with the Communists to fight the little devils' propaganda. And he was right about one thing: if the People's Liberation Army was part of a popular front, that front would come to reflect the views of the Communist Party.

After Nieh left the mosque, he went wandering through the streets and narrow *hutungs* of Peking. The scaly devils had set up a lot of their picture machines. Liu Han's images floated above every one of them, coupling with one man or another: usually Bobby Fiore, but not always. The little scaly devils turned up the sound at the moments when she neared and reached the Clouds and Rain, and also for the unctuous commentary of their Chinese lackey.

The propaganda piece did some of what the scaly devils wanted it to do. A lot of the men watching Liu Han being penetrated called her a bitch and a whore (just as Hsia Shou-Tao had, from what she'd said) and mocked the People's Liberation Army for having raised her to a position of leadership. "I know what position I'd like to raise her to," one wit cracked, and raised a loud laugh around that particular picture machine.

Not all the men reacted that way, though. Some did sympathize with her plight, and said so out loud. And Nieh found most interesting the reactions of the women who watched the record of Liu Han's degradation. Almost without exception, they used the same words: "Ohh, poor thing."

They would use those words not only among themselves, but also to their husbands and brothers and sons. The Chinese way of life shoved women into the background, but that didn't mean they had no way of making their opinions felt. If they thought the little scaly devils were oppressing Liu Han, they would let their men know about it—and, sooner or later, the opinions those men held would start to change, too.

The Party's counterpropaganda wouldn't hurt there, either. Nieh smiled. With any luck at all, the little scaly devils had wounded themselves in a way the Party couldn't have managed. And, he vowed, he'd give luck a hand.

☆ **VII** ☆

"All right, God damn it, where the hell is he?" That booming baritone, that look-out-world-here-I-am arrogance, could only have belonged to one man of Heinrich Jäger's acquaintance. He had not expected to hear from that one man while campaigning against the Lizards in western Poland.

He got to his feet, careful not to overturn the little aluminum stove on which his supper simmered. "Skorzeny!" he called. "What the devil are you doing here?"

"The devil's work, my lad; the devil's work," SS *Standartenführer* Otto Skorzeny answered, folding Jäger into a rib-crunching bearhug. Skorzeny towered over Jäger by fifteen centimeters, but dominated most men not because of his size but by sheer physical presence. When you fell under his spell, you wanted to charge out to do whatever he told you to, no matter how impossible the rational part of your brain knew it was.

Jäger had been on several missions with Skorzeny: in Russia, in Croatia, in France. He marveled that he remained in one piece after them. He marveled even more that Skorzeny did. He also set himself to resist whatever blandishments Skorzeny hurled his way. If you stood up to the SS man, you got respect. If you didn't, you got run over.

Skorzeny thumped his belly. The scar that furrowed his left cheek pulled up the corner of his mouth as he asked, "Got any food around these parts, or do you aim to starve me to death?"

"You're not wasting away," Jäger said, looking him over with a critical eye. "We have some stew—pork and turnips—and some ersatz coffee. Will they suit your majesty?"

"No truffled pheasant, eh? Well, stew will do. But fuck ersatz coffee and the dying horse that pissed it out." Skorzeny pulled a canteen off his belt, undid the stopper, and passed the canteen to Jäger. "Have a snort."

Jäger drank warily. With Skorzeny's sense of humor, you had to be wary. "Jesus," he whispered. "Where did you come by this?"

"Not a bad cognac, eh?" Skorzeny answered smugly. "Courvoisier VSOP five-star, smoother than the inside of a virgin's twat."

Jäger took another sip, this one with appropriate reverence, then handed the felt-covered aluminum flask back to Skorzeny. "I've changed my mind. I don't want to know where you found it. If you tell me, I'll desert and go there myself. Wherever it is, it's a nicer place than this."

"Which isn't saying one hell of a lot, when you get down to it," Skorzeny said. "Now, where's that stew?" When he'd filled the metal bowl from his own mess kit, he gulped the stuff down, then sent a shot of cognac after it. "Shame to chase anything so vile, but the hooch doesn't do me any good if I don't drink it, eh?" He gave Jäger a shot in the ribs with his elbow.

"Whatever you say," Jäger answered. If you let the SS man sweep you away, you were in trouble—he kept reminding himself of that. Of course, since Skorzeny was here, he was going to find himself in trouble anyway; Skorzeny brought it with him, along with heavenly cognac. What sort of trouble, now, that varied from mission to mission. Jäger got up and stretched as lazily as he could, then said, "Let's go for a little walk, shall we?"

"Oh, you just want to get me alone," Skorzeny said in a shrill, arch falsetto. The panzer crewmen still eating their suppers guffawed in delight. Gunther Grillparzer swallowed wrong and started to choke; somebody had to pound him on the back before he could breathe straight again.

"If I were that desperate, you big ugly lunk, I think I'd shoot myself first," Jäger retorted. The troopers laughed again. So did Skorzeny. He dished it out, but he could take it, too.

He and Jäger strode away from the encampment: not far enough to get lost, but out of earshot of the soldiers. Their boots squelched in mud. The spring thaw had done as much as the Lizards to slow the German advance. Off in a pond not far away, one of the first frogs of the new year let out a loud, mournful croak.

"He'll be sorry," Skorzeny said. "An owl will get him, or a heron." He sounded as if he thought the frog had it coming.

Jäger didn't care about frogs one way or the other. "The devil's work, you said. What sort of deviltry have you got in mind, and where do I fit into it?"

"Don't even know if you do or not," Skorzeny answered. "Have to see how things go. But as long as I was in the neighborhood, I thought I'd drop by and say hello." He bowed from the waist. "Hello."

"You're impossible," Jäger said with a snort. By the way Skorzeny beamed, he took that for a compliment. Holding onto his patience with both hands, Jäger went on, "Let's try it again. Why are you in the neighborhood?"

"I'm going to deliver a present, as soon as I figure out the best way to do it," the SS man said.

"Knowing the kind of presents you deliver, I'm sure the Lizards will be delighted to have this one," Jäger told him. "Anything I can do to tie a bow on the package, you know you have only to ask." There. He'd gone and said it. One way or another, odds were it would get him killed.

He waited for the SS *Standartenführer* to go into extravagant, probably obscene detail about the latest plan for making the Lizards' lives miserable. Skorzeny took a childish delight in his murderous schemes (Jäger got a sudden mental image of him as a child of six in *Lederhosen*, opening a package of tin soldiers; somehow the child Skorzeny in his mind had a scarred face, too). Now, though, he sent Jäger a hooded look before answering, "It's not for the Lizards."

"No?" Jäger raised an eyebrow. "Well, if it's for me, what are you doing giving me fair warning?" He suddenly sobered; officers who displeased the High Command had been known to disappear from the face of the earth as if they had never been. What had he done to displease anyone save the foe? "If you're carrying a pistol with one bullet in it, you'd better tell me why."

"Is *that* what you're thinking? *Gott im Himmel*, no!" Skorzeny held up his right hand as if taking an oath. "Nothing like that, I swear. Not you, not anybody you command or who commands you—no Germans at all, as a matter of fact."

"Well, all right, then," Jäger said in considerable relief. "So what are you getting all coy with me for? The enemies of the *Reich* are the enemies of the *Reich*. We'll smash them and go on."

Skorzeny's face grew unreadable again. "You say that now, it's not the song you've always sung. Jews are [the] *Reich, nicht wahr?*"

"If they weren't beforehand, we've certainly d[one] make them so," Jäger said. "Even so, we've had go[od]

from the ones in Lodz, keeping the Lizards from using the city as a staging point against us. When you get down to it, they're human beings, *ja*?"

"We've had cooperation from them?" Skorzeny said, not answering Jäger's question. "I'll tell you who's had cooperation from them: the Lizards, that's who. If the Jews hadn't stabbed us in the back, we'd hold a lot more of Poland than we do."

Jäger made a tired gesture. "Why do we need to get into all of that? You know what we were doing to the Jews in Poland and Russia. Is it any wonder they don't love us for the good Christians we are?"

"No, it's probably no wonder," Skorzeny said without any rancor Jäger could hear. "But if they want to play that game with us, they're going to have to pay the price. Now—do you want me to go on with what I have to say, or would you sooner not listen so you don't have to know a thing?"

"Go ahead," Jäger said. "I'm not an ostrich, to stick my head in the sand."

Skorzeny grinned at him. The scar on his cheek pulled half his face into a grimace that might have come from a gargoyle sitting somewhere high on a medieval cathedral—or maybe that was just Jäger's mind, pulling horror from the SS man's words: "I'm going to set off the biggest damned nerve-gas bomb the world has ever seen, and I'm going to do it right in the middle of the Lodz ghetto. So what do you think of that? Are you a colonel, or just a scoutmaster in the wrong uniform?"

"Fuck you, Skorzeny," Jäger said evenly. As the words came out of his mouth, he remembered a Jewish partisan who'd used that invitation about every other sentence. SS men had shot the Jew—Max, his name was—at a place called Babi Yar, outside of Kiev. They'd botched the job, or Max wouldn't have had the chance to tell his story. God only knew how many they hadn't botched.

"That's not an answer," Skorzeny said, as immune to insult as a Lizard panzer was to machine-gun bullets. "Tell me what you think."

"I think it's stupid," Jäger answered. "The Jews in Lodz have been helping us. If you start killing off the people who do that, you run out of friends in a hurry."

"Ahh, those bastards are playing both ends against the ~~~dle, and you know it as well as I do," Skorzeny said. "They ~~~hichever ass is closest to them. It doesn't matter one way or the other, anyhow. I've got my orders, and I'm going to carry them out."

Jäger came to attention and flipped up his right arm. *"Heil Hitler!"* he said.

He had to give Skorzeny credit: the big bruiser recognized it was sarcasm, not acquiescence. Not only that, he thought it was funny. "Come on, don't be a wet blanket," he said. "We've been through a lot together, you and I. You can give me a lot of help this time, too."

"Yes, I'd make a splendid Jew," Jäger said, deadpan. "How long do you suppose a circumcision takes to heal up?"

"You didn't used to be such a smartmouth," Skorzeny said, rocking back on his heels and sticking thumbs into trouser pockets so he looked like a young lout on a streetcorner. "Must be senility coming on, eh?"

"If you say so. How am I supposed to help, though? I've never been inside Lodz. In fact, the offensive steered wide around it so we wouldn't get bogged down in street fighting there. We can't afford to go losing panzers to Molotov cocktails and things like that; we lose too many of them to the Lizards as is."

"Yeah, that's the line you sent back to division, and division sent it back to army group headquarters, and the High Command bought it," Skorzeny said with a nod. "Bully for you. Maybe you'll get red stripes on your trousers like a General Staff officer."

"And it's worked, too," Jäger said. "I saw more street fighting in Russia than I ever wanted. Nothing in the world chews up men and machines like that, and we don't have them to waste."

"Ja, ja, ja," Skorzeny said with exaggerated patience. He leaned forward and glared at Jäger. "And I also happen to know that one of the reasons we swung around Lodz in two prongs is that you cut a deal with the Jewish partisans there. What do you have to say to that, Mr. General Staff Officer?"

It might have stopped snowing, but it was anything but warm. All the same, Jäger felt his face heat. If Skorzeny knew that, it was in an SS dossier somewhere . . . which did not bode well for his long-term survival, let alone his career. Even so, he answered as calmly as he could: "I say it was military necessity. This way, we have the partisans on our side and driving the Lizards crazy instead of the other way round. It's worked damned well, so you can take your 'I also happen' and flush it down the WC."

"Why? What does Winston Churchill want with i[...] said with a leer. The joke would have been funnier if [...]

hadn't been making it on the radio from the day Churchill became prime minister to the night the Lizards arrived. The SS man went on, "You have to understand, I don't really give a damn. But it does mean you have connections with the Jews. You ought to be able to use those to help me get my little toy right to the center of town."

Jäger stared at him. "And you pay me thirty pieces of silver afterwards, don't you? I don't throw away connections like that. I don't murder them, either. Why not ask me to betray my own men while you're at it?"

"Thirty pieces of silver? That's pretty good. Christ was a damn kike, too, remember. And a whole fat lot of good it did him. So." Skorzeny studied Jäger. "The more help we get from your little chums, the easier the job will be, and I'm in favor of easy jobs whenever I can get 'em. They pay me to risk my neck, but they don't pay me to stick it out when I don't have to."

This from a man who'd blown up a Lizard panzer by jumping onto it and throwing a satchel charge between turret and hull. Maybe Skorzeny called that a necessary sort of risk; Jäger had no way of knowing. He said, "You touch off a nerve-gas bomb in there, you're going to kill a lot of people who don't have thing one to do with the war."

This time, Skorzeny's laugh was rude. "You fought in Russia, same as I did. So what?" He thumped Jäger in the chest with a forefinger. "Listen and listen good. I'm going to do this with you or without you. It'd make my life easier if it was with you. But my life has been tough before. If it's tough again, believe me, I'll cope. So what do you say?"

"I don't say anything right now," Jäger answered. "I'm going to have to think this one over."

"Sure. Go ahead." Skorzeny's big head bobbed up and down in a parody of sweet reason. "Think all you want. Just don't take too long doing it."

The guard pointed a Sten gun at Moishe Russie's middle. "Come on, get moving," he said, his voice harsh and merciless.

Russie rose from the cot in his cell. "The Nazis put me in the ghetto, the Lizards put me in gaol," he said. "I never thought Jews would treat me the same way."

If he'd hoped to wound the guard, he was disappointed. "Life's ~ugh all over," the fellow answered indifferently. He gestured ~ the submachine gun. "Now put it in gear."

might have been an SS man. Moishe wondered if he'd

learned his military manner from the genuine article. He'd seen that in Poland, after the Jews and Poles helped the Lizards chase out the Germans. Quite a few Jews, suddenly become soldiers, imitated the most impressive, most ferocious human warriors they'd known. If you tried pointing that out to them, though, you were liable to get yourself killed. Moishe maintained a prudent silence here.

He didn't know exactly where *here* was. Somewhere in Palestine, of course, but he and his family had been brought in tied and blindfolded and concealed under straw. The outer walls of the compound were too high for him to see over them. He could tell he was in a town from the noises that came through the golden sandstone: smiths pounding on metal, wagons rattling by, the distant babel of a marketplace. Wherever he was, he was surely walking on soil mentioned in the Torah. Whenever he remembered that, awe prickled through him.

Most of the time, other things were on his mind. Chief among them was how to keep the Lizards from walking on this holy soil. He'd quoted the Bible at the Jewish underground leaders: *Thou trustest in the staff of this broken reed*. Isaiah had been talking about the Egyptians, and the Lizards were in Egypt now. Russie didn't want them to follow Moses across the Sinai and into Palestine.

Very few people cared about what he wanted, worse luck. The local Jews, fools that they were, reckoned the British here as oppressive as the Nazis in Poland—or so they said, anyhow. Some of them had escaped from Poland after the Nazis conquered it, so they should have known better.

"Turn," the guard said: unnecessarily, for Moishe knew the way to the interrogation chamber as well as a rat knew how to run through a familiar maze. He never got rewarded with a piece of cheese for doing it right, though; maybe his handlers hadn't heard of Pavlov.

When he got to the right doorway, the guard stood back and motioned for him to work the latch. That never failed to amuse him: his captors took him for a dangerous man who would seize a weapon and wreak havoc with it if he got the slightest chance. *If only it were so,* he thought wryly. Give him a swatter and he might be dangerous to a fly. Past that . . . past that, the members of the underground were letting their imaginations run away with them.

He opened the door, took one step into the room, and stopped in surprised dismay. There at the table, along with Begin and Stern and the other usual questioners, sat a Lizard. The alien swung an eye turret toward him. "This is the one? I have a hard time being sure," he said in fair German.

Moishe stared at him. The body paint he wore was far drabber than that which Moishe remembered, but no denying the voice was familiar. "Zolraag!"

"He knows me," the former Lizard governor of Poland said. "Either you have coached him well or he is indeed the male who gave the Race such a difficult time in Poland."

"He's Russie, all right," Stern said. He was a big, dark fellow, a fighter rather than a thinker if looks mattered, which wasn't always so. "He says we should steer clear of you, no matter what." He spoke German, too, with a Polish accent.

"And I say to you that we will give you quite a lot to have him in our claws again," Zolraag answered. "He betrayed us—he betrayed me—and he should pay for this betrayal." Lizards didn't have much in the way of facial expressions, but Moishe didn't like the way Zolraag looked or sounded. He hadn't thought the Race worried about such things as revenge, either. If he was wrong there, he would have been happier not knowing it.

"Nobody said anything about turning him over to you," Menachem Begin said in Yiddish. "That was not why we brought you here." He was short and slight, not a whole lot bigger than a Lizard himself. He was nothing much to look at, but when he spoke you had to take him seriously. He shook a finger at Zolraag. "We hear what you have to say, we hear what he has to say, and then we decide what to do."

"You would be well advised to take the Race and its desires more seriously," Zolraag answered, his voice cold. As he had back in Poland, he assumed his concerns were more important than mankind's simply because they were his. Had he been blond and blue-eyed instead of green–brown and scaly, he would have made a good SS man himself: the Race certainly had the notion of the *Herrenvolk* down solid.

He did not succeed in impressing Begin. "You would be well advised to remember where you are," the underground leader replied imperturbably. "We can always sell you to the British, and maybe get more from them for you than your people would give us for Russie here."

"I took this risk when I let you bring me up to this part of the continental mass," Zolraag said; he had courage, whatever you thought of him and his kind. "I still have hopes, though, of persuading you that aligning with the Race, the inevitable victors in this conflict, will serve you best in the long run."

Moishe spoke for the first time: "What he really hopes is to get back his old rank. His body paint is very plain these days."

"Yes, and that is your fault," Zolraag said with an angry hiss like that of a venomous serpent. "It was through you that the province of Poland passed from being peaceful to becoming restive, and you turned on us and blamed us for policies of similar nature to those you had previously praised."

"Bombing Washington was not the same as bombing Berlin," Moishe answered, picking up the old argument. "And now you cannot hold a rifle to my head to try to make me sing your praises and then use your machines to twist my words when I refuse. I was ready to die to tell the truth, and you would not let me. Of course I exposed you when I got the chance."

"Ready to die to tell the truth," Zolraag echoed. He swung his eye turrets toward the Jews who might lead Palestine into rebellion for his people and against the British. "You are sensible, rational Tosevites, sirs. You must see the fanaticism, the futility of this attitude."

Moishe started to laugh. He didn't intend to, but couldn't help himself. The degree to which Zolraag misunderstood people in general and Jews in particular was breathtaking. The folk who had given the world Masada, who had stubbornly stayed Jews when slaughtered for sport or for refusing to convert to Christianity . . . and he expected them to choose the path of expedience? No, Russie couldn't help but laugh.

Then Menachem Begin laughed, too, and then Stern, and then all the underground leaders. Even the guard with the Sten gun, at first glance as humorless a *mamzer* as was ever spawned, chuckled under his breath. The idea of Jews choosing rationality over martyrdom was too deliciously absurd to resist.

Now the underground leaders glanced at one another. How could you explain Zolraag's unintentional irony? Nobody tried. Maybe you couldn't explain it, not so it made sense to him. Didn't that show the essential difference between Lizards and human beings? Moishe thought so.

Before he could drive the point home, Stern said, "We will not turn Russie over to you, Zolraag. Get used to that idea. We take care of our own."

"Very well," the Lizard answered. "We also do this. Here I think your behavior may be more stubborn than necessary, but I comprehend it. Your mirth, however, I find beyond understanding."

"You would have to know more of our history for it to make sense to you," Moishe told him.

That set Zolraag to making unhappy-teakettle noises again. Russie hid a grin. He'd said that with malice aforethought. The Lizards had a history that reached far back into the depths of time, to the days when men still lived in caves and fire was the great new invention of the age. As far as they were concerned, mankind had no history to speak of. The idea that they should concern themselves with human ephemera hit a nerve.

Menachem Begin spoke to Zolraag: "Suppose we do rise against the British. Suppose you help us in the fight. Suppose that helps you come into Palestine afterwards. What do we get from it besides a new master to lord it over us in place of the master we have now?"

"Are you now as free as any Tosevites on this planet?" Zolraag asked, adding an interrogative cough to the end of the sentence.

"If we were, the British wouldn't be our masters," Stern answered.

"Just so," the Lizard said. "After the conquest of Tosev 3 is over, though, you will be raised to the same status as any other nation under us. You will have the highest degree of—what is the word?—autonomy, yes."

"Which is not much," Moishe put in.

"You be silent!" Zolraag said with an emphatic cough.

"Why?" Russie jeered when none of the Jewish underground leaders chose to back the Lizard. "I'm just being truthful, which is sensible and rational, isn't it? Besides, who knows if the conquest of Tosev 3 will ever be over? You haven't beaten us yet, and we've hurt you badly."

"Truth," Zolraag admitted, which disconcerted Moishe for a moment. The Lizard went on, "And among the Tosevite not-empires that has hurt us worst is Deutschland, which also hurt you Jews worst. Do you cheer on the Deutsche now where you fought them before?"

Russie tried not to show his wince. Zolraag might have had no notion of what the history of the Jews was like, but he knew mentioning the Nazis to Jews was like waving a red flag before a bull: he did it to take away their power of rational thought. Reckoning him a fool did not do.

"We are not talking about the Germans now," Moishe said. "We're talking about the British, who have treated Jews well on the whole, on the one hand, and your chances for conquering the world, which do not look as good as they might, on the other."

"Of course we shall conquer Tosev 3," Zolraag said. "The

Emperor has ordered it"—he looked down at the floor for a moment—"and it shall be done."

He didn't sound particularly sensible or rational himself there. What he sounded like was an ultrapious Jew who got everything he knew from the Torah and the Talmud and rejected all secular learning: his faith sustained him in the face of all obstacles. Sometimes that kept you going through bad times. Sometimes it blinded you to things you should see.

Moishe studied his captors. Would they see Zolraag's blind spot, or would their own blind them to it? He picked a different argument: "If you choose to deal with the Lizards, you'll always be a little fish next to them. They may think you're useful now, but what happens after they have Palestine and they don't need you any more?"

Menachem Begin showed his teeth in what was not a grin of amusement. "Then we start giving them a hard time, the same as we do the British now."

"This I believe," Zolraag said. "It would certainly follow the Polish pattern." Did he sound bitter? Hard to tell with a Lizard, but that would have been Moishe's guess.

"If the Race conquers the whole world, though, who will back you against us?" he asked Begin. "What can you hope to gain?"

Now Begin started to laugh. "We are Jews. No one will back us. We will gain nothing. And we will fight anyway. Do you doubt it?"

"Not even slightly," Moishe said. For a moment, captive and captor understood each other perfectly. Moishe had been Zolraag's captive, too. They had stared at each other across a gap of incomprehension wide as the black gulf of space that separated the Lizards' world from Earth.

Zolraag did not fully follow what was going on now, either. He said, "What is your answer, Tosevites? If you must, if there is fire for him in your innards because he is of your clutch of eggs, keep this Russie. But what do you say about the bigger question? Will you fight alongside us when we move forward here and punish the British?"

"Do you Lizards decide things on the spur of the moment?" Stern demanded.

"No, but we are not Tosevites, either," Zolraag answered with evident relish. "You do everything quickly, do you not?"

"Not everything," Stern said, chuckling a little. "This we have to talk about. We'll send you back safe—"

"I was hoping to bring an answer with me," Zolraag said. "This would not only help the Race but improve my own status."

"But we don't care about either of those, except insofar as they help us," Stern said. He nodded to Russie's guard. "Take him back to his room." He didn't call it a cell; even Jews used euphemisms to sugar-coat the things they did. Stern went on, "You can let his wife and son visit, or just his wife, if he'd rather. They aren't going anywhere."

"Right. Come on, you," the guard said to Moishe, as usual punctuating his orders with a jerk of the Sten gun's barrel. As they walked down the corridor toward the chamber—however you wanted to describe it—in which Russie was confined, the fellow added, "No, you aren't going anywhere—not alive, you're not."

"Thank you so much. You do reassure my mind," Moishe replied. For one of the rare times since the Jewish underground had stolen him from the British, he heard that hard-nosed guard laugh out loud.

Ice was still floating in the Moscow River. A big chunk banged into the bow of the rowboat in which Vyacheslav Molotov sat, knocking the boat sideways. "Sorry, Comrade Foreign Commissar," the fellow at the oars said, and put the rowboat back on its proper course upstream.

"It's all right," Molotov answered absently. Of course, the oarsman belonged to the NKVD. But he had such a heavy, bovine *okane*—a Gorky accent that turned *a*'s into *o*'s until he sounded as if he himself had been turned out to pasture—that no one, hearing him for the first time, could possibly take him seriously. A nice bit of *maskirovka*, that's what it was.

A couple of minutes later, another piece of ice ran into the boat. The NKVD man chuckled. "Bet you wish you'd taken a *panje* wagon to the *kolkhoz* now, eh, Comrade?"

"No," Molotov answered coldly. He waved a gloved hand over to the riverbank to illustrate why he said what he said. A *panje* wagon pulled by a *troika* of horses slowly struggled along. Even the Russian wagons, with their tall wheels and boatlike bottoms, had a tough time getting through the mud of the spring *rasputitsa*. The muddy season would vary in the fall, depending on how heavy the rains were. In spring, when a winter's worth of snow and ice melted, the mud was always thick enough to seem bottomless.

Not a bit put out at his abruptness, the rower chuckled again. When he wanted to, he showed skill with the oars, dodging more pieces of drift ice with almost a ballerina's adroitness. (Molotov thought of Anastas Mikoyan, caught by rain at a party to which he'd come without an umbrella. When the hostess exclaimed that he would get wet, he'd just smiled and said, "Oh, no, I'll dance between the raindrops." If any man could do it, Mikoyan was the one.)

Like a lot of riverside collective farms, *Kolkhoz* 118 had a rickety pier sticking out into the turbid brown water of the river. The NKVD boatman tied up the rowboat at the pier, then scrambled up onto it to help Molotov out. When Molotov started toward the farm building, the oarsman didn't follow him. The foreign commissar would have been astonished if he had. He might have been NKVD, but he surely didn't have the security clearance he'd need for this project.

Cows lowed, which made Molotov think again of the rower's intonation. Pigs grunted. They didn't mind mud—on the contrary. Neither did ducks and geese. Chickens struggled, pulling one foot out of the muck and then the other and looking down with little beady black eyes as if wondering why the ground kept trying to grab them.

Molotov wrinkled his nose. The *kolkhoz* had a fine barnyard odor, no doubt about that. Its buildings were typical for those of collective farms, too: unpainted and badly painted wood, all looking decades older than they were. Men in cloth caps, collarless shirts, and baggy trousers tucked into boots tramped here and there, some with pitchforks, some with shovels.

It was all *maskirovka*, carried out with Russian thoroughness. When Molotov rapped on the door to the barn, it opened quickly. "*Zdrast'ye*, Comrade Foreign Commissar," his welcomer said, closing the door behind him. For a moment, he was in complete darkness. Then the man opened the inner door of what might as well have been an airlock, and bright electric light from inside flooded into the chamber.

Molotov shed his coat and boots in there. Igor Kurchatov nodded approvingly. The nuclear physicist was about forty, with sharp features and a pointed chin beard that gave his handsome face almost a satanic aspect. "Hello, Comrade Foreign Commissar," he repeated, his tone somewhere between polite and fawning. Molotov had pushed his enterprise and had kept Stalin from gutting it when results flowed more slowly than he liked. Kurchatov and all the other physicists knew Molotov was the only man between them and the *gulag*. They were *his*.

"Good day," he answered, as always disliking the time polite small talk wasted. "How is progress?"

"We are working like a team of super-Stakhanovites, Vyacheslav Mikhailovich," Kurchatov answered. "We advance on many fronts. We—"

"Do you yet produce this plutonium metal, which will yield the large explosions the Soviet Union desperately requires?" Molotov interrupted.

Kurchatov's devilish features sagged in dismay. "Not yet," he admitted. His voice went high and shrill: "I warned you when this project began that it was a matter of years. The capitalists and fascists were ahead of us in technique when the Lizards came to Earth, and they remain ahead of us. We tried and failed to separate U-235 from U-238. The best chemical for this is uranium hexafluoride, which is as poisonous as mustard gas and hideously corrosive to boot. We do not have the expertise we need for that separation process. We have had no other choice but to seek to manufacture plutonium, which has also proved difficult."

"I am painfully aware of this, I assure you," Molotov said. "Iosef Vissarionovich is also painfully aware of it. But if the Americans succeed, if the Hitlerites succeed, why do you continue to fail?"

"Design of the requisite pile is one thing," Kurchatov answered. "There the American's arrival has already helped us. Having worked with one in full running order, Maksim Lazarovich has given us many valuable insights."

"I hoped he might," Molotov said. Learning that Max Kagan had reached *Kolkhoz* 118 was what had brought him up here. He hadn't yet told Stalin the Americans had chosen to send a clever Jew. Stalin was no Russian, but had a thoroughly Russian dislike for what he called rootless cosmopolites. Being married to a clever Jew himself, Molotov didn't. Now he went on, "This is one problem. What others have you?"

"The worst one, Comrade, is getting both the uranium oxide and the graphite in the nuclear pile free enough from impurities to serve our purposes," Kurchatov said. "There Kagan, however learned and experienced he is in his own field, cannot help us, much as I wish he could."

"You know the measures your producers are required to take to furnish you with materials of requisite purity?" Molotov asked. When Kurchatov nodded, Molotov asked another question: "The producers know they will suffer the highest form of punishment if they fail to meet your demands?" He'd scribbled VMN—for *vysshaya mera nakazamiya*—beside the names of plenty of enemies of the Revolution and the Soviet state, and they'd been shot shortly thereafter. Such deserved—and got—no mercy.

But Kurchatov said, "Comrade Foreign Commissar, if you liquidate these men, their less experienced successors will not deliver improved supplies to us. The required purities, you see, are on the very edge—perhaps just over the edge—of what Soviet chemistry and industry can achieve. We are all doing everything we can in the fight against the Lizards. Sometimes what we do is not enough. *Nichevo*—it can't be helped."

"I refuse to accept *nichevo* from an academician in a time of crisis, any more than I would accept it from a peasant," Molotov said angrily.

Kurchatov shrugged. "Then you will go back and tell the General Secretary to replace us, and good luck to you and the *rodina* with the charlatans who will take over this laboratory." He and his men were in Molotov's power, true, for Molotov held Stalin's wrath at bay. But, if Molotov exercised that power, he would hurt not only the physicists but the Soviet motherland. That made for an interesting and unpleasant balance between him and the laboratory staff.

He exhaled angrily, a show of temper as strong with him as pounding a shoe on a desk would have been for another man. "Have you any more problems standing between you and building these bombs?"

"Yes, one small one," Kurchatov answered with an ironic glint in his eye. "Once some of the uranium in the atomic pile is transmuted to plutonium, we have to get it out and shape it into the material required for a bomb—and we have to do all this without letting any radioactivity leak into the air or the river. We knew this already, and Maksim Lazarovich has been most insistent on it."

"Why is it a difficulty?" Molotov asked. "I confess, I am no physicist, to understand subtle points without explanation."

Kurchatov's smile grew most unpleasant. "This point is not subtle. A leak of radioactivity is detectable. If it is not only detectable but detected by the Lizards, this area will become much more radioactive shortly thereafter."

Molotov needed a moment to realize exactly what Kurchatov meant. When he did, he nodded: a single sharp up-and-down jerk of his head. "The point is taken, Igor Ivanovich. Can you bring Kagan here to me or take me to him? I wish to extend to him the formal thanks of the Soviet workers and peasants for his assistance to us."

That was business of a different sort. "Please wait here, Comrade Foreign Commissar. I will bring him. Do you speak English or German? No? Never mind; I will interpret for you." He hurried down along a white-painted corridor utterly alien to the rough-hewn exterior of the laboratory building.

Kurchatov returned a couple of minutes later with another fellow in a white lab coat in tow. Molotov was surprised at how young Max Kagan looked; he couldn't have been much past thirty. He was a medium-sized man with curly, dark brown hair and intelligent Jewish features.

Kurchatov spoke to Kagan in English, then turned to Molotov. "Comrade Foreign Commissar, I present to you Maksim Lazarovich Kagan, the physicist on loan from the Metallurgical Laboratory project of the United States."

Kagan stuck out his hand and vigorously pumped Molotov's. He spoke in voluble English. Kurchatov did the honors: "He says he is pleased to meet you, and that he aims to blow the Lizards to hell and gone. This is an idiom, and means about what you would think."

"Tell him I share his aspirations and hope they are realized," Molotov answered. He eyed Kagan and was bemused to find Kagan eyeing him back. Soviet scientists were properly deferential to the man who was second in the USSR only to the General Secretary of the Communist Party. To judge by Kagan's attitude, he thought Molotov was just another bureaucrat to deal with. In small doses, the attitude was bracing.

Kagan spoke in rapid-fire English, Molotov had no idea what he was saying, but his tone was peremptory. Kurchatov answered hesitantly in the same language. Kagan spoke some more, slamming a fist into an open palm to emphasize his point. Again, Kurchatov's answer sounded cautious. Kagan threw his hands in the air in obvious disgust.

"Tell me what he is saying," Molotov said.

"He is complaining about the quality of the equipment here, he is complaining about the food, he is complaining about the NKVD man who accompanies him whenever he goes outside—he attributes to the man unsavory sexual practices of which he can have no personal knowledge."

"In any case, he has strong opinions," Molotov remarked, hiding his amusement. "Can you do anything about the equipment of which he complains?"

"No, Comrade Foreign Commissar," Kurchatov answered. "It is the best available in the USSR."

"Then he will have to use it and make the best of it," Molotov said. "As for the others, this *kolkhoz* already has better food than most, but we shall see what we can do to improve it. And if he does not want the NKVD man to accompany him, the NKVD man will not do so."

Kurchatov relayed that to Max Kagan. The American answered at some length. "He will do his best with the equipment, and says he will design better," Kurchatov translated. "He is on the whole pleased with your other answers."

"Is that all?" Molotov asked. "It sounded like more. Tell me exactly what he said."

"Very well, Comrade Foreign Commissar." Igor Kurchatov spoke with a certain sardonic relish: "He said that, since I was in charge of this project, I ought to be able to take care of these matters for myself. He said I should be able to do more than wipe my own arse without a Party functionary's permission. He said that having the NKVD spy on scientists as if they were wreckers and enemies of the people would turn them into wreckers and enemies of the people. And he said that threatening scientists with the maximum punishment because they have not fulfilled norms impossible of fulfillment is the stupidest thing he has ever heard of. These are his exact words, Comrade."

Molotov fixed his icy stare on Max Kagan. The American glared back, too ignorant to know he was supposed to wilt. A little of his aggressive attitude was bracing. A lot of it loose in the Soviet Union would have been a disaster.

And Kurchatov agreed with Kagan. Molotov saw that, too. For now, the state and the Party needed the scientists' expertise. The day would come, though, when they didn't. Molotov looked forward to it.

If you were going to keep your clothes on, you couldn't have a whole lot more fun than riding a horse down a winding road through a forest in new springtime leaf. The fresh, hopeful green sang in Sam Yeager's eyes. The air had that magical, spicy odor you didn't get at any other season of the year: it somehow smelled alive and growing. Birds sang as if there was no tomorrow.

Yeager glanced over to Robert Goddard. If Goddard sensed the spring magic, he didn't show it. "You okay, sir?" Yeager asked anxiously. "I knew we should have put you in a buggy."

"I'm all right," Goddard answered in a voice thinner and raspier than Yeager was used to hearing from him. His face was more nearly gray than the pink it should have been. He wiped his forehead with his sleeve, then made a small concession to the evils the flesh is heir to: "Not much farther, eh?"

"No, sir," Sam answered, as enthusiastically as he was able. Actually, they had another day of hard riding ahead of them, maybe two days if Goddard didn't get over being poorly. "And when we do get there, we'll give the Lizards' stumpy little tails a hell of a tweak, won't we?"

Goddard's smile wasn't altogether exhausted. "That's the plan, Sergeant. How well it works remains to be seen, but I do have hopes."

"It's got to work, sir, doesn't it?" Yeager said. "Doesn't look like we're going to be able to hit the Lizards' spaceships any other way but long-range rockets. A lot of brave men have died trying, anyhow—that's a fact."

"So it is—a melancholy one," Goddard said. "So now we see what we can do. The only problem is, the aiming on these rockets could be a lot finer." He let out a wry chuckle. "It couldn't be much worse, when you get down to it—and that's another fact."

"Yes, sir," Yeager said. All the same, he still felt like somebody in the middle of a John Campbell story: invent the weapon one day, try it the next, and put it into mass production the day after that. Goddard's long-range rockets weren't quite like that. He'd had help on the design not only from the Lizards but also from the Germans, and they hadn't been built in a day any more than Rome was. But they had come along pretty darn quick, and Sam was proud to have had a hand in that.

As he'd feared, they didn't make it into Fordyce by sunset. That meant camping by the side of US 79. Yeager didn't mind for himself, but he worried about what it was doing to Goddard, even with sleeping bags and a tent among their gear. The rocket scientist needed all the pampering he could get, and, with the war on, he couldn't get much.

He was as game as they came, and didn't complain. He had some trouble choking down the rations they'd packed, but drank a couple of cups of the chicory brew that made do for coffee. He even made jokes about mosquitoes as he slapped at them. Sam joked, too, but wasn't fooled. When Goddard got into his sleeping bag after supper, he slept like a dead man.

Not even more of the chicory ersatz got him out of first gear the next morning, either. But, after he'd managed to heave himself up into the saddle, he said, "Today we give the Lizards a surprise." That seemed to hearten him where rest and not-quite-coffee hadn't.

Fordyce, Arkansas, bustled in a way Yeager had seen in few towns since the Lizards came. It boasted several lumber mills and cotton-ginning establishments and a casket factory. Wagons hauled away the output of the last-named establishment, which had never had slack time even during the lost days of peace and probably stayed busy round the clock these days.

The country south and west of Fordyce along US 79 looked to be a hunter's paradise: stands of oak and pine that had to be full of deer and turkey and who could say what all else. They'd given Sam a tommy gun before he set out from Hot Springs. Hunting with it wasn't what you'd call sporting, but when you were hunting for the pot sportsmanship went out the window anyhow.

Four or five miles outside of Fordyce, a fellow sat on the rusted hood of an abandoned Packard, whittling something out of a stick of pine. The guy had on a straw hat and beat-up overalls and looked like a farmer whose farm had seen a lot of better days, but he didn't have a drawl or a hillbilly twang in his voice when he spoke to Yeager and Goddard: "We been waitin' for youse," he said in purest Brooklyn.

"Captain Hanrahan?" Yeager asked, and the disguised New Yorker nodded. He led Goddard and Yeager off the highway into the woods. After a while, they had to dismount and tie their horses. A soldier in olive drab appeared as if from nowhere to look after the beasts. Sam worried about looking after Goddard. Tromping through the woods was not calculated to make him wear longer.

After about fifteen minutes, they came to a clearing. Hanrahan waved to something—a camouflaged shape—under the trees on the far side. "Dr. Goddard's here," he shouted. By the reverence in his voice, that might have been, *God's here*.

A moment later, Sam heard a sound he'd long since stopped taking for granted: a big diesel engine starting up. Whoever was inside the cabin let it get warm for a minute or two, then drove it out into the middle of the clearing. Things started happening very quickly after that. Soldiers dashed out to strip off the branch-laden tarp that covered the back of the truck.

Captain Hanrahan nodded to Goddard, then pointed to the rocket revealed when the tarp came off. "Dere's your baby, sir," he said.

Goddard smiled and shook his head. "Junior's been adopted by the U.S. Army. I just come visit to make sure you boys know how to take care of him. I won't have to do that much longer, either."

A smooth, silent hydraulic ram started raising the rocket from horizontal to vertical. It moved much more slowly than Sam would have liked. Every second they were out in the open meant one more second in which the Lizards could spot them from the air or from one of those instrument-laden artificial moons they'd placed in orbit around the Earth. A fighter plane had shot up the woods a couple of launches ago, and scared him into the quivering fidgets: only fool luck the rockets hadn't wrecked a lot of this scraped-together equipment.

As soon as the rocket was standing straight up, two smaller trucks—tankers—rolled up to either side of it. "Douse your butts!" a sergeant in coveralls shouted, though nobody was smoking. A couple of soldiers carried hoses up the ladder that was part of the launch frame. Pumps started whirring. Liquid oxygen went into one tank, 200-proof alcohol into the other.

"We'd get slightly longer range from wood alcohol, but good old ethanol is easier to cook up," Goddard said.

"Yes, sir," Hanrahan said, nodding again. "This way, the whole crew gets a drink when we're done, too. We'll have earned it, by God." *Oined* was what he really said. "And the Lizards over by Greenville, they get a hell of a surprise."

Ninety miles, Yeager thought, *maybe a few more.* Once it went off—if it didn't do anything stupid like blowing up on the launcher—it would cross the Mississippi River and land in Mississippi in the space of a couple of minutes. He shook his head. If that wasn't science fiction, what was it?

"Fueled!" the driver of the launch truck sang out—he had the gauges that let him see how the rocket was doing. The soldiers disconnected the hoses, climbed down the ladder, and got the hell out of there. The two fuel tankers went back into the woods.

The launcher had a rotating table at the base. It turned slightly, lining up the azimuth gyro with the planned course east to Greenville. The driver stuck his fist out the window and gave a thumbs-up: the rocket was ready to fly.

Goddard turned to Captain Hanrahan. "There—you see? You didn't need me here. I could have been back at Hot Springs, playing tiddlywinks with Sergeant Yeager."

"Yeah, when everything goes good, it goes great," Hanrahan agreed. "But when it's snafu, you like having the guy who dreamed up the gadget around, you know what I mean?"

"Sooner or later, you'll be doing it without me," Goddard said, absently scratching at the side of his neck. Sam looked at him, wondering how he'd meant that. Probably both ways—he knew he was a sick man.

Hanrahan took the statement at face value. "Whatever you say,

Doc. Now whaddaya say we get the hell out of here?" Before
Hanrahan could do that, he had to make a connection at the base
of the rocket. Then, trailing a wire after him, he loped for the
cover of the woods where the rest of the crew already waited.
Goddard's trot was slow but dogged. Sam stayed with him. When
they were out of the clearing, Hanrahan gave Goddard the control
box. "Here you go, sir. You wanna do the honors?"

"I've done it before, thanks." Goddard passed the box to Sam.
"Sergeant, why don't you take a turn?"

"Me?" Sam said in surprise. But why not? You didn't need to
know atomic physics to figure out how the control box worked. It
had one large red button, right in the middle. "Thank you, Dr.
Goddard." He pushed the button, hard.

Flame spurted from the base of the rocket, blue for a moment
then sun-yellow. The roar of the engine beat at Yeager's ears. The
rocket seemed to hang unmoving above the launcher for a
moment. Sam nervously wondered if they were far enough
away—when one of those babies blew, it blew spectacularly. But
it didn't blow. All at once, it wasn't hanging any more, it was
flying like an arrow, like a bullet, like nothing on God's green
earth. The roar sank down toward the merely unbearable.

The blast shield at the base of the launcher kept the grass from
catching fire. The driver sprinted out toward the cab of the truck.
The launcher sank back toward the horizontal once more.

"Now we get the hell outta here," Hanrahan said. "Come on, I'll
take youse back to your horses."

He set a brisk pace. Yeager needed no urging to keep up. Neither did Goddard, though he was breathing harshly by the time
they reached the soldier in charge of the animals. Yeager had just
swung one foot into the stirrup when a flight of helicopters buzzed
by overhead and started lashing the clearing from which the rocket
had flown and the surrounding woods with gunfire and little
rockets of their own.

None of the ordnance came close to him. He grinned at Goddard and Captain Hanrahan as the helicopters headed east, back
toward the Mississippi. "They don't like us," he said.

"Hey, don't blame me," Hanrahan said. "You're the guy shot
that thing off."

"Yeah," Yeager said, almost dreamily. "How about that?"

"This is unacceptable," Atvar declared. "That the Deutsch
Tosevites fire missiles at us is one thing. That some other Big

Uglies have now acquired the art presents us with severe difficulties."

"Truth, Exalted Fleetlord," Kirel said. "This one impacted uncomfortably close to the *17th Emperor Satla*, and would surely have destroyed it had the targeting been better." He paused, then tried to look on the bright side: "Like the Deutsch rockets, it is very inaccurate—more an area weapon than a pinpoint one."

"If they fire enough of them, that ceases to matter," Atvar snapped. "The Deutsche have killed a starship, though I don't believe their intelligence realizes as much: if they knew such a thing, they would boast of it. But those losses we absolutely cannot afford."

"Nor can we hope to prevent them altogether," Kirel said. "We have expended the last of our antimissile missiles, and close-in weapons systems offer only a limited chance of a target kill."

"I am all too painfully aware of these facts." Atvar felt uncomfortable, unsafe, on the surface of Tosev 3. His eye turrets nervously swiveled this way and that. "I know we are a long distance from the nearest sea, but what if it occurs to the Big Uglies to mount their missiles on those ships they use to such annoying effect? We have not been able to sink all of them. For all we know, a missile–armed ship may be approaching Egypt while we are holding this conversation."

"Exalted Fleetlord, this is indeed possible, but strikes me as unlikely," Kirel said. "We have enough genuine concerns to contemplate without inventing fresh ones."

"The Tosevites use missiles. The Tosevites use ships. The Tosevites are revoltingly ingenious. This does not strike me as an invented concern," Atvar said, adding an emphatic cough. "This whole North African region is as salubrious to us as any on the planet. If all of Tosev 3 were like it, it would be a far more pleasant world. I do not want our settlements here to come into danger from Big Ugly waterborne assaults."

"No male would, Exalted Fleetlord." Kirel drew back from the implied criticism he'd aimed at Atvar. "One way to improve our control over the area would be to annex the territory to the northeast of us, the region known as Palestine. I regret that Zolraag did not succeed in gaining the allegiance of the rebellious males there; they would reduce requirements for our own resources if they rose against the British."

"Truth," Atvar said, "but only part truth. Tosevite allies have a way of becoming Tosevite enemies. Look at the Mexicanos. Look at the Italianos. Look at the Jews and Poland—and are these Big Uglies not Jews, too?"

"They are, Exalted Fleetlord," Kirel replied. "How these Jews pop up in such widely separated areas is beyond my understanding, but they do."

"They certainly do, and they cause trouble wherever they appear, too," Atvar said. "Since the ones in Poland were so unreliable, I entertain no great hope that we shall be able to count on the ones in Palestine, either. They would not turn Moishe Russie over to Zolraag, for instance, which makes me doubt their good faith, however much they try to ascribe their failure to group solidarity."

"We may yet be able to use them, though, even if we cannot trust them," Kirel said, a sentiment the Race had employed with regard to a large variety of Big Uglies since coming to Tosev 3. The shiplord sighed. "A pity the Jews discovered the tracking device Zolraag planted in their conference chamber, or we could have swept down on the building that housed it and plucked Russie away from them."

"It is a pity, especially when the device was so small that their crude technology cannot come close to duplicating it," Atvar agreed. "They must be as suspicious of us as we are of them." His mouth dropped open in a wry chuckle. "They also have a nasty sense of humor."

"Truth, Exalted Fleetlord," Kirel said. "Finding that the tracker led directly to the largest British base in Palestine was—a disappointment."

Males of the Race had been saying that about a large variety of things since they came to Tosev 3, too.

When Mordechai Anielewicz left Lodz, as had been true when he'd left Warsaw, he was reminded that the Jews, however numerous they were in Poland, remained a small minority of its population. Most of them had guns now, and they could call on their militias, which could bring heavier weapons to bear, but they were thin on the ground.

That meant dealing with the Poles when he went out into the countryside, and dealing with the Poles made him nervous. A large majority of Poles had either done nothing or applauded when the Nazis shut the Jews away in big-city ghettos or massacred them in the towns and villages. A lot of those Poles hated the Lizards not for having driven out the Germans but for arming the Jews who'd helped them do it.

And so, when a message came into Lodz that a Polish peasant urgently needed to speak to him, Mordechai wondered if he was walking into a trap. Then he wondered who might be setting the trap, if it was such. The Poles might want his scalp. So might the Lizards. So, for that matter, might the Germans, if they wanted to rid the Jews of a fighting leader. And the Jews who worried about the Nazis more than the Lizards might want revenge on him for shipping David Nussboym off to the Russians.

Bertha Fleishman had spelled out all those possibilities in detail when the request for a meeting came in. "Don't go," she'd urged. "Think of all the things that can go wrong, and how few can go right."

He'd laughed. Back inside what had been the Jewish ghetto of Lodz, among his own people, laughter had come easily. "We didn't get out from under the Nazis' thumbs by being afraid to take chances," he'd said. "What's one more, among so many?" And so he'd prevailed, and so here he was, somewhere north of Lodz, not far from where Lizard control gave way to German.

And so here he was, regretting he'd come. Now, when the only people in the fields were Polish, everyone sent a stranger suspicious looks. He himself didn't look like a stereotypical Jew, but he'd seen on previous travels that he couldn't readily pass for a Pole among Poles, either.

"Fourth dirt road north of that miserable little town, go west, fifth farm on the left. Then ask for Tadeusz," he muttered to himself. He hoped he'd counted the roads rightly. Was that little track supposed to be one, or not? He'd find out. His horse was ambling toward the fifth farmhouse on the left.

A big burly blond man in overalls was forking beet tops into a manger for his cows. He didn't bat an eyebrow as Mordechai, German rifle slung over his shoulder, rode up. A Mauser identical to Anielewicz's leaned against the side of the barn. The fellow in overalls could grab it in a hurry if he had to. He stabbed the pitchfork into the ground and leaned on it. "You want something?" he asked, his deep voice wary but polite.

"I'm looking for Tadeusz," Anielewicz answered. "I'm supposed to tell him Lubomir says hello."

"Fuck hello," the Pole—presumably Tadeusz—said with a big, booming laugh. "Where's the five hundred zlotys he owes me?"

Anielewicz swung down off his horse: that was the recognition signal he was supposed to get back. He stretched. His back creaked. He rubbed at it, saying, "I'm a little sore."

"I'm not surprised. You ride like a clodhopper," Tadeusz said without rancor. "Listen, Jew, you must have all sorts of weird connections. Leastways, I never heard of any other clipcocks a German officer was trying to get hold of."

"A German officer?" For a moment, Mordechai simply stared. Then his wits started working again. "A panzer officer? A colonel?" He still didn't trust the big Pole enough to name names.

Tadeusz's head bobbed up and down, which made his bushy golden beard alternately cover and reveal the topmost brass fastener on his overalls. "That's the one," he said. "From what I gather, he would have come looking for you himself, except that would have given him away."

"Given him away to whom? The Lizards?" Mordechai asked, still trying to figure out what was going on.

Now Tadeusz's head went from side to side, and so did the tip of his beard. "I don't think so. Way I got the story, it's some other stinking Nazi he's worried about." The Pole spat on the ground. "To hell with all of 'em, I say."

"To hell with all of 'em is easy to say, but we have to deal with some of them, though God knows I wish we didn't," Anielewicz said. Off to the north and east, artillery fire rumbled. Mordechai pointed in that direction. "You see? That's the Germans, likely aiming at the railroad or the highway into Lodz. The Lizards have trouble getting supplies in there now, and a devil of a time fighting out of the place—not that we haven't done our bit as far as that goes."

Tadeusz nodded. Shaded by a shapeless, almost colorless cloth cap, his eyes—a startlingly bright blue—were very keen. Mordechai wondered if he'd been a peasant before the war broke out, or perhaps something like an army major. Under the German occupation, Polish officers had had plenty of incentive to make themselves invisible.

His suspicion gained intensity when Tadeusz said, "The Lizards won't just be having trouble bringing in military supplies, either. Your people will be getting hungry by and by."

"That's so," Mordechai admitted. "Rumkowski's noticed it—he's hoarding everything he can for the bad times ahead. The bastard will lick the boots of anybody over him, but he can smell trouble, I give the *alter kacker* that much."

Tadeusz had no trouble understanding the couple of words of Yiddish in the middle of the Polish conversation. "Not the worst thing for a man to be able to do," he remarked.

"No," Anielewicz said reluctantly. He tried to wrench matters back to those at hand: "Do you have any idea who this other Nazi is? If I knew that, I might have a better notion of why the panzer officer was trying to warn me. What do you know?" *What will you tell me?* If Tadeusz was a Polish officer lying low, he was liable to have the full measure of aristocratic contempt for Jews. If, on the other hand, he really was a peasant, he was even more liable to have a simple but even more vivid hatred running through his veins.

And yet, if that were so, he wouldn't have relayed Jäger's message in the first place. Mordechai couldn't let his own ingrained distrust of the Poles get in the way of the facts. Now Tadeusz tugged at his beard before answering, "You have to remember, I got this fourth-, maybe fifth-hand. I don't know how much of it to trust myself."

"Yes, yes," Anielewicz said impatiently. "Just tell me whatever you got, and I'll try and put the pieces together. This German could hardly rig up a field telephone and call right into Lodz, now could he?"

"Stranger things have happened," Tadeusz said, and Mordechai, remembering some of his own telephone calls out of the city, had to nod. The Pole went on, "All right, this is everything I got told: whatever's going to happen—and I don't know what that is—it's going to happen in Lodz, and it's going to happen to you Jews in Lodz. Word is, they've brought in some kind of an SS man with a whole bunch of notches on his gun to do the job."

"That's the craziest thing I ever heard of," Mordechai said. "It's not just that we're not doing anything to the Nazis: we're helping them, for God's sake. The Lizards haven't been able to do much of anything out of Lodz, and it isn't because they haven't tried."

Tadeusz looked at him with what he first took for scorn and then realized was pity. "I can give you two good reasons why the Nazis are doing what they're doing. For one thing, you're Jews, and then, for another thing, you're Jews. You know about Treblinka, don't you?" Without waiting for Anielewicz to nod, he finished, "They don't care about what you do; they care about what you are."

"Well, I won't say you're wrong," Anielewicz replied. He had a Polish Army canteen on his belt. He took it off, removed the stopper, and offered it to Tadeusz. "Here. Wash the taste of that out of your mouth."

The Pole's larynx worked as he took several long, blissful swallows. *Shikker iz ein goy,* ran through Mordechai's head: the gentile is a drunk. But Tadeusz stopped before the canteen was empty and handed it back to him. "If that's not the worst applejack I've ever drunk, I don't know what is." He thumped his belly; the sound was like someone hitting a thick, hard plank. "Even the worst, though, is a damn sight better than none."

Mordechai swigged from the canteen. The raw spirit charred its way down his gullet and exploded like a 105mm shell in his stomach. "Yeah, you could strip paint with just the fumes from that, couldn't you? But you're not wrong—as long as it has the kick, that's what you need." He could feel his skin flush and his heart start racing. "So what am I supposed to do when this SS man shows up in Lodz? Shooting him on the spot doesn't sound like the worst idea I've ever heard."

Tadeusz's eyes were slightly crossed. He'd taken a big dose on an empty stomach, and perhaps hadn't realized how strong the stuff was till he'd got outside it. People who drank a lot were like that sometimes: they were used to strong, so they didn't notice very strong till too late. The Pole's eyebrows drew together as he tried to gather his wits. "What else did your Nazi chum say?" he wondered aloud.

"He's no chum of mine," Anielewicz said indignantly. But maybe that wasn't true. If Jäger hadn't thought something lay between them, he would't have sent a message, even a garbled one, into Lodz. Anielewicz had to respect that, whatever he thought of the uniform Jäger wore. He took another cautious sip of applejack and waited to see if Tadeusz's brains would start working again.

After a while, they did. "Now I remember," the Pole said, his face lighting up. "I don't know how much to trust this, though—like I said, it came through a lot of mouths before it got to me." What came through his mouth was a loud and unmistakable hiccup. "God and the Virgin and the saints only know if it came through the way it was supposed to."

"Nu?" Mordechai said, trying to get Tadeusz moving forward once more instead of sideways.

"All right, all right." The Pole made pushing motions, as if to fend off his impatience. "If it came to me straight, what he said was that, next time you saw him, you shouldn't believe anything he told you, because he'd be lying through his teeth."

"He sent a message to tell me he'd be lying?" Anielewicz scratched his head. "What's that supposed to mean?"

"Not my problem, God be praised," Tadeusz answered. Mordechai glared at him, then turned, remounted his horse, and rode back toward Lodz without another word.

☆ **VIII** ☆

Leslie Groves couldn't remember the last time he'd been so far away from the Metallurgical Laboratory and its products. Now that he thought back on it, he hadn't been away from the project since the day he'd taken that load of plutonium stolen first from the Lizards and then from the Germans off the HMS *Seanymph*. Ever since then, he'd lived, breathed, eaten, and slept atomic weapons.

And now here he was well east of Denver, miles and miles away from worrying about things like graphite purity and neutron absorption cross sections (when he'd taken college physics, nobody had ever heard of neutrons), and making sure you didn't vent radioactive steam into the atmosphere. If you did, and if the Lizards noticed, you'd surely never get a second chance—and the United States would almost certainly lose the war.

But there were other ways to lose the war besides having a Lizard atomic bomb come down on his head. That was why he was out here: to help keep one of those other ways from happening. "Some vacation," he muttered under his breath.

"If you wanted a vacation, General, I hate to tell you, but you signed up with the wrong outfit," Lieutenant General Omar Bradley said. The grin on his long, horsey face took any sting from his words; he knew Groves did a platoon's worth of work all by his lonesome.

"Yes, sir," Groves answered. "What you've shown me impressed the living daylights out of me, I'll tell you that. I just hope it looks as tough to the Lizards as it does to us."

"You and me and the whole United States," Bradley answered. "If the Lizards punch through these works and take Denver, we're all in a lot of trouble. If they get close enough to put your facility under artillery fire, we're in a lot of trouble. Our job is to make

192

sure they don't, and to spend the fewest possible lives making sure of that. The people of Denver have seen enough."

"Yes, sir." Groves said again. "Back in 1941, I saw newsreels of women and kids and old men marching out from Moscow with shovels on their shoulders to dig tank traps and trenches to hold off the Nazis. I never dreamt then that the same thing would happen here in the States one day."

"Neither did I. Neither did anybody," Bradley said. He looked tough and worn, an impression strengthened by his Missouri twang and by the M-1 he carried in place of the usual officer's sidearm. He'd been a crack shot ever since the days when he went hunting with his father, and didn't let anyone forget it. Scuttlebutt had it that he'd used the M-1 to good effect, too, in the first counterattack against the Lizards in late 1942.

"We have more going for us than the Red Army did then," Bradley said. "We weren't just shoving dirt around." He waved to show what he meant, continuing, "The Maginot Line isn't a patch on these works. This is defense in depth, the way the Hindenburg Line was in the last war." He paused again, this time to cough. "Not that I saw the Hindenburg Line, dammit, but I did study the reports on it most thoroughly."

"Yes, sir," Groves said for the third time. He'd heard that Bradley was sensitive about not having gone Over There during World War I, and evidently the rumor machine had that one straight. He took a step up onto the parapet and looked around. "The Lizards'll stub their snouts if they run up against this, no doubt about it."

Bradley's voice went grim. "That's not an *if*, worse luck; it's a *when*. We won't stop 'em short of our works, not by the way they've broken out of Kansas and into Colorado. Lamar had to be evacuated the other day, you know."

"Yes, I'd heard that," Groves said. It had sent cold chills down his spine, too. "Looking at all this, though, I feel better than I did when the word came down."

What man could do to turn gently rising prairie into real defensive terrain, man had done. Trenches and deep, broad antitank ditches ringed Denver to the east for miles around. Great belts of barbed wire would impede Lizard infantry, if not armor. Concrete pillboxes had been placed wherever the ground was suitable. Some of them held machine guns; others provided aiming points for bazooka men.

Along with the antitank ditches, tall concrete teeth and stout steel posts were intended to channel Lizard armor toward the men with the rockets that could destroy it. If a tank tried to go over those obstacles instead of around them, it would present its weaker belly armor to the antitank guns waiting for just that eventuality. Stretches of the prairie looked utterly innocent but were in fact sown with mines enough to make the Lizards pay a heavy price for crossing them.

"It all looks grand, that it does," Bradley said. "I worry about three things, though. Do we have enough men to put into the works to make them as effective as they ought to be? Do we have enough munitions to make the Lizards say uncle if they strike us with everything they've got? And do we have enough food to keep our troops in the works day after day, week after week? The best answer I can up with for any of those is *I hope so*."

"Considering that any or all of them might be *no*, that's a damn sight better than it might be," Groves said.

"So it is, but it's not good enough." Bradley scratched his chin, then turned to Groves. "Your facilities have taken proper precautions?"

"Yes, sir," Groves answered. He was pretty sure Bradley already knew that, but even three-star generals sometimes needed reassuring. "As soon as the bombing in and around Denver picked up, we implemented our deception plan. We lit bonfires by our most important buildings, and under cover of the smoke we put up the painted canvas sheets that make them look like ruins from the air. We haven't had any strikes close by since, so for now it looks like the plan has paid off."

"Good," Bradley said. "It had better pay off. Your facility is why we'll fight to the last man to hold Denver, and you know it as well as I do. Oh, we'd fight for it anyway—God knows we don't want the Lizards stretching their hold all the way across the Great Plains—but with the Met Lab here, it's not a town we want to have, it's a town we have to have."

"Yes, sir, I understand that," Groves said. "The physicists tell me we'll have another little toy ready inside of a couple of weeks. We'll want to hold the Lizards away from Denver without using it, I know, but if it comes down to using it or losing the town—"

"I was hoping you would tell me something like that, General," Bradley answered. "As you say, we'll do everything we can to hold Denver without resorting to nuclear weapons, because the Lizards do retaliate against our civilian population. But if it comes down to a choice between losing Denver and taking every step we can to keep it, I know what the choice will be."

"I hope it doesn't come to that," Groves said. Bradley nodded.

Lizard planes screamed by. Antiaircraft guns hammered at them. Every once in a while, the guns brought down a fighter-bomber, too, but seldom enough that it wasn't much more than dumb luck. Bombs hit the American works; the blasts boxed Groves' ears.

"Whatever that was they hit, it'll take a lot of pick-and-shovel work to set it right again." Omar Bradley looked unhappy. "Hardly seems fair to the poor devils who have to do all the hard work to see the fruits of their labors go up in smoke that way."

"Destroying is easier than building, sir," Groves answered. *That's why it's easier to turn out a soldier than an engineer,* he thought. He didn't say that out loud. Giving the people who worked for you the rough side of your tongue could sometimes spur them on to greater effort. If you got your superior angry at you, though, he was liable to let you down when you needed him most.

Groves pursed his lips and nodded thoughtfully. In its own way, that was engineering, too.

Ludmila Gorbunova let her hand rest on the butt of her Tokarev automatic pistol. "You are not using me in the proper fashion," she told the leader of the guerrilla band, a tough, skinny Pole who went by the name of Casimir. To make sure he couldn't misunderstand it, she said it first in Russian, then in German, and then in what she thought was Polish.

He leered at her. "Of course I'm not," he said. "You still have your clothes on."

She yanked the pistol out of its holster: "Pig!" she shouted. "Idiot! Take your brain out of your pants and listen to me!" She clapped a hand to her forehead. "*Bozhemoi!* If the Lizards paraded a naked whore around Hrubieszów, they'd lure you and every one of your skirt-chasing cockhounds out of the forest to be slaughtered."

Instead of blowing up at her, he said, "You are very beautiful when you are angry," a line he must have stolen from a badly dubbed American film.

She almost shot him on the spot. *This* was what she'd got for doing that *kulturny* General von Brockdorff-Ahlefeldt a favor: a trip to a band of partisans who didn't have the wits to clear all the trees out of their landing strip and who hadn't the first clue how to employ the personnel who, for reasons often inscrutable to her, nonetheless adhered to their cause.

"Comrade," she said, keeping things as simple as she could, "I am a pilot. I have no working aircraft here." She didn't bother pointing out—what was the use?—that the partisans hadn't come up with a mechanic able to fix her poor *Kukuruznik*, which was to her the equivalent of failing kindergarten. "Using me as a soldier gives me less to do than I might otherwise. Do you know of any other aircraft I might fly?"

Casimir reached up under his shirt and scratched his belly. He was hairy as a monkey—*and not much smarter than one, either,* Ludmila thought. She expected he wouldn't answer her, and regretted losing her temper—regretted it a little, anyway, as she would have regretted any piece of tactics that could have been better. At last, though, he did reply: "I know of a band that either has or knows about or can get its hands on some sort of a German plane. If we get you to it, can you fly it?"

"I don't know," she said. "If it flies, I can probably fly it. You don't sound like you know much." After a moment, she added, "About this airplane, I mean. What kind is it? Where is it? Is it in working order?"

"I don't know what it is. I don't know if it is. Where? That I know. It is a long way from here, north and west of Warsaw, not far from where the Nazis are operating again these days. If you want to travel to it, this can probably be arranged."

She wondered if there was any such plane, or if Casimir merely wanted to be rid of her. He was trying to send her farther away from the *rodina*, too. Did he want her gone because she was a Russian? There were a few Russians in his band, but they didn't strike her as ideal specimens of Soviet manhood. Still, if the plane was where he said it was, she might accomplish something useful with it. She was long since convinced she couldn't do that here.

"Khorosho," she said briskly: "Good. What sort of guides and passwords will I need to get to this mysterious aircraft?"

"I will need some time to make arrangements," Casimir said. "They might go faster if you—" He stopped; Ludmila had swung up the pistol to point at his head. He did have nerve. His voice didn't waver as he admitted, "On the other hand, they might not."

"Khorosho," Ludmila said again, and lowered the gun. She hadn't taken off the safety, but Casimir didn't need to know that. She wasn't even very angry at him. He might not be *kulturny*, but he did understand *no* when he stared down a gun barrel. Some men—Georg Schultz immediately sprang to mind—needed much stronger hints than that.

Maybe having a pistol pointed at his face convinced Casimir that he really did want to be rid of Ludmila. Two days later, she and a pair of guides—a Jew named Avram and a Pole called Wladeslaw—headed north and west in a beat-up wagon pulled by a beat-up donkey. Ludmila had wondered if she ought to get rid of her Red Air Force gear, but seeing what the Pole and the Jew wore put an end to that notion. Wladeslaw might have been a Red Army man himself, though he carried a German *Gewehr* 98 on his back. And Avram's hooked nose and stringy, graying beard looked particularly out of place under the brim of a coal-scuttle helmet some *Wehrmacht* man would never need again.

As the wagon rattled on through the modest highlands south of Lublin, she saw how common such mixtures of clothing were, not just among partisans but for ordinary citizens—assuming any such still existed in Poland. And every other man and about every third woman carried a rifle or submachine gun. With only the Tokarev on her hip, Ludmila began to feel underdressed.

She also got a closer look at the Lizards than she'd ever had before: now a convoy of lorries rolling past and kicking up clouds of dust, now tanks tearing up the roads even worse. Had those tanks been in the Soviet Union, their machine guns would have made short work of a wagon and three armed people in it, but they rumbled by, eerily quiet, without even pausing.

In pretty good Russian—he and Wladeslaw both spoke the language—Avram said, "They don't know whether we're with them or against them. They've learned not to take chances finding out, too. Every time they make a mistake and shoot up people who had been their friends, they turn a lot of people who were for them against them."

"Why are there so many willing traitors to mankind in Poland?" Ludmila asked. The phrase from Radio Moscow sprang automatically to her lips; only after she'd said it did she wish she'd been more tactful.

Fortunately, it didn't irk either Wladeslaw or Avram. In fact, they both started to laugh. They both started to answer at the same time, too. With a flowery wave, Avram motioned for Wladeslaw to go on. The Pole said, "After you've lived under the Nazis for a while and under the Reds for a while, anything that isn't the Nazis or the Reds looks good to a lot of folks."

Now they'd gone and insulted her, or at least her government. She said, "But I remember Comrade Stalin's statement on the wireless. The only reason the Soviet Union occupied the eastern half of Poland was that the Polish state was internally bankrupt, the government had disintegrated, and the Ukrainians and Belorussians in Poland, cousins to their Soviet kindred, were left to the mercy of fate. The Soviet Union extricated the Polish people from war and enabled them to lead a peaceful life until fascist aggression took its toll on us all."

"That's what the wireless said, is it?" Avram said. Ludmila stuck out her chin and nodded stubbornly. She was primed and ready for a fine, bruising ideological debate, but Avram and Wladeslaw didn't feel like arguing. Instead, they howled laughter like a couple of wit-struck wolves baying at the moon. They pounded their fists down on their thighs and finally ended up embracing each other. The donkey flicked its ears in annoyance at their untoward carrying-on.

"What have I said that was so funny?" Ludmila inquired in tones of ice.

Avram didn't answer directly. Instead, he returned a question of his own: "Could I teach you Talmud in a few minutes?" She didn't know what Talmud was, but shook her head. He said, "That's right. To learn Talmud, you'd have to learn a whole new way of looking at the world and think only in that way—a new ideology, if you want to put it that way." He paused again. This time she nodded. He went on, "You already have an ideology, but you're so used to it, you don't even notice it's there. That's what's funny."

"But my ideology is scientific and correct," Ludmila said. For some reason, that started the Jew and the Pole on another spasm of laughter. Ludmila gave up. With some people, you simply could not have an intelligent discussion.

The land dropped down toward the valley of the Vistula. Kaziemierz Doly looked down on the river from high, sandy banks overgrown with willows whose branches trailed in the water and cut by a good many ravines. "Lovers come here in the springtime," Wladeslaw remarked. Ludmila sent him a suspicious look, but he let it go at that, so it probably hadn't been a suggestion.

Some of the buildings around the marketplace were large and had probably been impressive when they were whole, but several rounds of fighting had left most of them charred ruins. A synagogue didn't look much better than any of the other wreckage, but Jews were going in and out. Other Jews—armed guards—stood watch outside.

Ludmila caught Avram glancing over at Wladeslaw to see if he would say anything about that. He didn't. Ludmila couldn't tell whether that pleased the Jewish partisan or irked him. What passed for Polish politics was too complex for her to follow easily.

A ferryboat sent up a great cloud of soft-coal fumes as it carried the wagon across the Vistula. The country was so flat, it reminded Ludmila of the endless plain surrounding Kiev. Cottages with thatched roofs and with sunflowers and hollyhocks growing around them could have belonged to her homeland, too.

That evening, they stopped at a farmhouse by a pond. Ludmila didn't wonder how they'd found that particular house. Not only was it on the water, the Germans must have used it for target practice, for it was ringed by old, overgrown bomb craters, some of them, the deeper ones, on the way to becoming ponds themselves as groundwater seeped up into them.

No one asked or gave names there. Ludmila understood that; what you didn't know, you couldn't tell. The middle-aged couple who worked the farm with their swarm of children put her in mind of *kulaks*, the prosperous peasants who in the Soviet Union had resisted giving up their property to join the glorious egalitarian collective farm movement, and so had disappeared off the face of the earth when she was still a girl. Poland had not seen the same leveling.

The wife of the couple, a plump, pleasant woman who wore on her head a bright kerchief like a Russian *babushka*, cooked up a great pot of what she called *barszcz*: beet soup with sour cream, which, except for the caraway seeds stirred into it for flavor, might have come from a Russian kitchen. Along with it she served boiled cabbage, potatoes, and a spicy homemade sausage Ludmila found delicious but Avram wouldn't touch. "Jew," the woman muttered to her husband when Avram was out of earshot. They helped the partisans; that didn't mean they loved all of them.

After supper, Avram and Wladeslaw went out to sleep in the barn. Ludmila got the sofa in the parlor, an honor she wouldn't have been sorry to decline, as it was short and narrow and lumpy. She tossed and turned and almost fell off a couple of times in the course of an uncomfortable evening.

Toward sunset the next day, they crossed the Pilica River, a tributary of the Vistula, over a rebuilt wooden bridge and came into Warka. Wladeslaw waxed enthusiastic: "They make the best beer in Poland here." Sure enough, the air held the nutty tang of malt and hops. The Pole added, "Pulaski was born in Warka."

"And who is Pulaski?" Ludmila asked.

Wladeslaw let out a long, resigned sigh. "They don't teach you much in those Bolshevik schools, do they?" As she bristled, he went on, "He was a Polish nobleman who tried to keep the Prussians and the Austrians and you Russians from carving up our country. He failed." He sighed again. "We have a way of failing at such things. Then he went to America and helped the United States fight England. He got killed there, poor fellow. He was still a young man."

Ludmila had been on the point of calling—or at least thinking of—Pulaski as a reactionary holdover of the corrupt Polish feudal regime. But helping the revolutionary movement in the United States had surely been a progressive act. The curious combination left her without an intellectual slot in which to pigeonhole Pulaski, an unsettling feeling. This was the second time she'd left the confines of the USSR. On each trip, her view of the world had shown itself to be imperfectly adequate.

No doubt a Talmudic perspective would be even worse, she thought.

She consciously noticed what she'd been hearing for a while: a low, distant rumble off to the north and west. "That can't be thunder!" she exclaimed. The day was fine and bright and sunny, with only a few puffy white clouds drifting slowly across the sky from west to east.

"Thunder of a sort," Avram answered, "but only of a sort. That's Lizard artillery going after the Nazis, or maybe German artillery going after the Lizards. It's not going to be easy any more, getting where we're going."

"One thing I've learned," Ludmila said, "is that it's never easy, getting where you're going."

Avram plucked at his beard. "If you know that much, maybe those Bolshevik schools aren't so bad after all."

"Okay, listen up, people, because this is what we're going to do," Rance Auerbach said in the cool darkness of Colorado night. "Right now we're somewhere between Karval and Punkin Center." A couple of the cavalry troopers gathered round him chuckled softly. He did, too. "Yeah, they've got some great names for places 'round these parts. Before the sunset, scouts spotted Lizard outposts north and west of Karval. What we want to do is make 'em think there's a whole hell of a lot more than us between them and Punkin Center. We do that, we slow down this part of their drive on Denver, and that's the idea."

"Yeah, but Captain Auerbach, there *ain't* nothin' but us between them and Punkin Center," Rachel Hines said. She looked around in the darkness at the shapes of their companions. "There ain't that much left of us, neither."

"You know that, and I know that," Auerbach said. "As long as the Lizards don't know it, everything's swell."

His company—or the survivors thereof, plus the ragtag and bobtail of other broken units who'd hooked up with them— laughed some more. So did he, to keep up morale. It wasn't really funny. When the Lizards wanted to put on a blitzkrieg, they put one on that made the Nazis look like pikers. Since they started by pasting Lamar from the air, they'd ripped damn near halfway across Colorado, knocking out of their path everything that might have given them trouble. Auerbach was damned if he knew how anything could stop them before they hit the works outside of Denver. He'd got orders to try, though, and so he would.

Very likely, he'd die trying. Well, that was part of the job.

Lieutenant Bill Magruder said, "Remember, boys and girls, the Lizards have gadgets that let 'em see in the dark like cats wish they could. You want to keep under cover, use the fire from one group so they'll reveal their position and another group can attack 'em from a different direction. They don't play fair. They don't come close to playing fair. If we're going to beat 'em, we have to play dirty, too."

The cavalry wasn't going to beat 'em any which way. Auerbach knew that. Any of his troopers who didn't know it were fools. As hit-and-run raiders, though, they still might accomplish something useful.

"Let's mount up," he said, and headed for his own horse.

The rest of the company was dim shadows, jangling harness, the occasional cough from a man or snort from an animal. He didn't know this territory well, and worried about blundering into the Lizard pickets before he knew they were there. If that happened, he was liable to get his whole command chewed up without doing the cause a lick of good or the Lizards any harm.

But a couple of the men who rode along were farmers from these parts. They weren't in uniform. Had they been going up against a human foe, that could have got them shot if they were captured. The Lizards didn't draw those distinctions, though. And the farmers, in bib overalls, knew the country as intimately as they knew their wives' bodies.

One of them, a fellow named Andy Osborne, said, "We split here." Auerbach took it on faith that he knew where *here* was. Some of the company rode off under Magruder's command. Auerbach—and Osborne—took the rest closer to Karval. After a while, Osborne said, "If we don't dismount now, they're liable to spot us."

"Horseholders," Auerbach said. He chose them by lot before every raid. Nobody admitted to wanting the job, which held you out of the fighting while your comrades were mixing it up with Lizards. But it kept you safe, too—well, safer, anyhow—so you might crave it without having the nerve to say so out loud. Picking holders at random seemed the only fair way.

"We got a couple o' little ravines here," Osborne said, "and if we're lucky, we can sneak right on past the Lizards without them ever knowin' we're around till we open up. We manage that, we can hit Karval pretty damn hard."

"Yeah," somebody said, an eager whisper in the night. They had a mortar, a .50 caliber machine gun, and a couple of bazooka launchers with plenty of the little rockets they shot. Trying to kill Lizard tanks in the darkness was a bad-odds game, but one of the things they'd found out was that bazookas did a hell of a job of smashing up buildings, which weren't armored and didn't travel over the landscape on their own. Get close enough to a Lizard bivouac and who could say what you might do?

The mortar crew slipped off on their own, a couple of troopers with tommy guns along to give them fire support. They didn't have to get as close to Karval as the machine gunners and the bazooka boys did.

Auerbach slapped Osborne on the shoulder to signal him to guide them down the ravine that came closest to the little town. Along with the crews who served their fancy weapons, he and the rest of the men crouched low as they hustled along.

Off to the north somewhere, small-arms fire went *pop-pop-pop*. It sounded like firecrackers on the Fourth of July, and the flares that lit up the night sky could have been fireworks, too. But fireworks commonly brought cheers, not the muffled curses that came from the troopers. "Spotted 'em too soon," somebody said.

"And they'll be lookin' extra hard for us, too," Rachel Hines added with gloomy certainty.

As if to underscore her words, a flare mounted skyward from the low hilltop where the Lizard pickets were posted. "That's a good sign, not a bad one," Auerbach said. "They can't spy us with their funny gadgets, so they're trying out the old Mark One eyeball." He hoped he was right.

The troopers scuttled along down Osborne's wash. The flare fell, faded, died. In the north, a mortar opened up. That half of the company wasn't as close to Karval as it should have been, but it was doing what it could. *Crump! Crump!* If the bombs weren't landing in the little flyspeck of a town, they weren't missing by much, either.

Then Auerbach heard motor vehicles moving around inside Karval. His mouth went dry. Expecting to find the Lizards asleep at the switch didn't always pay off.

"This here's the end of the wash," Andy Osborne announced in a tone like doom.

Now Auerbach wished he'd laid Penny Summers when he had the chance. All his scruples had done was to give him fewer happy memories to hold fear at bay. He didn't even know what had happened to Penny. She'd been helping the wounded last he'd seen her, a day or so before a Lizard armored column smashed Lamar to bits. They'd evacuated the injured as best they could with horse-drawn ambulances—his States War ancestors would have sympathized with that ordeal. Penny was supposed to have gone out with them. He hoped she had, but he didn't know for sure.

"Okay, boys," he said out loud. "Mortar crew went off to the left. Machine gun to the right and forward. Bazookas straight ahead. Good luck to everybody."

He went forward with the two bazooka crews. They'd need all the fire support they could get, and the M-1 on his back had more range than a tommy gun.

The Lizard pickets behind them started firing. Troopers who'd stayed back with the mortar crew engaged the Lizards. Then another Lizard machine gun chattered, this one almost in Auerbach's face. He hadn't noticed the armored personnel carrier till it was nearly on top of him; Lizard engines were a lot quieter than the ones people built. He stretched himself flat in the dirt as bullets spattered dust and pebbles all around.

But that machine gun gave away the position of the vehicle on which it was mounted. One of the bazooka crew let fly at it. The rocket left the launcher with a roar like a lion. It trailed yellow fire as it shot toward the personnel carrier.

"Get the hell out of there!" Auerbach yelled at the two-man crew. If they missed, the enemy would just have to trace the bazooka's line of flight to know where they were.

They didn't miss. A Lizard tank's frontal armor laughed at the shaped-charge head of a bazooka round, but not an armored personnel carrier. Flame spurted from the stricken vehicle, lighting it up. Troopers with small arms opened up on it, potting the Lizard crew as they popped out of the escape hatches. A moment later, the deep stutter of the .50 caliber machine gun added itself to the nighttime cacophony.

"Keep moving! Come on, forward!" Auerbach screamed. "We gotta hit 'em inside Karval!" Behind him, his mortar crew started lobbing bombs at the hamlet. He was rooting for one of them to start a fire to illuminate the area. Lots of the Lizards were shooting back now, and they had a much better idea where his men were than the other way around. A nice cheery blaze would help level the playing field.

As if it were Christmas, he got his wish. A clapboard false front in Karval went up in yellow flames. By the way it burned, it had been standing and curing for a long time. Flames leaped to other false fronts along what had probably been the pint-sized main drag. Their lurid, buttery light revealed skittering Lizards like demons in hell.

From more than a mile outside of town, the heavy machine gun started blazing away at the targets the light showed. You couldn't count on any one bullet hitting any one target at a range like that, but when you threw a lot of bullets at a lot of targets, you had to score some hits. And, when a .50 caliber armor-piercing bullet hit a target of mere flesh and blood, that target (a nice bloodless word for a creature that thought and hurt like you) went down and stayed down.

Auerbach whooped like a red Indian when another Lizard armored personnel carrier brewed up. Then both bazooka crews started firing rockets almost at random into Karval. More fires sprouted. "Mission accomplished!" he shouted, though nobody could hear him, not even himself. The Lizards had to figure they were getting hit by something like an armored brigade, not a raggedy cavalry company.

The hammering of the guns hid the noise of the approaching helicopters till it was too late. The first warning of them Auerbach had was when they salvoed rockets at the bazooka crews. It seemed the Fourth of July all over again, but this time the fireworks were going the wrong way—from air to ground. That tortured ground seemed to erupt in miniature volcanoes.

Blast grabbed Auerbach, picked him up, and slammed him down again. Something wet ran into his mouth—blood from his nose, he discovered from the taste of iron and salt. He wondered if his ears were bleeding, too. If he'd been a little closer to one of those rockets—or maybe if he'd been inhaling instead of exhaling—he might have had his lungs torn to bits inside him.

He staggered to his feet and shook his head like a stunned prizefighter, trying to make his wits work. The bazookas weren't in operation any more. The .50 caliber machine gun turned its attention to the helicopters; its like flew in Army Air Force planes. He'd heard of machine guns bagging helicopters. But the helicopters could shoot back, too. He watched their tracers walk forward and over the machine-gun position. It fell silent.

"Retreat!" Auerbach yelled, for anyone who could hear. He looked around for his radioman. There was the fellow, not far away—dead, with the radio on his back blown to smithereens. Well, anybody who didn't have the sense to retreat when he was getting hit and couldn't hit back probably didn't deserve to live, anyhow.

He wondered where Andy Osborne was. The local could probably guide him back to the ravine—although, if helicopters started hitting you from above while you were in there, it would be a death trap, not a road to safety. A couple of the Lizard outposts were still firing, too. There weren't any roads to safety, not any more.

A shape in the night— He swung his Garand toward it before he realized it was a human being. He waved toward the northwest, showing it was time to head for home. The trooper nodded and said, "Yes, sir—we've got to get out of here." As if from a great distance, he heard Rachel Hines' voice.

Steering by the stars, they trotted in the right direction, more or less, though he wondered how they were going to find the horses some of the troopers were holding. Then he wondered if it would matter: those helicopters would chew the animals to dog food if they got there first.

They were heading that way, too, when the heavy machine gun started up behind them. With the crew surely dead, a couple of other men must have found it and started serving it. They had to have scored some hits on the helicopters, too, for the Lizard machines abandoned their course and swung back toward the .50 caliber gun.

The makeshift crew played it smart: as soon as the helicopters got close, they stopped firing at them. *No sense running up a SHOOT ME RIGHT HERE sign,* Auerbach thought as he stumbled on through the darkness. The Lizard helicopters raked the area where the machine gun hid, then started to leave. As soon as they did, the troopers opened up on them again.

They returned for another pass. Again, when they paused, the gunners on the ground showed they weren't done yet. One of the helicopters sounded ragged. He dared hope the armor-piercing ammunition had done it some harm. But it stayed in the air. When the helicopters finished chewing up the landscape this time, the machine gun didn't start up.

"Son of a bitch!" Rachel Hines said disgustedly. She swore like a trooper; half the time, she didn't notice she was doing it. Then she said, "Son of a bitch," in an altogether different tone of voice. The two hunting helicopters were swinging toward her and Auerbach.

He wanted to hide, but where could you hide from flying death that saw in the night? *Nowhere*, he thought, and threw his M-1 to his shoulder. He didn't have much chance of damaging the machines, but what he could do, he would. *If you're going to go down, go down swinging.*

The machine guns in the noses of both helicopters opened up. For a second or so, he thought they were beautiful. Then something hit him a sledgehammer blow. All at once, his legs didn't want to hold him up. He started to crumple, but he didn't know whether he hit the ground or not.

A guard threw open the door to Ussmak's tiny cell. "You— out," he said in the Russki language, which Ussmak was perforce learning.

"It shall be done," Ussmak said, and came out. He was always glad to get out of the cell, which struck him as poorly designed: had he been a Tosevite, he didn't think he would have been able to stand up or lie down at full length in it. And, for that matter, since Tosevites produced liquid as well as solid waste, the straw in the cell would soon have become a stinking, sodden mess for a Big Ugly. Ussmak did all his business over in one corner, and wasn't too badly inconvenienced by the lack of plumbing fixtures.

The guard carried a submachine gun in one hand and a lantern in the other. The lantern gave little light and smelled bad. Its odor reminded Ussmak of cooking; he wondered if it used some animal or plant product for fuel rather than the petroleum on which the Tosevites ran their landcruisers and aircraft.

He'd learned better than to ask such questions. It just got him into deeper trouble, and he was in quite enough already. As the guard led him toward the interrogation chamber, he called down mental curses on Straha's empty head. *May his spirit live an Emperorless afterlife,* Ussmak thought. On the radio, he'd sounded so sure the Big Uglies showed civilized behavior toward males they captured. Well, the mighty onetime shiplord Straha didn't know everything there was to know. That much Ussmak had found out, to his sorrow.

Waiting in the interrogation chamber, as usual, were Colonel Lidov and Gazzim. Ussmak sent the paintless interpreter a stare full of mixed sympathy and loathing. If it hadn't been for Gazzim, the Big Uglies wouldn't have got so much from him so fast. He'd yielded the base in Siberia intending to tell the males of the SSSR everything he could to help them: having committed treason, he was going to wallow in it.

But Lidov and the other males of the NKVD had assumed from the outset that he was an enemy bent on hiding things rather than an ally eager to reveal them. The more they'd treated him that way, the more they'd done to turn their mistake into truth.

Maybe Lidov was beginning to realize the error in his technique. Speaking without the translation of Gazzim (something he seldom did), he said, "I greet you, Ussmak. Here on the table is something that may perhaps make your day pass more pleasantly." He gestured toward the bowl full of brownish powder.

"Is that ginger, superior sir?" Ussmak asked. He knew what it was; his chemoreceptors could smell it across the room. The Russkis hadn't let him taste in—he didn't know how long. It seemed like forever. What he meant, of course, was, *May I have some?* The more he associated with the males of the NKVD, the less saying what he meant seemed like a good idea.

But Lidov was in an expansive mood today. "Yes, of course it is ginger," he answered. "Taste all you like."

Ussmak wondered if the Big Ugly was trying to drug him with something other than the powdered herb. He decided Lidov couldn't be. If Lidov wanted to give him another drug, he would go ahead and do it, and that would be that. Ussmak went over to the table, poured some ginger into the palm of his hand, raised the hand to his mouth, and tasted.

Not only was it ginger, it was lime cured, the way the Race liked it best. Ussmak's tongue flicked out again and again, till every speck of the precious powder on his hands was gone. The spicy taste filled not just his mouth, but his brain. After so long without, the herb hit him hard. His heart pounded; his breath gusted in and out of his lung. He felt bright and alert and strong and triumphant, worth a thousand of the likes of Boris Lidov.

Part of his mind warned him that feeling was a fraud, an illusion. He'd watched males who couldn't remember that die, confident their landcruisers could do anything and their Big Ugly opponents would not be able to hinder them in the slightest. If you didn't kill yourself through such stupidity, you learned to enjoy ginger without letting it enslave you.

But remembering that came hard, hard, in the middle of the exhilaration the drug brought. Boris Lidov's little mouth widened into the gesture the Tosevites used to show amiability. "Go ahead," he said. "Taste more."

Ussmak did not have to be invited twice. The worst thing about ginger was the black slough of despond into which you fell when a taste wore off. The first thing you wanted then was another taste. Usually, you didn't have one. But that bowl held enough ginger to keep a male happy for—a long time. Ussmak cheerfully indulged again.

Gazzim had one eye turret fixed on the bowl of powdered ginger, the other on Boris Lidov. Every line of his scrawny body showed Ussmak his terrible longing for the herb, but he did not make the slightest move toward it. Ussmak knew the depths of a male's craving. Gazzim had plainly sunk to those depths. That he was too afraid to try to take a taste said frightening things about what the Soviets had done to him.

Ussmak was used to suppressing the effects ginger had on him. But he hadn't tasted for a long time, and he'd just ingested a double dose of potent stuff. The drug was stronger than his inhibitions. "No, let us now give this poor addled male something to make him happy for a change," he said, and held the bowl of ginger right under Gazzim's snout.

"Nyet!" Boris Lidov shouted angrily.

"I dare not," Gazzim whispered, but his tongue was more powerful than he was. It leaped into the bowl, again and again and again, as if trying to make up for lost time by cramming a dozen tastes into one.

"No, I tell you," Lidov said again, this time in the language of the Race. He added an emphatic cough for good measure. When neither Ussmak nor Gazzim took the slightest notice of him, he strode forward and knocked the bowl out of Ussmak's hands. It shattered on the floor; a brownish cloud of ginger fogged the air.

Gazzim hurled himself at the male from the NKVD, rending him with teeth and claws. Lidov let out a bubbling shriek and reeled away, blood spurting from several wounds. He threw up one arm to protect his face. With the other hand, he grabbed for the pistol he wore on his belt.

Ussmak leaped at him, grabbing his right arm with both hands. The Big Ugly was hideously strong, but his soft, scaleless skin left him vulnerable; Ussmak felt his claws sink deep into Tosevite flesh. Gazzim might have been a wild thing. His jaws had a grip on Lidov's throat, as if he was going to feed on the male from the

NKVD. Along with the smell of the spilled ginger, Ussmak's chemoreceptors filled with the acrid tang of Tosevite blood. The combination brought him close to beasthood, too.

Lidov's shrieks grew fainter; his hand relaxed on the grip of the pistol. Ussmak was the one who drew it out of its holster. It felt heavy and awkward in his grip.

The door to the interrogation chamber opened. He'd expected that for some time, but the Big Uglies were too primitive to have television cameras monitoring such places. Gazzim screamed and charged at the guard who stood in the doorway. Blood dripped from his claws and his snout. Even armed, Ussmak would not have wanted to stand against him, not drug-crazed and insane as he was at that moment.

"Bozhemoi!" the Tosevite shouted. But he had extraordinary presence of mind. He brought up his submachine gun and fired a quick burst just before Gazzim got to him. The male of the Race crashed to the ground, twitching. He was surely dead, but his body hadn't quite realized it yet.

Ussmak tried to shoot at the guard. Though his chance of escape from this prison was essentially nil, he was a soldier with a weapon in his hand. The only problem was, he couldn't make the weapon fire. It had some kind of safety, and he couldn't figure out what it was.

As he fumbled, the muzzle of the Big Ugly's submachine gun swung to cover him. The pistol didn't even bear on the guard. In disgust, Ussmak threw down the Tosevite weapon, which clattered on the floor. He wondered dully if the guard would kill him out of hand.

Rather to his surprise, the fellow didn't. The sound of gunfire in the prison had drawn other guards on the run. One of them spoke a little of the language of the Race. "Hands high!" he yelled. Ussmak obeyed. "Move back!" the Tosevite said. Obediently, Ussmak stepped away from Boris Lidov, who lay in a pool of his own blood. *It looks the same as poor Gazzim's,* Ussmak thought.

A couple of guards hurried over to the fallen Soviet male. They spoke back and forth in their own guttural tongue. One of them looked toward Ussmak. Like any Big Ugly, he had to turn his whole flat face toward him. "Dead," he said in the language of the Race.

"What good would saying I'm sorry do, especially when I'm not?" Ussmak answered. None of the guards seemed to understand that, which was probably just as well. They talked some more among themselves. Ussmak waited for one of them to raise his firearm and start shooting.

That didn't happen. He remembered what Intelligence had said of the males of the SSSR: that they stuck to their orders almost as carefully as did the Race. From what he'd seen, that seemed accurate. Without orders, no one here was willing to take the responsibility for eliminating him.

Finally, the male who had led him to the interrogation chamber gestured with the muzzle of his weapon. Ussmak understood that gesture; it meant *come along*. He came. The guard led him back to his cell, as if after a normal interrogation. The door slammed behind him. The lock clicked.

His mouth fell open in amusement. *If I'd known that was all that would happen if I killed Lidov, I'd have done it a long time ago.* But he didn't think it was going to be all . . . oh, no. And, as the ginger euphoria leaked out of him and after-tasting depression set in, he wondered what the Russkis would do with him—to him—now. He could think of all sorts of unpleasant possibilities, and he was unpleasantly certain they could come up with even more.

Liu Han walked past the *Fa Hua Ssu*, the Temple of Buddha's Glory, and, just west of it, the wreckage of the Peking tramway station. She sighed, wishing the tramway station were not in ruins. Peking sprawled over a large area; the temple and the station were in the eastern part of the city, a good many *li* from her roominghouse.

Not far from the station was Porcelain Mouth Street, *Tz'u Ch'i K'ou*, whose clay was famous. She walked north up the street, then turned off onto one of the *hutungs*, Peking's innumerable lanes and alleys that branched from it. She was learning her way through the maze; she had to double back and retrace her steps only once before she found the *Hsiao Shih*, the Small Market.

Another name for that market, less often heard but always in the back of everyone's mind, was the Thieves' Market. From what Liu Han had been told, not everything in the market was stolen goods; some of the trash so loudly hawked had been legally acquired but was being sold here to create the illusion that the customer was getting a bargain.

"Brass plates!" "Cabbage!" "Chopsticks!" "Mah-jongg tiles!" "Noodles!" "Medicine to cure you of the clap!" "Piglets and fresh pork!" "Peas and bean sprouts!" The noise was deafening. Only by Peking standards could this be reckoned a small market. In most cities, it would have been the central emporium; all by itself, it seemed to Liu Han as big as the camp in which the little scaly devils had placed her after bringing her down from the airplane that never landed.

In the surging crowds, she was just one among many. Anonymity suited her. The kind of attention she got these days was not what she wanted.

A man selling fine porcelain cups that certainly looked as if they might have been stolen saw her, pointed, and rocked his hips back and forth. She walked over to him with a large smile on her face. He looked half eager, half apprehensive.

She made her voice high and sweet, like a singsong girl's. Still smiling, she said, "I hope it rots off. I hope it shrinks back into your body so you can't find it even if you've tied a string around its tiny little end. If you do find it, I hope you never, ever get it up."

He stared at her, his mouth falling open. Then he reached under the table that held his wares. By the time he'd pulled out a knife, Liu Han had a Japanese pistol pointed at his midsection. "You don't want to try that," she said. "You don't even want to think about trying that."

The man gaped foolishly, eyes and mouth wide and round as those of the goldfish in their ornamental ponds not far away. Liu Han turned her back and walked away. As soon as a few people got between her and him, he started screaming abuse at her.

She was tempted to go back and put a bullet in his belly, but shooting every man in Peking who mocked her would have wasted a lot of ammunition, and her peasant upbringing made her hate the idea of waste.

A minute later, another merchant recognized her. He followed her with his eyes but didn't say anything. By the standards she'd grown used to, that was a restrained response. She paid him the compliment of ignoring him.

Before, I had only Hsia Shou-Tao to worry about, she thought bitterly. *Thanks to the little scaly devils and their vile cinemas, I have hundreds.* A great many men had watched her yield to the desires of Bobby Fiore and the other men aboard the airplane that never came down. Having seen that, too many of them supposed she would be eager to yield to their desires. The little devils had succeeded in making her notorious in Peking.

Someone patted her backside from behind. She lashed out with a shoe and caught him in the shin. He howled curses. She didn't care. Notorious or not, she refused to vanish into a hole. The scaly devils had done their best to destroy her as an instrument of the

People's Liberation Army. If they succeeded, she would never see her daughter again.

She had no intention of letting them succeed.

They had made her an object of derision, as they'd planned. But they had also made her an object of sympathy. Women could tell that she'd been coerced in some of the films the little devils had taken of her. And the People's Liberation Army had mounted an aggressive propaganda campaign to educate the people of Peking, men and women alike, as to the circumstances in which she'd found herself. Even some men were sympathetic to her now.

Once or twice, she'd heard foreign devil Christian missionaries talking in their bad Chinese about martyrs. At the time, she hadn't understood the concept—what point to suffering when you didn't have to? These days, she was a martyr herself, and exploiting the role for all it was worth.

She came to the little stall of a woman who was selling carp that looked like ugly goldfish. She picked one up by the tail. "Are these fish fresh?" she asked dubiously.

"Just caught this morning," the woman answered.

"Why do you expect me to believe that?" Liu Han sniffed at the carp. In grudging tones, she said, "Well, maybe. What do you want for them?"

They haggled, but had trouble coming to an agreement. People watched them for a while, then went back to their own concerns when they didn't prove very interesting. Lowering her voice, the carp seller said, "I have the word you were looking for, Comrade."

"I hoped you would," Liu Han answered eagerly. "Tell me."

The woman looked around, her face nervous. "How you hear this must never be known," she warned. "The little scaly devils have no idea my nephew understands their ugly language as well as he does—otherwise they would not talk so freely around him."

"Yes, yes," Liu Han said with an impatient gesture. "We have put many like that in among them. We do not betray our sources. Sometimes we have even held off from making a move because the little scaly devils would have been able to figure out where we got the information. So you may tell me and not worry—and if you think I will pay your stinking price for your stinking fish, you are a fool!" She added the last in a loud voice when a man walked by close enough to eavesdrop on their conversation.

"Why don't you go away, then?" the carp seller shrilled. A moment later, she lowered her voice once more: "He says they will soon let the People's Liberation Army know they are willing to resume talks on all subjects. He is only a clerk, remember; he cannot tell you what 'all subjects' means. You will know that for yourself, though, won't you?"

"Eh? Yes, I think so," Liu Han answered. If the scaly devils meant what they said, they would return to talking about giving her back her daughter. The girl would be approaching two years old now, by Chinese reckoning: one for the time she'd spent in Liu Han's womb and the second for the time since her birth. Liu Han wondered what she looked like and how Ttomalss had been treating her. One day before too long, maybe, she'd find out.

"All right, I'll buy it, even if you are a thief." As if in anger, Liu Han slapped down coins and stalked away. Behind her angry façade, she was smiling. The carp seller was almost her own personal source of news; she didn't think the woman knew many others from the People's Liberation Army. She would get credit for bringing news of impending negotiations to the central committee.

With luck, that would probably be enough to ensure that she got her own seat on the committee. Nieh Ho-T'ing would want her back now; she was sure of that. And, once she had her seat, she would support Nieh's agenda—for a while. One of these days, though, she would have occasion to disagree with him. When she did, she'd have backing of her own.

She wondered how Nieh would take that. Would they be able to go on being lovers after they had political or ideological quarrels? She didn't know. Of one thing she was sure: she needed a lover less than she had before. She was her own person now, well able to face the world on her own two feet without requiring a man's support. Before the little scaly devils came, she hadn't imagined such a thing possible.

She shook her head. Strange that all the suffering the little devils had put her through had led her not only to be independent but to think she ought to be independent. Without them, she would have been one of the uncounted peasant widows in war-torn China, trying to keep herself from starving and probably having to become a prostitute or a rich man's concubine to manage it.

She passed by a man selling the conical straw hats both men and women wore to keep the sun off their faces. She had one back at the roominghouse. When the little scaly devils first began showing their vile films of her, she'd worn the hat a lot. With its front edge pulled low over her features, she was hardly recognizable.

Now, though, she walked through the streets and *hutungs* of Peking bareheaded and unashamed. A man leered at her as she left the Small Market. "Beware of revolutionary justice," she hissed. The fellow fell back in confusion. Liu Han walked on.

The little scaly devils had one of their movie machines playing on a streetcorner. There, bigger than life, Liu Han rode astride Bobby Fiore, her skin and his slick with sweat. The main thing that struck her, looking at her somewhat younger self, was how well fed and well rested she seemed. She shrugged. She hadn't been committed to the revolutionary cause yet.

A man looked from the three-dimensional image to her. He pointed. Liu Han pointed back at him, as if her finger were the barrel of a gun. He found something else to do—and found it in a hurry.

Liu Han kept walking. The little devils were still doing their best to discredit her, but they were also coming back to the negotiating table, and coming back to talk about all subjects. As far as she was concerned, that represented victory.

The year before, the little scaly devils hadn't been so willing to talk. The year before that, they hadn't talked at all, just swept all before them. Life was harder now for them than it had been, and they were starting to see that it might grow harder yet. She smiled. She hoped it would.

New fish came into camp utterly confused, utterly dismayed. That amused David Nussboym, who, having survived his first few weeks, was no longer a new fish but a *zek* among *zeks*. He was still reckoned a political rather than a thief, but the guards and the NKVD men had stopped using on him the blandishments they aimed at so many Communists caught in the web of the *gulag*:

"You're still eager to help the Party and the Soviet state, aren't you? Then of course you'll lie, you'll spy, you'll do whatever we say." The words were subtler, sweeter, but that was what they meant.

To a Polish Jew, the Party and the Soviet state were more attractive than Hitler's *Reich*, but not much. Nussboym had taken to using broken Russian and Yiddish among his fellow prisoners and answering the guards only in Polish too fast and slangy for them to understand.

"That's good," Anton Mikhailov said admiringly after yet another guard went off scratching his head at Nussboym's replies. "Keep it up and after a while they'll quit bothering you because they'll figure they won't be able to get any sense out of you anyway."

"Sense?" Nussboym rolled his eyes. "If you crazy Russians

wanted sense, you never would have started these camps in the first place."

"You think so, do you?" the other *zek* answered. "Try building socialism without the coal they get from the camps, and the timber, without the railroads *zeks* build and without the canals we dig. Why, without camps, the whole damn country would fall apart." He sounded as if he took a perverse pride in being part of such a vital and socially significant enterprise.

"Maybe it should fall apart, then," Nussboym said. "These NKVD bastards work everybody the way the Nazis work Jews. I've seen both now, and there isn't much to choose between them." He thought a moment. "No, I take that back. These are just labor camps. You don't have the kind of assembly-line murder the Nazis had started up just before the Lizards got there."

"Why murder a man when you can work him to death?" Mikhailov asked. "It's—what's the word I want?—it's inefficient, that's what it is."

"This—what we do here—you call this efficient?" Nussboym exclaimed. "You could train chimpanzees to do this."

The Russian thief shook his head. "Chimpanzees would fall over dead, Nussboym. They couldn't make 'em stand it. Their hearts would break and they'd die. They call 'em dumb animals, but they're smart enough to know when things are hopeless—and that's more than you can say about people."

"That's not what I meant," Nussboym said. "Look what they've got us doing now, these barracks we're making."

"Don't you bitch about this work," Mikhailov said. "Rudzutak was damn lucky to get it for our gang; it's a hell of a lot easier than going out to the forest and chopping down trees in the snow. This way you go back to your bunk half dead, not all the way."

"I'm not arguing about that," Nussboym said impatiently. Sometimes he wondered if he was a one-eyed man in the country of the blind. "Have you paid any attention to what we're building, though?"

Mikhailov looked around and shrugged. "It's a barracks. It's going up according to plan. The guards haven't said boo. As long as they're happy, I don't care. If they wanted me to make herring boats, I wouldn't complain about that, either. I'd make herring boats."

Nussboym threw down his hammer in exasperation. "Would you make herring boats that didn't hold herring?"

"Careful with that," his partner warned. "You break a tool and the guards will give you a stomping whether they can talk to you or not. They figure everybody understands a boot in the ribs, and they're mostly right. Would I make herring boats that didn't hold herring? Sure, if that's what they told me to do. You think I'm the one to tell 'em they're wrong? Do I look crazy?"

That sort of keep-your-head-down-and-do-what-you're-told attitude had existed in the Lodz ghetto. It didn't just exist in the *gulags*, it dominated. Nussboym felt like yelling, "But the Emperor has no clothes!" Instead, he picked up the hammer and drove a couple of nails into the frame of the bunk bed on which he and Mikhailov were working. He hit the nails as hard as he could, trying to relieve some of his frustration that way.

It didn't work. As he reached down into the bucket for another nail, he asked, "How would you like to sleep in these bunks we're making?"

"I don't like sleeping in the bunks we've got now," Mikhailov answered. "Give me a broad who'll say yes, though, and I don't care where you put me. I'll manage fine, thank you very much." He drove a nail himself.

"A broad?" Nussboym hesitated. "I hadn't thought of that."

His fellow *zek* stared at him in pity. "Then you're a fool, aren't you? They go and run up these new barracks. They put enough barbed wire between them and the ones we sleep in to keep the Nazis from crossing the border, and I hear we're supposed to get a trainload of 'special prisoners' before long. Do I have to draw you a picture, chum?"

"I hadn't heard about the special prisoners coming in," Nussboym said. He knew a lot of the gossip on the camp grapevine went right by him because his Russian really wasn't very good.

"Well, they are," Mikhailov said. "We'll be lucky even to catch a glimpse of 'em. The guards, though, they'll get fucked and sucked till they can't stand up straight, the stinking sons of bitches. The cooks, too, and the clerks—anybody with pull. You're just a regular *zek*, though, forget it."

Nussboym hadn't thought about women since he ended up in Soviet hands. No, that wasn't true: he hadn't thought about them in any concrete way, simply because he figured he wouldn't see any for a long, long time. Now—

Now he said, "Even for women, these bunks are awfully small and awfully close together."

"So the guards climb in and do it sideways instead of on top," Mikhailov said. "So what? It doesn't matter to them, they don't care what the broads think, and you're a stubborn kike, you know that?"

"I know that," Nussboym said; by the other's tone, it was almost a compliment. "All right, we'll get it done the way they tell us to. And if there are women here, we don't have to admit we made this stuff for them."

"Now you're talking," the other *zek* said.

The work gang met its norms for the day, which meant it got fed—not extravagantly, but almost enough to keep body and soul together. After his bread and soup, Nussboym stopped worrying about his belly for a little while. It had enough in it that it was no longer sounding an internal air-raid siren. He knew that klaxon would start up again all too soon, but had learned in Lodz to cherish these brief moments of satiety.

A lot of the other *zeks* had that same feeling. They sat around on their bunks, waiting for the order to blow out the lamps. When that came, they would fall at once into a deep, exhausted sleep. Meanwhile, they gossiped or read the propaganda sheets the camp muckymucks sometimes passed out (those generated plenty of new gossip, most of it sardonic or ribald) or repaired trousers and jackets, their heads bent close to the work so they could see what they were doing in the dim light.

Somewhere off in the distance, a train whistle howled, low and mournful. Nussboym barely noticed it. A few minutes later, it came again, this time unmistakably closer.

Anton Mikhailov sprang to his feet. Everybody stared at this unwonted display of energy. "The special prisoners!" the *zek* exclaimed.

Instantly, the barracks were in an uproar. Many of the prisoners hadn't seen a woman in years, let alone been close to one. The odds that they would be close to one now were slim. The barest possibility, though, was plenty to remind them they were men.

Going outside between supper and lights-out wasn't forbidden, though the weather was still chilly enough that it had been an uncommon practice. Now dozens of *zeks* trooped out of the barracks, Nussboym among them. The other buildings were emptying, too. Guards yelled, trying to keep the prisoners in some kind of order.

They had little luck. Like iron filings drawn to a magnet, the men made a beeline for the wire that separated their encampment from the new one. The barracks there were only half done, as no one knew better than Nussboym, but that, from everything he'd heard, was a typical piece of Soviet inefficiency.

"Look!" someone said with a reverent sigh. "They've put up a canopy to keep the poor darlings from getting the sun on their faces."

"And then they have them come in at night," somebody else added. "If that isn't the *gulag*, I don't know what is."

The train pulled to a stop a few minutes later, iron wheels screaming as they slid along the track. NKVD men with submachine guns and lanterns hurried up to the Stolypin cars that had carried the prisoners. When the doors opened, the first people off the cars were more guards.

"The hell with them," Mikhailov said. "We don't want to see their ugly mugs. We know all about what those bastards look like. Where are the broads?"

The way the guards were shouting and screaming at the prisoners to come out and hurry up about it set the *zeks* laughing fit to burst among themselves. "Better be careful, dears, or they'll send you to the front, and then you'll really be sorry," someone called in shrill falsetto.

A head appeared at the doorway to one of the Stolypin cars. The prisoners' breath went out in one long, anticipatory sigh. Then what was left of it went out again, this time in dozens of gasps of astonishment. A Lizard jumped out of the car and skittered toward the barracks, then another and another and another.

David Nussboym stared at them as avidly as if they were women. He spoke their language. He wondered if anyone else in the whole camp did.

☆ IX ☆

Mutt Daniels eyed the boat with something less than enthusiasm. "Damn," he said feelingly. "When they said they weren't shippin' us back to Chicago from Elgin, I reckoned they couldn't do no worse to us than what we seen there. Shows how blame much I know, don't it?"

"You got that right, Lieutenant," Sergeant Herman Muldoon said. "This whole mission, the way they talk about it, it's a 'deeply regret' telegram just waitin' to happen. Or it would be, I mean, if they still bothered sending those telegrams any more."

"That will be enough of that, gentlemen," Captain Stan Szymanski said. "They tapped us on the shoulder for this job, and we are going to do it."

"Yes, sir," Mutt said. The unspoken corollary to Szymanski's comment was, *or die trying*, which struck Mutt as likely. If it struck Szymanski as likely, too, he didn't let on. Maybe he was a good actor; that was part of being a good officer, same as it was for being a good manager. Or maybe Szymanski didn't really believe, not down deep, that his own personal private self could ever stop existing. If Szymanski was thirty yet, Mutt figured he was the King of England.

Mutt was getting close to sixty. The possibility of his own imminent extinction felt only too real. Even before the Lizards came, too many of the friends he'd had since the turn of the century and before had up and dropped dead on him, from heart disease or cancer or TB. Throw bullets and shell fragments into the mix and a fellow got the idea he was living on borrowed time.

"We'll have the advantage of surprise," Szymanski said.

Of course we will, Mutt thought. *The Lizards'll be surprised— hell, they'll be amazed—we could be so stupid.* He couldn't say that out loud, worse luck.

219

Captain Szymanski pulled a much-folded piece of paper out of his pocket. "Let's have a look at the map," he said.

Daniels and Muldoon crowded close. The map wasn't anything fancy from the Army Corps of Engineers. Mutt recognized it at once: it had come from a Rand McNally road atlas, the same kind of map bus drivers had used to get his minor-league teams from one little town to the next. He'd used them himself when the drivers got lost, which they did with depressing regularity.

Szymanski pointed. "The Lizards are holding the territory on the eastern side of the Illinois River, here. Havana, right on the eastern bank where the Spoon flows into the Illinois, is the key to their position along this stretch of the river, and they've got one of their prison camps right outside of town. Our objective is breaking in there and getting some of those people out. If we can do it here, maybe we'll be able to do it down at Cairo and even in St. Louis. If we're going to win this war, we have to break their grip on the Mississippi."

"Sir, let's us worry about doin' this here little one right," Mutt said. "We manage that, then the brass can start thinkin' big."

Herman Muldoon nodded vigorously. After a moment, so did Szymanski. "That makes sense," he said. "I've been promised that we'll have one hell of a diversion laid on when we go tonight. I don't mean just the stuff on the Spoon River, either. We already know about that; it's part of the basic plan. But this'll be something special. I know that much, even if they haven't told me what it'll be."

"Air support?" Muldoon asked, his voice eager. "When they have some, they don't want to talk about it, in case somebody gets nabbed and spills his guts."

"I don't know, and what I don't know I can't tell you," Szymanski answered. "If you want to make like that proves your point, go ahead. Don't go telling the troops that's what it is, though, because if it turns out not to be, their morale will suffer. Got it?"

"Yes, sir," Muldoon said. Mutt nodded. If there wasn't any air support, or some kind of pretty juicy diversion, a lot more than their morale would suffer. He didn't say anything about that. Szymanski was still a kid, but he wasn't a fool. He could figure things out for himself.

"Any more questions?" Szymanski asked. Mutt didn't say anything. Neither did Muldoon. The captain folded up the map again and stuck it back in his pocket. "Okay, then. We wait for nightfall and we do it." He got up and went off to brief his other platoon.

"He makes it sound easy," Mutt said. He peered out through the screen of willow branches that hung down into the water and—he devoutly hoped—kept the Lizards on the other side of the Illinois from figuring out what the Americans were up to.

Ducks quacked on the far side of the river. The marshes over there were a national wildlife refuge. Mutt wished he could row across with a shotgun instead of the tommy gun he was toting. There had been an observation post over there, on top of a steel tower a hundred feet high. That had given the game wardens a dandy view of poachers. These days, it would have given the Lizards a dandy view of the surrounding countryside, but it had been blown up in one round or another of the fighting over central Illinois.

Troops were scattered up and down the river, to escape detection if possible and to seem like routine patrols if they were spotted. Mutt and Muldoon made the rounds, telling the men what Szymanski had told them. It wasn't fresh news; they'd been getting ready for this mission quite a while now. Telling them one more time what they were supposed to do wasn't going to hurt, though. More times than he could count, Mutt had seen a ballplayer swing when he'd got the bunt sign or take when the hit and run was on. Somebody was still likely to foul up some way or other, even after a last go-round. Mutt had long since given up expecting perfection in men or their plans.

Twilight fell, then darkness. In the water, a fish leaped and fell back with a splash. Back when Mutt had gone through this country in his minor-league playing days, they'd taken more fish out of the Illinois than from any other river save the Columbia. It wasn't like that now, not with so many factories pouring filth into the water, but you could still do all right with a rod and reel, or even with a pole and a string and a hook.

Mutt looked down at his watch. The softly glowing numbers and hands told him it was a quarter to ten. "Into the boats," he whispered. "And quietly, God damn it, or we're dead meat before we even get goin'."

At exactly ten o'clock by his watch, he and the rest of the company started rowing down the Illinois toward Havana. The oars seemed to make a dreadful racket as they dipped into the water and splashed out again, but no Lizard machine guns opened up on the far side of the river. Mutt sighed with relief. He'd been afraid they were heading into a trap right from the start.

At 10:02, artillery and mortars and machine guns opened up on

Havana from the west and south. "Right on time," Mutt said; in the sudden chaos, noise from the boats mattered a lot less.

The Lizards reacted promptly, with artillery of their own and with small-arms fire. Daniels tried to gauge whether they were shifting troops from the camp, which was north of Havana, to meet the noisy, obvious threat the Americans were showing them. For his sake, he hoped they were.

A hot yellow glow sprang up in the southwest and swiftly spread toward Havana. Mutt wanted to whoop with glee, but had the good sense to keep his voice down: "They really went and did it, boys. They lit off the Spoon River."

"How many gallons of gas and oil did they pour into it before they lit a match?" somebody in the boat said. "How long could that stuff keep a tank running, or a plane?"

"I dunno," Mutt answered. "I figure they're usin' it against the enemy this way, too, an' if it rattles the Lizards so much that they forget to shoot at me, I ain't gonna complain. Now come on, boys, we gotta pull like bastards, get across the Illinois before the Spoon runs into it. We don't manage that"—he let out a wheezy chuckle—"our goose is cooked."

Little tongues of flame, drifting on the water, were already at the junction of the rivers and starting to flow down the Illinois. More floating fire followed. The Lizards didn't run gunboats along the river or anything like that, so the fire wasn't likely to do them any real harm, but it did draw their attention toward the Spoon and the territory west of it—and away from the boats sliding down the Illinois toward Havana from the north.

"Come on, pull hard, come on, come—" Mutt tumbled off his seat in the middle of a word when the boat ran hard aground. He came up laughing. If you made a fool of yourself in front of your men, you had to admit it. He jumped out onto the riverbank. Mud squelched under his boots. "Let's go break our boys outta stir."

He looked away from the burning Spoon River to let his eyes adapt to the darkness. That black shape there wasn't forest; the forest around it had been cut down. He waved an arm to urge his men after him and trotted toward the Lizards' prison camp.

Not too far away, Sergeant Muldoon was warning, "Spread out, you dumb bastards. You want 'em to go picking you off the easy way?"

The prison camp was designed more to keep people in than to keep them out. Nothing prevented the Americans from drawing close to the main gate, which lay on the northern side. Mutt, in fact, was beginning to think they could march right on in when a couple of Lizards did open up on them from a little guardhouse.

Grenades and submachine-gun fire quickly suppressed the opposition. "Come on, hurry up!" Mutt yelled all the same. "If those scaly sons of bitches had a radio, we're gonna get company up here pretty damn quick!"

Soldiers with wire cutters attacked the razor wire of the gateway. From inside the camp, men—and women—roused by the gunfire (Mutt hoped nobody, or at least not too many people, had stopped stray bullets) crowded up to the gate. As soon as there was a pathway out of the camp for them, they started pouring forth.

Captain Szymanski shouted, "Anybody who wants to go back to fighting the Lizards full time, come with us. Lord knows you'll be welcome. Otherwise, folks, scatter as best you can. We can use guerrillas, too, and a lot of people round about here will give you shelter and share what they've got. Good luck to you."

"God bless you, sir," a man called. More echoed that. Some people stuck close to their rescuers; others melted away into the night.

Firing picked up off to the south, and rapidly started getting closer. "Skirmish line forward!" Mutt called. "We gotta hold 'em off as long as we can, give people a chance to get away."

No sooner were the words out of his mouth than what sounded like a hell of a big bomb landed right next to the advancing Lizards. He looked around wildly; he hadn't heard any airplanes in the neighborhood. He still didn't, as a matter of fact. But a long rumble of cloven air came from the sky, then slowly faded: it was as if the explosive or whatever it was had arrived before word of its coming.

"That's got to be an American long-range rocket bomb," Captain Szymanski said. Whatever it was, the Lizards weren't steaming forward now the way they had been.

A few minutes later, another one of those rocket bombs went off, this one, by the sound of it, a couple of miles away from any of the fighting around Havana. The missiles didn't seem to be what you'd call accurate; they could have come down here as easily as on the Lizards. *But try stopping them,* Daniels thought. *Go ahead and try.*

In the darkness, he found Szymanski. "Sir, I think it's about time to get the hell out of here. We stay around tryin' to do more than we can, a lot of us'll end up dead."

"You're probably right, Lieutenant," the company commander

said. "No, you're certainly right." He raised his voice: "Back to the river, men!"

Piling into one of the boats—now crowded almost to sinking with rescued prisoners—felt very good to Mutt. Getting back across the Illinois, though, made him sweat big drops. If a Lizard helicopter came chattering by overhead just now, there wouldn't only be fire on the water: there'd be blood in it, too. Everybody understood that; the men at the oars pulled like maniacs as they got over to the west bank of the river.

Stumbling out of the boat and away, Mutt wondered if Sam Yeager had made the acquaintance of these fancy rockets (he also wondered, as he had ever since they'd separated outside Chicago, whether Sam was still alive to have met them). What with all the funny pulp magazines he'd always read, he'd be in better shape to make sense of this crazy new world than damn near anybody else.

"Not that anything makes sense any more," Daniels muttered, and set about getting his men under cover.

A coal-fired generator chugged, down in the basement of Dover College. David Goldfarb felt the throbbing in his bones. He could hear it, too, but didn't unless he made a conscious effort to do so. As long as it went on, lightbulbs shone, wireless sets played, radar worked, and he could pretend the world was as it had been back before the Lizards came.

When he remarked on that, Basil Roundbush said, "In my humble opinion"—he was about as humble as the Pope was Jewish, but at least he knew it—"playing those games doesn't much help. As soon as we leave the laboratory, the real world rudely steps up and kicks us in the teeth."

"Too right it does," Goldfarb said. "Even with every spare square inch of the island growing wheat and potatoes and mangel-wurzels, heaven only knows how we're going to feed everyone."

"Oh, indeed." Roundbush's mustache fluffed as he blew air out through it. "Rations were dreary enough when we were just fighting the Jerries. It's worse now—and the Yanks these days haven't the wherewithal to ship their surpluses over to us. For that matter, they haven't got surpluses any more, either, from all I've heard."

Goldfarb grunted and nodded. Then he took a video platter—the name that seemed to have stuck for the shimmering disks on which the Lizards stored sounds and pictures—and fed it into the captured machine that played it.

"What have you got there?" Roundbush asked.

"I won't know till I hit the switch that makes it play," Goldfarb answered. "I think they just dumped every video platter they could find into a crate and sent them all here. We get a few that are actually useful to us, and we get to label the ones that aren't and ship them on to people for whom they might come in handy."

"Bloody inefficient way of doing things," Roundbush grumbled, but he mooched over to see what the platter would yield. You never could tell. The British had captured a lot of them in the process of driving the Lizards off their island. Some were entertainments, some seemed to contain payrolls and such, and some were the Lizard equivalent of manuals. Those were the real prizes.

Goldfarb flicked the switch. Unlike the valves human electronics used, Lizard gadgets didn't need a minute or two to warm up before they started working. The screen showed the image of a Lizard tank. Having faced such beasts on the ground, Goldfarb had a wholesome respect for them. Nonetheless, they weren't what he was after.

He watched for a couple of minutes to confirm that the video platter was indeed a tank maintenance manual, then shut it off and made the player spit out the platter. After he'd done that, he wrapped it in a sheet of paper, on which he scribbled its subject. He picked up another one and fed it into the machine. It showed scenes of a city on the Lizards' home planet—whether it was a travelogue or a drama he couldn't tell.

"I hear some of these have been found with blue movies on them," Roundbush remarked as Goldfarb removed the video platter and labeled with its possible categories the paper he used to wrap it.

"Good heavens, who cares?" Goldfarb said. "Watching Lizards rut wouldn't get *my* juices flowing, I tell you that."

"You misunderstand, old chap," Roundbush answered. "I mean blue movies of our own kind of people. There's this one Chinese woman, I'm told, who shows up in a lot of them, and also in one where she's having a baby."

"Why do the Lizards care about that?" Goldfarb said. "We must be as ugly to them as they are to us. I'd bet it's a rumor the brass started to give us a reason to keep sifting through these bloody things."

Roundbush laughed. "I hadn't thought of that, and I shouldn't be the least bit surprised if you were right. How many more platters do you plan to go through this session?"

"Oh, perhaps another six or eight," Goldfarb said after a

moment's thought. "Then I'll have wasted enough time on them for a while, and I can go back to making little futile lunges at the innards of the radar set there." He pointed to the array of electronic components spread out over his workbench in what he hoped was a logical, sensible arrangement.

The first three video platters held nothing of any earthly use to him—nothing of any earthly use to anybody earthly, he thought. Two of them were nothing but endless columns of Lizard chicken scratches: most likely the mechanized equivalent of a division's worth of paybooks. The third showed a Lizard spaceship and some weird creatures who weren't Lizards. Goldfarb wondered if it was fact or the alien version of Buck Rogers or Flash Gordon two-reelers. Maybe some boffin would be able to figure it out. He couldn't.

He took out the platter and stuck in another one. As soon as it started to play, Basil Roundbush let out a whoop and thumped him on the back. There on the screen stood a Lizard in medium-fancy body paint disassembling a jet engine that lay on a large table in front of him.

Engines were Roundbush's speciality, not his own, but he watched with the RAF officer for a while. Even without understanding the Lizards' language, he learned a lot from the platter. Roundbush was frantically scribbling notes as he watched. "If only Group Captain Hipple could see this," he muttered several times.

"We've been saying that for a long time now," Goldfarb answered unhappily. "I don't think it's going to happen." He kept watching the video platter. Some of the animation and trick photography the Lizard instructor used to get his point across far outdistanced anything the Disney people had done in *Snow White* or *Fantasia*. He wondered how they'd managed several of the effects. However they did it, they took it as much for granted as he did—or rather, as he had—when he flicked a wall switch to make light come out of a ceiling fixture.

When the instructional film was over, Roundbush shook himself, as if he were a dog emerging from a chilly stream. "We definitely need to keep that one," he said. "Would be nice if we had the services of a Lizard prisoner, too, so we could find out what the blighter was actually saying. That business with the turbine blades, for instance—was he telling the technicians to fiddle with them or not to mess about with them under any circumstances?"

"I don't know," Goldfarb said. "We ought to find out, though, and not by experimenting, if we can help it." He made the player spit out the video platter, wrapped it and labeled it, and set it on a pile separate from the others. That done, he glanced at his wristwatch. "Good heavens, has it got round to seven o'clock already?"

"That it has," Roundbush answered. "Seeing as we've been here for something on the close order of thirteen hours, I'd say we've earned the chance to knock off, too. How say you?"

"I'd like to see what the rest of these platters are first," Goldfarb said. "After that, I'll worry about things like food."

"Such devotion to duty," Roundbush said, chuckling. "Among the things like food you'll be worrying about, unless I'm much mistaken, would be a pint or two at the White Horse Inn."

Goldfarb wondered whether his ears were hot enough to glow on their own if he turned out the lights. He tried to keep his voice casual as he answered, "Now that you mention it, yes."

"Don't be embarrassed, old man." Now Roundbush laughed out loud. "Believe me, I'm jealous of you. That Naomi of yours is a lovely girl, and she thinks the sun rises and sets on you, too." He poked Goldfarb in the ribs. "We shan't tell her any different, what?"

"Er—no," Goldfarb said, embarrassed still. He fed the remaining video platters he'd picked into the player, one at a time. He hoped none of them would prove to be about the care and feeding of radars. He even hoped none of them would be blue movies featuring Roundbush's probably legendary Chinese woman. He didn't tell his colleague that; Roundbush would have claimed someone was sprinkling saltpeter on his food.

He was in luck; a couple of minutes' watching was plenty to show him none of the platters was either relevant to his work or pornographic. As the player ejected the last of them, Basil Roundbush gently booted him in the backside. "Go on, old man. I'll keep the fires burning here, and try not to burn down the building while I'm about it."

With England on Double Summer Time, the sun was still in the sky when Goldfarb got outside. He swung aboard his bicycle and pedaled north toward the White Horse Inn. Like a lot of establishments these days, the pub had a bicycle guard outside to make sure the two-wheelers didn't pedal off of their own accord while their owners were within.

Inside, torches blazed in wall sconces. A hearty fire roared in the hearth. Since the place was packed with people, that left it hot and smoky. As it didn't have a generator chugging away, though, the blazes were necessary to give it light. A couple of chickens roasted above the hearth fire. Their savory smell made spit rush into Goldfarb's mouth.

He made his way toward the bar. "What'll it be, dearie?" Sylvia asked. Naomi was carrying a tray of mugs and glasses from table to table. She spotted Goldfarb through the crowd and waved to him.

He waved back, then said to Sylvia, "Pint of bitter, and are all the pieces from those birds spoken for yet?" He pointed toward the fireplace.

"No, not yet," the redheaded barmaid answered. "Which d'you fancy—legs or breasts?"

"Well, I think I'd like a nice, juicy thigh," he answered—and then caught the double entendre. Sylvia laughed uproariously at the look on his face. She poured him his beer. He raised the pint pot to his mouth in a hurry, not least to help mask himself.

"You're blushing," Sylvia chortled.

"I am not," he said indignantly. "And even if I was, you'd have the devil's own time proving it by firelight."

"So I would, so I would," Sylvia said, laughing still. She ran her tongue over her upper lip. Goldfarb was urgently reminded—as he was intended to be reminded—they'd been lovers not that long before. She might as well have been telling him, *See what you're missing?* She said, "I'll get you that chicken now." When she headed toward the fireplace, she put even more sway in her walk than she usually did.

Naomi came over a minute later. "What were you two laughing about?" she asked. To Goldfarb's relief, she sounded curious, not suspicious. He told her the truth; if he hadn't, Sylvia would have. Naomi laughed, too. "Sylvia is very funny," she said, and then, in a lower voice, "Sometimes, maybe, too much for her own good."

"Whose own good?" Sylvia asked, returning with a steaming chicken leg on a plate. "Has to be me. I tell too many jokes for my own good? Likely I do, by Jesus. But I'm not joking when I tell you that chicken's going to cost you two quid."

Goldfarb dug in his pocket for the banknotes. Prices had climbed dizzyingly high since the Lizard invasion, and his radarman's pay hadn't come close to keeping up. Even so, there were times when the rations he got grew too boring to stand.

"Besides," he said as he set the money on the bar, "what better have I got to spend it on?"

"Me," Naomi answered. Had that been Sylvia talking, the response would have been frankly mercenary. Naomi didn't really care that he couldn't spend like an air vice marshal. That was one of the things that made her seem wonderful to him. She asked, "Have you got more word of your cousin, the one who did the wireless broadcasts for the Lizards?"

He shook his head. "My family found that he lived through the invasion: that much I do know. But not long after that, he and his wife and their son might as well have dropped off the face of the earth. Nobody knows what's become of them."

"Somebody knows," Naomi said with conviction as Goldfarb dug into the chicken leg. "No one may be talking, but someone knows. In this country, people do not disappear for no reason. Sometimes I think you do not know how lucky you are that this is so."

"I know," Goldfarb said, and after a moment Naomi nodded, conceding the point. He smiled at her, even if crookedly. "What's the matter? Did you take me for an Englishman again?" Looking a little flustered, she nodded once more. He dropped into Yiddish to say, "If we win the war, and if I have children, or maybe grandchildren, they'll take that for granted. Me—" He shook his head.

"If you have children, or maybe grandchildren—" Naomi began, and then let it drop. The war had loosened everyone's standards, but she still wasn't what you'd call forward. Sometimes Goldfarb regretted that very much. Sometimes he admired it tremendously. Tonight was one of those nights.

"Let me have another pint, would you please?" he said. Sometimes quiet talk—or what they could steal of it while she was also busy serving other customers—was as good as anything else, maybe better.

He hadn't thought that with Sylvia. All he'd wanted to do with her was to get her brassiere off and her panties down. He scratched his head, wondering where the difference was.

Naomi brought him the bitter. He took a pull, then set the pot down. "Must be love," he said, but she didn't hear him.

Artillery was harassing the Race in a push north from their Florida base. The Big Uglies were getting smart about moving their guns before counterbattery fire found them, but they couldn't do much about attack from the air. Teerts had two pods of rockets mounted under his killercraft. They were some of the simplest weapons in the arsenal of the Race. They weren't even guided: if you saturated an area with them, that did the job. And, because they were so simple, even Tosevite factories could turn them out in large quantities. The armorers loved them these days, not least because they had plenty.

"I have acquired the assigned target visually," Teerts reported back to his commanders. "I now begin the dive on it."

Acceleration pressed him back in his seat. The Big Uglies knew he was there. Antiaircraft shells burst around his killercraft. Many more, he guessed, were bursting behind him. Try as they would, the Tosevites rarely gave jet aircraft enough lead when they fired at them. That helped keep the Race's pilots alive.

He fired a pod of the rockets. A wave of fire seemed to leap from the killercraft toward the artillery positions. The killercraft staggered slightly in the sky, then steadied. The autopilot pulled it out of the dive. He swung it around so he could inspect the damage he'd done. If he hadn't done enough, he'd make another pass with the second rocket pod.

That wouldn't be necessary, not today. "The target is destroyed," he said in some satisfaction. An antiaircraft gun was still popping away at him, but that didn't much matter. He went on, "Request new target."

The voice that answered wasn't his usual flight controller. After a moment, he recognized it all the same: it belonged to Aaatos, the male from Intelligence. "Flight Leader Teerts, we have a . . . bit of a problem."

"What's gone wrong now?" Teerts demanded. What felt like an eternity in Nipponese prisons—to say nothing of the ginger habit he'd developed there—had left him with no patience for euphemism.

"I'm glad you're airborne, Flight Leader," Aaatos said, apparently not wanting to give a straight answer. "Do you remember our talk not so long ago in that grassy area not far from the runways?"

Teerts thought back. "I remember," he said. Sudden suspicion blossomed in him. "You're not going to tell me the dark-skinned Big Uglies have mutinied against us, are you?"

"Evidently I don't have to," Aaatos said unhappily. "You were correct at the time to distrust them. I admit this." For a male from Intelligence to admit anything was an enormous concession. "Their unit was placed in line against American Big Uglies, and, under cover of a masking firefight, has allowed enemy Tosevites to infiltrate."

"Give me the coordinates," Teerts told him. "I still have a good supply of munitions, and adequate fuel as well. I gather I am to assume any Tosevites I see in the area are hostile to the Race?"

"That is indeed the operative assumption," Aaatos agreed. He paused, then went on, "Flight Leader, a question, if I may? You need not answer, but I would be grateful if you did. Our estimates were that these dark-skinned Big Uglies would serve us well and loyally in the role we had assigned to them. These estimates were not casually made. Our experts ran computer simulations of a good many scenarios. Yet they proved inaccurate and your casual concern correct. How do you account for this?"

"My impression is that our alleged experts have never had to learn what good liars the Big Uglies can be," Teerts answered. "They have also never been in a situation where, from weakness, they have to tell their interrogators exactly what those males most desire to hear. I have." Again, memories of his days in Nipponese captivity surged to the surface; his hand quivered on the killer-craft's control column. "Knowing the Tosevites' capacity for guile, and also knowing the interrogators were apt to be getting bad data on which to base their fancy simulations, I drew my own conclusions."

"Perhaps you would consider transferring to Intelligence," Aaatos said. "Such trenchant analyses would be of benefit to us."

"Flying a killercraft is also of benefit to the Race," Teerts answered, "especially at a time such as this."

Aaatos made no reply. Teerts wondered whether the male from Intelligence was chastened or merely insulted. He didn't much care. The analysts had made foolish assumptions, reasoned from them with undoubtedly flawless logic, and ended up worse off than if they'd done nothing at all. His mouth dropped open in a bitter laugh. Somehow, that left him unsurprised.

Smoke from burning forests and fields showed him he was nearing the site of the treason-aided American breakthrough. He saw several blazing landcruisers of the Race's manufacture, and more of the slower, clumsier ones the Big Uglies used. With those were advancing Tosevites, their upright gait and stiff motions making them unmistakable even as he roared past at high speed.

He loosed the second pod of rockets at the biggest concentration of Big Uglies he could find, then gained altitude to come round for another pass at them. The ground seemed to blaze with the little yellow flames of small-arms fire as survivors tried to bring him down. No one had ever denied that the Tosevites showed courage. Sometimes, though, courage was not enough.

Teerts dove for another firing run. Pillars of greasy black smoke marked the pyres of hydrocarbon-fueled vehicles; his first barrage had done some good. His fingerclaw stabbed the firing button at the top of the control column. He hosed down the area with cannon fire till warning lights told him he was down to his last thirty rounds. Doctrine demanded that he leave off at that point, in case he had to engage Tosevite aircraft on his way back to base. "The itch take doctrine," he muttered, and kept firing until the cannon had no more ammunition to expend.

He checked his fuel gauge. He was running low on hydrogen, too. Adding everything together, he wasn't much use on the battlefield any more. He headed back to the air base to replenish fuel and munitions both. If the Tosevite breakthrough wasn't checked by the time he got that done, they'd probably send him straight out again.

A male of the Race drove the fuel truck up to his killercraft, but two Big Uglies unreeled the hose and connected it to the couplings in the nose of his machine. More Big Uglies loaded cannon shells into his killercraft and affixed fresh rocket pods to two of the hardpoints below the wings.

The Tosevites sang as they worked, music alien to his hearing diaphragms but deep and rhythmic and somehow very powerful. They wore only leg coverings and shoes; their dark-skinned torsos glistened with cooling moisture under a sun that even Teerts found comfortable. He watched the Big Uglies warily. Males just like them had shown they were traitors. How was he supposed to be sure these fellows hadn't, say, arranged a rocket so it would blow up in the pod rather than after it was launched?

He couldn't know, not for certain, not till he used those rockets. There weren't enough males of the Race to do everything that needed doing. If they didn't have help from the Tosevites, the war effort would likely fail. If the Big Uglies ever fully realized that, the war effort would also likely fail.

He did his best to push such thoughts out of his mind. All the electronics said the killercraft was ready in every way. "Flight Leader Teerts reporting," he said. "I am prepared to return to combat."

Instead of the clearance and fresh orders he'd expected, the air traffic control male said, "Hold on, Flight Leader. We are generating something new for you. Stay on this frequency."

"It shall be done," Teerts said, wondering what sort of brain-addled fit had befallen his superiors now. There was a job right in front of his snout that badly needed doing, so why were they wasting their time and his trying to come up with something exotic?

Since he evidently wasn't going straight back into action, he dug out his vial of ginger from the space between the padding and the cockpit wall and had a good taste. With the herb coursing through him, he was ready to go out and slaughter Big Uglies even without his aircraft.

"Flight Leader Teerts!" The traffic control male's voice boomed in the audio button taped to Teerts' hearing diaphragm. "You are hereby detached from duty at this Florida air base and ordered to report to our forward base in the region known to the local Tosevites as Kansas, there to assist the Race in its attack on the center bearing the local name Denver. Flight instructions are being downloaded to your piloting computer as we speak. You will also require a drop tank of hydrogen. This will be provided to you."

Sure enough, a new truck came rolling up to Teerts' killercraft. A couple of males got out, lowered the droplet-shaped tank onto a wheeled cart with a winch, and hooked it up under the belly of the killercraft. As he listened to their clattering, he was heartily glad the Race didn't entrust that job to Big Ugly hirelings. The potential for disaster was much too high.

He let out a puzzled hiss. The Tosevites had scored a breakthrough on this front; he knew perfectly well that his bombardment hadn't halted them single-handedly. Yet the base commander was sending him away to serve on another front. Did that mean the Race was overwhelmingly confident of stopping the Big Uglies here, or that the attack on what was the name of the place?—Denver, the traffic-control male had called it, stood in desperate need of help? He couldn't very well ask, but he'd find out.

He checked the computer. Sure enough, it had the course information for the flight to Kansas. A good thing, too, because he didn't know where on this land mass the region was. The technicians finished installing the drop tank. They got back into their truck. It sped away.

"Flight Leader Teerts, you are cleared for takeoff," the traffic control male said. "Report to the Kansas forward base."

"It shall be done." Teerts gave the engine power and taxied down the runway toward the end.

Whenever George Bagnall went into the gloom of the *Krom* at Pskov these days, he felt his own spirits sinking into darkness, too. He wished Aleksandr German had never mentioned the possibility of sending him, Ken Embry, and Jerome Jones back to England. Before, he'd resigned himself to going on here in this godforsaken corner of the Soviet Union. But with even the slightest chance of getting home again, he found both the place and the work he did here ever more unbearable.

Inside the *Krom*, German sentries came to attention stiff as rigor mortis. Their Russian opposite numbers, most of them in baggy civilian clothes rather than uniforms that had been laundered too many times, didn't look as smart, but the submachine guns they carried would chew a man to pieces in short order.

Bagnall went up the stairs to Lieutenant General Kurt Chill's headquarters. The stairwell was almost black; neither occasional slit windows nor tallow lamps right out of the fourteenth century did much to show him where to put his feet. Every time he got up to the first floor, he thanked his lucky stars he hadn't broken his neck.

He found Embry up there ahead of him, shooting the breeze with Captain Hans Dölger, Chill's adjutant. As far as Bagnall could tell, Dölger didn't much fancy Englishmen, but he made a point of being correct and polite. As arguments in Pskov had a way of being settled with bullets as often as with words, politeness was a rarity worth noting.

Dölger looked up when Bagnall came in. *"Guten Tag,"* he said. "For a moment, I thought you might be one of the partisan brigadiers, but I know that was foolish of me. As well expect the sun to set in the east as a Russian to show up when he is scheduled."

"I think being late—or at least not worrying about being on time—is built into the Russian language," Bagnall answered in German. He'd done German in school, but had learned what Russian he had since coming to Pskov. He found it fascinating and frustrating in almost equal measure. "It has a verb form for doing something continuously and a verb form for doing something once, but pinning down the moment *right now* is anything but easy."

"This is true," Dölger said. "It makes matters more difficult. Even if Russian had the full complement of tenses of a civilized language, however, I am of the opinion that our comrades the partisan brigadiers would be late anyhow, simply because that is in their nature." A lot of Germans in Pskov, from what Bagnall had seen, had stopped automatically thinking of Russians as *Untermenschen*. Captain Dölger was not among their number.

Aleksandr German arrived twenty minutes late, Nikolai Vasiliev twenty minutes after him. Neither man showed concern, or even awareness of a problem. With the brigadiers in front of him, Captain Dölger was a model of military punctilio, no matter what he said about them behind their backs. Bagnall gave him points for that; he embodied some of the same traits as were found in a good butler.

Kurt Chill grunted when the Russians and the Englishmen who were supposed to lubricate Soviet-German relations entered his chamber. By the scraps of paper that littered his desk, he'd had plenty to keep him busy while he waited.

The meeting was the usual wrangle. Vasiliev and Aleksandr German wanted Chill to commit more *Wehrmacht* men to front-line fighting; Chill wanted to hold them in reserve to meet break-throughs because they were more mobile and more heavily armed than their Soviet counterparts. It was almost like a chess opening; for some time, each side knew the moves the other was likely to make, and knew how to counter them.

This time, grudgingly, urged along by Bagnall and Embry, Kurt Chill made concessions. "Good, good," Nikolai Vasiliev rumbled down deep in his chest, sounding like a bear waking up after a long winter's nap. "You Englishmen, you have some use."

"I am glad you think so," Bagnall said, though he wasn't par-ticularly glad. If Vasiliev thought them useful here, Aleksandr German probably did, too. And if Aleksandr German thought them useful here, would he help them get back to England, as he'd hinted he might?

Lieutenant General Chill looked disgusted with the world. "I still maintain that expending your strategic reserve will sooner or later leave you without necessary resources for a crisis, but we shall hope this particular use does not create that difficulty." His glance flicked to Bagnall and Embry. "You are dismissed, gentlemen."

He'd added that last word, no doubt, to irk the partisan briga-diers, to whom *gentlemen* should have been *comrades*. Bagnall refused to concern himself with fine points of language. He got up from his seat and quickly headed for the door. Any chance to get out of the gloom of the *Krom* was worth taking. Ken Embry fol-lowed him without hesitation.

Outside, the bright sunshine made Bagnall blink. During the winter, the sun seemed to have gone away for good. Now it stayed in the sky more and more, until, when summer came, it would hardly seem to leave. The Pskova River had running water in it again. The ice was all melted. The land burgeoned—for a little while.

In the marketplace not far from the *Krom*, the *babushkas* sat and gossiped among themselves and displayed for sale or trade eggs and pork and matches and paper and all sorts of things that should by rights long since have vanished from Pskov. Bagnall wondered how they came by them. He'd even asked, a couple of times, but the women's faces grew closed and impassive and they pretended not to understand him. *None of your business,* they said without saying a word.

Over on the edge of the city, a few scattered gunshots broke out. All through the marketplace, heads came up in alarm. "Oh, bloody hell," Bagnall exclaimed. "Are the Nazis and Bolshies hammering at each other again?" That had happened too often already in Pskov.

Gunshots came closer to the marketplace. So did a low roar that put Bagnall in mind of one of the Lizards' jet fighters, but seemed only a few feet off the ground. A long, lean, white-painted shape darted through the market square, dodged around the church of the Archangel Michael and the cathedral of the Trinity, and slammed into the *Krom.* The explosion knocked Bagnall off his feet, but not before he saw another white dart follow the course of its predecessor and hit the *Krom.* The second blast knocked Embry down beside him.

"Flying bombs!" the pilot bawled in his ear. He heard Embry as if from very far away. After the two blasts, his ears seemed wrapped in thick cotton batting. Embry went on, "They haven't bothered with the *Krom* in a long time. They must have found a traitor to let them know our headquarters was there."

A Russian, angry at having to serve alongside the Nazis? A *Wehrmacht* man, captured when trying to help Red Army troops he hated worse than any Lizard? Bagnall didn't know; he knew he never would know. In the end, it didn't matter. However it had happened, the damage was done.

He staggered to his feet and ran back toward the fortress that had been the core around which the town of Pskov grew. The great gray stones had been proof against arrows and muskets. Against high explosives precisely aimed, they were useless, or maybe worse than useless: when they toppled, they crushed those whom blast alone might have spared. During the Blitz—and how long ago that seemed!—unreinforced brick buildings in London had been death traps for the same reason.

Smoke began rising from the wreckage. The walls of the *Krom* were stone, but so much inside was wood . . . and every lamp in there was a fire that would spread given fuel. The lamps had been given fuel, all right.

The screams and groans of the wounded reached Bagnall's

ears, stunned though they were. He saw a hand sticking up between two blocks of stone. Grunting, he and Embry shoved one of those stones aside. Blood clung to the base of it and dripped. The German soldier who'd been crushed under there would never need help again.

Men and women, Russians and Germans, came running to rescue their comrades. A few, more alert than the rest, carried stout timbers to lever heavy stones off injured men. Bagnall lent the strength of his back and arms to one such gang. A stone went over with a crash. The fellow groaning beneath it had a ruined leg, but might live.

They found Aleksandr German. His left hand was crushed between two stones, but past that he hardly seemed hurt. A red smear beneath a nearby stone the size of a motorcar was all that was left of Kurt Chill and Nikolai Vasiliev.

Flames started peeping out between stones. The little crackling noise they made was in and of itself a jolly sound, but one that brought horror with it. Soldiers trapped in the rubble shrieked as fire found them before rescuers could. Smoke grew ever thicker, choking Bagnall, making his eyes run and his lungs burn as if they'd caught fire themselves. It was as if he was working inside a wood-burning stove. Every so often, too, he smelled roasting meat. Sickened—for he knew what meat that was—he struggled harder than ever to save as much, as many, as he could.

Not enough, not enough. Hand pumps brought water from the river onto the fire, but could not hold it at bay. The flames drove the rescuers away from those they would save, drove them back in defeat.

Bagnall stared at Ken Embry in exhausted dismay. The pilot's face was haggard and black with soot save for a few clean tracks carved by sweat. He had a burn on one cheek and a cut under the other eye. Bagnall was sure he looked no better himself.

"What the devil do we do now?" he said. His mouth was full of smoke, as if he'd had three packs of cigarettes all at once. When he spat to get rid of some of it, his saliva came out dark, dark brown. "The German commandant dead, one of the Russian brigadiers with him, the other one wounded—"

Embry wiped his forehead with the back of his hand. Since one was as filthy as the other, neither changed color. Wearily, the pilot answered, "Damned if I know. Pick up the pieces and go on as best we can, I suppose. What else is there to do?"

"Nothing I can think of," Bagnall said. "But oh, to be in England in the springtime—" That dream was gone, smashed as terribly as Aleksandr German's hand. What was left was the ruins of Pskov. Embry's answer was the best choice they had. It was still pretty lousy.

Air raid sirens screamed like the souls in the hell Polish Catholic priests took such delight in describing. Moishe Russie hadn't believed in eternal punishments of that sort. Now, after enduring air raids in Warsaw and London and wherever in Palestine this was, he wondered if hell wasn't real after all.

The door to his cell opened. The hard-faced guard he'd learned to loathe stood in the doorway. The fellow had a Sten gun in each hand. Even for him, that much weaponry struck Moishe as excessive. Then, to Russie's amazement, the guard handed him one of the weapons. "Here, take it," he said impatiently. "You're being liberated." As if to emphasize the point, he pulled a couple of magazines from his belt and gave them to Russie, too. By their weight, they were full. "Treat 'em like you would a woman," the guard advised. "They get bent up, especially at the top, and they won't feed right."

"What do you mean, I'm being liberated?" Moishe demanded, almost indignantly. Events had got ahead of him. Even with a weapon in his hands, he felt anything but safe. Would they let him out of his cell, let him walk round the corner, and then riddle him with bullets? The Nazis had played tricks like that.

The guard exhaled in exasperation. "Don't be stupid, Russie. The Lizards invaded Palestine without cutting any deals with us. Looks like they're going to win here, too, so we're making sure they see we're on the right side—we're giving the British all the trouble they want, all the trouble we can. But we don't have a deal over you with the Lizards, either. If they ask for you when the fighting's done, we don't want to be in a place where we have to say yes or no. You aren't ours, we don't have to. You get it now?"

In a crazy sort of way, Moishe did get it. The Jewish underground could have kept him while denying to the Lizards they were doing so, but that exposed them to the risk of being found out. "My family?" he asked.

"I'd have taken you to them by now, if you hadn't started banging your gums," the guard told him. He squawked indignant protest, which the other Jew ignored, turning his back and giving Moishe the choice of following or staying where he was. He followed.

He went down hallways he'd never seen before. Up till now, they'd always brought Rivka or Reuven to him, not the other way around. Turning a corner, he almost ran into Menachem Begin. The underground leader said, "*Nu*, you were right, Russie. The Lizards aren't to be trusted. We'll deal with them as best we can, and then we'll make their lives miserable. How does that sound?"

"I've heard worse," Moishe said, "but I've also heard better. You should have stood with the British against the Lizards from the beginning."

"And gone down with them? For they will go down. No, thank you."

Begin started to head down the hall. "Wait." Moishe called after him. "Before you turn me loose, at least tell me where I am."

The underground leader and the tough-looking guard both started to laugh. "That's right, you never did find out," Menachem Begin said. "Now it doesn't hurt us for you to know. You're in Jerusalem, Russie, not far from the one wall of the Temple that's still left standing." After an awkward half wave, he hurried away on whatever his own mission was.

Jerusalem? Moishe stood staring for a moment. The guard vanished round a corner before he noticed his charge wasn't coming after him. He stuck his head and upper body back into sight and waved impatiently. As if awakening from a dream, Moishe started moving again.

The guard took a key from his belt and used it to unlock a door like any other door. "What do you want?" Rivka exclaimed, her voice sharp with alarm. Then she saw Moishe behind the guard, who was both taller and broader than he. "What's going on?" she asked in an entirely different tone of voice.

She got a condensed version of the story the guard had given Moishe. He didn't know how much of it she believed. He didn't know how much of it he believed himself, although the submachine gun he carried was a potent argument for there being some truth to it. "Come on," the guard said. "You're getting out of here right now."

"Give us some money," Rivka said. Moishe shook his head in chagrin. He hadn't even thought of that. Evidently the guard had. He reached into a trouser pocket and pulled out a roll of bills that would have made a man rich before the war and now might keep him eating till he found work. Moishe handed the roll to Rivka. As the guard snorted, he bent to hug Reuven.

"Do you know where we are?" he asked his son.

"Palestine, of course," Reuven answered scornfully, as if wondering what was wrong with him.

"Not just Palestine—Jerusalem," Moishe said.

The guard snorted again, this time at Reuven's wide-eyed wonder. He said, "Out you go now, the lot of you." The strides with which he led them toward the street had made no concessions to the boy's short legs. Moishe grabbed Reuven's hand to help his son keep up.

How strange, he thought, *to be holding Reuven with one hand and a Sten gun in the other.* He'd wanted to fight the Lizards ever since they twisted his words in Poland. He had fought them, with medic's kit and with wireless broadcasts. Now he had a gun. Mordechai Anielewicz had convinced him that was not his best weapon, but it was better than nothing.

"Here." The guard slid back a bar from the front doors. The doors and the bar looked as if they could withstand anything short of a tank running into them. The guard grunted as he pushed the stout portals open wide enough for Moishe and his family to squeeze through. As soon as they were out on the street, he said, "Good luck," and closed the doors behind them. The scrape of the bar sliding back into place behind them sounded very final.

Moishe looked around. To be in Jerusalem without looking around—that seemed a sin. What he saw was chaos. He'd seen that before, in Warsaw. London hadn't shown him as much; the British had been under attack from the sky long before he got there, and had learned to cope as best they could . . . and, in any case, they were far more phlegmatic than Poles or Jews or Arabs.

The Russies walked a couple of blocks. Then someone shouted at them: "Get off the street, you fools!" Not until he was running for a doorway did Moishe realize the yell had been in English, not Yiddish or Hebrew. A khaki-clad soldier, ignoring his own advice, fired at the Lizard planes overhead.

"He can't knock them down, Papa," Reuven said seriously; his brief life had made him an expert on air raids. "Doesn't he know that?"

"He knows it," Moishe answered. "He's trying anyhow, because he is brave."

Bombs crashed down, not too close: the war had honed Moishe's ears, too. He heard sharp whistling in the sky, then more explosions. The wall against which he was leaning shook. "Those aren't bombs, Papa," Reuven exclaimed—yes, he was a connoisseur of such things. "That's artillery."

"You're right again," Moishe said. If the Lizards were landing artillery in Jerusalem, they couldn't be far away. He wanted to flee the city, but how? And where would he go?

A new set of shells landed, these nearer to him. Fragments

hissed through the air. What had been a house was suddenly transformed into a pile of rubble. An Arab woman with veil and headcloth and robes covering her down to her toes emerged from the building next door to it, running for new shelter like a beetle when the stone under which it huddles is disturbed. A shell landed in the street, only a few meters from her. After that, she didn't run. She lay and writhed and screamed.

"She's hurt bad," Reuven said in that alarmingly knowing way of his.

Moishe ran out to do what he could for her. Without medicines, without instruments, he knew how little that would be. "Be careful!" Rivka called after him. He nodded, but laughed a little under his breath. As if he could be careful now! That was up to the shells, not to him.

Blood pooled under the woman. She wailed in Arabic, which Moishe didn't understand. He told her he was a doctor—"medical student" didn't pack enough punch—using German, Yiddish, Polish, and English. She didn't follow any of them. When he tried to tear her robe to bandage a wound high up in her leg, she fought him as if she thought he was going to rape her right there. Maybe she did think that.

An Arab man came up. "What you do, Jew?" he asked in bad Hebrew, then in worse English.

"I'm a doctor. I try to help her." Moishe also spoke in both languages.

The man turned his words into rapid-fire Arabic. Halfway through, the woman stopped struggling. It wasn't because she acquiesced. Moishe grabbed for her wrist. He found no pulse. When he let her arm drop, the Arab man knew what that meant. *"Inshallah,"* he said, and then, in English, "The will of God. Good you try to help, Jew doctor." With a nod, he walked away.

Shaking his head, Russie went back to his family. Now, too late for the poor woman, the Lizard bombardment was easing. Staying close to the sides of buildings in case it picked up again, Moishe led his wife and son through the streets of Jerusalem. He didn't know just what he was looking for. He would have taken a way out of the city, a good shelter, or a glimpse of the Wailing Wall.

Before he got any of those, a spatter of small-arms fire broke out, no more than a few hundred meters away. "Are the Lizards here?" Rivka exclaimed.

"I don't think so," Moishe answered. "I think it's the Jewish underground rising against the British."

"Oy!" Rivka and Reuven said it together. Moishe nodded

mournfully. The shooting—rifles, submachine guns, machine guns, the occasional *pop!* of a mortar—spread like wildfire, fanning out in every direction. Inside a couple of minutes, the Russies were flat on their bellies in another doorway as bullets pinged and ricocheted all around.

Several British soldiers in tin hats and khaki tunics and shorts dashed up the street. One of them spotted Moishe and his family. He pointed his rifle at them and screamed, "Don't move or you're dead, you Jew bastards!"

That was when Moishe remembered the submachine gun that lay on the ground beside him. *So much for taking up arms,* he thought. "Take the gun," he told the Englishman. "You have us."

The soldier called, "Permission to take prisoners, sir?" That didn't mean anything to Russie for a moment. Then it sank in: if the man didn't get that permission, he was going to shoot them and go on about his business. Moishe got ready to reach for the Sten gun. If he was going to go down, he'd go down fighting.

But a fellow with a second lieutenant's single pips on his shoulder boards said, "Yes, take them back to the detention center. If we start murdering theirs, they'll slaughter ours, the buggers." He sounded weary and bitter beyond measure. Moishe hoped Rivka hadn't followed what he said.

The British soldier darted forward to grab the submachine gun. "On your feet!" he said. When Moishe rose, the soldier plucked the spare magazines from the waistband of his trousers. "Hands high! Those hands come down, you're dead—you, the skirt, the brat, anybody." Moishe said that in Yiddish so he was sure his wife and son got it. "March!" the Englishman barked.

They marched. The soldier led them into what looked as if it had been a market square. Now barbed wire and machine-gun positions all around turned it into a prisoner camp. To one side was a tall wall of large stones that looked to have been in place forever. Atop that wall stood a mosque whose golden dome was marred by a shell hole.

Moishe realized what that wall had to be just as the British soldier herded him and his family into the barbed-wire cage. There they stayed. The only sanitary arrangements were slop buckets by the barbed wire. Some people had blankets; most didn't. Toward noon, the guards distributed bread and cheese. The portions were bigger than those he'd known in the Warsaw ghetto, but not much. Water barrels had a common dipper. He scowled at that; it would make disease spread faster.

He and his family spent two miserable, chilly nights, sleeping huddled together on bare ground. Artillery shells fell all around, some alarmingly close. Had any landed inside the barbed-wire perimeter, the slaughter would have been gruesome.

On the morning of the third day, bigger explosions rocked Jerusalem. "The British are pulling out!" exclaimed someone who sounded as if he knew what he was talking about. "They're blowing up what they can't take with them." Moishe didn't know whether the fellow was right, not then, but before long the guards deserted their posts, taking machine guns with them.

They hadn't been gone more than a few minutes before other men carrying guns entered the square: fighters from the Jewish underground. The prisoners cheered themselves hoarse as their comrades released them from confinement.

But with the Jews came Lizards. Moishe stiffened: wasn't that one there by the gate Zolraag? And, at the same time as he recognized the Lizard, Zolraag recognized him. Zolraag hissed in excitement. "We want this one," he said, and added an emphatic cough.

"Progress at last!" Atvar said. A pleasant breeze blew off the sea toward him. He walked along the northern shore of the little triangular peninsula that separated Egypt from Palestine. The warmth, the sand, the stones put him in mind of Home. It was very pleasant country—and yet he'd had to come here by helicopter, for the Big Uglies didn't bother with roads leading away from their railroad.

Kirel paced beside him for a while without speaking: perhaps the shiplord was also thinking of the world he'd left behind for the sake of the greater glory of the Emperor. A couple of feathered flying creatures glided past the two males. They were nothing like the leather-winged fliers with which Atvar had been familiar before coming to Tosev 3, and reminded him this was an alien world. Males and females hatched here after the colonization fleet arrived would find these Tosevite animals normal, unexceptional. He didn't think he would ever grow used to them.

He didn't think he would ever grow used to Big Uglies, either. That didn't keep him from hoping to conquer their world in spite of everything. "Progress!" he repeated. "The most important centers of Palestine are in our hands, the drive against Denver advances most satisfactorily on the whole . . . and we may yet triumph."

For Kirel not to respond then would have implied he thought

the fleetlord mistaken. A male implied that at his peril these days. And so Kirel said, "Truth. In those areas, we do advance."

That, unfortunately, reminded Atvar of the many areas where the Race still did not advance: of Poland, where the Deutsche were being troublesome in the extreme; of China, where holding the cities and roads left the countryside a sea of rebellion—and where even control over the cities sometimes proved illusory; of the SSSR, where gains in the west were counterbalanced by Soviet advances in Siberia; of the central United States, where missiles were making starships vulnerable; of India, where Big Uglies weren't fighting much, but showed a willingness to die rather than yielding to the commands of the Race.

He hadn't come here to think about places like those, and resolutely shoved them to the back of his mind. Even with the ugly flying creatures to remind him it wasn't quite Home, it was a place to relax, enjoy decent—better than decent—weather, and make the best of things.

Resolutely sticking to that best, he said, "We also have the agitator Moishe Russie in custody at last, and his mate and their hatchling. We can either control him through them or take vengeance upon him for the manifold troubles he has caused us. This is also progress."

"Truth again, Exalted Fleetlord." Kirel hesitated, then went on, "Before punishing him as he deserves, it might be worthwhile to interrogate him, to learn exactly why he turned against us after his initial cooperation. Despite all his subsequent propaganda, this has never been completely clear."

"I want him punished," Atvar said. "Treason against the Race is the inexpiable crime."

That wasn't strictly true, not on Tosev 3. The Race maintained polite relations with Big Uglies who had turned on it and then professed friendship once more: antagonizing them for good would have caused more trouble than it solved. But conditions on Tosev 3 created ambiguity and doubts in a great many areas. Why should that one be any different? Atvar had stated the letter of the law.

Kirel said, "Punished he shall surely be, Exalted Fleetlord—but all in good time. Let us first learn all we can from him. Are we Big Uglies, to act precipitately and destroy an opportunity without first learning if we can exploit it? We shall be attempting to govern the Tosevites for thousands of years to come. What we learn from Russie may give us a clue as to how to do it better."

"Ah," Atvar said. "Now my chemoreceptors also detect the scent. Yes, perhaps that could be beneficial. As you say, he is in our hands, so punishment, while certain, need not be swift. Indeed, most likely he will view our exploitation of him as punishment in its own right. This world does its best to make me hasty. I must remember, now and again, to resist."

Mordechai Anielewicz had company as he approached the meeting with the Nazis: a squad of Jews with submachine guns and rifles. He wasn't supposed to bring along that kind of company, but he'd long since stopped worrying about what he was supposed to do. He did what needed doing.

He waved. His support squad vanished among the trees. If anything went wrong at the meeting, the Germans would pay. A couple of years before, Jewish fighters wouldn't have been so smooth about moving in the woods. They'd had practice since.

Anielewicz walked up the trail toward the clearing where he was supposed to confer with the Nazis and see what Heinrich Jäger had up his sleeve—or what he said he had up his sleeve. Since that talk with the Pole who called himself Tadeusz, Anielewicz was leery about believing anything the German might tell him. On the other hand, he would have been leery about believing Jäger without talking to Tadeusz, too.

As he'd been instructed, he paused before entering the clearing and whistled the first few bars of Beethoven's Fifth. He found that a curious choice for the Germans, since those bars made a Morse V-for-victory, the symbol of the anti-Nazi underground before the Lizards came. But, when somebody whistled back, he advanced up the forest track and out into the open space.

There stood Jäger, and beside him a tall, broad-shouldered man with a scar on his face and a glint in his eye. The scar made the big man's expression hard to read: Mordechai couldn't tell if that was a friendly grin or a nasty one. The German had on a private's tunic, but if he was a private, Anielewicz was a priest.

Jäger said, "Good day," and offered his hand. Mordechai took it: Jäger had always dealt fairly with him. The German panzer colonel said, "Anielewicz, here is Colonel Otto Skorzeny, who's given the Lizards more trouble than any ten men you could name."

Mordechai kicked himself for not recognizing Skorzeny. The German propaganda machine had pumped out plenty of material about him. If he'd done a quarter of what Gobbels claimed, he was indeed a hero on the hoof. Now he stuck out his hand and boomed, "Good to meet you, Anielewicz. From what Jäger says, you two are old friends."

"We know each other, yes, *Standartenführer*." Mordechai shook hands, but deliberately used Skorzeny's SS rank rather than the *Wehrmacht* equivalent Jäger had given. *I know what you are.*

So what? Skorzeny's eyes answered insolently. He said, "Isn't that sweet? How do you feel about giving the Lizards a boot in the balls they haven't got?"

"Them or you, it doesn't much matter to me." Anielewicz kept his voice light, casual. Skorzeny impressed him more than he'd expected. The man didn't seem to give a damn whether he lived or died. Mordechai had seen that before, but never coupled with so much relentless energy. If Skorzeny died, he'd make sure he had a lot of choice company.

He studied Anielewicz, too, doing his best to intimidate him with his presence. Mordechai stared back. If the SS man wanted to try something, he'd be sorry. He didn't try. He laughed instead. "All right, Jew, let's do business. I've got a little toy for the Lizards, and I could use some help getting it right into the middle of Lodz where it'll do the most good."

"Sounds interesting," Mordechai said. "So what is this toy? Tell me about it."

Skorzeny set a finger by the side of his nose and winked. "It's the biggest goddamn ginger bomb you ever did see, that's what. Not just the powdered stuff, mind you, but an aerosol that'll get all over everything in a huge area and keep the Lizards too drugged up to get into it for a long time." He leaned forward a little and lowered his voice. "We've tested it on Lizard prisoners, and it's the straight goods. It'll drive 'em out of their skulls."

"I bet it will," Anielewicz answered. *Sure it will, if he's telling the truth. Is he? If you were a mouse, would you let a cat carry cheese down into your hole?* But if Skorzeny was lying, he didn't show it at all. And if, by some odd chance, he was telling the truth, the ginger bomb would wreak all the havoc he said it would. Mordechai could easily imagine the Lizards battling one another in the streets because they were too full of ginger to think straight, or even to do much thinking at all.

He wanted to believe Skorzeny. Without Jäger's obscure warning, he thought he would have believed Skorzeny. Something about the SS man made you want to go in the direction he was pushing. Anielewicz had enough of that gift himself to recognize it in others—and Skorzeny had a big dose.

Anielewicz decided to prod a little, to see what lay behind the bluff, hearty façade. "Why the devil should I trust you?" he demanded. "When has the SS ever meant anything but trouble for Jews?"

"The SS means trouble for all enemies of the *Reich*." Pride rang in Skorzeny's voice. In his own way, he was—or seemed—honest. Anielewicz didn't know whether he preferred that or the hypocrisy he'd been expecting. Skorzeny went on, "Who now is the most dangerous enemy of the *Reich*? You kikes?" He shook his head. "Of course not. The Lizards are the most dangerous. We worry about them first and the rest of the shit later."

Before the Lizards came, the Soviet Union had been the most dangerous enemy of the *Reich*. That hadn't stopped the Nazis from building extermination camps in Poland, diverting resources they could have used to fight the Bolsheviks. Anielewicz said, "All right, suppose you drive the Lizards away from Lodz and Warsaw. What happens to us Jews then?"

Skorzeny spread his big hands and shrugged. "I don't make policy. I just kill people." Amazing that his grin could be disarming after he said something like that, but it was. "You don't want to be around us, though, and we don't want you around, so maybe we could ship you somewhere. Who knows? To Madagascar, maybe; they were talking about that before the Lizards came, but we didn't exactly own the seas." Now that twisted grin was wry. "Or maybe even to Palestine. Like I say, who the hell knows?"

He was glib. He was convincing. He was all the more frightening on account of that. "Why use this thing in Lodz?" Mordechai asked. "Why not at the front?"

"Two reasons," Skorzeny answered. "First, you get a lot more enemies in one place at concentration areas in the rear. And second, a lot of Lizards at the front have some protection against gas warfare, and that keeps the ginger out, too." He chuckled. "Ginger is gas warfare—happy gas, but gas."

Anielewicz turned to Heinrich Jäger. "What do you think of this? Will it work? If it was up to you, would you do it?"

Jäger's face didn't show much, but Jäger's face, from what Mordechai had seen, seldom showed much. He half regretted his words; he was putting on the spot the nearest thing he had to a friend and ally in the *Wehrmacht*. Jäger coughed, then said, "I've been on more missions with Colonel Skorzeny than I care to remember." Skorzeny laughed out loud at that. Ignoring him, Jäger went on, "I've never seen him fail when he sets himself a goal. If he says this will do the job, you'd better listen to him."

"Oh, I'm listening," Anielewicz said. He gave his attention back to Otto Skorzeny. "Well, *Herr Standartenführer*, what will you do if I tell you we don't want anything to do with this? Will you try to get it into Lodz anyhow?"

"*Aber natürlich*." Skorzeny's Austrian accent made him sound like an aristocrat from *fin de siècle* Vienna rather than a Nazi thug. "We don't give up easily. We'll do this with you or without you. It would be easier with you, maybe, and you Jews can put yourselves in our good graces by going along. Since we're going to win the war and rule Poland, doesn't that strike you as a good idea?"

Come on. Collaborate with us. Skorzeny wasn't subtle. Mordechai wondered if he had it in him to be subtle. He sighed. "Since you put it that way—"

Skorzeny slapped him on the back, hard enough to make him stagger. "Ha! I knew you were a smart Jew. I—"

Noise from the woods made him break off. Anielewicz quickly figured out what it was. "So you brought some friends along to the meeting, too? They must have bumped up against mine."

"I said you were a smart Jew, didn't I?" Skorzeny answered. "How soon can we get this moving? I don't like waiting around with my thumb up my arse."

"Let me get back to Lodz and make the arrangements to bring in your little package," Mordechai said. "I know how to get in touch with Colonel Jäger here, and he probably knows how to get in touch with you."

"Yes, probably." Jäger's voice was dry.

"Good enough," Skorzeny said. "Just don't take too damn long, that's all I have to tell you. Remember, with you or without you, this is going to happen. Those Lizards will be sorry about the day they crawled out of their eggs."

"You'll hear from me soon," Mordechai promised. He didn't want Skorzeny doing whatever he had in mind all by himself. The SS man was altogether too likely to succeed at it, whatever it was. It might make the Lizards sorry, but Anielewicz wouldn't have bet the Jews would care for it, either.

He whistled loudly, a cue for his men to head toward Lodz, then nodded to Jäger and Skorzeny and left the clearing. He was very thoughtful all the way back down there.

"How far do we trust the Germans?" he asked back at the fire station on Lutomierska Street. "How far *can* we trust the Germans, especially when one of them has told us not to?"

"Timeo Danaos et donas ferentes," Bertha Fleishman said. Mordechai nodded; he'd had a secular education, with Latin a good part of it. For those who didn't know their Virgil, Bertha translated: "I fear the Greeks, even bearing gifts."

"That's it exactly," Solomon Gruver said. The fireman was a battered, blunt-faced fellow who looked like a prizefighter and had been a sergeant in the Polish Army in 1939. He'd managed to conceal that from the Nazis, who probably would have liquidated him for it. It made him enormously useful to the Jewish underground: unlike most of its members, he hadn't had to learn matters military from scratch. He tugged at his bushy, gray-streaked beard. "Sometimes I think Nussboym had the right idea after all: better to live under the Lizards than with these Nazi *mamzrim* cracking the whip."

"Either way, we get the short end of the stick," Mordechai said. Heads bobbed up and down along the length of the table. "With the Nazis, it's just us who get the short end, but it's bloody short. With the Lizards, everybody gets it, but maybe not so bad as the Germans give it to us." He chuckled ruefully. "Some bargain, isn't it?"

"So what do we do?" Gruver demanded. This wasn't a military matter, or not strictly so. He let others lead—sometimes made others lead—in policy decisions, then weighed in with his own opinion, but was oddly shy about taking the lead himself.

Everybody looked at Anielewicz. Partly that was because he'd met the Germans, partly because people were used to looking at him. He said, "I don't think we have any choice but to take the thing from Skorzeny. That way, we have some control over it, no matter what it ends up being."

"The Trojan Horse," Bertha Fleishman suggested.

Mordechai nodded. "That's right. That's just what it's liable to be. But Skorzeny said he'd do it with us or without us. I believe him. We'd be making a big mistake if we ever took that man less than seriously. We'll take it now, we'll do our best to find out what it is, and go from there. Otherwise, he'd find some other way to sneak it into Lodz without our knowing—"

"You really think he could do that?" Gruver asked.

"I have talked with this man. I would not put anything past

him," Mordechai answered. "The only way we have a chance of getting away with this is pretending we're a pack of *schlemiels* who believe everything he says. Maybe then he'll trust us to do his dirty work for him and not look inside the Trojan Horse."

"And if it is the world's biggest ginger bomb, as he says?" somebody asked.

"Then we have a lot of Lizards getting into a king-sized brawl, right in the middle of Lodz," Mordechai said. "*Alevai omayn*, that's all we have."

"T-T-T-oma," the Tosevite hatchling said triumphantly, and looked right at Ttomalss. Its mobile face twisted into an expression that indicated pleasure.

"Yes, I am Ttomalss," the psychologist agreed. The hatchling had no control over its excretions, but it was learning to talk. The Big Uglies were a peculiar species indeed, as far as Ttomalss was concerned.

"T-T-T-oma," the hatchling repeated, and added an emphatic cough for good measure. Ttomalss wondered whether it really was putting stress on his name or just reproducing another word-like sound it knew.

"Yes, I am Ttomalss," he said again. If Big Uglies acquired language in a way at all similar to that which hatchlings of the Race used, hearing things over and over would help it learn. It was already showing itself to be a good deal more precocious than hatchlings of the Race as far as talking went: however it learned words, it learned them rapidly. But its coordination, or rather lack of same, set it apart from hatchlings still wet with the juices of their eggs.

He started to repeat his name once more, but the communicator squawked for attention. He went over to it and saw Ppevel staring out of the screen. "Superior sir," he said as he turned on the video so Ppevel could see him in turn. "How may I serve you, superior sir?"

The assistant administrator for the eastern section of the main continental mass wasted no time with polite small talk. He said, "Prepare the hatchling that came from the body of the Tosevite called Liu Han for immediate return to the surface of Tosev 3."

Ttomalss had known for some time that that blow might come. He still could not prevent a hiss of pain. "Superior sir, I must appeal," he said. "The hatchling is at the point of beginning to acquire language. To abandon the project involving it would be to cast aside knowledge that can be obtained in no other way, violating principles of scientific investigation the Race has traditionally employed regardless of circumstances." He knew no stronger argument than that.

"Tradition and Tosev 3 increasingly prove immiscible," Ppevel replied. "I repeat: prepare the hatchling for immediate return to Tosev 3."

"Superior sir, it shall be done," Ttomalss said miserably. Obedience was a principle the Race had traditionally followed, too. Even so, he went on, "I do protest your decision, and request"—he couldn't demand, not when Ppevel outranked him—"that you tell me why you made it."

"I will give you my reasons—or rather, my reason," the assistant administrator answered. "It is very simple: the People's Liberation Army is making life in China unbearable for the Race. Their most recent outrage, which took place just the other day, involved the detonation of several large-caliber artillery shells, and produced losses larger than we can afford to absorb. The males of the People's Liberation Army—and the one angry female whose hatchling you now have—have pledged to diminish such activities in exchange for the return of this hatchling. The bargain strikes me as being worth making."

"The female Liu Han is still high in the councils of this bandit grouping?" Ttomalss said glumly. He had been so certain his plan to disgrace the female would succeed. It had fit perfectly with what he thought he knew of Big Ugly psychology.

But Ppevel said, "Yes, she is, and still insistent on the return of the hatchling. It has become a political liability to us. Returning it to the Tosevite female Liu Han may transform that liability into a propaganda victory, and will have the effect of reducing military pressure on our forces in Peking. Therefore, for the third time, ready the hatchling for immediate return to Tosev 3."

"It shall be done," Ttomalss said sadly. Ppevel didn't hear that: he'd already broken the connection, no doubt so he wouldn't have to listen to any further objections from Ttomalss. That was rude. Ttomalss, unfortunately for him, was in no position to do anything about it except resent it.

He had to assume that when Ppevel said *immediate*, he meant it. He made sure the Tosevite hatchling had dry wrappings for its excretory orifices, and made sure those wrappings were snug around the hatchling's legs and midsection. The trip down would be in free fall; the last thing he wanted was bodily waste floating around in the shuttlecraft. The pilot wouldn't be delighted if that happened, either.

He wished he could do something about the hatchling's mouth. Big Uglies in free fall had been known to suffer reverse peristalsis, as if they were expelling poisonous material they had swallowed. The Race did not suffer similar symptoms. Ttomalss packed several clean waste cloths, just in case he'd need them.

While he worked, the hatchling cheerfully babbled on. The sounds it made these days were as close to the ones the Race used as it could come with its somewhat different vocal apparatus. Ttomalss let out another hissing sigh. He would have to start over with a new hatchling, and it would be years before he could learn all he wanted about Tosevite language acquisition.

Tessrek stopped in the doorway. He didn't undo the gate Ttomalss had rigged to keep the hatchling from wandering the corridor, but jeered over it: "You'll finally be getting rid of that horrible thing, I hear. I won't be sorry to see—and scent—the last of it, let me tell you."

Ppevel wouldn't have called Tessrek directly. He might well have called the male who supervised both Tessrek and Ttomalss, though, to make sure his orders were obeyed. That would have been all he needed to get rumors flying. Ttomalss said, "Go tend to your own research, and may it be treated as cavalierly as mine has."

Tessrek let his mouth fall open in a derisive laugh. "My research, unlike yours, is productive, so I have no fear of its being curtailed." He did leave then, and just as well, or Ttomalss might have thrown something at him.

Only a little later, a male in the red and silver body paint of a shuttlecraft pilot gave the gateway a dubious look with one eye turret. He speared Ttomalss with the other, saying, "Is the Big Ugly ready to travel, Researcher?" His tone warned, *It had better be*.

"It is," Ttomalss said grudgingly. He examined the other male's body paint again and added, even more grudgingly, "Superior sir."

"Good," the shuttlecraft pilot said. "I am Heddosh, by the way." He gave Ttomalss his name as if convinced the researcher should already have known it.

Ttomalss scooped up the Tosevite hatchling. That wasn't as easy as it had been when the creature was newly emerged from the body of the female Liu Han: it was much bigger now, and weighed much more. Ttomalss had to put down the bag of supplies he had with him so he could open the gate, at which point the hatchling nearly wriggled out of his arms. Heddosh emitted a derisive snort. Ttomalss glared at him. He had no idea of the difficulties involved in keeping this hatchling of another species alive and healthy.

Being taken to the shuttlecraft fascinated the hatchling. Several times on the journey, it saw something new and said, "This?"— sometimes with the interrogative cough, sometimes without.

"It speaks!" Heddosh said in surprise.

"Yes, it does," Ttomalss answered coldly. "It would learn to speak more if I were allowed to continue my experiment, too." Now the hatchling would have to acquire the horrible sounds of Chinese rather than the Race's elegant, precise, and (to Ttomalss) beautiful language.

The clanging noises the shuttlecraft airlock doors made frightened the hatchling, which clung tightly to Ttomalss. He soothed it as best he could, all the while trying to look on the bright side of things. The only bright side he found was that, until he could obtain another newly emerged Big Ugly hatchling, he would get enough sleep for a while.

More clangings signaled the shuttlecraft's freeing itself from the starship to which it had been attached. With centrifugal force no longer giving a simulacrum of gravity, the shuttlecraft went into free fall. To Ttomalss' relief, the hatchling showed no perceptible distress. It seemed to find the sensation interesting, perhaps even pleasant. Data showed that the female Liu Han had had the same reaction. Ttomalss wondered if it was hereditary.

There was a long-term research project, he thought. Maybe someone could start it after the conquest was safe and secure. He wondered if the day would ever come when the conquest was safe and secure. He'd never imagined the Race making concessions to the Tosevites in negotiations, as Ppevel was in yielding the hatchling to them. Once you started making concessions, where would you stop? That was a chilling thought, when you got down to it.

The shuttlecraft's rocket engine began to roar. Acceleration shoved Ttomalss back into his couch, and the hatchling against him. It squalled in fright. He comforted it again, even though its weight pressing on him made him far from comfortable. The hatchling had calmed before acceleration ended, and squealed with delight when free fall returned.

Ttomalss wondered if the Big Ugly female Liu Han could have done as well with the hatchling, even if she'd kept it since it emerged from her body. He had his doubts.

* * *

When Otto Skorzeny came back to the panzer encampment, he was grinning from ear to ear. "Brush the canary feathers off your chin," Heinrich Jäger told him.

The SS man actually did make brushing motions at his face. In spite of everything, Jäger laughed. Whatever else you could say about him, Skorzeny had style. The trouble was, there was so much else to say. "Off it went," Skorzeny boomed. "The Jews ate the story up like gumdrops, poor damned fools. They brought up their own wagon to carry the present, and they promised they'd sneak it past the Lizards. I figure they can do that, probably better than I could. And once they do—"

Jäger tipped back his head and slid his index finger across his throat. Chuckling, Skorzeny nodded. "When is the timer set for?" Jäger asked.

"Day after tomorrow," Skorzeny answered. "That'll give 'em plenty of time to get the bomb back to Lodz. Poor stupid bastards." He shook his head, perhaps even in genuine sympathy. "I wonder if anybody's ever done such a good job of committing suicide before."

"Masada," Jäger said, dredging the name up from the long-vanished days before the First World War, when he'd wanted to be a Biblical archaeologist. He saw it meant nothing to Skorzeny, and explained: "The whole garrison killed one another off instead of surrendering to the Romans."

"There'll be more of 'em done in now," the SS man said. "A lot more."

"*Ja,*" Jäger answered absently. He still couldn't tell whether Skorzeny hated Jews on his own hook or because he'd got orders to hate them. In the end, what did it matter? He'd go after them with the same genial ferocity either way.

Had the message got through to Anielewicz? Jäger had been wondering about that ever since the meeting he, Skorzeny, and the Jewish fighting leader had had in the forest. Anielewicz hadn't tipped his hand then. Had he got the message and then not believed it? Had he got it, believed it, and then been unable to convince his fellow Jews it was true?

No way to be sure, not from here. Jäger shook his head. He'd have a way to tell, soon enough. If the Jews in Lodz were snuffed out like so many candles day after tomorrow, he could figure somebody down there had decided he was lying.

Skorzeny had an animal alertness to him. "What's up?" he asked, seeing Jäger's head go back and forth.

"Nothing, really." The panzer colonel hoped his voice sounded casual. "Thinking about the surprise they'll have in Lodz—for a little while, anyhow."

"For a little while is right," Skorzeny said. "Stupid sheep. You'd think they'd know better than to trust a German, but no, they walked right into it." He bleated sardonically. "And the lambs' blood will go up on the doorposts of all the houses." Jäger stared; he hadn't imagined Skorzeny as a man who knew his Scripture. The SS *Standartenführer* chuckled again. "The *Führer* will have his revenge on the Jews, and who knows? We may even kill a few Lizards, too."

"We'd better," Jäger answered. "You go and rip the heart out of the human sector of Lodz and there's nothing to keep the scaly sons of bitches from staging out of it any more. They could hit the bases of our penetrations north and south of the city and cut us right off. That's too steep a price for the *Führer*'s revenge, you ask me."

"Nobody asked you, and the *Führer* doesn't think so," Skorzeny said. "He told me as much himself—he wants those Jews dead."

"How am I supposed to argue with that?" Jäger said. The answer was simple: he couldn't. So he'd set himself up to circumvent a personal order from the *Führer*, had he? Well, if anyone ever found out what he'd done, he was a dead man anyhow. They couldn't kill him any deader. *No, but they can take longer getting you dead,* he thought uneasily.

He threw himself flat on the ground almost before he consciously heard the shells whistling in from out of the east. Skorzeny sprawled there beside him, hands up to cover the back of his neck. Somewhere not far away, a wounded man was screaming. The bombardment went on for about fifteen minutes, then let up.

Jäger scrambled to his feet. "We've got to move camp now," he shouted. "They know where we are. We were lucky that time—far as I could tell, that was all ordinary ammunition coming, none of their special delights that spit mines all over the place so people and panzers don't dare go anywhere. They're short of those little beauties, by all the signs, but they will use 'em if they think they can make a profit. We won't let 'em."

He'd hardly finished speaking before the first panzer engines rumbled into life. He was proud of his men. Most of them were veterans who'd been through everything the Russians and the British and the Lizards could throw at them. They understood what needed doing and took care of it with a minimum of fuss and bother. Skorzeny was a genius raider, but he couldn't run a regiment like this. Jäger had his own talents, and they were not to be sneezed at.

While the regiment was shifting its base, he didn't have to think about the horror waiting to happen in Lodz, growing closer with every tick of a timer. Skorzeny was right: the Jews were fools to trust any German. Now the question was, which German had they been fools enough to trust?

The next day, he was too busy to worry about it. A Lizard counterattack drove the German forces west six or eight kilometers. Panzers in the regiment went from machinery to burnt and twisted scrap metal, a couple from the fire of Lizard panzer cannon, the rest because of the antipanzer rockets the Lizard infantry carried. The only Lizard panzer killed was taken out by a *Wehrmacht* private in a tree who dropped a Molotov cocktail down into the turret through the open cupola when the panzer clattered by below him. That happened toward sunset, and seemed to halt the Lizards' push all by itself. They didn't like losing panzers these days.

"We have to do better," he told his men as they ate black bread and sausage that night. "We got flank targets, but we weren't hitting them. Can't make many mistakes like that, not unless we want to get buried here."

"But, *Herr Oberst*," somebody said, "when they move, they can move so damned fast, they're by us before we have a chance to react."

"Good thing we had defense in depth, or they would have cracked us wide open," somebody else said. Jäger nodded, pleased at the way the troops were hashing things out for themselves. That was how German soldiers were supposed to operate. They weren't just ignorant peasants who followed orders without thinking about them, as Red Army men did. They had brains and imaginations, and used them.

He was about to curl up in his bedroll under his Panther when Skorzeny showed up in camp. The SS man was toting a jug of vodka he'd found God only knew where, and passed it around so everybody got a nip. It wasn't good vodka—the taste put Jäger in mind of stale kerosene—but it was better than no vodka.

"Think they're going to hit us again in the morning?" Skorzeny asked.

"Won't know for certain till then," Jäger answered, "but if I had to guess, I'd say no. They'd have kept pressing harder after it got dark if that was what they had in mind. These days, they push when they think they've found a weakness, but they ease up when we show strength."

"They can't afford the kind of losses they get when they go up against a strongpoint," Skorzeny said shrewdly.

"I think you're right." Jäger glanced over at the SS man in the darkness. "We could have used that nerve gas here at the front."

"Ahh, you'd say that even if things were quiet," Skorzeny retorted. "It's doing what it's supposed to be doing, right where it is." He grunted. "I want your wireless people to be alert for any intercepts they pick up about that, too. If the Lizards don't burn up the airwaves, I'll eat my hat."

"That's fine." Jäger yawned enormously. "Right now, I'm alert for sleep. You want to crawl in under here? Safest place you can be if they start shelling again. I know damn well you snore, but I suppose I can live with it."

Skorzeny laughed. Gunther Grillparzer said, "He's not the only one who snores—sir." Betrayed by his own gunner, Jäger settled in for the night.

Spatters of small-arms fire woke him a couple of times. They picked up at dawn, but, as he'd predicted, the Lizards were more interested in consolidating what they'd gained the day before than in pushing on against stiffening resistance.

Otto Skorzeny hadn't been kidding when he said he wanted the wireless men to stay alert. He made sure they did, hanging around them and regaling them with what seemed like an endless stream of dirty stories. Most of them were good dirty stories, too, and some were even new to Jäger, who'd thought he'd heard every story of that sort ever invented.

As morning gave way to afternoon, Skorzeny's temper began to wear thin. He paced through the camp, kicking up dirt and sending spring flowers flying. "Damn it, we should have intercepted something from the Jews or the Lizards in Lodz by now!" he stormed.

"Maybe they're all dead," Jäger suggested. The notion horrified him, but might ease Skorzeny's mind.

But the big SS man shook his head. "Too much to hope for. Somebody always lives through these things by one kind of fool luck or another." Jäger thought of Max, the foulmouthed Jew who'd lived through Babi Yar. Skorzeny was right. He went on with a muttered, "No, something's gone south somewhere."

"You think the timer didn't work the way it should have?" Jäger asked.

"I suppose it is possible," Skorzeny allowed, "but fry me for a *schnitzel* if I ever heard of one of them failing before. They aren't just foolproof, they're idiotproof, and the gadget had a backup. We send out a goody like that, we want to make sure it works as advertised." He chuckled. "That's what people who don't like us so well call German efficiency, eh? No, the only way that bomb could have failed would have been—"

"What?" Jäger said, though he had an idea as to what. "As you say, if it had a backup timer, it was going to go off."

"The only way that bomb could have failed—" Skorzeny repeated musingly. His gray eyes went very wide. "The only way that bomb could have failed would have been for that stinking little kike to pull the wool over my eyes, and dip me in shit if he didn't do it!" He clapped a hand to his forehead. "The bastard! The fucker! The nerve of him! Next time I see him, I'll cut off his balls one at a time." Then, to Jäger's amazement, he started to laugh. "He played me for a sucker. I didn't think any man alive could do that. I'd like to shake his hand—*after* he's castrated, not before. You think *stupid kike* and you take it for granted, and this is what it gets you. Jesus Christ!"

Also a Jew, Jäger thought, but he didn't say it. Instead, he asked, "What now? If the Jews in Lodz know what it is"—*and if they do, or guess, it's thanks to me, and how do I feel about that?*—"they've got their hands on something they can use against us."

"Don't I know it." Skorzeny sounded disgusted, maybe with the Jews, maybe with himself. He wasn't used to failing. Then he brightened. For a moment, he looked like his old, devilish self. "Maybe we can plaster the place with rockets and long-range artillery, hope to blow up the damned thing that way, at least deny the Jews the use of it." He made an unhappy clucking noise. "It's bloody long odds, though."

"Too true," Jäger said, as if sympathetically. "Those rockets pack a decent punch, but you can't tell for sure whether they'll hit the right town, let alone the right street."

"I wish we had some of the toys the Lizards know how to make," Skorzeny said, still discontented with the world. "They don't just hit the right street. They'll pick a room for you. Hell, they'll fly into a closet if that's what you want." He scratched at his chin. "Well, one way or another, those Jews are going to pay. And when they do, I'll be the one who collects." He sounded very sure of himself.

*   *   *

Off in the next room at the Army and Navy General Hospital in Hot Springs, there were so many car batteries that they'd had to reinforce the floor to take the weight. Among the Lizard gadgets they powered was the radio set taken from the shuttlecraft that had brought Straha down to Earth when he defected to the United States.

Now he and Sam Yeager sat in front of that radio, flipping from one frequency to another in an effort to monitor the Lizards' signals and find out what the Race was up to. Right now, they weren't picking up much anywhere. Straha had the leisure to turn to Yeager and ask, "How many of our males do you have engaged in the practice of espionage and signal gathering?"

"Numbers? Who knows?" Sam answered. If he had known, he wouldn't have told Straha. One of the things he'd had drilled into him was that you didn't tell anybody, human or Lizard, anything he didn't have to know. "But a lot of them, a lot of the time. Not many of us Big Uglies"—he used the Lizards' nickname for mankind unselfconsciously—"speak your language well enough to follow without help from one of you."

"You, Sam Yeager, I think you could succeed at this," Straha said, which made Sam feel damn good. He thought he could have gained even more fluency in the Lizards' language if he hadn't also had to spend time with Robert Goddard. On the other hand, he would have learned more about rockets if he hadn't had to spend time with Straha and the other Lizard POWs.

And he would have learned more about his baby son if he hadn't been in the Army. That would have kept Barbara happier, too; he worried about not seeing her enough. There weren't enough hours in a day, in a year, in a lifetime, to do all the things he wanted to do. That was true all the time, but trying to keep up during a war rubbed your nose in it.

Straha touched the frequency-advance toggle. The Lizard numbers in the display showed that the radio was now monitoring a frequency a tenth of a megacycle higher (or rather, something that worked out to be about an eighth of a megacycle—the Lizards naturally used their own units rather than those of mankind). A male's voice came out of the speaker.

Yeager leaned forward and listened intently. The Lizard was apparently in a rear area, and complaining about rockets falling nearby and disrupting resupply efforts for the troops pushing toward Denver. "That's good news," Sam said, scribbling notes.

"Truth," Straha agreed. "Your ventures into uncharted technology are paying a handsome profit for your species. If the Race were so innovative, Tosev 3 would long since have been con-quered—provided the Race had not blown itself to radioactive dust in innovative frenzy."

"You think that's what we would have done if you hadn't invaded?" Sam asked.

"It is certainly one of the higher probabilities," Straha said, and Yeager was hard-pressed to disagree with him. The ex-shiplord flipped to a new frequency. The Lizard talking now sounded angry as all get-out. "He is ordering the dismissal, demotion, and transfer of a local commander in a region called Illinois," Straha said. Yeager nodded. The Lizard went on, "Where is this Illinois place?"

Sam showed him on a map. He was listening, too. "Something about letting a pack of prisoners escape or get rescued or some-thing. The fellow who's cursing him is really doing quite a job, isn't he?"

"If said snout-to-snout, telling a male that someone shit in his egg before it hatched is guaranteed to start a fight," Straha said.

"I believe it." Sam listened to the radio some more. "They're moving that incompetent officer to—upstate New York." He wrote it down. "That's worth knowing. With luck, we'll be able to take advantage of his weaknesses over there, too."

"Truth," Straha said again, this time in bemused tones. "You Big Uglies aggressively exploit the intelligence you gather, and you gather great quantities of it. Do you do this in your own con-flicts as well?"

"Don't know," Yeager answered. "I've never been in a war before, and I'm only a little fellow in this one." He thought back to his ballplaying days, and to all the signs he and his teammates had stolen. Mutt Daniels was a genius at that kind of thing. He wondered how—and if—Mutt was doing these days.

Straha shifted to yet another frequency. An excited-sounding Lizard was relaying a long, involved message. "Ah, that is most interesting," Straha said when he was done.

"I didn't follow all of it," Sam confessed, embarrassed at having to say that after Straha had praised his grasp of the Lizards' tongue. "Something about ginger and calculator fraud, whatever that is."

"Not calculator fraud—computer fraud," Straha said. "I do not blame you for not understanding completely. You Big Uglies, while technically far more advanced than you have any business being, as yet have no real grasp of the potential of computing machines."

"Maybe not," Yeager said. "Sounds like we don't have any grasp of how to commit crimes with them, either."

Straha's mouth dropped open in amusement. "Committing the crime is easy. Males in the payroll section diverted payments to ginger purveyors into accounts of which only they and the purveyors—and, of course, the computers—were aware. Since no one else knew these accounts existed, no one not party to the secret could access them. The computers would not announce their presence; it was, in essence, a perfect scheme."

"We have a saying that there's no such thing as a perfect crime," Yeager remarked. "What went wrong with this one?"

Straha laughed again. "Nothing is accident-proof. A male in the accounting section who was not part of the miscreants' scheme was investigating a legitimate account. But he made a mistake in entering the number of that account and found himself looking at one of the concealed ones. He recognized it at once for what it was and notified his superiors, who began a larger investigation. Many males will find themselves in difficulties because of it."

"Hope you won't be angry if I tell you that doesn't make me too unhappy," Sam said. "Who would have thought the Race would turn out to have drug fiends? Makes you seem almost human—no offense."

"I shall endeavor to take none," Straha replied with dignity.

Yeager kept his face straight; Straha was getting pretty good at interpreting human expressions, and he didn't want the Lizard to see how funny he thought that was. He said, "I wonder if we have any way to use the news, maybe make some of your people think males who aren't ginger tasters really are. Something like that, anyhow."

"You have an evilly twisted mind, Sam Yeager," Straha said.

"Thank you," Sam answered, which made Straha first jerk both eye turrets toward him and then start to laugh as he understood it was a joke. Yeager went on, "You might talk with some of our propaganda people, maybe ask if they want you to broadcast about it. Who knows what kind of trouble you might stir up?"

"Who indeed?" Straha said. "I shall do that." It wasn't quite *It shall be done*, the Lizards' equivalent for *Yes, sir*, but it was more deference than Sam had ever got from Straha before. Little by little, he was earning respect.

When his shift was done, he started to go upstairs to see Barbara and Jonathan, but ran into Ristin and Ullhass in the hospital lobby. Those two Lizard POWs were old buddies; he'd captured them back in the summer of 1942, when the Lizard invasion was new and looked irresistible. By now, they seemed well on the way to becoming Americans, and wore their official U.S. prisoner-of-war red-white-and-blue body paint with considerable pride. They'd also picked up pretty good English over the last couple of years.

"Hey, Sam," Ristin said in that language. "Baseball this afternoon?"

"Yes," Ullhass echoed. "Baseball!" He added an emphatic cough.

"Maybe later—not now," Sam said, to which both Lizards responded with steam-whistle noises of disappointment. With their fast, skittery movements, they made surprisingly good middle infielders, and had taken to the game well. Their small size and forward-sloping posture gave them a strike zone about the size of a postage stamp, too, so they were good leadoff men— well, leadoff males—even if they seldom hit the ball hard.

"Good weather for a game," Ristin said, doing his best to tempt Sam. A lot of soldiers played ball when they were off duty, but Ristin and Ullhass were the only Lizards who joined in. With Yeager's endless years of bush-league experience, everybody was glad to see him out there, and people had put up with his Lizard pals for his sake. Now Ullhass and Ristin were starting to get noticed for the way they played, not for their scaly hides.

"Maybe later," Sam repeated. "Now I want to see my wife and son, if you don't mind too much." The Lizards sighed in resignation. They knew families mattered to Tosevites, but it didn't feel real to them, any more than Yeager understood in his gut how much their precious Emperor meant to them. He headed for the stairs. Ristin and Ullhass started practicing phantom double plays. Ristin, who mostly played second, had a hell of a fast pivot.

Up on the fourth floor, Jonathan was telling the world in no uncertain terms that he didn't care for something or other it had done to him. Listening to him yowl, Sam was glad the Lizards who lived up there weren't around to hear the racket. It sometimes drove him a little squirrely, and he was a human being.

The crying stopped, very suddenly. Sam knew what that meant: Barbara had given the baby her breast. Sam smiled as he opened the door to their room. He was fond of his wife's breasts, too, and figured the kid took after his old man.

Barbara looked up from the chair in which she was nursing Jonathan. She didn't seem as badly beat up as she had just after he was born, but she wasn't what you'd call perky, either. "Hello, honey," she said. "Shut the door quietly, would you? He may fall asleep. He's certainly been fussing as if he was tired."

Sam noted the precise grammar there, as he often did when his wife talked. He sometimes envied her fancy education; he'd left high school to play ball, though an insatiable curiosity had kept him reading this and finding out little fragmented pieces of that ever since. Barbara never complained about his lack of formal schooling, but it bothered him anyhow.

Sure enough, Jonathan did go to sleep. The kid was growing; he took up more room in the cradle now than he had when he was first born. As soon as Sam saw he would stay down after Barbara put him in there, he touched her on the arm and said, "I got a present for you, hon. Well, really it's a present for both of us, but you can go first with it. I've been saving it all morning long, so I figure I can last a little longer."

The buildup intrigued her. "What *do* you have?" she breathed.

"It's not anything fancy," he warned. "Not a diamond, not a convertible." They both laughed, not quite comfortably. It would be a long time, if ever, before you could start thinking about driving a convertible. He dug in his pocket and pulled out a new corncob pipe and a leather pouch of tobacco, then handed them to her with a flourish. "Here you go."

She stared as if she couldn't believe her eyes. "Where did you get them?"

"This colored guy came around early this morning, selling 'em," Sam answered. "He's from up in the northern part of the state, where they grow some tobacco. Cost me fifty bucks, but what the heck? I don't have a whole lot of things to spend money on, so why not?"

"It's all right with me. It's better than all right with me, as a matter of fact." Barbara stuck the empty pipe in her mouth. "I never smoked one of these before. I probably look like a Southern granny."

"Babe, you always look good to me," Yeager said. Barbara's expression softened. Keeping your wife happy was definitely worth doing—especially when you meant every word you said. He tapped at the tobacco pouch with his index finger. "You want me to load the pipe for you?"

"Would you, please?" she said, so he did. He had a Zippo, fueled now not by lighter fluid but by moonshine. He had no idea how he'd keep it going when he ran out of flints, but that hadn't happened yet. He flicked the wheel with his thumb. A pale, almost invisible alcohol flame sprang into being. He held it over the bowl of the pipe.

Barbara's cheeks hollowed as she inhaled. "Careful," Sam

warned. "Pipe tobacco's a lot stronger than what you get in cigarettes, and—" Her eyes crossed. She coughed like somebody in the last throes of consumption. "—you haven't smoked much of anything lately," he finished unnecessarily.

"No kidding." Her voice was a raspy wheeze. "Remember that bit in *Tom Sawyer*? 'First Pipes—"I've Lost My Knife,"' something like that. I know just how Tom felt. That stuff is *strong*."

"Let me try," Sam said, and took the pipe from her. He drew on it cautiously. He knew about pipe tobacco, and knew what any tobacco could do to you when you hadn't smoked for a while. Even taking all that into account, Barbara was right: what smoldered in that pipe was strong as the devil. It might have been cured and mellowed for fifteen, maybe even twenty minutes—smoking it felt like scraping coarse sandpaper over his tongue and the inside of his mouth. Spit flooded from every salivary gland he owned, including a few he hadn't known were there. He felt dizzy, almost woozy for a second—and he knew enough not to draw much smoke down into his lungs. He coughed a couple of times himself. "Wowie!"

"Here, give it back to me," Barbara said. She made another, much more circumspect, try, then exhaled. "God! That is to tobacco what bathtub gin was to the real stuff."

"You're too young to know about bathtub gin," he said severely. Memories of some pounding headaches came back to haunt him. He puffed on the pipe again himself. It wasn't a bad comparison.

Barbara giggled. "One of my favorite uncles was a part-time bootlegger. I had quite a high-school graduation party—from what I remember of it, anyway." She took the pipe back from Sam. "I'm going to need a while to get used to this again."

"Yeah, we'll probably be there just about when that pouch goes empty," he agreed. "God knows when that colored fellow will come through town again, if he ever does."

They smoked the bowl empty, then filled it again. The room grew thick with smoke. Sam's eyes watered. He felt loose and easy, the way he had after a cigarette in the good old days. That he also felt slightly nauseated and his mouth like raw meat was only a detail, as far as he was concerned.

"That's good," Barbara said meditatively, and punctuated her words with another set of coughs. She waved those aside. "Worth it."

"I think so, too." Sam started to laugh. "Know what we remind me of?" When Barbara shook her head, he answered his own question: "We're like a couple of Lizards with their tongues in the ginger jar."

"That's terrible!" Barbara exclaimed. Then she thought it over. "It *is* terrible, but you may be right. It is kind of like a drug—tobacco, I mean."

"You bet it is. I tried quitting a couple of times when I was playing ball—didn't like what it was doing to my wind. I couldn't do it. I'd get all nervous and twitchy and I don't know what. When you can't get any, it's not so bad: you don't have a choice. But stick tobacco in front of us every day and we'll go back to it, sure enough."

Barbara sucked on the pipe again. She made a wry face. "Ginger tastes better, that's for certain."

"Yeah, I think so, too—now," Sam said. "But if I'm smoking all the time, I won't think so for long. You know, when you get down to it, coffee tastes pretty bad, too, or we wouldn't have to fix it up with cream and sugar. But I like what coffee used to do for me when we had it."

"So did I," Barbara said wistfully. She pointed toward the cradle. "With him waking up whenever he feels like it, I could really use some coffee these days."

"We're a bunch of drug fiends, all right, no doubt about it." Yeager took the pipe from her and sucked in smoke. Now that he'd had some, it wasn't so bad. He wondered whether he ought to hope that Negro would come around with more—or for him to stay away.

The partisan leader, a fat Pole who gave his name as Ignacy, stared at Ludmila Gorbunova. "*You* are a pilot?" he said in fluent but skeptical German.

Ludmila stared back. Almost at sight, she had doubts about Ignacy. For one thing, almost the only way you could stay fat these days was by exploiting the vast majority who were thin, sometimes to the point of emaciation. For another, his name sounded so much like *Nazi* that just hearing it made her nervous.

Also in German, she answered, "Yes, I am a pilot. *You* are a guerrilla commander?"

"I'm afraid so," he said. "There hasn't been much call for piano teachers the past few years."

Ludmila stared again, this time for a different reason. *This* had been a member of the petty bourgeoisie? He'd certainly managed to shed his class trappings; from poorly shaved jowls to twin bandoliers worn crisscross on his chest to battered boots, he looked like a man who'd been a bandit all his life and sprang from a long line of bandits. She had trouble imagining him going through Chopin *études* with bored young students.

Beside her, Avram looked down at his scarred hands. Wladeslaw looked up to the top of the linden tree under which they stood. Neither of the partisans who'd accompanied her from near Lublin said anything. They'd done their job by getting her here. Now it was up to her.

"You have here an airplane?" she asked, deciding not to hold Ignacy's looks, name, or class against him. Business was business. If the Great Stalin could make a pact with the fascist Hitler, she could do her best to deal with a Schmeisser-toting piano teacher.

"We have an airplane," he agreed. Maybe he was trying to overcome distrust of her as a socialist and a Russian, for he went on with a detailed explanation: "It landed here in this area when the Lizards were booting out the Germans. We don't think anything was wrong with it except that it was out of fuel. We have fuel now, and we have a new battery which holds a charge. We have also drained the oil and the hydraulic fluid, and have replaced both."

"This all sounds good," Ludmila said. "What sort of airplane is it?" Her guess would have been an Me-109. She'd never before flown a hot fighter—or what had been a hot fighter till the Lizards came. She suspected it would be a merry life but a short one. The Lizards had hacked Messerschmitts and their opposite numbers from the Red Air Force out of the sky with hideous ease in the early days of their invasion.

But Ignacy answered, "It's a Fieseler 156." He saw that didn't mean anything to Ludmila, so he added, "They call it a *Storch*—a Stork."

The nickname didn't help. Ludmila said, "I think it would be better if you let me see the aircraft than if you talk about it."

"Yes," he said, and put his hands out in front of him, as if on an imaginary keyboard. He had been a piano teacher, sure enough. "Come with me."

The aircraft was about three kilometers from Ignacy's encampment. Those three kilometers of rough trail, like most of the landscape hereabouts, showed how heavy the local fighting had been. The ground was cratered; chunks of metal and burned-out hulks lay everywhere; and she passed a good many hastily dug graves, most marked with crosses, some with Stars of David, and some just left alone. She pointed at one of those. "Who lies under there? A Lizard?"

"Yes," Ignacy said again. "The priests, so far as I know, have not yet decided whether Lizards have souls."

Ludmila didn't know how to answer that, so she kept quiet. She didn't think she had a soul, not in the sense Ignacy meant. The things people too ignorant to grasp the truths of dialectical materialism could find over which to worry themselves!

She wondered where the alleged Fieseler 156 was hiding. They'd passed only a couple of buildings, and those had been too battered to conceal a motorcar, let alone an airplane. Ignacy led her up a small rise. He said, "We're right on top of it now." His voice showed considerable pride.

"Right on top of what?" Ludmila asked as he led her down the other side of the rise. He took her around to a third side—and then realization sank in. "*Bozhemoi!* You built a platform with the aircraft under it." That was *maskirovka* even the Soviets would have viewed with respect.

Ignacy heard the admiration in her voice. "So we did," he said. "It seemed the best way of concealing it we had available." To that she could only nod. They'd done as much work as the Red Air Force had outside Pskov, and they couldn't even fly the airplane they were hiding. The partisan leader pulled a candle out of one of the pockets of the *Wehrmacht* tunic he was wearing. "It will be dark in there with the earth and the timer and the nets blocking away the light."

She sent Ignacy a suspicious look. She'd had trouble from men when they got her alone in a dark place. She touched the butt of her Tokarev. "Don't try anything foolish," she advised him.

"If I tried nothing foolish, would I be a partisan?" he asked. Ludmila frowned but held her peace. Stooping, Ignacy held up an edge of the camouflage netting. Ludmila crawled under it. She in turn held it up so the Polish guerrilla could follow her.

The space under the camouflaged platform was too large for a single candle to do much to illuminate it. Ignacy walked over to the aircraft hidden there. Ludmila followed him. When the faint glow showed her what the aircraft was, her eyes got wide. "Oh, one of these," she breathed.

"You know it?" Ignacy asked. "You can fly it?"

"I know of it," she answered. "I don't know yet whether I can fly it. I hope I can, I will tell you so much."

The Fieseler *Storch* was a high-wing monoplane, not much bigger than one of her beloved *Kukuruzniks*, and not much faster, either. But if a *Kukuruznik* was a cart horse, a *Storch* was a trained Lipizzan. It could take off and land in next to no room at all; flying into a light breeze, it could hover in one place, almost like a Lizard helicopter. Ludmila took the candle from Ignacy and walked around the plane, fascinatedly studying the huge flaps, elevators, and ailerons that let it do its tricks.

From what she'd heard, not every *Storch* was armed, but this one carried two machine guns, one under the body, one in back of the pilot for an observer to fire. She set her foot in the mounting stirrup, opened the pilot-side door, and climbed up into the cockpit.

So much of it was glass that, although it was enclosed, she had a much better all-around view than she did in the open cabin of a *Kukuruznik*. She wondered how she'd like flying without the slipstream blasting her in the face. Then she brought the candle up to the instrument panel and studied it in amazement. So many dials, so many gauges . . . how were you supposed to do any flying if you tried to keep track of all of them at once?

Everything was finished to a much higher standard than she was used to. She'd seen that before with German equipment; the Nazis made their machines as if they were fine watches. The Soviet approach, contrariwise, was to turn out as many tanks and planes and guns as possible. If they were crude, so what? They were going to get destroyed anyhow.

"You can fly it?" Ignacy repeated as Ludmila, rather reluctantly, descended from the cabin.

"Yes, I really think I can," Ludmila answered. The candle was burning low. She and Ignacy started back out toward the netting under which they would leave. She glanced back at the *Storch*, hoping to be a rider worthy of her steed.

Soviet artillery boomed south of Moscow, flinging shells toward Lizard positions. Distantly, the reports reverberated even in the Kremlin. Listening to them, Iosef Stalin made a sour face. "The Lizards grow bolder, Vyacheslav Mikhailovich," he said.

Vyacheslav Molotov did not care for the implication behind the words. *It's your fault*, Stalin seemed to be saying. "As soon as we can produce another explosive-metal bomb, Iosef Vissarionovich, we shall remind them we deserve respect," he answered.

"Yes, but when will that be?" Stalin demanded. "These so-called scientists have been telling me lies all along. And if they don't move faster, they will regret it—and so will you."

"So will the entire Soviet Union, Comrade General Secretary," Molotov said. Stalin always thought everyone lied to him. A lot of the time, people did, simply because they were too afraid to tell him the truth. Molotov had tried to tell him that, after using the bomb made from the Lizards' explosive metal, the USSR would not be able to make any more for a long time to come. He hadn't wanted to listen. He seldom wanted to listen. Molotov went on, "It seems, however, that we shall soon have more of these weapons."

"I have heard this promise before," Stalin said. "I grow weary of it. *When* exactly will the new bombs appear in our arsenal?"

"The first by summer," Molotov answered. That made Stalin sit up and take notice, as he'd thought it would. He continued, "Work at the *kolkhoz* has made remarkable progress lately, I'm happy to report."

"Yes, Lavrenti Pavlovich tells me the same. I am glad to hear it," Stalin said, his expression hooded. "I will be gladder to hear it if it turns out to be true."

"It will," Molotov said. *It had better.* But now he began to believe that it would—and so, evidently, did Beria. Getting that American to *Kolkhoz* 118 had proved a master stroke. His presence and his ideas proved, sometimes painfully, just how far behind that of the capitalist West the Soviet nuclear research program had been. He took for granted both theory and engineering practice toward which Kurchatov, Flerov, and their colleagues were only beginning to grope. But, with his knowledge, the Soviet program was finally advancing at a decent pace.

"I am glad to hear we shall have these weapons," Stalin repeated, "glad for your sake, Vyacheslav Mikhailovich."

"I serve the Soviet Union!" Molotov said. He picked up the glass of vodka in front of him, knocked it back, and filled it again from the bottle that stood beside it. He knew what Stalin meant. If the workers and peasants of the Soviet Union did not soon have an explosive-metal bomb, they would soon have a new foreign commissar. He would get the blame for the failure, not Stalin's Georgian crony, Beria. Stalin was not allergic to scribbling the initials VMN on the case files of those marked for liquidation, any more than Molotov had been.

"When we have our second bomb, Comrade General Secretary," Molotov said, resolutely not thinking about what would happen—to the USSR and to him—if they didn't have it, "I recommend that we use it at once."

Stalin puffed on his pipe, sending up unreadable smoke signals. "With the first bomb, you advised against using it. Why now the change of mind?"

"Because when we used the first, we had no second with which to back it, and I feared that would become obvious," Molotov answered. "Now, though, by using the new bomb, we not only prove we do have it, but also give the promise of producing many more after it."

More nasty smoke rose. "There is method in this," Stalin said with a slow nod. "Not only does it serve warning on the Lizards, it also warns the Hitlerites we are not to be trifled with. And it sends the same signal to the Americans. Not bad, Vyacheslav Mikhailovich."

"First priority, as you say, is the Lizards." Molotov stuck strictly to the business at hand. He had not let Stalin see his fear at the threat he'd received, though the General Secretary surely knew it was there. He did not show his relief, either. Again, sham or not, Stalin could hardly be ignorant of it. He played his subordinates' emotions as if they were violin strings, and set one man against another like an orchestra conductor developing and exploiting opposing themes.

Now Stalin said, "In remembering the first priority, we must also remember it is not the only one. After the Lizards make peace with the *rodina*—" He stopped and puffed meditatively on the pipe.

Molotov was used to listening for subtle nuances in the General Secretary's speech. "After the Lizards make peace, Iosef Vissarionovich? Not, after the Lizards are defeated or exterminated or driven from this world?"

"Comrade Foreign Commissar, for your ears only, I do not think this within our power," Stalin said. "We shall use the bomb—if the scientists deign to give it to us. We shall destroy whatever concentration of Lizards we can with it. They, in turn, will destroy one of our cities: this is the exchange they make. We cannot win at this rate. Our goal now must be to convince the aliens they cannot win, either, but face only ruin if the war goes on."

"Under these circumstances, what terms do you intend to seek?" Molotov asked. *How long do you intend to honor them?* also came to mind, but he did not have the nerve to put that question to Stalin. The General Secretary was ruthlessly pragmatic; he'd wrung every bit of advantage he could from his pact with Hitler. The one thing he hadn't expected there was Hitler's outdoing him in ruthlessness and striking first. Any peace with the Lizards was liable to be similarly temporary.

"I want them out of the USSR," Stalin said, "beyond the frontiers of 22 June 1941. Past that, everything is negotiable. Let the fascists and capitalists dicker for their own countries. If they fail, I shall not lift a finger to help them. They would not help me, as you know."

Molotov nodded, first in agreement to that and then in slow consideration of the General Secretary's reasoning. It fit with what Stalin had done in the past. Rather than trying to foment world revolution, as the Trotskyites urged, Stalin had concentrated on building socialism in one country. Now he would take the same approach toward building independent human power.

"The Lizards are imperialists," Molotov said. "Can they be made to accept something less than their full, planned scope of conquest? This is my principal concern, Iosef Vissarionovich."

"We can make the Soviet Union not worth their having." By Stalin's tone, he was prepared to do exactly what he said. Molotov did not think the General Secretary was bluffing. He had the will to do such a thing if he was given the ability. The physicists were giving him that ability. Could the Lizard fleetlord match the General Secretary's driving will? The only humans Molotov had met who came up to that standard were Lenin, Churchill, and Hitler. Could Atvar come up to it? Stalin was betting the fate of his country that the alien could not.

Molotov would have been more confident had Stalin not so disastrously misjudged Hitler. He—and the USSR—had come close to perishing from that mistake. If he made a similar one against a foe with explosive-metal bombs, neither he, the Soviet Union, nor Marxism-Leninism would survive.

How to tell Stalin of his misgivings? Molotov drained the second glass of vodka. He could find no way.

☆ XI ☆

Out to the front again. If it hadn't been for the honor of the thing, Brigadier General Leslie Groves would have greatly preferred to stay back at the University of Denver and tend to his knitting: which is to say, making sure atomic bombs got made and the Lizards weren't any the wiser.

But when the general commanding the front ordered you to get your fanny out there, that was what you did. Omar Bradley, in a new-style pot helmet with three gold stars painted on it, pointed from his observation post out toward the fighting line and said, "General, we're hurting them, there's no two ways about that. They're paying for every inch of ground they take—paying more than they can afford, if our intelligence estimates are even close to being right. We're hurting them, as I said, but they keep taking inches, and we can't afford that at all. Do you understand what I'm saying?"

"Yes, sir," Groves answered. "We are going to have to use a nuclear device to stop them."

"Or two, or three, or as many as we have, or as many as it takes," Bradley said. "They must not break into Denver. That, right now, is our sine qua non."

"Yes, sir," Groves repeated. At the moment, he had one, count it, one atomic bomb ready for use. He would not have any more for several weeks. Bradley was supposed to know as much. In case he didn't, Groves proceeded to spell it out in large red letters.

Bradley nodded. "I do understand that, General. I just don't like it. Well, the first one will have to rock them back on their heels enough to buy us time to get the next built, that's all there is to it."

A flight of American planes, long hoarded against desperate need, roared by at treetop height. The P-40 Kittyhawks had ferocious shark mouths painted on their radiator cowlings. Wing

273

machine guns blazing, they shot up the Lizards' front-line positions. One of them took out an enemy helicopter, which crashed in flames.

Briefed against heroics that would get them killed, the pilots quickly turned for the run home. Two exploded in midair in quick succession, the second with a blast louder than the other racket on the battlefield. The rest made it back into American-held territory.

"Nice to see the Lizards on the receiving end for a change instead of dishing it out," Groves said.

Bradley nodded. "I hope those pilots can get down, get out of their planes, and get under cover before any Lizard rockets follow them home." He had a reputation for being a soldiers' general, for thinking of his men first. Groves felt a vague twinge of conscience that he hadn't done the same.

As if to show how the job should be done, a Lizard fighter dove on the American lines like a swooping eagle. Instead of talons, it used two pods full of rockets to rend its foes. Men—and a few women—with red crosses in white circles on helmets and armbands ran forward to take the wounded back to aid stations.

"The Lizards don't shoot at medics on purpose, do they?" Groves said. "They're better at playing by the rules than the Japs were."

"You can't say things like that any more. Japan is on our side now." A dry tone and a raised eyebrow warned that Bradley did not intend to be taken altogether seriously.

Another Lizard fighter pounded the American positions, this one close enough to Groves and Bradley that both men dove into a dugout to escape bomb fragments and cannon fire. Groves spat out mud. That wasn't the taste of war he got in his usual theater of operations. He wasn't used to looking down at himself and seeing a filthy uniform, either.

Bradley took it all in stride, although he wasn't used to real live combat himself. As calmly as if he were still standing upright, he said, "We'll want to site the bomb in an area where the Lizards are concentrating troops and matériel. In fact, we'll do our best to create such an area. The tricky part will be doing it so the Lizards don't notice what we're up to till too late."

"You tell me where you want it, sir, and I'll get it there for you," Groves promised, doing his best to match Bradley's aplomb. "That's how I earn my salary, after all."

"No one has anything but praise for the way you've handled your project, General," Bradley said. "When General Marshall—Secretary Marshall, I should say; his second hat takes precedence—sent me here to conduct the defense of Denver, he spoke very highly of you and of the cooperation I could expect from you. I haven't been disappointed, either."

Praise from George Marshall was praise indeed. Groves said, "We can get the bomb up to the front either by truck with reinforced suspension or by horse-drawn wagon, which is slower but might be less conspicuous. If we have to, I suppose we can send it up in pieces and assemble it where we'll set it off. The beast is five feet wide and more than ten feet long, so it comes in a hell of a big crate."

"Mm, I'll have to think about that," Bradley said. "Right now, I'm inclined to vote against it. If I understand correctly, if we lose any of the important parts, we could have all the rest and the thing still wouldn't work. Is that right?"

"Yes, sir," Groves answered. "If you try to start a jeep without a carburetor, you'd better hope you're not going farther than someplace you can walk."

Bradley had dirt all over his face, which made his grin seem brighter and more cheerful than it was. "Fair enough," he said. "We'll do everything we can to keep from having to use it—we've got a counterattack laid on for the Kiowa area, a little bit south of here, for which I have some hope. The Lizards had trouble on the plains southeast of Denver, and they still haven't fully reorganized in that sector. We may hurt them." He shrugged. "Or, on the other hand, we may just force them to concentrate and become more vulnerable to the bomb. We won't know till we try."

Groves brushed clinging dirt from his shirtfront and the knees of his trousers. "I'll cooperate in any way you require, sir." The words didn't come easy. He'd grown used to being the biggest military fish in the pond in Denver. But he could no more have defended it from the Lizards than Bradley could have ramrodded the Metallurgical Laboratory project.

Bradley waved for his adjutant, a fresh-faced captain. "George, take General Groves back to the University of Denver. He'll be awaiting our orders there, and prepared to respond to the situation however it develops."

"Yes, sir." George looked alarmingly clean and well pressed, as if mud knew better than to stick to him or his clothes. He saluted, then turned to Groves. "If you'll come with me, sir—"

He had a jeep waiting. Groves had hoped he would; his office was most of a day's ride away by horseback, and he was so heavy that neither he nor most horses enjoyed the process of equitation. He glanced skyward several times on the way back, though. The

Lizards made a point of shooting at motor vehicles and those who rode in them. He managed to return to the university campus unpunctured, for which he was duly grateful.

That evening, a great rumble of gunfire came from the southeast, with flashes lighting the horizon like distant lightning. Groves went up to the roof of the Science Building for a better view, but still could not see much. He hoped the barrage meant the Army was giving the Lizards hell and not the other way around.

The next morning, an aide woke him before the sun rose. "Sir, General Bradley on the telephone for you."

Groves yawned, rubbed his eyes, ran his hands through his hair, and scratched at his unruly mustache, which was tickling his nose. By the time he'd picked up the telephone, perhaps forty-five seconds after he'd been awakened, he sounded competent and coherent, even if he didn't feel that way yet. "Groves here."

"Good morning, General," Bradley said through static that came from the telephone rather than from Groves' fuzzy brain—or so he hoped, anyhow. "You remember that package we were discussing yesterday. It looks like we're going to need it delivered."

What felt like a jolt of electricity ran up Groves' spine. All at once, he wasn't sleepy any more. "Yes, sir," he said. "As I told you, we're ready. Ahh—will you want it all in one piece, or shall I send it by installments?"

"One piece would be sooner, wouldn't it?" Without waiting for an answer, Bradley went on, "You'd better deliver it that way. We'll want to open it as soon as we can."

"Yes, sir; I'll get right on it," Groves said, and hung up. He threw off his pajamas and started scrambling into his uniform, begrudging even that little time wasted. When Groves said he'd get right on something, he didn't mess around. He bulled past his aide without a *Good morning* and headed for the reprocessing plant, where the latest atomic bomb was stored. Soon enough, part of Colorado would go into the fire.

Liu Han's heart pounded as she approached the little scaly devils' pavilion that so marred the beauty of the island in the midst of the lake in the Forbidden City. Turning to Nieh Ho-T'ing, she said, "At last, we have a real victory against the little devils."

Nieh glanced over to her. "You have a victory, you mean. It matters little in the people's fight against imperialist aggression, except in the propaganda advantages we can wring from it."

"*I* have a victory," Liu Han conceded. She didn't look back at

Nieh. As far as she could see, he put ideology and social struggle even ahead of love, whether between a man and a woman or between a mother and a child. A lot of the members of the central committee felt the same way. Liu Han sometimes wondered if they were really human beings, or perhaps little scaly devils doing their best to impersonate people but not quite grasping what made them work.

Nieh said, "I hope you will not let your personal triumph blind you to the importance of the cause you also serve." He might have less in the way of feelings than an ordinary person— or might just keep those feelings under tighter rein— but he was far from stupid.

A little scaly devil pointed his automatic rifle at the approaching humans. In fair Chinese, he said, "You will enter the tent. You will let us see you bring no concealed weapons with you. You will pass through this machine here." He pointed to the device.

Liu Han had gone through it once before, Nieh Ho-T'ing many times. Neither of them had ever tried sneaking armaments through. Nieh had intelligence that the machine made a positively demonic racket if it did detect anything dangerous. So far, the People's Liberation Army hadn't found a way to fool it. Liu Han suspected that would come, sooner or later. Some very clever people worked for the Communist cause.

The machine kept quiet. Beyond it, another armed little devil said, "Pass on." His words were almost unintelligible, but no one could mistake the gesture he made with the barrel of the gun.

Inside the tent, the little scaly devil called Ppevel sat behind the table at which Liu Han had seen him before. Beside him sat another male with much plainer body paint: his interpreter. Ppevel spoke in his own hissing, popping language. The interpreter turned his words into Chinese: "You are to be seated." He pointed to the overstuffed chairs in front of Nieh and Liu Han. They were different from the ones that had been there on Liu Han's last visit, and perhaps implied higher status for the envoys of the People's Liberation Army.

Liu Han noticed that only peripherally. She had hoped to see Ttomalss sitting at the table with Ppevel, and had hoped even more to see her daughter. She wondered what the baby would look like, with her for a mother and the foreign devil Bobby Fiore for a father. Then a really horrible thought struck her: if the little devils wanted to substitute another baby of the right age and type for the one she had borne, how would she know?

The answer to that was simple and revolting: she wouldn't, not with any certainty. She muttered an inaudible prayer to the Amida

Buddha that such a thought had not occurred to the devils. Nieh Ho-T'ing, she knew, had no more use for the Amida Buddha than for any other god or demon, and did not think anyone else should, either. Liu Han shrugged. That was his ideology. She did not discern certain truth in it.

Ppevel spoke again. The interpreter translated: "We will return this hatchling to the female as a token of our willingness to give in exchange for getting. We expect in return a halt to your guerrilla attacks here in Peking of half a year. Is this the agreement?" He added an interrogative cough.

"No," Nieh Ho-T'ing answered angrily. "The agreement is for three months only—a quarter year." Liu Han's heart sank. Would she lose her daughter again for the sake of a quarter of a year?

Ppevel and the interpreter went back and forth in their own tongue. Then the interpreter said, "You will please pardon me. A quarter of a year for you people is the correct agreement. This is half a year for my people."

"Very well," Nieh said. "We are agreed, then. Bring out the girl child you stole as part of your systematic exploitation of this oppressed woman." He pointed to Liu Han. "And, though we did not agree, I tell you that you should apologize to her for the treatment she suffered at your hands, and also for the propaganda campaign of vilification you recently conducted against her in an effort to keep from returning the smallest victim of your injustice."

The interpreter translated that for Ppevel. The little devil with the fancy body paint spoke a single short sentence by way of reply, ending it with an emphatic cough. The interpreter said, "There is no agreement for the apology, so there shall be no apology."

"It's all right," Liu Han said softly to Nieh. "I don't care about the apology. I just want my baby back."

He raised an eyebrow and didn't say anything. She realized he hadn't made his demand for the apology for her sake, or at least not for her sake alone. He was working for the cause, trying to win a moral advantage over the scaly devils as he would have done over the Japanese or the Kuomintang clique.

Ppevel turned both his eye turrets away from the human beings, back toward an opening that led to the rear part of the large tent. He spoke in his own language. Liu Han's hands knotted into fists—she caught Ttomalss' name. Ppevel repeated himself. Ttomalss came out. He was carrying Liu Han's daughter.

For a moment, she couldn't see what the baby looked like— her eyes blurred with tears. "Give her to me," she said softly. The rage she'd expected to feel on confronting the little devil who'd stolen her child simply wasn't there. Seeing the little girl had dissolved it.

"It shall be done," Ttomalss answered in his own language, a phrase she understood. Then he switched to Chinese: "My opinion is that returning this hatchling to you is an error, that it would have served a far more useful purpose as a link between your kind and mine." That said, he angrily thrust the baby out at Liu Han.

"My opinion is that you would serve a more useful purpose as night soil than you do now," she snarled. The rage wasn't gone after all, merely suppressed. She snatched her daughter away from the scaly devil.

Now, for the first time, she took a good look at the little girl. Her daughter was not quite the same color as a purely Chinese baby would have been: her skin was a little lighter, a little ruddier. Her face was a little longer, a little more forward-thrusting, too, with a narrow chin that reminded Liu Han of Bobby Fiore's and laid to rest any fears that the little devils had switched children on her. The baby's eyes had the proper shape; they weren't round and staring like those of a foreign devil.

"Welcome back to your home, little one," Liu Han crooned, hugging her daughter tightly to her. "Welcome back to your mother."

The baby began to cry. It looked not to her but to Ttomalss, and tried to get away from her to go back to him. That look was like a knife in her heart. The sounds her daughter made were not like those of Chinese, nor even like those of the foreign devil language Bobby Fiore had spoken. They were the hisses and pops of the little scaly devils' hateful speech. Among them was an unmistakable emphatic cough.

Ttomalss spoke with what sounded like spiteful satisfaction: "As you see, the hatchling is now used to the company of males of the Race, not to your kind. Such language as it has learned is our language. Its habits are our habits. It looks like a Big Ugly, yes, but its thoughts are those of the Race."

Liu Han wished she had somehow smuggled a weapon into the tent. She would cheerfully have slain Ttomalss for what he'd done to her daughter. The baby kept twisting in her arms, trying to get away, trying to go back to the slavery with Ttomalss that was all it had ever known. Its cries dinned in her ears.

Nieh Ho-T'ing said, "What has been done can be undone. We shall reeducate the child as a proper human being. This will take time and patience, but it can be done and it shall be done." He spoke the phrase in Chinese.

"It shall be done." Liu Han used the little devils' language, throwing the words in Ttomalss' face and adding an emphatic cough of her own for good measure.

Her daughter stared up at her, eyes wide with wonder, at hearing her use words it understood. Maybe it would be all right after all, Liu Han thought. When she'd first met Bobby Fiore, the only words they'd had in common had been a handful from the speech of the little scaly devils. They'd managed, and they'd gone on to learn fair amounts of each other's languages. And babies picked up words at an astonishing rate once they began to talk. Nieh was right—before long, with luck, her daughter would pick up Chinese and would become a proper human being rather than an imitation scaly devil.

For now, she'd use whatever words she could to make the baby accept her. "All good now," she said in the little devils' language. "All good." She grunted out another emphatic cough to show how good having her daughter back was.

Again, the little girl gaped in astonishment. She gulped and sniffed and then made a noise that sounded like an interrogative cough. She might have been saying, "Is it *really*?"

Liu Han answered with one more emphatic cough. Suddenly, like the sun coming out from behind rain clouds, her daughter smiled at her. She began to cry, and wondered what the baby would make of that.

"Ready for takeoff," Teerts reported. A moment later, the air traffic control male gave him permission to depart. His killercraft roared down the runway and flung itself into the sky.

He was glad he'd climbed quickly, for an antiaircraft gun not far west of the Kansas air base threw several shells at him. The Race had been in nominal control of the area for some time, but the Big Uglies kept smuggling in weapons portable on the backs of their males or beasts and made trouble with them. It wasn't so bad here as he'd heard it was in the SSSR, but it wasn't a holiday, either.

He radioed the approximate position of the antiaircraft gun back to the air base. "We'll tend to it," the traffic control male promised. So they would—eventually. Teerts had seen that before. By the time they got around to sending out planes or helicopters or infantrymales, the gun wouldn't be there any more. But it would pop up again before long, somewhere not far away.

Nothing he could do about that. He flew west, toward the fighting outside of Denver. Now that he'd carried out several missions against the Tosevite lines outside the city, he understood why his superiors had transferred him from the Florida front to this one. The Big Uglies here had fortified their positions even more strongly than the Nipponese had outside Harbin in Manchukuo. They had more antiaircraft guns here, too.

He didn't like thinking about that. He'd been shot down outside Harbin, and still shuddered to remember Nipponese captivity. The Americans were said to treat captives better than the Nipponese did, but Teerts was not inclined to trust the mercies of any Tosevites, not if he could help it.

Before long, he spied the mountains that ridged the spine of this land mass like the dorsal shields of an *eruti* back on Home. Rising higher than any of the peaks were the clouds of smoke and dust from the fighting.

He contacted forward air control for guidance to the targets that most urgently needed hitting. "We are having success near the hamlet known to the Tosevites as Kiowa. The assault they launched in that area has failed, and they are ripe for a counterattack." The male gave Teerts targeting coordinates, adding, "If we break through here, we may be able to roll up their line. Strike them hard, Flight Leader."

"It shall be done," Teerts said, and swung his killercraft in the direction ordered.

For Rance Auerbach, the war was over. For a while there, he'd thought he was over. He'd wished he was, with a bullet in the chest and another in the leg. Rachel Hines had tried to drag him back to the American lines after he was hit. He remembered coming to in the middle of that, a memory he wouldn't have kept if he'd had any choice in the matter.

Then the Lizards, sallying out of Karval against the cavalry raiders he'd led, got close. He remembered blood bubbling from his nose and mouth as he'd croaked—he'd tried to yell—for Rachel to get the hell out of there. He'd figured he was done for anyhow, and why should they get her, too?

The one good memory he had from that dreadful time was the kiss on the cheek she'd given him: not an attention he would have wanted from most cavalry troopers. He hoped she'd got away. He didn't know whether she had or not; his lights had gone out again right about then.

Next thing he knew, he was in Karval, which was a hell of a mess after the shelling the Americans had given it. A harassed-looking human doctor was sprinkling sulfa powder into the wound in his thigh, while a Lizard who had red crosses in white circles added to his Lizardly body paint watched with two-eye-turreted fascination.

Auerbach had tried to raise his right arm to let the doc—and the Lizard who looked to be a doctor, too—know he was among those present. That was when he noticed the needle stuck in his vein and the tubing that led up to the plasma bottle a young woman was holding.

The motion was feeble, but the girl noticed it and exclaimed. He'd been too woozy to notice her face, which was masked anyhow, but he recognized her voice. He'd lost Rachel Hines, but now he'd found Penny Summers.

"You understand me?" the human doctor had asked. When he'd managed a quarter-inch's worth of nod, the fellow had gone on, "Just in case you're wondering, you're a POW, and so am I. If it weren't for the Lizards, odds are you'd be dead. They know more about asepsis than we'll learn in a lifetime. I think you're gonna make it. You'll walk again, too—after a while." At that moment, walking hadn't been the biggest thing on his mind. Breathing had seemed plenty hard enough.

Now that the Lizard armor had moved out of Karval, the aliens were using it as a center for wounded prisoners they'd taken. Pretty soon, the few battered buildings left in town weren't enough to hold everybody. They'd run up tents of a brilliant and hideous orange, one to a patient. Auerbach had been in one for several days now.

He didn't see the doctor as often as he had at first. Lizards came by to look him over several times a day. So did human nurses, Penny Summers as often as any and maybe more often than most. The first couple of times he needed it, he found the bedpan mortifyingly embarrassing. After that, he stopped worrying about it: it wasn't as if he had a choice.

"How'd they get you?" he asked Penny. His voice was a croaking whisper; he hardly had breath enough to blow out a match.

She shrugged. "We were evacuating wounded out of Lamar when the Lizards were comin' in. You know how that was—they didn't just come in, they rolled right on through. They scooped us up like a kid netting sunfish, but they let us go on takin' care of hurt people, and that's what I've been doin' ever since."

"Okay," he said, nodding. "Yeah, they seem to play by the rules, pretty much, anyhow." He paused to get some more air, then asked. "How's the war going?"

"Can't hardly tell," she answered. "Ain't no people around here with radios, none I know about, anyways. I'll say this much, though—they been shippin' a whole lot o' POWs back here lately. That's liable to mean they're winning, isn't it?"

"Liable to, yeah," he said. He wanted to cough, but held what little breath he had till the urge went away. He'd coughed once or twice already, and it felt as if his chest was going to rip to pieces. When he could speak again, he went on, "Do you know what kind of casualties they're taking?"

She shook her head. "No way for me to tell. They ship their own wounded back somewheres else."

"Ah," he said, then shook his head—carefully, because that pulled at the stitches that were holding him together. Boris Karloff might have had more when he played in *Frankenstein*, but not a whole lot. "Darned if I know why I'm even bothering to ask. It's going to be a long time before I'm able to worry about that kind of stuff."

He said it that way to keep from thinking it would never matter to him again. If his chest healed, if his leg healed, he'd eventually go to a real POW camp, and maybe there, however many months away that was, he could start planning how to escape. If his chest healed but his leg didn't, he wouldn't be going anywhere—nowhere fast, anyhow. If his leg healed but his chest didn't . . . well, in that case, they'd stick a lily in his hand and plant him.

Penny looked at him, looked down at the shiny stuff—it was like thick cellophane, but a lot tougher—the Lizards had used to cover the dirt on which they'd set up the tent, then back at him again. In a low voice, she said, "Bet you wish now you would have laid me when you had the chance."

He laughed, panted, laughed again. "You really want to know, I've been wishing that ever since the Lizards bombed Lamar. But look at me." His left arm worked, more or less. He gestured with it. "Not much I can do about that now, so why worry about it?"

"No, you can't, that's so." Penny's eyes kindled. She knelt beside the government-issue cot on which he was lying and flipped back the blanket. "But I can." She laughed as she took him in hand and bent over him. "If I hear anybody comin', I'll make like I was givin' you the bedpan."

He gasped when her mouth came down on him. He didn't know whether he'd rise. He didn't know whether he wanted to rise. Suddenly he understood how a woman had to feel when the guy she was with decided he was going to screw her then and there and she was too drunk to do anything about it.

Rise he did, in spite of everything. Penny's head bobbed up and down. He gasped again, and then again. He wondered if he was going to have enough air in him to come, no matter how good it felt . . . and her lips and teasing tongue felt as good—well, almost as good—as getting shot up felt bad.

She closed her hand around his shaft, down below her busy mouth, and squeezed him, hard. Not more than two heartbeats later, he shuddered and exploded. For a moment, purple spots swam before his eyes. Then the inside of the tent filled with light, so clear and brilliant it seemed to be—

The Lizard fighter-bomber broke off its attack run and began to gain altitude. Omar Bradley scratched at the little bandage on his nose; he'd had a boil there lanced a couple of days before. "I'm glad we're doing this with a radio signal to back up the wire," he said. "Lay you seven to two the bombs and rockets broke the link."

"My old man always told me never bet when I was liable to lose," Leslie Groves answered. "No flies on him."

"Not a one," Bradley agreed. "You've got the buttons right there, General. One of them had better work. You want to do the honors and push them?"

"You bet I do," Groves said. "I've been building these damn things for a hell of a long time now. About time I get to find out what they're like when they go off."

One of the ignition devices had an insulated wire coming out of it. The other one didn't. Groves' broad right thumb came down on one red button, his left on the other.

"Take that, you scaleless, egg-addled, stiff-jointed things!" Teerts cried as his rockets turned a stretch of Tosevite defenses into an oven where the meat would be diced and ground as it was roasted.

The Race's landcruisers were snouting forward even as he bombarded the Big Uglies. The Tosevites had made a mistake this time—they'd made their attack with inadequate resources, and not shifted over to the defensive fast enough when they ran out of steam. The Race's commanders, who'd learned alertness since coming to Tosev 3, were making them pay for it.

There wasn't even much in the way of antiaircraft fire in this sector. The Big Uglies had probably had a lot of guns overrun when the Race's counterattack went in. As Teerts began to climb back into the sky so he could return to the Kansas air base and rearm his killercraft, he decided he hadn't had such an easy mission since the early days of the conquest, well before the Nipponese captured him.

Sudden impossible swelling glare made the nictitating membranes slide over his eyes in a futile effort to protect them. The killercraft spun and flipped and twisted in the air, violently unstable in all three axes. The controls would not answer, no matter what Teerts did.

"No!" he shouted. "Not *twice*!" He stabbed a thumb toward the ejector button. The killercraft smashed into a hillside just before he reached it,

—real.

Penny Summers pulled back from him, gulping and choking a little, too. She took a long, deep breath, then said, "What the dickens do you suppose that is?"

"You mean you see it, too?" Auerbach said in his ruined voice. His heart was racing like a thoroughbred on Kentucky Derby day.

"Sure do." Penny flipped the blanket up over him again. "Like somebody fired up a new sun right outside the tent." She looked around. "Fading now, though."

"Yeah." The preternatural glow had lasted only a few seconds. When Auerbach first saw it, he'd wondered if it was a sign he was going to cash in his chips right then and there. It would have been a hell of a way to go, but he was glad he was still around. "What do you suppose it was?"

Before she answered, Penny scrubbed at her chin with a corner of the blanket. Then she said, "Couldn't begin to guess. Probably some damn Lizard thing, though."

"Yeah," Auerbach said again. He cocked his head to one side. There was some sort of commotion out in the streets of the growing tent city of wounded. He heard Lizards calling and shouting to one another, sounding like nothing so much as boilers with bad seams. "Whatever it was, they're sure excited about it."

"Will you look at that?" Leslie Groves said softly, craning his neck back to look up and up and up at the cloud whose top, now spreading out like the canopy of an umbrella, towered far higher into the sky than any of the Rockies. He shook his head in awe and wonder. The Lizard fighter plane burning not far away, normally cause for a celebration, now wasn't worth noticing. "Will you just *look* at that?"

"I'd heard what they were like," General Bradley answered.

"I've been through the ruins of Washington, so I know what they can do. But I never imagined the blast itself. Until you've seen it—" He didn't go on. He didn't need to go on.

"—and heard it," Groves added. They were some miles back toward Denver: the one thing you didn't want to be was too close to an atomic bomb when it went off. Even so, the roar of the blast had sounded like the end of the world, and the earth had jumped beneath Groves' feet. Wind tore past, then quickly stilled.

"I hope we pulled all our men back far enough so the blast didn't harm them," Bradley said. "Hard to gauge that, when we don't have enough experience with these weapons."

"Yes, sir," Groves said, and then, "Well, we're learning more all the time, and I expect we'll know quite a lot before this war is through."

"I'm very much afraid you're right, General," Bradley said, scowling. "Now we have to see where and how the Lizards will reply. The price we've paid to stop this drive is a city given over to the fire. I pray it will prove a good bargain in the end."

"So do I, sir," Groves replied. "But if we don't hold Denver, we can't hang on to the rest of the U.S.A."

"So I tell myself," Bradley said. "It lets me fall asleep at night." He paused. His features grew so grim and taut, Groves was easily able to imagine what he'd look like if he lived to eighty. "It lets me fall asleep," he repeated, "but it doesn't let me stay that way."

Atvar had been used to getting bad news up in his chamber aboard the *127th Emperor Hetto* or in the bannership's command center. Receiving it in this Tosevite room more or less adapted for the comfort of the Race was somehow harder. The furnishings and electronics were familiar. The design of the windows, the Tosevite cityscape he saw through them, the very size of the chamber—reminding him why the Race called Tosevites *Big* Uglies—all shouted at him that this was not his world, that he did not belong here.

"Outside Denver, is it?" he said dully, and stared at the damage estimates coming up on the computer screen. The numbers were still preliminary, but they didn't look good. The Americans, fighting ferociously from prepared positions, had already taken a heavy toll on his males. And now, just when he thought his forces had achieved a breakthrough—

"Exalted Fleetlord, they tricked us," Kirel said. "They conducted an attack in that sector, but so clumsily that they used themselves up in the process, leaving inadequate force to hold the line there. When the local commander sought to exploit what he perceived as a blunder—"

"It was a blunder. Indeed it was," Atvar said. "It was a blunder on our part. They are subtle, the Big Uglies, full of guile and deceit. They did not simply pull back and invite us forward, as they have with past nuclear weapons. We have warned our males against that. But no. They executed what seemed a legitimate if foolish tactical maneuver—and deceived us again."

"Truth," Kirel said, his voice as worn and filled with pain as that of the fleetlord. "How shall we avenge ourselves now? Destroying their cities does not seem to deter the Big Uglies from employing the nuclear weapons they build."

"Do you suggest a change in policy, Shiplord?" Atvar asked. That could have been a very dangerous question, one all but ordering Kirel to deny he'd suggested any such thing. It wasn't, not the way the fleetlord phrased it. He meant it seriously.

Even so, Kirel's voice was cautious as he answered, "Exalted Fleetlord, perhaps we might be wiser to respond in kind and destroy Tosevite military formations in the field against us. This may have more effect than our present policy of devastating civilian centers, and could hardly have less."

"That does appear to be truth." Atvar called up a situation map of the fighting in the United States. That let him banish the damage reports from the computer screen, if not from his mind. He pointed to the narrow peninsula stabbing out into the water in the southeastern region of the not-empire. "Here! This Florida place is made for such exploitation. Not only is the fighting on a confined front where nuclear weapons can be particularly effective, striking the Big Uglies in this area will also let us avenge ourselves on the dark-skinned Tosevites who treacherously feigned allegiance to us."

"May I, Exalted Fleetlord?" Kirel asked, approaching the computer. At Atvar's gesture of permission, he shifted the image to a more detailed map of the fighting front in Florida. He pointed. "Here, between this town called Orlando and the smaller one named . . . can it really be Apopka?"

His mouth fell open in surprised amusement. So did Atvar's. In the language of the Race, *apopka* meant "to create a bad smell." The fleetlord leaned forward to examine the map. "That does seem to be what the characters say, doesn't it? And yes, that is a likely spot for retaliation."

"Truth." Kirel pointed to the dispositions on the map. "The Americans have concentrated a good deal of armor hereabouts.

Let the bomb fall where you indicated—after our males withdraw just a bit too obviously. Perhaps we can lure the Tosevites with one of their own tricks."

"Exalted Fleetlord, it shall be done," Kirel said.

Nieh Ho-T'ing was glad the little scaly devils had finally stopped showing their pornographic films of Liu Han. They hadn't succeeded in destroying her usefulness to the cause of the People's Liberation Army, and, after they'd returned her daughter to her, there wasn't much point in continuing to portray her as a slut.

If anything, she'd gained prestige from their attacks on her. That had partly been Nieh's doing, through his showing how the films exposed not Liu Han's character but the little scaly devils' vicious exploitation of her when they had her in a situation where her only choice was to submit.

That proposition had proved persuasive to the people of Peking. The central committee, however, had been less impressed. Oh, they'd gone along with Nieh's arguments, because it redounded to their advantage to do so—and, indeed, Liu Han had gained prestige there, too. But they couldn't forget that she had been photographed in positions far beyond merely compromising. Since they couldn't blame her for that, they looked askance at Nieh for taking up with a woman who had done such things.

"Not fair," Nieh muttered under his breath. The complaints went unnoticed in the *hutung* down which he made his way. What with gossiping women, squealing children, yapping dogs, vendors crying the virtues of their nostrums and fried vegetables, and musicians hoping for coins, anything less than machine-gun fire would have drawn scant attention. And even machine-gun fire, provided it wasn't too close, went unremarked in Peking these days.

Nieh came out onto the *Liu Li Ch'ang*, the Street of the Glazed Tile Factory. It would have been a pleasant place to pass time had he had more leisure, for it was full of shops selling old books and other curios. Though he'd been born in the dying days of the Chinese Empire, and though he'd been thoroughly indoctrinated in Marxist-Leninist thought, he still maintained more respect for antiquarian scholarship than he sometimes realized.

Now, though, instead of going into one of those booksellers' establishments, he paused at the little devils' outdoor cinema device in front of it. Instead of leering at Liu Han as she let some man's potent pestle penetrate her, the crowd gaped at what looked like the mother of all explosions.

The smooth Chinese narrator for the newsreel—the same running dog who had so lovingly described Liu Han's degradation—said, "Thus does the Race destroy those who oppose it. This blast took place in the American province called Florida, after the foolish foreign devils provoked the merciful servants of the Empire beyond measure. Let it serve as a warning to all those who dare to offend our masters here in China."

From the fiery cloud of the bomb blast itself, the scene shifted to the devastation it wrought. A tank's cannon sagged down as if it were a candle that had drooped from being too close to the fire. Some of the ground looked as if the heat of the bomb had baked it into glass. Charred corpses lay everywhere. Some of the charred chunks of meat were not yet corpses, for they wriggled and moaned and cried out in their unintelligible language.

"I wouldn't want that happening to me," exclaimed an old man with a few long white whiskers sprouting from his chin.

"It happened to the little scaly devils, too," Nieh Ho-T'ing said. "The Americans used a bomb just like this one against them. This is the scaly devils' retaliation, but people can make these bombs, too." He was glad of that, even if the Americans were capitalists.

"Foreign devils can make these bombs, maybe, if what you say is true," the old man answered. "But can we Chinese do this?" He paused a moment to let the obvious answer sink in, then went on, "Since we can't we had better do what the little devils say here, eh?"

Several people nodded. Nieh glared at them and at the old man. "The little devils have never used that kind of bomb here, or even threatened to," he said. "And if we don't resist them, they'll rule us the same way the Japanese did—with fear and savagery. Is that what we want?"

"The little scaly devils, they'll leave you alone if you leave them alone," the old man said. Nieh resolved to find out who he was and arrange for his elimination; he was obviously a collaborator and a troublemaker.

A couple of people nodded again. But a woman spoke up: "What about that poor girl, the one they made do all those horrible things in front of their cameras? What had she done to them beforehand?"

The old man stared at her. He opened his mouth like a little devil laughing, but had far fewer teeth than the imperialist aggressors from the stars. While the fellow was still groping for a reply,

Nieh Ho-T'ing headed back toward the roominghouse where he lived.

When he got there, he found Hsia Shou-Tao sitting in the downstairs dining room, drinking tea with a pretty singsong girl whose green silk dress was slit to show an expanse of golden thigh. Hsia looked up and nodded to him, without the least trace of embarrassment. His self-criticism had not included any vows of celibacy, only a pledge to keep from bothering women who showed they were not interested in him. For the singsong girl, the transaction would be purely commercial. Nieh frowned anyhow. His aide had a way of letting pledges slip a finger's breadth at a time.

Nieh had other things on his mind at the moment, though. He trudged upstairs to the room he'd been sharing with Liu Han—and, lately, with her daughter, at last redeemed from the little scaly devils. As he climbed the stairs, he let out a small, silent sigh. That wasn't yet working out as well as Liu Han had imagined it would. In Nieh's experience, few things in life did. He had not found a good way to tell that to Liu Han.

He tried the door. It was locked. He rapped on it. "Who's there?" Liu Han called warily from within. She hadn't casually opened the door since the day Hsia Shou-Tao tried to rape her. But, when she heard Nieh's voice, she lifted the bar, let him in, and stepped into his arms for a quick embrace.

"You look tired," he said. What she looked was haggard and harassed. He didn't think he ought to say that to her. Instead, he pointed to her daughter, who sat over in a corner playing with a straw-stuffed doll made of cloth. "How is Liu Mei this afternoon?"

To his surprise and dismay, Liu Han started to cry. "I gave birth to her, and she is still frightened of me. It's as if she thinks she ought to be a little scaly devil, not a human being."

Liu Mei started to pull some of the stuffing out of the doll, which was far from new. "Don't do that," Liu Han said. Her daughter took no notice of her. Then she spoke a word in the little devils' language and added one of their coughs. The little girl stopped what she was doing. Wearily, Liu Han turned to Nieh. "You see? She understands their tongue, not Chinese. She cannot even make the right sounds for Chinese. What can I do with her? How can I raise her when she is like this?"

"Patience," Nieh Ho-T'ing said. "You must remember patience. The dialectic proves Communism will triumph, but says nothing with certainty as to when. The little scaly devils know nothing of the dialectic, but their long history gives them patience.

They had Liu Mei her whole life, and did their best to make her into one of them. You have had her only a few days. You must not expect her to change overnight for you."

"I know that—here." Liu Han tapped a finger against her forehead. "But my heart breaks every time she flinches from me as if I were a monster, and whenever I have to speak to her in a language I learned because I was a slave."

"As I said, you are not viewing this rationally," Nieh answered. "One reason you are not viewing it rationally is that you are not getting enough sleep. Liu Mei may not be a human child in every way but she wakes up in the night like one. He yawned. "I am tired, too."

Liu Han hadn't asked him to help take care of the baby. That she might had never occurred to him. Caring for a child was women's work. In some ways, Nieh took women and their place as much for granted as Hsia Shou-Tao did.

So did Liu Han, in some ways. She said, "I wish I had an easier time comforting her. I am not what she wants. She makes that quite plain." Her mouth twisted into a thin, bitter line. "What she wants is that little devil, Ttomalss. He did this to her. He should be made to pay for it."

"Nothing we can do about that, not unless we learn he's come down to the surface of the world again," Nieh said. "Not even the People's Liberation Army can reach into one of the scaly devils' ships high in the sky."

"The little devils are patient," Liu Han said in a musing tone of voice. "He will not stay up in his ship forever. He will come down to steal another baby, to try to turn it into a little scaly devil. When he does—"

Nieh Ho-T'ing would not have wanted her to look at him that way. "I think you are right," he said, "but he may not do that in China. The world is a larger place than we commonly think."

"If he comes, he will come to China." Liu Han spoke with the assurance of a man. "He speaks Chinese. I do not think he speaks any other human language. If he robs some poor woman, he will rob one from China."

Nieh spread his hands. "This is logical, I must say. What do you want us to do about it?"

"Punish him," she answered at once. "I will bring the matter before the central committee and get official approval for it."

"The central committee will not approve of an act of personal vengeance," he warned her. "Getting agreement to put the rescue of your child on the negotiation agenda was difficult enough, but this—"

"I think the motion will be approved," Liu Han said steadily. "I do not intend to present it as a matter of personal vengeance, but as a symbol that the little devils' oppression of mankind is not to be tolerated."

"Present it however you like," Nieh replied. "It is still personal vengeance. I am sorry, Liu Han, but I do not feel able to give you my own support in this matter. I have spent too much political capital for Liu Mei already."

"I will present the motion anyhow," Liu Han told him. "I have discussed it with several committee members. I think it will pass, whether you support it or not."

He stared at her. They'd worked well together, in bed and out, but he'd always been the dominant partner. And why not? He'd been an army chief of staff before the little scaly devils came and turned everything topsy-turvy, and she'd been nothing but a peasant woman and an example of the scaly devils' oppression. Everything she was in the revolutionary struggle, she was because of him. He'd brought her onto the central committee to give him more support. How could she turn against him?

By the look in her eye, she'd gained the backing she needed to get her motion adopted. She'd done that quietly, behind his back. Hsia Shou-Tao hadn't got wind of it, either. "You're good," he said in genuine admiration. "You're very good."

"Yes, I am," she said matter-of-factly, to herself as much as to him. Then her expression softened a little. "Thank you for putting me in a place where I've had the chance to show I could be."

She *was* very good. She was even letting him down easy, making sure he didn't stay angry at her. And she was doing it as a man would, with words, rather than using her body to win the point. He didn't think it was because she didn't fancy him any more; it was just another way for her to show him what she could do.

He smiled at her. She looked back in wary surprise. "The two of us will go far if we stick together," he said. She thought about that, then nodded. Only later did he wonder whether he would be guiding her down his track or she guiding him down hers.

The train groaned to a stop. Ussmak had never ridden on such a hideous conveyance in all his life. Back on Home, rail transport was fast, smooth, and nearly silent; thanks to magnetic levitation, trains never actually touched the rails over which they traveled. It wasn't like that here. He felt every crosstie, every rail joint, that jounced the train as it slowly chugged along. His landcruiser had had a smoother, more pleasant ride on the worst broken terrain than the train did in its own roadbed.

He let out a soft, sad hissing sigh. "If I'd had my wits about me, I never would have sunk my teeth into that Lidov creature. Ah, well—that's what ginger does to a male."

One of the other males jammed into the compartment with him, a riflemale named Oyyag, said, "At least you got to bite one of the stinking Big Uglies. Most of us just got squeezed dry and used up."

A chorus of agreement rose from the others. To them, Ussmak was a hero of sorts, precisely because he'd managed to strike a blow against the SSSR even after the local Big Uglies got him in their claws. It was an honor he could have done without. The Tosevites knew why he was on this train, too, and treated him worse because of it. As Oyyag had said, the Soviets had simply run out of questions to put to most of the captive males. Not Ussmak, though.

Two Big Uglies carrying automatic weapons opened the door to the compartment. "Out! Out!" they bawled in the Russkis' ugly language. That was a word Ussmak had learned. He hadn't learned many, but some of his fellows had been captive for a long time. They translated for those who, like him, were new-caught and innocent.

Out he went. The corridor was chilly. The Tosevites pressed back against the outer wall, making sure no males could come close and attack them. Nobody was foolhardy enough to try; no one who had any experience in the SSSR could doubt that the Big Uglies would cheerfully shoot any male who gave them the least bit of trouble.

The outer door at the far end of the railroad car was open. Ussmak made for it. He was used to being jammed into close quarters with many of his fellow males—he'd been a landcruiser crewmale, after all—but a little open space was welcome now and then, too. "Maybe they'll feed us better here than they did on the train," he said hopefully.

"Silence!" one of the weapon-toting guards bawled in the Russki language. He'd learned that command, too. He shut up.

If the corridor had been chilly, it was downright cold outside. Ussmak rapidly swiveled his eye turrets, wondering what sort of place this would be. It was certainly different from the battered city of Moskva, where he'd been brought after yielding up his base to the males of the SSSR. He'd got to see some on that journey, but he'd been a collaborator then, not a prisoner.

Dark green Tosevite trees grew in great profusion all around the open area where the train had halted. He opened his mouth a crack to let his tongue drink in their scent. It was tangy and spicy and almost put him in mind of ginger. He wished he had a taste—anything to take his mind off his predicament. He wouldn't try to attack these Big Ugly guards. Well, he didn't think he would, anyhow.

The Big Uglies' shouts and gestures sent him and his comrades in misery skittering through a gateway in a fence made of many strands of the fanged stuff Tosevites used in place of razor wire, and toward some rough buildings of new, raw timber not far away. Other, more weathered buildings lay farther off, separated from these by more wire with fangs. Big Uglies in stained and faded coverings stared toward him and his companions from the grounds around those old buildings.

Ussmak didn't have much chance to look at them. Guards yelled and waved some more to show him which way to go. Some held automatic weapons, too; others controlled snarling animals with mouths full of big, sharp yellow teeth. Ussmak had seen those Tosevite beasts before. He'd had one with an explosive charge strapped to its back run under his landcruiser, blow itself up, and blow a track off the armored fighting vehicle. If the Big Uglies could train them to do that, he was sure they could train them to run over and bite males of the Race who got out of line, too.

He didn't get out of line, literally or figuratively. Along with the rest of the males from the train, he went into the building to which he'd been steered. He gave it the same swift, eye-swiveling inspection he'd used on the terrain surrounding it. Compared to the box in which he'd been stored in the Moskva prison, compared to the packed compartment in which he'd ridden from that prison to this place, it was spacious and luxurious. Compared to any other living quarters, even the miserable Tosevite barracks he'd had to inhabit in Besançon, it gave squalor a new synonym.

There was a small open space in the center of this barracks, with a metal contraption in the middle of it. A guard used an iron poker to open a door on the device, then flung some black stones into the fire inside it. Only when he saw the fire did Ussmak realize the thing was supposed to be a stove.

Surrounding it were row on row of bunks, five and six spaces high, built to a size that conformed to the dimensions of the Race, not those of the Big Uglies. As males hurried to get spaces of their own, the impression of roominess the barracks had given disappeared. They would be desperately crowded in here, too.

A guard shouted something at Ussmak. He didn't know exactly what it meant, but he got moving, which seemed to satisfy the Big Ugly. He claimed a third-tier bunk in the second row of frames away from the stove. That was as close as he could get; he hoped it would be close enough. Having served in Siberia, he had an awed respect for the extremes Tosevite weather could produce.

The bunk's sleeping platform was of bare boards, with a single smelly blanket—probably woven from the hairs of some native beast, he thought with distaste—in case that joke of a stove did not put out enough warmth. That struck Ussmak as likely. Next to nothing the Tosevites did worked the way it was supposed to, except when intended to inflict suffering. Then they managed fine.

Oyyag scrambled up into the bunk above his. "What will they do with us, superior sir?" he asked.

"I don't know, either," Ussmak answered. As a former landcruiser driver, he did outrank the riflemale. But even males of the race whose body paint was fancier than his often awarded him that honorific salute now that they were captives together. None of them had ever led a mutiny or commanded a base after overcoming legitimate authority.

What they don't know is how much I wish I hadn't done it, Ussmak thought sadly, *and how much more I wish I hadn't yielded the base up to Soviet troops once it was in my claws.* Wishes did as much good as they usually did.

The barracks quickly filled with males. As soon as the last new arrivals found bunks—bunks so far away from the stove that Ussmak pitied them when night came—another male and two Big Uglies came into the doorway and stood there waiting to be noticed. As they were, the barracks slowly quieted.

Ussmak studied the newcomers with interest. The male of the Race carried himself like someone who was someone, though his body paint had been faded and abraded till little remained by which to judge his rank. The Tosevites with him presented an interesting contrast. One wore the type of cloth wrappings typical of the guards who had oppressed Ussmak ever since he went into captivity. The other, though, had the ragged accouterments of the males who had watched from the far side of the fanged-wire fence as Ussmak and his colleagues arrived. He'd also let the hair grow out on his face, which to Ussmak made him look even more scruffy than Tosevites normally did.

The male spoke: "I am Fsseffel. Once I was an infantry combat vehicle band commander. Now I am headmale of Race Barracks One." He paused; the Big Ugly with the fuzz on his face spoke in the Russki language to the one who wore the official-style cloth wrappings. *Interpreter,* Ussmak realized. He got the idea that a Big Ugly who understood his language might be a useful fellow with whom to become acquainted.

Fsseffel resumed: "Males of the Race, you are here to labor for the males of the SSSR. This will henceforth be your sole function." He paused to let that sink in, and for translation, then went on, "How well you work, how much you produce, will determine how well you are fed."

"That's barbarous," Oyyag whispered to Ussmak.

"You expect Big Uglies to behave like civilized beings?" Ussmak whispered back. Then he waved Oyyag to silence; Fsseffel was still talking—

"You will now choose for yourselves a headmale for this, Race Barracks Three. This male will be your interface with the Russki males of the People's Commissariat for the Interior, the Tosevite organization responsible for administration of this camp." He paused again to let the interpreter speak to the Big Ugly from the NKVD. "Choose wisely, I urge you." He tacked an emphatic cough onto that. "If you do not make a selection, one will be made for you, more or less at random. Race Barracks Two had this happen. Results have been unsatisfactory. I urge against such a course."

Ussmak wondered what sort of unsatisfactory results Fsseffel had in mind. All sorts of nasty possibilities occurred to him: starvation, torture, executions. He hadn't thought in terms like those before the mutiny. His frame of reference had changed since then, and not for the better.

Oyyag startled him by shouting, "Ussmak!" A moment later, half the males in the barracks were calling his name. They wanted him for headmale, he realized with something less than delight. That would bring him into constant contact with the Big Uglies, which was the last thing he wanted. He saw no good way to escape, though.

The Big Ugly with the hairy face said, "Let the male called Ussmak come forward and be recognized." He was as fluent in the language of the Race as any Tosevite Ussmak had heard. When Ussmak got down from his bunk and walked over to the door, the Big Ugly said, "I greet you, Ussmak. We will be working with each other in days to come. I am David Nussboym."

"I greet you, David Nussboym," Ussmak said, although he would rather not have made the Tosevite's acquaintance.

The breeze still brought the alien stink of Cairo to the scent receptors on Atvar's tongue. But it was a fine mild breeze, and the fleetlord was more prepared to tolerate Tosevite stinks now that he had succeeded in dealing the Big Uglies a heavy blow.

He called up the Florida situation map on one of the computers installed in his Tosevite lodging. "We've broken the Americans here," he told Kirel, pointing to the map. "The bomb created a gap, and we've poured through it. Now they flee before us, as they did in the early days of the conquest. Our possession of the peninsula seems assured."

"Truth, Exalted Fleetlord," Kirel said, but then tempered that by adding, "A pity the conquest does not proceed elsewhere as it did in the early days."

Atvar did not care to dwell on that unless forcibly reminded of it. After the Americans exploded their own nuclear device outside Denver, the Race's attack there had bogged down. It had already proved more expensive than calculations predicted, as attacks against Big Ugly strongpoints had a way of doing. The bomb had broken the southern prong of the attack, and weakened the center and north as well, because the local commander had shifted forces southward to help exploit what had looked like an opening. An opening it had been—the opening of a trap.

Kirel said, "Exalted Fleetlord, what are we to make of this latest communication from the SSSR? Its leadership is certainly arrogant enough, demanding that we quit its territory as a precondition for peace."

"That is—that must be—a loud bluff," Atvar replied. "The only nuclear weapon the SSSR was able to fabricate came from plutonium stolen from us. That the not-empire has failed to produce another indicates to our technical analysts its inability to do so. Inform the Big Ugly called Molotov and his master the Great Stalin—great compared to what?" the fleetlord added with a derisive snort, "—that the SSSR is in no position to make demands of us that it cannot enforce on the battlefield."

"It shall be done," Kirel said.

Atvar warmed to the subject: "In fact, the success of our retaliatory bomb once more makes me wonder if we should not employ these weapons more widely than we have in the past."

"Not in the SSSR, surely, Exalted Fleetlord," Kirel said in some alarm. "The broad expanse of land there is vulnerable to widespread radioactive pollution, and would otherwise be highly satisfactory for agriculture and herding for our colonists."

"In purely military terms, this would be a much more highly satisfactory campaign if we could ignore the requirements of the colonization fleet," Atvar answered resentfully. He sighed. "Unfortunately, we cannot. Were it not for the colonization fleet, this conquest fleet would have no point. The analysts agree with you: large-scale nuclear bombing of the SSSR, however tempting it would be to rid this planet of the Emperor-murdering clique now governing that not-empire, would create more long-term damage than the military advantage we would gain could offset."

"I have also studied these analyses," Kirel said, which raised Atvar's suspicions: was Kirel trying to prepare himself to wear a fleetlord's body paint? But he hadn't done anything about which Atvar could take exception, so the fleetlord waited for him to go on. He did: "They state that there are certain areas where nuclear weapons may successfully be employed in an offensive role without undue damage to the planet."

Atvar's suspicion diminished, not least because Kirel had agreed with him. He said, "If we do employ nuclear weapons on our own behalf rather than as retaliation for Tosevite outrages, we will also make ourselves appear less predictable and more dangerous to the Big Uglies. This may have a political effect out of proportion to the actual military power we employ."

"Again, Exalted Fleetlord, this is truth," Kirel said. "Letting the Big Uglies know we, too, can be unpredictable may prove, as you say, a matter of considerable importance for us."

"That is a vital point," Atvar agreed. "We cannot predict the actions of the Big Uglies even with all the electronics at our disposal, while they, limited as they are in such matters, often anticipate what we intend to do, with results all too frequently embarrassing for us."

Finding Kirel in accord with him, Atvar blanked the map of Florida and summoned another from the computer to take its place. "This large island—or perhaps it is a small continent, but let the planetologists have the final say there—lying to the southeast of the main continental mass had huge tracts of land ideally suited for settlement by the Race and little used by the Big Uglies, most of whose habitations cling to the damper eastern coast. Yet from those bases they continually stage annoying raids on us. All conventional efforts to suppress these raids have proved useless. This might prove the ideal site for nuclear intervention."

"Well said, Exalted Fleetlord," Kirel answered. "If we do strike those areas with nuclear weapons, most of the radioactive fallout they produce will be blown out to sea, and seas the size of those here on Tosev 3 undoubtedly can accommodate such with far less damage than the land."

"This planet has altogether too much sea in proportion to its land area," Atvar agreed. "The planetologists will spend centuries accounting for what makes it so different from Home and the worlds of the Rabotevs and Hallessi."

"Let them worry about such things," Kirel said. "Our job is to make certain they have the opportunity *to* worry."

"Now you have spoken well, Shiplord," Atvar said, and Kirel stretched out from the rather nervous posture he usually assumed around the fleetlord. Atvar realized he had not given his chief subordinate much in the way of praise lately. That was an error on his part: if they did not work well together, the progress of the conquest would be impeded—and too many things had already impeded the progress of the conquest. Atvar hissed out a sigh. "Had I any conception of the magnitude of the task involved in suppressing resistance on an industrialized world without destroying it in the process, I would have thought long and hard before accepting command."

Kirel didn't answer right away. Had Atvar declined the position, he most likely would have been appointed fleetlord. How much did he want to taste the job? Atvar had never been certain of that, which made his dealings with the shiplord of the conquest fleet's bannership edgier than they might have been. Kirel had never shown himself to be disloyal, but—

When the shiplord did speak, he dealt with the tactical situation under discussion, not with Atvar's latest remark: "Exalted Fleetlord, shall we then prepare to use nuclear weapons against these major Tosevite settlements on the island or continent or whatever it may be?" He leaned forward to read the toponyms on the map so as to avoid any possible mistakes. "Against Sydney and Melbourne, I mean?"

Atvar leaned forward, too, to check the sites for himself. "Yes, those are the ones. Begin preparations as expeditiously as possible."

"Exalted Fleetlord, it shall be done."

☆ **XII** ☆

As prisons went, the one Moishe Russie and his wife and son now inhabited wasn't bad. It even outdid the villa where the Jewish underground in Palestine had incarcerated them. Here, in what had been a fine hotel, he and his family got plenty of food and enjoyed both electricity and hot and cold running water. If not for bars on the windows and armed Lizard guards outside the door, the suite would have been luxurious.

Despite bars, the windows drew Moishe. He stared in endless fascination out across Cairo at the Nile and, beyond it, the Pyramids. "I never thought we would be like Joseph and come to Egypt out of Palestine," he said.

"Who will be our Moses and lead us out again?" Reuven asked.

Moishe felt a burst of pride: the boy was still so young, but already not just learning the great stories of the Torah but applying them to his own life. He wished he had a better answer to give his son than "I don't know," but he didn't want to lie to Reuven, either.

Rivka had a question much more to the point: "What will they do to us now?"

"I don't know that, either," Moishe said. He wished Rivka and Reuven hadn't come with him after Zolraag recognized him in the Jerusalem prison camp. Far too late now to do anything but wish, though. But he was vulnerable through them. Even back in Warsaw, the Lizards had threatened them to try to make him do what they wanted. His family's convenient disappearance had scotched that there. It wouldn't here. He'd been ready to let himself be killed rather than obey the Lizards. But letting his wife and son suffer—that was something else again.

A key turned in the lock, out in the hall. Moishe's heart beat faster. It was halfway between breakfast and lunchtime, not a

usual hour for the Lizards to bother him. The door opened. Zolraag came in. The former provincelord of Poland was wearing
more ornate body paint now than either of the times when Moishe
had seen him in Palestine. He hadn't returned to the almost rococo
splendor of his ornamentation back in his Warsaw days, but he
was gaining on it.

He stuck out his tongue in Moishe's direction, then reeled it
back in. "You will come with me immediately," he said in fair
German, turning *sofort* into a long, menacing hiss.

"It shall be done," Moishe answered in the language of the
Race. He hugged Rivka and kissed Reuven on the forehead, not
knowing whether he would see them again. Zolraag allowed that,
but made small, impatient noises, like a thick pot of stew coming
to a boil.

When Moishe came over to him, the Lizard rapped on the inner
surface of the door: the knob there had been removed. Zolraag
used a sequence of knocks different from any the Lizards had
employed before, presumably to keep the Russies from learning a
code, breaking out, and causing trouble. Not for the first time,
Moishe wished he and his family were as dangerous as the Lizards
believed they were.

Out in the hallway, four males pointed automatic weapons at
his midsection. Zolraag gestured for him to walk toward the stairwell. Two of the Lizard guards followed, both of them too far back
to let him whirl and try to seize their rifles—as if he would have
been *meshuggeh* enough to try.

Zolraag ordered him into a mechanical combat vehicle. The
guards got into it, too. One of them slammed the rear doors shut
behind him. The clang of metal striking metal had a dreadfully
final sound.

Zolraag spoke a single word into what looked like a microphone at the front of the troop compartment: "Go."

The combat vehicle clattered through the streets. Moishe got
only a limited view through the machine's firing ports. It was one
of the least pleasurable journeys of his life in any number of ways.
The seat on which he awkwardly tried to perch was made for a
male of the Race, not someone his size; his backside didn't fit it,
while his knees came up under his chin. It was hot in there, too,
hotter even than outside. The Lizards basked in the heat. Russie
wondered if he'd pass out before they got where they were going.

He glimpsed a marketplace that dwarfed any he'd seen in Palestine. Through the fighting vehicle's armor plate, he heard people

jeering and cursing at the Lizards—that, at least, is what he thought they were doing, though he knew not a word of Arabic. But if anything so gutturally incandescent wasn't cursing, it should have been. Whatever it was, Zolraag ignored it.

A few minutes later, the vehicle stopped. One of Moishe's guards opened the doors at the rear. *"Jude heraus,"* Zolraag said, which made the hair stand up on the back of Russie's neck.

They'd brought him to another hotel. The Lizards had fortified this one like the Maginot Line; when Moishe looked around, he saw enough razor wire, aliens with automatic weapons, and panzers and combat vehicles to hold off Rommel's *Afrika Korps* and the British who'd fought him . . . not that the Nazis or the British were going concerns in North Africa these days.

He didn't get much time for sightseeing. Zolraag said, "Come," the guards pointed their weapons at him, and he perforce came. The hotel lobby had ceiling fans. They weren't turning. The electric lights were on, so Moishe decided the fans were off because the Lizards wanted them off.

The lift worked, too. In fact, it purred upward more silently and smoothly than any on which Moishe had ever ridden. He didn't know whether it had always been like that or the Lizards had improved it after they conquered Cairo. It was, at the moment, the least of his worries.

When the lift doors opened, he found himself on the sixth floor, the topmost one. "Out," Zolraag said, and Moishe obeyed again. Zolraag led him along the hallway to a suite of rooms that made the one where the Russies were confined seem prisonlike indeed. A Lizard who wore strange body paint—the right side fairly plain, the left fancier than any Moishe had seen till now—spoke with Zolraag at the doorway, then ducked back into the suite.

He returned a moment later. "Bring in the Big Ugly," he said.

"It shall be done, adjutant to the fleetlord," Zolraag answered.

They spoke their own language, but Moishe managed to follow it. "The fleetlord?" he said, and was proud that, despite his surprise, he'd remembered to add an interrogative cough. The Lizards ignored him even so. He hadn't even thought the fleetlord was on the face of the Earth.

Atvar's body paint was like that of Pshing's left side, only all over. Other than that, he looked like a Lizard to Russie. He was able to tell one of the aliens from another, but only after he'd known him for a while.

Zolraag said, "Exalted Fleetlord, I present to you the Tosevite Moishe Russie, who is at last returned to our custody."

"I greet you, superior sir," Moishe said, as politely as he could: no point in insulting the chief Lizard over anything inconsequential.

He turned out to be wrong even so. " 'I greet you, *Exalted Fleetlord*,' " Zolraag said sharply. Moishe repeated the phrase, this time with the right honorific. "That is better," Zolraag told him.

Atvar, meanwhile, was studying him from head to toe, eye turrets swinging up and down independently of each other in the unnerving way Lizards had. The fleetlord spoke in his own language, too fast for Moishe to stay with him. Seeing that, Zolraag translated his words into German: "The exalted fleetlord wants to know if you are now satisfied as to the overwhelming power of the Race."

The word he used to translate *Race* into German was *Volk*. That raised Moishe's hackles all over again: the Nazis had used *Volk* for their own ends. He had to bring himself back under conscious control before answering, "Tell the fleetlord I am not. If the Race had overwhelming power, this war would have been over a long time ago."

He wondered if that would anger Atvar. He hoped not. He had to be careful about what he said, much less for his own sake than for Rivka's and Reuven's. To his relief, Atvar's mouth fell open. The Lizard's sharp little teeth and long, forked tongue were not delightful sights in and of themselves, but they meant the fleetlord was amused rather than annoyed.

"Truth," Atvar said, a word Russie knew. He nodded to show he understood. Atvar went on in the Lizards' speech, again too quickly for Moishe to keep up. Zolraag translated once more: "The exalted fleetlord has learned, from me among others, that you opposed having the Jews rise on our behalf when we entered Palestine. Why did you do this, when you supported us against the Germans in Poland?"

"Two reasons," Moishe said. "First, I know better now than I did then that you plan to rule all of mankind forever, and I cannot support that. Second, the Germans in Poland were slaughtering Jews, as you know. The British in Palestine were doing no such thing. Some of the Jews who back you there had escaped from Germany or from Poland. You seem more dangerous to me than the British do."

Zolraag translated that into the Lizards' hisses and pops and squeaks. Atvar spoke again, this time slowly, aiming his words directly at Moishe: "These other males who escaped do not think as you do. Why is this?"

Moishe did his best to answer in the language of the Race: "Other males see short. I look for long. In long, Race worse, British better." To show how strongly he believed that, he ended with an emphatic cough.

"It is good that you think of the long term. Few Big Uglies do," Atvar said. "It may even be that, from the point of view of a Big Ugly who does not wish to come under the rule of the Race, you are right." He paused and turned both eye turrets toward Moishe's face. "This will not help you, though."

The Lizards had replaced the human-made furniture in the suite with their own gear. It made the room in which Russie stood appear even larger than it really was. One of the many devices with blank glass screens lit up, suddenly showing a Lizard's face. The Lizard's voice came out of the machine, too. *A telephone with a cinema attachment,* Moishe thought.

By the way Atvar's adjutant jerked at whatever the message was, he might have stuck his tongue into a live electrical socket. He turned one eye turret back toward Atvar and said, "Exalted Fleetlord!"

"Not now, Pshing," Atvar replied with very human impatience.

But the adjutant—Pshing—kept talking. Atvar hissed something Russie didn't understand and whirled away from him toward the screen. As he did so, the Lizard's face disappeared from it, to be replaced by a great, mushroom-shaped cloud rising into the sky. Moishe gasped in horror. He'd seen one of those clouds on his way to Palestine, rising over what had been Rome.

The sound he made seemed to remind Atvar he was there. The fleetlord turned one eye turret toward Zolraag for a moment and snapped, "Get him out of here."

"It shall be done, Exalted Fleetlord," Zolraag said. He turned to Russie. "Go now. The exalted fleetlord has more important things with which to concern himself at the moment than one insignificant Big Ugly."

Moishe went. He said nothing until the infantry combat vehicle that had brought him to Atvar's headquarters started back toward the hotel in which he was imprisoned. Then he asked, "Where did that atomic bomb explode?"

Zolraag let out a hiss that made him sound like an unhappy samovar. "So you recognized it, did you? The place is part of this province of Egypt. I gather it has two names, in your sloppy Tosevite fashion. It is called both El Iskandariya and Alexandria. Do you know either of these names?"

"Someone bombed Alexandria?" Moishe exclaimed. "*Vay iz mir!* Who? How? You of the Race control all this country, don't you?"

"I thought we did," Zolraag answered. "Evidently not, yes? Who? We do not know. The British, taking revenge for what we did to Australia? We did not—do not—believe them to have weapons of this sort. Could they have borrowed one from the Americans?"

He sounded as if he meant the question seriously. Moishe made haste to reply: "I have no idea, superior sir."

"No?" Zolraag said. "Yet you broadcast for the British. We must investigate further." Ice ran up Russie's back. The Lizard went on, "The Deutsche, fighting us as best they could? We do not know—but when we learn which Big Uglies did this, they will pay a great price."

Something Zolraag had said got through to Moishe slower than it should have. "Australia, superior sir? What happened in Australia?"

"We destroyed two cities to secure our conquests there," the former Polish provincelord answered with chilling indifference before returning to a previous question: "How? We do not know that, either. We detected no airplanes, no missiles, no boats moving over the water. We do not believe the bomb could have been smuggled in by land, either; we would have found it in our searches of cargo."

"Not over water, not by air, not on land?" Moishe said. "That doesn't leave much. Did someone dig a tunnel and set the bomb *under* Alexandria?"

Zolraag made more horrified-teakettle noises, then burst out, "You Tosevites have not the technology to accomplish this!" That was when he figured out Russie had been offering a jest, however feeble. "Not funny, *Reb* Moishe," he said, and used an emphatic cough to show how unfunny it was.

Nobody had called Moishe *Reb* since he'd left Warsaw. Then he'd thought the Lizards had come in answer to his prayer to make the Nazis leave off persecuting the Jews in the ghetto they'd established. People had gained hope from that. Now he saw that the Lizards, while they didn't hate Jews in particular, were more dangerous for the rest of the world than the Nazis had dreamt of being. Two Australian cities, destroyed without provocation? No matter how sweltering the air inside the armored fighting vehicle, he shivered.

Heinrich Jäger peered down into the Panther's engine compartment. "Fuel-pump gasket again?" he growled. "God in heaven, how long does it take for them to get the fabrication right?"

Gunther Grillparzer pointed to the lot number stenciled in white paint on the black rubber gasket. "This is an old one, sir," he said. "Probably dates back to the first couple of months' production run."

That did little to console Jäger. "We're damned lucky the engine didn't catch fire when it failed. Whoever shipped it out to us ought to be horsewhipped."

"Ahh, give the dumb bastard a noodle and put somebody else in his job," Grillparzer said, using SS slang for a bullet in the back of the neck. He'd probably picked that up from Otto Skorzeny. He probably wasn't joking, either. Jäger knew how things worked in German factories these days. With so many German men at the front, a lot of people doing production work were Jews, Russians, Frenchmen, and other slave laborers subject to just that kind of punishment if they made the slightest mistake.

"Is the replacement a new one?" Jäger demanded.

Grillparzer checked the lot number. "Yes, sir," he answered. "We slap that in there, it shouldn't give us any trouble till—the next time, anyhow." On that optimistic note, he grabbed a screwdriver and attacked the fuel pump.

Off in the distance, a flight of rockets screamed away toward the Lizard lines. Jäger winced at the horrible noise. He'd been on the receiving end of Stalin-organ concertos when the Red Army lobbed *Katyushas* at the *Wehrmacht* before the Lizards came. If you wanted to tear up a whole lot of ground in a hurry, rockets were the way to do it.

They didn't bother Skorzeny at all. "Someone will be catching hell," he said cheerfully. Then, lowering his voice so only Jäger could hear, he went on, "Almost as good as the pasting we gave Alexandria."

"Ah, that was us, was it?" Jäger said, just as softly. Skorzeny—heard things. "The radio hasn't claimed it for the *Reich*."

"The radio bloody well isn't going to claim it for the *Reich*, either," the SS man answered. "If we take credit for it, one of our towns goes right off the map. Cologne, maybe, or Frankfurt, or Vienna. May happen anyway, but we're not going to brag and help it along, not when we can keep quiet and smile mysteriously,

if you know what I mean." Maybe his smile was intended to be
mysterious, but it ended up looking raffish.

Jäger asked, "Do you know how we did it? That's a mystery
to me."

"As a matter of fact, I do, but I'm not supposed to tell," Skorzeny said. Jäger picked a branch up off the ground and made as if
to hit him with it. Skorzeny chuckled. "Shit, I never have been any
good at doing what I'm supposed to. You know you can't fit one
of those bombs on a plane or a rocket, right?"

"Oh, yes," Jäger said. "Remember, I got involved in that project
deeper than I wanted to. You mad bastard, that was your fault, too.
If I hadn't been on that raid with you that snatched the explosive
metal from the Lizards—"

"—You'd have stayed a Soviet puppet and you'd probably be
dead by now," Skorzeny broke in. "If the Lizards didn't get you,
the Bolsheviks would have. But that's neither here nor there. We
didn't put it on a freighter, either, the way we did when we blasted
Rome. Hard to fool the Lizards the same way twice."

Jäger walked along, thinking hard. He scratched the side of his
jaw. He needed a shave. He had a straight razor, but scraping his
face without shaving soap hurt more than it was worth. At length,
he said, "We couldn't have sent it in overland. Insane even to
think about it. That leaves—nothing I can see."

"Nothing the Lizards can see, either." Skorzeny grinned an evil
grin. "They'd be tearing their hair if they had any. But I know
something they don't know." He almost chanted the words, as if
he were a little boy taunting the other children on the schoolyard.
He thumped his finger off Jäger's chest. "I know something you
don't know, too."

"That's all right," Jäger said. "I know I'm going to boot you in
the arse if you don't spill it. How did we burn the library at
Alexandria?"

Like most classical allusions, that one sailed past Skorzeny. He
answered the main question, though: "I know we have a new kind
of U-boat, that's what I know. Damned if I know how, but it can
do 450 kilometers submerged every centimeter of the way."

"God in heaven," Jäger said in genuine awe. "If the Lizards
hadn't come, we'd have swept the Atlantic clean with boats like
that." He scratched his jaw again, visualizing a map of the eastern
Mediterranean. "It must have sailed from—Crete?"

Skorzeny's blunt features registered a curious blend of respect
and disappointment. "Aren't you the clever chap?" he said. "Yes,

from Crete to Alexandria you can sail underwater—as long as you understand you won't sail back."

"Mm, yes, there is that." Jäger did some more mulling. "You couldn't tell the whole crew—there'd be a mutiny. But you could find a man you could rely on to press the button or flip the switch or whatever he had to do." He took off his black service cap in respect for the courage of that man.

"Has to be how they did it, all right," Skorzeny agreed. "One thing—he'd never know what hit him."

Jäger thought of the fireball he'd seen going up east of Breslau, the one that had stalled the Lizards' attack on the town. He tried to imagine being at the center of that fireball. "You're right," he said. "You might as well drop a man into the sun."

"That's what it would be like, sure enough," the SS man said. He walked along beside Jäger, whistling tunelessly between his teeth. After half a dozen paces or so, he asked, ever so casually, "Your Jewish chums down in Lodz send any messages back to you? They gloating that they got the better of me?"

"I haven't heard a word from them," Jäger answered truthfully. "I wouldn't be surprised if they'd stopped trusting Germans altogether after that bill of goods you tried selling them." And there, he thought, was a fine euphemism for a nerve-gas bomb. If you couldn't speak straight out about the things you did, maybe you shouldn't have done them. In pointed tones, he went on, "They are still keeping the Lizards from using Lodz as a staging point against us, in spite of everything."

"Goody for them," Skorzeny said with a fine sardonic sneer. He thumped Jäger on the back, hard enough that he almost went headlong into the trunk of a birch tree. "Not so long from now, that won't matter, either."

"No?" Apprehension trickled down Jäger's spine. Skorzeny *did* hear things. "Are they going to order us to try to reduce the town? I'm not sure we can do it—and even if we manage, street fighting'll play hob with our armor."

Skorzeny laughed, loud and long. From up in that birch tree, a squirrel chattered indignantly. "No, they're not going to stick your dick in the sausage machine, Jäger," he said. "How do I put it? If we can give the Lizards a present in Alexandria, we can give them and the Jews one in Lodz."

Jäger was a Lutheran. He wished he'd grown up Catholic. Crossing himself would have been a comfort. There could be no mistaking what Skorzeny meant. "How will you get it into Lodz?" he asked, genuinely curious. "The Jews will never trust you—trust us—again. They're liable to have warned the Poles, too. God, if they know what's in that bomb of yours, they're liable to have warned the Lizards."

"Fuck the Lizards. Fuck the Poles. And fuck the Jews, too," Skorzeny said. "I won't take anybody's help with this one. When the package gets here, I'll deliver it personally."

"You have to work," David Nussboym said in the language of the Lizards. He used an emphatic cough. "If you don't work, they'll starve you or they'll just kill you." As if to underscore his words, men with submachine guns surrounded Alien Prisoner Barracks Number 3.

The Lizards in the barracks hissed and squeaked and muttered among themselves. Their spokesman, the male called Ussmak, answered, "So what? For what they feed us, the work is impossibly hard. We starve anyhow. If they kill us quickly, it will all be over. Our spirits will join those of Emperors departed, and we will be at peace." He cast down his eyes. So did the rest of the Lizards who listened to the talk.

Nussboym had seen Lizards in Lodz do likewise when they spoke of their sovereign. They believed in the spirits of Emperors past as passionately as ultraorthodox Jews in God or good Communists in the dictatorship of the proletariat. They were also right about the rations they got. None of that mattered much to Nussboym. If he didn't get these Lizards working again, out he'd go to the timber-cutting detail he'd escaped when they arrived. The rations human woodchoppers got were made for slow starvation, too.

"What can the camp administrators do that would put you back to work?" he asked Ussmak. He was ready to make extravagant promises. Whether the NKVD men who ran the camp would keep them was another matter. But once the Lizards again got into the habit of working, they'd keep at it.

At lot of Lizards were naive and trusting by human standards. Ussmak proved he wasn't one of those. "They can leave. They can die," he answered, his mouth dropping open in a laugh surely sardonic.

"Truth," several males echoed from their crowded bunks.

"Fsseffel's gang is working as ordered," Nussboym said, trying another tack. "They are meeting norms in all areas." He didn't know whether that last bit was true or not, but Ussmak had no way to contest it: contact between his barracks hall and the one where

Fsseffel was headman had been cut off as soon as the males here began their strike.

"Because Fsseffel is a fool, do not think I am a fool, too," Ussmak replied. "We will not be worked to death. We will not be starved to death. Until we believe we will not be overworked or underfed, we will not do anything."

Nussboym glanced out toward the NKVD guards. "They could come in here, drag a few of you outside, and shoot you," he warned.

"Yes, they could," Ussmak agreed. "They would not get much work from the males they shot, though." He laughed again.

"I shall take your words to the commandant," Nussboym said. He meant that for a warning, too, but did not think Ussmak was impressed. The Lizard seemed to him to have more depths of bitterness than any male of the Race Nussboym had known in Poland. He might almost have been a human being. In Poland, of course, the Race had kept prisoners. Males had not been prisoners there.

When Ussmak declined to answer, Nussboym left the barracks. "Any luck?" one of the guards called to him in Russian. He shook his head. He did not like the scowl on the guard's face. He also did not like going back to the hodgepodge of Polish, Russian, and Yiddish he used to communicate with his fellow humans here in the camp. Making himself understood was sometimes easier in the Lizards' language.

The leader of the guards who surrounded the barracks was a gloomy captain named Marchenko. "Comrade Captain, I need to speak with Colonel Skriabin," Nussboym said.

"Maybe you do." Marchenko had some kind of accent—Ukrainian, Nussboym thought—that made him even harder to understand than most Russians. "But does he need to speak to you?" From him, that passed for wit. After a moment, scowling still, he nodded. "All right. Pass back into the old camp."

The camp administrative offices were better built, better heated, and far less crowded than the *zeks'* barracks. Half the people working there were *zeks*, though: clerks and orderlies and what have you. It was far softer work than knocking down pines and birches in the woods, that was certain. His fellow prisoners eyed Nussboym with glances half conspiratorial, half suspicious: in a way, he was one of them, but his precise status wasn't yet clear and might prove too high to suit a lot of them. The speed with which he won access to Skriabin prompted mutters among the file cabinets.

"What news, Nussboym?" the NKVD colonel asked. Nussboym was not important enough to rate first name and patronymic from the short, dapper little man. On the other hand, Skriabin understood Polish, which meant Nussboym didn't have to mumble along in his ugly makeshift jargon.

"Comrade Colonel, the Lizards remain stubborn," he said in Polish. As long as Skriabin called him by his surname, he couldn't address the colonel as Gleb Nikolaievich. "May I state an opinion as to why this is so?"

"Go ahead," Skriabin said. Nussboym wasn't sure just how smart he was. Shrewd, yes, of that there could be no doubt. But how much real intelligence underlay that mental agility was a different question. Now he leaned back in his chair, steepled his fingers, and gave Nussboym either his complete attention or a good facsimile of it.

"Their reasons, I think, are essentially religious and irrational," Nussboym said, "and for that reason all the more likely to be deeply and sincerely held." He explained about the Emperor-worship that suffused the Race, finishing, "They may be willing to martyr themselves to join with Emperors gone by."

Skriabin closed his eyes for a little while. Nussboym wondered if the NKVD man had listened at all, or if he would start to snore at any moment. Then, all at once, Skriabin laughed, startling him. "You are wrong," he said. "We can get them back to work—and with ease."

"I am sorry, Comrade Colonel, but I do not see how." Nussboym didn't like having to admit incapacity of any sort. The NKVD was only too likely to assume that, if he didn't know one thing, he didn't know anything, and so to dispense with his services. He knew things like that happened.

But Colonel Skriabin seemed amused, not angry. "Perhaps you are naive and innocent. Perhaps you are merely ignorant. Either one would account for your blindness. Here is what you will tell this Ussmak who thinks we cannot persuade him to do what the workers and peasants of the Soviet Union require of him—" He spoke for some little while, then asked, "Now do you see?"

"I do," Nussboym said with respect grudging but nonetheless real. Either Skriabin was very shrewd or genuinely clever.

He got no chance to think about which, for the NKVD man said, "Now march back there this instant and show that Lizard he cannot set his naked will against the historical dialectic impelling the Soviet Union ahead to victory."

"I shall go, Comrade Colonel," Nussboym said. He had his own opinions about the historical dialectic, but Skriabin hadn't asked him about them. With luck, Skriabin wouldn't.

Captain Marchenko glowered at Nussboym when he returned. It didn't faze him; Marchenko glowered at everyone all the time. Nussboym went into the barracks full of striking Lizards. "If you do not go back to work, some of you will be killed," he warned. "Colonel Skriabin is fierce and determined."

"We are not afraid," Ussmak said. "If you kill us, the spirits of Emperors past will watch over us."

"Will they?" David Nussboym asked. "Colonel Skriabin tells me many of you males here are mutineers who murdered your own officers. Even those who did not, have surely given secrets of the Race to the Soviet Union. Why would the Emperors want anything to do with your spirits?"

Appalled silence crashed down inside the rebellious barracks. Then the Lizards started talking among themselves in low voices, mostly too fast for Nussboym to follow. He got the drift, though: that was something the Lizards might have thought privately but had never dared speak aloud. He gave Skriabin credit for understanding the way the aliens' minds worked.

At last, Ussmak said, "You Big Uglies go straight for the killing shot, don't you? I have not abandoned the Empire, not in my spirit, but the Emperors may have abandoned me. This is truth. Dare I take the chance of finding out? Dare *we* take the chance of finding out?" He turned to the prisoners and put the question to them.

In Poland, the Lizards had derisively called democracy *snout-counting*. Here they were using something uncommonly like it to hash the matter out for themselves. Nussboym didn't say anything about that. He stood waiting till they were done arguing, and tried to follow the debate as best he could.

"We will work," Ussmak said. He sounded dull and defeated. "We do need more food, though. And—" He hesitated, then decided to go on: "If you can get us the herb ginger, it would help us through these long, boring days."

"I will put your requests to Colonel Skriabin," Nussboym promised. He didn't think the Lizards were likely to get more food. Nobody except the NKVD men, their trusties, and the cooks got enough to eat. Ginger was another story. If it drugged them effectively, they might get it.

He walked out of the barracks. "Well?" Captain Marchenko barked at him.

"The strike is over," he answered in Polish, then added a Ger-

man word to make sure the NKVD man got it: *"Kaputt."* Marchenko nodded. He still looked unhappy with the world, but he
didn't look like a man about to hose down the neighborhood with
his submachine gun, as he often did. He waved Nussboym back
toward the original camp.

As he returned, he saw Ivan Fyodorov limping back into camp,
accompanied by a guard. The right leg of Fyodorov's trousers was
red with blood; his axe must have slipped, out there in the woods.

"Ivan, are you all right?" Nussboym called.

Fyodorov looked at him, shrugged, then looked away. Nussboym's cheeks flamed. This wasn't the first time since he'd
become interpreter for the Lizards that he'd got the cold shoulder
from the men of his former work gang. They made it all too clear
he wasn't one of them any more. He hadn't been asked to rat on
them or anything of the sort, but they treated him with the same
mistrustful respect they gave any of the other *zeks* who went out of
their way to work with the camp administration.

I'm just being realistic, he told himself. In Poland, the Lizards
had been the power to propitiate, and he'd propitiated them. Only
a fool would have thought the Germans a better choice. Well, God
had never been shy about turning out fools in carload lots. That
was how he'd ended up here, after all. No matter where a man
was, he had to land on his feet. He was even serving mankind by
helping the NKVD get the most from the Lizards. He reported
what they wanted to Colonel Skriabin. Skriabin only grunted.

Nussboym wondered why he felt so lonely.

For the first time since George Bagnall had had the displeasure
of making his acquaintance, Georg Schultz had kitted himself out
in full German uniform rather than the motley mix of Nazi and
Bolshevik gear he usually wore. Standing in the doorway of the
house Bagnall, Ken Embry, and Jerome Jones shared, he looked
large and mean and menacing.

He sounded menacing, too. "You damned Englishmen, you had
better clear out of Pleskau while you have the chance." He gave
the German version of the name of the Russian town. "You don't
clear out now, don't bet anyone will let you next week. You
understand what I'm saying?"

Embry and Jones came up behind Bagnall. As if by chance, the
pilot casually held a Mauser, while the radarman bore a Soviet
PPSh 41 submachine gun. "We understand you," Bagnall said.
"Do you understand us?"

Schultz spat in the mud by the doorway. "Try and do some people a favor and this is the thanks I get."

Bagnall looked at Embry. Embry looked at Jones. Jones looked at Bagnall. They all started to laugh. "Why the devil would you want to do us a favor?" Bagnall demanded. "Far as I can tell, you want to see us dead."

"Me especially," Jones added. "I am not responsible for the fair Tatiana's affections, or for the shifts thereof." He spoke as he might have of blizzards or earthquakes or other ineluctable forces of nature.

"If you're dead, she can't yank your trousers down—that's so," Schultz said. "But if you're gone, she can't yank your trousers down, either. One way or another, you aren't going to be around long. I already told you that. You can clear out or you can end up dead—and you'd better figure out quick which one you aim to do."

"Who's going to kill us?" Bagnall said. "You?" He let his eyes flick back to his companions. "Good luck."

"Don't be a *Dummkopf*," Schultz advised him. "In real fighting, you three would just be—what do they say?—collateral damage, that's it. Nobody would know you were dead till you started to stink. And there's going to be real fighting, sure as hell. We're going to set this town to rights, is what we're going to do."

"Colonel Schindler says—" Bagnall began, and then stopped. Lieutenant General Chill's second-in-command made most of the right noises about maintaining Soviet-German cooperation, but Bagnall had got the impression he was just making noise. Chill had thought working with the Russians the best way to defend Pskov against the Lizards. If Schindler didn't—

"Ah, see, you're not so stupid after all," Schultz said, nodding in sardonic approval. "If somebody draws you a picture, you can tell what's on it. Very good." He clicked his heels, as if to an officer of his own forces.

"Why shouldn't we go off to Brigadier German with news like this?" Ken Embry demanded. "You couldn't stop us." He made as if to point his rifle at Schultz.

"What, you think the Russians are blind and deaf and dumb like you?" Schultz threw back his head and laughed. "We fooled 'em good in '41. They won't ever let us do that again. Doesn't matter." He rocked back on his heels, the picture of arrogant confidence. "We would have whipped 'em if the Lizards hadn't come, and we'll whip 'em here in Pleskau, too."

The first part of that claim was inherently unprovable. However much he didn't care for it, Bagnall thought the second part likely to be true. The Soviet forces in and around Pskov were ex-partisans. They had rifles, machine guns, grenades, a few mortars. The Nazis had all that plus real artillery and some armor, though Bagnall wasn't sure how much petrol they had for it. If it came to open war, the *Wehrmacht* would win.

Bagnall didn't say anything about that. Instead, he asked, "Do you think you're going to be able to keep the fair Tatiana"—*die schöne Tatiana*; it was almost a Homeric epithet for the sniper—"as a pet? I wouldn't want to fall asleep beside her afterwards, let me tell you."

A frown settled on Schultz's face like a rain cloud. Plainly, he hadn't thought that far ahead. In action, he probably let his officers do his thinking for him. After a moment, though, the cloud blew away. "She knows strength, Tatiana. When the forces of the *Reich* have shown themselves stronger than the Bolsheviks, when I have shown myself stronger than she is—" He puffed out his chest and looked manly and imposing.

The three RAF men looked at one another again. By their expressions, Embry and Jones were having as much trouble holding in laughter as Bagnall was. Tatiana Pirogova had been fighting the Germans since the war started, and only reluctantly went over to fighting the Lizards after they landed. If Schultz thought a Nazi win in Pskov would awe her into thinking him a German *Übermensch*, he was in for disappointment—probably painful, possibly lethal, disappointment.

But how could you tell him that? The answer was simple: you couldn't. Before Bagnall even started to figure out what to say, Schultz spoke first: "You have your warning. Do with it what you will. *Guten Tag.*" He did a smart about-turn and clumped away. Now that spring was truly here, he wore German infantry boots in place of the Russian felt ones everyone, regardless of politics, used during the winter.

Bagnall shut the door, then turned to his fellow Englishmen. "Well, what the devil are we supposed to do about *that*?"

"I think the first thing we do, no matter what Schultz said, is to go pay a visit to Aleksandr German," Jerome Jones said. "Knowing the Germans don't love you is rather different from knowing they aim to kick you in the ballocks one day soon."

"Yes, but after that?" Embry said. "I don't much care to scuttle out of here, but I'm damned if I'll fight for the Nazis and I'm not dead keen on laying my life on the line for the Bolshies, either."

That summed up Bagnall's feelings so well, he nodded instead of adding a comment of his own along those lines. What he did say was, "Jones is right. We'd best learn what German"—he put the hard *G* in there—"knows about what the Germans"—soft *G*—"are up to."

He got a rifle of his own before going out on the streets of Pskov. Embry and Jones carried their weapons. So did most of the men and a lot of the women in town: Nazis and Red Russians put him in mind of cowboys and Red Indians. This game, though, was liable to be bloodier.

They went through the marketplace to the east of the ruins of the *Krom*. Bagnall didn't like what he saw there. Only a handful of *babushkas* sat behind the tables, not the joking, gossiping throngs that had filled the square even through the winter. The goods the old women set out for sale were shabby, too, as if they didn't want to show anything too fine for fear of having it stolen.

Aleksandr German made his headquarters across the street from the church of Sts. Peter and Paul at the Buoy, on Ulitsa Vorovskogo north of the *Krom*. The Red Army soldiers who guarded the building gave the Englishmen suspicious looks, but let them through to see the commander.

The fierce red mustache German wore had given him the appearance of a pirate. Now, with his face thin and pale and drawn, the mustache seemed pasted on, like misplaced theatrical makeup. An enormous bandage still padded his crushed hand. Bagnall was amazed the surgeons hadn't simply amputated it; he couldn't imagine the ruined member ever giving the partisan brigadier as much use as he could have got from a hook.

He and Jerome Jones took turns telling German of Georg Schultz's warning. When they were through, the Soviet partisan officer held up his good hand. "Yes, I do know about this," he said in the Yiddish that came more naturally to him than did Russian. "The Nazi is probably right—the fascists and we will be fighting again before long."

"Which does no one but the Lizards any good," Bagnall observed.

Aleksandr German shrugged. "It doesn't even do them much good," he said. "They aren't going to come north and take Pskov, not now they're not. They've pulled most of their forces off this front to fight the Germans in Poland. We were fighting the fascists before the Lizards came, and we'll be fighting them after the Lizards go. No reason we shouldn't fight them while the Lizards are here, too."

"I don't think you'll win," Bagnall said.

German shrugged again. "Then we fade back into the woods and become the Forest Republic once more. We may not hold the town, but the Nazis will not hold the countryside." He sounded very sure of himself.

"Doesn't seem to leave much place for us," Jerome Jones said in Russian. Thanks to his university studies, he preferred that language to German; with Bagnall, it was the other way around.

"It does not leave much place for you," Aleksandr German agreed. He sighed. "I had thought to try to get you out of here. Now I shall not have the chance. But I urge you to leave before we and the Nazis start fighting among ourselves again. You did all you could to keep that from happening up until now, but Colonel Schindler is a less reasonable man than his late predecessor—and, as I say, the threat from the Lizards is less now, so we have not got that to distract us from each other. Make for the Baltic while you still can."

"Will you write us a safe-conduct?" Ken Embry asked him.

"Yes, certainly," the partisan brigadier said at once. "You should get one from Schindler, too." His face twisted. "You are Englishmen, after all, and so deserve fair treatment under the laws of war. If you were Russians—" He shook his head. "The other thing you need to remember is how little good a safe-conduct, ours or Schindler's, may do for you. If someone shoots at you from five hundred meters, you will not be able to present it to him."

Though that was true, it was not a topic on which Bagnall cared to dwell. Aleksandr German found a scrap of paper, dipped a pen into a bottle that smelled more of berry juice than of ink, and scribbled rapidly. He handed the document to Bagnall, who still read Cyrillic script only haltingly. Bagnall passed it to Jerome Jones. Jones skimmed through it and nodded.

"Good luck," Aleksandr German said. "I wish I had something more than that to offer you, but even it is in short supply here these days."

The three Englishmen were somber when they left the partisan brigadier. "Do you think we ought to get a *laissez-passer* from Schindler?" Embry asked.

"My guess is that we needn't bother," Bagnall answered. "The Germans around here are all soldiers, and all know who we are. That isn't true of the Russians, not by a long chalk. Our piece of paper may keep some peasants from slitting our throats one night while we're asleep in their haystack."

"Or, of course, it may not," Embry said, not wanting his

reputation for cynicism to suffer. "Still, I suppose we're better off with it."

"Pity we didn't bring all our food and ammunition along," Bagnall said. "We could have started off straightaway instead of having to go back to the house."

"It's not that far back," Jones said. "And after we recover the gear, I suggest we stay not upon the honor of our going. When both sides tell you you'd better hop it, you're a fool if you don't listen. And, except where the fair Tatiana is concerned"—he grinned ruefully—"Mrs. Jones raised no fools."

"You'll be free of her at last," Bagnall reminded him.

"So will I," he said, and then, "dammit."

A captain with a set of decorations as impressive as Basil Roundbush's rapped on the door frame of David Goldfarb's laboratory at Dover College. "Hullo," he said. "I have a present for you chaps." He turned and let out some grunts and hisses that sounded rather as if he were doing his best to choke to death. More funny noises came back at him. Then a Lizard walked into the room, its turreted eyes going every which way.

Goldfarb's first reaction was to grab for a pistol. Unfortunately, he wasn't wearing one. Roundbush was, and had it out with commendable speed. "No need for that," the much-decorated captain said. "Mzepps is quite tame, and so am I: Donald Mather, at your service."

After his first instant of surprise, Basil Roundbush had taken a good look at Mather's uniform. The pistol went back into its holster. "He's SAS, David," he said. "I expect he can protect us from a Lizard or two . . . dozen." He sounded more serious than he normally would have while making such a crack.

Goldfarb took a second look at Mather and concluded Roundbush *was* serious. The captain was a handsome chap in a blond, chisel-featured way, and seemed affable enough, but something about his eyes warned that getting on his wrong side would be a mistake—quite likely a fatal mistake. And he hadn't won those medals for keeping the barracks clean and tidy, either.

"Sir, what will we do with—Mzepps, did you say?" he asked.

"Mzepps, yes," Mather answered, pronouncing each *p* separately. "I expect he might be useful to you: he's a radar technician, you see. I'll stay around to interpret till the two of you understand each other well enough, then I'll be on my merry way. He does speak a little English now, but he's far from fluent."

"A radar technician?" Basil Roundbush said softly. "Oh,

David, you are a lucky sod. You know that, don't you? That peach of a girl, now a Lizard of your very own to play with." He rounded on Mather. "You don't happen to have a jet-engine specialist concealed anywhere about your person, do you? We have this lovely video platter here on how to service their bloody engines, and knowing what the words mean would help us understand the pictures."

Captain Mather actually did look up his sleeve. "Nothing here, I'm afraid." The dispassionate tone of the reply only made it more absurd. Mzepps spoke up in the Lizards' hissing language. Mather listened to him, then said, "He tells me he was kept with a couple of jet-engine men, er, Lizards, back in—well, you don't need to know that. Where he was before. They like it where they are, he says. Why was that, Mzepps?" He repeated the question in the Lizards' speech, listened to the answer, laughed, and reported back: "They like it because the bloke they're working with is hardly bigger than they are . . . Hullo! What's got into you two?"

Goldfarb and Roundbush had both let out yelps of delight. Goldfarb explained: "That has to be Group Captain Hipple. We both thought he'd bought his plot when the Lizards jumped on Bruntingthorpe with both feet. First word we've had he's alive."

"Ah. That is a good show," Mather said. He snapped his fingers and pointed at Goldfarb. "Something I was supposed to tell you, and I nearly forgot." He looked angry at himself: he wasn't supposed to forget things. "You're cousin to that Russie chap, aren't you?" Without waiting for Goldfarb's startled nod, he went on, "Yes, of course you are. I ought to let you know that, not so very long ago, I put him and his family on a boat bound for Palestine, on orders of my superiors."

"Did you?" Goldfarb said tonelessly. "Thank you for telling me, sir. Other than that—" He shook his head. "I got them out of Poland so the Lizards wouldn't do their worst to him, and now he's back in another country they've overrun. Have you heard any word of him since he got there?"

"I'm afraid not," Mather answered. "I've not even heard *that* he got there. You know how security is." He seemed faintly embarrassed. "I daresay I shouldn't have told you what I just did, but blood's thicker than water, what?"

"Yes." Goldfarb gnawed on his lower lip. "Better to know, I suppose." He wasn't sure he meant what he said. He felt helpless. But then, Mather might as easily have brought news that Moishe and Rivka and Reuven had been killed in a Lizard air raid on

London. There was still hope. Clinging to it, he said, "Well, we haven't much choice but to get on with it, have we?"

"Right you are," Mather said, and Goldfarb gathered he'd made a favorable impression. The SAS man went on, "Only way to keep from going mad is to carry on."

How very British, Goldfarb thought, half ruefully, half in admiration. "Let's find out what Mzepps knows about radars, and what he can tell us about the sets we've captured from his chums."

Before that first day's work with the Lizard prisoner was done, he learned as much in some areas as he had in months of patient—and sometimes not so patient—trial and error. Mzepps gave him the key to the color-coding system the Lizards used for their wires and electrical components: far more elaborate and more informative than the one with which Goldfarb had grown up. The Lizard also proved a deft technician, showing the RAF radarman a dozen quick tricks, maybe more, that made assembling, disassembling, and troubleshooting radars easier.

But when it came to actually repairing the sets, he was less help. Through Mather, Goldfarb asked him, "What do you do when this unit goes bad?" He pointed to the gadgetry that controlled the radar wavelength. He didn't know how it did that, but more cut and try had convinced him it did.

Mzepps said, "You remove the module and replace it with one in good working order." He reached into the radar. "See, it snaps in and out like this. Very easy."

It was very easy. From an accessibility standpoint, the Lizards' sets beat what the RAF made all hollow. The Lizards designed them so they not only worked but were also convenient to service. A lot of good engineering had gone into that. British engineers had just got to the point of being able to design radars that worked. Every time he looked at the cat's cradle of wires and resistors and capacitors and the rest of the electronics that made up the guts of an RAF set, Goldfarb was reminded that they hadn't yet concerned themselves with convenience.

But Mzepps hadn't quite grasped what he'd meant. "I see how you replace it, yes. But suppose you haven't got a replacement for the whole unit. Suppose you want to repair the part in it that's gone bad? How do you diagnose which part that is, and how do you fix it?"

Captain Mather put the revised question to the Lizard. "No can do," Mzepps said in English. He went on in his own language. Mather had to stop and ask more questions a couple of times. At last he gave Goldfarb the gist: "He says it really can't be done, old man. That's a unitary assembly. If one part of it goes, the whole unit's buggered for fair." Mzepps added something else. Mather translated again: "The idea is that it shouldn't break down to start with."

"If he can't fix it when it breaks, what the devil good is he?" Goldfarb said. As far as he was concerned, you had no business mucking about with electronics without some notion of the theory behind the way the machines worked—and if you understood the theory, you were halfway to being able to jury-rig a fix when something went wrong. And something would go wrong.

After a moment, he realized he wasn't quite fair. Plenty of people ran motorcars without knowing more about how they worked than where to put in the petrol and how to patch a punctured inner tube. Still, he wouldn't have wanted one of those people on his team if he were driving a race car.

Mzepps might have been thinking along with him. Through Captain Mather, the Lizard said, "The task of a technician is to know which unit is ailing. We cannot manufacture components for our sets on this planet, anyhow. Your technology is too primitive. We have to use what we brought with us."

Goldfarb imagined a Victorian expeditionary force stranded in darkest Africa. The British soldiers could cut a great swath through the natives—as long as their ammunition held out, their Maxim guns didn't break some highly machined part, their horses didn't start dying of sleeping sickness, and they didn't come down with malaria or yaws or whatever you came down with in darkest Africa (sure as hell, you'd come down with something). If that Victorian army was stuck there, without hope of rescue . . .

He turned to Donald Mather. "Do you know, sir, this is the first bit of sympathy I've ever felt for the Lizards."

"Don't waste it," Mather advised him. "They'd waste precious little on you, and that's the God's truth. They're a nasty set of foes, which only means we shall have to be nasty in return. Gas, these bombs . . . if we're not to go under, we must seize what spares we can."

That was inarguably true. Even so, Goldfarb didn't think Mather took his point. He glanced over at the SAS man. No, Mather didn't look to be the sort who'd appreciate argument by historical analogy or any such *pilpul*—not that he'd know that word, either.

"Ask Mzepps what he'll do when he and his scaly chums run out of spares," Goldfarb said.

"By then, we'll be beaten," Mather said after the Lizard was done with his noises. "That's still their propaganda line, in spite of the thrashing they took when they came over here."

"Can't expect them to go about saying they're doomed, I suppose," Goldfarb allowed. "But if our charming prisoner there still thinks we're going to be trounced, why is he being so cooperative here? He's helping grease the skids for his own people. Why not just name, rank, and pay number?"

"There's an interesting question." Mather made steam-engine noises at Mzepps. Goldfarb doubted he came up with many interesting questions on his own, not ones unrelated to the immediate task at hand. The Lizard prisoner replied at some length, and with some heat. Mather gave Goldfarb the essence of it: "He says we are his captors, so we have become his superiors. The Lizards obey their superiors the way Papists obey the Pope, only rather more so."

Goldfarb didn't know how well, or even if, Catholics obeyed the Pope. He didn't point out his ignorance to Mather. The SAS man was liable to have other aversions, including one to Jews. If he did, he didn't let it interfere with the way he did his job. Goldfarb was willing to settle for that. The world being as it was these days, it was more than you could count on getting.

"What sort of treatment does he get?" he asked Mather, pointing to Mzepps. "After he's done here, where does he go? How does he spend his time?"

"We've brought several Lizards into Dover to work with you boffins," Mather replied. That in itself surprised Goldfarb, who was used to thinking of people like Fred Hipple as boffins, not to having the label applied to himself. He supposed that, to a combat soldier like Mather, anyone who fought the war with slide rule and soldering iron rather than Sten gun and hand grenade counted as an intellectual sort. His bemusement made him miss part of the SAS man's next sentence: "—billeted them at a cinema house that was worthless otherwise with so little electricity in town. They get the same rations our troops do, but—"

"Poor devils," Goldfarb said with deep feeling. "Isn't that against the Geneva Convention? Being purposely cruel to prisoners, I mean."

Mather chuckled. "I shouldn't wonder. I was going to say, they get more meat and fish than we do, which isn't hard, I know. Signs are, they need it in their diet."

"So do I," Basil Roundbush said plaintively from across the room. "Oh, so do I. Can't you see me pining away for want of sirloin?" He let out a theatrical groan.

Captain Mather rolled his eyes and tried to carry on: "The ones who want it, we give ginger. Mzepps hasn't got that habit. They talk among themselves. Some of them have taken up cards and dice and even chess."

"Those can't be games anything like what they're used to," Goldfarb said.

"They have dice, Mzepps tell me. The others, I suppose, help fill up the time. We don't let them have any of their own amusements. Can't. Most of those are electric—no, you'd say electronic, what?—devices of one sort or another, and who knows but what they might build some sort of wireless from them."

"Mm, that's so." Goldfarb glanced over at Mzepps. "Is he happy?"

"I'll ask him." Mather did, then laughed. " 'Are you crazy?' he says." Mzepps spoke some more. Mather went on, "He says he's alive and fed and not being tortured, and all that's more than he expected when he was captured. He may not be dancing in the daisies, but he's got no kick coming."

"Fair enough," Goldfarb said, and went back to work.

Sergeant Herman Muldoon peered out through a glassless second-story window of the Wood House across Quincy, Illinois, down toward the Mississippi at the base of the bluffs. "That there," he declared, "is one hell of a river."

"This is a hell of a place, too," Mutt Daniels said. "Yeah, the windows are blown to smithereens, but the house itself don't hardly look no different than the way it did last time I was in this town, back about nineteen and seven."

"They made the joint to last, all right," Muldoon agreed. "You set stone blocks in lead, they ain't goin' anyplace. Bein' shaped like a stop sign don't hurt, neither, I guess: more chance to deflect a shell, less chance to stop one square." He paused. "What were you doin' here in 1907, Lieutenant, you don't mind my askin'?"

"Playin' ball—what else?" Mutt answered. "I started out number two catcher for the Quincy Gems in the Iowa State League—my first time ever in Yankee country, and Lord! was I lonesome. Number one catcher—his name was Ruddock, Charlie Ruddock—he broke his thumb second week in May. I hit .360 for a month after that, and the Gray's Harbor Grays, out in Washington State, bought my contract. The Northwestern League was Class B, two notches up from Quincy, but I was kinda sorry to leave just the same."

"How come?" Muldoon asked. "You ain't the kind of guy to turn down a promotion, Lieutenant, and I bet you never was."

Daniels laughed softly. He looked out toward the Mississippi, too. It *was* a big river here, but not a patch on what it would be when it got down to his home state, which shared its name. It hadn't had the Missouri or the Ohio or the Tennessee or the Red or a zillion other rivers join it, not yet.

Only a quarter of him was thinking about the Mississippi, though. The rest looked not so much across Quincy as across almost two thirds of a lifetime. More to himself than to Herman Muldoon, he said, "There was this pretty little girl with curly hair just the color o' ripe corn. Her name was Addie Strasheim, an' I can see the little dimple in her cheek plain as if it was yesterday. She was a sweetie, Addie was. I'd'a stayed here all season, likely tell I woulda married her if I coulda talked her pa into it."

"You get the chance, you oughta go lookin' for her," Muldoon said. "Town ain't been fought over too bad, and this don't look like the kind of place where a whole bunch of people pull up stakes and head for the big city."

"You know, Muldoon, for a pretty smart guy, you can be a natural-born damn fool," Mutt said. His sergeant grinned back at him, not in the least put out. Slowly, again half to himself, Daniels went on, "I was twenty-one then, she was maybe eighteen. Don't think I was the first boy who ever kissed her, but I reckon there couldn't have been more than a couple ahead of me. She's alive now, she's got old, same as me, same as you, same as everybody. I'd sooner think of her like she was, sweet as a peach pie." He sighed. "Hell, I'd sooner think of me like I was, a kid who thought a kiss was somethin' special, not a guy standin' in line for a fast fuck."

"World's a nasty place," Muldoon said. "You live in it, it wears you down after a while. War makes it worse, but it's pretty bad any old way."

"Ain't that the sad and sorry truth?" Mutt said.

"Here." Muldoon took his canteen off his belt and held it out to Mutt. "Good for what ails you."

"Yeah?" Nobody had ever offered Mutt water with a promise like that. He unscrewed the lid, raised the canteen to his lips, and took a swig. What came out was clear as water, but kicked like a mule. He'd had raw corn likker a time or three, but this stuff made some of the other moonshine he'd poured down feel like Jack Daniel's by comparison. He swallowed, coughed a couple of times, and handed the canteen back to Muldoon. "Good thing I ain't got me no cigarettes. I light a match and breathe in, I figure I'd explode."

"Wouldn't surprise me one damn bit," the sergeant said with a chuckle. He looked at his watch. "We better grab some sack time while we can. We start earnin' our pay again at midnight."

Daniels sighed. "Yeah, I know. An' if this goes just right, we push the Lizards back a quarter of a mile down the Mississippi. At that rate, we can have the whole damn river open about three weeks before Judgment Day." Once he got the complaints out of his system, he rolled himself up in a blanket and fell asleep in a minute and a half, tops.

As he was dozing off, he figured Captain Szymanski would have to kick him awake, because he was down for the count. But he woke up in good time without the help of the company commander's boot. Mosquitoes made sure of that. They came through the glassless windows of the Wood House buzzing like a flight of fighter planes, and they didn't chew him up a whole lot less than getting strafed would have.

He slapped at his hands and his face. He wasn't showing any other bare skin, but that was plenty for the mosquitoes. Come morning, he'd look like raw meat. Then he remembered the mission. Come morning, he was liable to *be* raw meat.

Muldoon was awake, too. They went downstairs together, a couple of old-timers still hanging on in a young man's world, a young man's game. Back when he was a kid fighting to hook onto a big-league job even for a little while, he'd resented—he'd almost hated—old geezers who hung on and hung on and wouldn't quit and give the new guys a chance. Now he was a geezer himself. When quitting meant going out feet first, you were less inclined to do it than when all you lost was your job.

Captain Szymanski was already down there in the big hall, telling the dogfaces what they were going to do and how they'd do it. They were supposed to know, but you didn't get anywhere taking brains for granted. Szymanski finished, "Listen to your lieutenant and your sergeant. They'll get you through." That made Mutt feel pretty good.

More mosquitoes buzzed outside. Crickets chirped. A few spring peepers peeped, though most of them had already had their season. The night was warm and muggy. The platoon tramped south toward the Lizards' forward positions. Boots clunked on pavement, then struck dirt and grass more quietly.

A couple of scouts halted the advancing Americans just north of Marblehead, the hamlet next down the river from Quincy. "Dig in," Mutt whispered through the sticky darkness. Entrenching tools were already biting into dirt. Daniels missed the elaborate trench networks of the First World War, but fighting nowadays moved too fast to make those practical in most places. Even a fox-hole quickly scraped out of the dirt was mighty nice to have some-times, though.

He tugged back the cuff of his sleeve to look at his watch. A quarter to twelve, the glowing hands said. He held it up to his ear. Yes, it was ticking. He would have guessed it a couple of hours later than that, and something gone wrong with the attack. "Time flies when you're havin' fun," he muttered.

No sooner had he lowered his arm than artillery opened up, off to the east of Quincy. Shells started slamming into Marblehead, some landing no more than a couple of hundred yards south of where he crouched. Nothing had gone wrong after all; he'd just been too keyed up to keep track of time.

"Let's go!" he shouted when his watch told him it was time. The barrage shifted at the same moment, plastering the southern half of Marblehead instead of the northern part. Lizard artillery was busy, too, but mostly with counterbattery fire. Mutt was glad the Lizards were shelling the American guns, not him.

"Over here!" a scout yelled. "We've got paths cut through their wire." The Lizards used stuff that was like nothing so much as a long, skinny double-edged razor blade. As far as he was con-cerned, it was even nastier than barbed wire. The plan had said there would be paths, but what the plan said didn't always have a lot to do with reality.

Lizards in Marblehead opened up on the Americans as they were coming through the wire. No matter how many traps you set, you wouldn't get all the rats. No matter how you shelled a place, you wouldn't clear out all the fighters. Mutt had been on the receiving end of barrages a lot worse than this one. He'd expected opposition, and here it was.

He blazed away with his tommy gun, then threw himself flat behind the overturned hulk of an old Model A. Mike Wheeler, the platoon BAR man, hosed down the town with his Browning Auto-matic Rifle. Daniels wished for Dracula Szabo, the BAR man in his old platoon. Dracula would have got right up there nose-to-snout with the Lizards before he let 'em have it.

His platoon's attack developed the Lizard position. The com-pany's other platoon moved on the town from the east a couple of minutes later. They knew where the enemy was holed up, and winkled the aliens out house by house. Some Lizards surrendered, some fled, some died. One of their medics and a couple of human corpsmen worked side by side on casualties.

A little fight, Mutt thought wearily. A few men killed—even fewer Lizards, by the look of things. Marblehead hadn't been heavily garrisoned. A few of the locals started sticking their heads out of whatever shelters they'd made to protect themselves from pieces of metal flying around with hostile intent.

"Not too bad," Herman Muldoon said. He pointed west, toward the Mississippi. "Another stretch of river liberated. We'll clear all the Lizards out a lot sooner than three weeks before Judgment Day like you said."

"Yeah," Daniels agreed. "Mebbe six weeks." Muldoon laughed, just as if Mutt had been kidding.

☆ **XIII** ☆

Liu Han turned and saw Liu Mei pick up a bayonet Nieh Ho-T'ing had been careless enough to leave on the floor. "No!" Liu Han shouted. "Put it down!" She hurried across the room to take the edged weapon away from her little daughter.

Before she got there, Liu Mei had dropped the bayonet. The baby stared up at her with wide eyes. She started to scold Liu Mei, then stopped. Her daughter had obeyed her when she yelled in Chinese. She hadn't had to speak the little scaly devils' language or use an emphatic cough to make the baby understand her.

She scooped up Liu Mei and squeezed her tight. Liu Mei didn't scream and squawk and try to get away, as she had when Liu Han first got her back from Ttomalss. Little by little, her daughter was becoming used to being a human being among other human beings, not a counterfeit little devil.

Liu Mei pointed to the bayonet. "This?" she asked in the little devils' tongue, complete with interrogative cough.

"This is a bayonet," Liu Han answered in Chinese. She repeated the key word: "Bayonet."

Liu Mei made a noise that might have been intended for *bayonet*, though it also sounded like a noise a scaly devil might have made. The baby pointed in the general direction of the bayonet again, let out another interrogative cough, and said, "This?" once more.

Liu Han needed a moment to realize that, in spite of the cough, the question itself had been in Chinese. "This is a bayonet," she said again. Then she hugged Liu Mei and gave her a big kiss on the forehead. Liu Mei hadn't known what to make of kisses when Liu Han got her back, which struck Liu Han as desperately sad. Her daughter was getting the idea now: a kiss meant you'd done something pleasing.

The baby laughed in reply. Liu Mei laughed, but seldom smiled. No one had smiled at her when she was tiny; the scaly devils' faces didn't work that way. That saddened Liu Han, too. She wondered if she would ever be able to make it up to Liu Mei.

She paused and sniffed, then, despite the baby's protests—Liu Mei, whatever else you could say about her, wasn't shy about squawking—put a fresh cloth around her loins after cleaning the night soil from them.

"Something goes through you," she told her daughter. "Is it enough? Are you getting enough to eat?"

The baby made squealing noises that might have meant anything or nothing. Liu Mei was old for a wet nurse now, and Liu Han's breasts, of course, were empty of milk because her child had been stolen from her so young. But Liu Mei did not approve of the rice powder and overcooked noodles and soups and bits of pork and chicken Liu Han tried to feed her.

"Ttomalss must have been feeding you from tins," Liu Han said darkly. Her mood only got angrier when Liu Mei looked alert and happy at hearing the familiar name of the little scaly devil.

Liu Han had eaten food from tins, too, when the little devils kept her prisoner aboard the airplane that never came down. Most of those tins had been stolen from Bobby Fiore's America or other countries that ate similar kinds of foods. She had loathed them, almost without exception. They were preferable to starving to death, but not, as far as she was concerned, greatly preferable.

But they were what Liu Mei had known, just as the scaly devils were the company she had known. The baby thought the food of China, which seemed only right and proper to Liu Han, tasted and smelled peculiar, and ate it with the same reluctance Liu Han had felt in eating canned hash and other horrors.

Foreign-devil food could still be found in Peking, though most of it was under the control of rich followers of the Kuomintang's counterrevolutionary clique or those who served as the scaly devils' running dogs—not that those two groups were inseparable. Nieh Ho-T'ing had offered to get some by hook or by crook so Liu Mei could have what she was used to.

Liu Han had declined when he first made the offer and every time since. She suspected—actually, she more than suspected; she was sure—one reason he'd made his proposal was to help keep the baby quiet through the night. She had a certain amount of sympathy with that, and certainly had nothing against a full night's sleep, but she was dedicated to the idea of turning Liu Mei back into a proper Chinese child as fast as she could.

She'd had that thought many times since she got her baby back. Now, though, she stared down at Liu Mei in a new way, almost as if she'd never seen the child before. Her program was the opposite of the one Ttomalss had had in mind: he'd been as intent on making Liu Mei into a scaly devil as Liu Han was on turning her daughter back into an ordinary, proper person. But both the little devil and Liu Han herself were treating Liu Mei as if she were nothing more than a blank banner on which they could draw characters of their own choosing. Wasn't a baby supposed to be something besides that?

Nieh wouldn't have thought so. As far as Nieh was concerned, babies were small vessels to be filled with revolutionary spirit. Liu Han snorted. Nieh was probably annoyed that Liu Mei wasn't yet planning bombings of her own and didn't wear a little red star on the front of her overalls. Well, that was Nieh's problem, not Liu Han's or the baby's.

Over a brazier in a corner of the room, Liu Han had a pot of *kao kan mien-erh*, dry cake powder. Liu Mei liked that better than the other common variety of powdered rice, *lao mi mien-erh* or old rice flour. She didn't like either one of them very much, though.

Liu Han went over and took the lid off the pot. She stuck in her forefinger and took it out smeared with a warm, sticky glob of the dry cake powder. When she brought the stuff over to Liu Mei, the baby opened her mouth and sucked the powdered rice off the finger.

Maybe Liu Mei was getting used to proper sorts of food after all. Maybe she was just so hungry that anything even vaguely edible tasted good to her right now. Liu Han understood how that might be from her own desperate times aboard the airplane that never came down. She'd eaten grayish-green tinned peas that reminded her of nothing so much as boiled dust. Perhaps in the same spirit of resignation, Liu Mei now took several blobs of *kao kan mien-erh* from Liu Han's finger and didn't fuss once.

"Isn't that good?" Liu Han crooned. She thought the dry cake powder had very little flavor of any sort, but babies didn't like strongly flavored food. So grandmothers said, anyhow, and if they didn't know, who did?

Liu Mei looked up at Liu Han and let out an emphatic cough. Liu Han stared at her daughter. Was she really saying she liked the dry cake powder today? Liu Han couldn't think of anything else that cough might mean. Although her daughter had still expressed herself in the fashion of a little scaly devil, she'd done it to approve of something not only earthly but Chinese.

"Mama," Liu Mei said, and then used another emphatic cough. Liu Han thought she would melt into a little puddle of dry-cake-flour mush, right there on the floor of her room. Nieh Ho-T'ing had been right: little by little, she was winning her daughter back from the scaly devils.

Mordechai Anielewicz looked at his companions in the room above the fire station on Lutomierska Street. "Well, now we have it," he said. "What do we do with it?"

"We ought to give it back to the Nazis," Solomon Gruver rumbled. "They tried to kill us with it; only fair we should return the favor."

"David Nussboym would have said we should give it to the Lizards," Bertha Fleishman said, "and not the way Solomon meant, but as a true gift."

"Yes, and because he kept saying things like that, we said good-bye to him," Gruver answered. "We don't need any more of such foolishness."

"Just a miracle we managed to get that hideous stuff out of the casing and into our own sealed bottles without killing anybody doing it," Anielewicz said: "a miracle, and a couple of those anti-dote kits the *Wehrmacht* men sold us, for when their own people started feeling the gas in spite of the masks and the protective clothes they were wearing." He shook his head. "The Nazis are much too good at making things like that."

"They're much too good at giving them to us, too," Bertha Fleishman said. "Before, their rockets would send over a few kilos of nerve gas at a time, with a big bursting charge to spread it around. But this ... we salvaged more than a tonne from that bomb. And they were going to have us place it so it hurt us worst. The rockets could come down almost anywhere."

Solomon Gruver's laugh was anything but pleasant. "I bet that Skorzeny pitched a fit when he found out he couldn't play us for suckers the way he thought he could."

"He probably did," Mordechai agreed. "But don't think he's done for good because we fooled him once. I never thought the *mamzer* would live up to the nonsense Göbbels puts out on the wireless, but he does. That is a man to be taken seriously no matter what. If we don't keep an eye on him all the time, he'll do something dreadful to us. Even if we do, he may yet."

"Thank God for your friend, the other German," Bertha said.

Now Anielewicz laughed—uncomfortably. "I don't think he's my friend, exactly. I don't think I'm his friend, either. But I let him live and I let him carry that explosive metal back to Germany, and so . . . I don't know what it is. Maybe it's just a stiff-necked sense of honor, and he's paying back a debt."

"There can be decent Germans," Solomon Gruver said reluctantly. That almost set Mordechai laughing again. If he had started, the laugh would have carried an edge of hysteria. He could imagine some plump, monocled Nazi functionary using that precise tone of voice to admit, *There can be decent Jews.*

"I still wonder if I should have killed him," Mordechai said. "The Nazis would have had a much harder time building their bombs without that metal, and God knows the world would be a better place without them. But the world wouldn't be a better place with the Lizards overrunning it."

"And here we are, still stuck in the middle between them," Bertha Fleishman said. "If the Lizards win, everyone loses. If the Nazis win, we lose."

"We'll hurt them before we go," Anielewicz said. "They've helped us do it, too. If they should come back, we won't let them treat us the way they did before. Not now. Never again. What was the last desire of my life before the Lizards came has been fulfilled. Jewish self-defense is a fact."

How tenuous a fact it was came to be shown a moment later, when a Jewish fighter named Leon Zelkowitz walked into the room where they were talking and said, "There's an Order Service district leader down at the entrance who wants to talk with you, Mordechai."

Anielewicz made a sour face. "Such an honor." The Order Service in the Jewish district of Lodz still reported to Mordechai Chaim Rumkowski, who had been Eldest of the Jews under the Nazis and was still Eldest of the Jews under the Lizards. Most of the time, the Order Service prudently pretended the Jewish fighters did not exist. That the Lizards' puppet police came looking for him now—he needed to find out what it meant. He got up and slung a Mauser over his shoulder.

The Order Service officer still wore his Nazi-issue trench coat and kepi. He wore his Nazi-issue armband, too: red and white, with a black *Magen David* on it; the white triangle inside the Star of David showed his rank. He carried a billy club on his belt. Against a rifle, that was nothing much.

"You wanted me?" Anielewicz was ten or twelve centimeters taller than the district leader, and used his height to stare coldly down at the other man.

"I—" The Order Service man coughed. He was chunky and

pale-faced, with a black mustache that looked as if a moth had landed on his upper lip. He tried again: "I'm Oskar Birkenfeld, Anielewicz. I have orders to take you to Bunim."

"Do you?" Anielewicz had expected a meeting with Rumkowski or some of his henchmen. To be summoned instead to meet with the chief Lizard in Lodz . . . something out of the ordinary was going on. He wondered if he should have this Birkenfeld seized and drop out of sight himself. He'd made plans to do that at need. Was the need here? Temporizing, he said, "Does he give me a safe-conduct pledge to and from the meeting?"

"Yes, yes," the Order Service man said impatiently.

Anielewicz nodded, his face thoughtful. The Lizards were perhaps better than human beings about keeping those pledges. "All right. I'll come."

Birkenfeld turned in what looked like glad relief. Maybe he'd expected Mordechai to refuse, and also expected to catch it from his own superiors. He started away with his shoulders back and a spring in his step, for all the world as if he were on a mission of his own rather than a puppet of puppets. Sad and amused at the same time, Anielewicz followed him.

The Lizards had moved into the former German administrative offices in the Bialut Market Square. *Only too fitting,* Anielewicz thought. Rumkowski's offices were in the next building over; his buggy, with its German-made placard proclaiming him Eldest of the Jews, sat in front of it. But Mordechai got only a glimpse of the buggy, for Lizard guards came forward to take charge of him. District Leader Birkenfeld hastily disappeared.

"Your rifle," a Lizard said to Anielewicz in hissing Polish. He handed over the weapon. The Lizard took it. "Come."

Bunim's office reminded Mordechai of Zolraag's back in Warsaw: it was full of fascinating but often incomprehensible gadgets. Even the ones whose purpose the Jewish fighting leader could grasp worked on incomprehensible principles. When the guard brought him into the office, for instance, a sheet of paper was silently issuing from a squarish box made of bakelite or something very much like it. The paper was covered with the squiggles of the Lizards' written language. It had to have been printed inside the box. As he watched, a blank sheet went inside; it came out with printing on it. How, without any sound save the hum of a small electric motor?

He was curious enough to ask the guard. "It is a *skelkwank* machine," the Lizard answered. "Is no word for *skelkwank* in this speech." Anielewicz shrugged. Incomprehensible the machine would remain.

Bunim turned one eye turret toward him. The regional sub-administrator—the Lizards used titles as impressively vague as any the Nazis had invented—spoke fairly fluent German. In that language, he said, "You are the Jew Anielewicz, the Jew leading Jewish fighters?"

"I am that Jew," Mordechai said. He wondered how angry the Lizards still were at him for helping Moishe Russie escape their clutches. If that was why Bunim had summoned him, maybe he shouldn't have admitted his name. But the way he'd been summoned argued against it. The Lizards didn't seem to want to seize him, but to talk with him.

Bunim's other eye turret twisted in its socket till the Lizard looked at him with both eyes, a sign of full attention. "I have a warning to deliver to you and to your fighters."

"A warning, superior sir?" Anielewicz asked.

"We know more than you think," Bunim said. "We know you Tosevites play ambiguous—is that the word I want?—games with us and with the Deutsche. We know you have interfered with our war efforts here in Lodz. We know these things, I tell you. Do not trouble yourself to deny them. It is of no use."

Mordechai did not deny them. He stood silent, waiting to see what the Lizard would say next. Bunim let out a hissing sigh, then went on, "You know also that we are stronger than you."

"This I cannot deny," Anielewicz said with wry amusement.

"Yes. Truth. We could crush you at any time. But to do this, we would have to divert resources, and resources are scarce. So. We have tolerated you as nuisances—is this the word I want? But no more. Soon we move males and machines again through Lodz. If you are interfering, if you are nuisances, you will pay. This is the warning. Do you understand it?"

"Oh, yes, I understand it," Anielewicz said. "Do you understand how much trouble you will have all through Poland, from Jews and Poles both, if you try to suppress us? Do you want nuisances, as you call them, all over the country?"

"We shall take this risk. You are dismissed," Bunim said. One eye turret swiveled to look out the window, the other toward the sheets of paper that had emerged from the silent printing machine.

"You come," the Lizard guard said in his bad Polish. Anielewicz came. When they got outside the building from which the Lizards administered Lodz, the guard returned his rifle.

Anielewicz went, thoughtfully. By the time he got back to the fire station on Lutomierska Street, he was smiling. The Lizards were not good at reading humans' expressions. Had they been, they would not have liked his.

Max Kagan spoke in rapid-fire English. Vyacheslav Molotov had no idea what he was saying, but it sounded hot. Then Igor Kurchatov translated: "The American physicist is upset with the ways we have chosen to extract plutonium from the improved atomic pile he helped us design."

Kurchatov's tone was dry. Molotov got the idea he enjoyed delivering the American's complaints. Translating for Kagan let him be insubordinate while avoiding responsibility for that insubordination. At the moment, Kagan and Kurchatov were both necessary—indeed, indispensable—to the war effort. Molotov had a long memory, though. One day—

Not today. He said, "If there is a quicker way to get the plutonium out of the rods than to use prisoners in that extraction process, let him acquaint me with it, and we shall use it. If not, not."

Kurchatov spoke in English. So did Kagan, again volubly. Kurchatov turned to Molotov. "He says he never would have designed it that way had he known we would be using prisoners to remove the rods so we could reprocess them for plutonium. He accuses you of several bloodthirsty practices I shall not bother to translate."

You enjoy hearing of them, though. Kurchatov was not as good as he should have been at concealing what he thought. "Have him answer my question," Molotov said. "Is there a quicker way?"

After more back-and-forth between the two physicists, Kurchatov said, "He says the United States uses machines and remote-control arms for these processes."

"Remind him we have no machines or remote-control arms."

Kurchatov spoke. Kagan replied. Kurchatov translated: "He says to remind you the prisoners are dying from the radiation in which they work."

"Nichevo," Molotov answered indifferently. "We have plenty to replace them as needed. The project will not run short, of that I assure him."

By the way Kagan's swarthy face grew darker yet, that was not the assurance he'd wanted. "He demands to know why the prisoners are not at least provided with clothing to help protect them from the radiation," Kurchatov said.

"We have little of such clothing, as you know perfectly well,

Igor Ivanovich," Molotov said. "We have no time to produce it in the quantities we need. We have no time for anything save manufacturing this bomb. For that, the Great Stalin would throw half the state into the fire—though you need not tell Kagan as much. How long now till we have enough of this plutonium for the bomb?"

"Three weeks, Comrade Foreign Commissar, perhaps four," Kurchatov said. "Thanks to the American's expertise, results have improved dramatically."

A good thing, too, Molotov thought. Aloud, he said, "Make it three; less time if you can. And results are what counts here, not method. If Kagan cannot grasp this, he is a fool."

When Kurchatov had translated that for Kagan, the American sprang to attention, clicked his heels, and stuck out his right arm in a salute Hitler would have been proud to get. "Comrade Foreign Commissar, I do not think he is convinced," Kurchatov said dryly.

"Whether he is convinced or not I do not care," Molotov answered. Inside, though, where it didn't show, he added an entry to the list he was compiling against Kagan. Maybe, when the war was over, the sardonic physicist would not find it so easy to go home again. But that was for later contemplation. For now, Molotov said, "What matters is that he continue to cooperate. Do you see any risk his squeamishness will imperil his usefulness?"

"No, Comrade Foreign Commissar. He is outspoken"— Kurchatov coughed behind his hand; Kagan was a lot more, a lot worse, than outspoken—"but he is also dedicated. He will continue to work with us."

"Very well. I rely on you to see that he does." *Your head will go on the block if he doesn't,* Molotov meant, and Kurchatov, unlike Kagan, was not so naive as to be able to misunderstand. The foreign commissar continued, "This center holds the future of the USSR in its hands. If we can detonate one of these bombs soon and then produce more in short order, we shall demonstrate to the alien imperialist aggressors that we can match their weapons and deal them such blows as would in the long run prove deadly to them."

"Certainly they can deliver such blows to us," Kurchatov replied. "Our only hope for preservation is to be able to match them, as you say."

"This is the Great Stalin's policy," Molotov agreed, which also meant it was how things were going to be. "He is certain that, once we have shown the Lizards our capacity; they will become more amenable to negotiations designed to facilitate their withdrawal from the *rodina*."

The foreign commissar and the Soviet physicist looked at each other, while Max Kagan stared at the two of them in frustrated incomprehension. Molotov saw one thought behind Kurchatov's eyes, and suspected the physicist saw the same one behind his, despite his reputation for wearing a mask of stone. It was not the sort of thing even Molotov could say. *The Great Stalin had better be right.*

Ttomalss' hiss carried a curious mixture of annoyance and enjoyment. The air in this Canton place was decently warm, at least during Tosev 3's long summers, but so moist that the researcher felt as if he were swimming in it. "How do you keep fungus from forming in the cracks between your scales?" he asked his guide, a junior psychological researcher named Saltta.

"Superior sir, sometimes you can't," Saltta answered. "If it's one of our fungi, the usual creams and aerosols do well enough in knocking it down. But, just as we can consume Tosevite foods, some Tosevite fungi can consume us. The Big Uglies are too ignorant to have any fungicides worthy of the name, and our medications have not proved completely effective. Some of the afflicted males had to be transported—in quarantine conditions, of course—to hospital ships for further treatment."

Ttomalss' tongue flicked out and wiggled in a gesture of disgust. A great deal of Tosev 3 disgusted him. He almost wished he could have been an infantrymale so he could have slaughtered Big Uglies instead of studying them. He didn't like traveling through Tosevite cities on foot. He felt lost and tiny in the crowd of Tosevites who surged through the streets all around him. No matter how much the Race learned about these noisy, obnoxious creatures, would they ever be able to civilize them and integrate them into the structure of the Empire, as they'd succeeded in doing with the Rabotevs and Hallessi? He had his doubts.

If the Race was going to succeed, though, they'd have to start with new-hatched Tosevites, ones that weren't set in their ways, to learn the means by which Big Uglies might be controlled. That was what he'd been doing with the hatchling that had come out of the female Liu Han's body . . . until Ppevel shortsightedly made him return it to her.

He hoped Ppevel would come down with an incurable Tosevite fungus infection. So much time wasted! So much data that would not be gathered. Now he was going to have to start all over with a new hatchling. It would be years before he learned anything worth having, and for much of the first part of this experiment, he would merely be repeating work he'd already done.

He would also be repeating a pattern of sleep deprivation he would just as soon have avoided. Big Ugly hatchlings emerged from the bodies of females in such a wretchedly undeveloped state that they hadn't the slightest idea about the difference between day and night, and made a horrendous racket whenever they felt like it. Why that trait hadn't caused the species to become extinct in short order was beyond him.

"Here," Saltta said as they turned a corner. "We are coming to one of the main market squares of Canton."

If the streets of the city were noisy, the market was cacophony compounded. Chinese Tosevites screamed out the virtues of their wares at hideous volume. Others, potential customers, screamed just as loud or maybe louder, ridiculing the quality of the merchants' stock in trade. When they weren't screaming, and sometimes when they were, they entertained themselves by belching, spitting, picking their teeth, picking their snouts, and digging fingers into the flesh-flapped holes that served them for hearing diaphragms.

"You want?" one of them yelled in the language of the Race, almost poking Ttomalss in an eye turret with a length of leafy green vegetable.

"No!" Ttomalss said with an angry emphatic cough. "Go away!" Not in the least abashed, the vegetable seller let out a series of the yipping barks the Big Uglies used for laughter.

Along with vegetables, the merchants in the market sold all sorts of Tosevite life forms for food. Because refrigeration hereabouts ranged from rudimentary to nonexistent, some of the creatures were still alive in jugs or glass jars full of seawater. Ttomalss stared at gelatinous things with a great many sucker-covered legs. The creatures stared back out of oddly wise-looking eyes. Other Tosevite life forms had jointed shells and clawed legs; Ttomalss had eaten those, and found them tasty. And still others looked a lot like the swimming creatures in Home's small seas.

One fellow had a box containing a great many legless, scaly creatures that reminded Ttomalss of the animals of his native world far more than did the hairy, thin-skinned life forms that dominated Tosev 3. After the usual loud haggling, a Big Ugly bought one of those creatures. The seller seized it with a pair of tongs and lifted it out, then used a cleaver to chop off its head. While the body was still writhing, the merchant slit open the animal's belly and scooped out the offal inside. Then he cut the body into finger-long lengths, dripped fat into a conical iron pan that sat above a charcoal-burning brazier, and began frying the meat for the customer.

All the while, instead of watching what he was doing, he kept his eyes on the two males of the Race. Nervously, Ttomalss said to Saltta, "He would sooner be doing that to us than to the animal that shares some of our attributes."

"Truth," Saltta said. "Truth, no doubt. But these Big Uglies are still wild and ignorant. Only with the passage of generations will they come to see us as their proper overlords and the Emperor" he lowered his eyes, as did Ttomalss—"as their sovereign and the solace of their spirits."

Ttomalss wondered if the conquest of Tosev 3 could be accomplished. Even if it was accomplished, he wondered if the Tosevites could be civilized, as the Rabotevs and Hallessi had been before them. It was refreshing to hear a male still convinced of the Race's power and the rightness of the cause.

North of the market, the streets were narrow and jumbled. Ttomalss wondered how Saltta found his way through them. The comfortable warmth was a little less here; the Big Uglies, for whom it was less comfortable, built the upper stories of their homes and shops so close together that they kept most of Tosev's light from reaching the street itself.

One building had armed males of the Race standing guard around it. Ttomalss was glad to see them; walking through these streets never failed to worry him. The Big Uglies were so— unpredictable was the kindest word that crossed his mind.

Inside the building, a Tosevite female held a newly emerged hatchling to one of the glands on her upper torso so it could ingest the nutrient fluid she secreted for it. The arrangement revolted Ttomalss; it smacked of parasitism. He needed all his scientific detachment to regard it with equanimity.

Saltta said, "The female is being well compensated to yield up the hatchling to us, superior sir. This should prevent any difficulties springing from the pair bonding that appears to develop between generations of Tosevites."

"Good," Ttomalss said. Now he could get on with his experimental program in peace—and if snivelers like Tessrek did not care for it, too bad. He switched to Chinese to speak to the Big Ugly female: "Nothing bad will happen to your hatchling. It will be well fed, well cared for. All its needs will be met. Do you understand? Do you agree?" He was getting ever more fluent; he even remembered not to use interrogative coughs.

"I understand," the female said softly. "I agree." But as she held out the hatchling to Ttomalss, water dripped from the corners of her small, immobile eyes. Ttomalss recognized that as a sign of insincerity. He dismissed it as unimportant. Compensation was the medicine to heal that wound.

The hatchling wiggled almost bonelessly in Ttomalss' grasp and let out an annoying squawk. The female turned her head away. "Well done," Ttomalss said to Saltta. "Let us take the hatchling back to our own establishment here. Then I shall remove it to my laboratory, and then the research shall begin. I may have been thwarted once, but I shall not be thwarted twice."

To make sure he was not thwarted twice, four guards accompanied him and Saltta back toward the Race's base in the little island in the Pearl River. From there, a helicopter would take him and the hatchling to the shuttlecraft launch site not far away—and from there, he would return to his starship.

Saltta retraced in every particular the route by which he had come to the female Big Ugly's residence. Just before he, Ttomalss, and the guards reached the marketplace with the strange creatures in it, they found their way forward blocked by an animal-drawn wagon as wide as the lane down which they were coming.

"Go back!" Saltta shouted in Chinese to the Big Ugly driving the wagon.

"Can't," the Big Ugly shouted back. "Too narrow to turn around. You go back to the corner, turn off, and let me go by."

What the Tosevite said was obviously true: he couldn't turn around. One of Ttomalss' eye turrets swiveled back to see how far he and his companions would have to retrace their steps. It wasn't far. "We shall go back," he said resignedly.

As they turned around, gunfire opened up from two of the buildings that faced the street. Big Uglies started screaming. Caught by surprise, the guards crumpled in pools of blood. One of them squeezed off an answering burst, but then more bullets found him and he lay still.

Several Tosevites in ragged cloth wrappings burst out of the buildings. They still carried the light automatic weapons with which they'd felled the guards. Some pointed those weapons at Ttomalss, others at Saltta. "You come with us right now or you die!" one of them screamed.

"We come," Ttomalss said, not giving Saltta any chance to

disagree with him. As soon as he got close enough to the Big Uglies, one of them tore the Tosevite hatchling from his arms. Another shoved him into one of the buildings from which the raiders had emerged. In the back, it opened onto another of Canton's narrow streets. He was hustled along through so many of them so fast, he soon lost any notion of where he was.

Before long, the Big Uglies split into two groups, one with him, the other with Saltta. They separated. Ttomalss was alone among the Tosevites. "What will you do with me?" he asked, fear making the words have to fight to come forth.

One of his captors twisted his mouth in the way Tosevites did when they were amused. Because he was a student of the Big Uglies, Ttomalss recognized the smile as an unpleasant one—not that his current situation made pleasant smiles likely. "We've liberated the baby you kidnapped, and now we're going to give you to Liu Han," the fellow answered.

Ttomalss had only thought he was afraid before.

Ignacy pointed to the barrel of the Fieseler *Storch*'s machine gun. "This is of no use to you," he said.

"Of course it's not," Ludmila Gorbunova snapped, irritated at the indirect way the Polish partisan leader had of approaching things. "If I'm flying the aircraft by myself, I can't fire it, not unless my arms start stretching like an octopus'. It's for the observer, not the pilot."

"Not what I meant," the piano-teacher-turned-guerrilla-chief replied. "Even if you carried an observer, you could not fire it. We removed the ammunition from it some time ago. We're very low on 7.92mm rounds, which is a pity, because we have a great many German weapons."

"Even if you had ammunition for it, it wouldn't do you much good," Ludmila told him. "Machine-gun bullets won't bring down a Lizard helicopter unless you're very lucky, and the gun is wrongly placed for ground attack."

"Again, not what I meant," Ignacy said. "We need more of this ammunition. We have a little through the stores the Lizards dole out to their puppets, but only a little is redistributed. So—we have made contact with the *Wehrmacht* to the west. If, tomorrow night, you can fly this plane to their lines, they will put some hundreds of kilograms of cartridges into it. When you return here, you will be a great help in our continued resistance to the Lizards."

What Ludmila wanted to do with the *Storch* was hop into it and fly east till she came to Soviet-held territory. If she somehow got it back to Pskov, Georg Schultz could surely keep it running. Nazi though he was, he knew machinery the way a jockey knew horses.

Schultz's technical talents aside, Ludmila wanted little to do with the *Wehrmacht*, or with heading west. Comrades in arms though the Germans were against the Lizards, her mind still shouted *enemies! barbarians!* whenever she had to deal with them. All of which, unfortunately, had nothing to do with military necessity.

"I take it this means you have petrol for the engine?" she asked, grasping at straws. When Ignacy nodded, she sighed and said, "Very well, I will pick up your ammunition for you. The Germans will have some sort of landing strip prepared?" The Fieseler-156 wouldn't need much, but putting down in the middle of nowhere at night wasn't something to anticipate cheerfully.

The dim light of the lantern Ignacy held showed his nod. "You are to fly along a course of 292 for about fifty kilometers. A landing field will be shown by four red lamps. You know what it means, this flying a course of 292?"

"I know what it means, yes," Ludmila assured him. "Remember, if you want your ammunition back, you'll also have to mark off a landing strip for my return." *And you'll have to hope the Lizards don't knock me down while I'm in the air over their territory, but that's not something you can do anything about—it's my worry.*

Ignacy nodded again. "We will mark the field with four white lamps. I presume you will be flying back the same night?"

"Unless something goes wrong, yes," Ludmila answered. That was a hair-raising business, but easier on the life expectancy than going airborne in broad daylight and letting any Lizard who spotted you take his potshots.

"Good enough," Igancy said. "The *Wehrmacht* will expect you to arrive about 2330 tomorrow night, then."

She glared at him. He'd made all the arrangements with the Nazis, then come to her. Better he should have had her permission before he went off and talked with the Germans. Well, too late to worry about that now. She also realized she was getting very used to operating on her own, as opposed to being merely a part of a larger military machine. She never would have had such resentments about obeying a superior in the Red Air Force: she would have done as she was told, and never thought twice about it.

Maybe it was that the Polish partisans didn't strike her as being military enough to deserve her unquestioned obedience. Maybe it was that she felt she didn't really belong here—if her U-2 hadn't cracked up, if the idiot guerrillas near Lublin hadn't forgotten an extremely basic rule about landing strips—

"Make sure there aren't any trees in the middle of what's going to be my runway," she warned Ignacy. He blinked, then nodded for a third time.

She spent most of the next day making as sure as she could that the *Storch* was mechanically sound. She was uneasily aware she'd never be a mechanic of Schultz' class, and also uneasily aware of how unfamiliar the aircraft was. She tried to make up for ignorance and unfamiliarity with thoroughness and repetition. Before long, she'd learn how well she'd done.

After dark, the partisans took the netting away from one side of the enclosure concealing the light German plane. They pushed the *Storch* out into the open. Ludmila knew she didn't have much room in which to take off. The Fieseler wasn't supposed to need much. She hoped all the things she'd heard about it were true.

She climbed up into the cockpit. When her finger stabbed the starter button, the Argus engine came to life at once. The prop spun, blurred, and seemed to disappear. The guerrillas scattered. Ludmila released the brake, gave the *Storch* full throttle, and bounced toward two men holding candles who showed her where the trees started. They grew closer alarmingly fast, but when she pulled back on the stick, the *Storch* hopped into the air as readily as one of its feathered namesakes.

Her first reaction was relief at flying again at last. Then she realized that, compared to what she was used to, she had a hot plane on her hands now. That Argus engine generated more than twice the horsepower of a U-2's Shvetsov radial, and the *Storch* didn't weigh anywhere near twice as much as a *Kukuruznik*. She felt like a fighter pilot.

"Don't be stupid," she muttered to herself, good advice for a pilot under any circumstances. In the Fieseler's enclosed cabin, she could hear herself talk, which had been all but impossible while she was flying *Kukuruzniks*. She wasn't used to being airborne without having the slipstream blast her in the face, either.

She stayed as low to the ground as she dared; human-built aircraft that got up much above a hundred meters had a way of reaching zero altitude much more rapidly than their pilots had intended. Flying behind the lines, that worked well. Flying over them, as she discovered now, was another matter. Several Lizards opened up on the *Storch* with automatic weapons. The noise bullets made hitting aluminum was different from that which came when they penetrated fabric. But when the *Storch* didn't tumble out of the sky, she took fresh hope that its designers had known what they were doing.

Then she passed the Lizards' line and over into German-held Poland. A couple of Nazis took potshots at her, too. She felt like hauling out her pistol and shooting back.

Instead, she peered through the night for a square of four red lanterns. Sweat that had nothing to do with a warm spring night sprang out on her face. She was so low she might easily miss them. If she couldn't spot them, she'd have to set down anywhere and then no guessing how long the Germans would take to move the ammunition from their storage point to her aircraft, or whether the Lizards would notice the *Storch* and smash it on the ground before the ammo got to it.

Now that she was flying over human-held terrain, she let herself gain a few more meters' worth of altitude. There! Off to the left, not far. Her navigation hadn't been so bad after all. She swung the *Storch* through a gentle bank and buzzed toward the marked strip.

As she got close to it, she realized it seemed about the size of a postage stamp. Would she really be able to set the *Storch* down in such a tiny space? She'd have to try, that was certain.

She eased off on the throttle and lowered the aircraft's huge flaps. The extra resistance they gave her cut into her airspeed astonishingly fast. Maybe she could get the *Storch* down in one piece after all. She leaned over and looked down through the cockpit glasshouse, almost feeling for the ground.

The touchdown was amazingly gentle. The *Storch*'s landing gear had heavy springs to take up the shock of a hard descent. When the descent wasn't hard, you hardly knew you were on the ground. Ludmila killed the engine and tromped hard on the brake. Almost before she knew it, she was stopped—and she still had fifteen or twenty meters of landing room to spare.

"Good. That was good," one of the men holding a lantern called to her as he approached the Fieseler. The light he carried showed his toothy grin. "Where did a pack of ragtag partisans come up with such a sharp pilot?"

At the same time as he was speaking, another man—an officer by his tone—called to more men hidden in the darkness: "Come on, you lugs, get those crates over here. You think they're going to move by themselves?" He sounded urgent and amused at the same time, a good combination for getting the best from the soldiers under his command.

"You Germans always think you're the only ones who know

anything about anything," Ludmila told the *Wehrmacht* man with the lantern.

His mouth fell open. She'd heard that meant something among the Lizards, but for the life of her couldn't remember what. She thought it was pretty funny, though. The German soldier turned around and exclaimed, "Hey, Colonel, would you believe it? They've got a girl flying this plane."

"I've run into a woman pilot before," the officer answered. "She was a very fine one, as a matter of fact."

Ludmila sat in the unfamiliar seat of the *Storch*. Her whole body seemed to have been dipped in crushed ice — or was it fire? She couldn't tell. She stared at the instrument panel—all the gauges hard against the zero pegs now—without seeing it. She didn't realize she'd dropped back into Russian till the words were out of her mouth: "Heinrich . . . is that you?"

"Mein Gott," the officer said quietly, out there in the cricket-chirping darkness where she could not see him. She thought that was his voice, but she hadn't seen him for a year and a half, and never for long at any one stretch. After a moment, he tried again: "Ludmila?"

"What the hell is going on?" asked the soldier with the lantern.

Ludmila got out of the Fieseler *Storch*. She needed to do that anyhow, to make it easier for the Germans to get the chests of ammunition into the aircraft. But even as her feet thumped down onto the ground, she felt she was flying far higher than any plane could safely go.

Jäger came up to her. "You're still alive," he said, almost severely.

The landing lamp didn't give enough light. She couldn't see how he looked, not really. But now that she was looking at him, memory filled in the details the light couldn't: the way his eyes would have little lines crinkling at the corners, the way one end of his mouth would quirk up when he was amused or just thinking hard, the gray hair at his temples.

She took a step toward him, at the same time as he was taking a step toward her. That left them close enough to step into each other's arms. "What the *hell* is going on?" the soldier with the lantern repeated. Ludmila ignored him. Jäger, his mouth insistent on hers, gave no sign he even heard.

From out of the night, a big, deep German voice boomed, "Well, this is sweet, isn't it?"

Ludmila ignored that interruption, too. Jäger didn't. He ended the kiss sooner than he should have and turned toward the man who was coming up—in the night, no more than a large, looming shadow. In tones of military formality, he said, "*Herr Standartenführer*, I introduce to you Lieutenant—"

"Senior Lieutenant," Ludmila broke in.

"—Senior Lieutenant Ludmila Gorbunova of the Red Air Force. Ludmila"—the formality broke down there—"this is *Standartenführer* Otto Skorzeny of the *Waffen* SS, my—"

"Accomplice." Now Skorzeny interrupted. "You two are old friends, I see." He laughed uproariously at his own understatement. "Jäger, you sneaky devil, you keep all sorts of interesting things under your hat, don't you?"

"It's an irregular sort of war," Jäger answered, a little stiffly. Being "old friends" with a Soviet flier was likely to be as destructive to a *Wehrmacht* man's career—and maybe to more than that—as having that sort of relationship with a German had been dangerous for Ludmila. But he didn't try to deny anything, saying, "You've worked with the Russians, too, Skorzeny."

"Not so—intimately." The SS man laughed again. "But screw that, too." He chucked Jäger under the chin, as if he were an indulgent uncle. "Don't do anything I wouldn't enjoy." Whistling a tune that sounded as if it was probably salacious, he strolled back into the night.

"You—work with him?" Ludmila asked.

"It's been known to happen," Jäger admitted, his voice dry.

"How?" she said.

The question, Ludmila realized, was far too broad, but Jäger understood what she meant by it. "Carefully," he answered, which made better sense than any reply she'd expected.

Mordechai Anielewicz had long since resigned himself to wearing bits and pieces of German uniforms. There were endless stocks of them in Poland, and they were tough and reasonably practical, even if not so well suited to winter cold as the ones the Russians made.

Dressing head to foot in *Wehrmacht* gear was something else again, he discovered. Taking on the complete aspect of the Nazi soldiers who had so brutalized Poland gave him a thrill of superstitious dread, no matter how secular he reckoned himself. But it had to be done. Bunim had threatened reprisals against the Jews if they tried to block Lizard movements through Lodz. Therefore, the attack would have to come outside of town, and would have to seem to come from German hands.

Solomon Gruver, also decked out in German uniform, nudged

him. He had greenery stuck onto his helmet with elastic bands, and was almost invisible in the woods off to the side of the road. "They should hit the first mines soon," he said in a low voice distorted by his gas mask.

Mordechai nodded. The mines were German, too, with casings of wood and glass to make them harder to detect. A crew charged with repairing the highway had done just that . . . among other things. Over this stretch of a couple of kilometers, the Lizards would have a very bumpy ride indeed.

As usual, Gruver looked gloomy. "This is going to cost us a lot of men no matter what," he said, and Anielewicz nodded again. Doing favors for the Germans was nothing he loved, especially after what the Germans had tried to do to the Jews of Lodz. But this favor, while it might help Germans like Heinrich Jäger, wouldn't do Skorzeny or the SS any good. So Anielewicz hoped.

He peered through the eye lenses of his own gas mask toward the roadway. The air he breathed tasted flat and dead. The mask made him look like some pig-snouted creature as alien as any Lizard. It was German, too—the Germans knew all about gas warfare, and had been teaching it to the Jews even before the Lizards came.

Whump! The harsh explosion announced a mine going off. Sure enough, a Lizard lorry lay on its side in the roadway, burning. From the undergrowth to either side of the road, machine guns opened up on it and on the vehicles behind it. Farther off, a German mortar started lobbing bombs at the Lizard convoy.

A couple of mechanized infantry combat vehicles charged off the road to deal with the raiders. To Anielewicz's intense glee, they both hit mines almost at once. One of them began to burn; he fired at the Lizards who emerged from it. The other slewed sideways and stopped, a track blown off.

The weapon with which Anielewicz hoped to do the most damage, though, involved no high explosives whatever: only catapults made with lengths of inner tube and wax-sealed bottles full of an oily liquid. As he and Gruver had learned, you could fling a bottle three hundred meters with old rubber like that, and three hundred meters was plenty far enough. From all sides, bottles of captured Nazi nerve gas rained down on the stalled head of the Lizard column. Still more landed farther down its length once the head had stalled. They didn't all break, but a lot of them did.

Lizards started dropping. They weren't wearing masks. The stuff could nail you if it got on your skin, too. Since they wore only body paint, the Lizards were also at a disadvantage there—not that ordinary clothing was any sure protection. Mordechai had heard that the Germans made special rubber-impregnated uniforms for their troops who dealt with gas all the time. He didn't know for certain whether it was true. It sounded typically German in its thoroughness, but wouldn't you stew like a chicken in a pot if you had to fight cooped up in a rubber uniform for more than an hour or two at a stretch?

"What do we do now?" Gruver asked, pausing to shove another clip into his *Gewehr* 98.

"As soon as we've thrown all the gas we brought, we get out," Anielewicz answered. "The longer we hang around, the better the chance the Lizards will capture some of us, and we don't want that."

Gruver nodded. "If we can, we have to bring our dead away, too," he said. "I don't know how smart the Lizards are about these things, but if they're smart enough, they can figure out we're not really Nazis."

"There is that," Mordechai agreed. The last time he'd been reminded of the obvious difference, Zofia Klopotowski had thought it was funny. Consequences springing from it would be a lot more serious here.

The catapult-propelled bottles of nerve gas had a couple of advantages over more conventional artillery: neither muzzle flash nor noise gave away the positions of the launchers. Their crews kept flinging bottles till they were all gone.

After that, the Jewish fighters pulled away from the road, their machine guns covering the retreat. They had several rendezvous points in the area: farms owned by Poles they could trust (*Poles we hope we can trust,* Mordechai thought as he neared one of them). There they got back into more ordinary clothes and stashed weapons of greater firepower than rifles. These days in Poland, you might as well have been naked as go out in public without a Mauser on your shoulder.

Mordechai slipped back into Lodz from the west, well away from the direction of the fighting. It wasn't long past noon when he strolled into the fire station on Lutomierska Street. Bertha Fleishman greeted him outside the building: "They say there was a Nazi raid this morning, just a couple of kilometers outside of town."

"Do they?" he answered gravely. "I hadn't heard, though there was a lot of gunfire earlier in the day. But then, that's so about one day in three."

"It must have been that what's-his-name—Skorzeny, that's it,"

Bertha said. "Who else would be crazy enough to stick his nose in the wasps' nest?"

While they were standing there talking, the Order Police district leader who'd taken Anielewicz to Bunim approached the fire station. Oskar Birkenfeld still carried only a truncheon, and so waited respectfully for the rifle-toting Anielewicz to notice him. When Mordechai did, the man from the Order Police said, "Bunim requires your presence again, immediately."

"Does he?" Anielewicz said. "Whatever for?"

"He'll tell you that," Birkenfeld answered, sounding tough—or as tough as he could when so badly outgunned. Anielewicz looked down his nose at him without saying anything. The Order Service man wilted, asking weakly, "Will you come?"

"Oh, yes, I'll come, though Bunim and his puppets could stand to learn better manners," Mordechai said. Birkenfeld flushed angrily. Mordechai patted Bertha Fleishman on the shoulder. "I'll see you later."

At his Bialut Market Square offices, Bunim stared balefully at Anielewicz. "What do you know of the Deutsche who severely damaged our advancing column this morning?"

"Not much," he answered. "I'd just heard it was a Nazi attack when your pet policeman came to fetch me. You can ask him about it after I go; he heard me get the news, I think."

"I shall ascertain this," Bunim said. "So you deny any role in the attack on the column?"

"Am I a Nazi?" Anielewicz said. "Bertha Fleishman, the woman I was talking with when Birkenfeld found me, thinks that Skorzeny fellow might have had something to do with it. I don't know that for a fact, but I've heard talk he's here in Poland somewhere, maybe to the north of Lodz." If he could do the SS man a bad turn, he would.

"Skorzeny?" Bunim flipped out his tongue but did not waggle it back and forth, a sign of interest among the Lizards. "Exterminating that one would be a whole clutch of eggs' worth of ordinary Tosevites like you."

"Truth, superior sir," Mordechai said. If Bunim wanted to think he was bumbling and harmless, that was fine with him.

The Lizard said, "I shall investigate whether these rumors you report have any basis in fact. If they do, I shall bend every effort to destroying the troublesome male. Considerable status would accrue to me on success."

Mordechai wondered whether that last was intended for him or if Bunim was talking to himself. "I wish you good luck," he said, and, despite having led the raid on that column moving north against the Germans, he meant what he told the Lizard.

"Now we're cooking with gas!" Omar Bradley said enthusiastically as he sat down in Leslie Groves' office in the Science Building at the University of Denver. "You said the next bomb wouldn't be long in coming, and you meant it."

"If I told lies about things like that, you—or somebody—would throw my fanny out of here and bring in a man who delivered on his promises," Groves answered. He cocked his head to one side. Off in the distance, artillery still rumbled. Denver did not look like falling, though, not now. "And you, sir, you've done a hell of a job defending this place."

"I've had good help," Bradley said. They both nodded, pleased with each other. Bradley went on, "Doesn't look like we'll have to use that second bomb anywhere near here. We can try moving it someplace else where they need it worse."

"Yes, sir. One way or another, we'll manage that," Groves said. The rail lines going in and out of Denver had taken a hell of a licking, but there were ways. Break the thing down into pieces and it could go out on horseback—provided all the riders got through to the place where you needed all the pieces.

"I figure we will," Bradley agreed. He started to reach into his breast pocket, but arrested the motion halfway through. "All this time and I still can't get used to going without a smoke." He let out a long, weary exhalation. "That should be the least of my worries—odds are I'll live longer because of it."

"Certainly seem longer, anyhow," Groves said. Bradley chuckled, but sobered in a hurry. Groves didn't blame him. He too had bigger worries than tobacco. He voiced the biggest one: "Sir, how long can we and the Lizards keep going tit for tat? After a while, there won't be a lot of places left, if we keep on trading them the way we have been."

"I know," Bradley said, his long face somber. "Dammit, General, I'm just a soldier, same as you. I don't make policy, I just carry it out, best way I know how. Making it is President Hull's job. I'll tell you what I told him, though, if you want to hear it."

"Hell, yes, I want to hear it," Groves answered. "If I understand what I'm supposed to be doing, figuring out how to do it gets easier."

"Not everybody thinks that way," Bradley said. "A lot of

people want to concentrate on their tree and forget about the forest. But for whatever you think it's worth, my view is that the only fit use for the bombs we have is to make the Lizards sit down at the table and talk seriously about ending this war. Any peace that lets us preserve our bare independence is worth making, as far as I'm concerned."

"Our bare independence?" Groves tasted the words. "Not even all our territory? That's a hard peace to ask for, sir."

"Right now, I think it's the best we can hope to get. Considering the Lizards' original war aims, even getting that much won't be easy," Bradley said. "That's why I'm so pleased with your efforts here. Without your bombs, we'd get licked."

"Even with them, we're getting licked," Groves said. "But we aren't getting licked fast, and we are making the Lizards pay like the dickens for everything they get."

"That's the idea," Bradley agreed. "They came here with resources they couldn't readily renew. How many of them have they expended? How many do they have left? How many more can they afford to lose?"

"Those are the questions, sir," Groves said. "*The* questions."

"Oh, no. There's one other that's even more important," Bradley said. Groves raised an interrogative eyebrow. Bradley explained: "Whether *we* have anything left by the time *they* start scraping the bottom of the barrel."

Groves grunted. "Yes, sir," he said.

Nuclear fire blossomed above a Tosevite city. Seen from a reconnaissance satellite, the view was beautiful. From up at the topmost edges of the atmosphere, you didn't get the details of what a bomb did to a city. Riding in a specially protected vehicle, Atvar had been through the ruins of El Iskandariya. He'd seen firsthand what the Big Uglies' bomb had done there. It wasn't beautiful, not even slightly.

Kirel had not made that tour, though of course he had viewed videos from that strike and others, by both the Race and the Tosevites. He said, "And so we retaliate with this Copenhagen place. Where does it end, Exalted Fleetlord?"

"Shiplord, I do not know where it ends or even if it ends," Atvar answered. "The psychologists recently brought me a translated volume of Tosevite legends in the hope they would help me—would help the Race as a whole—better understand the foe. The one that sticks in my mind tells of a Tosevite male fighting an imaginary monster with many heads. Every time he cut one off, two more grew to take its place. That is the predicament in which we presently find ourselves."

"I see what you are saying, Exalted Fleetlord," Kirel said. "Hitler, the Deutsch not-emperor, has been screaming over every radio frequency he can command about the vengeance he will wreak on us for what he calls the wanton destruction of a Nordic city. Our semanticists are still analyzing the precise meaning of the term *Nordic*."

"I don't care what it means," Atvar snapped petulantly. "All I care about is carrying the conquest to a successful conclusion, and I am no longer certain we shall be able to accomplish that."

Kirel stared at him with both eyes. He understood why. Even when things seemed grimmest, he had refused to waver from faith in the ultimate success of the Race's mission. He had, he admitted to himself, repeatedly been more optimistic than the situation warranted.

"Do you aim to abandon the effort, then, Exalted Fleetlord?" Kirel asked, his voice soft and cautious. Atvar understood that caution, too. If Kirel didn't like the answer he got, he was liable to foment an uprising against Atvar, as Straha had done after the first Tosevite nuclear explosion. If Kirel led such an uprising, it was liable to succeed.

And so Atvar also answered cautiously: "Abandon it? By no means. But I begin to believe we may not be able to annex the entire land surface of this world without suffering unacceptable losses, both to our own forces and to that surface. We must think in terms of what the colonization fleet will find when it arrives here and conduct ourselves accordingly."

"This may involve substantive discussions with the Tosevite empires and not-empires now resisting us," Kirel said.

Atvar could not read the shiplord's opinion of that. He was not sure of his own opinion about it, either. Even contemplating it was entering uncharted territory. The plans with which the Race had left Home anticipated the complete conquest of Tosev 3 in a matter of days, not four years—two of this planet's slow turns around its star—of grueling warfare with the result still very much in the balance. Maybe now the Race would have to strike a new balance, even if it wasn't one in the orders the Emperor had conferred upon Atvar before he went into cold sleep.

"Shiplord, in the end it may come to that," he said. "I still hope it does not—our successes in Florida, among other places, give me reason to continue to hope—but in the end it may. And what have you to say to that?"

Kirel let out a soft, wondering hiss. "Only that Tosev 3 has changed us in ways we could never have predicted, and that I do not care for change of any sort, let alone change inflicted upon us under such stressful circumstances."

"I do not care for change, either," Atvar answered. "What sensible male would? Our civilization has endured for as long as it has precisely because we minimize the corrosive effect of wanton change. But in your words I hear the very essence of the difference between us and the Big Uglies. When we meet change, we feel it is inflicted on us. The Tosevites reach out and seize it with both hands, as if it were a sexual partner for which they have developed the monomaniacal passion they term *love*." As well as he could, he reproduced the word from the Tosevite language called English: because it was widely spoken and even more widely broadcast, the Race had become more familiar with it than with most of the other tongues the Big Uglies used.

"Would Pssafalu the Conqueror have negotiated with the Rabotevs?" Kirel asked. "Would Hisstan the Conqueror have negotiated with the Hallessi? What would their Emperors have said if word reached them that our earlier conquests had not achieved the goals set for them?"

What he was really asking was what the Emperor would say when he learned the conquest of Tosev 3 might not be a complete conquest. Atvar said, "Here speed-of-light works with us. Whatever he says, we shall not know about it until near the time when the colonization fleet arrives, or perhaps even a few years after that."

"Truth," Kirel said. "Until then, we are autonomous."

Autonomous, in the language of the Race, carried overtones of *alone* or *isolated* or *cut off from civilization*. "Truth," Atvar said sadly. "Well, Shiplord, we shall have to make the best of it, for ourselves and for the Race as a whole, of which we are, and remain, a part."

"As you say, Exalted Fleetlord," Kirel answered. "With so much going on in such strange surroundings at so frenetic a pace, keeping that basic fact in mind is sometimes difficult."

"Is frequently difficult, you mean," Atvar said. "Even without the battles, there are so many irritations here. That psychological researcher the Big Uglies in China have kidnapped . . . They state it is in reprisal for his studies of a newly hatched Tosevite. How can we do research on the Big Uglies if our males go in fear of having vengeance taken on them for every test they make?"

"It is a problem, Exalted Fleetlord, and I fear it will only grow worse," Kirel said. "Since we received word of this kidnapping, two males have already abandoned ongoing research projects on the surface of Tosev 3. One has taken his subjects up to an orbiting starship, which is likely to skew his results. The other has also gone aboard a starship, but has terminated his project. He states he is seeking a new challenge." Kirel waggled his eye turrets, a gesture of irony.

"I had not heard that," Atvar said angrily. "He should be strongly encouraged to return to his work: if necessary, by kicking him out the air lock of that ship."

Kirel's mouth fell open in a laugh. "It shall be done, Exalted Fleetlord."

"Exalted Fleetlord!" The image of Pshing, Atvar's adjutant, suddenly filled one of the communicator screens in the fleetlord's chamber. It was the screen reserved for emergency reports. Atvar and Kirel looked at each other. As they'd just said, the conquest of Tosev 3 was nothing but a series of emergencies.

Atvar activated his own communications gear. "Go ahead, Adjutant. What has happened now?" He was amazed at how calmly he brought out the question. When life was a series of emergencies, each individual crisis seemed less enormous than it would have otherwise.

Pshing said, "Exalted Fleetlord, I regret the necessity of reporting a Tosevite nuclear explosion by a riverside city bearing the native name Saratov." After a moment in which he swiveled one eye turret, perhaps to check a map, he added, "This Saratov is located within the not-empire of the SSSR. Damage is said to be considerable."

Atvar and Kirel looked at each other again, this time in consternation. They and their analysts had been confident the SSSR had achieved its one nuclear detonation with radioactives stolen from the Race, and that its technology was too backwards to let it develop its own bombs, as had Deutschland and the United States. Once again, the analysts had not known everything there was to know.

Heavily, Atvar said, "I acknowledge receipt of the news, Adjutant. I shall begin the selection process for a Soviet site to be destroyed in retaliation. And, past that"—he looked toward Kirel for a third time, mindful of the discussion they'd been having—"well, past that, right now I don't know what we shall do."

☆ **XIV** ☆

The typewriter spat out machine-gun bursts of letters: *clack-clack-clack, clack-clack-clack, clackety-clack*. The line-end bell dinged. Barbara Yeager flicked the return lever; the carriage moved with an oiled whir to let her type another line.

She stared in dissatisfaction at the one she'd just finished. "That ribbon is getting too light to read any more," she said. "I wish they'd scavenge some fresh ones."

"Not easy to come by anything these days," Sam Yeager answered. "I hear tell one of our foraging parties got shot at the other day."

"I heard something about that, but not much," Barbara said. "Was it the Lizards?"

Sam shook his head. "Nothing to do with the Lizards. It was foragers out from Little Rock, after the same kinds of stuff our boys were. There's less and less stuff left to find, and we aren't making much these days that doesn't go straight out the barrel of a gun. I think it'll get worse before it gets better, too."

"I know," Barbara said. "The way we get excited over little things now, like that tobacco you bought—" She shook her head. "And I wonder how many people have starved because crops either didn't get planted or didn't get raised or couldn't get from the farm to a town."

"Lots," Sam said. "Remember that little town in Minnesota we went through on the way to Denver? They were already starting to slaughter their livestock because they couldn't bring in all the feed they had to have—and that was a year and a half ago. And Denver's going to go hungry now. The Lizards have tromped on the farms that were feeding it, and wrecked the railroads, too. One more thing to put on their bill, if we ever get around to giving it to them."

"We're lucky to be where we are," Barbara agreed. "It gets down to that, we're lucky to be anywhere."

"Yeah." Sam tapped a front tooth with a fingernail. "I've been lucky I haven't broken a plate, too." He reached out and rapped on the wooden desk behind which Barbara sat. "Way things are now, a dentist would have a heck of a time fixing my dentures if anything did break." He shrugged. "One more thing to worry about."

"We've got plenty." Barbara pointed to the sheet of paper in the typewriter. "I'd better get back to this report, honey, not that anybody'll be able to read it when I'm through." She hesitated, then went on, "Is Dr. Goddard all right, Sam? When he gave me these notes to type up, his voice was as faint and gray as the letters I'm getting from this ribbon."

Sam wouldn't have put it that way, but Sam hadn't gone in for literature in college, either. Slowly, he answered, "I've noticed it for a while now myself, hon. I think it's getting worse, too. I know he saw some of the docs here, but I don't know what they told him. I couldn't hardly ask, and he didn't say anything." He corrected himself: "I take that back. He did say one thing: 'We've gone far enough now that no one man matters much any more.' "

"I don't like the sound of that," Barbara said.

"Now that I think about it, I don't, either," Sam said. "Sort of sounds like a man writing his own what-do-you-call-it—obituary—doesn't it?" Barbara nodded. Sam went on, "Thing is, he's right. Pretty much everything we've done with rockets so far has come out of his head—either that or we've stolen it from the Lizards or borrowed it from the Nazis. But we can go on without him now if we have to, even if we won't go as fast or as straight."

Barbara nodded again. She patted the handwritten originals she was typing. "Do you know what he's doing here? He's trying to scale up—that's the term he uses—the design for the rockets we have so they'll be big enough and powerful enough to carry an atomic bomb instead of TNT or whatever goes into them now."

"Yeah, he's talked about that with me," Sam said. "The Nazis have the same kind of project going, too, he thinks, and they're liable to be ahead of us. I don't think they have a Lizard who knows as much as Vesstil, but their people were making rockets a lot bigger than Dr. Goddard's before the Lizards came. We're doing what we can, that's all. Can't do more than that."

"No." Barbara typed a few more sentences before she came to the end of a page. She took it out and ran a fresh sheet into the typewriter. Instead of going back to the report, she looked up at

Sam from under half-lowered eyelids. "Do you remember? This is what I was doing back in Chicago, the first time we met. You brought Ullhass and Ristin in to talk with Dr. Burkett. A lot of things have changed since then."

"Just a few," Sam allowed. She'd been married to Jens Larssen then, though already she'd feared he was dead: otherwise, she and Sam never would have got together, never would have had Jonathan, never would have done a whole lot of things. He didn't know about literature or fancy talk; he couldn't put into graceful words what he thought about all that. What he did say was, "It was so long ago that when you asked me for a cigarette, I had one to give you."

She smiled. "That's right. Not even two years, but it seems like the Middle Ages, doesn't it?" She wrinkled her nose at him. "I'm the one who feels middle-aged these days, but that's just on account of Jonathan."

"Me, I'm glad he's old enough now that you feel easy about letting the mammies take care of him during the day," Sam said. "It frees you up to do things like this, makes you feel useful again, too. I know that was on your mind."

"Yes, it was," Barbara said with a nod that wasn't altogether comfortable. She lowered her voice. "I wish you wouldn't call the colored women that."

"What? Mammies?" Sam scratched his head. "It's what they are."

"I know that, but it sounds so—" Barbara groped for the word she wanted and, being Barbara, found it. "So antebellum, as if we were down on the plantation with the Negroes singing spirituals and doing all the work and the kind masters sitting around drinking mint juleps as if they hadn't the slightest idea their whole social system was sick and wrong—and so much of what was wrong then is still wrong now. Why else would the Lizards have given guns to colored troops and expected them to fight against the United States?"

"They sure were wrong about that," Sam said.

"Yes, some of the Negroes mutinied," Barbara agreed, "but I'd bet not all of them did. And the Lizards wouldn't have tried it in the first place if they hadn't thought it would work. The way they treat colored people down here . . . Do you remember some of the newsreels from before we got into the war, the ones that showed happy Ukrainian peasants greeting the Nazis with flowers because they were liberating them from the Communists?"

"Uh-huh," Sam said. "They found out what that was worth pretty darn quick, too, didn't they?"

"That's not the point," Barbara insisted. "The point is that the Negroes here could have greeted the Lizards the same way."

"A good many of them did." Sam held up a hand before she could rhetorically rend him. "I know what you're getting at, hon: the point is that so many of 'em didn't. Things down here would have been mighty tough if they had, no two ways about it."

"Now you understand," Barbara said, nodding. She always sounded pleased when she said things like that, pleased and a little surprised: he might not have a fancy education, but it was nice that he wasn't dumb. He didn't think she knew she was using that tone of voice, and he wasn't about to call her on it. He was just glad he could come close to keeping up with her.

He said, "Other side of the coin is, whatever the reasons are, these colored women—I won't call 'em mammies if you don't want me to—they can't do the job you're doing right now. Since they *are* on our side, shouldn't we give 'em jobs they *can* do, so the rest of us can get on with doing the things they can't?"

"That isn't just," Barbara said. But she paused thoughtfully. Her fingernails clicked on the home keys of the typewriter, enough to make the type bars move a little but not enough to make them hit the paper. At last, she said, "It may not be just, but I suppose it's practical." Then she did start typing again.

Sam felt as if he'd just laced a game-winning double in the ninth. He didn't often make Barbara back up a step in any argument. He set a fond hand on her shoulder. She smiled up at him for a moment. The clatter of the typewriter didn't stop.

Liu Han cradled the submachine gun in her arms as if it were Liu Mei. She knew what she had to do with it if Ttomalss got out of line: point it in his direction and squeeze the trigger. Enough bullets would hit him to keep him from getting out of line again.

From what Nieh Ho-T'ing had told her, the gun was of German manufacture. "The fascists sold it to the Kuomintang, from whom we liberated it," he'd said. "In the same way, we shall liberate the whole world not only from the fascists and reactionaries, but also from the alien aggressor imperialist scaly devils."

It sounded easy when you put it like that. Taking revenge on Ttomalss had sounded easy, too, when she'd proposed it to the central committee. And, indeed, kidnapping him down in Canton had proved easy—as she'd predicted, he had returned to China to steal some other poor woman's baby. Getting him up here to

Peking without letting the rest of the scaly devils rescue him hadn't been so easy, but the People's Liberation Army had managed it.

And now here he was, confined in a hovel on a *hutung* not far from the roominghouse where Liu Han—and her daughter—lived. He was, in essence, hers to do with as she would. How she'd dreamed of that while she was in the hands of the little scaly devils. Now the dream was real.

She unlocked the door at the front of the hovel. Several of the people begging or selling in the alleyway were fellow travelers, though even she was not sure which ones. They would help keep Ttomalss from escaping or anyone from rescuing him.

She closed the front door after her. Inside, where no one could see it from the street, was another, stouter, door. She unlocked that one, too, and advanced into the dim room beyond it.

Ttomalss whirled. "Superior female!" he hissed in his own language, then returned to Chinese: "Have you decided what my fate is to be?"

"Maybe I should keep you here a long time," Liu Han said musingly, "and see how much people can learn from you little scaly devils. That would be a good project, don't you think, Ttomalss?"

"That *would* be a good project for you. You would learn much," Ttomalss agreed. For a moment, Liu Han thought he had missed her irony. Then he went on, "But I do not think you will do it. I think instead you will torment me."

"To learn how much thirst you can stand, how much hunger you can stand, how much pain you can stand—that would be an *interesting* project, don't you think, Ttomalss?" Liu Han purred the words, as if she were a cat eyeing a mouse it would presently devour—when it got a little hungrier than it was now.

. She'd hoped Ttomalss would cringe and beg. Instead, he stared at her with what, from longer experience with the scaly devils than she'd ever wanted, she recognized as a mournful expression. "We of the Race never treated you so when you were in our claws," he said.

"No?" Liu Han exclaimed. Now she stared at the little devil. "You didn't take my child from me and leave my heart to break?"

"The hatchling was not harmed in any way—on the contrary," Ttomalss replied. "And, to our regret, we did not fully understand the attachment between the generations among you Tosevites. This is one of the things we have learned—in part, from you yourself."

He meant what he said, Liu Han realized. He didn't think he

had been wantonly cruel—which didn't mean he hadn't been cruel. "You scaly devils took me up in your airplane that never landed, and then you made me into a whore up there." Liu Han wanted to shoot him for that alone. "Lie with this one, you said, or you do not eat. Then it was lie with that one, and that one, and that one. And all the time you were watching and taking your films. And you say you never did me any harm?"

"You must understand," Ttomalss said. "With us, a mating is a mating. In the season, male and female find each other, and after time the female lays the eggs. To the Rabotevs—one race we rule—a mating is a mating. To the Hallessi—another race we rule—a mating is a mating. How do we know that, to Tosevites, a mating is not just a mating? We find out, yes. We find out because of what we do with people like you and the Tosevite males we bring up to our ship. Before that, we did not know. We still have trouble believing you are as you are."

Liu Han studied him across a gap of incomprehension as wide as the separation between China and whatever weird place the little scaly devils called home. For the first time, she really grasped that Ttomalss and the rest of the little devils had acted without malice. They were trying to learn about people and went ahead and did that as best they knew how.

Some of her fury melted. Some—but not all. "You exploited us," she said, using a word much in vogue in the propaganda of the People's Liberation Army. Here it fit like a sandal made by a master shoemaker. "Because we were weak, because we could not fight back, you took us and did whatever you wanted to us. That is wrong and wicked, don't you see?"

"It is what the stronger does with the weaker," Ttomalss said, hunching himself down in a gesture the little devils used in place of a shrug. He swung both eye turrets toward her. "Now I am weak and you are strong. You have caught me and brought me here, and you say you will use me for experiments. Is this exploiting me, or is it not? Is it wrong and wicked, or is it not?"

The little scaly devil was clever. Whatever Liu Han said, he had an answer. Whatever she said, he had a way of twisting her words against her—she wouldn't have minded listening to a debate between him and Nieh Ho-T'ing, who was properly trained in the dialectic. But Liu Han had one argument Ttomalss could not overcome: the submachine gun. "It is revenge," she said.

"Ah." Ttomalss bowed his head. "May the spirits of Emperors past look kindly upon my spirit."

He was waiting quietly for her to kill him. She'd seen war and its bloody aftermath, of course. She'd had the idea for bombs that had killed and hurt and maimed any number of little scaly devils—the more, the better. But she had never killed personally and at point-blank range. It was, she discovered, not an easy thing to do.

Angry at Ttomalss for making her see him as a person of sorts rather than an ugly, alien enemy, angry at herself for what Nieh would surely have construed as weakness, she whirled and left the chamber. She slammed the inner door after her, made sure it was locked, then closed and locked the outer door, too

She stamped back toward the roominghouse. She didn't want to be away from Liu Mei a moment longer than absolutely necessary. With every word of Chinese the baby learned to understand and to say, she defeated Ttomalss all over again.

From behind her, a man said, "Here, pretty sister, I'll give you five dollars Mex—real silver—if you'll show me your body." He jingled the coins suggestively. His voice had a leer in it.

Liu Han whirled and pointed the submachine gun at his startled face. "I'll show you this," she snarled.

The man made a noise like a frightened duck. He turned and fled, sandals flapping as he dashed down the *hutung*. Wearily, Liu Han kept on her way. Ttomalss was smaller than the human exploiters she'd known (she thought of Yi Min the apothecary, who'd taken advantage of her as ruthlessly as any of the men she'd had the displeasure to meet in the airplane that never landed save only Bobby Fiore), he was scalier, he was uglier, he was—or had been—more powerful.

But was he, at the bottom, any worse?

"I just don't know," she said, and sighed, and kept on walking.

"This is bloody awful country," George Bagnall said, looking around. He, Ken Embry, and Jerome Jones no longer had Lake Peipus and Lake Chud on their left hand, as they had through the long slog north from Pskov. They'd paid a chunk of sausage to an old man with a rowboat to ferry them across the Narva River. Now they were heading northwest, toward the Baltic coast.

The forests to the east of Pskov were only a memory now. Everything was flat here, so flat that Bagnall marveled at the lakes' and rivers' staying in their beds and not spilling out over the landscape. Embry had the same thought. "Someone might have taken an iron to this place," he said.

"Someone did," Jones answered: "Mother Nature, as a matter of fact. In the last Ice Age, the glaciers advanced past here for

Lord knows how many thousand years, then finally went back. They pressed down the ground like a man pressing a leaf under a board and a heavy rock."

"I don't much care what did it," Bagnall said. "I don't fancy it, and that's that. It's not just how flat it is, either. It's the color—it's off, somehow. All the greens that should be bright are sickly. Can't blame it on the sun, either, not when it's in the sky practically twenty-four hours a day."

"We aren't very far above lake level," Embry said. "We can't be very far above sea level. I wonder how far inland the salt has soaked. That would do something to the plants, I daresay."

"There's a thought," Bagnall said. "Always nice having an explanation for things. I've no idea whether it's the proper explanation, mind you, but any old port in a storm, what?"

"Speaking of which—" Embry took out a map. "As best I can tell, we're about ten miles from the coast." He pointed northwest. "That great plume of smoke over there, I think, is from the great industrial metropolis of Kohtla-Jarve." He spoke with palpable irony; had it not been for the name of the place beside it, he would have taken the dot on the map for a flyspeck.

"Must be something going on in whatever-you-call-it," Jerome Jones observed, "or the Lizards wouldn't have pounded it so hard."

"I don't think that's war damage," Ken Embry said. "The volume of smoke is too steady. We've seen it for the past day and a half, and it's hardly changed. I think the Germans or the Russians or whoever controls the place have lighted off a big smudge to keep the Lizards from looking down and seeing what they're about."

"Whatever it is, at the moment I don't much care," Bagnall said. "My question is, are we likelier to get a boat if we saunter blithely into Kohtla-Jarve or if we find some fishing village on the Baltic nearby?"

"Would we sooner deal with soldiers or peasants?" Jones asked.

Bagnall said, "If we try to deal with peasants and something goes wrong, we can try to back away and deal with the soldiers. If something goes wrong dealing with the soldiers, though, that's apt to be rather final."

His companions considered for the next few steps. Almost in unison, they nodded. Embry said, "A point well taken, George."

"I feel rather Biblical, navigating by a pillar of smoke," Jerome

Jones said, "even if we're steering clear of it rather than steering by it."

"Onward," Bagnall said, adjusting his course more nearly due north, so as to strike the Baltic coast well east of Kohtla-Jarve and whatever whoever was making there. As he had been many times, Bagnall was struck by the vastness of the Soviet landscape. He supposed the Siberian steppe would seem even more huge and empty, but Estonia had enough land and to spare sitting around not doing much. It struck him as untidy. The Englishmen would walk past a farm with some recognizable fields around it, but soon the fields would peter out and it would be just—land again till the next farm.

That they were approaching the Baltic coast didn't make the farms come any closer together. Bagnall began to wonder if they'd find a little fishing village when they got to the sea. Hardly anyone seemed to live in this part of the world.

One advantage of traveling at this time of year was that you could keep going as long as you had strength in you. At around the latitude of Leningrad, the sun set for only a couple of hours each night as the summer solstice approached, and never dipped far enough below the horizon for twilight to end. Even at midnight, the northern sky glowed brightly and the whole landscape was suffused with milky light. As Ken Embry said that evening, "It's not nearly so ugly now— seems a bit like one of the less tony parts of fairyland, don't you think?"

Distances were hard to judge in that shadowless, almost sourceless light. A farmhouse and barn that had seemed a mile away not two minutes before were now, quite suddenly, all but on top of them. "Shall we beg shelter for the night?" Bagnall said. "I'd sooner sleep in straw than unroll my blanket on ground that's sure to be damp."

They approached the farmhouse openly. They'd needed to display Aleksandr German's safe-conduct only a couple of times; despite their worries, the peasants had on the whole been friendly enough. But they were still a quarter of a mile from the farmhouse, as best Bagnall could judge, when a man inside shouted something at them.

Bagnall frowned. "That's not German. Did you understand it, Jones?"

The radarman shook his head. "It's not Russian, either. I'd swear to that, though I don't quite know what it is." The shout came again, as unintelligible as before. "I wonder if it's Estonian,"

Jones said in a musing voice. "I hadn't thought anyone spoke Estonian, the Estonians included."

"We're friends!" Bagnall shouted toward the house, first in English, then in German, and last in Russian. Had he known how to say it in Estonian, he would have done that, too. He took a couple of steps forward.

Whoever was in the farmhouse wanted no uninvited guests. A bullet cracked past above Bagnall's head before he heard the report of the rifle whose flash he'd seen at the window. The range was by no means extreme; maybe the strange light fooled the fellow in there into misjudging it.

Though not an infantryman, Bagnall had done enough fighting on the ground to drop to that ground when someone started shooting at him. So did Ken Embry. They both screamed, "Get down, you fool!" at Jones. He stood gaping till another bullet whined past, this one closer than the first. Then he, too, sprawled on his belly.

That second shot hadn't come from the farmhouse, but from the barn. Both gunmen kept banging away, too, and a third shooter opened up from another window of the house. "What the devil did we start to walk in on?" Bagnall said, scuttling toward a bush that might conceal him from the hostile locals. "The annual meeting of the Estonian We Hate Everyone Who Isn't Us League?"

"Shouldn't be a bit surprised," Embry answered from behind cover of his own. "If these are Estonians, they must have taken us for Nazis or Bolsheviks or similar lower forms of life. Do we shoot back at them?"

"I'd sooner retreat and go around," Bagnall said. Just then, though, two men carrying rifles ran out of the barn and toward some little trees not far away to the right. He flicked the safety off his Mauser. "I take it back. If they're going to hunt us, they have to pay for the privilege." He brought the German rifle with the awkward bolt up to his shoulder.

Before he could fire, three more men sprinted from the back of the farmhouse toward an outbuilding off to the left. Ken Embry shot at one of them, but the light was as tricky for him as it was for the Estonians. All three of them safely made it to the outbuilding. They started shooting at the RAF men. A couple of bullets kicked up dirt much too close to Bagnall for his liking.

"Bit of a sticky wicket, what?" Jerome Jones drawled. Neither the hackneyed phrase nor the university accent disguised his concern. Bagnall was worried, too. *Bugger worried,* he told himself—

I'm bloody petrified. There were too many Estonians out there, and they too obviously meant business.

The two men in the house and the one still in the barn kept shooting at the Englishmen, making them keep their heads down. Under cover of their fire and that of the fellow behind the outbuilding, the two Estonians in the trees scooted forward and farther to the right, heading for some tall brush that would give them cover.

Bagnall snapped off a couple of shots at them as they ran, to no visible effect. "They're going to flank us out," he said in dismay.

Then another rifle spoke, from behind him and to his right. One of the running men dropped his weapon and crashed to earth as if he'd been sapped. That unexpected rifle cracked again. The second runner went down, too, with a cry of pain that floated over the flat, grassy land.

He tried to crawl to cover, but Bagnall fired twice more at him. One of the bullets must have hit, for the fellow lay quiet and motionless after that.

One of the Estonians behind the outbuilding popped up to shoot. Before he could, the rifleman behind the RAF men squeezed off another round. The Estonian crumpled. He must have dropped his rifle, for it fell where Bagnall could see it. "We have a friend," he said. "I wonder if he's Russian or German." He looked back over his shoulder, but couldn't see anyone.

The man in the farmhouse who'd fired first—or perhaps someone else using the same window—fired again. At what seemed the same instant, the marksman behind Bagnall also fired. An arm dangled limply from the window till it was dragged back inside.

"Whoever that is back there, he's a bloody wonder," Embry said. The Estonians evidently thought the same thing. One of them behind the outbuilding waved a white cloth. "We have a wounded man here," he called in oddly accented German. "Will you let us take him back to the house?"

"Go ahead," Bagnall said after a moment's hesitation. "Will you let us back up and go around you? We didn't want this fight in the first place."

"You may do that," the Estonian answered. "Maybe you are not who we thought you were."

"Maybe you should have found out about that before you tried blowing our heads off," Bagnall said. "Go on now, but remember, we have you in our sights—and so does our friend back there."

Still waving the cloth, the Estonian picked up his fallen comrade's rifle and slung it on his back. He and his hale companion dragged the wounded man toward the farmhouse. By the limp way he hung in their arms, he was badly hurt.

While they did that, Bagnall and his companions crawled backwards, not fully trusting the truce to which they'd agreed. But the Estonians in the house and barn evidently wanted no more of them. Bagnall realized he was withdrawing in the direction of the rifleman who'd bailed them out of that tight spot. Softly, he called, *"Danke sehr,"* and then, to cover all bases, *"Spasebo."*

"Nye za chto—you're welcome," came the answer: he'd guessed right the second time. That wasn't what made his jaw drop foolishly, though. He'd expected whatever answer he got to be baritone, not creamy contralto.

Jerome Jones yelped like a puppy with its tail caught in a door. "Tatiana!" he exclaimed, and went on in Russian, "What are you doing here?"

"Never mind that now," the sniper answered. "First we go around that house full of anti-Soviet reactionaries, since you Englishmen were foolish enough to give them quarter."

"How do you know they aren't anti-fascist patriots?" Embry asked in a mixture of German and Russian.

Tatiana Pirogova let out an annoyed snort. "They are Estonians, so they must be anti-Soviet." She spoke as if stating a law of nature. Bagnall didn't feel inclined to quarrel with her, not after what she'd just done for them.

She didn't say anything else as she led the RAF men on a long loop around the farmhouse. It went slowly; none of them dared stand while they might still be in rifle range. The house and barn, though, remained as silent as if uninhabited. Bagnall wished they had been.

At last, cat-wary, Tatiana got to her feet. The Englishmen followed her lead, grunting with relief. "How did you come upon us at just the right moment?" Bagnall asked her, taking her rising as giving him leave to speak.

She shrugged. "I left two days after you. You were not traveling very fast. And so—there I was. In half an hour's time—less, maybe—I would have hailed you if the shooting had not started."

"What about—Georg Schultz?" Jerome Jones asked—hesitantly, as if half fearing her reply.

She shrugged again, with magnificent indifference. "Wounded— maybe dead. I hope dead, but I am not sure. He is strong." She spoke with grudging respect. "But he thought he could do with me as he pleased. He was wrong." She patted the barrel of her telescopically sighted rifle to show how wrong he was.

"What will you do now?" Bagnall asked her.

"Get you safe to the sea," she answered. "After that? Who knows? Go back and kill more Germans around Pskov, I suppose."

"Thank you for coming this far to look after us," Bagnall said. Odd to think of Tatiana Pirogova, sniper extraordinaire (had he been inclined to doubt that, which he wasn't, the affair at the farmhouse would have proved her talents along those lines), with a mother-hen complex, but she seemed to have one. Now he hesitated before continuing, "If we can lay hold of a boat, you're welcome—more than welcome—to come to England with us."

He wondered if she'd get angry; he often wondered that when he dealt with her. Instead, she looked sad and—most unlike the Tatiana he thought he knew—confused. At last she said, "You go back to your *rodina*, your motherland. So that is right for you. But this"—she stamped a booted foot down on the sickly green grass—"this is my *rodina*. I will stay and fight for it."

The Estonians she'd shot had thought this particular stretch of ground was part of their motherland, not hers. The Germans in Kohtla-Jarve undoubtedly thought of it as an extension of their *Vaterland*. All the same, he took her point.

He nodded off toward the west, toward the smoke that never stopped rising from Kohtla-Jarve. "What do they make there, that they have to keep it hidden from the Lizards no matter what?" he asked.

"They squeeze oil out of rocks in some way," Tatiana answered. "We have been doing that for years, we and then the reactionary Estonian separatists. I suppose the fascists found the plants in working order, or they may have repaired them."

Bagnall nodded. That made sense. Petroleum products were doubly precious these days. Any place the Germans could get their hands on such, they would.

"Come," Tatiana said, dismissing the Germans as a distraction. She set off with a long, swinging stride that was a distraction in itself and gave some justification to her claim the RAF men traveled slowly.

They reached the Baltic a couple of hours later. It looked unimpressive: gray water rolling up and back over mud. Even so, Jerome Jones, imitating Xenophon's men, called out, *"Thalassa! Thalassa!"* Bagnall and Embry both smiled, recognizing the allusion. Tatiana shrugged it off. Maybe she thought it was English. To her, that tongue was as alien as Greek.

Perhaps half a mile to the west, a little village squatted by the sea. Bagnall felt like cheering when he saw a couple of fishing boats pulled up onto the beach. Another, despite the early hour, was already out on the Baltic.

Dogs barked as the RAF men and Tatiana came into the village. Fishermen and their wives stepped out of doors to stare at them. Their expressions ranged from blank to hostile. In German, Bagnall said, "We are three English fliers. We have been trapped in Russia for more than a year. We want to go home. Can any of you sail us to Finland? We do not have much, but we will give you what we can."

"Englishmen?" one of the fishermen said, with the same strange accent the Estonian fighters had had. Hostility melted. "I will take you." A moment later, someone else demanded the privilege.

"Didn't expect to be quarreled over," Embry murmured as the villagers hashed it out. The fellow who'd spoken first won the argument. He ducked back into his home, reemerging with boots and knitted wool cap, then escorted them to his boat.

Tatiana followed. As the RAF men were about to help drag the boat into the water, she kissed each of them in turn. The villagers muttered among themselves in incomprehensible Estonian. A couple of men guffawed. That was understandable. So were the loud sniffs from a couple of women.

"You're certain you won't come with us?" Bagnall said. Tatiana shook her head yet again. She turned around and tramped south without looking back. She knew what she intended to do, and had to know the likely consequences of it.

"Come," the fisherman said. The RAF men scrambled aboard with him. The rest of the villagers finished pushing the boat into the sea. He opened the fire door to the steam engine and started throwing in wood and peat and what looked like chunks of dried horse manure. Shaking his head, he went on, "Ought to burn coal. Can't get coal. Burn whatever I get."

"We know a few verses to that song," Bagnall said. The fisherman chuckled. The boat had probably been slow burning its proper fuel. It was slower now, and the smoke that poured from its stack even less pleasant than the smudges from Kohtla-Jarve. But the engine ran. The boat sailed. Barring the Lizards' strafing them from the air, Finland was less than a day away.

"Oh, Jäger, dear," Otto Skorzeny said in scratchy falsetto. Heinrich Jäger looked up in surprise; he hadn't heard Skorzeny come up. The SS man laughed at him. "Stop mooning over that

Russian popsy of yours and pay attention. I need something from you."

"She isn't a popsy," Jäger said. Skorzeny laughed louder. The panzer colonel went on, "If she were a popsy, I don't suppose I'd be mooning over her."

The half admission got through to Skorzeny, who nodded. "All right, something to that. But even if she's the Madonna, stop mooning over her. You know our friends back home have sent us a present, right?"

"Hard not to know it," Jäger agreed. "More of you damned SS men around than you can shake a stick at, every stinking one of them with a Schmeisser and a look in his eye that says he'd just as soon shoot you as give you the time of day. I'll bet I even know what kind of present it is, too." He didn't say what kind of present he thought it was, not because he believed he might be wrong but from automatic concern for security.

"I'll bet you do," Skorzeny said. "Why shouldn't you? You've known about this stuff as long as I have, ever since those days outside Kiev." He said no more after that, but it was plenty. They'd stolen explosive metal from the Lizards in the Ukraine.

"What are you going to do with—it?" Jäger asked cautiously.

"Are you thick in the head?" Skorzeny demanded. "I'm going to blow the kikes in Lodz to hell and gone, is what I'm going to do, and their chums the Lizards, and all the poor damned Poles in the wrong place at the wrong time." He laughed again. "There's the story of Poland in a sentence, *nicht wahr*? The poor damned Poles, in the wrong place at the wrong time."

"I presume you have authorization for this?" Jäger said, not presuming any such thing. If anybody could lay hands on an atomic bomb for his own purposes, Otto Skorzeny was the man.

But not this time. Skorzeny's big head went up and down. "You bet your arse I do: from the *Reichsführer-SS* and straight from the *Führer* himself. Both of 'em in my attaché case. You want to gape at fancy autographs?"

"Never mind." In a way, Jäger was relieved—if Himmler and Hitler had signed off on this, at least Skorzeny wasn't running wild . . . or no wilder than usual, at any rate. Still— "Strikes me as a waste of a bomb. There's nothing threatening coming out of Lodz. Look what happened the last time the Lizards even tried sending something up our way through the town: it got here late and chewed up, thanks to what happened down there."

"Oh, yes, the Jews did us a hell of a favor." Skorzeny rolled his eyes. "When they hit the Lizards, the bastards all wore German uniforms, so they didn't get blamed for it—we did. I did in particular, as a matter of fact. The Lizards bribed a couple of Poles with scope-sighted rifles to come up here and go Skorzeny-hunting to see if they could pay me back."

"You're still here," Jäger noted.

"You noticed that, did you?" Skorzeny made as if to kiss him on the cheek. "You're such a clever boy. And both the Poles are dead, too. It took a while—we know to the zloty how big their payoff was." His smile showed teeth; maybe he was remembering how the Poles perished. But then he looked grim. "Lieutenant-Colonel Brockelmann is dead, too. Unlucky son of a whore happened to be about my size. One of the Poles blew off the top of his head from behind at about a thousand meters. Damn fine shooting, I must say. I complimented the fellow on it as I handed him his trigger finger."

"I'm sure he appreciated that," Jäger said dryly. Associating with Skorzeny had rubbed his nose in all the uglier parts of warfare, the parts he hadn't had to think about as a panzer commander. Mass murder, torture . . . he hadn't signed up for those. But they were part of the package whether he'd signed up for them or not. Was destroying a city where the people were doing the *Reich* more good than harm? Was their being Jews reason enough? Was their having piqued Skorzeny for not letting him destroy them on his first try reason enough? He'd have to think about that—and he couldn't waste too much time doing it, either. Meanwhile, he asked, "So what am I supposed to do about all this? What's the favor you have in mind? I've never been into Lodz, you know."

"Oh, yes, I know that." Skorzeny stretched like a tiger deciding he was too full to go hunting right now. "If you had been in Lodz, you'd be talking with the *Sicherheitsdienst* or the *Gestapo* now, not me."

"I've talked with them before." Jäger shrugged, trying not to show the stab of alarm he felt.

"I know that, too," Skorzeny answered. "But they would be asking more—pointed questions this time, and using more pointed tools. Never mind all that. I don't want you to go into Lodz." The tiger became more alert. "I'm not sure I'd trust you to go into Lodz. I want you to lay on a diversionary attack, make the Lizards look someplace else, while I trundle on down the road with my band of elves and make like St. Nicholas."

"Can't do it tomorrow, if that's what you have in mind," Jäger answered promptly—and truthfully. "Every time we fight, it hurts us worse than the Lizards, a lot worse. You know that. We're sort of putting things back together here right now, bringing up new panzers, new men, getting somewhere close—well, closer—to establishment strength. Give me a week or ten days."

He expected Skorzeny to blow up, to demand action yesterday if not sooner. But the SS man surprised him—Skorzeny spent a lot of time surprising him—by nodding. "That's fine. I still have some arrangements of my own to work out. Even for elves, hauling in a bloody big crate takes a bit of planning. I'll let you know when I need you." He thumped Jäger on the back. "Now you can go back to thinking about your Russian with her clothes off." He walked away, laughing till he wheezed.

"What the devil was all that in aid of, sir?" Gunther Grillparzer asked.

"The devil indeed." Jäger glanced toward the panzer gunner, whose eyes followed Skorzeny as if he were some cinema hero. "He's found some new reasons for getting a bunch of us killed, Gunther."

"*Wunderbar!*" Grillparzer said with altogether unfeigned enthusiasm, leaving Jäger to contemplate the vagaries of youth. He came up with a twisted version of the Book of Ecclesiastes: *vagary of vagaries, all is vagary.* It seemed as good a description of real life as the more accurate reading.

"Ah, good to see you, Vyacheslav Mikhailovich," Iosef Stalin said as Molotov entered his Kremlin office.

"And you, Comrade General Secretary," Molotov answered. Stalin had a purr in his voice that Molotov hadn't heard in a long time: not since just after the previous Soviet atomic bomb, as best he could remember. The last time he'd heard it before that was when the Red Army threw the Nazis back from the gates of Moscow at the end of 1941. It meant Stalin thought things were looking up for the time being.

"I presume you have again conveyed to the Lizards our non-negotiable demand that they cease their aggression and immediately withdraw from the territory of the peace-loving Soviet Union," Stalin said. "Perhaps they will pay more attention to this demand after Saratov."

"Perhaps they will, Iosef Vissarionovich," Molotov said. Neither of them mentioned Magnitogorsk, which had ceased to exist shortly after Saratov was incinerated. Measured against the blow dealt the Lizards, the loss of any one city, even an important industrial center like Magnitogorsk, was a small matter. Molotov went on, "At least they have not rejected the demand out of hand, as they did when we made it on previous occasions."

"If once we get them to the conference table, we shall defeat them there," Stalin said. "Not only does the dialectic predict this, so does their behavior at all previous conferences. They are too strong for us to drive them from the world altogether, I fear, but once we get them talking, we shall free the Soviet Union and its workers and peasants of them."

"I am given to understand they have also received withdrawal demands from the governments of the United States and Germany," Molotov said. "As those are also powers possessing atomic weapons, the Lizards will have to hear them as seriously as they hear us."

"Yes." Stalin filled a pipe with *makhorka* and puffed out a cloud of acrid smoke. "It is the end for Britain, you know. Were Churchill not a capitalist exploiter, I might have sympathy for him. The British did a very great thing, expelling the Lizards from their island, but what has it got them in the end? Nothing."

"They could yet produce their own atomic weapons," Molotov said. "Underestimating them does not pay."

"As Hitler found, to his dismay," Stalin agreed. For his part, Stalin had underestimated Hitler, but Molotov did not point that out. Stalin sucked meditatively on the pipe for a little while before going on, "Even if they make these bombs for themselves, Vyacheslav Mikhailovich, what good does it do them? They have already saved their island without the bombs. They cannot save their empire with them, for they have no way of delivering them to Africa or India. Those will stay in the Lizards' hands from this time forward."

"A cogent point," Molotov admitted. You endangered yourself if you underestimated Stalin's capacity. He was always brutal, he could be naive, foolish, shortsighted. But when he was right, as he often was, he was so breathtakingly right as to make up for the rest.

He said, "If the German fascists persuade the Lizards to withdraw from territory that had been under their occupation before the aliens invaded, it will be interesting to see how many of those lands eagerly return to Nazi control."

"Much of the land the fascists occupied was ours," Molotov said. "The Lizards did us a favor by clearing them from so much of it." Nazi-held pockets persisted in the north and near the Romanian frontier, and Nazi bands one step up from guerrillas still ranged over much of what the Germans had controlled, but those were manageable problems, unlike the deadly threats the fascists had posed and the Lizards now did.

Stalin sensed that, too, saying, "Personally, I would not be brokenhearted to see the Lizards remain in Poland. With peace, better them on our western border than the fascists: having made a treaty, they are more likely to adhere to it."

He had underestimated Hitler once; he would not do it twice. Molotov nodded vigorously. Here he agreed with his superior. "With the Nazis' rockets, with their gas that paralyzes breathing, with their explosive-metal bombs, and with their fascist ideology, they would make most unpleasant neighbors."

"Yes." Stalin puffed out more smoke. His eyes narrowed. He looked through Molotov rather than at him. It was not quite the hooded look he gave when mentally discarding a favorite, consigning him to the *gulag* or worse. He was just thinking hard. After a while, he said, "Let us be flexible, Vyacheslav Mikhailovich. Let us, instead of demanding withdrawal before negotiations, propose a cease-fire in place while negotiations go on. Perhaps this will work, perhaps it will not. If we are no longer subject to raids and bombings, our industry and collective farms will have the chance to begin recovery."

"Shall we offer this proposal alone, or shall we try to continue to maintain a human popular front against the alien imperialists?" Molotov asked

"You may consult with the Americans and Germans before transmitting the proposal to the Lizards," Stalin said with the air of a man granting a great boon. "You may, for that matter, consult with the British, the Japanese, and the Chinese—the small powers," he added, dismissing them with a wave of his hand. "If they are willing to make the Lizards the same offer at the same time, well and good: we shall go forward together. If they are unwilling . . . we shall go forward anyway."

"As you say, Comrade General Secretary." Molotov was not sure this was the wisest course, but imagining von Ribbentrop's face when he got the despatch announcing the new Soviet policy—and, better yet, imagining von Ribbentrop's face when he had to bring Hitler the news—came close to making it all worthwhile. "I shall begin drafting the telegram at once."

Heinrich Jäger was getting to be a pretty fair horseman. The accomplishment filled him with less delight than it might have under other circumstances. When you had to climb on a horse to go back and visit corps headquarters, that mostly proved you didn't have enough petrol to keep your utility vehicles operational. Since the *Wehrmacht* barely had enough petrol to keep its panzers operational, the choice lay between visiting corps headquarters on a bay mare or on shank's mare. Riding beat the devil out of walking.

The road through the forest forked. Jäger urged the mare south, down the right-hand fork. That was not the direct route back to his regiment. One of the good things—one of the few good things—about riding a horse as opposed to a *Volkswagen* was that you did it by yourself, without a driver. Jäger didn't want anyone to know he was turning down the right-hand fork. If anyone found out, in fact, he would soon be having intimate discussion with the SS, the SD, the *Gestapo*, the *Abwehr*, and any other security or intelligence service that could get its hands (to say nothing of assorted blunt, sharp, heated, and electrically conductive instruments) on him.

"Why am I doing this?" he said in the middle of forest stillness broken only by the distant rumble of artillery. The mare answered with a snort.

He felt like snorting himself. He did know the answer: partly the debt he felt to Anielewicz personally, partly that Anielewicz and his Jewish fighters had kept their side of the bargain they'd made with him and didn't deserve incineration, partly the way his stomach knotted whenever he thought about what the forces of the *Reich* had done to the Jews of eastern Europe before the Lizards came—and were still doing to the Jews remaining in the territory they controlled. (He remembered all too vividly the Jewish and homosexual prisoners who worked on the atomic pile under *Schloss Hohentübingen* till they died, which seldom took long.)

Was all that reason enough to violate his military oath? The head of the SS and the *Führer* himself had authorized Skorzeny to visit atomic fire upon Lodz. Who was Colonel Heinrich Jäger to say they were wrong?

"A man," he said, answering the question no one had asked aloud. "If I can't live with myself, what good is anything else?"

He sometimes wished he could turn off his mind, could numb himself to everything that happened in war. He knew a good many officers who were aware of the horrors the *Reich* had committed in the east but who refused to think about them, who sometimes even refused to admit they were aware of them. Then there was Skorzeny, who knew but didn't give a damn. Neither path suited Jäger. He was neither an ostrich, to stick his head in the sand, nor a Pharisee, to pass by on the other side of the road.

And so here he was riding down this side of this road, a sub-machine gun on his knee, alert for Lizard patrols, German patrols, Polish brigands, Jewish brigands ... anyone at all. The fewer people he saw, the better he liked it.

His nerves jumped again when he came out of the forest into open farm country. Now he was visible for kilometers, not just a few meters. Of course, a lot of men got around on horseback these days, and a lot of them were in uniform and carried weapons. Not all of those were soldiers, by any means. The times had turned Poland as rough as the cinema made the America Wild West out to be. Rougher—the cowboys didn't have machine guns or panzers.

His eyes swiveled back and forth. He still didn't see anybody. He rode on. The farm wasn't far. He could leave his message, boot the mare up into a trot, and be back with his regiment at the front only an hour or so later than he should have been. Given how erratic any sort of travel was these days, no one would think twice over that.

"Here we go," he said softly, recognizing the well-kept little grove of apple trees ahead. Karol would pass the word to Tadeusz, Tadeusz could get it to Anielewicz, and that would be that.

Everything was quiet ahead. Too quiet? The hair prickled up on the back of Jäger's neck. No chickens ran in the yard, no sheep bleated, no pigs grunted. For that matter, no one was in the fields, no toddlers played by the house. Like a lot of Poles, Karol was raising a great brood of children. You could always spot them—or hear them, anyhow. Not now, though.

His horse snorted and sidestepped, white showing around her eyes. "Steady," Jäger said, and steady she was. But something had spooked her. She was walking forward, yes, but her nostrils still flared with every breath she took.

Jäger sniffed, too. At first he noted nothing out of the ordinary. Then he too smelled what was bothering the mare. It wasn't much, just a faint whiff of corruption, as if a *Hausfrau* hadn't got round to cooking a joint of beef until it had stayed in the icebox too long.

He knew he should have wheeled the horse around and ridden out of there at that first whiff of danger. But the whiff argued that the danger wasn't there now. It had come and gone, probably a couple of days before. Jäger rode the ever more restive mare up to the farmhouse and tied her to one of the posts holding up the front porch. As he dismounted, he flipped the change lever on his Schmeisser to full automatic.

Flies buzzed in and out through the front door, which was

slightly ajar. Jäger kicked it open. The sudden noise made the mare quiver and try to run. Jäger bounded into the house.

The first two bodies lay in the kitchen. One of Karol's daughters, maybe seven years old, had been shot execution-style in the back of the neck. His wife lay there, too, naked, on her back. She had a bullet hole between the eyes. Whoever had been here had probably raped her a few times, or more than a few, before they'd killed her.

Biting his lip, Jäger walked into the parlor. Several more children sprawled in death there. The visitors had served one of them, a little blond of about twelve whom Jäger remembered as always smiling, the same way they had Karol's wife. The black bread he'd had for breakfast wanted to come back up. He clamped his jaw and wouldn't let it.

The door to Karol's bedroom gaped wide, like his wife's legs, like his daughter's. Jäger walked in. There on the bed lay Karol. He had not been slain neatly, professionally, dispassionately. His killers had taken time and pains on their work. Karol had taken pain, too, some enormous amount of it, before he was finally allowed to die.

Jäger turned away, partly sickened, partly afraid. Now he knew who had visited this farmhouse before him. They'd signed their masterpiece, so to speak: on Karol's belly, they'd burned in the SS runes with a redhot poker or something similar. The next interesting question was, how much had they asked him before they finally cut out his tongue? He didn't know Jäger's name—the panzer colonel called himself Joachim around here—but if he'd described Jäger, figuring out who he was wouldn't take the SS long.

Whistling tunelessly, Jäger went outside, unhitched the mare, and rode away. Where to ride troubled him. Should he flee for his life? If he could get to Lodz, Anielewicz and the Jews would protect him. That was loaded with irony thick enough to slice, but it was also probably true.

In the end, though, instead of riding south, he went north, back toward his regiment. Karol and his family had been dead for days now. If the SS did know about him, they would have dropped on him by now. And, never mind the Jews, he still had the war against the Lizards to fight.

When he did get back to the regimental encampment, Gunther Grillparzer looked up from a game of skat and said, "You look a little green around the gills, sir. Everything all right?"

"I must have drunk some bad water or something," Jäger

answered. "I've been jumping down off this miserable creature"—he patted the horse's neck—"and squatting behind a bush about every five minutes, all the way back from corps headquarters." That accounted not only for his pallor but also for getting back here later than he should have.

"The galloping shits are no fun at all, sir," the panzer gunner said sympathetically. Then he guffawed and pointed to Jäger's mare. "The galloping shits! Get it, sir? I made a joke without even noticing."

"Life is like that sometimes," Jäger said. Grillparzer scratched his head. Jäger just led away the horse. He'd ridden it a long way; it needed seeing to. Grillparzer shrugged and went back to his card game.

Nieh Ho-T'ing and Hsia Shou-Tao passed the little scaly devils' inspection and were allowed into the main part of the tent on the island in the lake at the heart of the Forbidden City. "Good of you to invite me here with you today," he said, "instead of—" He stopped.

Instead of your woman, the one I tried to rape. Nieh completed the sentence, perhaps not exactly as his aide would have. Aloud, he answered, "Liu Mei has some sort of sickness, the kind babies get. Liu Han asked the central committee for permission to be relieved of this duty so she could care for the girl. Said permission having been granted—"

Hsia Shou-Tao nodded. "Women need to look after their brats. It's one of the things they're good for. They're—" He stopped again. Again, Nieh Ho-T'ing had no trouble coming up with a likely continuation. *They're also good for laying, which causes the brats in the first place.* But Hsia, while he might have thought that, hadn't come out and said it. His reeducation, however slowly it proceeded, was advancing.

"Liu Han has all sorts of interesting projects going on," Nieh said. Hsia Shou-Tao nodded once more, but did not ask him to amplify that. Where women were not involved, Hsia was plenty clever. He would not allude to the whereabouts of the scaly devil Ttomalss where other little devils might hear.

Nieh had thought that by this time he would be delivering small pieces of Ttomalss to the little devils one at a time. It hadn't worked out that way. The capture of the little devil who'd stolen Liu Han's child had gone off as planned—better than planned— but she hadn't yet taken the ferocious revenge she and Nieh had anticipated. He wondered why. It wasn't as if she'd become a Christian or anything foolish like that.

A couple of chairs were the only articles of human-made furniture inside the tent. Nieh and Hsia sat down in them. A moment later, the little scaly devil named Ppevel and his interpreter came out and seated themselves behind their worktable. Ppevel let loose with a volley of hisses and pops, squeaks and coughs. The interpreter turned them into pretty good Chinese: "The assistant administrator, eastern region, main continental mass, notes that one of you appears to be different from past sessions. Is it Nieh Ho-T'ing or Liu Han who is absent?"

"Liu Han is absent," Nieh answered. The little devils had as much trouble telling people apart as he did with them.

Ppevel spoke again: "We suspect a link between her and the disappearance of the researcher Ttomalss."

"Your people and mine are at war," Nieh Ho-T'ing answered. "We have honored the truce we gave in exchange for Liu Han's baby. We were not required to do anything more than that. Suspect all you like."

"You are arrogant," Ppevel said.

That, coming from an imperialist exploiter of a little scaly devil, almost made Nieh Ho-T'ing laugh out loud. He didn't; he was here on business. He said, "We have learned that you scaly devils are seriously considering cease-fires without time limits for discussion of your withdrawal from the territory of the peace-loving Soviet Union and other states."

"These requests are under discussion," Ppevel agreed through the interpreter. "They have nothing to do with you, however. We shall not withdraw from China under any circumstances."

Nieh stared at him in dismay. He had been ordered by Mao Tse-Tung himself to demand China's—and, specifically, the People's Liberation Army's—inclusion in such talks. Having the little scaly devils reject that out of hand before he could even propose it was a jolt. It reminded Nieh of the signs the European foreign devils had put up in their colonial parks: NO DOGS OR CHINESE ALLOWED.

"You shall regret this high-handed refusal," he said when he could speak again. "What we have done to you is but a pinprick beside what we might do."

"What you might do is a pinprick beside the damage from an explosive-metal bomb," Ppevel replied. "You have none. We are strong enough to hold down this land no matter what you do. We shall."

"If you do, we'll make your life a living hell," Hsia Shou-Tao burst out hotly. "Every time you step out on the street, someone may shoot at you. Every time you get into one of your cars or trucks or tanks, you may drive over a mine. Every time you travel between one city and another, someone may have a mortar zeroed on the road. Every time you bring food into a city, you may have to see if it is poisoned."

Nieh wished his aide hadn't given the little devils such bald threats. Liu Han would have known better; she was, as Nieh had discovered to his own occasional discomfiture, a master at biding her time till she was ready to attack a target full force. But Nieh did not disagree with the sentiments Hsia had expressed.

Ppevel remained unimpressed. "How is this different from what you are doing now?" he demanded. "We hold the centers of population, we hold the roads between one of them and another. Using these, we can control the countryside."

"You can try," Nieh Ho-T'ing told him. That was the recipe the Japanese had used in occupying northeastern China. It was almost the only recipe you could use if you lacked the manpower—or even the devilpower—to occupy a land completely. "You will find the price higher than you can afford to pay."

"We are a patient people," Ppevel answered. "In the end, we shall wear you down. You Big Uglies are too hasty for long campaigns."

Nieh Ho-T'ing was used to thinking of the Europeans and Japanese as hasty folk, hopelessly out of their depth in dealing with China. He was not used to being perceived as a blunt, unsubtle barbarian himself. Pointing a finger at Ppevel, he said, "You will lose more fighters here in China than you would from an explosive-metal bomb. You would do better to negotiate a peaceful withdrawal of your forces now than to see them destroyed piecemeal."

"Threats are easy to make," Ppevel said. "They are harder to carry out."

"Conquests are sometimes easy to make, too," Nieh replied. "They are harder to keep. If you stay here, you will not be facing the People's Liberation Army alone, you know. The Kuomintang and the eastern devils—the Japanese—will struggle alongside us. If the war takes a generation or longer, we shall accept the necessity."

He was sure he spoke the truth about the Kuomintang. Chiang Kai-shek had betrayed the Chinese revolution, but he was as wily a politician as any in the land. Even after the Japanese invaded, he'd saved the bulk of his strength for the conflict against the People's Liberation Army, just as Mao had conserved force to use against him. Each of them recognized the need for protracted war to gain his own objectives.

What the Japanese would do was harder to calculate. Without a doubt, though, they hated the little scaly devils and would fight them ferociously, even if without any great political acumen.

Ppevel said, "As I told you before, we are going to keep this land. Your threats we ignore. Your pinpricks we ignore. We recognize only true force. You are far too backward to build an explosive-metal bomb. We have no need to fear you or anything you might do."

"Maybe we cannot build one," Hsia Shou-Tao hissed, "but we have allies. One of these bombs might yet appear in a Chinese city."

This time, Nieh felt like patting Hsia on the back. That was exactly the right thing to say. Nieh knew—he did not think Hsia did—that Mao had sent Stalin a message, asking for the use of the first bomb the Soviet Union did not urgently require in its own defense.

The interpreter translated. Ppevel jerked in his chair as if he'd sat on something sharp and pointed. "You are lying," he said. Yet the interpreter's Chinese sounded uncertain. And Nieh did not think Ppevel sounded confident, either. He wished after all that he'd had Liu Han along; she would have been better at gauging the little devil's tone.

"Are we lying when we say we have allies?" Nieh replied. "You know we are not. The United States was allied with the Kuomintang and the People's Liberation Army against the Japanese before you scaly devils came here. The Soviet Union was allied with the People's Liberation Army against the Kuomintang. Both the U.S.A. and the USSR have explosive-metal bombs."

He thought the chances that one of those bombs would make its way to China were slim. But he did not have to let Ppevel know that. The more likely the little devil reckoned it to be, the better the bargain the People's Liberation Army would get.

And he'd rocked Ppevel too. He could see as much. The high-ranking scaly devil and his interpreter went back and forth between themselves for a couple of minutes. Ppevel finally said, "I still do not altogether believe your words, but I shall bring them to the attention of my superiors. They will pass on to you their decision on whether to include you Chinese in these talks."

"For their own sake and for yours, they had best not delay," Nieh said, a monumental bluff if ever there was one.

"They will decide in their own time, not in yours," Ppevel answered. Nieh gave a mental shrug: not all bluffs worked. He recognized a delaying tactic when he saw one. The little devils would discuss and discuss—and then say no. Ppevel went on, "The talks between us now are ended. You are dismissed, pending my superiors' actions."

"We are not your servants, to be dismissed on your whim," Hsia Shou-Tao said, anger in his voice. But the interpreter did not bother translating that; he and Ppevel retreated into the rear area of the enormous orange tent. An armed little devil came into what Nieh thought of as the conference chamber to make sure he and Hsia departed in good time.

Nieh was thoughtful and quiet till he and his aide left the Forbidden City and returned to the raucous bustle of the rest of Peking: partly because he needed to mull over what Ppevel had so arrogantly said, partly because he feared the little scaly devils could listen if he discussed his conclusions with Hsia Shou-Tao anywhere close to their strongholds.

At last he said, "I fear we shall have to form a popular front with the Kuomintang and maybe even with the Japanese as well if we are to harass the little devils to the point where they decide staying in China is more trouble than it's worth."

Hsia looked disgusted. "We had a popular front with the Kuomintang against the Japanese. It was just noise and speeches. It didn't mean much in the war, and it didn't keep the counter-revolutionaries from harassing us, too."

"Or we them," Nieh said, remembering certain exploits of his own. "Maybe this popular front will be like that one. But maybe not, too. Can we truly afford the luxury of struggle among ourselves while we also combat the little scaly devils? I have my doubts."

"Can we convince the Kuomintang clique and the Japanese to fight the common enemy instead of us and each other?" Hsia retorted. "I have my doubts of that."

"So do I," Nieh said worriedly. "But if we cannot, we will lose this war. Who will come to our rescue then? The Soviet Union? They share our ideology, but they have been badly mauled fighting first the Germans and then the scaly devils. No matter what we told Ppevel, I do not think the People's Liberation Army will get an explosive-metal bomb from the USSR any time soon."

"You're right there," Hsia said, spitting in the gutter. "Stalin kept the treaty he made with Hitler till Hitler attacked him. If he makes one with the little scaly devils, he will keep it, too. That leaves us fighting a long war all alone."

"Then we need a popular front—a true popular front," Nieh Ho-T'ing said. Hsia Shou-Tao spat again, perhaps at the taste of the idea. But, in the end, he nodded.

☆ **XV** ☆

"Armor-piercing!" Jäger barked as the Panther's turret traversed—not so fast as he wished it would move—to bear on the Lizards' mechanized infantry combat vehicle. He was hull-down behind a rise and well screened by bushes; the Lizards hadn't a clue his panzer was there.

"Armor-piercing!" Gunther Grillparzer echoed, his face pressed up against the sight for the Panther's long 75mm cannon.

Karl Mehler slapped the discarding-sabot round into the breech of the gun. "Nail 'em, Gunther," the loader said.

Grillparzer fired the panzer's main armament. To Jäger, who stood head and shoulders out of the cupola, the roar was like the end of the world. He blinked at the glare of the meter-long tongue of flame that shot from the muzzle of the gun. Down inside the turret, the brass shell casing fell to the floor of the panzer with a clang.

"Hit!" Grillparzer shouted exultantly. "They're burning."

They'd better be burning, Jäger thought. Those discarding-sabot rounds could punch through the side armor on a Lizard panzer. If they didn't wreck the more lightly protected combat vehicles, they wouldn't be worth using.

"Fall back," he said over the intercom to Johannes Drucker. The driver already had the Panther in reverse. He backed down the rear slope of the rise and continued in reverse to the next pre-selected firing position, this one covering the crestline to attack any Lizard vehicles that pursued too aggressively.

Other panzers of the regiment were also blasting away at any Lizard targets they could find. Infantrymen lurked among trees and in ruined buildings, waiting with their rocket launchers to assail Lizard armor. Lizard foot soldiers had been doing that to

German panzers since the invasion began. Having the where-withal to return the compliment was enjoyable.

Overhead, artillery shells made freight-train noises as they came down on the Lizards. The *Wehrmacht* had pushed the line several kilometers eastward over the past couple of days. The Lizards didn't seem to have been looking for an attack north of Lodz, and Jäger's losses, though still dreadful, were lighter than they might have been.

"I hope they're good and bloody well diverted," he muttered under his breath. He hadn't been much better prepared to make the attack than the Lizards were to receive it. How well he succeeded was for all practical purposes irrelevant, anyhow. As long as the Lizards paid full attention to him, he was doing his job.

Very quietly, down to the south, Otto Skorzeny was smuggling an atomic bomb into Lodz. Jäger didn't know just how the SS man and his chums were doing it. He didn't want to know. He didn't want them to do it, either, but he had no say about that.

He wondered if he'd managed to get word into the city. The fellow he'd contacted didn't seem nearly so reliable as Karol: he was furtive and frightened, half rabbit, half weasel. He was also alive, however, a good reason to prefer him to the late farmer.

Gunther Grillparzer made a disgusted noise. "They aren't rushing up to skewer themselves on our guns, the way they used to," he said. "Took 'em long enough to learn, didn't it? The British were quicker, down in North Africa. Hell, even the Russians were quicker, and that's saying something."

Off to the right, a Lizard antipanzer rocket got a Panzer IV between concealed firing positions. It brewed up, flame spurting from every hatch and a perfect black smoke ring shooting out through the open cupola. None of the five crewmen escaped.

Then Lizard artillery started landing around the German panzers. Jäger considered that a signal to halt the attack for the day. The Lizards weren't so prodigal in their use of the special shells that spat mines as they had been when the war was new, but they did still throw them about from time to time. He didn't care to lose half a company's worth of panzers to blown tracks.

The men were just as glad to bivouac. As Gunther Grillparzer got a little cookfire going, he turned to Johannes Drucker and asked, "Ever get the feeling you've lived too long already?"

"Don't talk like a dumbhead," the driver answered. "You just had a goose walk over your grave, that's all."

"Maybe you're right," Grillparzer said. "I hope so. Jesus,

though, every time we fight the Lizards, I don't believe I'm going to come through in one piece."

Otto Skorzeny had a way of materializing out of thin air, like a genie from the *Arabian Nights*. "You're a young man yet," he said. "One piece a day shouldn't be enough to satisfy you."

"I didn't expect to see you here so soon," Jäger said as the panzer crewmen snickered.

"Hell, don't give me that—you didn't expect to see me at all," Skorzeny said with a laugh. "But I needed to give you the news and I couldn't very well put it on the wireless, so *hier steh' ich—here I stand.*" He struck a pose perhaps meant to be clerical. Jäger was hard-pressed to imagine anyone who seemed less like Martin Luther. The SS man nudged him. They walked away from the cookfire and the big, friendly bulk of the Panther. In a low voice, Skorzeny went on, "It's in place."

"I figured it had to be," Jäger answered. "Otherwise you'd still be down in Lodz. But how the devil did you manage it?"

"We have our methods," Skorzeny said, not sounding much like Sherlock Holmes, either. "Enough ginger for the Lizards, enough gold pieces for the Poles." He laughed. "Some of them may even live to spend their loot—but not many." Merely being himself, he was as frightening a man as Jäger had ever known.

"When does it go off?" he asked.

"When I get orders to touch it off," Skorzeny said. "Now that it's in place, all my chums in the fancy black uniforms will go on home. It'll be my show. And do you know what?" He waited for Jäger to shake his head before continuing, "I'm really looking forward to it, too."

No, he was never more frightening than when he sounded like Skorzeny.

The rubble behind which Mutt Daniels sprawled had once been the chimney to a prosperous farmhouse about halfway between Marblehead and Fall Creek, Illinois. He glanced over to Herman Muldoon, who was sprawled behind some more of those red bricks. "We don't go forward any way a-tall," he said, "we don't clear the Lizards off the Mississippi till the week *after* Judgment Day."

"Yeah," Muldoon agreed mournfully. "They don't much want to be moved, do they?"

"Not hardly," Mutt said. Everything had gone fine till the U.S. Army tried to push south from Marblehead. They'd gone a couple of miles and stalled. A double handful of Shermans and a few older Lees had supported the attack, too. A couple of the Shermans were still running, but the powers that be had got leery about putting them any place where the Lizards could shoot at them. In a way, Mutt understood that. In another, he didn't. What point having tanks if you were afraid to use 'em?

Over to his right, behind the burned-out carcass of one of those Lees, a mortar team started lobbing bombs at the Lizard lines a few hundred yards south of the farmhouse. *Whump! Whump! Whump!* Those little finned shells didn't have much in the way of range, but they could throw a lot of explosive and steel fragments in a hurry.

The Lizards wasted no time replying. Mutt hunkered down and dug himself into the ground with his entrenching tool. Those weren't only mortar bombs whistling in; the Lizards were shooting real cannon, too, and probably from a range at which American guns couldn't reply.

Under cover of that bombardment, Lizard infantry skittered forward. When Mutt heard the platoon BAR start chattering, he stuck his head up and blazed away with his tommy gun. He didn't know whether any of the Lizards got hit or not. The BAR might well nail 'em at those ranges, but he'd just be lucky if he wounded one of the aliens. Still, they dove for cover and stopped advancing, which was the point of shooting early and often.

"Haven't seem 'em try to move up on us in a while," Muldoon yelled through the din.

"Me neither," Daniels said. "They been happy enough on the defensive for a while. An' you know somethin' else? I was pretty much happy to have 'em that way my own self."

"Yeah," Muldoon said. A big shell landed close by a couple of seconds later, showering both men with dirt and leaving them stunned and half deafened.

Mutt glanced back into a foxhole about twenty yards away to make sure his radioman was still in one piece. The kid was still moving and wasn't screaming, so Daniels figured nothing irreparable had happened to him. He wondered if he was going to have to call for mustard-gas shells to hold the Lizards back.

He was about to yell to the radioman when the Lizards' barrage let up. He peered suspiciously over the bricks. What sort of trick were they trying to play? Did they think they could catch the Americans all so deep in their holes that they wouldn't notice attackers till those attackers were in among them? If they didn't know better than that after more than two years of hard fighting, they damned well should have.

But the Lizards, having tried one advance, weren't pushing forward again. Small-arms fire from their side of the line had died away, too. "Made their point, I guess," Mutt said under his breath.

"Hey, Lieutenant, take a gander at that!" Herman Muldoon pointed out toward the Lizards' lines. Something white was waving on the end of a long stick. "They want a parley or somethin'."

"Pick up their wounded, mebbe," Daniels said. "I dickered that kind o' deal with 'em once or twice. Wouldn't mind doin' it again: they make a truce, they keep it for as long as they say they're gonna." He raised his voice. "Hold fire, boys! I'm gonna go out there an' parley with them scaly sons of bitches." He turned to Muldoon as the Americans' guns fell silent. "You got anything white, Herman?"

"Still got a snotrag, believe it or not." Muldoon pulled the handkerchief out of his pocket with no small pride; not many dogfaces could match it these days. It wasn't very white, but Mutt supposed it would do. He looked around for something to fix it to. When he didn't find anything, he cussed for a couple of seconds and then stood up, waving the hanky over his head. The Lizards didn't shoot at him. He walked out into the debatable ground between the two forces. A Lizard holding his own flag of truce came toward him.

He hadn't gone very far before the radioman hollered, "Lieutenant! Lieutenant Daniels, sir!"

"Whatever it is, Logan, it's gonna have to wait," Mutt called back over his shoulder. "I got business here."

"But, sir—"

Mutt ignored the call and kept walking. If he turned around and went back now, the Lizards were liable to figure he'd changed his mind about the cease-fire and start shooting at him. The alien with the white flag approached to within maybe ten feet of him, then stopped. So did Mutt. He nodded politely; as a soldier, he had nothing but respect for the Lizards. "Second Lieutenant Daniels, U.S. Army," he said. "You speak English?"

"Yessss." The Lizard drew the word out into a long hiss, but Mutt had no trouble understanding him. *Good thing, too,* he thought: he didn't know word one of Lizard talk. The alien went on, "I am Chook, small-unit group leader, conquest fleet of the Race."

"Pleased to meet you, Chook. Our ranks match, pretty much."

"Yess, I think so also," the Lizard said. "I come to tell you, there is cease-fire between conquest fleet of the Race and your U.S. Army."

"We can do that," Mutt agreed. "How long do you want the truce to last? Till nightfall, say? That'll give both sides plenty of time to bring in whoever's hurt and let us have a bit of a blow—a little rest," he added, thinking the Lizard was liable not to know slang—"afterwards, too."

"You not understand, Second Lieutenant Daniels," Chook said. "Is cease-fire between conquest fleet of the Race and your U.S. Army. Whole U.S. Army, whole part of conquest fleet here. Declared by Atvar, fleetlord of conquest fleet. Agree by not-emperor of your U.S. Army, whatever him name be. Cease-fire in place for now: not move forward, not move back. No set time to ending of cease-fire. You hear, Second Lieutenant Daniels? You understand?"

"Yeah," Mutt answered absently. "Jesus." He didn't know the last time he'd felt like this. November 1918, maybe, but he'd been expecting that cease-fire. This was a bolt from the blue. He turned and hollered, loud as he could: "Logan!"

"Sir?" The radioman's voice came back thin and tiny over a hundred fifty yards of ground.

"We got a cease-fire with these Lizards?"

"Yes, sir. I was trying to tell you, sir, I just got the word when—"

Mutt turned back to Chook. The Lizard had already given him the word. He spoke formally to Chook, to make sure the alien knew he had it straight: "I hear you, Small-Unit Group Leader Chook. I understand you, too. We got us a cease-fire in place here, just like all over the U.S. of A, no time limit."

"Truth," Chook said. "This what we have. This cease-fire not only for you. Is also for SSSR"—Mutt needed a second to figure out he meant Russia—"and for Deutschland." After going Over There, Daniels got that one fast.

"Lordy," Mutt said in an awed voice. "You pile that all together, it's half the world, pretty much." He noticed something else, too. "You made truces with the countries that bombed you back when you bombed 'em."

"Truth," Chook said again. "Are we fools, to waste cease-fire on empires we have beaten?"

"Look at things from your end o' the stick and I guess maybe you got a point," Mutt admitted. He wondered what was going to happen to England. Chook hadn't said a thing about the limeys, and Mutt had admired them ever since he'd seen them in action in

France in the war that was supposed to end war. Well, the Lizards had tried invading them once, and got a clout in the snout for their trouble. Maybe they'd learned a lesson.

Chook said, "You are good fighters, you Big Uglies. I tell you that much. It is truth. We come to Toscv 3—this planet, this world—we think we will win and win fast. We not win fast. You fight good."

"You're no slouches your own selves." Mutt half turned. "One of your boys, he shot me right there." He indicated his left nether cheek.

"I am lucky. I am not shot. Many males who are my friends, they are shot," Chook said. Mutt nodded. He knew about that. Every front-line soldier knew about that. Chook said, "We are fighters, you and I." Mutt nodded again. Chook let loose with a hissing sigh, then went on, "I think now one time, now another time, fighters of Race, fighters at the tips of the tongue of the fight, these males more like Big Uglies at tips of tongue of fight than like other males far away. You hear, Second Lieutenant Daniels? You understand?" He made a funny coughing noise after each question.

"Small-Unit Group Leader Chook, I hear you real good," Mutt said. "I understand you real good, too. What do you say when something is just right? You say 'truth,' don't you? That there's truth, Chook."

"Truth," Chook agreed. He spoke into something not much bigger than a paperback book. Back at his line, Lizards started standing up and poking their noses out of cover. *He's got a radio right there with him,* Mutt realized, *and so do all his troops. Ain't that a hell of a thing? Wish we could do the like.*

He turned around and waved to his own men. One by one, they stood up, too. Of them all, Herman Muldoon was the last fellow to show himself. Mutt didn't blame him a bit. He'd been shot at so many times by now, he probably had trouble believing this wasn't some sort of trick. Mutt would have, too, if he hadn't already been standing out here all vulnerable in case the Lizards did aim to pull off something sneaky.

Warily, still holding weapons, humans and Lizards approached each other. Some of them tried to talk back and forth, though Chook's males knew a lot less English than he did, and few Americans had much in the way of Lizard lingo. That was okay. You didn't need a whole lot of talking to get across the idea that you weren't trying to kill anybody right now, even if you had been a few minutes before. Mutt had seen that on truces in no-man's-land in France in 1918. Only a few of his buddies had been able to talk with the *Boches*, but they'd got on well enough.

Of course, back then the Yanks (Daniels remembered how irate he'd been to find the French considering him a Yankee) and *Boches* had swapped smokes and rations when they met. He'd traded rations only once; as far as he was concerned, it was a miracle the Germans fought so damn hard on the slop they got to eat.

He didn't figure he'd see anything like that here now. The Lizards didn't smoke, and their rations were nastier than anything the *Boches* had had. But when he looked around, he saw some of his guys trading something with the aliens. What the devil did they have that the Lizards wanted?

Chook was watching that, too, his eye turrets twisting every which way while his head hardly moved. Mutt wondered if he'd stop this unofficial commerce. Instead, after a minute or so, he said, "You, Second Lieutenant Daniels, have any of the fruit or small cakes with what you Big Uglies call *ginger* in them?"

A lightbulb went on in Mutt's head. He'd heard the Lizards had a hell of a yen for the stuff. " 'Fraid I don't, Small-Unit Group Leader," he said, and it *was* too bad—no telling what sort of interesting stuff a Lizard might have to trade. "Looks like some of my boys do, though."

As he spoke, he wondered why some of his boys were carrying around stuff with ginger in it. The only answer that came to mind was that they'd already been doing some trading with the Lizards on the sly. Any other time, that would have made him furious. When you looked at it after a cease-fire, though, how could you get excited about it?

"Yess. Truth," Chook said. With an eager spring in his skittering stride, he hurried off to find out what the Americans did have for sale. Behind his back, Mutt Daniels smiled.

Fluffy white clouds floated lazily across a blue sky. The sun was high and, if not hot, pleasantly warm. It was a fine day for walking hand in hand with the girl you—loved? David Goldfarb hadn't used the word with Naomi Kaplan, not out loud, but he thought it more and more often these days.

Naomi's thoughts, on the other hand, seemed focused on politics and war, not love. "But you are in the RAF," she said indignantly. "How could you not know whether we have got a cease-fire with the Lizards or have not got any such thing?"

He laughed. "How could I not know? Nothing simpler: they

don't tell me. I don't need to know to do my job, which is a good enough reason for not telling. All I know is what I want to know: I've not heard any Lizard aircraft—nor heard *of* any Lizard aircraft—over England since the cease-fire with the Yanks, the Russians, and the Nazis."

"Then it is a cease-fire," Naomi insisted. "It must be a cease-fire."

Goldfarb shrugged. "Maybe it is and maybe it's not. I admit, I don't know of any of our planes heading off to bomb the Continent, either, but we've not done much of that lately anyhow; the loss rate got too beastly high to bear. Maybe it's one of those informal arrangements: you don't hurt me and I shan't hurt you, but we'll not put anything in writing for fear of admitting we're doing whatever it is we're doing—or not doing."

Naomi frowned. "This is not right. This is not proper. This is not orderly." At that moment, she sounded very German. Goldfarb would sooner have bitten through his tongue than said so out loud. She went on, "The Lizards' agreements with the other nations are formal and binding. Why not with us?"

"I told you I don't know anything for certain," Goldfarb said. "Will you listen to my guess?" When she nodded, he went on, "The Americans, the Russians, and the Nazis have all used super-bombs of the same type the Lizards have. We've not done that. In their eyes, maybe we don't deserve a truce because we've not done it. But when they tried invading us, they found we weren't a walkover. And so they leave us alone without saying they're doing it."

"This is possible, I suppose," Naomi admitted after some serious thought. "But it is still not orderly."

"Maybe not," he said. "No matter what it is, though, I'm glad not to hear the air-raid sirens go off every day, or twice a day, or every hour on the hour."

He waited to see if Naomi would say such an irregular schedule of raids was disorderly, too. Instead, she pointed to the bright red breast of a robin streaking through the air after a dragonfly. "That's the only kind of aircraft I want to see in the sky."

"Hmm," Goldfarb said. "I am partial to a nice flight of Meteors, but I'd be stretching things if I didn't say you had a point."

They walked on for a while, not talking, glad of each other's company. It was very quiet. A bee buzzed from flower to flower in a field by the side of the road. Goldfarb noticed both the sound and the field without any vegetables growing in it: it had to be one of the few such so close to Dover.

Apparently apropos of nothing in particular, Naomi remarked, "My father and mother like you, David."

"I'm glad," he answered, which was true enough. Had Isaac and Leah Kaplan not liked him, he wouldn't be out walking with their daughter now. "I like them, too." That was also true to a large degree: he liked them about as well as a young man could like the parents of the girl he was courting.

"They think you have a serious mind," Naomi went on.

"Do they?" Goldfarb said, a little more cautiously now. If by serious-minded they meant he wouldn't try to seduce their daughter, they didn't know him as well as they thought they did. He'd already tried that. Maybe they knew Naomi, though, because it hadn't worked. And yet he hadn't gone off in a huff because she wouldn't sleep with him. Did that make him serious-minded? Maybe it did. He realized he had to say something more. "I think it's good they don't worry about where I'm from—or where my mother and father are from, I should say."

"They think of you as an English Jew," Naomi answered. "So do I, as a matter of fact."

"I suppose so. I was born here," Goldfarb said. He didn't think of himself as an English Jew, though, not when his parents had fled here from Warsaw on account of pogroms before the First World War. German Jews had a way of looking down their noses at their Eastern European cousins. If Naomi met his parents, it would be quite plain they weren't what she thought of as English Jews. If— Thoughtfully, he went on, "My father and mother would like you, too. If I get leave and you can get a day off from the pub, would you like to go up to London and meet them?"

"I would like that very much," she replied. Then she cocked her head to one side and looked over at him. "How would you introduce me?"

"How would you like me to introduce you?" he asked. But Naomi shook her head; that one wasn't for her to answer. *Fair enough,* he thought. He went on for another couple of paces before trying a slightly different question: "How would you like me to introduce you as my fiancée?"

Naomi stopped in her tracks. Her eyes went very wide. "You mean this?" she asked slowly. Goldfarb nodded, though his stomach felt as it sometimes had up in a Lancaster taking violent evasive action. Naomi said, "I would like this very much," and stepped into his arms.

The kiss she gave him nailed his stomach firmly back in place, though it made his head spin. When one hand of his closed softly on her breast, she didn't pull away. Instead, she sighed and held him tighter. Emboldened, he slid his other down from the small of her back to her right buttock—and, with a twirl as neat as a jitterbug dancer's, she twisted away from him.

"Soon," she said. "Not yet. Soon. We tell my parents. I meet your mother and father—and my mother and father will want to do the same. We find a rabbi to marry us. Then." Her eyes glittered. "And I tell you this—you will not be the only one who is impatient."

"All right," he said. "Maybe we ought to go tell your father and mother now." He turned and started toward Dover. The faster he cleared obstacles out of the way, the sooner she wouldn't use that little twirl. His feet didn't seem to touch the ground all the way back to the city.

Mordechai Anielewicz's voice came out flat as the Polish plain, hard as stone: "I don't believe you. You're lying."

"Fine. Whatever you say." The Polish farmer had been milking a cow when Anielewicz found him. He turned away from the Jewish fighting leader and back to the business at hand. *Siss! Siss! Siss!* Jets of milk landed in the dented tin pail. The cow tried to walk off. "Stay here, you stupid bitch," the Pole growled.

"But see here, Mieczyslaw," Mordechai protested. "It's impossible, I tell you. How could the Nazis have smuggled an explosive-metal bomb into Lodz without us or the Lizards or the Polish Home Army knowing about it?"

"I don't know anything about how," Mieczyslaw answered. "I hear tell they've done it. I'm supposed to tell you somebody stayed at Lejb's house in Hrubieszów. Does that mean anything to you?"

"Maybe it does, maybe it doesn't," Anielewicz said with as much equanimity as he could muster. He didn't want the Pole to know how shaken he was. Heinrich Jäger had stayed with a Jew named Lejb, all right, back when he was carrying explosive metal from the Soviet Union to Germany. The message had to be authentic, then; who else would know about that? It wasn't even the sort of thing he'd have been likely to mention in a report. Cautiously, Mordechai asked, "What else have you heard?"

"It's somewhere in the ghetto," Mieczyslaw told him. "Don't have any idea where, so don't waste time asking. Hadn't been for the cease-fire, all you kikes'd probably be toasting your toes in hell by now."

"I love you, too, Mieczyslaw," Anielewicz said. The Pole

chuckled, not in the least put out. Mordechai kicked at the dirt. "*Gottenyu!* That man has balls the size of an elephant. The *chutzpah* it takes to try something like that—and the luck you need to get away with it . . ."

"What man is that?" Mieczyslaw asked. Mordechai didn't answer him. He hardly heard him. How had Skorzeny sneaked an explosive-metal bomb past everybody and into Lodz? How had he got it into the Jewish quarter? How had he got out again afterwards? All good questions, the only trouble being that Mordechai had answers for none of them.

One other question, of course, overrode all of those. *Where was the bomb?*

He worried at it every step of the way back to Lodz, like a man worrying with his tongue at a piece of gristle stuck between two molars. The gristle was still stuck when he strode into the fire station of Lutomierska Street. Solomon Gruver was fiddling with the fire engine's motor. "Why the long face?" he asked, looking up from his work.

He wasn't the only man in earshot. The last thing Anielewicz wanted to do was spread panic through the ghetto. "Come on upstairs with me," he said, as casually as he could.

Gruver's long face turned somber. With his bushy eyebrows, harsh features, and thick, graying beard, he generally looked grim. When he felt grim, he looked as if his best friend had just died. He put down his wrench and followed Mordechai up to the room where the leaders of the Jewish fighters commonly met.

On the stairwell, he said quietly, "Bertha's up there. She picked up something interesting—what it is, I don't know—and she's passing it along. Is whatever you've got something she can know about?"

"It's something she'd better know about," Anielewicz answered. "If we can't deal with it ourselves, we may have to let Rumkowski's gang of *tukhus-lekhers* know it, too, and maybe even the Lizards, though that's the last thing I want to do."

"*Oy!*" Those eyebrows of Gruver's twitched. "Whatever it is, it must be bad."

"No, not bad," Mordechai said. Gruver gave him a quizzical look. "Worse," he explained as they got to the top of the stairs. Gruver grunted. Every time Anielewicz lifted his foot off the worn linoleum of the floor, he wondered if he would live to set it down again. That was not in his hands, not any more. If Otto Skorzeny pushed a button or flicked a switch on a wireless transmitter, he would cease to be, probably so fast he wouldn't realize he was dead.

He laughed. Solomon Gruver stared at him. "You're carrying news like this and you find something funny?"

"Maybe," Anielewicz answered. Skorzeny had to be one frustrated SS man right this minute. He'd risked his life getting that bomb into Lodz (Anielewicz, who'd despised him on sight, knew how much courage that had taken), but his timing was bad. He couldn't touch it off now, not without destroying the shiny new cease-fire between the Lizards and the *Reich*.

A couple of serious-looking Jewish men came out of the meeting room. "We'll take care of it," one of them promised Bertha Fleishman.

"Thank you, Michael," she said, and started to follow them out. She almost ran into Anielewicz and Gruver. "Hello! I didn't expect to see you two here."

"Mordechai ran into something interesting," Solomon Gruver said. "What it is, God knows, because he's not talking." He glanced over to Mordechai. "Not talking yet, anyhow."

"Now I am," Anielewicz said. He walked into the meeting room. When Gruver and Bertha Fleishman had followed him inside, he closed the door and, with a melodramatic touch, locked it. That made Bertha's eyebrows fly up, as Gruver's had before.

Mordechai spoke for about ten minutes, relaying as much as Mieczyslaw had told him. As he passed it on, he realized how little it was. When he was finished, Gruver looked at him and said, "I don't believe a word of it. It's just the damned Nazis trying to pull our chains and make us run around like chickens in the farmyard." He shook his head, repeating, "I don't believe a word."

"If it hadn't been this Jäger who sent us the message, I wouldn't believe it, either," Anielewicz said. "If it hadn't been for him, you know, the nerve-gas bomb would have done us in." He turned to Bertha. "What do you think?"

"As far as I can see, whether it's true or not doesn't matter," she answered. "We have to act as if it is, don't we? We can't really afford to ignore it."

"*Feh!*" Gruver said in disgust. "We'll waste all sorts of time and effort, and what will we come up with? Nothing, I tell you."

"*Alevai omayn* you're right and there's nothing to find," Mordechai said. "But suppose—just suppose—you're wrong and there is a bomb. Then what? Maybe we find it. That would be good; with a bomb of our own, we could tell the Lizards and Nazis both where to head in. Maybe the Lizards find it, and use it as an excuse to blow up some city somewhere—look what happened to Copenhagen. Or maybe we don't find it and the Lizards don't find it. Suppose the truce talks break down? All Skorzeny has to do is get on the wireless and—"

Solomon Gruver grimaced. "All right. You made your point, damn you. Now all we have to do is try to find the *verkakte* thing—if, like I say, it's there to be found in the first place."

"It's somewhere here, in our part of the city," Anielewicz said, as he had before. "How could the SS man have got it here? Where would he have hidden it if he did?"

"How big is it?" Bertha asked. "That will make a difference in where he might have put it."

"It can't be small; it can't be light," Anielewicz answered. "If it were, the Germans would load these bombs into airplanes or onto their rockets. Since they don't do that, the bombs can't be something they'd leave behind a kettle in your kitchen."

"That makes sense," Gruver admitted. "It's one of the few things about this miserable business that does. Like you say, it narrows down the places where the bomb is liable to be . . . if there is a bomb." He stubbornly refused to acknowledge that was anything more than an *if*.

"Around the factories," Bertha Fleishman said. "That's one place to start."

"One place, yes," Gruver said. "A big one place. Dozens of factories here, all through the ghetto. Straw boots, cartridge casings, rucksacks—we were making all sorts of things for the Nazis, and we're still making most of them for the Lizards. So where around the factories would you have us start?"

"I'd sooner not start with them," Anielewicz said. "As you say, Solomon, they're too big to know where to begin. We may not have much time; it probably depends on how soon the Lizards and the Nazis quarrel. So where's the likeliest place that SS *mamzer* would have hidden a big bomb?"

"From what you say about him, would he have picked the likeliest place?" Solomon Gruver asked.

"If he didn't, we're going to be in even more trouble than I already think we are," Mordechai answered. "But I think, I hope, I pray this time he didn't. He couldn't have spent much time in Lodz. He'd have wanted to hide this thing for a little while, escape, and then set it off. It wouldn't have needed to stay hidden very long or be hidden very well. But then the cease-fire came along and complicated his life—and maybe saved ours."

"If this isn't all a load of *dreck* to make us spin our wheels," Gruver said.

"If," Anielewicz admitted.

"I know one other place we ought to check," Bertha Fleishman said: "the cemetery and the ghetto field south of it."

Gruver and Anielewicz both looked at her. The words hung in the air of the dingy meeting room. "If I were doing the job, that's *just* where I'd put it," Mordechai exclaimed. "Can't think of a better place—quiet at night, already plenty of holes in the ground—"

"Especially in the ghetto field," Bertha said, catching fire at a suggestion she had first made casually. "That's where so many mass graves are, from when the sickness and starvation were so bad. Who would pay any special attention to one more hole in the ground there?"

"Who would notice anybody coming to dig one more hole in the ground in the middle of the night?" Solomon Gruver's big head bobbed up and down. "Yes, if it's anywhere, that's where we need to start looking."

"I agree," Mordechai said. "Bertha, that's wonderful. If you're not right, you deserve to be." He frowned after he said that, working it through to make sure he'd really given her the compliment he'd intended. To his relief, he decided he had.

She smiled back at him. When she smiled, she wasn't plain and anonymous any more. She still wasn't pretty, not in any ordinary sense of the word, but her smile gave her an odd kind of beauty. She quickly sobered. "We'll need to have fighters along, not just diggers," she said. "If we do find this hideous thing, people are going to want to take it away from us. As far as that goes, Lizards are people here."

"You're right again," Anielewicz said. "Draining the nerve gas out of the Nazi bomb made us dangerous nuisances. If we have this bomb, we won't be nuisances. We'll have real power."

"Not while it sits in a hole in the ground," Gruver said. "As long as it's there, the most we can do is blow ourselves up with our enemies. That's better than Masada, but it's not good. It's not good enough. If we can get the bomb out and put it where we want it, now—that's good. For us, anyhow."

"Yes," Mordechai breathed. Visions of might floated through his head—hurting the Lizards and getting the Nazis blamed for it, smuggling the bomb into Germany and taking real revenge for what the *Reich* had done to the Jews of Poland. Reality intervened, as reality has a way of doing. "There's only the one bomb—if there's any bomb there at all. We have to find it, and we have to get it out of the ground if it's there—you're right on both counts, Solomon—before we can even think about what to do with it."

"If we go with half the fighters in the ghetto, other people will know we're after something, even if they don't know what," Gruver said. "We don't want that, do we? Find it first, then see if we can get it out without raising a fuss. If we can't—" He shrugged.

"We'll walk through the cemetery and the ghetto field," Anielewicz declared—if he was commander here, he *would* command. "If we find something, then we figure out what to do next. And if we don't find anything"—he too shrugged, wryly—"then we figure out what to do next."

"And when someone asks us what we're doing there, what do we tell him?" Gruver asked. He was good at finding problems, not so good at solutions.

It was a good question. Anielewicz scratched his head. They had to say something, and something both innocuous and convincing. Bertha Fleishman said, "We can tell people we're looking for areas where no one is buried, so we can dig in those places first in case we have to fight inside the city."

Anielewicz chewed on that, then nodded, as did Solomon Gruver. Mordechai said, "It's better than anything I could have come up with. It might not even be a bad idea for us to do that one of these days, though there are so many graves there I'd bet there isn't much open space to be had."

"Too many graves," Bertha said quietly. Both men nodded again.

The cemetery and the ghetto field next to it lay in the northeastern corner of the Jewish district of Lodz. The fire station on Lutomierska Street was in the southwest, two, maybe two and a half kilometers away. It started to drizzle as Mordechai, Bertha, and Solomon Gruver tramped across the ghetto. Anielewicz looked gratefully up at the heavens; the rain would give them more privacy than they might have had otherwise.

A white-bearded rabbi chanted the burial service over a body wrapped in a sheet; wood for coffins had long since become a luxury. Behind him, amid a small crowd of mourners, stood a stooped man with both hands pressed up to his face to hide his sobs. Was it his wife going into the increasingly muddy ground? Mordechai would never know.

He and his companions paced among the headstones—some straight, some tilting drunkenly—looking for freshly turned earth.

Some of the grass in the cemetery was knee high; it had been poorly tended ever since the Germans first took Lodz, almost five years before.

"Would it fit in an ordinary grave?" Gruver asked, pausing before one that couldn't have been more than a week old.

"I don't know," Anielewicz answered. He paused. "No. Maybe I do. I've seen regular bombs the size of a man. Airplanes can carry those. What the Germans have has to be bigger."

"We're wasting our time here, then," the fireman said. "We should go down to the ghetto field, where the mass graves are."

"No," Bertha Fleishman said. "Where the bomb is—that doesn't have to look like a grave, you know. They could have made it seem as if they'd repaired the sewer pipes or something of that sort."

Gruver scratched at his chin, then finally nodded. "You're right."

An old man in a long black coat sat by one of the graves, a battered fedora pulled down low over his face against the drizzle. He closed the prayerbook he'd been reading and put it in his pocket. When Mordechai and his friends went by, the fellow nodded but did not speak.

A walk through the cemetery didn't show any new excavations of any sort bigger than ordinary graves. Gruver had an I-told-you-so look in his eye as he, Mordechai, and Bertha headed south into the ghetto field.

Grave markers got fewer there, and many of them, as Solomon Gruver had said, marked many corpses thrown into one pit: men, women, and children dead of typhus, of tuberculosis, of starvation, perhaps of broken hearts. Grass grew on a lot of those mounds, too. Things were not so desperate now. With the Nazis gone, times had improved all the way up to hard, and burials were by ones, not by companies at a time.

Bertha paused in front of one of the large interments: the board that was all the marker the poor souls down there would ever get had fallen over. When she stooped to straighten it, she frowned. "What's this?" she said.

Mordechai couldn't see what "this" was till he came close. When he did, he whistled softly under his breath. A wire whose insulator was the color of old wood ran the length of the board, held to it by a couple of nails pounded in and bent over. The nails were rusted, so they didn't stand out. The wire stopped at the top of the memorial board, but kept going from the bottom. There, it disappeared into the ground.

"Wireless aerial," he muttered, and yanked at it. It didn't want to come out. He pulled with all his strength. The wire snapped, sending him stumbling backwards. He flailed his arms to keep from falling. "*Something's* under there that doesn't belong," he said.

"Can't be," Solomon Gruver rumbled. "The ground's not torn up the way it . . ." His voice trailed away. He got down on his hands and knees, heedless of what the wet grass would do to his trousers. "Will you look at this?" he said in tones of wonder.

Mordechai Anielewicz got down beside him. He whistled again. "The grass has been cut out in chunks of sod and then replaced," he said, running his hand along one of the joins. If it had rained harder and melted the mud, that would have been impossible to notice. In genuine admiration, Anielewicz murmured, "They made a jigsaw puzzle and put it back together here when they were done."

"Where's the dirt?" Gruver demanded, as if Anielewicz had stolen it himself. "I don't care if they didn't bury the thing deep, they were going to have some left over—and they would have spilled it to either side of the grave as they were digging."

"Not if they set canvas down first and tossed the spoil onto that," Mordechai said. Gruver stared at him. He went on, "You have no idea how thorough the Nazis can be when they do something like this. Look at the way they camouflaged their antenna wire. They don't take chances on having something this important spotted."

"If the board hadn't fallen over—" Bertha Fleishman said in a dazed voice.

"I'll bet it was like that when the SS bastards got here," Anielewicz told her. "If you hadn't had the keen eyes to notice the aerial—" He made silent clapping motions and smiled at her. She smiled back. She really was quite extraordinary when she did that, he thought.

"Where's the dirt?" Solomon Gruver repeated, intent on his own concerns and not noticing the byplay between his comrades. "What did they do with it? They couldn't have put it all back."

"You want me to guess?" Mordechai asked. At the fireman's nod, he went on, "If I were running the operation, I would have loaded it onto the wagon they used to bring in the bomb and hauled it away. Throw canvas over it and nobody would think twice."

"I think you're right. I think that's just what they did." Bertha

Fleishman looked over to the detached wire. "The bomb can't go off now?"

"I don't think so," he answered. "Or, anyhow, they can't set it off by wireless now, which is good enough for us. If they hadn't needed the aerial, they wouldn't have put it there."

"Thank God," she said.

"So," Gruver said, sounding as if he still didn't believe it. "We have a bomb of our own now?"

"If we can figure out how to fire it," Anielewicz said. "If we can get it out of here without the Lizards' noticing. If we can move it so that if, God forbid, we have to, we can fire it without blowing ourselves right out of this world. If we can do all that, we have a bomb of our own now."

Sweat burst from Rance Auerbach's forehead. "Come on, darling," Penny Summers breathed. "You can do it. I know you can. You done it before, remember? Come on—big strong man like you can do whatever he wants."

Auerbach gathered himself, gasped, grunted, and, with an effort that took everything he had in him, heaved himself upright on his crutches. Penny clapped her hands and kissed him on the cheek. "Lord, that's hard," he said, catching his breath. Maybe he was light-headed, maybe just too used to lying flat on his back, but the ground seemed to quiver like pudding under him.

His arms weren't strong, either; supporting so much of his weight with his armpits was anything but easy. His wounded leg didn't touch the ground, and wouldn't for a long time yet. Getting around with one leg and two crutches felt like using an unsteady photographic tripod instead of his proper equipment.

Penny took a couple of steps back from him, toward the opening of the Lizards' shelter tent. "Come on over to me," she said.

"Don't think I can yet," Auerbach answered. This was only the third or fourth time he'd tried the crutches. Starting to move on them was as hard as getting an old Nash's motor to turn over on a snowy morning.

"Oh, I bet you can." Penny ran her tongue across her lips. She'd gone from almost completely withdrawn to just as brazen with next to nothing in between. When he had time to think, Auerbach wondered if they were two sides of the same coin. He didn't have time to think right this second. Penny went on, "You come on over to me now, and tonight I'll . . ." What she said she'd do would have sent a man hurt a lot worse than Auerbach over to her in nothing flat, maybe less. He let himself fall forward, hopped on his good leg, brought the crutches up to help keep his balance, straightened, did it again, and found himself by her side.

From outside the tent, a dry voice said, "That's the best incentive for physical therapy I've ever heard." Auerbach almost fell down. Penny squeaked and turned the color of the beets that grew so widely in Colorado.

By the way his own face heated, Auerbach was pretty sure he was the same color. "Uh, sir, it's not—" he began, but then his tongue stumbled to a halt even more readily than his poor damaged carcass had.

The doctor stepped into the tent. He was a young fellow, a stranger, not one of the Lizards' POW medicos. He looked from Auerbach to Penny Summers and back again. "Look, folks, I don't care if it is or it isn't—none of my business any which way. If it makes you get up and walk, soldier, that's what matters to me." He paused judiciously. "In my professional opinion, an offer like that would make Lazarus get up and walk."

Penny blushed even redder than she had before. Auerbach had had more experience with Army docs. They did their level best to embarrass you, and their level best was usually pretty damn good. He said, "Uh—who are you, sir?" The doctor had gold oak leaves on his shoulder straps.

"My name's Hayward Smithson—" The doctor paused. Rance gave his own name and rank. After a minute, Penny Summers stammered out her name, too, her right one; Auerbach wouldn't have been surprised to hear her come up with an alias on the spot. Major Smithson went on, "Now that the cease-fire's in place, I'm down from Denver inspecting the care the Lizards have been giving to wounded prisoners. I see you've got a set of government-issue crutches there. Good."

"Yes, sir," Auerbach said. His voice was still weak and thin and raspy as all get out, as if he'd smoked about fifty packs of Camels in the last hour and a half. "I got 'em day before yesterday."

"They came in a week ago," Penny said, "but Rance—uh, Captain Auerbach—he wasn't able to do much in the way of moving around till just the other day."

Auerbach waited for Smithson to make a crack about Penny's having done most of the moving before then, but, to his relief, Smithson had mercy. Maybe nailing her again would have been too much like shooting fish in a barrel. Instead, the doctor said, "You took one in the chest and one in the leg, eh, and they've pulled you through?"

"Yes, sir," Auerbach said. "They've done their best by me, the Lizards and the people they've got helping them. Sometimes I've felt kind of like a guinea pig, but I'm here and on my pins—well, on one pin, anyway—instead of taking up space in the graveyard back of town."

"More power to you, Captain," Smithson said. He pulled a spiral-bound notebook and a fountain pen out of his pocket and scribbled a note to himself. "I have to say, I've been favorably impressed with what I've seen of the Lizards' facilities. They've done what they could for the men they've captured."

"They've treated me okay," Auerbach said. "Firsthand, that's all I can tell you. I got outside this tent yesterday for the very first time."

"What about you, Miss, uh, Summers?" Major Smithson asked. "Captain Auerbach's not the only patient you've nursed back to health, I expect."

Auerbach devoutly hoped he was the only patient Penny had nursed back to health that particular way. He didn't think she noticed the possible double entendre there, and was just as well pleased she didn't. Seriously, she answered, "Oh, no, sir. I get all over this encampment. They do their best. I really think so."

"That's also the impression I've had," Smithson said, nodding. "They do their best—but I think they're overwhelmed." He sighed wearily. "I think the whole world is overwhelmed."

"Are there *that* many wounded, sir?" Auerbach asked. "Like I said, I haven't seen much outside of this tent except through the doorflap since they put me here, and nobody's told me there's all that many wounded POWs here in Karval." He sent Penny a look that might have been accusing. To the other nurses, to the harassed human doctors, to the Lizards, he was just another injured POW; he'd thought he meant something to her.

But Smithson said, "It's not just wounded soldiers, Captain. It's—" He shook his head and didn't try to explain. Instead, he went on, "You've been upright a good while now. Why don't you come outside and have a look for yourself? You'll have a doctor at your elbow, and who knows what Miss Summers will do for you or to you or with you after that?"

Penny blushed for a third time. Auerbach wished he could give the doctor a shot in the teeth for talking about a lady that way in front of her, but he couldn't. And he was curious about what was happening in the world beyond the tent, and he had been standing here a while without keeling over. "Okay, sir, lead on," he said, "but don't lead too fast, on account of I'm not going to win any races on these things."

Hayward Smithson and Penny held the tent flaps open so he could come out and look around. He advanced slowly. When he got out into the sunshine, he stood blinking for a moment, dazzled by its brilliance. And some of the tears that came to his eyes had nothing to do with the sun, but with his own delight at being unconfined, if only for a little while.

"Come along," Smithson said, positioning himself to Auerbach's left. Penny Summers immediately put Rance between her and the doctor. A slow procession, they made their way along the open track the Lizards had left between the rows of tents sheltering wounded men.

Maybe there weren't *that* many wounded men, but it still made for a pretty fair tent city. Every so often, Auerbach heard a man moaning inside one of those domes of the bright orange slick stuff the Lizards used. Once, a doctor and nurse hurried into one a good ways away on the dead run. That didn't look good, not even slightly. Smithson clicked his tongue between his teeth.

The way he'd been talking, though, half of Denver might have been here, and that didn't look to be so. Auerbach was puzzled till he came to the intersection of his lane with one that ran perpendicular to it. He hadn't come so far before. When you looked down that crossroad in one direction, you saw what was left of the tiny town of Karval: in two words, not much. When you looked the other way, you got a different picture.

He couldn't guess how many refugees inhabited the shantytown out beyond the Lizards' neat rows of tents. "It's like a brand-new Hooverville," he said, staring in disbelief.

"It's worse than a Hooverville," Smithson said grimly. "Most Hoovervilles, they had boxes and boards and sheet metal and what have you to build shacks with. Not much of that kind of stuff here in the middle of nowhere. But people have come anyhow, from miles and miles around."

"I've watched that happen," Penny said, nodding. "There's food and water here for prisoners, so people come and try to get some. When the Lizards have anything left over, they give a little. That's more'n people can get anywheres else, so they keep comin'."

"Lord," Auerbach said in his ruined voice. "It's a wonder they haven't tried coming into the tents and stealing what the Lizards wouldn't give 'em."

"Remember that gunfire the other night?" Penny asked. "A

couple of 'em was tryin' just that. The Lizards shot 'em down like they was dogs. I don't reckon any more folks'll try sneakin' in where the Lizards don't want 'em to."

"Sneaking up on the Lizards isn't easy anyhow," Dr. Smithson said.

Auerbach looked down at himself, at the much-battered excuse for a carcass he'd be dragging around for the rest of his life. "Matter of fact, I found out about that. Sneaking away from 'em's not so easy, either."

"They have Lizard doctors in Denver, looking out for their people that we caught?" Penny asked.

"Yes—it's all part of the cease-fire," Smithson answered. "I almost wish I could have stayed in town to watch them work, too. If we don't keep fighting them, they're going to push our medicine forward a hundred years in the next ten or fifteen, we have so much to learn." He sighed. "But this is important work, too. We may even be able to set up a large-scale prisoner exchange, wounded men for wounded Lizards."

"That would be good," Auerbach said. Then he looked over at Penny, whose face bore a stricken expression. She wasn't a wounded prisoner. He turned his head back toward Smithson. "Would the Lizards let noncombatants out?"

"I don't know," the doctor answered. "I can understand why you'd want to find out, though. If this comes off—and there are no guarantees—I'll see what I can do for you. How's that?"

"Thank you, sir," Auerbach said, and Penny nodded. Auerbach's gaze went toward the canvas tents and old wagons and shelters of brush housing the Americans who'd come to Karval to beg for crumbs of the Lizards' largesse. Thinking about that brought home like a kick in the teeth what the war had done to the country. He looked down at himself. "You know something? I'm not so bad off after all."

The buzz of a human-built airplane over Cairo sent Moishe Russie hurrying to the windows of his hotel-room cell for a glimpse. Sure enough, there it was, painted lemon yellow as a mark of truce. "I wonder who's in that one," he said to Rivka.

"You've said Molotov is already here," she answered, "so that leaves von Ribbentrop"—she and her husband both donned expressions redolent of distaste—"and the American foreign minister, whatever his name is."

"Marshall," Moishe said. "And they call him Secretary of State, for some reason." He soaked up trivia, valuable or not, like a sponge; the book-learning in medical school had come easy for him because of that. Had his interest lain elsewhere, he would have made a formidable *yeshiva-bucher*. He turned back to the window. The yellow airplane was lower now, coming in for a landing at the airfield east of town. "That's not a Dakota. Marshall would fly in one of those, I think. So it's probably a German plane."

Rivka sighed. "If you see Ribbentrop, tell him every Jew in the world wished a *kholeriyeh* on him."

"If he doesn't know that by now, he's pretty stupid," Moishe said.

"Tell him anyway," his wife said. "You get a chance like that, you shouldn't waste it." The drone of the motors faded out of hearing. Rivka laughed, a little uneasily. "That used to be a sound you took for granted. Hearing it here, hearing it now—it's very strange."

Moishe nodded. "When the truce talks started, the Lizards tried to insist on flying everyone here in their own planes. I suppose they didn't want the Nazis—or anyone else—sending a plane full of bombs instead of diplomats. Atvar was very confused when the Germans and the Russians and the U.S.A. all said no. The Lizards haven't really figured out what all negotiating as equals means. They've never had to do it before; they're used to dictating."

"It shall be done," Rivka said in the aliens' hissing language. Anyone who was around them long learned that phrase. She dropped back into Yiddish: "That's the way they think. It's about the only way they think."

"I know," Moishe answered. He made as if to pound his head against the wall. "*Oy*, do I know."

Through loudspeakers, the muezzins called the faithful to prayer. Cairo slowed down for a little while. Another bright yellow airplane flew low over the city, making for the airport. "That is a Dakota," Rivka said, coming up to stand by Moishe. "So—Marshall?—is here, too, now."

"So he is," Moishe answered. He felt as if he were setting up a game of chess with a friend back in Warsaw, and had just put the last couple of pieces where they belonged. "Now we see what happens next."

"What will you tell Atvar if he summons you to ask what you think of these people?" Rivka asked.

Moishe used a few clicks and pops himself. "The exalted fleet-lord? You mean, besides *geh in drerd*?" Rivka gave him a dangerous look, one that meant, *Stop trying to be funny*. He sighed and went on, "I don't know. I'm not even sure why he keeps bringing me in to question me. I wasn't—"

Rivka made urgent shushing motions. Moishe shut up. He'd started to say something like, *I wasn't anywhere near the caliber of those people*. Rivka was right. The Lizards surely monitored everything he said. If they hadn't figured out for themselves how small a fish he was, no point telling them. Being thought more important than he was might improve both his treatment and his life expectancy.

And sure enough, a couple of hours later Zolraag walked into the hotel room and announced, "You are summoned to the quarters of the exalted fleetlord Atvar. You will come immediately."

"It shall be done, superior sir," Moishe answered. The Lizards certainly hadn't bothered learning to negotiate with him as an equal. They told him where to go and what to do, and he perforce did it.

The guards didn't seem quite so eager to shoot him if he so much as stumbled as they had when the Lizards first brought him to Cairo. They still turned out for him full force, though, and transported him from hither to yon and back again in one of their armored personnel carriers, as uncomfortable a mode of travel for a human being as any ever invented.

While they were on their way to Atvar's headquarters, Zolraag remarked, "Your insights into the political strategies likely to be utilized are of interest to the exalted fleetlord. Having headed a not-empire yourself, you will be prepared to empathize with these other Tosevite males."

"That's certainly better than being shot," Moishe said gravely. He was glad he'd had practice holding his face straight. Yes, he'd headed up the Jews of Poland for a little while after the Lizards came, till he found he could no longer stand to obey them. To imagine that that put him in the same class as Hitler and Hull and Stalin—well, if you could imagine that, you had a vivid and well-stocked imagination. From what he'd gathered, anything smaller than the entire surface of a planet was too small for the Lizards to bother making what they reckoned subtle distinctions in size. The distinctions were anything but subtle to him, but he—thank God!—was not a Lizard.

Atvar rounded on him as soon as he came into the machine-strewn suite the fleetlord occupied. "If we make an agreement with these males, is it your judgment they will abide by it?" he demanded, using Zolraag to translate his words into Polish and German.

This to a man who'd watched Poland carved up between Germany and the USSR after they'd made their secret agreement, and then watched them go to war against each other less than two years later in spite of the agreement still formally in force. Picking his words with care, Moishe answered, "They will—so long as they see keeping the agreement as being in their interest."

The fleetlord made more mostly unintelligible noises. Again, Zolraag interpreted for him: "You are saying, then, that these Tosevite males are altogether unreliable?"

By any standard with which the Lizard was familiar, the answer to that had to be *yes*. Moishe didn't think putting it so baldly would help end the fighting. He said, "You have much to offer that would be in their interest to accept. If you and they can agree upon terms for your males' leaving their countries, for instance, they would probably keep any agreements that would prevent the Race from coming back."

As he'd seen with Zolraag's efforts in Warsaw, the Lizards had only the vaguest notions of diplomacy. Things that seemed obvious even to a human being who had no governmental experience—to Moishe himself, for instance—sometimes struck the aliens with the force of revelation when they got the point. And sometimes, despite genuine effort, they didn't get it.

As now: Atvar said, "But if we yield to the demands of these importunate Tosevites, we encourage them to believe they are our equals." After a moment, he added, "And if they believe themselves equal to us, soon they will come to think they are superior."

That last comment reminded Moishe the Lizards weren't fools; they might be ignorant of the way one nation treated with another, but they weren't stupid. Ignoring the difference could be deadly dangerous. Carefully, Moishe said, "What you have already done should make it plain to them that they are not your superiors. And what they have done to you should show you that you are not so much superior to them as you thought you were when you came to this world. When neither side is superior, isn't talking better than fighting?"

After Zolraag had translated what he'd said, Atvar fixed Russie with what certainly looked like a baleful stare. The fleetlord said, "When we came to Tosev 3, we thought you Big Uglies would still be the spear-flinging barbarians our probes of this planet had shown you to be. We discovered very soon we were not so superior as we had thought we would be when we went into cold sleep.

It is the most unpleasant discovery the Race has ever known." He added an emphatic cough.

"Nothing stays the same here, not for long," Moishe said. Some of the Polish Jews had tried to pretend time had stopped, to live their lives as they had before the Enlightenment and the Industrial Revolution blew across Europe. They'd even thought they were succeeding—till the Nazis brought all the worst parts of the modern world to bear against them.

Moishe had spoken with more than a little pride. That wasn't what he touched off in the fleetlord. Atvar replied in considerable agitation: "This is what is wrong with you Tosevites. *You are too changeable.* Maybe we can make peace with you as you are now. But will you be as you are now when the colonization fleet reaches this world? It is to be doubted. What will you be? What will you want? What will you know?"

"I have no answers to these questions, Exalted Fleetlord," Moishe said quietly. He thought of Poland, which had had a large army, well trained to fight the sort of war fought on that frontier a generation before. Against the *Wehrmacht*, the Poles had fought with utmost bravery and utmost futility—and had gone down to ignominious defeat in a couple of weeks. While they weren't looking, the rules had changed.

"I have no answers to these questions, either," Atvar said. Unlike the Polish army, he at least sensed the possibility of change. It frightened him even more than it had frightened the pious Jews who tried to turn their backs on Voltaire and Darwin and Marx, Edison and Krupp and the Wright brothers. The fleetlord went on, "I have to be certain this world will be intact and ready for settlement by the males and females of the colonization fleet."

"The question you must ask yourself, Exalted Fleetlord," Moishe said, "is whether you would sooner have part of the world ready for settlement than all of it in ruins."

"Truth," Atvar said. "But there is also another question: if we let you Tosevites retain part of the land surface of this world on your own terms now, for what will you use that base between now and the arrival of the colonization fleet? Do we end one war now but lay the eggs for another, larger one later? You are a Tosevite yourself; your people have done little but fight one war after another. How do you view this?"

Moishe supposed he should have been grateful the fleetlord was using him for a sounding board rather than simply disposing of him. He *was* grateful, but Atvar had given him another essentially unanswerable question. He said, "Sometimes war does lead to war. The last great war we fought, thirty years ago now it started, sowed the seeds for this one. But a different peace might have kept the new war from happening."

"Might," the fleetlord echoed unhappily. "I cannot afford *might*. I must have certainty, and there is none on this world. Even you Big Uglies cannot come into concord here. Take this Poland where you lived, where Zolraag was provincelord. The Deutsche claim it because they had it when the Race came to Tosev 3. The SSSR claims half of it because of an agreement they say the Deutsche violated. And the local Tosevites claim it belongs to neither of these not-empires, but to them alone. If we leave this Poland place, to whom shall we in justice restore it?"

"Poland, Exalted Fleetlord, is a place I hope you do not leave," Moishe said.

"Even though you did everything you could to undermine our presence there?" Atvar said. "You may have the egg, Moishe Russie, or you may have the hatchling. You may not have both."

"I understand that," Moishe said, "but Poland is a special case."

"All cases on Tosev 3 are special—just ask the Big Uglies involved in them," Atvar answered. "One more reason to hate this world."

☆ XVI ☆

Vyacheslav Molotov gulped down yet another glass of iced tea, pausing halfway through to swallow a couple of salt tablets. The heat of Cairo was unbelievable, enervating, even deadly dangerous: one of his aides, an NKVD colonel named Serov, who spoke the Lizards' language as fluently as any human being in the Soviet Union, had collapsed of heatstroke, and was now recovering in an air-conditioned hospital suite the English had set up to treat similarly afflicted folk of their own nation.

Neither the Semiramis Hotel, in which the Soviet delegation and other human diplomats were staying, nor Shepheard's, in which the negotiations were being conducted, enjoyed the benefits of air-conditioning. Here, the Soviets kept enough fans going at all times to make paperweights mandatory to prevent a blizzard of documents from blowing around the suite. Even if it did move, the air the fans blew remained hot.

No fans blew during the negotiations. The Lizards, as Molotov had discovered to his dismay when he was first flown up to one of their spaceships to discuss the war with their fleetlord, reveled in heat. Before Colonel Serov was rendered *hors de combat*, he'd reported that the Lizards here continually talked about how fine the weather was—almost like their home, they said.

As far as Molotov was concerned, they were welcome to it.

He reached in the drawer and pulled out a dark blue necktie. As he fastened the collar button of his shirt, he allowed himself a small, martyred sigh: here in Cairo, he envied the Lizards their body paint. Knotting the tie, he reflected that he still had an advantage over most of his colleagues. His neck was thin, which let air circulate under his shirt. A lot of the Soviets were beefy types, with double chins and rolls of fat at their napes. For them, closed collar and cravat were even worse torment.

Just for a moment, he wondered how the USSR's Lizard prisoners enjoyed the labor camps northeast of Leningrad and up in the northern reaches of Siberia. He wondered how they would enjoy them come February.

"As much as I enjoy Cairo now," he murmured, checking in the dresser mirror to make sure the tie was straight. Satisfied, he put on his hat and went downstairs to wait for the Lizard vehicle that would take him to today's negotiating session.

His interpreter, a birdlike little man named Yakov Donskoi, was pacing about the hotel lobby. He brightened on seeing Molotov arrive. "Good morning, Comrade Foreign Commissar," he said. With Molotov here, he had a set place to be and set things to do.

"Good morning, Yakov Beniaminovich," Molotov answered, and looked pointedly at his wristwatch. The Lizards were . . .

Exactly at the appointed hour, an armored personnel carrier pulled up in front of the hotel. He kept expecting the Lizards to be late, and they never were. Donskoi said, "I have been down for some time. Von Ribbentrop left about forty minutes ago, Marshall about twenty. Before that, I do not know."

The Lizards did not transport human diplomats together. Molotov supposed that was to keep them from conferring with one another. The tactic had its advantages for them. The humans didn't dare speak too freely among themselves at the hotel, either. The NKVD had swept Molotov's room for listening devices. He was sure the *Gestapo*, the OSS, and other intelligence agencies had done likewise for their principals' quarters. He was equally sure they hadn't found everything there was to find. The Lizards had too long a lead on humanity in that kind of technology.

He turned to Donskoi. "Tell the Lizards it would be *kulturny* if they provided seats in this machine suitable to the shape of our fundaments."

Donskoi addressed the Lizard with the fanciest body paint not in his own language but in English, the human tongue in which the talks were being conducted. It was the native tongue of George Marshall and Anthony Eden, while von Ribbentrop and Shigenori Togo were fluent in it. Eden and Togo were not formal conference participants, but the Lizards had let them come and sit in.

The Lizard replied to Donskoi in English that sounded to Molotov not much different from the alien's native tongue. The interpreter, however, made sense of it: that was his job. He translated for Molotov: "Strukss says no. He says we should be honored they deign to talk with us at all, and that we have no business asking for anything more than they provide."

"Tell him he is *nye kulturny*," Molotov said. "Tell him he is an ignorant barbarian, that even the Nazis whom I hate know more of diplomacy than his people, that his superior will hear of his insolence. Tell him in just those words, Yakov Beniaminovich."

Donskoi spoke in English. The Lizard made horrible spluttering noises, then spoke English himself. Donskoi said, "He says, with the air of one granting a great concession, he will see what arrangements can be made. I take this to mean he will do as you say."

"Ochen khorosho," Molotov said smugly. In some ways, the Lizards were very much like his own people: if you convinced one of them you had superior status, he would grovel, but he would ride roughshod over you if he thought himself of the higher rank.

The armored vehicle—far quieter and less odorous than its human-made equivalent would have been—pulled to a stop in front of Shepheard's Hotel, where Atvar made his headquarters. Molotov found it amusing and illuminating that the Lizard should choose for his own the hotel that had had the highest status under the British colonialist regime.

He got out of the Lizard personnel carrier with nothing but relief; not only was the seat wrong for his backside, it was even hotter in there than on the street. Strukss led him and Yakov Donskoi to the meeting room, where the other human representatives sat sweltering as they waited for Atvar to condescend to appear. George Marshall drank from a glass of iced tea and fanned himself with a palm-frond fan he'd probably brought from home. Molotov wished he'd thought to bring or acquire such a convenience himself. Marshall's uniform remained crisp, starchy.

Through Donskoi, Molotov asked the Egyptian servant hovering in the corner of the room for iced tea for himself. The servant, not surprisingly, was fluent in English. With a bow to Molotov—who kept his face still despite despising such self-abnegation—he hurried away, soon to return with a tall, sweating glass. Molotov longed to press it to his cheek before he drank, but refrained. A fan was suitably decorous; that was not.

Atvar came in a few minutes later, accompanied by a Lizard in far less elaborate body paint: his interpreter. The human delegates rose and bowed. The Lizard interpreter spoke to them in English that seemed more fluent than that which Strukss used. Yakov

Donskoi translated for Molotov: "The fleetlord recognizes the courtesy and thanks us for it."

Von Ribbentrop muttered something in German, a language Donskoi also understood. "He says they should show us more courtesy now, and they should have shown us more courtesy from the beginning."

Like a lot of the things the Nazi foreign minister said, that was both true and useless. Von Ribbentrop was on the heavyset side and, with his tight collar and fair skin, looked rather like a boiled ham with blue eyes. As far as Molotov was concerned, he had the wits of a boiled ham, too, but the interests of the popular front kept him from saying so.

Donskoi translated word for word as Eden asked Atvar, "Am I to construe that my presence means the Race extends the same cease-fire to Great Britain as to my cobelligerents who sit at this table with me?"

The handsome Englishman—Churchill's alter ego—had asked that question before, without getting a straight answer for it. Now Atvar spoke. The Lizard interpreter, having already translated Eden's question, turned the fleetlord's reply into English: "The fleetlord says in his generosity the truce applies to you in your island. It does not apply to any of the other lands of your empire across the seas from you and this island."

Anthony Eden, though not bad at keeping his face straight, was not in Molotov's class. The Soviet foreign minister had no trouble seeing his anguish. As Stalin had predicted, the British Empire was dead, having been pronounced so by a child-sized green-brown creature with sharp teeth and swiveling eye turrets. *In spite of your heroics, the dialectic consigns you to the ash-heap of history,* Molotov thought. *Even absent the Lizards, it would have happened soon.*

George Marshall said, "For us, Fleetlord, the cease-fire is not enough. We want you off our soil, and we are prepared to hurt your people more if you don't leave of your own free will and be quick about it."

"The German *Reich* expresses this same demand," von Ribbentrop declared, sounding pompous even when Molotov did not understand his words till they were translated. Sweating and blustering, he went on, "The *Führer* insists on the full restoration of all territory under the benevolent dominion of the *Reich* and its allied states, including Italy, at the time of your people's arrival from the depths of space."

As far as Molotov was concerned, no territory had been under the *benevolent* dominion of the *Reich*. That, however, was not his primary concern. Before Atvar could reply to von Ribbentrop, he spoke up sharply: "Much of the territory claimed by the Germans was illegally seized from the peace-loving workers and peasants of the Soviet Union, to whom, as Comrade Stalin, the General Secretary of the Communist Party of the USSR, rightly requires, it must be restored."

"If you Tosevites cannot settle where the boundaries of your empires and not-empires lie, why do you expect us to do it for you?" Atvar demanded.

Von Ribbentrop turned to glare at Molotov, who looked back stonily. The two of them might have been allied against the Lizards, but were not and would never be friends.

"Perhaps," Shigenori Togo said, "this situation being so irregular, both human states might agree to allow the Race to continue to possess some territory between them, serving as a buffer and aiding in the establishment and maintenance of peace all over our world."

"Subject to negotiation of the precise territory to be retained, this may in principle be acceptable to the Soviet Union," Molotov said. Given the Germans' prowess not merely with explosive-metal bombs but also with nerve gas and long-range guided rockets, Stalin wanted a buffer between the Soviet border and fascist Germany. "Since the Race is already in Poland—"

"No!" von Ribbentrop interrupted angrily. "This is not acceptable to the *Reich*. We insist on a complete withdrawal, and we will go back to war before we accept anything less. So the *Führer* has declared."

"The *Führer* has declared a great many things," Anthony Eden said with relish. " 'The Sudetenland is the last territorial claim I have to make in Europe,' for instance. That a declaration is made does not necessarily test its veracity."

"When the *Führer* promises war, he delivers," von Ribbentrop replied, a better comeback than Molotov had looked for from him.

George Marshall coughed, then said, "If we are throwing quotations around, gentlemen, let me give you one from Ben Franklin that fits the present circumstances: 'We must all hang together, or assuredly we shall all hang separately.' "

To Molotov, Yakov Donskoi murmured the translation, then added, "The pun in English I cannot reproduce in Russian."

"Never mind the pun," Molotov answered. "Tell them for me that Franklin is right, and that Marshall is right as well. If we are to be a popular front against the Lizards, a popular front we must be, which removes the pleasure of sniping at one another." He waited till Donskoi had rendered that into English, then went on, for the interpreter's ears alone, "If I am to be deprived of the pleasure of telling von Ribbentrop what I think of him, I want no one else to enjoy it—but you need not translate that."

"Yes, Vyacheslav Mikhailovich," the interpreter said dutifully. Then he stared at the foreign commissar. Had Molotov made a joke? His face denied it. But then, Molotov's face always denied everything.

Ussmak lifted the axe, swung it, and felt the jar as the blade bit into the tree trunk. Hissing with effort, he pulled it free, then swung again. At this rate, felling the tree would take about forever, and he would end up starving for no better reason than that he could not satisfy the quotas the Big Uglies of the SSSR insisted on setting for males of the Race.

Those quotas were the same ones they set for their own kind. Before this ignominious captivity, when Ussmak had thought of the Big Uglies, the *ugly* part was uppermost in his mind. Now he realized how much the *big* mattered. All the tools the guards gave him and his fellow males were designed for their kind, not his. They were large and heavy and clumsy in his hands. The males of the SSSR did not care. Unending toil on not enough food was making prisoners die off one after another. The guards did not care about that, either.

A brief moment's fury made Ussmak take a savage hack at the tree. "We should have kept on refusing to work and made them kill us that way," he said. "They mean for us to die anyhow."

"Truth," said another male nearby. "You were our headmale. Why did you give in to the Russkis? If we had hung together, we might have got them to do what we wanted. More food for less work sounds good to me." Like Ussmak, he had lost so much flesh, his skin hung loose on his bones.

"I feared for our spirits," Ussmak said. "I was a fool. Our spirits will be lost here soon enough no matter what we do."

The other male paused a moment in his own work—and a guard raised a submachine gun and growled a warning at him. The guards didn't bother learning the language of the Race—they expected you to understand them, and woe betide you if you didn't. The male picked up his axe again. As he swung it, he said, "We could try another work stoppage."

"We could, yes," Ussmak said, but his voice sounded hollow even to himself. The males of Barracks Three had tried once and failed. They would never come together as a group enough to try again. Ussmak was morbidly certain of it.

This was what he had bought for mutiny against his superiors. No matter how addled he had thought them, even their worst was a hundred, a thousand, a million times better than the superiors for whom he now toiled. Had he known then what he knew now— His mouth dropped open in a bitter laugh. That was what old males always told young ones just embarking on their lives. Ussmak wasn't old, not even counting the time he'd spent in cold sleep traveling to Tosev 3. But he had a hard-won store of bitter knowledge acquired too late.

"Work!" the guard snapped in his own language. He didn't add an emphatic cough; it was as if he'd only made a suggestion. Ignoring that suggestion, though, might cost you your life.

Ussmak hammered away at the tree trunk. Chips flew, but the tree refused to fall. If he didn't chop it down, they were liable to leave him out here all day. The star Tosev stayed in the sky almost all the time here at this season of the Tosevite year, but still could not warm the air much past cool.

He hit two more solid strokes. The tree tottered, then toppled with a crash. Ussmak felt like cheering. If the males quickly sawed the trunk into the sections the guards required, they might yet gain—almost—enough to eat.

Emboldened, he used his halting Russki to ask the guard, "Cease-fire truth is?" The rumor had reached the camp with a fresh batch of Big Ugly prisoners. Maybe the guard would feel well enough inclined to him for having cut down the tree to give him a straight answer.

And so it proved: the Big Ugly said, *"Da."* He took some crumbled leaves from a pouch he wore on his belt, rolled them in a piece of paper, lighted one end, and sucked in smoke at the other. The practice struck Ussmak as corrosive to the lung. It couldn't possibly have been so pleasant, so enjoyable, as, say, tasting ginger.

"We go free?" Ussmak asked. The Tosevite prisoners said that could happen as part of a cease-fire. They knew far more about such things than Ussmak did. All he could do was hope.

"Chto?" the guard said: "What? You go *free?*" He paused to suck more smoke and to blow it out in a harsh white cloud. Then he paused again, this time to make the barking noises Big Uglies used for laughter. "Free? You? *Gavno!*" Ussmak knew that meant some sort of bodily waste, but not how it applied to his question. The guard proceeded to make it perfectly, brutally, clear: "You go

free? *Nyet!* Never!" He laughed louder, the Tosevite equivalent of laughing wider. As if to reject the very idea, he leveled his sub-machine gun at Ussmak. "Now work!"

Ussmak worked. When at last the guards suffered the males of the Race to return to their barracks, he trudged back with dragging stride: half exhaustion, half despair. He knew that was dangerous. He'd already seen males who'd lost hope give up and die in short order. But knowing something was dangerous was different from being able to keep from doing it.

They had made their work norm for the day. The ration of bread and salted sea creature the Big Uglies doled out was not enough to keep them going through another day of grinding toil, but it was what they got.

Ussmak toppled into his hard, comfortless bunk as soon as he had eaten. Sleep dropped over him like a thick, smothering black curtain. He knew he would not be fully recovered when the males were routed out come morning. Tomorrow would be just the same as today had been, maybe a little worse, not likely to be any better.

So would the day after that, and the day after that, and the day after *that*. Free? Once more, the guard's barking laughter seemed to reverberate from his hearing diaphragms. As sleep overcame him, he thought how sweet never waking up would be.

Ludmila Gorbunova looked to the west, not in the hopes of catching a glimpse of the evening star (in any case, Venus was lost in the skirts of the sun) but longingly nonetheless.

From right beside her elbow, a voice said, "You would fly another mission into the *Wehrmacht* lines in a moment, wouldn't you?"

She jumped; she hadn't heard Ignacy come up. She also felt no small anger and embarrassment. Wearing her heart on her sleeve was the last thing she wanted to do, especially when it was given to a Nazi panzer colonel. *A* German *panzer colonel*, she thought, correcting herself. That sounded better to her—and besides, could any man who called a medal he'd won "Hitler's fried egg" be a dedicated fascist? She doubted it, though she knew her objectivity was suspect.

"You do not answer me," Ignacy said.

She wanted to pretend the guerrilla leader hadn't spoken, but she couldn't very well do that. Besides, since his Russian was better than anyone else's hereabouts, ignoring him would cut her off from the person to whom she could most readily speak. So she replied with something that was true but not responsive: "What I want does not much matter. With the cease-fire in place between the Germans and the Lizards, I will have no occasion to fly over there, will I? If the Germans have any sense, they will not do anything to make the Lizards lose patience with them and start fighting again."

"If the Germans had any sense, would they be Germans?" Ignacy returned. Ludmila would not have cared to take piano lessons from such a cynical man; perhaps the war had revealed to him his true calling. After pausing a moment to let the jab sink in, he went on, "The Germans will, I think, encourage unrest in the parts of Poland they do not control."

"Do you really?" Ludmila embarrassed herself all over again by how eager she sounded.

Ignacy smiled. It was not altogether pleasant, that curl of lips, not in a plump face in a land full of thin ones, not when it didn't quite light up his eyes. She hadn't told him anything of her meeting with Jäger; as far as she was concerned, that was her business and nobody else's. But whether she'd told him or not, he seemed to have drawn his own conclusions, most of them disconcertingly accurate. He said, "As a matter of fact, I am trying to arrange—ever so discreetly, of course—to get my hands on some German antitank rockets. Would you be interested in transporting those if I succeed?"

"I will do whatever is required to bring victory to the workers and peasants of Poland against the alien imperialists," Ludmila answered. Sometimes taking refuge in the rhetoric she'd learned from childhood was comforting. Using it also gave her more chance to think. She said, "Are you certain flying those rockets in would be the best way to get them? Moving them along back roads and paths might be easier and safer."

Ignacy shook his head. "The Lizards have been patrolling rear areas much more aggressively than they did when they fought major battles along the front. Also, the Nazis do not want anyone capturing antitank rockets that could be shown to have entered Poland after the cease-fire began. That might give the Lizards the excuse they need to end the truce. But if you flew the rockets back here without having them noticed on the ground, we could use them as we like: who could prove when we acquired them?"

"I see," Ludmila said slowly, and she did. The Nazis had an interest in playing it close to the vest, while Ignacy, she suspected, didn't know how to play it any other way. "And what happens if I am shot down trying to deliver the rockets to you?"

"I shall miss both you and the aircraft," the guerrilla leader answered. She gave him a dirty look. He stared back, his face bland and blank. She got the idea he wouldn't miss her much, even if she did give him an air force of sorts. She wondered if he wanted to get her airborne to be rid of her, but soon decided that was foolish. He could pick many more direct ways of disposing of her, ones that didn't involve the precious Fieseler *Storch*.

The nod he gave her was almost a bow: a bourgeois affectation he'd preserved even here in a setting most emphatically prole-tarian. "Be assured I shall let you know the instant I have word that this plan goes forward, that I have persuaded the German authorities here there is no danger to it. And now I leave you to enjoy the beauties of the sunset."

It *was* beautiful, even if she bridled at the way he said that. Crimson and orange and brilliant gold filled the sky; drifting clouds seemed to be aflame. And yet, though the colors were those of fire and blood, they didn't make her think of war. Instead, she wondered what she ought to be doing when, in a few short hours, the sun rose again. Where was her life going, tomorrow and next month and next year?

She felt torn in two. Part of her wanted to go back to the Soviet Union in any way she could. The pull of the *rodina* was strong. But she also wondered what would become of her if she returned. Her dossier already had to be suspect, because she was known to have associated with Heinrich Jäger. Could she justify going off to a foreign country—a country under occupation by the Lizards and the Nazis—at the behest of a German general? She'd been in Poland for months, too, without making any effort to come back till now. If the NKVD happened to be in a suspicious mood, as the NKVD so often happened to be (the nasty, skinny face of Colonel Boris Lidov flashed in front of her mind), they'd ship her to a *gulag* without a second thought.

The other half of her wanted to run to Jäger, not away from him. She recognized the impracticalities there, too. The Nazis had the *Gestapo* instead of the NKVD. They wouldn't just be looking at Jäger through a magnifying glass, either. They'd rake her over the coals, too, maybe more savagely than the People's Commissariat for the Interior would. She tried to imagine what happened to Nazis who fell into the NKVD's hands. That same sort of shud-dersome treatment had to await Soviet citizens in the grip of the *Gestapo*.

Realistically, she couldn't go east. As realistically, she couldn't go west, either. That left staying where she was, also an unpalat-able choice. Ignacy was hardly the sort of leader she'd follow into battle with a song on her lips (though if she did, she thought wryly, she'd better sing in tune).

As she stood and thought and watched, gold faded out of the sky. Now the horizon was orange, with crimson creeping down the dome of heaven toward it. Some of the clouds, off in the east, were just floating dumplings, not fire incarnate. Night was coming.

Ludmila sighed. "What I'd really like," she said, though nothing and no one was likely to pay her any heed, "is to go off somewhere—maybe by myself, maybe, if he wants, with Heinrich—and forget this whole war and that it ever started." She laughed. "And while I'm wishing for that, why don't I wish for the moon from out of the sky, too?"

Ttomalss paced back and forth on the concrete floor of his cell. His toeclaws clicked over the hard, rough surface. He wondered how long he would take to wear a groove in the floor, or maybe even wear through it so he could dig a hole in the dirt below and escape.

That depended on how thick the concrete was, of course. If the Tosevites had put down only a thin layer of the stuff, he shouldn't need more than, oh, three or four lifetimes.

Not much light came in through the small, narrow windows of the cell. Those windows were set too high for him to see out through them, and too high for any Big Ugly to see in. He had been told that if he raised an outcry, he would be shot without a chance to explain or make amends. He believed the warning. It was very much in character for the Tosevites.

He'd tried to keep track of days by scratching tally marks in the wall. It hadn't worked. He'd forgotten a day, or thought he had, and then scratched two marks instead of one the next morning, only to decide, afterwards, that maybe he hadn't forgotten after all, which rendered his makeshift calendar inaccurate and therefore useless. All he knew now was that he'd been here . . . forever.

"Sensory deprivation," he said. If no one outside could hear him, he was allowed to talk to himself. "Yes, sensory deprivation: that is the experiment the accursed female Liu Han has in mind for me. How long can I experience nothing and still keep my wits unaddled? I do not know. I hope I do not find out."

Was a slow descent into madness, watching yourself take each step down the road, preferable to being quickly killed? He didn't know that, either. He was even beginning to wonder whether he would have preferred to suffer the physical torment against which the Big Uglies, proving their barbarity, had no scruples. If thinking you'd sooner be tortured wasn't a step on the road to madness, what was?

He wished he'd never gone into cold sleep aboard a starship, wished he'd never seen Tosev 3, wished he'd never turned his eye turrets toward Liu Han, wished he'd never watched the hatchling emerge all slimy and bloody and disgusting from the genital opening between her legs, and wished—oh, how he wished!— he'd never taken that hatchling to see what he could learn from it.

Those wishes weren't going to come to fruition, either. He cherished them all the same. No one could deny they were utterly rational and sensible, the products of a mind fully in touch with reality.

He heard a sharp, metallic click and felt the building in which he was confined vibrate ever so slightly. He heard footfalls in the chamber outside his door, and heard the outer door to the building close. Someone fumbled at the lock that confined him. It opened, too, with a click different from that of the one on the outer door.

With a squeak of hinges that needed oil, the inner door swung open. Ttomalss all but quivered with joy at the prospect of seeing, speaking with, anyone, even a Big Ugly. "Superior—female," he said when he recognized Liu Han.

She did not answer right away. She carried a submachine gun in one hand and her hatchling on her other hip. Ttomalss had trouble knowing the hatchling was the creature he had studied. When the little Tosevite had been his, he'd put no cloths on it except the necessary ones around its middle that kept its wastes from splashing indiscriminately all over his laboratory area.

Now— Now Liu Han had decked the hatchling in shiny cloth of several bright colors. The hatchling also wore bits of ribbon tied in its black hair. The adornment struck Ttomalss as foolish and unnecessary; all he'd ever done was make sure the hair was clean and untangled. Why bother with anything more?

The hatchling looked at him for some time. Did it remember? He had no way to know; his research had been interrupted before he could learn such things—and, in any case, he couldn't be sure how long he'd been imprisoned here.

"Mama?" the hatchling said—in Chinese, without an interrogative cough. A small hand went out to point toward Ttomalss. "This?" Again, it spoke in the Tosevite language, without any hint it had begun to learn that of the Race.

"This is a little scaly devil," Liu Han answered, also in Chinese. She repeated herself: "Little scaly devil."

"Little scaly devil," the hatchling echoed. The words were not pronounced perfectly, but even Ttomalss, whose own Chinese was far from perfect, had no trouble understanding them.

"Good," Liu Han said, and twisted her rubbery face into the expression Big Uglies used to convey amiability. The hatchling did not give that expression back. It hadn't done that so much in the latter part of the time when Ttomalss had had it, perhaps because it had had no models to imitate. Liu Han's grimace left her features. "Liu Mei hardly smiles," she said. "For this I blame you."

Ttomalss realized the female had given the hatchling a name reminiscent of her own. *Family relationships are critical among Tosevites,* he reminded himself, becoming for a moment a researcher once more, not a captive. Then he saw Liu Han was waiting for his reply. Relying on the patience of a Big Ugly waiting with a submachine gun did not do. He said, "It may be so, superior female. Perhaps the hatchling needed a pattern for this expression. I cannot smile, so I could not be that pattern. We do not learn these things until we encounter them."

"You should not have had to learn them," Liu Han answered. "You should not have taken Liu Mei from me in the first place."

"Superior female, I wish I had not taken the hatchling," Ttomalss said, and backed that with an emphatic cough. The hatchling—*Liu Mei,* he reminded himself—stirred in Liu Han's arms, as if reminded of something it had once known. Ttomalss went on, "I cannot undo what I did, though. It is too late for that."

"It is too late for many things," Liu Han said, and he thought she meant to kill him on the spot. Then Liu Mei wiggled again. Liu Han looked down at the small Tosevite that had come from her body. "But it is not too late for all things. Do you see how Liu Mei is becoming a proper human person, wearing proper human clothes, speaking proper human language?"

"I see that, yes," Ttomalss answered. "She is very—" He didn't know how to say *adaptable* in Chinese, and cast around for a way to get across what he meant: "When the way she lives changes, she changes with it, very fast." Tosevite adaptability had addled the Race ever since the conquest fleet came to Tosev 3. Ttomalss saw no reason to be surprised at one more example.

Even in the gloomy little cell, Liu Han's eyes glittered. "Do you remember when you gave me back my baby, you gloated because you had raised it as a little scaly devil and it would not become a proper human being? That is what you said."

"I seem to have been wrong," Ttomalss said. "I wish I had

never said any such thing. We of the Race are always finding out we do not know as much about you Tosevites as we thought we did. That is one of the reasons I took the hatchling: to try to learn more."

"One of the things you have learned is that you should not have done it," Liu Han snapped.

"Truth!" Ttomalss exclaimed, and used another emphatic cough.

"I brought Liu Mei here to show you how wrong you were," Liu Han said. "You little scaly devils, you do not like to be wrong." Her tone was mocking; Ttomalss had learned enough of the way Tosevites spoke to be sure of that. She went on, mocking still, "You were not patient enough. You did not think enough about what would happen when Liu Mei was among proper human beings for a while."

"Truth," Ttomalss said again, this time quietly. What a fool he had been, to scoff at Liu Han without regard for possible consequences. As the Race had so often with the Big Uglies as a whole, he had underestimated her. And, as the Race had, he was paying for it.

"I will tell you something else," Liu Han said—if it wasn't going to be sensory deprivation, apparently she would do everything she could to make him feel dreadful. "You scaly devils have had to agree to talks of peace with several nations of human beings, because you were being so badly hurt in the fighting."

"I do not believe you," Ttomalss said. She was his only source of information here—why shouldn't she tell all sorts of outrageous lies to break his morale?

"I do not care what you believe. It is the truth even so," Liu Han answered. Her indifference made him wonder if perhaps he'd been wrong—but it might have been intended to do that. She continued, "You little devils still go on oppressing China. Before too much time has passed, you will learn this too is a mistake. You have made a great many mistakes, here and all over the world."

"It may be so," Ttomalss admitted. "But I make no mistakes here." He lifted a foot and brought it down on the concrete floor. "When I can do nothing, I can make no mistakes."

Liu Han let out several barks of Tosevite laughter. "In that case, you will stay a perfect male for a long time." Liu Mei started to fuss. Liu Han jiggled the hatchling back and forth, calming it more readily than Ttomalss had ever managed. "I wanted to show you how very wrong you were. Think of that as part of your punishment."

"You are more clever than I ever thought," Ttomalss said bitterly. Was it worse to contemplate nothing or his own stupidity? He did not know, not yet. Here in this cell, he expected he would have plenty of time to find out.

"Tell this to the other little devils—if I ever let you go," Liu Han said. She backed out of the chamber, keeping him covered with the submachine gun till she had shut the door. The click of the lock closing over the hasp had a dreadfully final sound. A moment later, he heard her close the outer door, too.

He stared after her. If she ever let him go? He realized she had told him that precisely to have it prey on his mind. Would she? Wouldn't she? Could he persuade her? If he could, how? Worrying about it would addle his mind, but how could he keep from worrying about it?

She was *much* more clever than he'd ever thought.

Sam Yeager stood on first base after cracking a single to left. In a seat in back of the first-base dugout, Barbara clapped her hands.

"Nice poke," said the first baseman, a stocky corporal named Grabowski. "But then, you played ball, didn't you? Pro ball, I mean."

"Years and years," Sam answered. "I'd be doing it yet if the Lizards hadn't come. I've got full dentures, top and bottom, so the Army wouldn't touch me till everything went to hell in a handbasket."

"Yeah, I've heard other guys say the same kind of thing," Grabowski answered, nodding. "But you're used to playing in a fancy park like this, is what I was getting at."

Yeager hadn't thought of Ban Johnson Field as a fancy park. It was just a ballyard, like hundreds of other minor-league parks he'd been through: covered grandstand, bleachers out in back of left and right, advertisements pasted on the boards of the outfield fences—faded, peeling, tattered advertisements now, because nobody in Hot Springs was advertising much of anything these days.

Grabowski went on, "Hell, for me this is like what the Polo Grounds must feel like. City parks're as hot a ball as I ever played."

"All depends on how you look at things," Sam said.

Crack! The guy up behind him hit a bouncer to short. Sam lit out for second full tilt. In a pickup game like this, you couldn't be sure the shortstop would make the play. But he did. He shoveled the ball to second, smooth as you please.

Ristin, who was playing second base, brushed the bag with one foot, then got it between him and the oncoming Yeager. The Lizard dropped down sidearm for the throw to first, giving Sam the choice between sliding and taking the ball right between the eyes. Sam hit the dirt. The ball thumped into Grabowski's mitt when the GI who'd hit the grounder was still a stride from the bag. "Yer out!" yelled the dogface making like an ump.

Yeager got up and brushed off his chinos. "Pretty double play," he told Ristin before he trotted off the field. "Can't turn 'em any better than that."

"I thank you, superior sir," Ristin answered in his own language. "This is a good game you Tosevites play."

When Sam got back to the bench, he grabbed for a towel and wiped his sweaty face. You played ball in Hot Springs in summertime, you might as well have played *in* the hot springs.

"Yeager! Sergeant Sam Yeager!" somebody called from the stands. It didn't sound like somebody from the crowd—if you called three, four dozen people a crowd. It sounded like somebody looking for him.

He stuck his head out of the dugout. "Yeah? What is it?"

A fellow with a first lieutenant's silver bar on each shoulder said, "Sergeant, I have orders to fetch you back to the hospital right away."

"Yes, sir," Sam said, glad the lieutenant wasn't getting shirty about the casual way he'd answered. "Let me get out of my spikes and into street shoes." He did that in a hurry, telling his teammates, "You'll have to find somebody else for left now." He took off his baseball cap and stuck his service cap on his head. He wished his pants weren't dirty, but he couldn't do anything about that now.

"Shall I come, too?" Barbara asked as he climbed up into the stands and headed toward the lieutenant. She shifted Jonathan from her lap to her shoulder and started to get up.

But Yeager shook his head. "You may as well stay, hon," he answered. "They wouldn't be looking for me like this if they didn't have some kind of duty in mind." He saw the officer had his hands on his hips, a bad sign. "I better get moving," he said, and did just that.

They went back to the Army and Navy General Hospital at a fast walk that was close to a trot. Ban Johnson Field was in Whittington Park, out at the west end of Whittington Avenue. They went past the old Catholic school on Whittington, down past Bathhouse Row on Central, and over Reserve to the hospital.

"What's gone wrong, anyhow?" Yeager asked as they went inside.

The lieutenant didn't answer, but hustled him along to the offices reserved for top brass. Sam didn't like that. He wondered if he was in trouble and, if he was, how much trouble he was in. The farther down the row of fancy offices they got, the bigger he figured the trouble might be.

A door with a frosted glass windowpane had a cardboard sign taped to it: BASE COMMANDANT'S OFFICE. Yeager gulped. He couldn't help it. "Hawkins, sir," the lieutenant said, saluting a captain sitting at a desk full of papers. "Reporting with Sergeant Yeager as ordered."

"Thank you, Hawkins." The captain got up from his desk. "I'll tell Major General Donovan he's here." He ducked into the office behind the antechamber. When he emerged a moment later, he held the door open. "Go on in, Sergeant."

"Yes, sir." Yeager wished to high heaven the lieutenant had given him a chance to clean up a little before he presented himself to a two-star general. Even if they did call Donovan "Wild Bill," he wasn't likely to appreciate sweat and grime and an aroma that clearly announced Yeager had been running around in hot, muggy weather.

No help for that now, though. Sam walked through the door, which the adjutant closed behind him. Saluting, he said, "Sergeant Samuel Yeager, sir, reporting as ordered."

"At ease, Sergeant," Donovan said as he returned the salute. He was a fit sixty, more or less, with blue eyes and the map of Ireland on his face. He had a couple of cans' worth of fruit salad on his chest. One of those ribbons was blue, with white stars. Yeager's eyes widened slightly. You didn't pick up a Congressional Medal of Honor for playing jacks. Before he got over that surprise, Donovan gave him another one, saying in fluent Lizard talk, "I greet you, Tosevite male who so well understands the males of the Race."

"I greet you, superior sir," Yeager answered automatically, using the same language. He dropped back into English to continue, "I didn't know you knew their lingo, sir."

"I'm supposed to know everything. That's my job," Donovan answered, without the slightest hint he was joking. He made a wry face. "Can't be done, of course. It's still my job. Which is why I sent for you."

"Sir?" Yeager said. *I don't know from nothin'.*

Donovan shuffled through papers on his desk. When he found

the one he wanted, he peered at it through the bottoms of his bifocals. "You were transferred here from Denver, along with your wife and the two Lizards Ullhass and Ristin. That right?" Without waiting for Yeager's answer, he went on, "That was before you started making an infielder out of Ristin, hey?"

"Uh, yes, sir," Sam said. Maybe Donovan *did* know everything.

"Okay," the general said. "You were attached to that Denver project for a good long while, weren't you? Even when they were back in Chicago. That right?" This time, he did let Sam nod before continuing, "Which means you probably know more about atomic bombs than anybody else in Arkansas. That right?"

"I don't know about *that*, sir," Yeager said. "I'm no physicist or anything like that. Uh, sir, am I allowed to talk about this stuff with you? They worked real hard on keeping it a secret."

"You're not only allowed to, you're ordered to—by me," Donovan answered. "But I'm glad to see you concerned with security, Sergeant, because I'm going to tell you something you are absolutely forbidden to mention outside this room, except as I may later direct. Have you got that?"

"Yes, sir," Sam said. By the way the base commandant spoke, he'd get a blindfold if he messed that one up; nobody'd bother wasting a cigarette on him.

"Okay," Donovan repeated. "By now, you're probably wondering what the hell is going on and why I dragged you in here. That right?" No answer seemed necessary. Donovan charged ahead: "Reason's real simple—we just got one of these atomic bombs delivered here, and I want to know as much about it as I can find out."

"*Here*, sir?" Sam stared.

"That's what I told you. It set out from Denver before the cease-fire was announced, and after that it just kept going. Makes sense when you think about it, hey? Thing must have come on one devil of a roundabout route to get here at all. They weren't about to stop it halfway, leave it somewhere in no-man's-land for the Lizards to find if they got lucky. It's our baby now."

"Okay, sir, I see that, I guess," Yeager answered. "But didn't some people from Denver come with it, people who know all about it?"

"They did like hell," Donovan said. "Security again—you don't want people like that captured. Thing came with typed instructions on how to arm it, a timer, and a radio transmitter. That's it. Orders boiled down to get it to a target, back away, run like hell, and fire when ready, Gridley."

Donovan would have been just about starting to shave when that Spanish-American War slang entered the language; Sam hadn't heard anybody use it for years. He said, "I'll tell you whatever I can, sir, but like I said before—uh, as I said before" (which was what he got for being married to Barbara) "I don't know everything there is to know."

"And as I told you, Sergeant, that's *my* job, not yours. So talk." Donovan leaned forward in his chair, ready to listen intently.

Sam told him everything he knew about the theory and practice of atomic bombs. Some of that was gleaned from science articles in the regretted *Astounding* from the days before the Lizards came; more came from what he remembered of interpreting for Enrico Fermi and the other Metallurgical Laboratory physicists and from what he'd picked up while they talked among themselves.

Donovan took no notes. At first, that irked Yeager. Then he realized the general didn't want to put anything in writing anywhere. That told him how seriously Donovan was taking the whole business.

When he ran down, Donovan nodded thoughtfully and said, "Okay, Sergeant; thanks very much. That clears up one of my major worries: I don't have to worry about the damn thing going off under my feet, any more than I do with any other piece of ordnance. I didn't *think* so, but with a weapon that new and that powerful, I wasn't what you'd call eager to risk my neck on what might have been my own misunderstanding."

"That makes sense to me, sir," Yeager agreed.

"Okay. Next question: you're in the rocket business, too, with Goddard. Can we load this thing on a rocket and shoot it where we want it to go? It weighs ten tons, give or take a little."

"No, sir," Sam answered at once. "Next rocket we make that'll throw one ton'll be the first. Dr. Goddard's working on ways to scale up what we've got, but . . ." His voice trailed away.

"But he's sick, and who knows how long he'll last?" Donovan finished for him. "And who knows how long it'll take to build a big rocket even if it gets designed, hey? Okay. Any chance of making atomic bombs small enough to go on the rockets we have? That'd be the other way to solve the problem."

"I plain don't know, sir. If it can be done, I bet they're working on it back in Denver. But I have no idea whether they can do it or not."

"Okay, Sergeant. That's a good answer," Donovan said. "If I told you how many people try to make like bigshots and pretend they know more than they do— Well, hell, I don't need to burden you with that. You're dismissed. If I need to pick your brain some more about this miserable infernal device, I'll call you again. I hope I don't."

"I hope you don't, too," Sam said. "That'd mean the cease-fire broke down." He saluted and left Donovan's office. The major general hadn't gigged him about his uniform after all. *Pretty good fellow,* he thought.

The German major at the port of Kristiansand shuffled through an enormous box of file cards. "Bagnall, George," he said, pulling one out. "Your pay number, please."

Bagnall rattled it off in English, then repeated it more slowly in German.

"Danke," said the major—his name was Kapellmeister, though he had a singularly unmusical voice. "Now, Flight Engineer Bagnall, have you violated in any way the parole you furnished to Lieutenant-Colonel Höcker in Paris year before last? Have you, that is, taken up arms against the German *Reich* in pursuance of the war existing between Germany and England prior to the coming of the Lizards? Speak only the truth; I have the answer before me."

"No, I have not," Bagnall answered. He almost believed Kapellmeister; that a Nazi officer in an out-of-the-way Norwegian town could, at the pull of a card, come up with the name of the man to whom he'd given that parole, or even the fact that he'd given such a parole, struck him as Teutonic efficiency run mad.

Apparently satisfied, the German scribbled something on the card and stuck it back in the file. Then he went through the same rigmarole with Ken Embry. Having done that, he pulled out several more cards and rattled off the names on them—the names of the Lancaster crewmen with whom Embry and Bagnall had formerly served—at Jerome Jones before asking, "Which of the above are you?"

"None of the above, sir," Jones replied, and gave his own name and pay number.

Major Kapellmeister went through his file. "Every third Englishman is named Jones," he muttered. After a couple of minutes, he looked up. "I do not find a Jones to match you, however. Very well. Before you may proceed to England, you must sign a parole agreeing not to oppose the German *Reich* in arms at any further time. If you are captured while you violate or after you have violated the terms of the parole, it will go hard for you. Do you understand?"

"I understand what you said," Jones answered. "I don't understand why you said it. Aren't we allies against the Lizards?"

"There is at present a cease-fire between the *Reich* and the Lizards," Kapellmeister answered. His smile was unpleasant. "There may eventually be a peace. At that time, our relations with your country will have to be defined, would you not agree?"

The three Englishmen looked at one another. Bagnall hadn't thought about what the cease-fire might mean in purely human terms. By their expressions, neither had Embry or Jones. The more you looked at things, the more complicated they got. Jones asked, "If I don't sign the parole, what happens?"

"You will be treated as a prisoner of war, with all courtesies and privileges extended to such prisoners," the German major said.

Jones looked unhappier yet. Those courtesies and privileges were mighty thin on the ground. "Give me the bloody pen," he said, and scrawled his name on the card Kapellmeister handed him.

"Danke schön," Major Kapellmeister said when he returned card and pen. "For now, as you rightly point out, we are allies, and you have been treated as such thus far. Is this not so?" Jones had to nod, as did Bagnall and Embry. The journey across German ally Finland, Sweden (neutral but ever so polite to German wishes), and German-held Norway had been fast, efficient, and as pleasant as such a journey could be in times of hardship.

As Kapellmeister disposed of the card, Bagnall had a vision of copies of it making journeys of their own, to every hamlet where Nazi soldiers and Nazi bureaucrats stood guard. If Jerome Jones ever stepped off the straight and narrow anywhere the *Reich* held sway, he was in trouble.

Once the parole was in his hands and in his precious file box, though, the major went from testy to affable. "You are free now to board the freighter *Harald Hardrada*. You are fortunate, in fact. Loading of the ship is nearly complete, and soon it will sail for Dover."

"Been a long time since we've seen Dover," Bagnall said. Then he asked, "Do the Lizards make a habit of shooting up ships bound for England? They haven't got a formal cease-fire with us, after all."

Kapellmeister shook his head. "It is not so. The informal truce they have with England appears to prevent them from doing this."

The three Englishmen left his office and walked down to the

dock where the *Harald Hardrada* lay berthed. The docks smelled of salt and fish and coal smoke. German guards stood at the base of the gangplank. One of them ran back to Kapellmeister to check whether the RAF men were to be allowed aboard. He came back waving his hand, and the rest of the guards stood aside. The inefficiency the Germans showed there made Bagnall feel better about the world.

He had to share with his comrades a cabin so small it lacked only a coat of red paint to double as a telephone box, but that didn't bother him. After so long away from England, he would cheerfully have hung himself on a hatrack to get home.

That didn't mean he wanted to spend much time in the cabin, though. He went back out on deck as soon as he'd pitched his meager belongings on a bunk. Uniformed Germans were rolling small, sealed metal drums up the gangplank. When the first one got to the *Harald Hardrada*, one of the soldiers tipped it onto its flat end. It was neatly stenciled, NORSK HYDRO, VEMORK.

"What's in there?" Bagnall asked, pointing. By now, his German was fluent enough that, for a few words or a few sentences at a time, he could be mistaken for a native speaker, though not one from his listener's home region, whatever that happened to be.

The fellow in the coal-scuttle helmet grinned at him. "Water," he answered.

"If you don't want to tell me, then just don't say," Bagnall grumbled. The German laughed at him and set the next barrel, identically stenciled, on its end beside the first. Irked, Bagnall stomped away, his feet clanging on the steel plates of the deck. The Nazi, damn him, laughed louder.

He and his comrades stowed away the barrels somewhere down in the cargo hold, where Bagnall didn't have to look at them. He told the story to Embry and Jones, both of whom chaffed him without mercy for letting a German get the better of him.

Thick, black coal smoke poured from the stack of the *Harald Hardrada* as it pulled out of Kristiansand harbor for the journey across the North Sea to England. Even if Bagnall was going home, it was a voyage he could have done without. He'd never been airsick, not in the worst evasive maneuvers, but the continual pounding of big waves against the freighter's hull sent him springing for the rail more than once. His comrades didn't twit him for that. They were right there beside him. So were some of the sailors. That made him feel, if not better, at least more resigned to his fate: *misery loves company* had a lot of truth to it.

Lizard jets flew over the freighter a couple of times, so high that their vapor trails were easier to see than the aircraft themselves. The *Harald Hardrada* had ack-ack guns mounted at bow and stern. Along with everyone else aboard, Bagnall knew they were essentially useless against Lizard planes. But the Lizards did not come down for a closer look or on a strafing run. Cease-fires, formal and otherwise, held.

Bagnall had spied several cloudbanks off to the west, identifying each in turn as England: he was seeing with a landlubber's eye, and one half blinded by hope. Before long, the clouds would shift and destroy his illusion. Then at last he caught sight of something out there that did not move or dissolve.

"Yes, that is the English coast," a sailor answered when he asked.

"It's beautiful," Bagnall said. The Estonian coast had gained beauty because he was sailing away from it. This one did so because he was approaching. Actually, the two landscapes looked pretty much alike: low, flat land slowly rising up from a sullen sea.

Then, off in the distance, he spotted the towers of Dover Castle, right down by the ocean. That made the homecoming feel real in a way it hadn't before. He turned to Embry and Jones, who stood beside him. "I wonder if Daphne and Sylvia are still at the White Horse Inn."

"Can but hope," Ken Embry said.

"Amen," Jones echoed. "Would be nice to have a lady friend who wouldn't just as soon shoot you down as look at you, let alone sleep with you." His sigh was full of nostalgia. "I remember there are women like that, though it's been so long I'm beginning to forget."

A tug came out to help nudge the *Harald Hardrada* up against a pier in a surprisingly crowded harbor. As soon as she'd been made fast in her berth with lines fore and aft, as soon as the gangplank snaked across to the dock, a horde of tweedy Englishmen with the unmistakable look of boffins swarmed aboard at a dead run and besieged every uniformed German they could find with a single question, sometimes in English, sometimes in German: "Where is it?"

"Where's what?" Bagnall asked one of the men.

Hearing an undoubtedly British voice, the fellow answered without hesitation: "Why, the water, of course."

Bagnall scratched his head.

* * *

One of the cooks ladled soup into David Nussboym's bowl. He sank the ladle all the way down to the bottom of the big iron pot. It came out full of cabbage leaves and bits of fish. The ration loaf he handed Nussboym was full weight or even a trifle over. It was still black bread, coarse and hard to chew, but it was warm from the oven and smelled good. His tea was made from local roots and leaves and berries, but the glass the cook gave him had plenty of sugar, so it was palatable enough.

And he had plenty of room in which to eat. Clerks and interpreters and other politicals got fed ahead of the common run of *zek*. Nussboym recalled with distaste the mob scenes in which he'd had to defend with his elbows the space in which he was sitting, and recalled a couple of times when he'd been elbowed off a bench and onto the planks of the floor.

He dug in. With every mouthful of soup, well-being flowed through him. It was almost as if he could feel himself being nourished. He sipped at his tea, savoring every morsel of dissolved sugar that flowed over his tongue. When your belly was full, life looked good—for a while.

"*Nu*, David Aronovich, how do you like talking with the Lizards?" asked Moisei Apfelbaum, Colonel Skriabin's chief clerk. He spoke in Yiddish to Nussboym but used his name and patronymic anyhow, which would have been an affectation anywhere in the USSR but seemed particularly absurd in the *gulag*, where patronymics fell by the wayside even in Russian.

Nevertheless, Nussboym imitated his style: "Compared to freedom, Moisei Solomonovich, it is not so much. Compared to chopping logs in the woods—" He did not go on. He did not have to go on.

Apfelbaum nodded. He was a skinny little middle-aged fellow, with eyes that looked enormous behind steel-rimmed spectacles. "Freedom you do not need to worry about, not here. The *gulag* has worse things than logging, believe me. A man could be unlucky enough to dig a canal. One can be unlucky, as I say, or one can be clever. Good to be clever, don't you think?"

"I suppose so," Nussboym answered. The clerks and cooks and trusties who made the *gulag* function—for the whole system would have fallen apart in days if not hours had the NKVD had to do all the work—were better company in many ways than the *zeks* of the labor gang to which he'd formerly been attached. Even if a lot of them were dedicated Communists (*plus royaliste que le roi* ran through his mind, for they upheld the principles of Marx and Engels and Lenin after other men espousing those same principles had sent them here), they were for the most part educated men, men with whom he had far more in common than the common criminals who were the dominant force in his work gang.

He did easier work now. He got more food for it. He should have been—well, not happy; you'd have to be *meshuggeh* to be happy here—as contented as he could be in the context of the *gulag*. He'd always been a man who believed in getting along with authority, whatever authority happened to be: the Polish government, the Nazis, the Lizards, now the NKVD.

But when the *zeks* with whom he'd formerly worked were shambling out to the forest for another day of toil, the looks they gave him chilled his blood. *Mene, mene, tekel upharsin* floated up from his days at the *cheder—thou art weighed in the balance, and art found wanting*. He felt guilty for having it easier than his former comrades, although he knew intellectually that interpreting for the Lizards made a far greater contribution to the war effort than knocking down yet another pine or birch.

"You are not a Communist," Apfelbaum said, studying him through those greatly magnified eyes. Nussboym shook his head, admitting it. The clerk said, "Yet you remain an idealist."

"Maybe I do," Nussboym said. He wanted to add, *What business is it of yours?* He kept his mouth shut, though; he was not such a fool as to insult a man who had such easy, intimate access to the camp commandant. The calluses on his hands were starting to soften, but he knew how easily he could once more grow accustomed to the feel of axehandle and saw grip.

"This will not necessarily work to your advantage," Apfelbaum said.

Nussboym shrugged. "If everything worked to my advantage, would I be here?"

Apfelbaum paused to sip at his glass of ersatz tea, then smiled. His smile was charming, so much so that Nussboym distrusted it at sight. The clerk said, "Again, I remind you that there are worse things than what you have now. You have not even been required to denounce any of the men of your old gang, have you?"

"No, thank God," Nussboym said. He hurriedly added, "Not that I ever heard any of them say anything that deserved denunciation." After that, he devoted himself to his bowl of soup. To his relief, Apfelbaum did not press him further.

But he was not altogether surprised when, two days later, Colonel Skriabin summoned him to his office and said, "Nussboym, we have heard a rumor that concerns us. I wonder if you can tell me whether there is any truth to it."

"If it concerns the Lizards, Comrade Colonel, I will do everything in my power," Nussboym said, hoping to deflect the evil moment.

He had no luck. Perhaps he had not really expected to have any luck. Skriabin said, "Unfortunately, it does not. It is reported to us that the prisoner Ivan Fyodorov has on more than one occasion uttered anti-Soviet and seditious sentiments since coming to this camp. You knew this man Fyodorov, I believe?" He waited for Nussboym to nod before going on, "Can there be any truth to this rumor?"

Nussboym tried to make a joke of it: "Comrade Colonel, can you name me even one *zek* who has *not* said something anti-Soviet at one time or another?"

"That is not the issue," Skriabin said. "The issue is discipline and examples. Now, I repeat myself: have you ever heard the prisoner Fyodorov utter anti-Soviet and seditious sentiments? Answer yes or no." He spoke in Polish and kept his tone light and seemingly friendly, but he was as inexorable as a rabbi forcing a *yeshiva-bucher* through the explication of a difficult portion of the Talmud.

"I don't really remember," Nussboym said. When *no* was a lie and *yes* was trouble, what were you supposed to do? *Temporize* was all that came to mind.

"But you said everyone said such things," Skriabin reminded him. "You must know whether the man Fyodorov was a part of everyone or an exception."

Damn you, Moisei Solomonovich, Nussboym thought. Aloud, he said, "Maybe he was, but maybe he wasn't, too. As I told you, I have trouble remembering who said what when."

"I have never noticed this trouble when you speak of the Lizards," Colonel Skriabin said. "You are always most accurate and precise." He thrust a typewritten sheet of paper across the desk to Nussboym. "Here. Just sign this, and all will be as it should."

Nussboym stared at the sheet in dismay. He could make out some spoken Russian, because many of the words were close to their Polish equivalents. Staring at characters from a different alphabet was something else again. "What does it say?" he asked suspiciously.

"That on a couple of occasions you did hear the prisoner Ivan Fyodorov utter anti-Soviet sentiments, nothing more." Skriabin held out a pen to him. He took it but did not sign on the line helpfully provided. Colonel Skriabin looked sorrowful. "And I had such hope for you, David Aronovich." His voice tolled out Nussboym's name and patronymic like a mourning bell.

With a couple of quick jerks that had almost nothing to do with his brain, Nussboym signed the denunciation and shoved it back at Skriabin. He realized he should have shouted at Skriabin the second the NKVD man tried to get him to betray Fyodorov. But if you'd always believed in getting along with authority, you didn't think of such things till that first fateful second had passed, and then it was too late. Skriabin took the paper and locked it in his desk.

Nussboym got another full bowl of soup at supper that night. He ate every drop of it, and every drop tasted like ashes in his mouth.

☆ **XVII** ☆

Atvar wished he had acquired the habit of tasting ginger. He needed something, anything, to fortify himself before going in to resume dickering with a chamber full of argumentative Big Uglies. Turning both eye turrets toward Kirel, he said, "If we are to have peace with the Tosevites, it appears we shall have to make the most of the concessions upon which they originally insisted."

"Truth," Kirel said in a melancholy voice. "They are certainly the most indefatigable argufiers the Race has ever encountered."

"That they are." Atvar twisted his body in distaste. "Even the ones with whom we need not conduct actual negotiations—the British and the Nipponese—go on with their unending quibbles, while two Chinese factions both insist they deserve to be here, though neither seems willing to admit the other does. Madness!"

"What of the Deutsche, Exalted Fleetlord?" Kirel asked. "Of all the Tosevite empires and not-empires, theirs seems to be presenting the Race with the greatest number of difficulties."

"I admire your gift for understatement," Atvar said acidly. "The envoy from Deutschland seems dim even for a Tosevite. The not-emperor he serves is, by all appearances, as addled as an unfertilized egg left half a year in the sun—or do you know a better way to interpret his alternating threats and cajolery?" Without waiting for an answer, the fleetlord went on, "And yet, of all these Tosevite empires and not-empires, the Deutsche may well be the most technologically advanced. Can you unravel this paradox for me?"

"Tosev 3 is a world full of paradoxes," Kirel replied. "Among so many, one more loses its capacity to surprise."

"This is also a truth." Atvar let out a weary, hissing sigh. "One or another of them is liable to prove a calamity, I fear. I admit I do not know which one, though, and very much wish I did."

Pshing spoke up: "Exalted Fleetlord, the time appointed for continuation of these discussions with the Tosevites is now upon us."

"Thank you, Adjutant," Atvar said, though he felt anything but grateful. "They are a punctual species, that much I will say for them. Even after so long in the Empire, the Hallessi would show up late for their own cremations if they could." His mouth dropped open in wry amusement. "Now that I think on it, so would I, if I could."

Regretfully, Atvar turned his eye turrets away from the males of his own kind and, with his interpreter, entered the chamber where the Tosevite representatives awaited him. They rose from their seats as he entered, a token of respect. "Tell them to sit down so we can get on with it," Atvar said to the interpreter. "Tell them politely, but tell them." The translator, a male named Uotat, turned his words into English.

The Tosevites returned to their chairs again, in their usual pattern. Marshall, the American male, and Eden, his British counterpart, always sat close together, though Eden was not really a formal participant in these talks. Then came Molotov, from the SSSR, and von Ribbentrop, of Deutschland. Like Eden, Togo of Nippon was more an observer than a negotiator.

"We begin," Atvar said. The Tosevite males leaned forward, away from the rigidly upright position they preferred most of the time and toward one more like that the Race used. This was, Atvar had learned, a sign of interest and attention. He went on, "In most cases, we have agreed in principle to withdraw from the territory controlled at the time of our arrival on Tosev 3 by the U.S.A., the SSSR, and Deutschland. We have done this in spite of claims we have received from several groups of Big Uglies offering the view that the SSSR and Deutschland did not rightfully possess some of these territories. Your not-empires are the ones strong enough to treat with us; this gives your claims priority."

Von Ribbentrop sat straight again and brushed an imaginary speck of dust from the material of the outer cloth covering of his torso. "He is smug," Uotat said to Atvar, using an eye turret to point to the Deutsch envoy.

"He is a fool," Atvar replied, "but you need not tell him that; if you are a fool, you derive no profit from hearing as much. I now resume with the matter at hand. . . . Because we are gracious, we also agree to withdraw our males from the northern territory that seems to be not quite a part of either the U.S.A. or Britain."

The toponym escaped him; Marshall and Eden supplied it together: "Canada."

"Canada, yes," Atvar said. The simple truth was that most of the place was too cold to be worth much to the Race under any circumstances. Marshall also seemed to think it was for all practical purposes part of the U.S.A., though it had a separate sovereignty. Atvar did not fully understand that, but it was to him a matter of small import.

"Now to the issue on which these talks paused in our last session," Atvar said: "the issue of Poland."

"Poland in its entirety must be ours!" von Ribbentrop said loudly. "No other solution is possible or acceptable. So the *Führer* has declared." (Uotat added, "This is the title of the Deutsch not-emperor." "I know," Atvar answered.) "I have no room whatever for discussion on this matter."

Molotov spoke. He was the only Tosevite envoy who did not use English. His interpreter translated for Uotat: "This view is unacceptable to the workers and farmers of the SSSR, who have an immediate claim on the eastern half of this region, one which I personally brokered with the Deutsch foreign minister, and also a historic claim to the entire country."

Atvar turned his eye turrets away from both contentious Big Uglies. Neither of them would budge on the issue. Atvar tried a new tack: "Perhaps we could let the Poles and the Jews of Poland form new not-empires of their own, between those of your not-emperors."

Molotov did not reply. Von Ribbentrop, unfortunately, did: "As I have said, the *Führer* finds this intolerable. The answer is no."

The fleetlord wanted to let loose with a long, hissing sigh, but refrained. The Big Uglies were undoubtedly studying his behavior as closely as he and his staff of researchers and psychologists were examining theirs. He tried a different course: "Perhaps, then, it is appropriate for the Race to remain sovereign over this place called Poland." In saying that, he realized he was meeting the ambitions of the Tosevite Moishe Russie. It wasn't what he'd had in mind, but he saw now that Russie did indeed understand his fellow Big Uglies.

"This may in principle be acceptable to the Soviet Union, depending on the precise boundaries of said occupation," Molotov said. In a low voice, Uotat added his own comment to that: "The Tosevites of the SSSR find the Deutsche no more pleasant neighbors than we do."

"Truth," Atvar said, amused but unwilling to show it to the Big Uglies.

Von Ribbentrop turned his head and looked at Molotov for several seconds before giving his attention back to Atvar. If that wasn't anger the Deutsch representative was displaying, all the Race's studies of Tosevite gestural language were worthless. But von Ribbentrop spoke without undue passion: "I am sorry to have to keep repeating myself, but this is not acceptable to Deutschland or to the *Führer*. Poland had been under and should return in its entirety to Deutsch sovereignty."

"That is not acceptable to the Soviet Union," Molotov said.

"The Soviet Union had control over not a particle of Polish soil at the time when—the situation changed," von Ribbentrop retorted. He turned back to Atvar. "Poland must be returned to Deutschland. The *Führer* has made it absolutely clear he will accept nothing less, and warns of the severest consequences if his just demands are not met."

"Does he threaten the Race?" Atvar asked. The Deutsch envoy did not reply. Atvar went on, "You Deutsche should remember that you hold the smallest amount of territory of any party to these talks. It is conceivable that we could destroy you without wrecking the planet Tosev 3 to the point where it would be unsuitable for the colonization fleet when it arrives. Your intransigence here is liable to tempt us to make the experiment."

That was partly bluff. The Race did not have the nuclear weapons available to turn all Deutsch-controlled territory to radioactive slag, however delightful the prospect was. The Big Uglies, however, did not know what resources the Race had and what it did not.

Atvar hoped, then, his threat would strike home. Marshall and Togo bent over the papers in front of them and both began to write furiously. The fleetlord thought that might represent agitation. Eden and Molotov sat unmoving. Atvar was used to that from Molotov. This was his first prolonged dealing with Eden, who struck him as competent but who was also in a weak bargaining position.

Von Ribbentrop said, "Then the war may resume, Fleetlord. When the *Führer* states his determination in regard to any issue, you may take it as certain that he means what he says. Am I to inform him that you flatly reject his reasonable requirement? If I do so, I warn you that I cannot answer for what will happen next."

His short, blunt-tipped tongue came out and moistened the everted mucus membranes that ringed his small mouth. That was, the Race's researchers insisted, a sign of nervousness among the Big Uglies. But why was von Ribbentrop nervous? Because he was running a bluff himself, at the orders of his not-emperor? Or because he feared the Deutsch leader really would resume the war if his insistence on having Poland was rejected?

Atvar picked his words with more care than he would have imagined possible when speaking to a Tosevite: "Tell this male that his demand for all of Poland is refused. Tell him further that, as far as the Race is concerned, the cease-fire between our forces and those of the Deutsche may continue while we address other issues. And tell him that, if the Deutsche are the first to break the cease-fire, the Race will retaliate forcefully. Do you understand?"

"Yes, Fleetlord, I understand," von Ribbentrop replied through Uotat. "As I have said, the *Führer* is not in the habit of making threats he does not mean. I shall convey your response to him. Then we shall all await his reply." The Big Ugly licked those soft, pink lips again. "I am sorry to say it, but I do not think we will be waiting long."

Major Mori handed Nieh Ho-T'ing a cup filled with gently steaming tea. "Thank you," Nieh said, inclining his head. The Japanese was, by his standards, acting courteously. Nieh still thought of him as an imperialist eastern devil, but one could be polite about such things.

Mori returned the half bow. "I am unworthy of your praise," he answered in his rough Chinese. The Japanese hid their arrogance behind a façade of false humility. Nieh preferred dealing with the little scaly devils. They made no bones about what they were.

"Have you decided which course would be most expedient for you to take?" Nieh asked. Looking around the Japanese camp, he thought that should be obvious. The eastern devils were ragged and hungry and starting to run low on the munitions that were their only means of coercing supplies from the local peasants. The arrival of the little scaly devils had cut them off from the logistics train that ran back to Japan. They were better disciplined than a band of bandits, but not much stronger.

But after their major nodded, he did not give the reply Nieh had hoped to hear: "I must tell you we cannot join what you call the popular front. The little devils do not formally stop their war against us, but they also do not fight us now. If we attack them here, who can say what that will provoke them to elsewhere in the world?"

"You join with them, in effect, against the progressive forces of the Chinese people."

Major Mori laughed at him. He stared. He had thought of many possible reactions from the Japanese, but had not expected that one. Mori said, "You have made an alliance with the Kuomintang, I see. That must be what transforms them from reactionary counterrevolutionary running dogs into progressives. A nice magic trick, I must say."

A mosquito buzzed down and bit Nieh on the back of one wrist. Smashing it gave him a moment to collect his thoughts. He hoped he was not turning red enough for the Japanese to notice. At last, he said, "Compared to the little scaly devils, the reactionaries of the Kuomintang are progressive. I admit it, though I do not love them. Compared to the little devils, even you Japanese imperialists are progressive. I admit that, too."

"*Arigato,*" the major said, giving him a politely sardonic seated bow.

"We have worked together against the scaly devils before." Nieh knew he was pleading, and knew he should not plead. But the Japanese, man for man, were better soldiers than either the troops of the People's Liberation Army or the forces of the Kuomintang. Having Mori's detachment as part of the local popular front would give the little scaly devils a great deal of added grief. And so Nieh went on, "The artillery shells with which you supplied me were put to good use, and caused the little devils many casualties."

"Personally, I am glad this is so," Mori replied. "But at the time you got those shells from me, the little devils and Japan were at war with each other. That does not now seem to be the case. If we join in attacks against the scaly devils and are identified, any chance of peace may be destroyed. I will not do that without a direct order from the Home Islands, no matter what my feelings are."

Nieh Ho-T'ing got to his feet. "I will return to Peking, then." Unspoken was the warning that, if the Japanese kept him from returning or shot him, they would find themselves rather than the little devils the focus of Chinese efforts from then on.

Even though he was but an eastern devil, Mori had enough subtlety to catch the warning. He too rose, and bowed once more to Nieh. "As I say, I wish you personal good luck against the little scaly devils. But, when set against the needs of the nation, personal wishes must give way."

He would have phrased it differently had he been a Marxist-

Leninist, but the import was the same. "I bear you no personal ill-will, either," Nieh said, and left the Japanese camp in the countryside for the hike back to Peking.

Dirt scuffed under his sandals as he trudged along. Crickets chirped in the undergrowth. Dragonflies skimmed by, darting and twisting with maneuvers impossible for any fighter plane. Farmers and their wives bent their backs in fields of wheat and millet, endlessly weeding. Had Nieh been an artist instead of a soldier, he might have paused a while to sketch.

What he was thinking about, though, had nothing to do with art. He was thinking Major Mori's Japanese had lingered close by Peking too long already. The little scaly devils, if they ever thought to do it, could use the Japanese against the popular front in the same way the Kuomintang had used warlord forces against the People's Liberation Army. That would let the little devils fight the Chinese without committing their own troops to the effort.

He had nothing personal against the Japanese major, no. But, because he respected Mori as a soldier, he found him all the more worrisome: he had the potential to be more dangerous. With the razor-sharp logic of the dialectic, that led to an ineluctable conclusion: Major Mori's pocket would have to be liquidated as soon as possible.

"It might even work out for the best," Nieh said aloud: no one to hear him but for a couple of ducks paddling in a pond. If the little scaly devils were subtle enough to understand indirect hints, the disappearance of possible allies would give them the idea that the popular front would not only prosecute a campaign against them, but would do so vigorously.

He reached Peking in the middle of the night. Off in the distance, gunfire rattled. Someone was striking a blow for the progressive cause. "What are you doing here at this hour?" a human gate guard asked.

"Coming in to see my cousin." Nieh showed a false identity card, and handed the guard a folded banknote with it.

The guard returned the card, but not the money. "Pass in, then," he said gruffly. "But if I see you coming around again so late, I am going to decide you're a thief. Then it will go hard for you." He brandished a spiked truncheon, reveling in his tiny authority.

Nieh had all he could do not to laugh in the fellow's face. Instead, he ducked his head as if in fright and hurried past the guard into Peking. The roominghouse was not far away.

When he got there, he found Liu Han chasing Liu Mei around the otherwise empty dining room. Liu Mei was squealing with glee. She thought it a wonderful game. Liu Han looked about ready to fall over. She shook a finger at her daughter. "You go to sleep like a good girl or maybe I will give you back to Ttomalss."

Liu Mei paid no attention. By Liu Han's weary sigh, she hadn't expected Liu Mei to pay any attention. Nieh Ho-T'ing said, "What will you do with the little scaly devil called Ttomalss?"

"I don't know," Liu Han said. "It's good to have you back, but ask me hard questions another time. Right now I'm too tired to see straight, let alone think straight." She ran and kept Liu Mei from overturning a chair on top of herself. "Impossible daughter!" Liu Mei thought it was funny.

"Has the scaly devil been punished enough?" Nieh persisted.

"He could never be punished enough, not for what he did to me, not for what he did to my daughter, not for what he did to Bobby Fiore and other men and women whose names I do not even know," Liu Han said fiercely. Then she calmed somewhat. "Why do you ask?"

"Because it may be useful, before long, to deliver either the little devil himself or his body to the authorities his kind have set up here in Peking," Nieh answered. "I wanted to know which you would prefer."

"That would be a decision for the central committee, not for me alone," Liu Han said, frowning.

"I know." Nieh watched her more warily than he'd ever expected when they first met. She'd come so far from the peasant woman grieving over her stolen child she'd been then. When class was ignored, when ability was allowed, even encouraged, to rise as in the People's Liberation Army, astonishing things sometimes happened. Liu Han was one of those astonishments. She hadn't even known what the central committee was. Now she could manipulate it as well as a Party veteran. He said, "I have not discussed the matter before the committee. I wanted to learn your opinion first."

"Thank you for thinking of my personal concerns," she said. She looked through Nieh for a little while as she thought. "I do not know," she went on. "I suppose I could accept either, if it helped our cause against the little scaly devils."

"Spoken like a woman of the Party!" Nieh exclaimed.

"Perhaps I would like to join," Liu Han said. "If I am to make myself all I might be here, I should join. Is that not so?"

"It is so," Nieh Ho-T'ing agreed. "You shall have instruction, if that is what you want. I would be proud to instruct you myself, in fact." Liu Han nodded. Nieh beamed. Bringing a new member into the Party gave him the feeling a missionary had to have on bringing a new convert into the church. "One day," he told her, "your place will be to give instruction, not to receive it."

"That would be very fine," Liu Han said. She looked through him again, this time perhaps peering ahead into the future. Seeing her so made Nieh nervous: did she see herself ordering him about?

He started to smile, then stopped. If she kept progressing at the rate she had thus far, the notion wasn't so unlikely after all.

The clop of a horse's hooves and the rattle of a buggy's iron tires always took Leslie Groves back in time to the days before the First World War, when those noises had been the normal sound of getting from one place to another. When he remarked on that, Lieutenant General Omar Bradley shook his head. "It's not quite right, General," he said. "Back in those days, the roads this far outside of town wouldn't have been paved."

"You're right, sir," Groves admitted. He didn't often yield points to anyone, not even to the nuclear physicists who sometimes made the Metallurgical Laboratory such a delight to administer, but this one he had to concede. "I remember when a little town felt medium-sized and a medium-sized one felt like a big city because they'd paved all the streets downtown."

"That's how it was," Bradley said. "You didn't have concrete and asphalt all over the place, not when I was a boy you didn't. Dirt roads were a lot easier on a horse's hooves. It was an easier time, a lot of ways." He sighed, as any man of middle years will when he thinks back on the days of his youth.

Almost any man. Leslie Groves was an engineer to the core. "Mud," he said. "Dust. Lap robes, so you wouldn't be filthy by the time you got where you were going. More horse manure than you could shake a stick at. More flies, too. Give me a nice, enclosed Packard with a heater on a good, flat, straight stretch of highway any old time."

Bradley chuckled. "You have no respect for the good old days."

"To hell with the good old days," Groves said. "If the Lizards had come in the good old days, they'd have smashed us to bits so fast it wouldn't even have been funny."

"There I can't argue with you," Bradley said. "And going out to a two-hole Chick Sale with a half-moon window wasn't much fun in the middle of winter." He wrinkled his nose. "Now that I think back on it, it wasn't much fun in hot weather, either." He laughed out loud. "Yeah, General, to hell with the good old days. But what

we've got now isn't the greatest thing since sliced bread, either."
He pointed ahead to show what he meant.

Groves hadn't been out to the refugee camp before. He knew of
such places, of course, but he'd never had occasion to seek them
out. He didn't feel guilty about that; he'd had plenty to do and then
some. If he hadn't done what he'd done, the U.S.A. might well
have lost the war by now, instead of sitting down with the Lizards
as near equals at the bargaining table.

That didn't make the camp any easier to take. He'd been
shielded from just how bad war could be for those who got stuck
in the gears. Because the Met Lab was so important, he'd always
had plenty to eat and a roof over his head. Most people weren't so
lucky.

You saw newsreels of things like this. But newsreels didn't usually show the worst. The people in newsreels were black and
white, too. And you didn't smell them. The breeze was at his back,
but the camp smelled like an enormous version of the outhouses
Bradley had mentioned all the same.

People in newsreels didn't come running at you like a herd of
living skeletons, either, eyes enormous in faces with skin stretched
drum-tight over bones, begging hands outstretched. "Please!"
came the call, again and again and again. "Food, sir?" "Money,
sir?" "Anything you've got, sir?" The offers the emaciated women
made turned Groves' ears red.

"Can we do anything more for these people than we're doing,
sir?" he asked.

"I don't see what," Bradley answered. "They've got water here.
I don't know how we're supposed to feed them when we don't
have food to give."

Groves looked down at himself. His belly was still ample. What
there was went to the Army first, not to refugees and to people
from Denver whose jobs weren't essential to the war effort. That
made good, cold, hard logical sense. Rationally, he knew as much.
Staying rational wasn't easy, not here.

"With the cease-fire in place, how soon can we start bringing in
grain from up north?" he asked. "The Lizards won't be bombing
supply trains the way they used to."

"That's so," Bradley admitted, "but they gave the railroads a
hell of a pasting when they made their big push on the city. The
engineers are still trying to straighten things out. Even when the
trains start rolling, though, the other question is where the grain'll
come from. The Lizards are still holding an awful lot of our bread-

basket. Maybe the Canadians'll have some to spare. The scaly bastards haven't hit them as hard as they did us, seems like."

"They like warm weather," Groves said. "There are better places to find it than north of Minnesota."

"You're right about that," Bradley said. "But watching people starve, right here in the middle of the United States, that's a damned hard thing to do, General. I never thought I'd live to see the day when we had to bring in what little we do have with armed guards to keep it from being stolen. And this is on our side of the line. What's it like in territory the Lizards have held for the last couple of years? How many people have died for no better reason than that the Lizards didn't give a damn about trying to feed them?"

"Too many," Groves said, wanting to quantify that but unable to with any degree of certainty. "Hundreds of thousands? Has to be. Millions? Wouldn't surprise me at all."

Bradley nodded. "Even if the Lizards do pull out of the U.S.A. and leave us alone for a while—and that's the most we can hope for—what kind of country will we have left? I worry about that, General, quite a lot. Remember Huey Long and Father Coughlin and the Technocrats? A man with nothing in his belly will listen to any sort of damn fool who promises him three square meals a day, and we've got a lot of people with nothing in their bellies."

As if to underscore his words, three horse-drawn wagons approached the refugee camp. Men in khaki who wore helmets surrounded the supply wagons on all sides. About half of them carried tommy guns; the rest had rifles with fixed bayonets. The surge of hungry people toward the wagons halted at a respectful distance from the troops.

"Hard to give shoot-to-kill orders to keep starving people from mobbing your food wagons," Bradley said glumly. "If I hadn't, though, the fast and the strong would get food, nobody else but. Can't let that happen."

"No, sir," Groves agreed. Under the hard and watchful eyes of the American soldiers, their fellow citizens lined up to get the tiny handfuls of grain and beans the quartermasters had to dole out. By comparison, Depression soup kitchens had been five-star restaurants with blue-plate specials. The food then had been cheap and plain, but there'd always been plenty of it, once you swallowed enough of your pride to take charity.

Now . . . Watching the line snake forward, Groves realized he'd been so busy working to save the country that General Bradley's question never once crossed his mind: what sort of country was he saving?

The more he looked around the refugee camp, the less he liked the answers he came up with.

For once in his life, Vyacheslav Molotov had to fight with every fiber of his being to maintain his stiff face. *No!* he wanted to scream at Joachim von Ribbentrop. *Let it go, you fool! We have so much of what we came here for. If you push too hard, you'll be like the greedy dog in the story, that dropped its bone into the river trying to grab the one its reflection was holding.*

But the German foreign minister got up on his hind legs and declared, "Poland was part of the German *Reich* before the coming of the Race to this world, and therefore must return to the *Reich* as part of the Race's withdrawal from our territory. So the *Führer* has declared."

Hitler, actually, was quite a lot like the dog in the fable. All he understood was taking; nothing else seemed real to him. Had he only been content to stay at peace with the Soviet Union while he finished Britain, he could have gone on fooling Stalin a while longer and then launched his surprise attack, thereby contending with one foe at a time. He hadn't waited. He couldn't wait. He'd paid for it against the USSR. Didn't he see he'd have to pay far more against the Lizards?

Evidently he didn't. There was his foreign minister, mouthing phrases that would have been offensive to human opponents. Against the Lizards, who were vastly more powerful than Germany, those phrases struck Molotov as clinically insane.

Through his interpreter, Atvar said, "This proposal is unacceptable to us because it is unacceptable to so many other Tosevites with concerns in the region. It would merely prove a generator of future strife."

"If you do not immediately cede Poland to us, it will prove a generator of present strife," von Ribbentrop blustered.

The Lizards' fleetlord made a noise like a leaking inner tube. "You may tell the *Führer* that the Race is prepared to take the chance."

"I shall do so," von Ribbentrop said, and stalked out of the Shepheard's Hotel meeting room.

Molotov wanted to run after him, to call him back. *Wait, you fool!* was the cry that echoed in his mind. Hitler's megalomania might drag everyone else down along with Germany. Even the nations with explosive-metal bombs and poison gas weren't much more than large nuisances to the Lizards. Until they could deliver their weapons somewhere other than along the front line with the aliens, they could not threaten them on equal terms.

The Soviet foreign commissar hesitated. Did von Ribbentrop's arrogance mean the Hitlerites had such a method? He didn't believe it. Their rockets were better than anyone else's, but powerful enough to throw ten tonnes across hundreds, maybe thousands, of kilometers? Soviet rocket scientists assured him the Nazis couldn't be that far ahead of the USSR.

If they were wrong . . . Molotov didn't care to think about what might happen if they were wrong. If the Germans could throw explosive-metal bombs hundreds or thousands of kilometers, they were as likely to throw them at Moscow as at the Lizards.

He checked his rising agitation. If the Nazis had such rockets, they would not be so insistent about holding on to Poland. They could launch their bombs from Germany and then scoop up Poland at their leisure. This time, the scientists had to be right.

If they were right . . . Hitler was reacting from emotion rather than reason. What was Nazi doctrine but perverted romanticism? If you wanted a thing, that meant it should become yours, and that meant you had the right—even the duty—to go out and take it. If anyone had the gall to object, you ran roughshod over him. Your will was all that mattered.

But if a man a meter and a half tall who weighed fifty kilos wanted something that belonged to a man two meters tall who weighed a hundred kilos and tried to take it, he'd end up with a bloody nose and broken teeth, no matter how strong his will was. The Hitlerites didn't see that, though their assault on the USSR should have taught it to them.

"Note, Comrade Fleetlord," Molotov said, "that the German foreign minister's withdrawal does not imply the rest of us refuse to work out our remaining differences with you." Yakov Donskoi turned his words into English; Uotat translated the interpreter's comments into the language of the Lizards.

With a little luck, the aliens would smash the Hitlerites into the ground and save the USSR the trouble.

"Jäger!" Otto Skorzeny shouted. "Get your scrawny arse over here. We've got something we need to talk about."

"You mean something besides your having the manners of a bear with a toothache?" Jäger retorted. He didn't get up. He was busy darning a sock, and it was hard work, because he had to hold it farther away from his face than he was used to. These past couple of years, his sight had begun to lengthen. You fell apart even if you didn't get shot. It just happened.

"Excuse me, your magnificent Coloneldom, sir, my lord von Jäger," Skorzeny said, loading his voice with sugar syrup, "would you be so generous and gracious as to honor your most humble and obedient servant with the merest moment of your ever so precious time?"

Grunting, Jäger got to his feet. "All the same to you, Skorzeny, I like 'Get your scrawny arse over here' better."

The SS *Standartenführer* chuckled. "Figured you would. Come on. Let's go for a walk."

That meant Skorzeny had news he didn't feel like letting anyone else hear. And that, presumably, meant all hell was going to break loose somewhere, most likely somewhere right around here. Almost plaintively, Jäger said, "I was enjoying the cease-fire."

"Life's tough," Skorzeny said, "and it's our job to make it tougher—for the Lizards. Your regiment's still the thin end of the wedge, right? How soon can you be ready to hit our scaly chums a good one right in the snout?"

"We've got about half our Panthers back at corps repair center for retrofitting," Jäger answered. "Fuel lines, new cupolas for the turrets, fuel pump gaskets made the right way, that kind of thing. We took advantage of the cease-fire to do one lot of them, and now that it's holding, we're doing the other. Nobody told me—nobody told anybody—it was breaking down."

"I'm telling you," the SS man said. "How long till you're up to strength again? You need those Panthers, don't you?"

"Just a bit, yes," Jäger said with what he thought was commendable understatement. "They should all be back here in ten days—a week, if somebody with clout goes and leans on the corps repair crews."

Skorzeny bit his lip. "*Donnerwetter!* If I lean on them hard, you think they'd have your panzers up here at the front inside five days? That's my outer limit, and I haven't got any discretion about it. If they aren't here by then, old chum, you just have to go without 'em."

"Go where?" Jäger demanded. "Why are you giving me orders? And not my division commander, I mean?"

"Because I get *my* orders from the *Führer* and the *Reichsführer-SS*, not from some tinpot major general commanding a measly corps," Skorzeny answered smugly. "Here's what's going to happen as soon as you're ready to motor and the artillery boys are set to do their part, too: I blow Lodz to kingdom come, and you—and everybody else—gets to hit the Lizards while they're still trying to figure out what's going on. The war is back, in other words."

Jäger wondered if his message to the Jews of Lodz had got through. If it had, he wondered if they'd been able to find the bomb the SS man had hidden there somewhere. And those were the least of his worries: "What will the Lizards do to us if we blow up Lodz? They took out one of our cities for every bomb we used during the war. How many will they slag if we use one of those bombs to break a cease-fire?"

"Don't know," Skorzeny said. "I do know nobody asked me to worry about it, so I bloody well won't. I have orders to blast Lodz in the next five days, so a whole raft of big-nosed kikes are going to get themselves fitted for halos along with the Lizards. We have to teach the Lizards and the people who suck up to 'em that we're too nasty to mess with—and we will."

"Blowing up the Jews will teach the Lizards something?" Jäger scratched his head. "Why should the Lizards give a damn what happens to the Jews? And with whom are we at war, the Jews or the Lizards?"

"We're sure as hell at war with the Lizards," Skorzeny answered, "and we've always been at war with the Jews, now haven't we? You know that. You've pissed and moaned about it enough. So we'll blow up a bunch of kikes *and* a bunch of Lizards, and the *Führer* will be so happy he'll dance a little jig, the way he did when the frog-eaters gave up in 1940. So—five days maximum. You'll be ready to roll by then?"

"If I have my panzers back from the workshops, yes," Jäger said. "Like I said, though, somebody will have to lean on the mechanics."

"*I'll* take care of that," the SS man promised with a large, evil grin. "You think they won't hustle with me holding their toes to the fire?" Jäger wouldn't have bet against his meaning that literally. "Other thing is, I'll make it real plain that if they don't make me happy, they'll tell Himmler why. Would you rather deal with me or with the little schoolmaster in his spectacles?"

"Good question," Jäger said. Taken as a man, Skorzeny was a lot more frightening than Himmler. But Skorzeny was just Skorzeny. Himmler personified the organization he led, and that organization invested him with a frightfulness of a different sort.

"The answer is, if you had your choice, you wouldn't want to get either one of us mad at you, let alone both, right?" Skorzeny said, and Jäger had to nod. The SS *Standartenführer* went on, "As soon as the bomb goes off, you roll east. Who knows? The Lizards are liable to be so surprised, you may end up visiting your Russian girlfriend instead of the other way round. How'd you like that?" He rocked his hips forward and back, deliberately obscene.

"I've heard ideas I liked less," Jäger answered, his voice dry.

Skorzeny boomed laughter. "Oh, I bet you have. I just bet you have." Out of the blue, he found a brand-new question: "She a Jew, that Russian of yours?"

He asked very casually, as a sergeant of police might have asked a burglary suspect where he was at eleven o'clock one night. "Ludmila?" Jäger said, relieved he was able to come back with the truth: "No."

"Good," the SS man said. "I didn't think so, but I wanted to make sure. She won't be mad at you when Lodz goes up, then, right?"

"No reason she should be," Jäger said.

"That's fine," Skorzeny said. "Yes, that's fine. You be good, then. Five days, remember. You'll have your panzers, too, or somebody will be sorry he was ever born." He headed back toward camp, whistling as he went.

Jäger followed more slowly, doing his best not to show how thoughtful he was. The SS had taken that Polish farmer apart, knowing he was involved in passing news on to the Jews in Lodz. And now Skorzeny was asking whether Ludmila was Jewish. Skorzeny couldn't know anything, not really, or Jäger wouldn't still be at the head of his regiment. But suspicions were raising their heads, like plants pushing up through dead leaves.

Jäger wondered if he could get word into Lodz by way of Mieczyslaw. He decided he didn't dare take the chance, not now. He hoped the Jews already had the news, and that they'd found the bomb. That hope sprang partly from shame at what the *Reich* had already done to them and partly from fear of what the Lizards would do to Germany if an atomic bomb went off in territory they held while truce talks were going on. To say he didn't think they'd be pleased was putting it mildly.

From the moment Jäger first met Mordechai Anielewicz, he'd seen the Jews had themselves a fine leader in him. If he knew Skorzeny had secreted the bomb in Lodz, he'd have moved heaven and earth to come up with it. Jäger had done his damnedest to make sure the Jew knew.

Five days from now, Skorzeny would press his button or

whatever it was he did. Maybe a new sun would seem to rise, as it had outside Breslau. And maybe nothing at all would happen.

What would Skorzeny do then?

Walking around out in the open with Lizards in plain sight felt unnatural. Mutt Daniels found himself automatically looking around for the nearest shell hole or pile of rubble so he'd have somewhere to take cover when firing broke out again.

But firing didn't break out. One of the Lizards raised a scaly hand and waved at him. He waved back. He'd never been in a cease-fire quite like this one. Back in 1918, the shooting had stopped because the *Boches* threw in the sponge. Neither side had given up here. He knew fighting could pick up again any old time. But it hadn't yet, and maybe it wouldn't. He hoped it wouldn't. By now, he'd had enough fighting to last any three men a couple of lifetimes each.

A couple of his men were taking a bath in a little creek not far away. Their bodies weren't quite so white and pale as they had been when the cease-fire started. Nobody'd had a chance to get clean for a long time before that. When you were in the front lines, you stayed dirty, mostly because you were liable to get shot if you exposed your body to water and air. After a while, you didn't notice what you smelled like: everybody else smelled the same way. Now Mutt was starting to get used to not stinking again.

From out of the north, back toward Quincy, came the sound of a human-made internal-combustion engine. Mutt turned around and looked up the road. Sure as hell, here came one of those big Dodge command cars officers had been in the habit of using till gas got too scarce for them to go gallivanting around. Seeing one again was a sure sign the brass thought the cease-fire would last a while.

Sure as hell, a three-star banner fluttered from the aerial of the command car. The fellow who stood in back of the pintle-mounted .50 caliber machine gun had three stars painted on his helmet, too. He also had a bone-handled revolver on each hip.

"Heads up, boys," Mutt called. "That there's General Patton coming to pay us a call." Patton had a name for being a tough so-and-so, and for liking to show off, to let everybody know how tough he was. Daniels hoped he wouldn't prove it by squeezing off a couple of belts of ammo in the Lizards' direction.

The command car rolled to a halt. Even before the tires had stopped turning, Patton jumped out and came up to Mutt, who happened to be standing closer to the Lizards than anybody else.

Mutt drew himself to attention and saluted, thinking the Lizards would be crazy if they didn't have somebody with a bead drawn on this aggressive-looking newcomer. Trouble was, if they started shooting at Patton, they'd be shooting at him, too.

"At ease, Lieutenant," Patton said in a gravelly voice. He pointed across the lines toward a couple of Lizards who were busy doing whatever Lizards did. "So there is the enemy, face-to-face. Ugly devils, aren't they?"

"Yes, sir," Mutt said. "Of course, they say that about us, too, sir—call us Big Uglies, I mean."

"Yes, I know. Beauty is in the eye of the beholder, or so they say. In *my* eye, Lieutenant, those are ugly sons of bitches, and if they think me ugly, well, by God, I take it for a compliment."

"Yes, sir," Daniels said again. Patton didn't seem inclined to start shooting up the landscape, for which he was duly grateful.

"Are they adhering to the terms of the cease-fire in this area?" the general demanded—maybe he *would* start the war up again if the answer turned out to be no.

But Mutt nodded. "Sure are, sir. One thing you got to give the Lizards: they make an agreement, they stick by it. More'n the Germans and the Japs and maybe the Russians ever learned."

"You sound like a man who speaks from experience, Lieutenant . . . ?"

"Daniels, sir." Mutt almost laughed. He was Patton's age, more or less. If you didn't have experience by the time you were pushing sixty, when the devil would you? But that probably wasn't what the general meant. "I went through the mill around Chicago, sir. Every time we dickered a truce with the Lizards for picking up wounded and such, they stuck right with it. They may be bastards, but they're honorable bastards."

"Chicago." Patton made a sour face. "That wasn't war, Lieutenant, that was butchery, and it cost them dear, even before we used our atomic weapon against them. Their greatest advantage over us was speed and mobility, and what did they do with it? Why, they threw it away, Lieutenant, and got bogged down in endless street fighting, where a man with a tommy gun is as good as a Lizard with an automatic rifle, and a man with a Molotov cocktail can put paid to a tank that would smash a dozen Shermans in the open without breaking a sweat. The Nazis fought the same way in Russia. They were fools, too."

"Yes, sir." Daniels felt like one of the kids he'd managed listening to him going on about the best time to put on the hit-and-run. Patton knew war the way he knew baseball.

The general was warming to his theme, too: "And the Lizards don't learn from their mistakes. If they hadn't come, and if the Germans had broken through to the Volga, do you suppose they would have been stupid enough to try and take Stalingrad house by house? Do you, Lieutenant?"

"Have to doubt it, sir," said Mutt, who'd never heard of Stalingrad in his life.

"Of course they wouldn't! The Germans are sensible soldiers; they learn from their mistakes. But after we drove the Lizards back from Chicago winter before last, what did they do? They slogged straight on ahead again, right back into the meat grinder. And they paid. That's why, if these talks go the way they look to be going, they're going to have to evacuate the whole U.S.A."

"That'd be wonderful, sir, if it happens," Mutt said.

"No, it wouldn't," Patton said. "Wonderful would be killing every one of them or driving them off our world here altogether." One thing you had to give him, Mutt realized: he didn't think small. He went on, "Since we can't do that, worse luck, we're going to have to learn to live with them henceforward." He pointed across to the Lizards. "Has fraternization after the cease-fire been peaceful in this area, Lieutenant?"

"Yes, sir," Daniels said. "Sometimes they come over and—I guess you'd call it talk shop, sir. And sometimes they want ginger. I reckon you know about that."

"Oh, yes," Patton said with a chuckle. "I know about that. It was good to find out we weren't the only ones with vices. For a while there, I did wonder. And when they get their ginger, what do they use to pay for it?"

"Uh," Mutt said. You couldn't tell a lieutenant general *uh*, though, so he continued, "This and that, sir. Souvenirs, sometimes: stuff that doesn't mean anything to them, like us trading beads to the Indians. Medical-kit supplies sometimes, too. They got self-stick bandages that beat our kind all hollow."

Patton's pale eyes glittered. "They ever trade—liquor for their ginger, Lieutenant? Has that ever happened?"

"Yes, sir, that's happened," Mutt allowed cautiously, wondering if the sky would fall on him in the next moment.

Patton's nod was slow. His eyes still held Daniels. "Good. If you'd told me anything different, I'd know you were a liar. The Lizards don't like whiskey—I told you they were fools. They'll drink rum. They'll even drink gin. But scotch, bourbon, rye? They won't touch 'em. So if they can forage up something they don't want and trade it for something they do, they think they're getting the good half of the deal."

"We haven't had any trouble with drunk and rowdy, sir," Mutt said, which was close enough to true to let him come out with it straight-faced. "I ain't tried to stop 'em from takin' a nip when they come off duty, not since the cease-fire, but they got to be ready to fight all the time."

"You look like a man who's seen a thing or two," Patton said. "I won't complain about the way you're handling your men so long as they're combat-ready, as you say. The Army isn't in the business of producing Boy Scouts, is it, Lieutenant Daniels?"

"No, sir," Mutt said quickly.

"That's right," Patton growled. "It's not. Which is not to say—which is not to say for a moment—that neatness and cleanliness aren't of importance for the sake of discipline and morale. I'm glad to see your uniform so tidy and in such good repair, Lieutenant, and even gladder to see those men over there bathing." He pointed to the soldiers in the creek. "Too often, men at the front lines think Army regulations no longer apply to them. They are mistaken, and sometimes need reminding of it."

"Yes, sir," Daniels said, knowing how filthy he and his uniform had been till he finally took the time to spruce up a couple of days earlier. He was glad Herman Muldoon wasn't anywhere around—one look at Muldoon and Patton (whose chin was neatly shaved, whose uniform was not only clean but showed creases, and whose spit-shined shoes gave off dazzling reflections) would have flung him in the brig.

"From the look of things, Lieutenant, you have a first-rate outfit here. Keep 'em alert. If our talks with the Lizards go as the civilian authorities hope, we'll be moving forward to reclaim the occupied areas of the United States. And if they don't, we'll grab the Lizards by the snouts and kick 'em in the tail."

"Yes, sir," Mutt said again. Patton sent a final steely-eyed glare over toward the Lizards, then jumped back into the command car. The driver started the motor. Acrid exhaust belched from the pipe. The big, clunky Dodge rolled away.

Mutt let out a sigh of relief. He'd survived a lot of contact with the Lizards, and now he'd survived contact with his own top brass, too. As any front-line soldier would attest, your own generals could be at least as dangerous to you as the enemy.

Liu Han listened with more than a little annoyance to the men of the central committee discussing how they would bring over to the side of the People's Liberation Army the large number of peasants who flooded into Peking to work for the little scaly devils in the factories they kept open.

The annoyance must have been visible; Hsia Shou-Tao stopped in the middle of his presentation on a new propaganda leaflet to remark, "I am sorry we seem to be boring you."

He didn't sound sorry, except perhaps sorry she was there at all. He hadn't displayed that kind of scornful arrogance since before he'd tried to rape her. Maybe the lesson he'd got then, like most lessons, wore off if it wasn't repeated till it stuck.

"Everything I have heard is very interesting to me," Liu Han replied, "but do you think it really would catch the interest of a peasant with nothing more in his mind than filling his belly and the bellies of his children?"

"This leaflet has been prepared by propaganda specialists," Hsia said in condescending tones. "How do you presume to claim you know more than they?"

"Because I was a peasant, not a propaganda specialist," Liu Han retorted angrily. "If someone came up to me and started preaching like a Christian missionary about the dictatorship of the proletariat and the necessity of seizing the means of production, I wouldn't have known what he was talking about, and I wouldn't have wanted to learn, either. I think your propaganda specialists are members of the bourgeoisie and aristocracy, out of touch with the true aspirations of the workers and especially of the peasants."

Hsia Shou-Tao stared at her. He had never taken her seriously, or he would not have tried to force himself upon her. He hadn't noticed how well she'd picked up the jargon of the Communist Party; she relished turning that complex, artificial set of terms against those who had devised it.

From across the table, Nieh Ho-T'ing asked her, "And how would you seek to make his propaganda more effective?" Liu Han weighed with great care the way her lover—who was also her instructor in Communist Party lore—spoke. Nieh was Hsia's longtime comrade. Was he being sarcastic to her, supporting his friend?

She decided he wasn't, that the question was sincerely meant. She answered it on that assumption: "Don't instruct new-come peasants in ideology. Most of them will not comprehend enough of what you are saying. Tell them instead that working for the little devils will hurt people. Tell them the things they help the scaly devils make will be used against their relatives who are still back in the villages. Tell them that if they do work for the scaly devils, they and their relatives will be liable to reprisals. These are things they can understand. And when we firebomb a factory or murder workers coming out of one, they will see we speak the truth."

"They will not, however, be indoctrinated," Hsia pointed out, so vehemently that Liu Han got the idea he'd written most of the leaflet she was criticizing.

She looked across the table at him. "Yes? And so what? Most important is keeping the peasants from working for the little devils. If it is easier to keep them from doing that without indoctrinating them, then we shouldn't bother trying. We do not have the resources to waste, do we?"

Hsia stared at her, half in anger, half in amazement. Liu Han might have been an ignorant peasant a year before, but she wasn't any more. Could others be quickly brought up to her level of political consciousness, though? She doubted that. She had seen the revolutionary movement from the inside, an opportunity most would never enjoy.

Nieh said, "We can waste nothing. We are settling in for a long struggle, one that may last generations. The little scaly devils wish to reduce us all to the level of ignorant peasants. This we cannot permit, so we must make the peasantry ideologically aware at some point in our program. Whether that point is the one under discussion, I admit, is a different question."

Hsia Shou-Tao looked as if he'd been stabbed. If even his old friend did not fully support him— "We shall revise as necessary," he mumbled.

"Good," Liu Han said. "Very good, in fact. Thank you." Once you'd won, you could afford to be gracious. But not too gracious: "When you have made the changes, please let me see them before they go to the printer."

"But—" Hsia looked ready to explode. But when he glanced around the table, he saw the other central committee members nodding. As far as they were concerned, Liu Han had proved her ability. Hsia snarled, "If I give you the text, will you be able to read it?"

"I will read it," she said equably. "I had better be able to read it, wouldn't you say? The workers and peasants for whom it is intended will not be scholars, to know thousands of characters. The message must be strong and simple."

Heads again bobbed up and down along the table. Hsia Shou-Tao bowed his own head in surrender. His gaze remained black as a storm cloud, though. Liu Han regarded him thoughtfully. Trying to rape her had not been enough to get him purged even from the central committee, let alone from the Party. What about obstructionism? If he delayed or evaded giving her the revised wording for the leaflet, as he was likely to do, would that suffice?

Part of her hoped Hsia would fulfill his duty as a revolutionary. The rest burned for a chance at revenge.

Atvar paced back and forth in the chamber adapted—not quite well enough—to the needs of the Race. His tailstump quivered reflexively. Millions of years before, when the presapient ancestors of the Race had been long-tailed carnivores prowling across the plains of Home, that quiver had distracted prey from the other end, the end with the teeth. Would that the Big Uglies could have been so easily distracted!

"I wish we could change our past," he said.

"Exalted Fleetlord?" The tone of Kirel's interrogative cough said the shiplord of the conquest fleet's bannership did not follow his train of thought.

He explained: "Had we fought among ourselves more before the unified Empire formed, our weapons technology would have improved. When it came time to duplicate those antique weapons for conquests of other worlds, we would have had better arms. What was in our data banks served us well against the Rabotevs and Hallessi, and so we assumed it always would. Tosev 3 has been the crematorium of a great many of our assumptions."

"Truth—undeniable truth," Kirel said. "But if our own internecine wars had continued longer and with better weapons, we might have exterminated ourselves rather than successfully unifying under the Emperors." He cast his eyes down to the soft, intricately patterned woven floor covering.

So did Atvar, who let out a long, mournful hissing sigh. "Only the madness of this world could make me explore might-have-beens." He paced some more, the tip of his tailstump jerking back and forth. At last, he burst out, "Shiplord, are we doing the right thing in negotiating with the Big Uglies and for all practical purposes agreeing to withdraw from several of their not-empires? It violates all precedent, but then, the existence of opponents able to manufacture their own atomic weapons also violates all precedent."

"Exalted Fleetlord, I believe this to be the proper course, painful though it is," Kirel said. "If we cannot conquer the entire surface of Tosev 3 without damaging great parts of it and having the Big Uglies damage still more, best we hold some areas and await the arrival of the colonization fleet. We gain the chance to reestablish ourselves securely and to prepare for the safe arrival of the colonists and the resources they bring."

"So I tell myself, over and over," Atvar said. "I still have trouble being convinced. Seeing how the Tosevites have improved their own technology in the short time since we arrived here, I wonder how advanced they will be when the colonization fleet finally reaches this world."

"Computer projections indicate we will retain a substantial lead," Kirel said soothingly. "And the only other path open to us, it would appear, is the one Straha the traitor advocated: using our nuclear weapons in prodigal fashion to smash the Big Uglies into submission— which also, unfortunately, involves smashing the planetary surface."

"I no longer trust the computer projections," Atvar said. "They have proved wrong too often; we do not know the Big Uglies well enough to model and extrapolate their behavior with any great hope of accuracy. The rest, however, is as you say, with the ironic proviso that the Tosevites care much less about the destruction of major portions of their world than we do. That has let them wage unlimited warfare against us, while we of necessity held back."

" 'Has let them'?" Kirel said. " 'Held back'? Am I to infer, Exalted Fleetlord, you purpose a change in policy?"

"Not an active one, only reactive," Atvar answered. "If the Deutsche, for example, carry out the threats their Leader has made through this von Ribbentrop creature and resume nuclear warfare against us, I shall do as I warned and thoroughly devastate Deutsch-held territory. That will teach whatever may be left of the Deutsche that we are not to be trifled with, and should have a salutary effect on the behavior of other Tosevite not-empires."

"So it should, Exalted Fleetlord," Kirel agreed. He was too tactful to remark on how closely the plan resembled the one Straha had advocated, for which the fleetlord silently thanked him. Instead, he continued, "I cannot imagine the Deutsch Tosevites taking such a risk in the face of our clear and unmistakable warnings, however."

"As a matter of fact, neither can I," Atvar said. "But, with the Big Uglies, the only certain thing is uncertainty."

Heinrich Jäger looked around with something approaching wonder. He could not see all the panzers and other armored fighting vehicles in his regiment, of course; they were concealed along the front on which they were to attack. But he'd never expected to come so close to establishment strength, never expected to be so fully loaded with both petrol and ammunition.

He leaned out of the cupola of his Panther and nodded to Otto Skorzeny. "I wish we weren't doing this, but if we do it, we'll do it well."

"Spoken like a soldier," said an SS man standing near Skorzeny. The boys in the black shirts had drifted back up to the front line over the past few days. If Lizard intelligence was up to keeping track of their movements, Jäger would be feeding his regiment into a sausage machine. He didn't think the Lizards were that smart, and hoped he was right. The SS man went on, "It is every officer's duty, just as it is that of every soldier, to obey the commands of his superiors and of the *Führer* without question, regardless of his personal feelings."

Jäger stared down at the jackbooted ignoramus in silent scorn. Take his words to the logical extreme and you'd turn the *Wehrmacht* into a bunch of automata as inflexible as the Russians or the Lizards. If you got orders that made no sense, you questioned them. If they still didn't make sense, or if they led you into an obvious catastrophe, you ignored them.

You needed guts to do it. You put your career on the line when you disobeyed orders. But if you could convince your superiors you'd been right, or that the orders you'd got showed no real understanding of the situation in front of you, you'd survive. You might even get promoted.

Jäger, now, hadn't just disobeyed orders. If you wanted to look at things in a particular light, he'd given aid and comfort to the enemy. Any SS man who found out about what he'd done would look at it in that particular light.

For his part, he studied the weedy little fellow standing there beside Skorzeny. Had he dropped his pants and enjoyed himself with Karol's wife, or maybe with his young daughter, while a couple of others held her down? Was he the one who'd carved SS runes into the Polish farmer's belly? And what, in his agony, had Karol said? Was this smiling chap just waiting for the bomb to go off before he arrested Jäger and started carving runes into him?

Skorzeny glanced down at his wristwatch. "Soon now," he said. "When it goes up, we move, and the signal goes out to our armies on the other fronts, too. The Lizards will be sorry they didn't give in to our demands."

"Yes, and what happens afterwards?" Jäger asked as he had before, still hoping he could talk Skorzeny out of pushing the fateful button. "We can be sure the Lizards will destroy at least one city of the German *Reich*. They've done that every time anyone used an explosive-metal bomb against them in war. But this isn't just war—it's breaking a cease-fire. Aren't they liable to do something worse?"

"I don't know," Skorzeny said cheerfully. "And you know what else? I don't give a fuck, either. We've been over this ground already. The job the *Führer*'s given me is kicking the Lizards and the Jews in the balls, just as hard as I can. That's what I'm going to do, too. Whatever happens afterwards, it damn well happens, that's all, and I'll worry about it then."

"That is the National Socialist way of thought," the other SS man declared, beaming at Skorzeny.

Skorzeny wasn't looking back on him. The *Standartenführer*'s eyes were on Jäger instead, up there in the cupola (the engineers and mechanics had been right—it was a vastly improved cupola) of the Panther. Without giving his black-shirted colleague a hint of what he was thinking, he made his opinion plain to the panzer colonel. If it wasn't, *What a load of pious crap,* Jäger would have eaten his service cap.

And yet, even if Skorzeny didn't give a damn about the slogans under which he fought, they remained valid for him. Hitler flew him like a falcon at chosen foes. And, like a falcon, he didn't worry about where he was flying or for what reasons, only about how to strike the hardest blow when he got there.

That wasn't enough.

Jäger had fought the same way himself, till he'd had his eyes forcibly opened to what Germany had done to the Jews in the lands it had overrun, and to what it would have done had the arrival of the Lizards not interrupted things. Once your eyes were opened, shutting them again wasn't easy. Jäger had tried, and failed.

He'd also—cautiously—tried to open the eyes of some other officers, Skorzeny among them. Without exception, everybody else had stayed willfully blind, not wanting to see, not wanting to discuss. He understood that. He even sympathized with it. If you refused to notice the flaws of your superiors and your country, you could go on about your daily routine a lot more easily.

As long as he was fighting just the Lizards, Jäger had no trouble suppressing his own doubts, his own worries. Nobody could doubt for even a moment that the Lizards were deadly foes not only to Germany but to all mankind. You did what you had to do to stop them. But the explosive-metal bomb in Lodz didn't have only the Lizards in mind. It didn't even have the Lizards primarily in mind.

Skorzeny knew as much. He'd set it there after the nerve-gas bomb he'd intended for the Jews of Lodz failed. It was his—and Germany's—revenge on the Jews for thwarting him once.

Try as Jäger would, he couldn't stomach that.

Skorzeny walked away, whistling. When he came back, he was wearing a pack like the one a wireless operator carried. In fact, it undoubtedly was a wireless operator's pack. The handset that went with it, though, was anything but standard issue. It had only two elements: a bar switch and a large red button.

"I make the time 1100 hours," Skorzeny said after yet another glance at his watch.

The other SS man brought his right wrist up toward his face. "I confirm the time as 1100 hours," he said formally.

Skorzeny giggled. "Isn't this fun?" he said. The other SS man stared at him: that wasn't in the script. Jäger just snorted. He'd seen too many times that Skorzeny was indifferent to the script. The big SS man flipped the bar switch 180 degrees. "The transmitter is now active," he said.

"I confirm that the transmitter has been activated," the other SS man droned.

And then Skorzeny broke the rules again. He reached up and gave Jäger the handset, asking, "Do you want to do the honors?"

"Me?" Jäger almost dropped it. "Are you out of your mind? Good God, no." He handed the device back to Skorzeny. Only after he'd done so did he realize he *should* have dropped it, or else contrived to smash it against the side of the panzer.

"All right, don't let it worry you," Skorzeny said. "I can kill my own dog. I can kill a whole great lot of sons of bitches." His thumb came down hard on the red button.

☆ **XVIII** ☆

Even had the weather been cool, Vyacheslav Molotov would have been steaming as he stood around in the lobby of the Semiramis Hotel waiting for a Lizard armored personnel carrier to convey him to Shepheard's.

"Idiocy," the Soviet foreign commissar muttered to Yakov Donskoi. Where von Ribbentrop was concerned, he did not bother holding his scorn in check. "Idiocy, syphilitic paresis, or both. Probably both."

Von Ribbentrop, waiting for his own armored personnel carrier, might well have been in earshot, but he didn't speak Russian. Had he spoken Russian, Molotov would have changed not a word. The interpreter glanced over to the German foreign minister, then, almost whispering himself, replied, "It is most irregular, Comrade Foreign Commissar, but—"

Molotov waved him to silence. "But me no buts, Yakov Beniaminovich. Since we came here, the Lizards have convened all our sessions, as is only proper. For that arrogant Nazi to demand a noon meeting—" He shook his head. "I thought it was mad dogs and Englishmen who went out in the noonday sun, not a mad dog of a German."

Before Donskoi could say anything to that, several personnel carriers pulled up in front of the hotel. The Lizards didn't seem happy about ferrying all the human diplomats to Shepheard's at the same time, but von Ribbentrop hadn't given them enough notice of this meeting upon which he insisted for them to do anything else.

When the negotiators reached Atvar's headquarters, Lizard guards made sure Molotov did not speak to Marshall or Eden or Togo before entering the meeting room. They also made sure he

465

did not speak to von Ribbentrop. That was wasted labor; he had nothing to say to the German foreign minister.

Precisely at noon, the Lizard fleetlord came into the meeting room, accompanied by his interpreter. Through that male, Atvar said, "Very well, speaker for the not-empire of Deutschland, I have agreed to your request for this special session at this special time. You will now explain why you made such a request. I listen with great attentiveness."

It had better be good, was what he meant. Even through two interpreters, Molotov had no trouble figuring that out. Von Ribbentrop heard it through only one, so it should have been twice as clear to him.

If it was, he gave no sign. "Thank you, Fleetlord," he said as he got to his feet. From the inside pocket of his jacket, he pulled out a folded sheet of paper and, as portentously as he could, unfolded it. "Fleetlord, I read to you a statement from Adolf Hitler, *Führer* of the German *Reich*."

When he spoke Hitler's name, his voice took on a reverence more pious than the Pope (back before the Pope had been blown to radioactive dust) would have used in mentioning Jesus. But then, why not? Von Ribbentrop thought Hitler was infallible; when he'd made the German-Soviet nonaggression pact the fascists had so brutally violated, he'd declared to the whole world, "The *Führer* is always right." In such opinions, unlike diplomacy, he lacked the duplicity needed to lie well.

Now, in pompous tones, he went on, "The *Führer* declares that, as the Race has intolerably occupied territory rightfully German and refuses to leave such territory regardless of the illegitimacy of that occupation, the *Reich* is fully justified in taking the strongest measure against the Race, and has now initiated those measures. We—"

Molotov knew a sinking sensation at the pit of his stomach. So the Nazi had had a reason for summoning everyone. The fascist regime had launched another sneak attack and was now, in a pattern long familiar, offering some trumped-up rationale for whatever its latest unprovoked act of aggression had been.

Sure enough, von Ribbentrop continued, "—have emphasized our legitimate demands by the detonation of this latest explosive-metal bomb, and by the military action following it. God will give the German *Reich* the victory it deserves." The German foreign minister refolded the paper, put it away, and shot out his right arm in the Nazi salute. "*Heil* Hitler!"

Anthony Eden, Shigenori Togo, and George Marshall all looked as shaken as Molotov felt. So much for the popular front: Hitler had consulted with no one before resuming the war. He and, all too likely, everyone else would have to pay the price.

Uotat finished hissing and popping and squeaking for Atvar. Molotov waited for the Lizard fleetlord to explode, and to threaten to rain down hideous destruction on Germany for what it had just done. The foreign commissar would have faced that prospect with considerable equanimity.

Instead, Atvar directed only a few words to the interpreter, who said, "The exalted fleetlord tells me to tell you he is looking into this statement." As Uotat spoke, the fleetlord left the room.

He came back a few minutes later, and spoke several sentences to the translator. One by one, Uotat turned them into English. As he did so, Donskoi translated them into Russian for Molotov: "The exalted fleetlord wonders why the negotiator for the not-empire of Deutschland has had us come here to listen to a statement bearing no resemblance to any sort of reality. No atomic explosion has occurred in or near Deutschland. No atomic explosion, in fact, has occurred anywhere on Tosev 3. No unusual military activity of any sort by Deutsch forces is noted. The exalted fleetlord asks whether your brain is addled, spokesmale von Ribbentrop, or that of your *Führer*."

Von Ribbentrop stared at Atvar. Along with the other human negotiators, Molotov stared at von Ribbentrop. Something had gone spectacularly wrong somewhere: that much was obvious. But what? And where?

Otto Skorzeny pressed down on the red button till his thumbnail turned white with the pressure. Heinrich Jäger waited for the southern horizon to light up with a brief new sun, and for the artillery barrage that would follow. Over the intercom, he spoke quietly to Johannes Drucker. "Be ready to start the engine."

"Jawohl, Herr Oberst," the panzer driver answered.

But the new sun did not rise. The mild Polish summer day continued undisturbed. Skorzeny jammed his thumb down on the button again. Nothing happened. "Christ on His cross," the SS man muttered. Then, when that proved too weak to satisfy him, he ground out, "Goddamned motherfucking son of a shit-eating bitch." He tried the transmitter one more time before throwing it to the ground in disgust. He turned to the blackshirt beside him. "Get me the backup unit. *Schnell!*"

"Jawohl, Herr Standartenführer!" The other SS officer dashed

away, to return in short order with a pack and transmitter identical to the ones that had failed.

Skorzeny flipped the activating switch and pressed the red button on the new transmitter. Again the bomb in Lodz failed to explode. "Shit," Skorzeny said wearily, as if even creative obscenity were more trouble than it was worth. He started to smash the second transmitter, but checked himself. Shaking his head, he said, "Something's fucked up somewhere. Go and broadcast EGGPLANT on the general-distribution frequencies."

"EGGPLANT?" The other SS man looked like a dog watching a juicy bone being taken away. "Must we?"

"Bet your arse we must, Maxi," Skorzeny answered. "If the bomb doesn't go off, we don't move. The bomb hasn't gone off. Now we have to send out the signal to let the troops know the attack's on hold. We'll send KNIFE as soon as it goes up. Now move, damn you! If some overeager idiot opens up because he didn't get the *halt* signal, Himmler'll wear your guts for garters."

Jäger had never imagined an SS officer named Maxi. He'd never imagined anybody, no matter what his name was, could move so fast. "What now?" he asked Skorzeny.

He'd seldom seen the big, bluff Austrian indecisive, but that was the only word that fit. "Damned if I know," Skorzeny answered. "Maybe some sexton or whatever the kikes call them spotted the aerial hooked up to the grave marker and tore it loose. If that's all it is, a simple reconnection would get things going again without much trouble. If it's anything more than that, if the Jews have their hands on the bomb . . ." He shook his head. "That could be downright ugly. For some reason or other, they don't exactly love us." Even his laugh, usually a great fierce chortle, rang hollow now.

For some reason or other. That was as close as Skorzeny would come to acknowledging what the *Reich* had done to the Jews. It was closer than a lot of German officers came, but it was not close enough, not as far as Jäger was concerned. He said, "What are you going to do about it?"

Skorzeny looked at him as if he were the idiot. "What do you think I'm going to do? I'm going to shag ass down to Lodz and make that fucker work, one way or the other. Like I say, I hope the problem's just with the aerial. But if it's not, if the Jews really did get wind of this some kind of way, I'll manage just fine, thank you very much."

"You can't be thinking of going by yourself," Jäger exclaimed. "If the Jews do have it"—he didn't know himself, not for sure—

"they'll turn you into a *blutwurst* quick as boiled asparagus." The classics sometimes came in handy in the oddest ways.

Skorzeny shook his head again. "You're wrong, Jäger. It'll be a—what do the RAF bastards call it?—a piece of cake, that's what. There's a cease-fire on, remember? Even if the kikes have stolen the bomb, they won't be guarding it real hard. Why should they? They won't know we know they've got it, because they can't figure we'd try and set it off in the middle of a truce." His leer had most of its old force back. "Of course not. We're good little boys and girls, right? Except for one thing: I'm not a good little boy.

"Mm, I'd noticed that," Jäger said dryly. Now Skorzeny's laugh was full of his wicked vinegar—he recovered fast. He was also damned good at thinking on his feet; every word he said sounded reasonable. "When are you leaving?"

"Soon as I change clothes, get some rations, and take care of a couple of things here," the SS man answered. "If the bomb goes up, it'll give those scaly sons of bitches a kick in the teeth they'll remember for a long time." In absurdly coquettish fashion, he fluttered his fingers at Jäger and tramped away.

From the cupola of the Panther, Jäger stared after him. With his unit on full battle alert, how the devil was he supposed to get away and get word to Mieczyslaw so he could pass it on to Anielewicz by whatever roundabout route he used? The answer was simple, and stared Jäger in the face: he couldn't. But if he didn't, he worried not just about thousands of Jews going up in a toadstool-shaped cloud of dust, but also about Germany. What *would* the Lizards visit on the *Vaterland* for touching off an atomic bomb during a truce? Jäger didn't know. He didn't want to find out, either.

From down in the turret of the Panther, Gunther Grillparzer said, "No show today after all, Colonel?"

"Doesn't look that way," Jäger answered, and then took a chance by adding, "Can't say I'm sorry, either."

To his surprise, Grillparzer said, "Amen!" The gunner seemed to think some kind of explanation was needed there, for he went on, "I hold no brief for kikes, mind you, sir, but it ain't like they're our number-one worry right now, you know what I mean? It's the Lizards I really want to boot in the arse, not them. They're all going to hell anyway, so I don't hardly have to worry about 'em."

"Corporal, as far as I'm concerned, they can sew red stripes on your trousers and put you on the General Staff," Jäger told him. "I think you've got better strategic sense than most of our top planners, and that's a fact."

"If I do, then God help Germany," Grillparzer said, and laughed.

"God help Germany," Jäger agreed, and didn't.

The rest of the day passed in lethargic anticlimax. Jäger and his crew climbed out of their Panther with nothing but relief: you rolled the dice every time you went up against the Lizards, and sooner or later snake eyes stared back at you. Sometime during the afternoon, Otto Skorzeny disappeared. Jäger pictured him slouching toward Lodz, a pack on his back, and very likely makeup over the famous scar. Could he hide that devilish gleam in his eye with makeup, too? Jäger had his doubts.

Johannes Drucker disappeared for a while, too, but he came back in triumph, with enough kielbasa for everybody's supper that night. "Give that man a Knight's Cross!" Gunther Grillparzer exclaimed. Turning to Jäger, he said with a grin, "If you're going to put me on the General Staff, sir, I might as well enjoy myself, *nicht wahr?*"

"Warum denn nicht?" Jäger said. "Why not?"

As twilight deepened, they got a fire going and stuck a pot over it to boil the sausage. The savory steam rising from the pot made Jäger's mouth water. When he heard approaching footsteps, he expected them to come from the crew of another panzer, drawn by the smell and hoping to get their share of meat.

But the men coming up to the cookfire weren't in panzer black, they were in SS black. *So Maxi and his friends aren't above scrounging,* Jäger thought, amused. Then Maxi drew a Walther from his holster and pointed it at Jäger's midsection. The SS men with him also took out their pistols, covering the rest of the startled panzer crewmen.

"You will come with me immediately, Colonel, or I will shoot you down on the spot," Maxi said. "You are under arrest for treason against the *Reich.*"

"Exalted Fleetlord," Moishe Russie said. He was getting used to these sessions with Atvar. He was even coming to look forward to them. The more useful Atvar thought him now, the less likely he and his family were to have to pay for his earlier strokes against the Lizards. And guessing with the diplomats of the great powers was a game that made chess look puerile. He was, apparently, a better guesser than most of the Lizards. That kept the questions coming, and let him find out how the negotiations fared, which had a fascination of its own: he was privy to knowledge only a handful of humans possessed.

Atvar spoke in his own language. Zolraag turned these words into the usual mix of German and Polish: "You are of course familiar with the Tosevite not-emperor Hitler, and hold no good opinion of him—I take it this remains correct?"

"Yes, Exalted Fleetlord." Moishe added an emphatic cough.

"Good," Atvar said. "I judge you more likely, then, to give me an honest opinion of his actions than you would those of, say, Churchill: solidarity with your fellow Big Uglies will be less of an issue in Hitler's case. Is this also correct?"

"Yes, Exalted Fleetlord," Moishe repeated. Thinking of Hitler as his fellow human being did not fill him with delight. Whatever you had to say against them, the Lizards had shown themselves to be far better people than Adolf Hitler.

"Very well," Atvar said through Zolraag. "Here is my question: how do you judge the conduct of Hitler and von Ribbentrop when the latter summoned me to announce the detonation of an atomic bomb and the resumption of warfare by Deutschland against the Race, when in fact no such detonation and no such warfare—barring a few more cease-fire violations than usual—in fact took place?"

Moishe stared. "This really happened, Exalted Fleetlord?"

"Truth," Atvar said, a word Russie understood in the Lizards' language.

He scratched his head as he thought. For all he knew, that might have made him uncouth in Atvar's eyes. But then, he was a Big Ugly, so was he not uncouth in Atvar's eyes by assumption? Slowly, he said, "I have trouble believing von Ribbentrop would make such a claim knowing it to be untrue and knowing you could easily learn it was untrue."

"That is perceptive of you," the fleetlord said. "When the spokesmale for Hitler did make the claim, I immediately investigated it and, finding it false, returned to inform him of the fact. The unanimous opinion of our psychologists is that my statement took him by surprise. Here: observe him for yourself."

At Atvar's gesture, Zolraag activated one of the little screens in the chamber. Sure enough, there stood von Ribbentrop, looking somewhere between arrogant and afraid. A Lizard the screen did not show spoke to him in hissing English. The German foreign minister's eyes widened, his mouth dropped open, a hand groped for the edge of the table.

"Exalted Fleetlord, that is a surprised man," Moishe declared.

"So we thought," Atvar agreed. "This raises the following question: is the delivery of false information part of some devious scheme on Hitler's part, or was the information intended to be true? In either case, of course, von Ribbentrop would have believed it accurate as he delivered it."

"Yes." Moishe scratched his head again, trying to figure out what possible benefit Hitler might have derived by deliberately deceiving his foreign minister into threatening the Lizards. For the life of him, he couldn't come up with any. "I have to believe the Germans intended to attack you."

"This is the conclusion we have also drawn, although we warned them they would suffer severely if they made any such attacks," Atvar said. "It is unsettling, distinctly so: somewhere on our frontier with Hitler's forces, or perhaps beyond that frontier, there is probably a nuclear weapon that for whatever reason has failed of ignition. We have searched for such a weapon, but have not discovered it. After El Iskandariya, it is by no means certain we would discover it. Now: will Hitler be willing to accept failure and resume talks, or will he seek to detonate the bomb after all?"

Being asked to peer inside Hitler's brain was rather like being asked to debride gangrenous tissue: revolting but necessary. "If the Germans find any way to detonate the bomb, my guess is that they will," Moishe said. "I have to say, though, that's only a guess."

"It accords with the predictions our researchers have made," Atvar said. "Whether this makes it accurate, only time will show, but I believe you are giving me your best and most reasoned judgment here."

"Truth, Exalted Fleetlord," Moishe said in the language of the Race.

"Good," the Lizard answered. "I am of the opinion that we previously tried to exploit you too broadly, and, as with any misused tool, this caused difficulties we would not have had if we kept you within limits appropriate to your situation. This appears to be the source of a large portion of your enmity toward us and your turning against us."

"It's certainly a source of some of it," Moishe agreed. That was the closest to understanding him the Lizards had ever come, at any rate, and vastly preferable to their equating his actions with treason, as they had been doing.

"If a knife breaks because it is used as a pry bar, is that the fault of the knife?" Atvar resumed. "No, it is the fault of the operator. Because your service, Moishe Russie, has improved when you are properly used, I grow more willing to overlook past transgressions. When these negotiations between the Race and the Tosevites are completed, perhaps we shall establish you in the area where you were recaptured—"

"The exalted fleetlord means Palestine," Zolraag put in on his own. "These names you give places have caused us considerable difficulty, especially where more than one name applies to the same place."

Atvar resumed: "We shall establish you there, as I was saying, with your female and hatchling, and, as necessary, consult with you on Tosevite affairs. We shall do a better job of recognizing your limits henceforward, and not force you to provide information or propaganda you find distasteful. Would you accept such an arrangement?"

They wanted to set him up in Palestine—in the Holy Land— with his family? They'd use him as an expert on humanity without coercing him or humiliating him? Cautiously, he said, "Exalted Fleetlord, my only worry is that it sounds too good to be true."

"It is truth," the fleetlord answered. "Have you not seen, Moishe Russie, that when the Race makes an agreement, it abides by what it agrees?"

"I have seen this," Moishe admitted. "But I've also seen the Race ordering rather than trying to agree."

The fleetlord's sigh sounded surprisingly human. "This has proved far less effective on Tosev 3 than we would have desired. We are, accordingly, trying new methods here, however distasteful innovation is for us. When the males and females of the colonization fleet arrive, they will undoubtedly have a great many sharp things to say about our practices, but we shall be able to offer them a large portion of a viable planet on which to settle. Considering what might have happened here, this strikes me as an acceptable resolution."

"I don't see how I could disagree, Exalted Fleetlord," Moishe said. "Sometimes not everyone can get everything he wants from a situation."

"This has never before happened to the Race," Atvar said with another sigh.

Moishe went from the world-bestriding to the personal in the space of a sentence: "When you settle me and my family in Palestine, there is one other thing I would like."

"And what is this?" the fleetlord asked.

Russie wondered if he was pushing his luck too far, but pressed ahead anyhow: "You know I was studying to become a doctor before the Germans invaded Poland. I'd like to take up those studies again, not just with humans but with males of the Race. If there is peace, we'll have so much to learn from you . . ."

"One of my principal concerns in making a peace with you Big Uglies is how much you will learn from us, and what sorts of things," Atvar said. "You have learned too much already. But in medicine I do not suppose you will become a great danger to us. Very well, Moishe Russie, let it be as you say."

"Thank you, Exalted Fleetlord," Moishe said. Some American in a film had once used an expression that sounded so odd when dubbed literally into Polish, Moishe had never forgotten it: *come up smelling like a rose*. If Atvar stayed by the terms of the agreement, he'd somehow managed to do exactly that. "A rose," he muttered. "Just like a rose."

"Moishe Russie?" Atvar asked, with an interrogative cough: Zolraag hadn't been able to make sense of the words.

"It is a bargain, Exalted Fleetlord," Moishe said, and hoped the rose didn't prove to have too many thorns.

Straha leaned away from the microphone and took off his earphones, which didn't fit well over his hearing diaphragms anyhow. "Another broadcast," he said, turning an eye turret toward Sam Yeager. "I do not see the necessity for many more, not with talks between the Race and you Big Uglies progressing so well. You cannot imagine how you must have horrified stodgy old Atvar, to get him to talk with you at all."

"I'm glad he did, finally," Sam said. "I've had a bellyful of war. This whole world has had a bellyful—two bellyfuls—of war."

"Half measures of any sort do not appear to succeed on Tosev 3," Straha agreed. "Had it been I in the fleetlord's body paint, we would have tried sooner and harder to batter you Tosevites into submission."

"I know that." Yeager nodded. The refugee shiplord had never made any great secret of his preference for the stick over the carrot. Sam remembered the American atomic bomb sitting somewhere here in Hot Springs, surely no more than a few hundred yards from this stuffy little studio. He couldn't tell Straha about the bomb, of course; General Donovan would nail his scalp to the wall if he pulled a boner like that. What he did say was, "With three not-empires making atomic bombs, you'd have had a hard time stopping all of them."

"Truth there, too, of course." Straha sighed. "When peace comes—if peace comes—what becomes of me?"

"We won't give you back for the Race to take vengeance on you," Sam told him. "We've already said as much to your people in Cairo. They didn't much like it, but they've agreed."

"Of this much I am already aware," Straha answered. "So I shall live out my life among you, the Tosevites of the U.S.A. And how am I to pass my time while I am doing this?"

"Oh." Sam started to see what the refugee was driving at. "Some males of the Race fit in fine with us. Vesstil's taught us an amazing lot about rocket engineering, and Ristin—"

"Has for all practical purposes turned into a Big Ugly," Straha said with acid in his voice.

"When you think about where he is, what's he supposed to do?" Sam asked.

"He is a male of the Race. He should have the dignity to remember that fact," Straha replied.

After a second, Sam figured out what the Lizard reminded him of: a snobby Englishman looking down his nose at a countryman who'd "gone native" in Tanganyika or Burma or somewhere like that. He'd seen enough jungle movies with that as part of the story. Only trouble was, he couldn't say as much to Straha, not without insulting him further. Instead, he said, "Maybe if we get a peace, we'll get a"—he had to fumble around to get across the idea he wanted, but finally did—"an amnesty along with it."

"For the likes of Ristin, there will surely be an amnesty," Straha said. "He shall have it, though he does not require it to enjoy his life. For the likes of Vesstil, there also may be an amnesty. Vesstil has taught you much—this is truth, Sam Yeager, as you say. But he came among you Tosevites at my order. He was my shuttlecraft pilot: when I ordered, his duty was to obey, and obey he did. Despite the aid he has furnished you, he may be forgiven. But for me, Sam Yeager, of amnesty there shall be none. I tried to remove the fleetlord Atvar, to keep him from losing the war to you Tosevites. I failed—and so did he, for is the war won? Do you think he will let me enter any land the Race holds after peace comes—if peace comes? It would but remind him I was right to doubt him, and that the conquest failed. No. If I am to live, it must be among you Big Uglies."

Sam slowly nodded. Traitors didn't get to go home again: that looked to be the same among Lizards as it was with people. If Rudolf Hess flew back to Germany from England, would Hitler welcome him with open arms? Not likely. But Hess, in England, was at least among his fellow human beings. Here in Hot Springs, Straha was as trapped among aliens as a human tool of the Lizards who spent the rest of his days with them—or, more accurately still, spent the rest of his days on Home.

"We'll do everything we can to make you comfortable," Yeager promised.

"So your leaders and you have assured me from the start," Straha replied. "And, so far as is in your power, so you have done. I cannot complain of your intentions. But intentions go only so far, Sam Yeager. If peace comes, I shall remain here, remain an analyst of the Race and propagandist for this not-empire. Is this not the high-probability outcome?"

"Truth," Sam said. "You've always earned your place here. Don't you want to go on doing that?"

"I shall—it is the best I can do. But you fail to understand," Straha said. "I shall stay here, among you Tosevites. Some other males, surely, will also stay. And we shall build our tiny community, for we shall be all of the Race we have. And we shall have to turn our eye turrets toward what the rest of the Race is doing here on Tosev 3, and study it for the leaders of this not-empire, and never, ever be a part of it. How to live with that loneliness? Can it be done? I shall have to learn."

"I apologize," Yeager said. "I did not see all of it." Back before the Germans conquered France, every once in a while you used to read stories in the papers about the doings of Russian emigrés in Paris. If any of them were left alive these days, they would have sympathized with Straha: there they were, on the outside looking in, while the great bulk of their countrymen went about building something new. If that wasn't hell, it had to be a pretty fair training ground.

Straha sighed. "Before long, too, in the scale of things the Race commonly uses, the colonization fleet will reach this world. Egg clutches will be incubated. Will any be mine? It is to laugh." His mouth fell open.

Some of the Russian emigrés had Russian wives, others sweethearts. The ones who didn't could look for willing Frenchwomen. Straha didn't miss lady Lizards the way a man missed women: out of sight (or rather, out of scent) really was out of mind for him. But, again, he'd be watching the Race as a whole move along, and he wouldn't be a part of it.

"Shiplord, that's hard," Sam said.

"Truth," Straha said. "But when I came down to this not-empire, I did not ask that life be easy, only that it continue. Continue it has. Continue it will, in the circumstances I chose for myself. I shall likely have a long time to contemplate whether I made the correct decision."

Sam wanted to find the right thing to say, but for the life of him could not come up with anything.

Mordechai Anielewicz walked casually past the factory that, up until a few months before, had housed workers turning out winter coats for the Lizards. Then one of the Nazis' rocket bombs had scored a direct hit on the place. It looked like any other building that had taken a one-tonne bomb hit: like the devil. The only good thing was that the rocket had come down during the night shift, when fewer people were working.

Anielewicz looked around. Not many people were on the street. He tugged at his trousers, as if adjusting them. Then he ducked behind one of the factory's shattered walls; any man might have done the same to get some privacy in which to ease himself.

From deeper in the ruins, a voice spoke in Yiddish: "Ah, it's you. We don't like people coming in here, you know."

"And why is that, Mendel?" Mordechai asked dryly.

"Because we're sitting on an egg we hope we don't ever have to hatch," the guard answered, his own tone less collected than he probably would have liked.

"As long as it's in our nest and not the one the Germans laid for it," Anielewicz answered. Getting it out of the ghetto field had been an epic in itself, and not one Mordechai ever wanted to repeat. The bomb had not been buried deep, or he and his comrades never would have budged it. As things were, the gaping hole in the ground that marked its presence had remained for the Lizards to spot when morning came. Fortunately, the cover story—that the corpses in that grave were suspected to have died of cholera, and so had to be exhumed and burned— had held up. Like most Lizards, Bunim was squeamish about human diseases.

Mordechai peered out from the gloom inside the ruined factory. None of the people who had been on the street was looking back. Nobody seemed to have taken any notice that he hadn't come out after going in there for privacy's sake. He walked farther into the bowels of the building. The way back twisted and went around piles of brick and tumbledown interior walls, but, once out of sight of the street, was free of rubble.

There, sitting in its oversized crate on a reinforced wagon, rested the bomb the Nazis had buried in the ghetto field. It had taken an eight-horse team to get it here; they'd need another eight horses to get it out, if they ever had to. One of the reasons Mordechai had chosen to hide the bomb here was the livery stable round the corner. Eight of the sturdiest draft horses the Jewish underground could find waited there, ready to be quickly brought over here in case of emergency.

As if by magic, a couple of Schmeisser-toting guards appeared from out of the shadows. They nodded to Anielewicz. He set his hand on the wagon. "When we have the chance, I want to get this damned thing out of Lodz altogether, take it someplace where there aren't so many Lizards around."

"That would be good," said one of the guards, a skinny, walleyed fellow named Chaim. "Put it somewhere without so many people around, too. Everybody who isn't one of us could be one of—them."

He didn't specify who *they* were. Likely he didn't know. Mordechai didn't know, either, but he had the same worries Chaim did. The enemy of your enemy wasn't your friend here— he was just an enemy of a different flavor. Anybody who found out the bomb was here—Lizards, Poles, Nazis, even the Jews who followed Mordechai Chaim Rumkowski (*and wasn't that an odd juxtaposition of names?* Anielewicz thought)—would try to take it away and take advantage of it.

Anielewicz rapped gently on the crate again. "If we have to, we can play Samson in the temple," he said.

Chaim and the other guard both nodded. That other fellow said, "You're sure the Nazis can't set it off by wireless?"

"Positive, Saul," Anielewicz answered. "We made certain of that. But we have the manual detonator not far away." Both guards nodded; they knew where it was. "God forbid we have to use it, that's all."

"Omayn," Chaim and Saul said together.

"See anything unusual around here?" Mordechai asked, as he did every time he came to check on the bomb. As they always did, the guards shook their heads. The job of guarding the crate was turning into routine for them; neither was a man of much imagination. Anielewicz knew he had more than was good for him.

He made his way out toward the street, pausing to ask Mendel the question he'd just put to Saul and Chaim. Mendel affirmed that he hadn't seen anything out of the ordinary, either. Anielewicz told himself he was worrying over nothing: nobody but the Jewish underground (and the Nazis, of course) knew the bomb had come into Lodz, and nobody but his own people knew where it was now. The Nazis wouldn't have tried to set it off, not with their cease-fire with the Lizards still holding.

He'd told himself that a great many times. He still had trouble believing it. After almost five years of war, first against the Germans and then sometimes against the Germans and Lizards both, he had trouble believing any counsel of safety.

As he emerged onto the street, he fumbled at his trousers to show why he had gone back behind the wall, then looked up and down to see if anyone was taking any special notice either of him or of the wrecked factory building. He didn't spot anyone like that, so he started up the street.

There maybe fifteen meters ahead of him, striding along briskly, was a tall, broad-shouldered man with light brown hair. The fellow turned a corner. Anielewicz followed, not thinking much of him except that his black coat was too short: it flapped halfway down his calves instead of at his ankles as it should have. Not many men in Lodz were so big, which no doubt explained why the fellow couldn't find a coat to fit him. He lacked only six or eight centimeters of two meters' height.

No, Anielewicz hadn't seen many men that size in the ghetto. Big, beefy men, because they needed more food, had a way of dying faster on bad rations than small men did. But Anielewicz had seen a man about that tall some time in the not too distant past. He frowned, trying to remember when and where. One of the Polish farmers who sometimes passed information on to the Jews? It had been outside of Lodz: he was fairly sure of that.

All at once, he started to run. When he got to the corner at which the tall man had turned, he paused, his head swiveling this way and that. He didn't see the fellow. He walked over to the next corner, where he peered both ways again. Still no sign of the man. He kicked at a paving stone in frustration.

Could that have been Otto Skorzeny on the streets of the Lodz ghetto, or was he starting at shadows? The SS man had no rational reason to be here, so Anielewicz tried to convince himself he'd spied someone else of about the same size and build.

"It's impossible," he muttered under his breath. "If the Nazis blow up Lodz in the middle of peace talks, God only knows what the Lizards will drop on their heads: reap the wind, sow the whirlwind. Not even Hitler's that *meshuggeh*."

As with his earlier, more general fears, he had trouble dismissing this one. When you got right down to it, who could say just how *meshuggeh* Hitler was?

* * *

David Goldfarb and Basil Roundbush climbed off their bicycles and made their eager way toward the White Horse Inn like castaways struggling up to the edge of a desert oasis. "Pity we can't bring Mzepps with us," Roundbush remarked. "Do the poor blighter good to have a night out, don't you think?"

"Me?" Goldfarb said. "I've given up thinking for the duration."

"Commendable attitude," Roundbush said with a nod. "Keep that firmly in mind, lad, and you'll go far—though thinking about not thinking does rather spoil the exercise, eh?"

Goldfarb had the sense not to get stuck in that infinite regress. He opened the door to the White Horse Inn and was greeted by a cloud of smoke and a roar of noise. Basil Roundbush shut the door after them. As soon as he'd done so, Goldfarb pushed aside the black cloth curtains that screened off the short entryway and went inside.

He blinked at the bright electric lamps. "I liked the place better when it was all torchlight and hearthfire," he said. "Gave it more atmosphere: you felt Shakespeare or Johnson might drop in for a pint with you."

"If Johnson dropped in, it would be for more than one, and that's a fact," Roundbush said. "All the fires did take one back to the eighteenth century, I must say. But remember, old boy, the eighteenth century was a filthy, nasty place. Give me electricity every day."

"They seem to be doing just that," Goldfarb said, making his way toward the bar. "Amazing how quickly you can get a system of electricity up and running again when you're not being bombed round the clock."

"Makes a bit of a difference," Roundbush agreed. "I hear the blackout regulations will be going soon, if this truce holds up." He waved to Naomi Kaplan, who stood behind the bar. She smiled and waved back, then turned up the wattage of that smile when she spotted the shorter Goldfarb behind him. Roundbush chuckled. "You are a lucky fellow. I hope you know it."

"You'd best believe I do," Goldfarb said, so enthusiastically that Roundbush laughed again. "And if I didn't, my family would tell me too often to let me forget." His parents and siblings approved of Naomi. He'd been certain they would. To his great relief, she approved of them, too, though their crowded East End flat was far from the upper-middle-class comforts she'd known growing up in Germany before Hitler made life there impossible.

They found a narrow opening at the bar and squeezed in to widen it. Roundbush slapped silver on the damp, polished wood.

"Two pints of best bitter," he said to Naomi, and then set out more coins: "And one for yourself, if you've a mind to."

"Thank you, no," she said, and pushed those back at the RAF officer. The others she scooped into the cash box under the bar. Goldfarb wished she didn't have to work here, but she was making much better money than he was. The landlord of the White Horse Inn could raise prices to keep up with the inflation galloping through the British economy, and raise wages almost as much. Goldfarb's meager RAF salary ran several bureaucratic lurches behind. He would have thought it a princely sum when he enlisted in 1939; what had been princely now left him a pauper.

He gulped down his pint and bought a round in return. Naomi let him get her a pint, too, which set Basil Roundbush to making indignant noises through his mustache.

They were just lifting the pint pots when someone behind Goldfarb said, "Who's your new chum, old man?"

Goldfarb hadn't heard those Cantabrian tones in a long time. "Jones!" he said. "I haven't seen you in so long, I'd long since figured you'd bought your plot." Then he got a good look at Jerome Jones' companions, and his eyes went even wider. "Mr. Embry! Mr. Bagnall! I didn't know they'd declared this old home week."

Introductions followed. Jerome Jones blinked with surprise when Goldfarb presented Naomi Kaplan as his fiancée. "You lucky dog!" he exclaimed. "You found yourself a beautiful girl, and I'd lay two to one she's neither a sniper nor a Communist."

"Er—no," David said. He coughed. "Would I be wrong in guessing you've not had a dull time of it this past little while?"

"Not half dull," the other radarman said with unwonted sincerity. He shivered. "Not half." Goldfarb recognized that tone of voice: someone trying hard not to think about places he'd been and things he'd done. The more he looked at it, giving up thought for the duration seemed a good scheme.

Sylvia came back to the bar carrying a tray crowded with empty pint pots. "Good Lord," she said, staring at the new arrivals. "Look what the breeze blew in." Of itself, her hand went up to smooth her hair. "Where the devil have you lads been? I thought—" She'd thought the same thing Goldfarb had, but didn't want to say it out loud.

"Beautiful, romantic Pskov." George Bagnall rolled his eyes to show how seriously the adjectives were meant to be taken.

"Where's whatever-you-call-it?" Sylvia asked, beating everyone else to the punch.

"If you draw a line from Leningrad to Warsaw, you won't be

far off," Bagnall answered. That let Goldfarb put it on his mental map.

Jerome Jones added, "And all the time we were there, the only thing sustaining us was the thought of the White Horse Inn and the sweet, gentle, lovely lasses working here."

Sylvia looked down under her feet. "Fetch me a dustpan," she said to Naomi. "It's getting pretty deep in here." She turned back to Jones. "You're even cheekier than I recall." He grinned, not a bit abashed. Looking him, Embry, and Bagnall over with a critical eye, Sylvia went on, "You must be the lot who were in here last week looking for me. I was in bed with the influenza."

"I never thought to be jealous of a germ," Jones said. Sylvia planted an elbow in his ribs, hard enough to lift him off his feet. She went on behind the bar, emptying the tray of the pints it had carried, and started filling fresh ones.

"Where's Daphne?" Ken Embry asked.

"She had twin girls last month, I hear," Goldfarb answered, which effectively ended that line of inquiry.

"I do believe I'd kill for a bit of beefsteak," Bagnall said, in a tone of voice implying that wasn't meant altogether as a joke. "One thing I've found since we got here is that we're on even shorter commons than they are on the Continent. Black bread, parsnips, cabbage, spuds—it's like what the Germans were eating the last winter of the Great War."

"You want beefsteak, sir, you may have to kill," Goldfarb said. "A man who has a cow stands watch over it with a rifle these days, and it seems rifles are easy to come by for bandits, too. Everybody got a rifle when the Lizards came, and not all of them were turned back in, not by a long chalk. You'll hear about gunfights over food in the papers or on the wireless."

Sylvia nodded emphatic agreement to that. "Might as well be the Wild West, all the shooting that goes on these days. Chicken, now, we might come up with, and there's fish about, seeing as we're by the ocean. But beef? No."

"Even chicken costs," Basil Roundbush said. Goldfarb had been thinking the same thing, but hadn't said it, though with his tiny pay he had more justification than the officer. But, when you were a Jew, you thought three times before you let others perceive you as cheap.

Jerome Jones slapped himself in the hip pocket. "Money's not the biggest worry in the world right now, not with eighteen months' pay dropped on me all at once. More money than I thought I'd get, too. How many times have they raised our salaries while we were gone?"

"Three or four," Goldfarb answered. "But it's not as much money as you think. Prices have gone up a lot faster than pay. I was just thinking that a few minutes ago." He glanced down the bar toward Naomi, who had just set a pint pot in front of a slicker-clad fisherman. His shoulders heaved up and down in a silent sigh. It would be so good to get her out of here and live on his pay—except he could barely do that himself, and two surely couldn't."

He caught his fiancée's eye. She came back over with a smile. "A round for all my friends here," he said, digging into his pocket to see what banknotes lay crumpled there.

By immemorial custom, everyone would buy a round after that. He'd want a radar mounted on the front of his bicycle by the time he had to go back to barracks, but he expected he'd manage. He'd have a thick head come morning, but he'd manage that, too. Beefsteak might be thin on the ground, but they'd never yet run short on aspirin tablets.

The Tosevite negotiators rose respectfully when Atvar entered the chamber where they waited. He flicked one eye turret toward Uotat. "Give them the appropriate greetings," he said to Uotat.

"It shall be done, Exalted Fleetlord," the translator answered, and switched from the beautiful, precise language of the Race to the mushy ambiguities of the Big Ugly tongue called English.

One after another, the Tosevites replied, Molotov of the SSSR through his own interpreter. "They say the usual things in the usual way, Exalted Fleetlord," Uotat reported.

"Good," Atvar said. "I am in favor of their doing any usual thing in any usual way. On this planet, that is in and of itself unusual. And speaking of the unusual, we now return to the matter of Poland. Tell the speaker from Deutschland I am most displeased over his recent threat of renewed combat, and that the Race will take unspecified severe measures should such threats reoccur in the future."

Again, Uotat spoke English. Von Ribbentrop replied in the same language. "Exalted Fleetlord, he blames errors in decoding the instructions from his not-emperor for that unseemly lapse of a few days ago."

"Does he?" Atvar said. "After the fact, a male may blame a great many things, some of which may even have some connection to the truth. Tell him it was as well he was mistaken. Tell him his not-empire would have suffered dreadful damage had he proved correct."

This time, von Ribbentrop replied at some length, and apparently with some heat. "He denies that Deutschland needs to fear the Empire and the Race. He says that, as the Race has been dilatory in these negotiations, his not-empire is within its rights to resume conflict at a time and in a manner of its choosing. He does regret having misinformed you at that time and in that manner, however."

"Generous of him," the fleetlord remarked. "Tell him we have not been dilatory. Point out to him that we have the essentials of agreement with the SSSR and with the U.S.A. Tell him it is the intransigent attitude of his own not-emperor over Poland that has led to this impasse."

Again Uotat translated. Von Ribbentrop let out several yips of Tosevite laughter before answering. "He says that any agreement with the SSSR is of less worth than the sheet of paper on which its terms are stated."

Even before von Ribbentrop had finished, Molotov began speaking in his own language, which to Atvar sounded different from English but no more beautiful. Molotov's interpreter spoke to Uotat, who spoke to Atvar: "He accuses the Deutsche of violating agreements they have made, and cites examples. Do you want the full listing, Exalted Fleetlord?"

"Never mind," Atvar told him. "I have heard it before, and can retrieve the data whenever necessary."

Von Ribbentrop spoke again. "He points out, Exalted Fleetlord, that the SSSR has a long frontier with China, where conflict against the local Big Uglies continues. He also points out that one Chinese faction is ideologically akin to the faction ruling the SSSR. He asks how we can imagine the males of the SSSR will not continue to supply their fellow factionalists with munitions even after reaching agreement with the Race."

"That is an interesting question," Atvar said. "Ask Molotov to answer."

Molotov did, and took a while doing it. Though Atvar could not understand his language any more than he could English, he noted a difference in style between the representatives of Deutschland and the SSSR. Von Ribbentrop was histrionic, dramatic, fond of making little points into big ones. Molotov took the opposite approach: the fleetlord did not know what he was saying, but it sounded soporific. His face was almost as still as that of a male of the Race, which, for a Big Ugly, was most unusual.

Uotat reported, "The male Molotov states that a large number of Soviet weapons and munitions are already in China; they were sent there to aid the Chinese, or one faction of them, in their struggle against Nippon prior to our arrival here. He further states that, because of this, the SSSR cannot be held liable if such weapons and munitions are discovered in China."

"Wait," Atvar said. "The SSSR and Nippon were not at war with each other when we came to this miserable mudball. Yet Molotov admits to aiding a Chinese faction against the Nipponese?"

"He does, Exalted Fleetlord," the translator replied.

"Then ask him why we should not expect the SSSR to supply the Chinese with arms against us, with whom his not-empire also would not be at war."

Uotat spoke. Molotov answered. His interpreter relayed his words to Uotat, and Uotat to Atvar: "He says that, unlike the Nipponese, the Race would have both the power and the interest to punish any such violations."

Such breathtaking cynicism made the fleetlord let out a sharp hiss. Nevertheless, the approach was realistic enough to make dealing possible. "Tell him violations *will* be punished," he said, and added an emphatic cough.

"He acknowledges your concern," Uotat said after Atvar had spoken.

"How good of him to do so," Atvar said. "And now, back to the matter of Poland, which appears to be the principal concern remaining before us here." As he spoke, he wondered if that would be true in the long run. China had a much larger area and many more Big Uglies living in it than Poland did. It also had a long frontier with the SSSR that even the Race's technology would have a hard time sealing. Sooner or later, the males of the SSSR would try to cheat and then deny they'd done it. He could feel that coming.

The male from Britain spoke up: "A moment, please." He was polite; he waited for Uotat to gesture for him to continue before going on, "I must reiterate that His Majesty's government, while acknowledging the Race's conquest of large portions of our empire, cannot consider any sort of formal recognition of these conquests without in return obtaining a cease-fire identical in formality and dignity to the ones to which you have agreed with the United States, the Soviet Union, and Germany."

"So long as the conquest is real, whether you recognize it does not matter," Atvar replied.

"A great deal of history contradicts you," Eden said.

As far as Atvar was concerned, Tosev 3 did not have a great deal of history. He did not say that; it only nettled the Big Uglies. What he did say was, "You must know why Britain is not in the same class as the not-empires you named."

"We have no atomic weapons," the British male answered. "And you must know that is not necessarily a permanent condition."

For a moment, Atvar was tempted to grant the British the formal cease-fire they craved on the spot, if for no other reason than to inhibit their nuclear research program. But he held silent: with three Tosevite not-empires already in possession of atomic weapons, what did one more matter, even if the British could make good on the warning? "Poland," he said.

"Is and must be ours," von Ribbentrop declared.

"Nyet." Atvar understood that word without any help from the interpreters; Molotov used it so much, it had become unmistakable.

"The Race shall, for the time being, retain possession of those parts of Poland it now holds," the fleetlord said. "We shall continue discussion with Deutschland, with the SSSR, and even with the Poles and Jews, in an effort to find a solution satisfactory to all parties."

"General Secretary Stalin has instructed me to acquiesce in this," Molotov said.

"The *Führer* does not, will not, and cannot agree," von Ribbentrop said.

"I warn you and the *Führer* once more: if you resume your war against the Race, and especially if you resume it with nuclear weapons, your not-empire will suffer the most severe consequences imaginable," Atvar said.

Von Ribbentrop did not answer, not to bellow defiance, not even to acknowledge he'd heard. The only thing that worried Atvar worse than a blustering, defiant Big Ugly was a silent one.

Ludmila Gorbunova pressed the self-starter of the Fieseler *Storch*. The Argus engine came to life at once. She was not surprised. German machinery worked well.

Ignacy waved to her. She nodded back as she built up revolutions. She would have had to push the *Storch* hard to get it airborne before it rammed the trees ahead. Her old U-2 could never have taken off in so short a space.

She nodded again. More partisans bent to remove the blocks of wood in front of the light plane's wheels. At the same time, Ludmila released the brake. The *Storch* bounded forward. When she pulled back on the stick, its nose came up and it sprang into the air. She could see the trees through the cockpit glasshouse: dark shapes down there, almost close enough to reach out and touch. The Poles whose candles had marked the edge of the forest for her now blew them out.

She buzzed along steadily, not wanting to gain much altitude. As long as she was on the Lizard side of the line, she might be shot down as an enemy. Ironic that she'd have to make it to German-held territory to feel safe,

Safe wasn't all she hoped she'd feel. By the coordinates, she was returning to the same landing strip she'd used before. With luck, Heinrich Jäger would be there waiting for her.

Off to the right, muzzle flashes blazed in the darkness. Something hit the side of the fuselage, once, with a sound like a stone clattering off a tin roof. Ludmila gave the *Storch* more throttle, getting out of there as fast as she could.

That complicated her navigation. If she was going faster, she needed to fly for less time. How much less? She worked the answer out in her head, decided she didn't like it, and worked it out again. By the time she discovered where she'd gone wrong the first time, a glance at her watch warned her it was time to start looking around for the landing strip.

She hoped she wouldn't have to do a search spiral. The Germans were liable to start shooting at her if she buzzed around for too long, and the spiral might take her back over Lizard-held territory if it got too big.

There! As usual, the lanterns marking the landing strip were small and dim, but she spotted them. Lowering the enormous flaps on the *Storch* killed airspeed almost as if she were stepping on the brakes on the highway. The light plane jounced to a stop well within the area the lanterns marked off.

Ludmila flipped up the cockpit door. She climbed out onto the wing, then jumped down to the ground. Men came trotting up toward the *Storch*. In the darkness, she couldn't be sure if any of them was Jäger.

They recognized her before she could make out who they were. "There—you see, Gunther?" one of them said. "It *is* the lady pilot." He gave the word the feminine ending, as Jäger sometimes did, as she had so often heard Georg Schultz do (she wondered what might have happened to Schultz and Tatiana, but only for a moment: as far as she was concerned, they deserved each other).

"*Ja*, you were right, Johannes," another German answered. "Only goes to show nobody can be wrong *all* the time." A couple of snorts floated out of the night.

Gunther, Johannes— "You are the men from Colonel Jäger's panzer, not so?" Ludmila called quietly. "Is he—is he here, too?" No point pretending she didn't care; they couldn't help knowing about her and Jäger.

The panzer crewmen stopped in their tracks, almost as if they'd run into an invisible wall. "No, he's not here," one of them—Gunther, she thought—answered. He spoke hardly above a whisper, as if he didn't want his words to go beyond the span of the *Storch*'s wings.

Ice ran down Ludmila's back. "Tell me!" she said. "Is he hurt? Is he dead? Did it happen before the cease-fire started? Tell me!"

"He's not dead—yet," Gunther said, even more softly than before. "He's not even hurt—yet. And no, it didn't happen in the fighting with the Lizards. It happened three days ago, as a matter of fact."

"*What* happened?" Ludmila demanded.

Maddeningly, Gunther fell silent. After a moment when Ludmila felt like yanking out her pistol and extorting answers at gunpoint, if need be, the crewman named Johannes said, "Miss, the SS arrested him."

"*Bozhemoi,*" Ludmila whispered. "Why? What could he have done? Was it on account of me?"

"Damned if we know," Johannes said. "This weedy little SS pigdog came up, pointed a gun at him, and marched him away. Stinking blackshirt bastard—who does he think he is, arresting the best commander we've ever had?"

His crewmen muttered profane agreement. It would have been loud profane agreement, except they were all veterans, and wary of letting anyone outside their circle know their thoughts.

One of them said, "Come on, boys, we're supposed to be loading ammo into this miserable little plane."

"It has to be because of me," Ludmila said. She'd always worried the NKVD would descend on her because of Jäger; now, instead, his nation's security forces had seized him on account of her. That struck her as frightful and dreadfully unfair. "Is there any way to get him free?"

"From the SS?" said the crewman who'd just urged getting the 7.92mm rounds aboard the *Storch*. He sounded incredulous; evidently the Nazis invested their watchdogs with the same fearsome, almost supernatural powers the Russian people attributed to the NKVD.

But the tankman called Gunther said, "Christ crucified, why not? You think Skorzeny would sit around on his can and let anything happen to Colonel Jäger, no matter who'd grabbed him? My left nut he would! He's an SS man, yes, but he's a real soldier, too, not just a damned traffic cop in a black shirt. Shit, if we can't break the colonel out, we don't deserve to be panzer troopers. Come on!" He was aflame with the idea.

That cautious crewman spoke up again: "All right, what if we do break him out? Where does he go after that?"

No one answered him for a couple of seconds. Then Johannes let out a noise that would have been a guffaw if he hadn't put a silencer on it. He pointed to the Fieseler *Storch*. "We'll break him out, we'll stick him on the plane, and the lady pilot can fly him the hell out of here. If the SS has its hooks in him, he won't want to stick around anyhow, that's for damn sure."

The other panzer crewmen crowded around him, pumping his hand and pounding him on the back. So did Ludmila. Then she said, "Can you do this without danger to yourselves?"

"Just watch us," Johannes said. He started away from the *Storch*, calling, "The pilot's got engine troubles. We're going to get a mechanic." And off they went, tramping through the night with sudden purpose in their stride.

Ludmila, left by herself, thought about loading some of the German ammunition into the *Storch* herself. In the end, she decided not to. She might want every gram of power the light plane had, and extra weight aboard would take some away.

A cricket chirped, somewhere out in the darkness. Waiting stretched. Her hand went to the butt of the Tokarev she wore on her hip. If shooting broke out, she'd run toward it. But, except for insects, the night stayed silent.

One of the *Wehrmacht* men who marked out the landing strip with lanterns called to her: *"Alles gut, Fräulein?"*

"Ja," she answered. *"Alles gut."* How much of a liar was she?

Booted feet trotting on dirt, coming closer fast . . . Ludmila stiffened. All she could see, out there in the grass-scented night, were moving shapes. She couldn't even tell how many till they got close. One, two, three, four . . . five!

"Ludmila?" Was it? It was! Jäger's voice.

"Da!" she answered, forgetting her German.

Something glittered. One of the panzer men with Jäger plunged a knife into the dirt again and again—to clean it, maybe—before he set it back in the sheath on his belt. When he spoke, he proved to have Gunther's voice: "Get the colonel out of here, lady pilot. We didn't leave any eyes to see who we were"—his hand caressed the hilt of the knife again, just for a moment—"and everybody here is part of the regiment. Nobody'll rat on us—we did what needed doing, that's all."

"You're every one of you crazy, that's all," Jäger said, warm affection in his voice. His crewman crowded round him, pressing his hand, hugging him, wishing him well. That would have told Ludmila everything she needed to know about him as an officer, but she'd already formed her own conclusions there.

She pointed to the dim shapes of the ammunition crates. "You'll have to get rid of those," she reminded the tankmen. "They were supposed to come with me."

"We'll take care of it, lady pilot," Gunther promised. "We'll take care of everything. Don't you worry about it. We may be criminals, *ja*, but by Jesus we're not half-assed criminals." The other tankers rumbled low-voiced agreement.

Ludmila was willing to believe German efficiency extended to crime. She tapped Jäger on the shoulder to separate him from his comrades, then pointed to the open door of the Fieseler *Storch*. "Get in," she said. "Take the rear seat, the one with the machine gun."

"We'd better not have to use it," he answered, hooking a foot in the stirrup at the bottom of the fuselage that let him climb up onto the wing and into the cockpit. Ludmila followed. She pulled down the door and dogged it shut. Her finger stabbed at the self-starter. The motor caught. She watched the soldiers scatter, glad she hadn't had to ask one to spin the prop for her.

"Have you got your belt on?" she asked Jäger. When he said yes, she let the *Storch* scoot forward across the field: the acceleration might have shoved her passenger out of his seat if he hadn't been strapped in place.

As usual, the light plane needed only a handful of ground on which to take off. After one last hard bump, it sprang into the air. Jäger leaned to one side to peer down at the landing strip. So did Ludmila, but there wasn't much to see. Now that they were airborne, the fellows with the lanterns had doused them. She supposed—she hoped—they were helping Jäger's crewmen get the ammunition either under cover or back into the regimental store.

Over her shoulder, she asked him, "Are you all right?"

"Pretty much so," he answered. "They hadn't done much of the strongarm stuff yet—they weren't sure how big a traitor I am." He laughed bitterly, then amazed her by going on, "A lot bigger than they ever imagined, I'll tell you that. Where are we going?"

Ludmila was swinging the *Storch* back toward the east. "I was going to take you to the partisan unit I've been with for a while. No one will try and come after you there, I shouldn't think; we'll have a good many kilometers between us and German-held territory. Is that good enough?"

"No, not nearly," he said, again surprising her. "Can you fly me down to Lodz? If you like, you can let me out of the airplane and go back to the partisans yourself. But I have to go there, no matter what."

"Why?" She could hear the hurt in her own voice. Here at last they had the chance to be together and stay together and . . . "What could be so important in Lodz?"

"That's a long story," Jäger said, and then proceeded to compress it with a forceful brevity that showed his officer's discipline. The more he talked, the wider Ludmila's eyes got—no, the SS hadn't arrested him on account of her, not at all. He finished, "And so, if I don't get back into Lodz, Skorzeny is liable to blow up the town and all the people and Lizards in it. And if he does that, what becomes of the cease-fire? What becomes of the *Vaterland*? And what becomes of the world?"

Ludmila didn't answer for a few seconds. Then, very quietly, she said, "Whatever you call yourself, you weren't a traitor." She gained a little altitude before swinging the *Storch* in a rightward bank. Numbers spun round the dial of the compass on the instrument panel till it steadied on south-southeast. "We'll both go to Lodz," Ludmila said.

☆ **XIX** ☆

Ttomalss must have slept through the opening of the outer door to the building that confined him. The sharp click of the lock to the inner door, though, brought him up to his feet from the hard floor, his eye turrets swiveling wildly as he tried to see what was going on. Next to no light came through the narrow window that illuminated and ventilated his cell.

Fear coursed through him. The Big Uglies had never come here at night before. Like any male of the Race, he found a break in routine threatening in and of itself. This particular change, he suspected, would have felt ominous even to a Tosevite.

The door opened. Not one but three Big Uglies came in. Each carried in one hand a lantern burning some smelly fat or oil and in the other a submachine gun. The lanterns were primitive: much the sort of tools the Race had expected the natives of Tosev 3 to possess. The submachine guns, unfortunately, were not.

In the dim, flickering light, Ttomalss needed a moment to recognize Liu Han. "Superior female!" he gasped when he did. She did not answer right away, but stood looking at him. He commended his spirit to Emperors past, confident they would care for it better than the Race's authorities had protected his body while he lived.

"Be still!" Liu Han snapped. Ttomalss waited for the weapon in her hand to stitch him full of holes. Instead of shooting him, though, she set it on the floor. She pulled out something she had tucked into the waist of her cloth leg-covering: a sack made of coarse, heavy fabric.

While the two males with her kept their submachine guns pointed at Ttomalss, Liu Han came up to him and pulled the sack down over his head. He stood frozen, not daring to resist. *If they shoot me now, I will not see the guns go off before the bullets strike,* he thought. Liu Han tied the bag closed around his neck, not quite tight enough to choke off his breath.

"Can he see?" one of the males asked. Then the fellow spoke directly to Ttomalss: "Can you see, miserable scaly devil?"

Miserable Ttomalss was. "No, superior sir," he answered truthfully.

Liu Han shoved him. He almost fell over. When he recovered, she put a hand in the middle of his back. "You walk in the directions I choose for you," she said, first in Chinese and then in the language of the Race. "Only in those directions." She used an emphatic cough.

"It shall be done," Ttomalss gasped. Maybe they were just taking him out to shoot him somewhere else. But if they were, wouldn't they have told him as much, so they could enjoy his terrified anticipation? Big Uglies were dreadfully sophisticated when it came to inflicting pain.

Liu Han shoved him again, lightly this time. He walked forward till she said, "Go left," and emphasized that by moving the hand on his back in the appropriate way. He turned to the left. Why not? In the sphere of blackness in which he moved, one direction was as good as another. A little later, Liu Han said, "Go right." Ttomalss went right.

He had not known where he was when he set out. Had he known, he soon would have become hopelessly lost. He turned right and left and right and left tens of times, with what seemed to him random intervals and choices. The streets of Peking were very quiet. He guessed it was somewhere between the middle of the night and dawn, but could not be certain.

At last, Liu Han said, "Stop." Ttomalss did, in apprehension. Was this the moment? Was this the place? Liu Han untied the cord fastening the cloth sack over his head. She said, "Count to one hundred, out loud, slowly, in your language. Then lift off the hood. If you lift it before you reach one hundred, you will die at once. Do you understand?"

"Y-Yes, superior female," Ttomalss quavered. "It shall be done. One . . . two . . . three . . ." He went on, as steadily as he could: "Ninety-eight . . . ninety-nine . . . one hundred." As he reached for the sack, he waited for bullets to tear into him. He yanked the cloth from his head in a quick, convulsive gesture.

No one shot him. His eye turrets scanned all around. He was alone, at the mouth of one of Peking's innumerable little *hutungs.* He threw down the sack. The soft *thwap!* it made hitting the ground was the only sound that reached his hearing diaphragms.

Ever so cautiously, he stepped out into the street onto which the *hutung* opened.

To his amazement, he recognized it. It was the Lower Slanting Street, in Chinese the *Hsia Hsieh Chieh*. And there stood the ruins of the *Ch'ang Ch'un Ssu*, the Temple of Everlasting Spring. He knew how to get back to the Race's headquarters in the center of Peking. He did not know if he would be allowed to do so, but he knew he had to try. The Lower Slanting Street even led in the right direction.

Before long, he ran into a patrol of males of the Race. Where the Tosevites had let him go, the patrol almost shot him before recognizing him as one of their own. *That* would have been an irony on which to end his career! But when he told them who he was, they hurried him off to the thoroughly fortified citadel the Race retained in what had been the Forbidden City.

He was pleased to find his arrival important enough to justify rousing Ppevel. Soon the assistant administrator, eastern region, main continental mass, came into the chamber where Ttomalss was enjoying proper food for the first time in ever so long and said, "I am glad to see you at liberty once more, Researcher. The Tosevites informed us yesterday they would release you, but they are not always reliable in their assertions, as you know."

"Truth, superior sir—as I know too well," Ttomalss said with an emphatic cough. "Did they say *why* they were releasing me? To me, they never gave a reason." Without waiting for an answer, he dug into the plate of fried worms the cooks had given him. Even though they'd been desiccated for the trip to Tosev 3 and then reconstituted, they were still a taste of Home.

Ppevel said, "By their messages, partly as a goodwill gesture and partly as a warning: typical of the Big Uglies to try to do both at once." As if to give his words a different sort of emphatic cough, a rattle of gunfire broke out, off in the distance. He went on, "They say this shows us they can move at will through this city and other cities in this not-empire, releasing whom they will, taking whom they will, killing whom they will. They warn us the struggle to integrate China into the Empire will fail."

Before coming down to the surface of Tosev 3, perhaps even before his kidnapping, Ttomalss would have found that laughable, ludicrous. Now— "They are determined, superior sir, and they are both ingenious and surprisingly well armed. I fear they may trouble us for years, maybe generations, to come."

"It could be so," Ppevel admitted, which surprised Ttomalss. He said, "While I was a captive, the female Liu Han claimed the

Race had granted certain Tosevite not-empires a cease-fire. Can this be so?"

"It can. It is," Ppevel said. "These are the not-empires capable of producing their own nuclear weapons and desperate enough to use them against us. China—all of its factions—has no such weapons, and is excluded from the cease-fire. This offends the Chinese, or so it would seem, and so they redouble their annoyances in an effort to be included."

"The Race—treating with barbarous Tosevites as if they were equals?" Ttomalss looked up toward the ceiling in wonder and dismay. "Even from your mouth, superior sir, I have trouble believing it."

"It is truth nonetheless," Ppevel answered. "Even with these Chinese, we have negotiated, as you know, though we have not granted them the concessions the other not-empires have gained. We shall share dominion of this planet with the Tosevites until the colonization fleet arrives. Perhaps we shall share it after the colonization fleet arrives. I would not care to guess as to that. It is the fleetlord's decision, not mine."

Ttomalss' head reeled, almost as if he had ingested too much of the Tosevite herb so many males found alluring. So much had changed while he lay in captivity! He would have to work hard to adapt himself, always unsettling to the Race. He said, "We shall need more than ever, then, to seek to understand the essential nature of the Big Uglies."

"Truth," Ppevel agreed. "When you are physically recovered from your ordeal, Researcher, we shall obtain for you, with the greatest discretion possible, a new Tosevite hatchling, with which you can resume your interrupted work."

"Thank you, superior sir," Ttomalss said, his voice far more hollow than he would have expected. After what had happened to him with the last hatchling—with Liu Mei, he made himself remember—the work that had once consumed him now seemed liable to be more dangerous than it was worth. "With your generous permission, superior sir, I shall carry on this research back aboard a starship laboratory rather than here on the surface of Tosev 3."

"That may well be arranged," Ppevel said.

"Thank you, superior sir," Ttomalss repeated. He hoped the distance between the surface and the cleanness of open space would protect him from Big Uglies wild for revenge because of their familial and sexual structure. He hoped so—but he was not so confident of it as he had been in the days when Tosev 3 was new and conquest had seemed certain to be quick and easy. He cherished that certainty, and knew he would never have its like again.

Patients and refugees crowded around the Lizard with the fancy body paint and the hand-held electrified megaphone. Rance Auerbach moved up slowly and carefully—the only way of moving he had—to get as good a vantage point as he could. Since so many other people had as much trouble moving as he did, he got up pretty close, almost to the gun-toting guards around the speaker.

He looked around for Penny Summers and spotted her on the opposite side of the crowd. He waved to her, but she didn't see him.

The electrified megaphone made flatulent noises. Somewhere close by, a child laughed. Then, in pretty fair English, the Lizard began to speak: "We leave this place now. The Race and the government of this not-empire here, the United States, we make agreement now. No more fight. The Race to leave the land of the United States. That include this place, this Karval, Colorado, too."

He couldn't go on, not right away. A buzz ran through the crowd, and then a cheer. A woman started singing "God Bless America." Inside the second line of the song, everybody there was singing with her. Tears stung Auerbach's eyes. The Lizards were leaving! They had won. Even getting shot up suddenly seemed worth it.

When the singing stopped, the Lizard resumed: "You free now, yes." More cheers rang out. "We go now." Auerbach cut loose with a Rebel yell: more of a coughing yip than the wild shriek he'd wanted, but good enough. The Lizard went on, "Now you free, now we go—now we not have to take care for you no more. We go, we leave not-empire of United States to take care for you now. They do it or nobody do it. We go now. That is all."

The Lizard guards had to gesture threateningly with their weapons before the people would clear aside and let them and the speaker out. For a few dreadful seconds, Auerbach was afraid they would start shooting. With people packed so tight around them, that would have been a slaughter.

He made his halting way toward Penny Summers. This time, she did spot him, and moved, far more nimbly than he could, to meet him. "What did that scaly bastard mean, exactly?" she asked. "Way he was talking, it sounded like the Lizards are just gonna up and leave us on our own."

"They couldn't do that," Auerbach said. "There's what?—thousands of people here, and a lot of 'em—me, for instance—

aren't what you'd call good at getting around. What are we supposed to do, walk to the American lines up near Denver?" He laughed at the absurdity of the notion.

But the Lizards didn't think it was absurd. They piled into trucks and armored personnel carriers and rolled out of Karval that afternoon, heading east, back toward wherever their spaceships were parked. By the time the sun went down, Karval was an altogether human town again.

It was a good-sized human town, too, and one utterly without government of any sort. The Lizards had taken as many of the supplies as they could load into their vehicles. Fights broke out over what was left. Penny managed to get hold of some hard biscuits, and shared them with Rance. They made his belly rumble a little less than it would have without them.

Off to the left, not quite far enough away from his convalescent tent to be out of earshot, somebody said, "We ought to string up all the stinking bastards who kissed the Lizards' butts while they was here. String 'em up by the balls, matter of fact."

Auerbach shivered, not so much because of what the fellow said as at the calm, matter-of-fact way he said it. In Europe, they'd called people who'd gone along with the Nazis, people like Quisling, collaborators. Auerbach had never figured anybody would need to worry about collaborators in the U.S.A., but he didn't know everything there was to know, either.

Penny said, "There's gonna be trouble. Anybody who's got a score to settle against somebody else will say they went along with the Lizards. Who's gonna be able to sort out what's true and what ain't? Families will be feuding a hundred years from now on account o' this."

"You're probably right," Rance said. "But there's going to be trouble sooner than that." He was thinking like a soldier. "The Lizards may have pulled out of here, but the Army hasn't pulled in. We'll eat Karval empty by tomorrow at the latest, and then what do we do?"

"Walk toward Denver, I reckon," Penny answered. "What else can we do?"

"Not much," he said. "But walk—what? A hundred miles, maybe?" He gestured toward the crutches that lay by his cot. "You might as well go on without me. I'll meet you there in a month, maybe six weeks."

"Don't be silly," Penny told him. "You're doin' a lot better than you were."

"I know, but I'm not doing well enough."

"You will be," she said confidently. "Besides, I don't want to leave you, darling." She blew out the one flickering candle that lit the inside of the tent. In the darkness, he heard cloth rustle. When he reached out toward her, his hand brushed warm, bare flesh. A little later, she rode astride him, groaning both in ecstasy and, he thought, in desperation, too—or maybe he was just guessing she felt the same thing he did. Afterwards, not bothering to dress, she slept beside him in the tent.

He woke before sunrise, and woke her, too. "If we're going to do this," he said, "we'd better get started early as we can. That way we can go a long way before it gets too hot, and lie up during the hottest part of the day."

"Sounds good to me," Penny said.

The eastern sky was just going pink when they set out. They were far from the first to leave Karval. Singly and in small groups, some people were making their way north along one of the roads that led out of town, others along the westbound road, and a few hearty souls, splitting the difference, heading northwest cross-country. Had Auerbach been in better shape, he would have done that. As things were, he and Penny went west: the Horse River was likelier to have water in it still than any of the streams they would cross heading north.

He was stronger and better on his crutches than he had been, but that still left him weak and slow. Men and women passed Penny and him in a steady stream. Refugees from Karval stretched out along the road as far as he could see.

"Some of us are going to die before we get to Denver," he said. The prospect upset him much less than it would have before he got wounded. He'd had a dress rehearsal for meeting the Grim Reaper; really doing it couldn't be a whole lot worse.

Penny pointed up to the sky. The wheeling black specks up there weren't Lizard airplanes, or even Piper Cubs. They were buzzards, waiting with the patient optimism of their kind. Penny didn't say anything. She didn't need to. Rance wondered if one of those buzzards would gnaw his bones.

He needed two days to get to the Horse. Had its bed been dry, he knew he wouldn't have got much farther. But people crowded the bank, down where the river passed under Highway 71. The water was warm and muddy, and there, not twenty feet away, some idiot was pissing into the stream. Auerbach didn't care about any of it. He drank till he was full, he splashed his face, he soaked his head, and then he took off his shirt and soaked that, too. As it dried, it would help keep him cool.

Penny splashed water on her blouse. The wet cotton molded itself to her shape. Auerbach would have appreciated that more had he not been so deadly weary. As things were, he nodded and said, "Good idea. Let's get going."

They headed north up Highway 71, and reached Punkin Center early the next morning. They got more water there. A sad-eyed local said, "Wish we could give you some eats, folks—you look like you could use 'em. But the ones ahead o' you done et us out of what we had. Good luck to you."

"I told you to go on without me," Auerbach said. Penny ignored him. One foot and two crutches at a time, he wearily plodded north.

By the end of that afternoon, he figured the buzzards were out tying napkins around their necks, getting ready for a delicious supper of sunbaked cavalry captain. If he fell over and died, he figured Penny could speed up and might make it to Limon before the heat and the dry and the hunger got her.

"I love you," he croaked, not wanting to die with things left unspoken.

"I love you, too," she answered. "That's why I'm gonna get you through."

He laughed, but, before he could tell her how big a joke that was, he heard cheering up ahead. He pointed, balancing for a moment on one foot and one crutch. "That's an Army wagon," he said in glad disbelief. The horses were the most beautiful animals he'd ever seen.

The wagon was already full, but the soldiers gave him and Penny canteens and crackers and scooted people around to make room in back. "We'll get you up to the resettlement center," one of them promised, "and they'll take care of you there."

That took another couple of days, but there were supply depots all the way. Auerbach spent his time wondering what the resettlement center would be like; the soldiers didn't talk much about it. When they finally got there, he found out why: it was just another name for a refugee camp, one dwarfing the squalid, miserable place outside Karval.

"How long will we have to stay here?" he asked a harried clerk who was handing Penny bedding for two and directing her to an enormous olive-drab communal tent, one of many all in a row.

"God knows, buddy," the corporal answered. "The war may be stopped, but this ain't no Easy Street. Ain't gonna be for a long time, neither. Welcome to the United States, new and not so improved model. With luck, you won't starve."

"We'll take that," Penny said, and Auerbach had to nod. Together, they set off to acquaint themselves with the new United States.

In his green undershirt and black panzer man's trousers, Heinrich Jäger didn't look badly out of place on the streets of Lodz. Lots of men wore odds and ends of German uniform, and, if his was in better shape than most, that meant little. His colonel's blouse, on the other hand, he'd ditched as soon as he jumped out of the *Storch*. A *Wehrmacht* officer was not a popular thing to be, not here.

Ludmila strode along beside him. Her clothes—a peasant tunic and a pair of trousers that had probably once belonged to a Polish soldier—were mannish, but no one save a particularly nearsighted Lizard could have mistaken her for the male of the species, even with an automatic pistol on her hip. Neither pants nor sidearm drew any special notice. A lot of women wore trousers instead of skirts or dresses, and a surprising number—most but not all of them Jewish-looking—carried or wore firearms.

"Do you know Lodz at all?" Ludmila asked. "Do you know how to find—the person we're looking for?" She was too sensible to name Mordechai Anielewicz where anyone might overhear his name.

Jäger shook his head. "No and no, respectively." He kept his voice low; nobody who spoke German, *Wehrmacht* officer or not, was likely to be popular in Lodz these days, not with Jews, not with Poles, and not with Lizards, either. "I expect we'll find him, though. In his own way, he's a big man here."

He thought about asking a policeman. He had a couple of different brands from which to choose: Poles in dark blue uniforms and Jews with armbands left over from German administration and with kepis that made them look absurdly like French *flics*. That didn't strike him as a healthy idea, though. Instead, he and Ludmila kept walking north up Stodolniana Street till they came to what had to have been the Jewish quarter. Even now, it was brutally crowded. What it had been like under the *Reich* was something Jäger would sooner not have contemplated.

Many more of those comic-opera Jewish policemen were on the street in that part of town. Jäger kept right on ignoring them and hoping they would extend him the same courtesy. He nodded to a fellow with a wild mop of hair and a big, curly reddish beard who carried a Mauser, had another slung over his shoulder, and wore crisscross bandoliers full of brass cartridges: a Jewish bandit if ever there was one, and as such a man likely to know where Anielewicz could be found. "I'm looking for Mordechai," he said.

The Jew's eyes widened slightly at his clear German. "*Nu?* Are you?" he said, using Yiddish, perhaps to see if Jäger could follow. Jäger nodded again to show he could. The Jewish fighter went on, "So you're looking for Mordechai. So what? Is he looking for you?"

"As a matter of fact, yes," Jäger answered. "Does the name Skorzeny mean anything to you?"

It did. The fighter stiffened. "You're him?" he demanded, and made as if to point the rifle he carried at Jager. Then he checked himself. "No. You can't be. He's supposed to be taller than I am, and you're not."

"You're right." Jäger pointed to Ludmila. "*She's* really Skorzeny."

"Ha," the Jew said. "A funny man. All right, funny man, you can come with me. We'll see if Mordechai wants to see you. See both of you," he amended, seeing how close Ludmila stuck to Jäger.

As it happened, they didn't have to go far. Jäger recognized the brick building they approached as a fire station. His escort spoke in Polish to a gray-bearded man tinkering with the fire engine. The fellow answered in the same language; Jäger caught Anielewicz's name but no more. Ludmila said, "I think they said he's upstairs, but I'm not sure."

She proved right. The Jew made his companions precede him, a sensible precaution Jäger would also have taken. They went down the hall to a small room. Mordechai Anielewicz sat at a table there with a plain woman. He was scribbling something, but stopped when the newcomers arrived. "Jäger!" he exclaimed. "What the devil are you doing here?"

"You know him?" The ginger-bearded Jew sounded disappointed. "He knows something about Skorzeny, he says."

"I'll listen to him." Anielewicz glanced at Ludmila. "Who's your friend?"

She answered for herself, with manifest pride: "Ludmila Vadimovna Gorbunova, Senior Lieutenant, Red Air Force."

"Red Air Force?" Anielewicz's lips silently shaped the words. "You have the oddest friends, Jäger—her and me, for instance. What would Hitler say if he knew?"

"He'd say I was dead meat," Jäger answered. "Of course, since I was already under arrest for treason, he's already said that, or his bully boys have. Right now, I want to keep him from blowing up

Lodz, and maybe keep the Lizards from blowing up Germany to pay him back. For better or worse, it still is my fatherland. Skorzeny doesn't care what happens next. He'll touch that thing off for no better reason than because someone told him to."

"You were right," the woman beside Anielewicz said. "You did see him, then. I thought you were worrying over every little thing."

"I wish I had been, Bertha," he replied, worry and affection warring in his voice. He turned his attention back to Jäger. "I didn't think ... anybody"—he'd probably been about to say something like *even you damned Nazis*, but forbore—"would explode the bomb in the middle of truce talks. Shows what I know, doesn't it?" His gaze sharpened. "You were arrested for treason, you say? *Gevalt!* They found you were passing things to us?"

"They found out I was, yes," Jäger answered with a weary nod. Since his rescue, things had happened too fast for him to take them all in at once. For now, he was trying to roll with each one as it hit. Later, if there was a later and it wasn't frantic, he'd do his best to figure out what everything meant. "Karol is dead." One more memory he wished he didn't have. "They didn't really have any idea how much I was passing on to you. If they'd known a tenth part of it, I'd have been in pieces on the floor when my boys came to break me out—and if my boys knew a tenth part of it, they never would have come."

Anielewicz studied him. Quietly, the younger man said, "If it hadn't been for you, we wouldn't have known about the bomb, it would have gone off, and God only knows what would have happened next." He offered the words as if in consolation for Jäger's having been rescued by his men when they didn't know what he'd truly done; he understood, with a good officer's instinctive grasp, how hard that was to accept.

"You say you saw Skorzeny?" Jäger asked, and Anielewicz nodded. Jäger grimaced. "You must have found the bomb, too. He said it was in a graveyard. Did you move it after you found it?"

"Yes, and that wasn't easy, either," Anielewicz said, wiping his forehead with a sleeve to show how hard it was. "We pulled the detonator, too—not just the wireless switch, but the manual device—so Skorzeny can't set it off even if he finds it and even if he gets to it."

Jäger held up a warning hand. "Don't bet your life on that. He may come up with the detonator you yanked, or he may have one of his own. You never want to underestimate what he can do. Don't forget: I've helped him do it."

"If he has only a detonator for use by the hand," Ludmila said in her slow German, "would he not be blowing himself up along with everything else? If he had to, would he do that?"

"Good question." Anielewicz looked from her to Jäger. "You know him best." He made that an accusation. "*Nu?* Would he?"

"I know two things," Jäger answered. "First one is, he's liable to have some sort of scheme for setting it off by hand and escaping anyhow—no, I have no idea what, but he may. Second one is, you didn't just make him angry, you made him furious when his nerve-gas bomb didn't go off. He owes you one for that. And he has his orders. And, whatever else you can say about him, he's a brave man. If the only way he can set it off is to blow himself up with it, he's liable to be willing to do that."

Mordechai Anielewicz nodded, looking unhappy. "I was afraid you were going to say that. People who will martyr themselves for their cause are much harder to deal with than the ones who just want to live for it." His chuckle held little humor. "The Lizards complain too many people are willing to become martyrs. Now I know how they feel."

"What will you do with us now that we are here?" Ludmila asked.

"That is another good question," said the woman—Bertha—sitting by Anielewicz. She turned to him, fondly; Jäger wondered if they were married. She wore no ring, whatever that meant. "What shall we do with them?"

"Jäger is a soldier, and a good one, and he knows Skorzeny and the way his mind works," the Jewish fighting leader said. "If he had not been reliable before, he would not be here now. Him we will give a weapon and let him help us guard the bomb."

"And what of me?" Ludmila demanded indignantly; Jäger could have guessed she was going to do that. Her hand came to rest on the butt of her automatic pistol. "I am a soldier. Ask Heinrich. Ask the Nazis. Ask the Lizards."

Anielewicz held up a placatory hand. "I believe all this," he answered, "but first things first." Yes, he was a good officer, not that Jäger found that news. He knew how to set priorities. He also knew how to laugh, which he did now. "And you will probably shoot me if I try to separate you from Colonel Jäger here. So. All right. *Wehrmacht*, Red Air Force, a bunch of crazy Jews—we are all in this together, right?"

"Together," Jäger agreed. "Together we save Lodz, or together we go up in smoke. That's about how it is."

A male shook Ussmak. "Get up, headmale! You must get up," Oyyag said urgently, adding an emphatic cough. "That is the signal for rousing. If you do not present yourself, you will be punished. The whole barracks will be punished because of your failing."

Ever so slowly, Ussmak began to move. Among the Race, superiors were supposed to be responsible for inferiors and to look out for their interests. So it had been for millennia uncounted. So, on Home, it no doubt continued to be. Here on Tosev 3, Ussmak was an outlaw. That weakened his bonds of cohesion to the group, though some of them were mutineers, too. Even more to the point, he was a starved, exhausted outlaw. When you were less than convinced your own life would long continue—when you were less than convinced you wanted it to continue—group solidarity came hard.

He managed to drag himself to his feet and lurch outside for the morning inspection. The Tosevite guards, who probably could not have stated their correct number of thumbs twice running without luck on their side, had to count the males of the Race four times before they were satisfied no one had grown wings and flown away during the night. Then they let them go in to breakfast.

It was meager, even by the miserable standards of the prison camp. Ussmak did not finish even his own small portion. "Eat," Oyyag urged him. "How can you get through another day's work if you do not eat?"

Ussmak had his own counterquestion. "How can I get through another day's work even if I do eat? Anyhow, I am not hungry."

That set the other male hissing in alarm. "Headmale, you must report to the Big Ugly physicians. Perhaps they can give you something to improve your appetite, to improve your condition."

Ussmak's mouth fell open. "A new body, perhaps? A new spirit?"

"You cannot eat?" Oyyag said. Ussmak's weary gesture showed he could not. His companion in misery, who was every bit as thin as he was, hesitated, but not for long. "May I consume your portion, then?" When Ussmak did not at once say no, the other male gulped down the food.

As if in a dream, Ussmak shambled out to the forest with his work gang. He drew an axe and went slowly to work hacking down a tree with pale bark. He chopped at it with all his strength, but made little progress. "Work harder, you," the Tosevite guard watching him snapped in the Russki language.

"It shall be done," Ussmak answered. He did some more chopping, with results equally unsatisfactory to the guard. When he first came to the camp, that would have left him quivering with fear. Now it rolled off his skinny flanks. They had put him here. Try as they would, how could they do worse?

He shambled back to camp for lunch. Worn as he was, he could eat little. Again, someone quickly disposed of his leftovers. When, too soon, it was time to return to the forest, he stumbled and fell and had trouble getting up again. Another male, aided him, half guiding, half pushing him out toward the Tosevite trees.

He took up his axe and went back to work on the pale-barked tree. Try as he would, he could not make the blade take more than timid nips at the trunk. He was too weak and too apathetic for anything more. If he did not chop it down, if the work gang did not saw it into the right lengths of wood, they would fall short of their norm and would get only penalty rations. *So what?* Ussmak thought. He hadn't been able to eat a regular ration, so why should he care if he got less?

All the other males would get less, too, of course. He could not care about that, either. A proper male of the Race would have; he knew as much. But he'd begun to get detached from the rest of the Race when a Tosevite sniper killed Votal, his first landcruiser commander. Ginger had made things worse. Then he'd lost another good landcruiser crew, and then he'd led the mutiny for which he'd had such hope. And the results of that had been . . . this. No, he was no proper male, no longer.

He was so tired. He set down the axe. *I'll rest for a moment,* he thought.

"Work!" a guard shouted.

"Gavno?" Ussmak said, adding an interrogative cough. Grudgingly, the Big Ugly swung aside the muzzle of his weapon and bobbed his head up and down to grant permission. The guards let you evacuate your bowels—most of the time. It was one of the few things they did let you do.

Stumbling slowly away from the tree, Ussmak went behind a screen of bushes. He squatted to relieve himself. Nothing happened—not surprising, not when he was so empty inside. He tried to rise, but instead toppled over onto his side. He took a breath. A little later, he took another. Quite a bit later, he took one more.

Of themselves, the nictitating membranes slid across his eyes. His eyelids drooped, closed. In those last moments, he wondered if Emperors past would accept his spirit in spite of all he had done. Soon, he found out what he would find out.

When the Lizard didn't come out of the bushes after taking a shit, Yuri Andreyevich Palchinsky went in after it. He had to scuffle around to find it, and it would not come out when he called. "Stinking thing will pay," he muttered.

Then he did find it, by tripping over it and almost falling on his face. He cursed and drew back his foot to give it a good kick, but didn't. Why bother? The damn thing was already dead.

He picked it up, slung it over his shoulder—it didn't weigh anything to speak of—and carried it back toward the camp. Off to one side was a trench in which to toss the ones who starved or worked themselves to death this week. In went the latest body, on top of a lot of others.

"We're liable to fill this one up before it's time to dig next week's," Palchinsky muttered. He shrugged. That wasn't his worry. The work gang was. He turned his back on the mass grave and headed out to the woods.

"We have shown we can be merciful," Liu Han declared. "We have let one little scaly devil go back to his kind in spite of his crimes against the workers and peasants." *I have let him go in spite of his crimes against me,* she added to herself. *Let no one say now that I cannot put the interests of the Party, the interests of the People's Liberation Army, above my own.* "In a few days, the truce to which we agreed with the scaly devils expires. They still refuse to make us party to the larger cease-fire. We shall show them we can be strong as dragons, too. They will become sorry enough to make concessions."

She sat down. The men of the Peking central committee put their heads together, discussing what she had said and how she said it. Nieh Ho-T'ing murmured something to a newcomer, a handsome, plump-cheeked man whose name she hadn't caught. The man nodded. He sent Liu Han an admiring glance. She wondered if he was admiring her words or her body. She stared back steadily, measuring him with her eyes. *Country bumpkin,* she decided, forgetting for a moment how recently she had been a peasant with no politics whatever.

Sitting on Nieh's other side was Hsia Shou-Tao. He got to his feet. Liu Han had been sure he would. If she said the Yangtze flowed from west to east, he would disagree because she had said it.

Nieh Ho-T'ing raised a warning finger, but Hsia plunged ahead anyhow: "Zeal is important to the revolutionary cause, but so is caution. Through too much aggressiveness, we are liable to force the little devils into strong responses against us. A campaign of low-level harassment strikes me as a better plan, one more likely to yield the results we desire, than going at once from truce to all-out war."

Hsia looked around the room to see what sort of reaction he'd received. Several men were nodding, but others, among them four or five upon whom he'd counted, sat silent and stony. Liu Han smiled inside while keeping her own features impassive. As was her way, she'd prepared this ground before she began to fight on it. Had Hsia Shou-Tao an ounce of sense, he would have realized that beforehand. Learning of it now, the hard way, made his face take on almost the rictus of agony it had worn when Liu Han kneed him in the private parts.

To her surprise, the bumpkinish fellow by Nieh Ho-T'ing spoke up: "While war and politics cannot be divorced for a single instant, still it is sometimes necessary to remind the foe that power springs ultimately from the barrel of a gun. The little scaly devils, in my view, must be forcibly shown that their occupation is temporary and shall in the end surely fail. Thus, as Comrade Liu has so ably stated, we shall strike them a series of hard blows the instant the truce expires, gauging our subsequent actions on their response."

He didn't talk like a bumpkin; he talked like an educated man, perhaps even a poet. And now, up and down the table, heads bobbed in approval of his words. Liu Han saw more was involved there than how well he'd spoken: he had authority here, authority everyone acknowledged without question. She wished she'd learned what his name was.

"As usual, Mao Tse-Tung analyzes clearly," Nieh Ho-T'ing said. "His viewpoint is most reasonable, and we shall carry out our program against the little scaly devils as he directs."

Again, the members of the Peking central committee nodded as if a single puppeteer controlled all their heads. Liu Han nodded along with everyone else. Her eyes were wide with amazement, though, as she stared at the man who headed the revolutionary cause throughout China. Mao Tse-Tung had thought well of something *she* said?

He looked back at her, beaming like Ho Tei, the fat little god of luck in whom proper Communists did not believe but whom Liu Han had trouble dismissing from her mind. Yes, he'd approved of her words. His face said that clearly. And yes, he was looking at her as a man looks at a woman: not crudely, as Hsia Shou-Tao did when he all but spread her legs with his eyes, but unmistakably all the same.

She wondered what she ought to do about that. She'd already had doubts about her attachment to Nieh Ho-T'ing, doubts both ideological and personal. She was a little surprised to note Mao's interest; a lot of the central committee members, probably most of them, lusted after revolution more than after women. Hsia was a horrible example of why that rule worked well. But Mao was surely a special case.

She'd heard he was married. Even if he did want her, even if he did bed her, she was certain he wouldn't leave his wife for her: some sort of actress, if she remembered rightly. How much influence could she gain as a mistress, and was that enough to make the offer of her body worthwhile? Had she felt no spark, she wouldn't have considered the notion for an instant; thanks to the scaly devils, she'd had far too much of coupling with men she did not want. But she'd thought Mao attractive before she had any idea who he was.

She smiled at him, just a little. He smiled, too, politely. Nieh Ho-T'ing noticed nothing. He tended to be blind that way; she sometimes thought she was more a convenience for him than a proper lover. The foreign devil Bobby Fiore had shown far more consideration for her as a person.

What to do, then? Part of that, of course, depended on Mao. But Liu Han, with a woman's ancient wisdom, knew that, if she showed herself to be interested, he would probably lie down beside her.

Did she want to do that? Hard to be sure. Would the benefits outweigh the risks and annoyances? She didn't have to decide right away. The Communists thought in terms of years, five-year plans, decades of struggle. The little scaly devils, she'd learned, thought in decades, centuries, millennia. She hated the little devils, but they were too powerful to be dismissed as stupid. Viewed from their perspective, or even that of the Party, leaping ahead with a seduction before you worked out the consequences was foolish, nothing else but.

She smiled at Mao again. It might well not matter, anyhow, not today. Who could guess how long he'd be here? She'd never seen him in Peking before, and might not see him again any time soon. But he likely would come back: that only stood to reason. When he did, she wanted him to remember her. By then, whenever *then* was, she would have made up her mind. She had plenty of time. And, whichever way she decided, the choice would be *hers*.

Mordechai Anielewicz had played a lot of cat-and-mouse games since the Nazis invaded Poland to open the Second World War. In every one of them, though, against the Germans, against the Lizards, against what Mordechai Chaim Rumkowski thought of as the legitimate Jewish administration of Lodz, playing the Germans and Lizards off against each other, he'd been the mouse, operating against larger, more powerful foes.

Now he was the cat, and finding he didn't much care for the role. Somewhere out there, Otto Skorzeny was lurking. He didn't know where. He didn't know how much Skorzeny knew. He didn't know what the SS man was planning. He didn't like the feeling one bit.

"If you were Skorzeny, what would you do?" he asked Heinrich Jäger. Jäger was, after all, not only a German but a man who'd worked closely with the commando extraordinaire. Asking a German felt odd, anyhow. Intellectually, he knew Jäger was no Jew-butcher. Emotionally . . .

The panzer colonel scratched his head. "If I were in charge instead of Skorzeny, I'd lie low till I knew enough to strike, then hit quick and hard." He chuckled wryly. "But whether that's what he'll do, I couldn't begin to tell you. He has his own way of getting things done. Sometimes I think he's daft—till he brings it off."

"Nobody's set eyes on him since I did," Anielewicz said, frowning. "He might have fallen off the face of the earth—though that'd be too much to ask for, wouldn't it? Maybe he is lying low."

"He can't do that for too long, though," Jäger pointed out. "If he finds out where the bomb is, he'll try to set it off. It's late already, of course, and a major attack hinges on it. He won't wait."

"We've taken out the detonator," Mordechai said. "It's not in the bomb any more, though we can get it to the bomb in a hurry if we have to."

Jäger shrugged. "That shouldn't matter. If Skorzeny didn't bring another one, he's a fool—and a fool he's not. Besides which, he's an engineer; he'd know how to install it." An engineering student himself, Anielewicz grimaced. He wanted nothing in common with the SS man.

Ludmila Gorbunova asked, "Will he have men he can recruit here in Lodz, or is he all alone in this city?"

Anielewicz looked to Jäger. Jäger shrugged again. "This town was under the rule of the *Reich* for some time before the Lizards came. Are there still Germans here?"

"From the days when it was Litzmannstadt, you mean?" Mordechai asked, and shook his head without waiting for an answer. "No, after the Lizards came, we made most of the Aryan colonists pack up and go. The Poles did the same thing with them. And do you know what? We don't miss the Germans a bit, either."

Jäger looked at him steadily. Anielewicz felt himself flushing. If any man alive was entitled to score points off a German soldier, he was. A German soldier, yes, but not *this* German soldier. If it hadn't been for *this* German soldier, he wouldn't be here *to* score points. He had to remember that, no matter how hard it was.

"Not many Germans, eh?" Jäger said matter-of-factly. "If any are left, Skorzeny will find them. And he'll probably have connections among the Poles. They don't like you Jews, either."

Was he trying to score points, too? Mordechai couldn't be sure. Even if he was, that didn't make him wrong. Ludmila said, "But the Poles, if they help Skorzeny, they'll be blowing themselves up, too."

"You know that," Jäger said. "I know that. But the Poles don't necessarily know it. If Skorzeny says, 'Here, I have a big bomb hidden that will blow up all the Jews but not you,' they're liable to believe him."

"He's a good liar?" Anielewicz asked, trying to get more of a feel for his opponent than he could from the unending propaganda the *Reich* pumped out about Skorzeny.

But Jäger might have been part of Göbbels' propaganda mill. "He's good at everything that has to do with being a raider," he answered with no trace of irony, then proceeded to give an example: "He went into Besançon, for instance, with a sack of ginger to bribe the Lizards, and he came out driving one of their panzers."

"I do not believe this," Ludmila said, before Anielewicz could. "I heard it reported on German shortwave wireless, but I do not believe it."

"It's true whether you believe it or not," Jäger said. "I was there. I saw his head sticking up out of the driver's hatch. I didn't believe he could do it, either; I thought he was going in there to commit suicide, nothing more. I was wrong. I have never underestimated him since."

Anielewicz took that evaluation, which he found almost too depressing to contemplate, to Solomon Gruver and Bertha Fleishman. Gruver's mouth turned down at the corners, making him look even gloomier than he usually did. "He can't be that good," the former sergeant said. "If he were that good, he'd be God, and he isn't. He's just a man."

"We have to put our ears to the ground among the Poles," Bertha said. "If anything is going on with them, we need to hear about it fast as we can."

Mordechai sent her a grateful look. She took this whole business as seriously as he did. Given the levelheadedness she usually displayed, that was a sign it needed to be taken seriously.

"So we listen. So what?" Gruver said. "If he's that good, we won't hear anything. We won't spot him unless he wants to be spotted, and we won't know what he's up to till he decides to hit us."

"All of which is true, and none of which means we can stop trying," Anielewicz said. He slammed his open hand into the side of the fire engine. That hurt his hand more than the engine. "If only I'd been certain I recognized him! If only I'd come out of—where I came out of—a few seconds earlier, so I could have seen his face. If, if, if—" It ate at him.

"Even thinking he was in Lodz put us on alert," Bertha said. "Who knows what he might have done if he'd got here without our knowing it?"

"He turned a corner," Anielewicz said, running it through his mind again like a piece of film from the cinema. "He turned a corner, and then another one, very quickly. The second time, I had to guess which way he'd gone, and I guessed wrong."

"Don't keep beating yourself over the head with it, Mordechai," Bertha said. "It can't be helped now, and you did everything you could."

"That's so," Gruver rumbled. "No doubt about it."

Anielewicz hardly heard him. He was looking at Bertha Fleishman. She'd never called him by his first name before, not that he remembered. He would have remembered, too; he was certain of that.

She was looking at him, too. She flushed a little when their eyes met, but she didn't look away. He'd known she liked him well enough. He liked her well enough, too. Except when she smiled, she was plain and mousy. He'd been to bed with women far prettier. He suddenly seemed to hear Solomon Gruver's deep voice again, going, *So what?* Gruver-that-wasn't had a point. He'd bedded those women and enjoyed himself doing it, but he hadn't for an instant thought of spending his life with any of them. Bertha, though . . .

"If we live through this—" he said. The five words made a complete sentence, if you knew how to listen to them.

Bertha Fleishman did. "Yes. If we do," she replied: a complete answer.

The real Solomon Gruver seemed less attentive to what was going on around him than the imaginary one inside Anielewicz's head. "If we live through this," he said, "we're going to have to do something better with that thing we have than leaving it where it is. But if we move it now, we just draw attention to it, and that lets this Skorzeny *mamzer* have his chance."

"That's all true, Solomon—every word of it," Mordechai agreed solemnly. Then he started to laugh. A moment later, so did Bertha.

"And what is so funny?" Gruver demanded with ponderous dignity. "Did I make a joke and, God forbid, not know it?"

"God forbid," Anielewicz said, and laughed harder.

As George Bagnall and Ken Embry walked to Dover College, jet engines roared overhead. Bagnall's automatic reaction was to find the nearest hole in the ground and jump into it. With an effort, he checked himself and looked upward. For once, the thinking, rational part of his brain had got it right: those were Meteors up there, not Lizard fighter-bombers.

"Bloody hell!" Embry burst out; conditioned reflex must nearly have got the better of him, too. "We've only been gone a year and a half, but it feels as though we've stepped back into 1994, not 1944."

"Doesn't it just," Bagnall agreed. "They were flying those things when we left, but not many of them. You don't see Hurricanes at all any more, and they're phasing out Spitfires fast as they can. It's a brave new world, and no mistake."

"Still a place for bomber crew—for the next twenty minutes, anyhow," Embry said. "They haven't put jets on Lancs, not yet they haven't. But everything else they have done—" He shook his head. "No wonder they sent us back to school. We're almost as obsolete as if we'd been flying Sopwith Camels. Trouble is, of course, we haven't been flying *anything*."

"It's even worse for Jones," Bagnall said. "We're still flying the same buses, even if they have changed the rest of the rules. His radars are starting to come from a different world: literally."

"Same with our bomb-aiming techniques," Embry said as they climbed the poured-concrete steps and strode down the corridor toward their classroom.

The lecturer there, a flight lieutenant named Constantine Jordan, was already scribbling on the blackboard, though it still lacked a couple of minutes of the hour. Bagnall looked around as he took his seat. Most of his classmates had a pale, pasty look to them; some were in obvious if stifled pain. That made sense—besides the rarities like Bagnall and Embry, the people who'd been out of service long enough to require refresher courses were the ones who'd been badly wounded. A couple had dreadful scars on their faces; what lay under their uniforms was anyone's guess, though not one Bagnall cared to make.

An instant before the clock in the bell tower chimed eleven, Flight Lieutenant Jordan turned and began: "As I noted at the end of yesterday's session, what the Lizards call *skelkwank* bids fair to revolutionize bomb aiming. *Skelkwank* light, unlike the ordinary sort"—he pointed up to the electric lamps—"is completely organized, you might say. It's all of the same frequency, the same amplitude, the same phase. The Lizards have several ways of creating such light. We're busy working on them to see which ones we can most readily make for ourselves. But that's largely beside the point. We've captured enough generators of *skelkwank* light to have equipped a good many bombers with them, and that's why you're here."

Bagnall's pencil scurried across the notebook. Every so often, he'd pause to shake his hand back and forth to wring out writer's cramp. All this was new to him, and all vital—now he was able to understand the term he'd first met in Pskov. Amazing, all the things you could do with *skelkwank* light.

Jordan went on, "What we do is, we illuminate the target with a *skelkwank* lamp. A sensor head properly attuned to it manipulates the fins on the bomb and guides it to the target. So long as the light stays on the target, the guidance will work. We've all seen it used against us more often than we'd fancy. Again, we're operating with captured sensor heads, which are in limited supply, but we're also exploring ways and means to manufacture them. Yes, Mr. McBride? You have a question?"

"Yes, sir," replied the flying officer who'd raised his hand. "These new munitions are all very well, sir, but if we're flying against the Lizards, how do we approach the target closely enough to have some hope of destroying it? Their weapons can strike us at much greater range than that at which we can respond. Believe me, sir, I know that." He was one of the men who had scar tissue slagging half his face.

"It is a difficulty," Jordan admitted. "We are also seeking to copy the guided rockets with which the Lizards have shot down so many of our aircraft, but that's proving slower work, even with the assistance of Lizard prisoners."

"We'd best not fight another war with them any time soon, is all I can say," McBride answered, "or we'll come out of it with no pilots left at all. Without rockets to match theirs, we're hors d'oeuvres, nothing better."

Bagnall had never thought of himself as a canapé, but the description fit all too well. He wished he could have gone up against the *Luftwaffe* with a Lancaster armed with *skelkwank* bombs and rockets to swat down the *Messerschmitts* before they bored in for the kill. After a moment, he realized he might fly with those weapons against the Germans one day. But if he did, the Germans were liable to have them, too.

Flight Lieutenant Jordan kept lecturing for several minutes after the noon bells rang. Again, that was habit. At last, he dismissed his pupils with the warning, "Tomorrow you'll be quizzed on what we've covered this past week. Those with poor marks will be turned into toads and sent hopping after blackbeetles. Amazing what technology can do these days, is it not? See you after lunch."

When Bagnall and Embry went out into the corridor to head to the cafeteria for an uninspiring but free meal, Jerome Jones called to them, "Care to dine with my chum here?"

His chum was a Lizard who introduced himself in hissing English as Mzepps. When Bagnall found out he'd been a radar technician before his capture, he willingly let him join the group. Talking civilly with a Lizard felt odd, even odder than his first tense meeting with that German lieutenant-colonel in Paris, barely days after the RAF had stopped going after the Nazis.

Despite Mzepps' appearance, though, the Lizard soon struck him as a typical noncommissioned officer: worried about his job, but not much about how it fit into the bigger picture. "You Big Uglies, you all the time go why, why, why," he complained. "Who cares why? Just do. Why not important. Is word? Yes, important."

"It never has occurred to him," Jones remarked, "that if we didn't go why, why, why all the time, we should have been in no position to fight back when he and his scaly cohorts got here."

Bagnall chewed on that as he and Ken Embry headed back toward Flight Lieutenant Jordan's class. He thought about the theory Jordan was teaching along with the practical applications of what the RAF was learning from the Lizards. By everything Mzepps had said, the Lizards seldom operated that way themselves. *What* mattered more to them than *why*.

"I wonder why that is," he murmured.

"Why what is?" Embry asked, which made Bagnall realize he'd spoken aloud.

"Nothing, really," he answered. "Just being—human."

"Is that a fact?" Embry said. "You couldn't prove it by me." The RAF men in the lecture hall stared at them as they walked through the doors. As far as Bagnall knew, no one had ever done that laughing before.

A sunbeam sneaking through the slats of a Venetian blind found Ludmila Gorbunova's face and woke her. Rubbing her eyes, she sat up in bed. She wasn't used to sleeping in a bed, not any more. After blankets on the ground, a real mattress felt decadently soft.

She looked around the flat Mordechai Anielewicz had given her and Jäger. The plumbing wasn't all it might have been, the wallpaper was peeling after years of neglect—Anielewicz had apologized for that. People in Lodz, it seemed, were always apologizing to outsiders for how bad things were. They didn't seem that bad to Ludmila. She was slowly starting to think the problem was different standards of comparison. They were used to the way things here had been before the war. She was used to Kiev. What that said—

She stopped worrying about what that said, because her motion woke Jäger up. He came awake quickly and completely. She'd seen that, the last couple of nights. She had the same trick. She hadn't had it before the war started. She wondered if Jäger had.

He reached up and set a hand on her bare shoulder. Then he surprised her by chuckling. "What is funny?" she asked, a little indignantly.

"This," he answered, waving at the flat. "Everything. Here we are, two people who for love of each other have run away from all the things we used to think important. We can't go back to them, ever again. We are—what do the diplomats say?—stateless persons, that's what we are. It's like something out of a cheap novel." As he had a way of doing, he quickly sobered. "Or it would be, if it weren't for the small detail of the explosive-metal bomb cluttering up our lives."

"Yes, if it weren't." Ludmila didn't want to get out of bed and get dressed. Here, naked between the sheets with Jäger, she too could pretend love had been the only thing that brought them to Lodz, and that treason and fear not only for the city but for the whole world had had nothing to do with it.

With a sigh, she did get up and start to dress. With a matching sigh an octave deeper, Jäger joined her. They'd only just finished putting on their clothes when somebody knocked on the door. Jäger chuckled again; maybe he'd had amorous thoughts, too, and also set them aside. They would have had to answer the door anyhow. Now, at least, they weren't interrupted.

Jäger opened it, as warily as if he expected to find Otto Skorzeny waiting in the hallway. Ludmila didn't see how that was possible, but she hadn't seen how a lot of Skorzeny's exploits Jäger talked about were possible, either.

Skorzeny wasn't out there. Mordechai Anielewicz was, a Mauser slung over his shoulder. He let it slide down his arm and leaned it against the wall. "Do you know what I wish we could do?" he said. "I wish we could get word to the Lizards—just as a rumor, mind you—that Skorzeny was in town. If they and their puppets were looking for him, too, it would hold his feet to the fire and make him do something instead of lying back and letting us do all the running around."

"You haven't done that, have you?" Jäger said sharply.

"I said I wished I could," Anielewicz answered. "No, if the Lizards find out Skorzeny's here, they're going to start wondering what he's doing here—and they'll start looking all over for him. We can't afford that, which leaves first move up to him: he has the white pieces, sure enough."

"You play chess?" Ludmila asked. Outside the Soviet Union, she'd found, not so many people did. She had to use the Russian word; she didn't know how to say it in German.

Anielewicz understood. "Yes, I play," he answered. "Not as well as I'd like, but everyone says that."

Jäger kept his mind on the business at hand: "What *are* you doing—as opposed to the things you're reluctantly not doing, I mean?"

"I understood you," Anielewicz answered with a wry grin. "I've got as many men with guns on the street as I can afford to put there, and I'm checking with every landlord who won't run straight to the Lizards to find out if he's putting up Skorzeny. So far—" He snapped his fingers to show what he had so far.

"Have you checked the whorehouses?" Jäger asked. That was another German word Ludmila didn't know. When she asked about it and he explained, she thought at first he'd made a joke. Then she realized he was deadly serious.

Mordechai Anielewicz snapped his fingers again, this time in annoyance. "No, and I should have," he said, sounding angry at himself. "One of those would make a good hideout for him, wouldn't it?" He nodded to Jäger. "Thanks. I wouldn't have thought of that myself."

Ludmila wouldn't have thought of it, either. The world outside the Soviet Union had corruptions new to her, along with its luxuries. *Decadent,* she thought again. She shook her head. She'd have to get used to it. No going back to the *rodina,* not now, not ever, not unless she wanted endless years in the *gulag* or, perhaps more likely, a quick end with a bullet in the back of the head. She'd thrown away her old life as irrevocably as Jäger had his. The question remained, could they build a new one together here, this being the sole remaining choice?

If they didn't stop Skorzeny, that answer was depressingly obvious, too.

Anielewicz said, "I'm going back to the fire station: I have to ask some questions. I haven't worried much about the *nafkehs*—the whores," he amplified when he saw Ludmila and Jäger didn't catch the Yiddish word, "but somebody will know all about 'em. Men are men—even Jews." He looked a challenge at Jäger.

The German, to Ludmila's relief, didn't rise to it. "Men are men," he agreed mildly. "Would I be here if I didn't think so?"

"No," Anielewicz said. "Men are men—even Germans, maybe." He touched a finger to the brim of the cloth cap he wore, reslung his rifle, and hurried away.

Jäger sighed. "This isn't going to be easy, however much we wish it would. Even if we stop Skorzeny, we're exiles here." He laughed. "We'd be a lot worse off than exiles, though, if the SS got its hooks in me again."

"I was just thinking the same thing," Ludmila said. "Not about the SS, but about the NKVD, I mean." She smiled happily. If two people thought the same thing at the same time, that had to mean they were well matched. But for herself, Jäger was all she had left in the world; not believing the two of them were well matched would have left her desolately lonesome. Her eyes slipped to the bed. Her smile changed, ever so slightly. They were well matched there, that was certain.

Then Jäger said, "Well, not surprising. We haven't got much else to think about here, have we? There's us—and Skorzeny."

"Da," Ludmila said, disappointed out of the German she'd mostly been speaking and back into Russian. What she'd taken as a good sign was to Jäger merely a commonplace. How sad that made her showed how giddy she was feeling.

On the table lay a chunk of black bread. Jäger went into the kitchen, came back with a bone-handled knife, and cut the chunk in two. He handed Ludmila half of it. Without the slightest trace of irony, he said, "German service at its finest."

Was he joking? Did he expect her to take him literally? She wondered as she ate her breakfast. That she didn't know and couldn't guess with any real confidence of being right bothered her: it reminded her how little she truly knew of the man she'd helped rescue and whose fate she'd linked with her own. She didn't want to be reminded of that—very much the contrary.

When she'd flown away with him, he'd come straight out of the hands of the SS. He hadn't had a weapon then, of course. Anielewicz had given him a Schmeisser after he got to Lodz, a sign the Jewish fighting leader trusted him perhaps further than he was willing to admit to himself. Jäger had spent a lot of time since with oil and brushes and cloth, getting the submachine gun into what he reckoned proper fighting condition.

Now he started to check it yet again. Watching how intent his face grew as he worked made Ludmila snort, half in annoyance, half in fascination. When he didn't look up, she snorted again, louder. That distracted him enough to make him remember she was there. She said, "Sometimes I think you Germans ought to marry machines, not people. Schultz, your sergeant—you act the same way he did."

"If you take care of your tools, as you should, they take proper care of you when you need them." Jäger spoke as automatically as if he were reciting the multiplication table. "If what you need them for is keeping yourself alive, you'd better take care of them, or you'll be too dead to kick yourself for not doing it."

"It's not that you do it. It's *how* you do it, like there is nothing in the world but you and the machine, whatever it is, and you are listening to it. I have never seen Russians do this," Ludmila said. "Schultz was the same way. He thought well of you. Perhaps he was trying to be like you."

That seemed to amuse Jäger, who checked the action of the cocking handle, nodded to himself, and slung the Schmeisser over his shoulder. "Didn't you tell me he'd found a Russian lady, too?"

"Yes. I don't think they got on as well as we do, but yes." Ludmila hadn't told him how much time Schultz had spent trying to get her trousers down as well as Tatiana's. She didn't intend to tell him that. Schultz hadn't done it, and she hadn't—quite—had to smash him across the face with the barrel of her pistol to get him to take his hands off her.

Jäger said, "Let's go to the fire station ourselves. I want to tell

Anielewicz something. It's not just whorehouses—Skorzeny might be taking shelter in a church, too. He's an Austrian, so he's a Catholic—or he was probably raised as one, anyhow; he's about the least godly man I know. But that's one more place, or set of places, to look for him."

"You have all sorts of ideas." Ludmila would not have thought of anything that had to do with religion. Here, though, that outmoded notion proved strategically relevant. "It is worth checking, I think, yes. The part of Lodz that is not Jewish is Catholic."

"Yes." Jäger headed for the door. Ludmila followed. They walked downstairs hand in hand. The fire station was only a few blocks away—go down the street, turn onto Lutomierska, and you were there.

They went down the street. They were about to turn onto Lutomierska when a great thunderclap, a noise like the end of the world, smote the air. For a dreadful moment, Ludmila thought Skorzeny had touched off his bomb in spite of everything they'd done to stop him.

But then, as glass blew out of windows that had held it, she realized she was wrong. This explosion had been close by. She'd seen an explosive-metal bomb go off. Had she been so near one of those blasts, she would have been dead before she realized anything had happened.

People were screaming. Some ran away from the place where the bomb had gone off, others toward it to help the wounded. She and Jäger were among the latter, pushing past men and women trying to flee.

Through stunned ears, she caught snatches of horrified comments in Yiddish and Polish: "—horsecart in front—" "—just stopped there—" "—man went away—" "—blew up in front of—"

By then, she'd come close enough to see the building in front of which the bomb had blown up. The fire station on Lutomierska Street was a pile of rubble, through which flames were beginning to creep. *"Bozhemoi,"* she said softly.

Jäger was looking at the dazed and bleeding victims, grim purpose on his face. "Where's Anielewicz?" he demanded, as if willing the Jewish fighting leader to emerge from the wreckage. Then he spoke another word: "Skorzeny."

☆ XX ☆

The Lizard named Oyyag dipped his head in a gesture of submission he'd learned from the NKVD. "It shall be done, superior sir," he said. "We shall meet all norms required of us."

"That is good, headmale," David Nussboym answered in the language of the Race. "If you do, your rations will be restored to the normal daily allotment." After Ussmak died, the Lizards of Alien Prisoner Barracks Three had fallen far below their required labor quotas, and had gone hungry—or rather, hungrier—on account of it. Now, at last, the new headmale, though he'd had no great status before his capture, was starting to whip them back into shape.

Oyyag, Nussboym thought, would make a better headmale for the barracks than Ussmak had. The other Lizard, perhaps because he'd been a mutineer, had tried to make waves in camp, too. If Colonel Skriabin hadn't found a way to break the hunger strike he'd started, no telling how much mischief and disruption in routine he might have caused.

Oyyag swiveled his eye turrets rapidly in all directions, making sure none of the other males in the barracks was paying undue attention to his conversation with Nussboym. He lowered his voice and spoke such Russian as he had: "This other thing, I do. I do it, you do like you say."

"Da," Nussboym said, wishing he were as sure he could deliver on his promise as he sounded.

Only one way to find out whether he could or not. He left the barracks hall and headed for the camp headquarters. Luck was with him. When he approached Colonel Skriabin's office, the commandant's secretary was not guarding the way in. Nussboym stood in the doorway and waited to be noticed.

Eventually, Skriabin looked up from the report he'd been

writing. Trains were reaching the camp more reliably now that
the cease-fire was in place. With paper no longer in short supply,
Skriabin was busy catching up on all the bureaucratic minutiae
he'd had to delay simply because he couldn't record the relevant
information.

"Come in, Nussboym," he said in Polish, putting down his pen.
The smudges of ink on his fingers told how busy he'd been. He
seemed glad of the chance for a break. Nussboym nodded to himself. He'd hoped to catch the colonel in a receptive mood, and here
his hope was coming true. Skriabin pointed to the hard chair in
front of his desk. "Sit down. You have come to see me for a
reason, of course." *You'd better not be wasting my time,* was what
he meant.

"Yes, Comrade Colonel." Nussboym sat gratefully. Skriabin
was in a good mood; he didn't offer the chair at every visit, nor did
he always speak Polish instead of making Nussboym work
through his Russian. "I can report that the new Lizard headmale is
cooperative in every way. We should have far less trouble from
Barracks Three than we've known in the past."

"This is good." Skriabin steepled his inky fingers. "Is it the only
thing you have to report?"

Nussboym made haste to reply: "No, Comrade Colonel."
Skriabin nodded—had he been interrupted just for that, he would
have made Nussboym regret it. The interpreter went on, "The
other matter, though, is so delicate, I hesitate to bring it to your
attention." He was glad he was able to use Polish with Skriabin; he
could never have been subtle enough in Russian.

"Delicate?" The camp commandant raised an eyebrow. "We
seldom hear such a word in this place."

"I understand. This, however"—Nussboym looked back over
his shoulder to make certain the desk out there remained unoccu-
pied—"concerns your secretary, Apfelbaum."

"Does it?" Skriabin kept his voice neutral. "All right. Go on.
You have my attention. What about Apfelbaum?"

"Day before yesterday, Comrade Colonel, Apfelbaum and I
were walking outside Barracks Three with Oyyag, discussing
ways the Lizard prisoners could meet their norms." Nussboym
picked his words with great care. "And Apfelbaum said everyone's life would be easier if the Great Stalin—he used the title sar-
castically, I must say—if the Great Stalin worried as much about
how much the Soviet people ate as he did about how hard they
worked for him. That is exactly what he said. He was speaking
Russian, not Yiddish, so Oyyag could understand, and I had

trouble following him, so I had to ask him to repeat himself. He did, and was even more sarcastic the second time than the first."

"Is that so?" Skriabin said. Nussboym nodded. Skriabin scratched his head. "And the Lizard heard it, too, you say, and understood it?" Nussboym nodded again. The NKVD colonel looked up to the boards of the ceiling. "He will, I suppose, make a statement to this effect?"

"If it is required of him, Comrade Colonel, I think he would," Nussboym replied. "Would it be? Perhaps I should not have mentioned it, but—"

"*But* indeed," Skriabin said heavily. "I suppose you now think it necessary to file a formal written denunciation against Apfelbaum."

Nussboym feigned reluctance. "I would really rather not. As you recall when I denounced one of the *zeks* with whom I formerly worked, this is not something I care to do. It strikes me as—"

"Useful?" Skriabin suggested. Nussboym looked back at him with wide eyes, glad the NKVD man could not see his thoughts. No, they hadn't put him in charge of this camp by accident. He reached into his desk and pulled out a fresh form headed with incomprehensible Cyrillic instructions. "Write out what he said—Polish or Yiddish will do. That way, we will have it on file. I suppose the Lizard would talk about this to all and sundry. You would never do such a thing yourself, of course."

"Comrade Colonel, the idea would never enter my mind." Nussboym put shocked innocence into his voice. He knew he was lying, as did Colonel Skriabin. But, like any game, this one had rules. He accepted a pen and wrote rapidly. After scrawling his signature at the bottom of the denunciation, he handed the paper back to Skriabin.

He supposed Apfelbaum would come back with a denunciation of his own. But he'd picked his target carefully. Skriabin's clerk would have a hard time getting his fellow politicals to back any accusations he made: they disliked him because of the way he sucked up to the commandant and the privileges he got because he was Skriabin's aide. The ordinary *zeks* despised him—they despised all politicals. And he didn't know any Lizards.

Skriabin said, "From another man, I might think this denunciation made because he wanted Apfelbaum's position."

"You could not possibly say that of me," Nussboym answered. "I could not fill his position, and would never claim I could. If the camp functioned in Polish or Yiddish, then yes, you might say that about me. But I do not have enough Russian to do his job. All I want is to let the truth be known."

"You are the soul of virtue," Skriabin said dryly. "I note, however, that virtue is not necessarily an asset on the road to success."

"Indeed, Comrade Colonel," Nussboym said. *Be careful,* the NKVD man was telling him. He intended to be careful. If he could shake Apfelbaum loose from his job, get him sent off to some harder camp in disgrace, everyone here would move up. His own place would improve. Now that he'd acknowledged he was in effect a political and cast his lot with the camp administration, he thought he might as well take as much advantage of the situation as he could.

After all, if you didn't look out for yourself, who was going to look out for you? He'd felt miserable after Skriabin had made him sign the first denunciation, the one against Ivan Fyodorov. This one, though, this one didn't bother him at all.

Offhandedly, Skriabin said, "A train bringing in new prisoners will arrive tomorrow. A couple of cars' worth, I am given to understand, will be women."

"That is most interesting," Nussboym said. "Thank you for telling me." Women who knew what was good for them accommodated themselves to the powerful people in the camp: first to the NKVD men, then to the prisoners who could help make their lives tolerable . . . or otherwise. The ones who didn't know what was good for them went out and cut trees and dug ditches like any other *zeks*.

Nussboym smiled to himself. Surely a man as . . . practical as he could find some equally . . . practical woman for himself— maybe even one who spoke Yiddish. Wherever you were, you did what you could to get by.

A Lizard with a flashlight approached the campfire around which Mutt Daniels and Herman Muldoon sat swapping lies. "That is you, Second Lieutenant Daniels?" he called in pretty good English.

"This here's me," Mutt agreed. "Come on over, Small-Unit Group Leader Chook. Set yourself down. You boys are gonna be pullin' out tomorrow mornin'—did I hear that right?"

"It is truth," Chook said. "We are to be no more in the Illinois place. We are to move out, first back to main base in Kentucky, then out of this not-empire of the United States. I tell you two things, Second Lieutenant Daniels. The first thing is, I am not sorry to go. The second thing is, I come here to say good-bye."

"That's mighty nice of you," Mutt said. "Good-bye to you, too."

"A sentimental Lizard," Muldoon said, snorting. "Who woulda thunk it?"

"Chook here ain't a bad guy," Daniels answered. "Like he said when we got the truce the first time, him and the Lizards he's in charge of got more in common with us than we do with the brass hats way back of the line."

"Yeah, that's right enough," Muldoon answered, at the same time as Chook was saying, "Truth," again. Muldoon went on, "It was like that Over There, wasn't it? Us and the Germans in the trenches, we was more like each other than us and the fancy Dans back in Gay Paree, that's for damn sure. Show those boys a louse and they'd faint dead away."

"I have also for you a question, Second Lieutenant Daniels," Chook said. "Does it molest you to have me ask you this?"

"Does it what?" Mutt said. Then he figured out what the Lizard was talking about. Chook's English was pretty good, but it wasn't perfect. "No, go ahead and ask, whatever the hell it is. You and me, we've got on pretty good since we stopped tryin' to blow each other's heads off. Your troubles, they look a lot like my troubles, 'cept in a mirror."

"This is what I ask, then," Chook said. "Now that this war, this fighting, this is done, what do you do?"

Herman Muldoon whistled softly between his teeth. So did Mutt. "That's the question, okay," he said. "First thing I do, I reckon, is see how long the Army wants to keep me. I ain't what you'd call a young man." He rubbed his bristly chin. Most of those bristles were white, not brown.

"What do you do if you are not a soldier?" the Lizard asked. Mutt explained about being a baseball manager. He wondered if he would have to explain about baseball, too, but he didn't. Chook said, "I have seen Tosevites, some almost hatchlings, some larger, playing this game. You were paid for guiding a team of them?" He added an interrogative cough. When Mutt agreed that he was, the Lizard said, "You must be highly skilled, to be able to do this for pay. Will you again, in time of peace?"

"Damfino," Daniels answered. "Who can guess what baseball's gonna look like when things straighten out? I guess maybe the first thing I do, I ever get out of the Army, I go home to Mississippi, see if I got me any family left."

Chook made a puzzled noise. He pointed west, toward the great river flowing by. "You live in a boat? Your home is on the Mississippi?" Mutt had to explain about the difference between the Mississippi River and the state of Mississippi. When he was through, the Lizard said, "You Big Uglies, sometimes you have more than one name for one place, sometimes you have more than one place for one name. It is confused. I tell no great secret to say once or twice attacks go wrong on account of this."

"Maybe we'll just have to call every town in the country Jonesville," Herman Muldoon said. He laughed, happy with his joke.

Chook laughed, too, letting his mouth fall open so the firelight shone on his teeth and on his snaky tongue. "You do not surprise me, you Tosevites, if you do this very thing." He pointed to Daniels. "Before you become a soldier, then, you command base-ball men. You are a leader from hatching?"

Again, Mutt needed a moment to understand the Lizard. "A born leader, you mean?" Now he laughed, loud and long. "I grew up on a Mississippi farm my own self. There was nigger share-croppers workin' bigger plots o' land than the one my pappy had. I got to be a manager on account of I didn't want to keep walkin' behind the ass end of a mule forever, so I ran off an' played ball instead. I was never great, but I was pretty damn good."

"I have heard before these stories of defiance of authority from Tosevites," Chook said. "They are to me very strange. We have not any like them among the Race."

Mutt thought about that: a whole planet full of Lizards, all doing their jobs and going on about their lives for no better reason than that somebody above them told them that was what they were supposed to do. When you looked at it that way, it was like what the Reds and the Nazis wanted to do to people, only more so. But to Chook, it seemed like water to a fish. He didn't think about the bad parts, just about how it gave his life order and meaning.

"How about you, Small-Unit Group Leader?" Daniels asked Chook. "After you Lizards pull out of the U.S. of A, what do you do next?"

"I go on being a soldier," the Lizard answered. "After this cease-fire with your not-empire, I go on to some part of Tosev 3 where no truce is, I fight more Big Uglies, till, soon or late, the Race wins there. Then I go to a new place again and do the same. All this for years, till colonization fleet comes."

"So you were a soldier from the git-go, then?" Mutt said. "You weren't doin' somethin' else when your big bosses decided to invade Earth and just happened to scoop you up so as you could help?"

"That would be madness," Chook exclaimed. Maybe he was taking Mutt too literally—and maybe he wasn't. He went on, "A hundred and five tens of years ago, the 63rd Emperor Fatuz, who reigned then and now helps watch spirits of our dead, he set forth a Soldier's Time."

Mutt could hear the capital letters thudding into place, but didn't know what exactly they meant. "A Soldier's Time?" he echoed.

"Yes, a Soldier's Time," the Lizard said. "A time when the Race needed soldiers, at first to train the males who would go with the conquest fleet, and then, in my own age group and that just before mine, the males who would make up the fleet."

"Wait a minute." Mutt held up a stubby, bent forefinger. "Are you tryin' to tell me that when it's not a Soldier's Time, you Lizards, you don't have any soldiers?"

"If we are not building a conquest fleet to bring a new world into the Empire, what need do we have for soldiers?" Chook returned. "We do not fight among us. The Rabotevs and Hallessi are sensible subjects. They are not Tosevites, to revolt whenever they like. We have the data to make males into soldiers when the Emperor"—he looked down at the ground—"decides we need them. For thousands of years at a time, we do not need. Is it different with you Big Uglies? You fought your own war when we came. Did you have soldiers in a time between wars?"

He sounded as if he were asking whether they picked their noses and then wiped their hands on their pants. Mutt looked at Muldoon. Muldoon was already looking at him. "Yeah, we've been known to keep a soldier or two around while we're not fightin'," Mutt said.

"Just in case we might need 'em," Muldoon added, his voice dry.

"This is wasteful of resources," Chook said.

"It's even more wasteful not to keep soldiers around," Mutt said, "on account of if you don't and the country next door does, they're gonna whale the stuffing out of you, take what used to be yours, an' use it for their own selves."

The Lizard's tongue flicked out, wiggled around, and flipped back into his mouth. "Ah," he said. "Now I have understanding. You are always in possession of an enemy next door. With us of the Race, it is a thing of difference. After the Emperors"—he looked down again—"made all Home one under their rule, what need had we of soldiers? We had need only in conquest time. Then the reigning Emperor"—and again—"declared a Soldier's Time. After the ending of the conquest, we needed soldiers no more. We pensioned them, let them die, and trained no new ones till the next time of need."

Mutt let out a low, soft, wondering whistle. In a surprisingly good Cockney accent, Herman Muldoon sang out, "Old soldiers never die. They only fade away." He turned to Chook, explaining, "With us, that's just a song. I heard it Over There during the last big war. You Lizards, though, sounds like you really mean it. Ain't that a hell of a thing?"

"We mean it on Home. We mean it on Rabotev 2. We mean it on Halless 1," Chook said. "Here on Tosev 3, who knows what we mean? Here on Tosev 3, who knows what anything means? Maybe one day, Second Lieutenant Daniels, we fight again."

"Not with me, you don't," Mutt said at once. "They let me out of the Army, they ain't never gettin' me back in. An' if they do, they wouldn't want what they got. I done had all the fightin' that's in me squeezed out. You want to mix it up down line, Small-Unit Group Leader Chook, you got to pick yourself a younger man."

"Two younger men," Sergeant Muldoon agreed.

"I wish to both of you good fortune," Chook said. "We fighted each other. Now we do not fight and we are not enemies. Let it stay so." He turned and skittered out of the circle of yellow light the campfire threw.

"Ain't that somethin'?" Muldoon said in wondering tones. "I mean, ain't that just somethin'?"

"Yeah," Mutt answered, understanding exactly what he was talking about. "If they ain't got a war goin' on, they don't have any soldiers, neither. Wish we could be like that, don't you?" He didn't wait for Muldoon's nod, which came as automatically as breathing. Instead, he went on, voice dreamy, "No soldiers a-tall, not for hundreds—shitfire, maybe thousands, all I know—of years at a time." He let out a long sigh, wishing for a cigarette.

"Almost makes you wish they won the war, don't it?" Muldoon said.

"Yeah," Mutt said. "Almost."

Whatever Mordechai Anielewicz was lying on, it wasn't a feather bed. He pulled himself to his feet. Something wet was running down his cheek. When he put his hand against it, the palm came away red.

Bertha Fleishman sprawled in the street, in amongst the tumbled bricks from which he had just arisen. She had a cut on her leg and another one, a nasty one, on the side of her head that left her scalp matted with blood. She moaned: not words, just sound. Her eyes didn't quite track.

Fear running through him, Mordechai stooped and hauled her upright. His head was filled with a hissing roar, as if a giant high-pressure air hose had sprung a leak right between his ears. Through that roar, he heard not only Bertha's moan but the screams and cries and groans of dozens, scores, maybe hundreds of injured people.

If he'd walked another fifty meters closer to the fire station, he wouldn't have been injured. He would have been dead. The realization oozed slowly through his stunned brain. "If I hadn't stopped to chat with you—" he told Bertha.

She nodded, though her expression was still faraway. "What happened?" Her lips shaped the words, but they had no breath behind them—or maybe Anielewicz was even deafer than he thought.

"Some kind of explosion," he said. Then, later than he should have, he figured out what kind of explosion: "A bomb." Again, he seemed to be thinking with mud rather than brains, because he needed several more seconds before he burst out, "Skorzeny!"

The name reached Bertha Fleishman, where nothing had before it. *"Gottenyu!"* she said, loud enough for Anielewicz to hear and understand. "We have to stop him!"

That was true. They had to stop him—if they could. The Lizards had never managed it. Anielewicz wondered if anyone could. One way or the other, he was going to find out.

He looked around. There in the chaos, using a bandage from the aid kit he wore on his belt, squatted Heinrich Jäger. The old Jew who held out a mangled hand to him didn't know he'd been a *Wehrmacht* panzer colonel, or care. And Jäger, by the practiced, careful way he worked, didn't worry about the religion of the man he was helping. Beside him, his Russian girlfriend—another story about which Anielewicz knew less than he would have liked— was tying what looked like an old wool sock around a little boy's bloody knee.

Anielewicz tapped Jäger on the shoulder. The German whirled around, snatching for the submachine gun he'd set down on the pavement so he could help the old man. "You're alive," he said, relaxing a little when he realized who Mordechai was.

"I think so, anyhow." Anielewicz waved at the hurly-burly all around. "Your friend plays rough."

"This is what I told you," the German answered. He looked around, too, but only for a moment. "This is probably a diversion—probably not the only one, either. Wherever the bomb is, you'd better believe Skorzeny's somewhere close by."

As if on cue, another explosion rocked Lodz. This one came from the east; gauging the sound, Anielewicz thought it had gone off not far from the ruined factory sheltering the stolen weapon. He hadn't told Jäger where that factory was, not quite trusting him. Now he had no more choice. If Skorzeny was around there, he'd need all the help he could get.

"Let's go," he said. Jäger nodded, quickly finished the bandaging job, and grabbed the Schmeisser. The Russian girl—the Russian pilot—Ludmila—drew her pistol. Anielewicz nodded. They started off. Mordechai looked back toward Bertha, but she'd slumped down onto the pavement again. He wished he had her along, too, but she didn't look able to keep up, and he didn't dare wait. The next blast wouldn't be a fire station. It wouldn't be whatever building had gone up in the latest explosion. It would be Lodz.

Nothing was left of the fire station. Petrol flames leaped high through the wreckage—the fire engine was burning. Mordechai kicked a quarter of a brick as hard as he could, sending it spinning away. Solomon Gruver had been in there. Later on—if he lived—he'd grieve.

The Mauser thumped against his shoulder as he trotted along. It didn't bother him; he noticed it only at odd moments. What did bother him was how little ammunition jingled in his pockets. The rifle bore a full five-round clip, but he didn't have enough cartridges to refill that clip more than once or twice. He hadn't expected to fight today.

"How are you fixed for ammunition?" he asked Jäger.

"Full magazine in the weapon, one more full one here." The German pointed to his belt. "Sixty rounds altogether."

That was better, but it wasn't as good as Mordechai had hoped. You could go through the magazine of a submachine gun in a matter of seconds. He reminded himself Jäger was a panzer colonel. If a German soldier—a German officer, no less—didn't maintain fire discipline, who would?

Maybe nobody. When bullets started cracking past your head, maintaining discipline of any sort came hard.

"And I, I have only the rounds in my pistol," Ludmila said.

Anielewicz nodded. She was coming along. Jäger seemed to think she had every right to come along, but Jäger was sleeping with her, too, so how much was his opinion worth? Enough that Anielewicz didn't feel like bucking it, not when anybody who wouldn't run away at the sound of a gunshot was an asset. She'd been in the Red Air Force and she'd been a partisan here in Poland, so maybe she'd be useful after all. His own fighters had shown him some women could do the job—and some men couldn't.

He passed a good many of his own fighters as he hurried with Jäger and Ludmila toward the ruined factory. Several shouted questions at him. He gave only vague answers, and did not ask any of the men or women to join. None of them was privy to the secret of the explosive-metal bomb, and he wanted to keep the circle of those who were as small as possible. If he stopped Skorzeny, he didn't want to have to risk playing a game of Samson in the temple with the Lizards afterwards. Besides, troops who didn't know what they were getting into were liable to cause more problems than they solved.

A couple of Order Service policemen also recognized him and asked him where he was going. Them he ignored. He was used to ignoring the Order Service. They were used to being ignored, too. Men who carried truncheons were polite to men with rifles and submachine guns: either they were polite, or their loved ones (assuming Order Service police had any loved ones, a dubious proposition) said *Kaddish* over new graves in the cemetery.

Jäger was starting to pant. "How far is it?" he asked on the exhale. Sweat streamed down his face and darkened his shirt at the back and under the arms.

Anielewicz was *shvitzing*, too. The day was hot and bright and clear, pleasant if you were just lounging around but not for running through the streets of Lodz. *This couldn't have happened, say, in fall?* he thought. Aloud, though, he answered, "Not much farther. Nothing in the ghetto is very far from anything else. You Nazis didn't leave us much room here, you know."

Jäger's mouth tightened. "Can't you leave that alone when you talk to me? If I hadn't got through to you, you'd have been dead twice by now."

"That's true," Mordechai admitted. "But it only goes so far. How many thousands of Jews died here before anyone said anything?" He gave Jäger credit. The German visibly chewed on that for a few strides before nodding.

A cloud of smoke was rising. As Mordechai had thought from

the sound, it was close to the place where the bomb lay concealed. Somebody shouted to him, "Where's the fire engine?"

"It's on fire itself by now," he answered. "The other explosion you heard was the fire station." His questioner stared at him in horror. When he had time, he figured he would be horrified, too. What would the ghetto do for a fire engine from now on? He grunted. If they didn't stop Skorzeny, *from now on* would be a phrase without meaning.

He rounded another corner, Jäger and Ludmila beside him. Almost, then, he stopped dead in his tracks. The burning building housed the stable that held the heavy draft horses he'd gathered to move the bomb in case of need. Fire trapped the horses in their stalls. Their terrified screams, more dreadful than those of wounded women, dinned in his ears.

He wanted to go help the animals, and had to make himself trot past them. People who didn't know what he did were trying to get the horses out of the stable. He looked to make sure none of the bomb guards were there. To his relief, he didn't see any, but he knew he might well have. When that thought crossed his mind, he was suddenly certain Skorzeny hadn't bombed the building at random. He'd tried to create a distraction, to lure the guards away from their proper posts.

"That SS pal of yours, he's a real *mamzer*, isn't he?" he said to Jäger.

"A what?" the panzer man asked.

"A bastard," Anielewicz said, substituting a German word for a Yiddish one.

"You don't know the half of it," Jäger said. "Christ, Aniele-wicz, you don't know a tenth part of it."

"I'm finding out," Mordechai answered. "Come on, we go round this last corner and then we're there." He yanked the rifle from his shoulder, flipped off the safety, and chambered the first round from the clip. Jäger nodded grimly. He also had his Schmeisser ready to fire. And Ludmila had been carrying her little automatic in her hand all along. It wasn't much, but better than nothing.

At the last corner, they held up. If they went charging around it, they were liable to be walking straight into a buzz saw. Ever so cautiously, Mordechai looked down the street toward the dead factory. He didn't see anyone, not with a quick glance, and he knew where to look. In the end, though, whether he saw anyone didn't matter. They had to go forward. If Skorzeny was ahead of them . . . With luck, he'd be busy at the bomb. Without luck—

He glanced over to Jäger. "Any better idea of how many little friends Skorzeny is liable to have with him?"

The panzer colonel's lips skinned back from his teeth in a mirthless grin. "Only one way to find out, isn't there? I'll go first, then you, then Ludmila. We'll leapfrog till we get to where we're going."

Mordechai resented his taking over like that, even if the tactic did make good sense. "No, I'll go first," he said, and then, to prove to himself and Jäger both that it wasn't bravado, he added, "You've got the weapon with the most firepower. Cover me as I move up."

Jäger frowned, but nodded after a moment. He slapped Anielewicz lightly on the shoulder. "Go on, then." Anielewicz dashed forward, ready to dive behind a pile of rubble if anyone started shooting from inside the factory. No one did. He hurled himself into a doorway that gave him some cover. No sooner had he done so than Jäger ran past him, bent double and dodging back and forth. He might have been a panzer man, but he'd learned somewhere to fight on foot. Anielewicz scratched his head. The German was old enough to have fought in the last war. And who but he could say what all he'd done in this one?

Ludmila ran by both of them. She chose a doorway on the opposite side of the street in which to shelter. While she paused there, she shifted the pistol to her left hand so she could shoot from that position without exposing much of her body to return fire. She knew her business, too, then.

Anielewicz sprinted past her, up to within ten or twelve meters of the hole in the wall that led into the ruined factory. He peered in, trying to pierce the gloom. Was that someone lying still, not far inside? He couldn't be certain, but it looked that way.

Behind him, booted feet thumped on the pavement. He hissed and waved; Heinrich Jäger saw him and ducked into the doorway where he was standing. "What's wrong?" the German asked, breathing hard.

Anielewicz pointed. Jäger narrowed his eyes, squinting ahead. The lines that came out when he did that said he was indeed old enough to have fought in the First World War. "That's a body," he said, just as Ludmila came up to crowd the narrow niche in front of the door. "I'd bet anything you care to name it isn't Skorzeny's body, either."

"No, thanks," Mordechai said. "I don't have much, but what I've got, I'll keep." He drew in a deep breath. That took some effort. *Nerves,* he thought; he hadn't run that far. He pointed again.

"If we can make it up to that wall, we go in there and then head for the bomb along the clear path that leads into the middle of the building. Once we're at the wall, nobody can shoot at us without giving us a clear shot back at him."

"We go, then," Ludmila said, and ran for the wall. She made it. Muttering under his breath, Jäger followed. So did Anielewicz. Ever so cautiously, he peered into the factory. Yes, that was a sentry lying there—his rifle lay beside him. His chest wasn't moving.

Mordechai tried to take another deep breath himself. His lungs didn't seem to want to work. Inside his chest, his heart stumbled. He turned back toward Jäger and Ludmila. It had been shadowy inside the wrecked factory. He'd expected that. But here, too, on a bright, sunny day, he saw his comrades only dimly. He looked up at the sun. Staring at it didn't hurt his eyes. He looked back to Ludmila. Her eyes were very blue, he thought, and then realized why: her pupils had contracted so much, he could barely see them at all.

He fought for another hitching breath. "Something's—wrong," he gasped.

Heinrich Jäger had watched the day go dark around him without thinking much of it till Anielewicz spoke. Then he swore loudly and foully, while fear raced through him. He was liable to have killed himself and the woman he loved and all of Lodz out of sheer stupidity. You couldn't see nerve gas. You couldn't smell it. You couldn't taste it. It would kill you just the same.

He yanked open the aid kit he'd used to bandage the wounded old Jew. He had—he thought he had—five syringes, one for himself and each man in his panzer crew. If the SS had taken those out when they'd arrested him— If they'd done that, he was dead, and he wouldn't be the only one.

But the blackshirts hadn't. They hadn't thought to paw through the kit and see what was inside. He blessed them for their inefficiency.

He took out the syringes. "Antidote," he told Ludmila. "Hold still." All at once, speaking was an effort for him, too: the nerve gas was having its way. A few more minutes and he would have quietly keeled over and died, without ever figuring out why he was dead.

Ludmila, for a wonder, didn't argue. Maybe she was having trouble talking and breathing, too. He jabbed the syringe into the meat of her thigh, as he'd been trained, and pressed down on the plunger.

He grabbed another syringe. "You," he told Anielewicz as he yanked off its protective cap. The Jewish fighting leader nodded. Jäger hurried to inject him; he was starting to turn blue. If your lungs didn't work and your heart didn't work, that was what happened to you.

Jäger threw down the second syringe. Its glass body shattered on the pavement. He heard that, but had trouble seeing it. Working as much by touch as by sight, he got out another syringe and stabbed himself in the leg.

He felt as if he'd held a live electrical wire against his flesh. It wasn't well-being that rushed through him; instead, he was being poisoned in a different way, one that fought the action of the nerve gas. His mouth went dry. His heart pounded so loud, he had no trouble hearing it. And the street, which had gone dim and faint as the nerve gas squeezed his pupils shut, all at once seemed blindingly bright. He blinked. Tears filled his eyes.

To escape the hideous glare, he ducked inside the factory. There, in real shadows, the light seemed more tolerable. Mordechai Anielewicz and Ludmila followed. "What was that stuff you shot us with?" the Jew asked, his voice a whisper.

"The antidote for nerve gas—that's all I know," Jäger answered. "They issued it to us in case we had to cross areas we'd already saturated while we were fighting the Lizards—or in case the wind shifted when we didn't expect it to. Skorzeny must have brought along gas grenades, or maybe just bottles full of gas, for all I know. Throw one in, let it break, give yourself a shot while you're waiting, and then go in and do what you were going to do."

Anielewicz looked down at the dead body of the sentry. "We have nerve gas now, too, you know," he said. Jäger nodded. Anielewicz scowled. "We're going to have to be even more careful with it than we have been—and we've taken casualties from it." Jäger nodded again. With nerve gas, you couldn't be too careful.

"Enough of this," Ludmila said. "Where is the bomb, and how do we get to it and stop Skorzeny without getting killed ourselves?"

Those were good questions. Jäger couldn't have come up with better if he'd thought for a week, and he didn't have a week to waste thinking. He glanced over to Anielewicz. If anybody had the answers, the Jewish fighting leader did.

Anielewicz pointed into the bowels of the building. "The bomb is there, less than a hundred meters away. See the opening there, behind the overturned desk? The path isn't straight, but it's clear. One of you, maybe both of you, should go down it. It's the only way you'll get there fast enough to be useful. Me, I set this place up. There's another way to get to the bomb. I'll take that—and we see what happens then."

Jäger was used to sending others out to create distractions for him to exploit. Now he and Ludmila were the distraction. He couldn't argue with that, not when Anielewicz knew the ground and he didn't. But he knew the people who created distractions were the ones likely to get expended when the shooting started. If his mouth hadn't already been dry from the antidote, it would have gone that way.

Anielewicz didn't wait for him and Ludmila to argue. Like any good commander, he took being obeyed for granted. Pointing one last time to the upside-down desk, he slipped away behind a pile of rubble.

"Stay in back of me," Jäger whispered to Ludmila.

"Chivalry is reactionary," she said. "You have the better weapon. I should lead and draw fire." In strictly military terms, she was right. He'd never thought strictly military terms would apply to the woman he loved. But if he failed here out of love or chivalry or whatever you wanted to call it, he failed altogether. Reluctantly, he waved Ludmila ahead.

She didn't see the motion, because she'd already started moving forward. He followed, close as he could. As Anielewicz had said, the path wound but was easy enough to use. With his pupils dilated by the nerve gas antidote, he could see exactly where to place each foot to make the least possible noise.

What he thought was about halfway to the bomb, Ludmila stopped in her tracks. She pointed round the corner. Jäger came up far enough to see. A Jewish guard lay dead there, one hand still on his rifle. Ever so carefully, Jäger and Ludmila stepped over him and moved on.

Up ahead, Jäger heard tools clinking on metal, a sound with which he'd become intimately familiar while serving on panzers. Normally, that was a good sound, promising that something broken would soon be fixed. Something broken would soon be fixed now, too. Here, though, the sound of ongoing repair raised the hair at the back of his neck.

He made a mistake then—brushing against some rubble, he knocked over a brick. It fell to the ground with a crash that seemed hideously loud. Jäger froze, cursing himself. *That's why you didn't stay in the infantry, you clumsy son of a whore.*

He prayed Skorzeny hadn't heard the brick. God wasn't listening. The handicraft noises stopped. A burst of submachine gun fire came in their place. Skorzeny couldn't see him, but didn't care. He was hoping ricochets would do the job for him. They almost did. A couple of bouncing bullets came wickedly close to Jäger as he threw himself flat.

"Give up, Skorzeny!" he shouted, wriggling forward with Ludmila beside him. "You're surrounded!"

"Jäger?" For one of the rare times in their acquaintance, he heard Skorzeny astonished. "What are you doing here, you kike-loving motherfucker? I thought I put paid to you for good. They should have hanged you from a noose made of piano wire by now. Well, they will. One day they will." He fired another long burst. He wasn't worried about spending ammunition. Bullets whined around Jäger, striking sparks as they caromed off bricks and wrecked machines.

Jäger scuttled toward him anyhow. If he made it to the next heap of bricks, he could pop up over it and get a decent shot. "Give up!" he yelled again. "We'll let you go if you do."

"You'll be too dead to worry about it, whether I give up or not," the SS man answered. Then he paused again. "No, maybe not. You should be dead already, as a matter of fact. Why the hell aren't you?" Now he sounded friendly, interested, as if they were hashing it out over a couple of shots of schnapps.

"Antidote," Jäger told him.

"Isn't that a kick in the balls?" Skorzeny said. "Well, I'd hoped I'd get out of here in one piece, but—" The *but* was punctuated by a potato-masher hand grenade that spun hissing through the air and landed five or six meters behind Jäger and Ludmila.

He grabbed her and folded both of them into a tight ball an instant before the grenade exploded. The blast was deafening. Hot fragments of casing bit into his back and legs. He grabbed for his Schmeisser, sure Skorzeny would be following hard on the heels of the grenade.

A rifle shot rang out, then another one. Skorzeny's submachine gun chattered in reply. The bullets weren't aimed at Jäger. He and Ludmila untangled themselves from each other and both rushed to that pile of bricks.

Skorzeny stood swaying like a tree in the breeze. In the gloom, his eyes were enormous, and all pupil: he'd given himself a stiff dose of nerve-gas antidote. Right in the center of the ragged old shirt he wore was a spreading red stain. He brought up his Schmeisser, but for once didn't seem sure what to do with it, whether to aim at Anielewicz or at Jäger and Ludmila.

His foes had no such hesitation. Anielewicz's rifle and Ludmila's pistol cracked at the same instant in which Jäger squeezed off a burst. More red flowers blossomed on Skorzeny's body. The breeze in which he swayed became a gale. It blew him over. The submachine gun fell from his hands. His fingers groped toward it, pulling hand and arm after them as they struggled from one rough piece of ground to the next, a centimeter and a half farther on. Jäger fired another burst. Skorzeny twitched as the bullets slammed into him, and at last lay still.

Only then did Jäger notice the SS man had pried several planks off the big crate that held the explosive-metal bomb. Under them, the aluminum skin of the device lay exposed, like that of a surgical patient revealed by an opening in the drapes. If Skorzeny had already set the detonator in there—

Jäger ran toward the bomb. He got there a split second ahead of Anielewicz, who was in turn a split second ahead of Ludmila. Skorzeny had removed one of the panels from the skin. Jäger peered into the hole thus exposed. With his pupils so dilated, he had no trouble seeing the hole was empty.

Anielewicz pointed to a cylinder a few centimeters in front of his left foot. "That's the detonator," he said. "I don't know if it's the one we pulled or if he brought it with him, the way you said he might. It doesn't matter. What matters is that he didn't get to use it."

"We won." Ludmila sounded dazed, as if she was fully realizing for the first time what they'd done, what they'd prevented.

"Nobody will put the detonator in this bomb any time soon," Anielewicz said. "Nobody will be able to get close to it and keep living, not for a while, not without the antidote, whatever that is. How long does the gas persist, Jäger? You know more about it than anyone else around here."

"It's not exposed to bright sun. What's left of the roof will keep rain off. It should last a good while. Days, certainly. Weeks, maybe," Jäger answered. He still felt keyed up, ready to fight. Maybe that was the aftermath of battle. Maybe, too, it was the antidote driving him. Anything that made his heart thump like that probably scrambled his brains, too.

"Can we go out of here now?" Ludmila asked. She looked frightened; the antidote might have been turning her to flight, not fight.

"We'd better get out of here, I'd say," Anielewicz added. "God only knows how much of that gas we're taking in every time we breathe. If there's more of it than the antidote can handle—"

"Yes," Jäger said, starting toward the street. "And when we do get out, we have to burn these clothes. We have to do it ourselves, and we have to bathe and bathe and bathe. You don't need to breathe this gas for it to kill you. If it touches your skin, that will do the job—slower than breathing it, but just about as sure. We're dangerous to anyone around us till we decontaminate."

"Lovely stuff you Germans turn out," Anielewicz said from behind him.

"The Lizards didn't like it," Jäger answered. The Jewish fighting leader grunted and shut up.

The closer Jäger got to the street, the brighter the glare became, till he squeezed his eyes almost shut and peered through a tiny crack between upper and lower lids. He wondered how long his pupils would stay dilated and then, relentlessly pragmatic, wondered where in Lodz he could come up with a pair of sunglasses.

He strode past the outermost dead Jewish sentry, then out onto the street, which seemed to him awash in as much brilliance as if the explosive-metal bomb had gone off. The Jews probably would have to cordon off a couple of blocks around the wrecked factory on one pretext or another, just to keep people from inadvertently poisoning themselves as they walked by.

Ludmila emerged and stood beside him. Through his half-blind squint, he saw hers. He didn't know what was going to happen next. He didn't even know whether, as Anielewicz had suggested, they'd ended up breathing more nerve gas than their antidote could handle. If the day started going dim instead of brilliant, he still had two syringes left in his aid kit. For three people, that made two-thirds of a shot apiece. Would he need it? If he did, would it be enough?

He did know what wouldn't happen next. Lodz wouldn't go up in a fireball like a new sun. The Lizards wouldn't aim their concentrated wrath at Germany—not on account of that, anyhow. He wouldn't go back to the *Wehrmacht*, nor Ludmila to the Red Air Force. Whatever future they had, whether hours or decades, was here.

He smiled at her. Her eyes were almost closed, but she saw him and smiled back. He saw that, very clearly.

Atvar had heard the buzzing racket of Tosevite aircraft a great many times through sound recordings, but only rarely in person. He turned one eye turret toward the window of his suite. Sure enough, he could see the clumsy, yellow-painted machine climbing slowly into the sky. "That is the last of them, is it not?" he said.

"Yes, Exalted Fleetlord, that one bears away Marshall, the negotiator from the not-empire of the United States," Zolraag replied.

"The talks are complete," Atvar said, sounding disbelieving even to himself. "We are at peace with large portions of Tosev 3." *No wonder I sound disbelieving,* he thought. *We have peace here, but peace without conquest. Who would have imagined that when we set out from Home?*

"Now we await the arrival of the colonization fleet, Exalted Fleetlord," Zolraag said. "With its coming, with the permanent establishment of the Race on Tosev 3, begins the incorporation of this whole world into the Empire. It will be slower and more difficult than we anticipated before we came here, but it shall be done."

"That is also my view, and why I agreed to halt large-scale hostilities for the time being," Atvar said. He turned one eye turret toward Moishe Russie, who still stood watching the Big Ugly aircraft shrink in the distance. To Zolraag, he went on, "Translate for him what you just said, and ask his opinion on the matter."

"It shall be done," Zolraag said before shifting from the language of the Race to the ugly, guttural grunts he used when speaking to the Tosevite.

Russie made more grunts by way of reply. Zolraag turned them into words a person could understand: "His answer is not altogether germane, Exalted Fleetlord. He expresses relief that the negotiator from Deutschland departed without embroiling the Race and the Tosevites in fresh warfare."

"I confess to a certain amount of relief on this score myself," Atvar said. "After that pompous pronouncement the Big Ugly issued which proved to be either a bluff or a spectacular example of Deutsch incompetence—our analysis there is still incomplete—I did indeed anticipate renewed combat. But the Tosevites apparently decided to be rational instead."

Zolraag translated for Russie, whose reply made his mouth fall open in amusement. "He says expecting the Deutsche to be rational is like expecting good weather in the middle of winter: you may get it, yes, for a day or two, but most of the time you will be disappointed."

"Expect anything from either Tosevites or Tosevite weather

and most of the time you will be disappointed—though you need not translate that," the fleetlord answered. Russie was looking at him with what he thought was alertness; he remembered the Big Ugly did know some of the language of the Race. Atvar shrugged mentally; Russie already had a good notion of his opinion of Tosevites. He said, "Tell him that, sooner or later, his people will be subjects of the Emperor."

Zolraag dutifully told him. Russie did not answer, not directly. Instead, he went back to the window and stared out once more. Atvar felt only annoyance: the Tosevite aircraft was long gone by now. But Russie still kept looking out through the glass without saying anything.

"What is he doing?" Atvar snapped at last, patience deserting him.

Zolraag put the question. Through him, Moishe Russie replied, "I am looking across the Nile at the Pyramids."

"Why?" Atvar said, irritated still. "What do you care about these—what were they?—these large funerary monuments, is that it? They are massive, yes, but barbarous even by Tosevite standards."

"My ancestors were slaves in this country three, maybe four thousand years ago," Russie told him. "Maybe they helped build the Pyramids. That's what our legends say, though I don't know if it's true. Who cares about the ancient Egyptians now? They were mighty, but they are gone. We Jews were slaves, but we're still here. How can you know what will happen from what is now?"

Now Atvar's mouth fell open. "Tosevite pretensions to antiquity always make me laugh," he said to Zolraag. "Hear how the Big Ugly speaks of three or four thousand years—six or eight thousand of ours—as if it were a long time in historic terms. We had already absorbed both the Rabotevs and the Hallessi by then, and some of us were beginning to think about the planets of the star Tosev: day before yesterday, in the history of the Race."

"Truth, Exalted Fleetlord," Zolraag said.

"Of course it is truth," Atvar said, "and it is why in the end we shall triumph, our setbacks because of the Big Uglies' unexpected technological sophistication notwithstanding. We are content to progress one small step at a time. There are whole Tosevite civilizations, as Russie just said, which moved forward at the usual Big Ugly breakneck clip—and then failed utterly. We do not have this difficulty, nor shall we ever. We are established, even if on only part of the world. With the arrival of the colonization fleet, our presence shall become unassailably permanent. We then have only to wait for another Tosevite cultural collapse, extend our influence over the area where it occurs, and repeat the process until no section of the planet remains outside the Empire's control."

"Truth," Zolraag repeated. "Because of Tosevite surprises, the conquest fleet might not have accomplished quite everything the plan back on Home called for." Kirel could not have been more cautious and diplomatic than that. Zolraag continued, "The conquest, however, does go on, just as you said. What, in the end, does it matter if it takes generations rather than days?"

"In the end, it matters not at all," Atvar replied. "History is on our side."

Vyacheslav Molotov coughed. The last T-34 had rumbled through Red Square a good while before, but the air was still thick with diesel fumes. If Stalin noticed them, he gave no sign. He chuckled in high good humor. "Well, Vyacheslav Mikhailovich, it wasn't quite a victory parade, not the sort I would have wanted after we'd finished crushing the Hitlerites, for instance, but it will do, it will do."

"Indeed, Comrade General Secretary," Molotov said. Stalin, for once, had been guilty of understatement. Molotov had gone to Cairo expecting to have nothing but trouble because of the intransigent stand Stalin required him to take. But if Stalin had disastrously misread Hitler's intentions, he'd gauged the Lizards aright.

"The Lizards have adhered in every particular to the agreement you forged with them," Stalin said: displays of martial might such as the one just past made him happy as a boy playing with lead soldiers. "They have everywhere removed themselves from Soviet soil: with the exception of the formerly Polish territory they elected to retain. And there, Comrade Foreign Commissar, I have no fault to find with you."

"For which I thank you, Iosef Vissarionovich," Molotov answered. "Better to have borders with those who keep agreements than with those who break them."

"Exactly so," Stalin said. "And our mopping up of German remnants on Soviet soil continues most satisfactorily. Some areas in the southern Ukraine and near the Finnish border remain troublesome, but, on the whole, the Hitlerite invasion, like that of the Lizards, can be reckoned a thing of the past. We move forward once more, toward true socialism."

He dug in a trouser pocket and took out his pipe, a box of matches, and a leather tobacco pouch. Opening the pouch, he filled the pipe from it, then lighted a match and held it to the bowl of the pipe. His cheeks hollowed as he sucked in breath to get the pipe going. Smoke rose from the bowl; more leaked from his nostrils and one corner of his mouth.

Molotov's nose twitched. He'd expected the acrid reek of *makhorka*, which, as far as he was concerned, was to good tobacco what diesel fumes were to good air. What Stalin was smoking, though, had an aroma rich and flavorful enough to slice and serve on a plate for supper.

"A Turkish blend?" he asked.

"As a matter of fact, no," Stalin answered. "An American one: a gift from President Hull. Milder than I quite care for, but good of its kind. And there will be Turkish again, in short order. Once we have the northern coast of the Black Sea fully under our control, sea traffic will resume, and we can also begin rail shipments by way of Armenia and Georgia." As he usually did when he mentioned his homeland, he gave Molotov a sly look, as if daring him to make something of his ancestry. Never one for foolhardy action, Molotov knew much better than that. Stalin took another puff, then went on, "And we shall have to work out arrangements for trade with the Lizards, too, of course."

"Comrade General Secretary?" Molotov said. Stalin's leaps of thought often left logic far behind. Sometimes that brought great benefits to the Soviet state: his relentless industrialization, much of it beyond the range of Nazi bombers, might have saved the USSR when the Germans invaded. Of course, the invasion, when it came, would have been better handled had Stalin's intuition not convinced him that everyone who warned him of it was lying. You couldn't tell in advance what the intuition was worth. You had to sit back and await results. When the Soviet state was on the line, that grew nerve-racking.

"Trade with the Lizards," Stalin repeated, as if to a backwards child. "The regions they occupy will not produce everything they need. We shall supply them with raw materials they may lack. Being socialists, we shall not be good capitalists, and we shall lose greatly on the exchanges—so long as we obtain their manufactured goods in return."

"Ah." Molotov began to see. This time, he thought, Stalin's intuition was working well. "You want us to begin copying their methods and adapting them for our own purposes."

"That is right," Stalin said. "We had to do the same thing with the West after the Revolution. We had a generation in which to catch up, or they would destroy us. The Nazis struck us a hard blow, but we held. Now, with the Lizards, we have—mankind has—paid half the world in exchange for most of another generation."

"Until the colonization fleet comes," Molotov said. Yes, logic backed intuition to give Stalin solid reasons for trading with the Lizards.

"Until the colonization fleet comes," Stalin agreed. "We need more bombs of our own, we need rockets of our own, we need calculating machines that almost think, we need ships that fly in space so they cannot look down upon us without our looking down upon them as well. The Lizards have these things. The capitalists and fascists are on their way to them. If we are left behind, they will bury us."

"Iosef Vissarionovich, I think you are right," Molotov said. He would have said it whether he thought Stalin right or wrong. Had he actually thought him wrong, he would have started looking for ways and means to ensure that the latest pronunciamento was diluted before it took effect. That was dangerous, but sometimes necessary: where would the Soviet Union be now had Stalin liquidated everyone in the country who knew anything about nuclear physics? *Under the Lizards' thumb,* Molotov thought.

Stalin accepted Molotov's agreement as no more than his due. "Of course I am," he said complacently. "I do not see how we can keep the colonization fleet from landing, but the thing we must remember—this above all else, Vyacheslav Mikhailovich—is that it will bring the Lizards fresh numbers, but nothing fundamentally new."

"True enough, Comrade General Secretary," Molotov said cautiously. Again, Stalin had got ahead of him on the page.

This time, though, intuition had nothing to do with it. While Molotov was dickering with the Lizards, Stalin must have been working through the implications of their social and economic development. He said, "It is inevitable that they would have nothing fundamentally new. Marxist analysis shows this must be so. They are, despite their machines, representatives of the ancient economic model, relying on slaves—with them partly mechanical, partly the other races they have subjugated—to produce for a dependent upper class. Such a society is without exception highly conservative and resistant to innovation of any sort. Thus we can overcome them."

"That is nicely argued, Iosef Vissarionovich," Molotov said, his admiration unfeigned. "Mikhail Andreyevich could not reason more trenchantly."

"Suslov?" Stalin shrugged. "He made some small contributions to this line of thought, but the main thrust of it, of course, is mine."

"Of course," Molotov agreed, straight-faced as usual. He wondered what the young Party ideologist would say to that, but had no intention of asking. In any case, it did not matter. No matter who had formulated the idea, it supported what Molotov had believed all along. "As the dialectic demonstrates, Comrade General Secretary, history is on our side."

Sam Yeager strolled down Central Avenue in Hot Springs, savoring the summer weather. One of the things he savored about it was being able to escape it every now and then. The sign painted on the front window of the Southern Grill said, OUR REFRIGERATED AIR-CONDITIONING IS WORKING AGAIN. The wheeze and hum of the machinery and fan backed up the claim.

He turned to Barbara. "Want to stop here for some lunch?"

She looked at the sign, then took one hand off the grip of Jonathan's baby carriage. "Twist my arm," she said. Sam gave it a token twist. "Oh, mercy!" she cried, but not very loud, because Jonathan was asleep.

Sam held the door open for her. "Best mercy I know of." He followed her into the restaurant.

That took them out of Hot Springs summer in a hurry. The air-conditioning was refrigerated, all right; Sam felt as if he'd walked into Minnesota November. He wondered if his sweat would start freezing into tiny icicles all over his body.

A colored waiter in a bow tie appeared as if by magic, menus under his arm. "You jus' follow me, Sergeant, ma'am," he said. "I'll take you to a booth where you can park that buggy right alongside."

Sam slid onto the maroon leatherette of the booth with a sigh of contentment. He pointed to the candle on the table, then to the electric lights in the chandelier overhead. "Now the candle is a decoration again," he said. "You ask me, that's the way it's supposed to be. Having to use candles for light when we didn't have anything better—" He shook his head. "I didn't like that."

"No, neither did I." Barbara opened her menu. She let out a squeak of surprise. "Look at the prices!"

With some apprehension, Sam did just that. He wondered if he'd suffer the embarrassment of having to walk out of the Southern Grill. He had maybe twenty-five bucks in his wallet; Army pay hadn't come close to keeping up with jumping prices. The only reason he'd figured he could eat out once in a while was that he got most of his meals for nothing.

But Barbara hadn't said which way prices had gone. Everything was down about a third from what he'd expected, and a hand-written addendum boasted of cold Budweiser beer.

He remarked on that when the waiter returned to take his order and Barbara's. "Yes, sir, first shipment from St. Louis," the colored man replied. "Just got in yesterday, matter of fact. We're startin' to see things now we ain't seen since the Lizards came. Things is lookin' up, that they is."

Sam glanced at Barbara. When she nodded, he ordered Budweiser for both of them. The red-white-and-blue labels made them smile. The waiter poured the beers with great ceremony. Barbara lifted her glass on high. "Here's to peace," she said.

"I'll drink to that." Sam matched action to word. He swallowed the first swig of beer, then thoughtfully smacked his lips. He drank again, and was even more thoughtful. "You know, hon, after drinking mostly home brews and such the last couple of years, I'll be darned if I don't like 'em better. More flavor to 'em, you know what I mean?"

"Oh, good," Barbara said. "If I were the only one who thought that, I'd figure it was just because I didn't know anything about beer. It doesn't mean I can't drink this, though." She proved as much. "And it is good to see the Budweiser bottle again—as if an old friend were back from the war."

"Yeah." Yeager wondered how Mutt Daniels was doing, and about all the other Decatur Commodores who'd been riding the train with him when the Lizards strafed it in northern Illinois.

The waiter set a hamburger in front of him and a roast-beef sandwich before Barbara. Then, with a flourish, he put a full bottle of Heinz catsup on the table between them. "This got here this morning," he said. "Y'all are the first ones to use it."

"How about that?" Sam said. He pushed it over toward Barbara so she could have first crack at it. It acted like catsup—it didn't want to come out of the bottle. When it did pour, too much came out: except, after most of two years without, how could there be too much?

After he'd anointed the hamburger, Sam took a big bite. His

eyes widened. Unlike the Budweiser, he found no disappointment there. "Mm-mm," he said with his mouth full. "That's the McCoy."

"Mm-hmm," Barbara agreed, with as much enthusiasm and as few manners.

Sam disposed of the hamburger in a few bites, then slathered more catsup on the grits that took the place of french fries. He didn't usually do that. In fact, nobody he knew did that; a proper Southerner who saw him perpetrating such an atrocity would probably ride him out of town on a rail. He didn't care, not today. He wanted every bite of the sweet-sour tomato tang he could get, and any excuse was a good one. When Barbara did the same thing, he grinned in vindication.

"Another beer?" the waiter asked as he picked up their plates.

"Yes," Sam said after glancing at Barbara again. "But why don't you make it a local special this time? I'm glad to see the Budweiser, but it's not as good as I remembered."

"You're about the fo'th person to say that today, sir," the Negro remarked. "I'll be right back with the pride of Hot Springs."

He had just set the local brews—altogether a deeper, richer amber than Budweiser's—before Sam and Barbara when Jonathan woke up and started to fuss. Barbara took him out of the carriage and held him, which calmed him down. "You were a good boy—you let us eat lunch," she told him. She checked. "You're even dry. Pretty soon I'll give you lunch, too." Now she looked over at Sam. "And pretty soon, maybe, I'll be able to start giving him formula in a bottle. That should be one of the things that come back pretty fast."

"Uh-huh," Sam said. "Way things work, it'll probably start showing up right about the time he can start drinking regular milk." He grinned at his son, who was groping for Barbara's bottle of beer. She pushed it safely out of reach. Jonathan started to cloud up, but Sam made a silly face at him, so he decided to laugh instead. Sam let his features relax. "What a crazy world he'll grow up in."

"I only hope it's a world where he *can* grow up," Barbara said, setting a hand on top of the baby's head. Jonathan tried to grab it and stuff it into his mouth. Jonathan tried to grab everything and stuff it into his mouth these days. Barbara went on, "What with the bombs and the rockets and the gas—" She shook her head. "And the Lizards' colonization fleet will get to Earth when he's only a young man. Who can guess what things will be like then?"

"Not you, not me, not anybody," Sam said. "Not the Lizards, either." The colored waiter set the check on the table. Sam dug his wallet out of his hip pocket and pulled out a ten, a five, and a couple of singles, which left the fellow a nice tip. Barbara put Jonathan back into the buggy. As she started wheeling the baby toward the door, Sam finished his thought: "We'll just have to wait and see what happens, that's all."

AUTHOR'S NOTE AND ACKNOWLEDGMENTS

The text of *Worldwar: Striking the Balance* corrects a couple of small errors that appear in the hardback edition of *Worldwar: Upsetting the Balance*.

For helping to spot mistakes and helping with the research that went into this series, I want to thank Arlan Andrews, Greg Edington, John Filpus, Stanley Foo, David Hulan, Damon Knight, Dal Koger, Mike McManus, and Bill Seney. Errors, of course, remain my own.

HOW FEW REMAIN

The dramatic new novel by
HARRY TURTLEDOVE

The Master of Alternate History

In 1862, key Confederate orders nearly fell into Union hands. But those orders were saved, the Rebels swept into Pennsylvania, smashed the Army of the Potomac, and assured Southern independence.

A generation later, America writhed once more in the throes of battle. Furious over the annexation of key Mexican territory, the U.S. again declared war on the Confederacy, and in 1881 the fragile peace was shattered.

This new war was fought on a lawless frontier where the blue and gray battled not only each other but the Apache, the outlaw, and even the redcoat. For along with France, England entered the fray on the side of the South.

Out of this tragic struggle emerged historic figures. A disgraced Abraham Lincoln crisscrossed the nation championing Socialist ideals. Cocky Theodore Roosevelt bickered with George Custer. Confederate General Stonewall Jackson again soared to the heights of military genius, while the North struggled to find a leader who could prove his equal.

Thanks to such journalists as Samuel Clemens, the nation witnessed the clash of human dreams and passions in this, a Second War Between the States.

Published by Del Rey Books.
Available at a bookstore near you.